All That Matters

All That Matters

L.H. Burruss

This book is dedicated to my children:
Thomas, Jefferson, Frances, Alice, and Carmella.

"So hear my words with faith and passion,
For what I say to you is true,
And when you find the one you might become,
Remember part of me is you..."
- Lyle Lovett – Simple Song

PART ONE

WATER

"Those boys down in Gloucester they call Guineamen are some of the best watermen on this bay. My father and I tonged right beside one this last fall and if we tonged thirty bushels between us, he'd tong fifty by himself."

From *The Watermen of the Chesapeake Bay*
by J.H. Whitehead III

PROLOGUE

1956

They headed out of Sarah's Creek in the early light of dawn, the old Chesapeake Bay deadrise work boat gliding easily along through the calm water.

As they cleared the mouth of the creek, James Walker shoved the *Mary Anne's* throttle forward, and she raised her bow and headed out into the broad York River.

James's younger brother Edward, sitting on the fantail, huddled against the cold in an old Navy pea coat and watched James light another cigarette from the butt of the one he had been smoking. "Sounds good, don't she, Bubbie?" James said to him, and Edward smiled and nodded, then looked back at the widening wake. It was still dark enough that he could see splotches of phosphorescent glow in the churning water just astern.

He pulled the tattered pea coat more tightly around him in a futile effort to ward off the cold breeze. Then he gave up and walked forward, stepping over the long wooden handles of the oyster tongs and ducking beneath the culling board to stand beside his brother.

Edward saw that James was gazing ashore at one of the houses on the riverbank in Little Richmond; the one where James' girlfriend Evelyn lived.

"You going to marry her, James?" Edward asked.

His brother shot him a cold glance, then looked ashore again, took a drag off his cigarette, and flicked it overboard. "Ain't no way her daddy's gonna let her marry a damn waterman," James said. "Especially one as poor as me."

"Shit, Bubba," Edward said. "We ain't poor."

James brought the *Mary Anne* around the channel marker and looked at the boy. He started to say something to his younger brother about cussing, but thought, What the hell; he's old enough.

Instead, he reached over and raised the wooden lid of the engine box. "You see that new engine?" he said. "It took every bit of money the bank would loan me to buy it; that and the new coat of copper paint on the bottom of this rotten tub."

"She ain't a rotten tub!" Edward said, and he stroked the top of the gunwale. Their father had built the sturdy, straight-stemmed work boat with his own hands before James was born, and had labored aboard her six days a week from then until he died.

"Anyway," Edward added, "I'll help you make that money back and a lot more, before I go back to school."

James gave him a look of disdain and said, "Shi-it, boy. In two weeks? You're out of your mind. We'll be lucky to tong enough oysters to make the first payment, the money you get for a bushel of the damn things these days." He dropped the engine-box cover down, then grinned and said, "Unless you know where there's an oyster bed that's got a pearl in every one."

Edward frowned, picked up a rusty bolt from the deck, and threw it overboard. "I was thinking I wouldn't go back to school after Christmas holidays," he said. "I can help you the rest of oyster season, and run crab pots with you all summer. I can always go back to school in the fall."

James stared at him for a time. Maybe that was a good idea. If they could tong enough oysters the rest of the season to keep ahead of the bank payments, and had a decent summer of crabbing, maybe they'd be all right. Edward could go back to school after that, and... But, no, it didn't work that way. Once the boy quit, he would never go back. None of them ever did. Hell, most of the watermen from the marshes of Guinea Neck had dropped out of school by the time they were sixteen.

Anyway, James had promised their mother before she died that he'd see to it that Edward finished school, so that was that. He scowled at the boy and said, "You even *mention* quittin' school again, boy, and I'll throw your scrawny ass overboard!"

"I didn't say quit! I said I'd just wait till the fall to go back."

"Never happen!" James said. "Now get in there and make us a pot of coffee."

Edward looked at him a moment longer, then nodded and ducked into the pilot house.

The small, cramped cabin on the bow of the boat was just large enough for a crew of two or three to crowd into to get out of the weather. Storage lockers ran along each side of the cabin, and also served as benches, or they could be used for cramped bunks, if needed.

Between the lockers was a small table with the coffee pot and a single gas burner on it. Edward filled the pot with water and spooned some coffee grounds into the basket, then lit the burner and set the pot on it. He sat down to wait for it to boil, holding his hands near the gas flame to warm them and whistling to himself.

He was elated that James wouldn't let him quit school, because Edward Walker loved learning; he loved the discovery of old facts and new ideas, and how to put them into proper English. He loved the challenges of mathematics and science. And he especially loved history, because he would always imagine himself as one of the men involved in the things he learned about; the great voyages of discovery, the explorations deep into unknown lands, the defining battles of history. And so much of that history had occurred in his native Gloucester County or nearby; Jamestown colony, the saga of Pocahontas, and Bacon's rebellion; Yorktown, Williamsburg and Richmond, the capital of the Confederacy, and the Virginia battlefields where much of the Civil War was fought.

Astern and off to starboard were his favorite of all those historic places; the battlefields of Gloucester and Yorktown where American independence was assured in the autumn of 1781. In Gloucester, at the battle of the Hook, Lauzun's Legion and Mercer's Virginians had defeated the dreaded Tarleton, assuring the surrender in Yorktown two weeks later of Cornwallis and his army, and an hour after that in Gloucester, the last surrender of British forces in America.

Edward Walker pressed his face against the starboard porthole. He could see the Yorktown Victory Monument in the growing light, rising above the trees of the historic little village. He imagined himself there a century-and-three-quarters earlier:

He was at the front of Alexander Hamilton's battalion, moving silently forward toward Redoubt Number Ten to lead the assault against the British troops entrenched there. Off to the left, he could see the dark figures of a French battalion moving against the other redoubt that anchored the British left.

Now they attacked, struggling up the slippery mud walls, some of the men hacking through the sharpened log fraises to open a way in as the British fired a volley from their muskets into the Americans at point blank range. The men on either side of him fell screaming to the bottom of the trench, but not Edward; he scrambled through a gap and up to the top of the redoubt wall, slashing and jabbing with his bayonet, redcoat after redcoat crumpling to earth before him. And when it was over, Hamilton stood beside him, surveying the fallen enemy and saying, "Well done, Walker! General Washington will hear of this!" And then a few days later, the great moment of surrender, with the army of the Lord Cornwallis, banners furled, marching between the files of American and French victors, and the hero of the battle, Edward Walker, standing between Washington and Lafayette while the British band played The World Turned Upside Down.

A beautiful girl in a dazzling white dress stands nearby, watching him. He looks into her adoring eyes, and she smiles, and later, she meets him alone on the high banks above the river. They're under the spreading branches of a giant oak, the ground beneath it covered with moss. She moves into his arms and they kiss passionately, then fall gently to the soft moss, and his hands begin to...

"EDWARD! Damn it, boy, are you asleep in there? You gonna bring me a cup of coffee, or not?"

Edward jumped up and bumped his head on an overhead brace. "Ow! Damn!" he muttered, rubbing his head with one hand and pressing the bulge in his trousers down with the other. Then he poured two mugs of coffee from the bubbling pot, backed out of the pilot house into the cold, and handed a mug to James.

A jet fighter, navigation lights blinking, flew over on the way to nearby Langley Field, and James looked up at it, a dark, faraway look clouding his face as he watched it disappear. Edward studied his older brother, sipping his coffee in silence.

James, twelve years Edward's senior, had been drafted in the early days of the Korean War, and had spent most of his time in the Army serving in Korea as an infantryman. And he had never been the same since. He had been so carefree before he left - the first to make a joke when things got tense, the one who was always laughing. But no more. Now, something as simple as a jet fighter flying overhead would plunge him into these dark moods. Yet he would never talk about the Army, or the war. Other people would mention it, and he would seem to draw into himself, and ignore them.

Edward felt that it was unfair of his brother to keep it to himself. He had been some kind of a hero - several of the other Guinea watermen had said so. And Edward had found some medals in his brother's dresser drawer one day, which seemed to prove it. But he had been afraid to mention that fact to James, not only because he had no business rummaging around in his brother's belongings, but because he was afraid it would send him into one of these moods.

Still, they were brothers, and Edward felt he deserved to know, so he said, "What was it like, James? The war, I mean."

His brother's face took on that same dark look that shrouded it whenever the war was mentioned.

"Cold," James replied, shivering at the thought. He jumped down off the engine box and took a cigarette out of the pack in his pocket. "Anyway, it doesn't matter."

He walked astern and stood facing aft, smoking his cigarette and thinking his own thoughts for awhile.

It continued to lighten up to the east. Day was breaking.

They tonged oysters all morning. James did most of it, deftly feeling the bottom of the river with the scissors-like twenty-two-foot long tongs until he felt a big cluster, then trapping them in the basket of the tongs, and hauling them up hand-over-hand to dump the load of shellfish onto the culling board.

When the pile of oysters was fairly high, young Edward would heft his tongs onto the fantail and jump from the washboard where they stood to do the work, down onto the deck. He would quickly cull through the pile, throwing the oysters that were big enough to keep into a pile on the deck, and tossing the empty shells and undersized oysters overboard. Then he would climb back up onto the washboard, where James was still methodically, powerfully working his long pair of twenty-twos.

Now and then he would haul in the anchor and direct Edward to move the boat slowly a short distance while he felt the bottom with his tongs for a richer part of the bed to anchor over.

Edward welcomed such breaks, because the difficult labor of tonging was taking its toll on him. His arms and back ached, and his hands were blistering.

The brothers spoke little while they worked, and even when they broke for lunch, they didn't talk much. They sat up on the engine box and watched the crew of the other work boats as they wolfed down their lunch; a can of corned beef hash and half a loaf of white bread each, washed down with Pepsi Cola.

When they finished eating, James looked at the pitifully small pile of oysters and shook his head. "It ain't much, is it, boy?" he said.

"We'll do better this afternoon," Edward said. "And even better next week, when I'm back in shape for tonging."

"No," James said and shook his head again. "No, the oysters just ain't there no more."

"Yeah, they are, Bubba," Edward said. "This is just a poor bed. We'll find 'em. And when we do, we'll fill this son of a bitch to the

gunnels." He hoped so, because if the oysters were nearly gone, he might yet have to quit school and work to help pay off the bank loan.
James watched him hop back up on the washboard and take up his twenty-twos. He let the smooth handles of the tongs slide through his hands until the basket hit bottom, then felt around the dying shellfish bed in search of oysters.

Edward Walker worked beside his brother on through the afternoon, ignoring the pain. It was hard work, and it was cold. But it was honest work, and his family had been doing it for generations, and Edward supposed they would continue to do it for generations to come.

ONE

1965

Ed Walker sat on the porch of the little clapboard house where he was raised, looking out across the marshes of Guinea Neck to the York River. The sun was just coming up, but there were already several work boats out on the water, and it reminded him of his days with his brother James aboard the *Mary Anne*. Then he turned and looked in the marsh at the rotting skeleton of the old work boat his father had built, and thought, *No, those days are long gone now. God, so much has changed since then.*

His brother and Evelyn had eloped eight years earlier, and after struggling unsuccessfully for several years to earn a living on the water, James had finally given up and agreed to go into the real estate business with Evelyn's father. It was a good decision; they made a small fortune speculating on waterfront property along the York River and the Mobjack Bay.

Best of all, though, was the fact that, with Evelyn's encouragement and his own desire and hard work, Ed had graduated from high school with honors and won a scholarship to William and Mary College.

During his first two years there, he had pursued a degree in marine biology, intent upon learning all he could about the ecology of the lower Chesapeake and the marine life that had once been so abundant in the Bay. His aim at the time had been to learn how it might be rejuvenated; how the oysters and endangered species of fin fish might be not only saved, but brought back to their earlier abundance so that he and his cousins and their sons and grandsons could harvest them as their forefathers had done for three hundred years.

But Ed Walker had changed, too, and so had his goals. He was no longer fascinated by the subject of biology, for he understood now how the fauna and flora of the earth and her oceans evolved, grew, reproduced, and died. His thirst for an understanding of the creatures of the sea was quenched, and mankind became the object of his curiosity: man, with his ability to reason, to invent, to communicate; man's history, man's psychology, man's tendencies to love and to hate, to create art, and to destroy his fellow man. All these things seemed to matter more, especially after the earth-shaking day in November of 1963 when President Kennedy was shot to death. Like so many young people of that time, JFK's assassination affected Ed Walker and his values immensely; it shattered a dream and made him wonder, *Why?*

In the midst of his junior year, he changed his major to history, the field in which he felt the greatest lessons of mankind could be learned.

He read Shirer's *Rise and Fall of the Third Reich*, and it stunned him, held him fascinated by the brutality, the submissiveness, the cruel inventiveness of which man had so recently been capable. How, he wondered, could Adolph Hitler and Jack Kennedy have existed on one planet within the same lifetime? Within his *own* lifetime? How could the likes of Lester Maddox emerge two centuries later from a system founded by men like Thomas Jefferson? How? Why? Where was mankind headed?

He found himself deeply affected by the World War I and its poets; Brooke and Owen and Blunden and Sassoon, those poet-soldiers who seemed to understand the full breadth of man, from his capacity for unparalleled beauty to his capacity for such ceaseless, senseless slaughter as they had endured in the First World War. But what of the Second World War - that Holy Crusade against Hitler and the Axis enemies? And what of communism, the present brutality that was enslaving the mind and creativity of man in increasing numbers? What was it President Kennedy had said in his inaugural address? *"Let every nation know, whether it wishes us well or ill, that we shall pay any price, bear any burden, meet any hardship, support any friend, oppose any foe, in order to assure the survival and the success of liberty.*"

The more he studied, the more Ed Walker found himself believing that Americans, as free men of the strongest nation on earth, had a sacred responsibility to help others avoid the cruel bondage of communism; the enslavement of their minds, the denial of their right to reason and to make choices; their right to freedom.

In the spring of 1965, Ed Walker's senior year at William and Mary, he finally made up his mind about what he wanted to do when he finished college.

The history of man is largely the history of his wars, and some young men feel incomplete until they have been tested by its fires. It is, to some of them, the great adventure, the true test of ideals, the ultimate challenge.

War. It is recalled by veteran- politicians as proof of their strength and loyalty. It is glorified, much of the time, in print and on film. And even when its horrors are described, it often leaves young men feeling challenged by it, curious about how *they* would perform in battle.

In the spring of 1965, the opportunity to meet that challenge, to satisfy that curiosity, was readily available to the young men of America.

In some cases, the decision was made for them by the Selective Service System - an appropriate name for a system that selectively allowed military service to be deferred by those with the means to stay in college, or the political pull to find other reasons for avoiding their government's call, while the less fortunate were selected to serve.

For others, the decision sprang from family tradition, or the example of boyhood buddies, or from broken love affairs. But whatever the reasons, and regardless of the degree of willingness with which they did so, they went. Edward Allen Walker had decided to become one of them.

When the Army recruiters visited the William and Mary campus that spring, Ed wove his way through the handful of protesters outside the auditorium and listened as the recruiters explained the College Option Program.

If he could pass a battery of written tests and an interview by a board of officers, he could enlist with a guaranteed option to attend the Infantry Officer Candidate School at Fort Benning, Georgia. And they didn't give a damn whether his degree was in history, or marine biology, or basket weaving - they would take him just the same.

While he was at home for spring break shortly after that, he was helping his brother James mend the few crab pots he would use to catch enough crabs for family meals.

They were sitting on the dock at James and Evelyn's new house on Sarah's Creek when James, without looking up, asked, "So, what are you going to do with all that education, now that you're about finished with it, Bubba?" He was hoping to hear his brother say he had finally made the decision to join him in the booming real estate business.

Ed looked at him for a long moment, wondering what his response would be when he told James his plans. He recalled the aged look James had brought back with him from his war a dozen years earlier, and the bitter comments he usually spat out when he was reminded of it. But Ed felt it would be different for himself. It was a different war. And he would be a commissioned officer.

Finally, he answered his brother's question. "I've been thinking about that this whole school year," he said. "I've decided to go into the Army. As an officer."

James stopped what he was doing, looked hard into Ed's eyes, then scratched his chin with the pliers he was using to repair the wire mesh crab pot. His face was expressionless, and he went back to repairing the crab pot before he said, "Well, at least you won't freeze your ass off - not in Vietnam."

Neither of them said anything else for a long time, until James eventually broke the silence. "I'll be damned. An officer, eh?"

"Yeah, James, an officer. An Infantry officer."

Once more, James worked silently on the crab pot for a time, thinking. Then he said, "You know, Edward, I had a lot of different officers in Korea - some good, some bad. Most of the good ones didn't last long."

He had finished the last of the crab pots, and now he stacked it atop the others, lit two cigarettes, and handed one to Ed. He looked up at the sky and sighed, remembering, then he said, "The best officer I ever worked for was this one Yankee lieutenant; a guy named Grange - Dave Grange. He had been a rifleman himself in World War Two, and he knew what he was doing. Kept things simple. I mean, he stuck to the basics. Nothing fancy. Just plain, simple soldiering, like keeping your weapons clean and your feet dry. And everybody in his platoon had better know his sector of fire. And he'd better maintain noise and light discipline."

James took a deep draw of his cigarette as Ed listened attentively. He stared deep into the water as he continued talking. "Yeah, you kept your stuff straight with old Lieutenant Grange. And you carried your share of the load, or you were in for an ass whipping from Sergeant Bodecker. He was the platoon sergeant, a big ol' boy from Alabama. Dumb as a clam shell, but hard as one, too. All Grange had to say was something like, 'Sergeant Bodecker, it doesn't look to me like Smith is filling his share of sandbags,' and the next thing you knew, Smith and Bo would disappear for a little bit and Smith would come back with a fat lip. But I'll tell you what; he'd fill twice as many sandbags as anybody else, at least for awhile."

James took a last drag of his cigarette and flicked the butt into the creek, then continued. "I remember once, the chinks attacked all night; I mean the *whole* damn night. After they pulled back in the morning, and we got our wounded back to the rear, what did Grange do?

"'Prepare the platoon for inspection, Sergeant Bodecker,' he says. And then and there, with the whole goddam slope in front of us littered with gooks, we fall in for inspection. I thought he was nuts, at first. We were so tired we could hardly stand up. But he looked us over real good, and told us how we'd done fine, so far. Then he redistributed weapons and ammo, and sent us back to our foxholes.

"Good thing he did, too," James continued, "'cause the gooks came back that afternoon, and all night again, and we barely hung on. Next morning, he fell us in for inspection again. Bodecker was dead, so he fell us in himself - what there was left of us. We got a little more ammo, and he shuffled us and our weapons around again. And, sure as hell, here come the chinks again. Grange got shot himself, that night.

"Next morning, when the new lieutenant showed up with some other replacements, we were standing in ranks, prepared for inspection. 'What are you men doing standing in formation?' the new butter bar asks, and somebody says, 'Hell, sir, we're Second Platoon. We *always* stand inspection after we've been killing gooks all night!'"

James shook his head, then mumbled, "Ol' Dave Grange." He looked up at Ed and studied his face, then put a hand on his kid brother's shoulder and said, "Well, if you're gonna be an officer, Bubba, be a good one. A lot of guys' lives are going to depend on it."

Young Edward Walker looked his brother in the eye. "I will, James," he said. I'll try."

Mary McClanahan awoke with a start, and for a moment she didn't know where she was. Then she saw the old photograph of Ed Walker's parents on the wall of the bedroom, and remembered. She was in the little house that had once been their home.

The old place was seldom used anymore. Now and then, James would have some of his fishing buddies in for a card game, or Ed and some of his college friends would come over from Williamsburg for the weekend. But lately, Ed and Mary had used the house as they had the night before; a place to explore each other and the mysteries of lovemaking.

She could smell coffee, so she swung her naked body out of bed.

God, her parents would kill her if they knew she was here. It would be bad enough even if they thought she was sexually involved with one of the well-to-do prospective husbands her mother had been parading before her since she started college two years earlier. But a Guinea waterman? They would be furious. And it made little difference that he was going to make something of himself; "*He isn't our kind*," or, "*His family has no background*," is what they would say. Of course, what they *really* meant was that he had no money.

But what the heck, she thought as she brushed her hair, *I'm not going to marry him, for heaven's sake. Anyway, he's leaving soon; he's made this foolish commitment to go into the Army and off to Vietnam.*

He had told Mary so the night before and she frowned and said, "I can't believe you're going to waste a good education like that, Ed. What good is there in working so hard for a college degree if all you're going to do with your life is risk it in the *Army*, of all things?"

Ed returned the frown an said, "It's not *all* I'm going to do with my life, Mary. It's just for a couple of years. Anyway, it's... well, it's my *duty*. Just like it was your father's. And my brother's."

She gave him a distasteful look and said, "Duty. You sound like my father. Duty. Freedom. *Baloney*. I mean, it's not like there's a Hitler threatening to take over the world, or to kill millions of people again. What duty do we have to go interfere with a bunch of Orientals fighting over their rice crops, or whatever it is they're fighting about?"

"Well," he said, "that's where you're wrong, Mary. It *is* about millions of people's lives. It's about stemming the tide of communism; about people living in freedom instead of the slavery that communism brings. It's..."

"Oh, sure! Communism. Now you *really* sound like my father. My father and Joe McCarthy. And Ed Walker. The commies don't stand a chance."

"Don't make fun of me, Mary," he said softly. "I know what I'm doing, and why I'm doing it."

She stared at him for a time. He was obviously serious so she stifled the urge to ridicule his idealism, and instead she said, "Well, maybe it's just something a woman can't understand."

He smiled and said, *"Vive la difference,"* and pulled her to him, and they dropped the subject and returned to their lovemaking.

Now Mary went into the kitchen and poured herself a cup of coffee, then joined him on the porch. He pulled her onto his lap, and they kissed. Then he said, "You'll come to see me, won't you, Mary?" "Where?"

"At Fort Benning, when I'm in OCS. They have a big dance after the eighteenth week."

"That's a long way off, Ed," she said. "You'll probably have forgotten about me by then."

He turned her face toward his and looked into the beautiful, amber-flecked blue eyes that had first attracted him to her and said, "No, Mary McClanahan, I won't forget you. Not ever. I'll love you for the rest of my life." And then he scooped her up and carried her to the bedroom.

An hour later, Mary McClanahan turned off Route 17 into the lane that led through the two thousand acres of Broad Marsh Plantation to the colonnaded ante-bellum house that was her home.

She felt guilty, not so much for lying to her parents, whom she had told that she was going to spend the night in Williamsburg with a girlfriend, but because she would not let Ed Walker come there. Not yet, because she knew what her father's response would be; he would forbid her from ever seeing Ed again. Maybe after he had earned a commission as an Army officer, because that would mean a lot to her father, who had himself been an officer in the Second World War. But not yet.

TWO

"Man, I haven't felt this relaxed since we started OCS," Rocco DeCalesta declared. He and Ed Walker were sitting with their backs resting against an old live oak in the woods of the sprawling Army base at Fort Benning, Georgia.

"Me either," Ed replied, and glanced around the area. Most of the other officer candidates were also sitting on the ground, leaning against the trees behind the bleachers at Fort Benning's land navigation instruction site. At least half of the young men were asleep.

It was a rare moment of relaxation for the members of the Infantry Officer Candidate Course. For the previous four-and-a-half months they had spent at least eighteen hours a day hurrying to do something; rushing to shave and shower, running to the physical training area or the obstacle course or the mess hall. Or hurrying to get their boots spit-shined and their floors and brass uniform insignia and helmet liners polished before inspection. And when they weren't rushing, they were sitting in bleachers at outdoor training sites or at desks in the classrooms of Infantry Hall, fighting to stay awake. They were nearly worn out from it.

The only reason they were being allowed to relax now, they knew, was that for some reason the land navigation instructors were not present when the company arrived at the training site; that and the fact that only the senior tactical officer of 55th Company, First Lieutenant Moore, was there with them. He had sent Second Lieutenant Black, one of the company's junior tactical officers, off to find out why the instructors were not there. Had Black or any of the other junior tacs been present, the officer candidates knew, they would no doubt be doing pushups or conducting police call in search of cigarette butts, or something else with little other purpose than to keep them busy.

Ed looked over at Lieutenant Moore and studied him. He was only in his late twenties, but he looked much older standing there leaning against a pine tree, smoking a cigarette and staring off into the distance. He seems to do that a lot, Ed thought. It reminded him of his brother James.

And then he looked at the big black and gold First Cavalry Division patch on Moore's right shoulder and thought, *No wonder.*

Joe Moore had only recently returned from duty with the division in Vietnam after being wounded in the brutal and desperate fight at Landing Zone X-ray in the Ia Drang Valley.

It was the U.S. forces' first major battle against the North Vietnamese Army, and one of the initial duties Moore had been given by the OCS Company commander when he took over as the senior tac was to brief the officer candidates on the Ia Drang operation.

The presentation began very formally. Lieutenant Moore used a map to brief the overall situation on the ground the November day that his battalion was inserted by helicopter into the Valley of Death. He referred often to his notes at first, and it sounded to the candidates as if they were in for just another stilted, acronym-laden lecture on military history. But then the memories came back to him, and Moore forgot his notes. His voice lost its rigid tone, and it softened as his eyes took on a distant look. He spoke, in no apparent order, of noise and fear and blood; of loneliness and courage and death. He told of tall grass so thick that nearly everyone in it felt alone; as if all there was of the world was the small patch of grass where you stood. Then he told of that grass suddenly raked by machine gun fire and explosions. He mentioned two-hundred-pound men trying to hide behind inch-thick saplings, and blood so thick that it made the ground slippery, and the maddening wails of the wounded when the morphine ran out. He spoke of men shot once, and twice, and three times, and still fighting because the only other alternative was to be overrun and killed. He told of the command of platoons passing from dead lieutenants to severely-wounded platoon sergeants, to already-injured squad leaders. He mumbled about teenaged draftees earning ninety-nine dollars a month, and artillery tubes getting so hot that they split, and taxi drivers delivering telegraphed death notifications to wives and mothers in the middle of the night. He talked about men lying wounded in the elephant grass, their last realization being that the North Vietnamese were laughing as they walked among the young Americans and finished them off one-by-one with shots to the head.

He spoke for the better part of an hour before he paused. When he did, it was as quiet as death in the classroom - officer candidates and tactical officers alike frozen in silent awe at what they had heard. And finally, Lieutenant Moore said, "We lost about three hundred men in the Ia Drang Valley. If you check your history, you'll see that no regiment on either side lost that many men at the battle of Gettysburg. But we killed *thousands* of North Vietnamese. Thousands. So I guess we won... Now, what are your questions?"

There were no questions, even though many of the men wanted to ask, "But, sir, what did *you* do?" because he hadn't mentioned himself once. Not once.

They all knew that what Moore had told them was the truth, because you couldn't make up a story like that; nobody would believe it. And you couldn't invent a tale that powerful.

The company took on a greater sense of seriousness after Moore's lecture. Now they understood what they were in for, most of them did. The following day, five of the officer candidates had quit the course.

Rocco DeCalesta was speaking to Ed Walker, but Ed hadn't been listening, so he said, "What did you say, Rocco?"

"I said, are you sure Sharon is as good looking as you claim, or are you just telling me that to get a date for your girl's room mate?"

Ed looked at Rocco and smiled. "Just like Natalie Wood, Rock. I promise."

DeCalesta sighed and closed his eyes, then mumbled, "Man, I hope you're not lying to me, Walker. One more week. I can hardly wait."

Ed and Rocco had first met in adjacent barber chairs at the induction center in Fort Jackson, South Carolina, eight months earlier. Together, they had endured four months of basic and advanced training in infantry skills, and now, four months of intense regimentation in the Infantry Officer Candidate School. But relief was in sight; in another week, they would "turn blue."

Blue Day. Senior status. The big parade, and the dance, and the weekend off. And best of all, as far as Officer Candidate Edward Walker was concerned, the presence of Mary McClanahan.

He closed his eyes and remembered their last night in the old house in Guinea and said, "Eight months. I can hardly wait either, Rock."

Neither man had been on leave since the day they were sworn into the Army. Ed was disappointed that he had been unable to see Mary for so long, but the lack of time off suited Rocco DeCalesta just fine. The Italian-American had only joined the Army to avoid a pre-arranged marriage to a chubby distant cousin from the Old Country. If he was lucky, Rocco said, he wouldn't have any leave until after he got back from Vietnam; by then, maybe his fat cousin and her family, who were still in Italy, would have given up on him, and she would be married to someone else.

But his father had other ideas. To ensure that his son remained true to his betrothed, he was sending Rocco's sister Maria to be his date for the Blue Day weekend. That way, the old man figured, his son couldn't violate the pact with his cousin's family.

But Rocco had other ideas, too, and his buddy Ed Walker had agreed to help. Rocco's sister, Maria, was coming to Blue Day weekend, all right - but not to be escorted by her brother. Officer Candidate Mike Burns had agreed to escort her, and Ed had arranged a date for Rocco with Mary's college room mate, Sharon Miller. Ed had no idea what Sharon actually looked like, but he knew it didn't really matter; after eight months without even *seeing* a woman up close, Rocco DeCalesta was sure to think she was beautiful.

Ed was just imagining how the first moments in the motel room with Mary would be when his reverie was broken by the sound of a jeep approaching and his friend Rocco muttering, "Aw, shit. Here he comes."

"He" was Rocco's platoon tactical officer, Second Lieutenant Chuck Black.

Black had it in for Rocco DeCalesta. He was the sort of tactical officer whom all the candidates disliked - arrogant, humorless, tactless. Rocco, on the other hand, seemed always to be ready with a laugh and a joke. The result was that they got along like oil and water and seemed constantly to be sparring. But Black, of course, had the upper hand, and he used his powers as a tactical officer insidiously, assessing Rocco unreasonable numbers of demerits during inspections, constantly watching him to catch any mistake so that he could make Rocco do pushups or give him more demerits, and just generally making life miserable for him. Yet the more he pushed, the more determined DeCalesta was to not yield to him.

Now Lieutenant Black pulled into the training site, jumped out of the jeep, and glared around the area at the officer candidates, a few of whom were already getting to their feet. "What *is* this, gentlemen? A picnic? I thought this was an officer candidate class! On your feet! Get on your feet and fall in!" he ordered.

As the company of officer candidates scrambled into formation, Black looked inquisitively at Lieutenant Moore, who was staring at him with an almost imperceptible sneer. Then Moore turned and walked to the jeep and without even waiting for an explanation about why the instructors weren't present, he got in and drove away.

"Sir," the student company commander reported to Lieutenant Black, "the company is formed!"

Black returned his salute and said, "Well, candidates, it looks as if we have a bit of a problem here. *Someone...*" and he turned and watched Lieutenant Moore drive away, then turned back to the officer candidates. "Someone failed to notify the land navigation committee of our schedule change."

They all knew that it was the responsibility of Moore, as the senior tactical officer, to coordinate such changes. But few if any of them appreciated Black's snide remark.

"Sir! Candidate DeCalesta!" Rocco shouted, indicating he wished to be recognized.

Lieutenant Black glared at him for a moment, then said, "Yes, candidate? What is it?"

"Sir, perhaps the '*someone*' you refer to has more important things on his mind; things like the Ia Drang Valley."

Black continued to glare at DeCalesta for a time before his face broke into a toothy, phony smile. "Perhaps so, candidate. And perhaps such lapses are why there were so many men killed there."

There was a murmur of disbelief at the comment, but Black ignored it. "Well," he said, "since there are no instructors here, and no transportation; and since this is Infantry OCS, and it's only about twenty miles back to the barracks, I suppose we should do what the infantry does best."

They walked the twenty-one miles in just over five hours, and after a hurried meal in the mess hall, changed into fresh uniforms and formed up again for Blue Day parade practice.

Lieutenant Black twice required DeCalesta to drop out of formation en route to the parade field and knock out twenty-five pushups each time. He claimed that Rocco was out of step, which he was not. But the anticipation of meeting Sharon and of achieving senior status the next day had put Rocco in high spirits, so he took the unwarranted harassment in stride and complied with Black's orders without complaint.

The parade practice went well. They were proud of the way they marched, and they had reason to be. They were lean and fit and they stood tall; they looked good and they knew it. And they were about to become "third lieutenants" of infantry in the best army in the world, and most of them were more proud of that fact than they were of anything else they had ever accomplished in their young lives.

     *   *   *

There she is, Ed thought to himself. He was in the front rank of the platoon, but he was unable to look at the bleachers on either side of the reviewing stand until they had moved to the ready line and aligned themselves in perfect order.

When the company commander ordered, "Ready, *front!*" Ed snapped his head back to the front again and his eyes went straight to Mary. She was wearing a hat, as was her college roommate, Sharon, seated beside her. On the other side of her was a hatless young woman with long, dark hair. Rocco's sister, Ed correctly surmised.

The company moved up to the final line, the colors were honored with the National Anthem, and the reviewing officer made a few terse remarks about duty, honor, and country. Then he directed, "Pass in review," and the company of future officers executed the review with a degree of precision that made even the officers from West Point nod in approval.

After it was over, and after a final admonition to "hold down on the PDAs," - public displays of affection - the senior tactical officer declared, "Dismissed!"

Ed thought that the brief kiss Mary gave him when he reached her was the sweetest of his life.

"Hi, handsome," she said.

"God, you're beautiful, Mary," he replied, studying her amber-flecked blue eyes. "I've missed you."

Mary introduced him to Maria DeCalesta, an olive-skinned beauty with thick, dark hair that hung all the way to her waist, and Ed turned and looked for Rocco. He was twenty yards away, doing push ups for some reason or the other, probably contrived, as Lieutenant Black stood over him.

"That son of a bitch," Ed mumbled under his breath, then saw Mike Burns hovering nearby. "Mike! Come meet your date," Ed called. He introduced Burns to Maria, who said, "Hello, Mike. It's kind of you to agree to be my blind date."

All Burns could say in response was, "Wow!"

The new senior candidates had only a few minutes to spend with the girls before they had to return to the barracks to prepare for the evening's activities, so Mary agreed that the trio of young women would go back to the motel, get ready for the dance, and pick the men up at the parking lot outside the barracks.

"Hey, Rocco, thanks a million for setting me up with your sister," Mike Burns said as they moved back to where the student company commander was ordering them to fall in.

"No sweat," DeCalesta replied. "Just make sure you keep your hands off her, or I'll cut your balls off."

Ed laughed at the comment, then asked, "Hey, why did Black drop you for pushups awhile ago?"

"I walked by him without saluting," DeCalesta said, smiling. "Did it on purpose. I knew the prick would drop me for it."

"He's not supposed to drop you when you're in dress greens," Burns said.

"Exactly," Rocco said. "I heard the senior tac ripping his ass for it when I was walking away."

"Well, be careful, Rock," Ed warned. "We've still got five weeks to go."

"Yep," DeCalesta said, "five weeks. Then *I'll* be a second lieutenant, too, and I can knock the hell out of him."

When they met their dates in the parking lot that evening, each of the three senior candidates thought his was the prettiest girl at Fort Benning. They all were indeed lovely in their elegant evening gowns.

They passed through the reception line, behaving as perfect gentlemen in accordance with the classes in courtesy they had received as junior candidates.

Lieutenant Black leered at the senior candidates' dates when they were introduced to him as they moved through the reception line. When the senior tactical officer introduced Maria as he handed her off to Black, the next officer in line, Black said, "Miss *DeCalesta*? Well,

well." He looked her up and down, then his face broke into its phony, toothy smile and he leered at her until she pulled her hand away.

After dinner, when the dancing had begun, the bachelor officers were making the rounds from table to table, now and then asking one of the candidates' good-looking dates to dance. Most complied.

Lieutenant Black showed up at the table Ed and Mary, Rocco and Sharon, and Mike and Maria had been occupying. Ed and Rocco were dancing with their dates, and Mike had excused himself to go to the men's room.

"Would you like to dance, Miss DeCalesta?" her brother's tormentor asked.

Maria felt it would be inappropriate to refuse, and agreed to do so. The lieutenant led her to a corner of the dance floor away from where her brother was dancing, and away from the head table where the senior officers were seated.

Everything might have been all right if Rocco had not looked in that direction when he did. But he happened to notice his sister dancing just as the lieutenant reached down and gave Maria's buttocks a squeeze. She immediately backed out of his grip and turned to go back to her table, but it was too late. Rocco had seen what happened. He broke away from Sharon and hurried toward Black.

Mary saw Sharon's eyes following him, her hand to her open mouth, and stopped dancing. By the time that Ed Walker turned and saw what the young women were watching, there was nothing he could do. Rocco DeCalesta reached Lieutenant Black and floored him with a powerful, roundhouse punch.

"Oh, Jesus," Ed muttered, rushing in that direction, "No, Rocco. No!"

Everyone on the dance floor stopped, and even the band faltered when they saw the lieutenant crumple to the floor. Rocco walked to where his sister was standing, took her by the hand, and started out of the ballroom. Ed caught up with him at the door.

"Jesus, Rocco! What the hell happened?" he asked, catching his friend by the arm.

DeCalesta pulled his arm away from Ed's grip and said, "What does it look like? I cold-cocked the son of a bitch."

"But why?"

"Because he grabbed my sister's butt, that's why. What the hell was I supposed to do?"

Ed looked at Maria. Tears were streaming down her face, and she said, "Oh, Rocco, you didn't have to hit him. What will they do to you?"

Both candidates knew what they would do. They would dismiss Officer Candidate DeCalesta from OCS, and he would spend the remainder of his term of service as an enlisted soldier in an infantry unit. That was the least they would do; they might court martial him, as well.

Yes, they might also discipline the lieutenant when they found out what had happened. But that wouldn't save Rocco DeCalesta. He was as good as gone, and he and his comrades-in-arms knew it. The senior tactical officer, First Lieutenant Moore, appeared just then and said, "Candidate DeCalesta, report to the company orderly room immediately."

Rocco looked at him, still holding Maria's arm. "No, sir," he said. "I'm going to take my sister to her hotel first."

"Don't add an AWOL charge to the trouble you're already in, Rocco," the lieutenant said. It was the first time either of the candidates had ever heard the officer address someone by his first name. He turned to Ed and said, "What happened, Walker? Did you see it?"

"Black got fresh with Rocco's sister, sir," Ed said. "What was he supposed to do?"

"You know what he was supposed to do," Moore responded, then asked, "Did you see it?"

"Well, no sir, but..."

Moore looked at Maria and asked, "Is that what happened, Miss DeCalesta?"

"Yes," she said.

"Well, I apologize then. And I assure you that Lieutenant Black will be held accountable."

"What about my brother?"

Moore looked at Rocco. "You're in some trouble, Rocco. Big trouble. You should have reported it to me. But please, don't make it worse. Go straight to the orderly room. I'll see what I can do."

Lieutenant Clements, another of the company's tactical officers, showed up and motioned Moore aside.

Ed said, "You'd better go, Rock. I'll make sure Maria is looked after, OK? I'll take the girls back to the motel, then come right back to the company." He put his arm around his friend's shoulder and said, "Man, you shouldn't have let him get to you - not in front of all those people."

"What would you have done?" DeCalesta asked.

Ed looked him in the eye and said, "The same goddam thing."

Lieutenants Moore and Clements finished their brief parlay, and Moore said to the two officer candidates, "I'm afraid we've got a problem, men."

"What do you mean, sir?" Ed asked.

"Black has a different version. He says she took his hand and, well, and *put* it on her rear."

"I did no such thing," Maria said at the same time that Rocco spat, "He's a lying son of a bitch!"

Lieutenant Moore looked at Rocco, then Maria, then back at Rocco and said, "Look, someone else must have seen what happened. I'm sure Captain Ross will have an investigation to find out. Anyway, it's already the word of a good candidate and his sister against Bl... *Lieutenant* Black. Now, Candidate DeCalesta, report to the company orderly room."

The incident ruined the Blue Day dance for those who counted Rocco DeCalesta as a friend and those who disliked his platoon tactical officer, Lieutenant Black. That included most of the company.

Ed and Mike Burns were allowed to leave immediately with

the three girls, and when they reached the hotel, Ed left them in the care of Burns, indicating he would return there as soon as he could.

Lieutenants Moore and Clements were the only ones in the company when Ed got to the orderly room. "Where's Rocco, sir?" he asked Moore.

"Already gone to the holding company," Moore said.

"Holding company? I thought you were going to try to help him, sir."

"We will," Clements offered. "Maybe we can get him recycled to a later class. But you don't punch out your tac and stay in the same company, candidate. Not in *any* case."

Ed shook his head. It wasn't fair. There was a lot about OCS that wasn't fair.

"And what about Lieutenant Black?" he asked. "*He's* the one who should be in the holding company, if you ask me."

"We *didn't* ask you, candidate," Clements said. "But he'll be gone, too, regardless of the results of the investigation Captain Ross holds tomorrow." He smiled, then added, "You don't get your ass whipped by an officer candidate and stay in the same class, either."

Ed surveyed the two lieutenants, resplendent in the dress blue uniforms they had worn to the dance. They were good men, and fair. They'd do what they could for Rocco, he was sure of that.

By the time he got back to the hotel, Maria and Sharon had said goodnight to Mike Burns and gone to bed. Ed Walker and Mary McClanahan went to the room next door.

Sometime later, his uniform folded neatly across a chair and Mary's evening dress and frilly underthings strewn about the floor, Ed pulled Mary's naked body more tightly to him and said, "I love you, Mary."

"I love you, too," she whispered, rolling atop him.

A week later, after the company commander's investigation was completed and the results forwarded up the chain of command,

Lieutenant Black received orders to the Republic of Vietnam, a letter of reprimand in his official file.

Specialist Four Rocco DeCalesta was sent to parachute training, after which he was to report to the 82nd Airborne Division's replacement company at Fort Bragg, North Carolina. He would not be allowed to return to officer candidate school.

"It's not fair," Ed said when he got the news from First Lieutenant Moore.

"*Life* is not fair, Candidate Walker," Moore replied. "It's like President Kennedy once said: 'Life is unfair. Some men go to war and get killed or wounded, and some men never go at all. Life is unfair.'

THREE

Sam Hagen leaned forward in the saddle, looking over the broad valley called Jackson Hole. Beyond the valley floor where elk herds come to winter, the majestic, jagged spires of the Grand Tetons towered into the sky, their peaks outlined in orange by the setting June sun.

Surely there was no more beautiful sight than this, except perhaps the same vista in winter, when eight thousand elk migrated in to spend the season, and snow covered the spacious valley and the hills and clung to the firs and all but the steepest spires of the Tetons.

For twenty years he had watched these sunsets, and it seemed that each season of each year some new and spectacular combination of clouds and light and snow or foliage combined to form a sight more beautiful than any he had seen before. And always, across the way, those awesome peaks towering nearly two miles above the valley.

Now he wondered if he would ever see them again. Tomorrow, Sergeant Sam Hagen, United States Army Special Forces, was leaving Wyoming to return to Fort Bragg, North Carolina, where orders promoting him to sergeant and sending him to Vietnam awaited. He would have a few months at Fort Bragg for premission training before his assignment to the war zone, but he would not return to these mountains and this valley before he left. For several more minutes, he watched the Grand Tetons turn deep purple as darkness began to replace the setting sun, then reined his horse around and started down the trail to the ranch.

It was nearly dark when he got to his father's grave. It sat alone on a knoll above the corral and the cluster of buildings that were the center of activity at the Wounded Elk Ranch. Sam halted his horse and sat awhile staring at the slab of marble and mound of stones beneath which his father lay. Or more correctly, his father, a grouse, and the old man's favorite shotgun.

Sam had put the gun and the bird there the day of the funeral, before the dirt was shoveled in. He was standing with his mother and sister at the front of the funeral gathering, listening to a long-winded preacher go on and on about his father, when he heard a grouse in the clump of brush across the dirt track from the knoll. He eased out of the crowd, lifted the shotgun from the back of his battered pickup, and moved toward the brush. He killed the grouse as soon as it got up, the preacher's words replaced by murmurs from the crowd at the sound of the shotgun's blast.

Sam retrieved the bird and walked back to the grave, the crowd parting and staring at him as he walked up to the hole, then threw the grouse and the shotgun in atop the coffin.

Then he turned to face them.

"None of you really knew him," he said. "You didn't know him, and you didn't give a damn for him - especially you, preacher. So why don't you just get the hell out of here and leave us alone?" He looked at his mother and sister and added, "All of you."

The preacher started to say something, but Sam's mother halted him with a hand on his arm, and then she turned and led the way down the track to the ranch house, the others following and casting looks of dismay back at Sam.

One woman remained behind. It was Jeanne, the aging barmaid from the Camp Creek Inn down at Hoback Junction, his father's girlfriend of the last few years. She was the last person to have seen him alive, when he left her trailer to return to the ranch one morning at daybreak. He died a few minutes after that when his pickup truck skidded on a patch of ice and plunged into the rapids of the Snake River.

She looked into the hole at the coffin, the grouse, and the old shotgun, then smiled at Sam and said, "He would have liked that."

Then she picked up a handful of rocky soil and threw it into the hole, and followed the others down the hill.

That had been three years ago. Now, Sam Hagen looked at the mound of stones and threw them a half salute.

"I'll see ya," he said, and headed for the stables.

His father had bought the Wounded Elk ranch when he returned from the Pacific after World War II, forsaking the successful stucco and plastering business Sam's grandfather had established in Los Angeles. At the ranch, he ran a small herd of cattle, bred horses to sell to the increasingly popular mountain resorts and dude ranches in the Grand Tetons-Yellowstone area, and served as a hunting guide for big game hunters in the mountains around Jackson Hole.

Sam's mother, also a native of Los Angeles, had long ago tired of life at the ranch, and for the past ten years had spent more time at her parents' home in LA than she did in Wyoming. When Sam's sister Jan entered UCLA shortly before their father's death, his mother moved to the city for good.

His mother had sold the ranch shortly after the funeral, but Sam stayed on there, taking care of the place for the new owners, a group of wealthy sportsmen from back east. And then one day he stopped in at the recruiting office in Jackson, as much out of idle curiosity as anything else.

The Army recruiter was a Green Beret just back from Vietnam, where he had been a member of a long range reconnaissance outfit, patrolling the mountainous jungles of Vietnam and Laos with a handful of other men. When he learned Sam was a hunting guide, he said, "Hagen, you'd be ideal for Special Forces, doing the same kind of thing I was doing over there. We could really use a man like you."

Sam thought of what his father had done twenty-five years earlier; joined the service, fought a jungle war, then came to these mountains. He had always said he was a better man for it.

Sam might well be drafted soon anyway, the recruiter pointed out. And Sam Hagen didn't want to be like those punk friends of his sister's in southern California or like the sons of the Wounded Elk's new owners, who sat in college dodging the draft and taking part in protest marches. He was like his father, not them. He was an American, and he was proud of it, and of what he had been taught that meant.

He signed on without another thought, and after making his way through the training posts and courses that led to his becoming a Special Forces light weapons specialist, Sam had volunteered for duty in the Republic of Vietnam.

His orders came through quickly, for that had been only two weeks ago, just before he came home to Wyoming on leave.

He'd spent much of the past two weeks riding alone on the familiar trails that led deep into the mountains, enjoying the sight of the high meadows bursting into bloom, fishing the mountain lakes and streams when he was hungry, watching the moose and elk and bighorn sheep, making camp some nights in whatever valley or on whatever ridge he happened to find himself at sunset.

He hadn't even considered going to Los Angeles on leave to see his mother and sister. He cared for neither his mother's city nor her way of life, and since Jan had come up during spring break with her dope and her newly-vulgar mouth and her seeming readiness to screw everybody she met, he didn't care much for her, either.

The things he loved were here in Wyoming; his cowboy buddies, his horses, the wildlife, the mountains, the valleys and their swift, cold rivers. And those magnificent sunsets behind the spires of the incomparable Grand Tetons.

He unsaddled the old appaloosa who had been his favorite horse for many years, and patted him on the neck. "I'll miss you, old buddy," he said. "But I won't see you again."

Sam had told his friend Scott to take old Jack out in the fall and kill him for bear bait. It was better that way than leaving him there to wither away in the corral and die.

He smacked the horse on the haunch, and Jack swayed out into the corral with the other horses.

Sam heaved a bale of hay over the fence for them, and Jack came over to get some of it. Sam reached through the fence and patted him once more.

"I'll see you on the other side, old Jack," he said, then turned and walked to his pickup truck. He took one final look at the horse, then headed to town for a last few beers with his cowboy buddies.

      *   *   *

The surf fishing just below the Cape Hatteras lighthouse at Cape Point wasn't bad, considering the wind was up and the water somewhat rough and dirty. But there were enough bluefish hitting to make it interesting, and Ed Walker and Sam Hagen each caught a puppy drum of around six or seven pounds weight.

Rocco DeCalesta caught a couple of small blues and then gave up, preferring to sit on the beach and drink Hamms beer as he watched the others fish.

Ed kept checking his watch and Rocco smiled when he saw him do so. He knew Ed was anxious for four o'clock to arrive because he was supposed to meet Mary McClanahan up the beach at the lighthouse then.

Old Ed, Rocco thought as he studied the new lieutenant. He was the only one of Rocco's former OCS classmates who had bothered to get in touch with him after they were commissioned, even though more than a dozen of them had ended up at Fort Bragg. And it was just like Ed to have quickly made friends with Sam Hagen, a sergeant in Ed's Special Forces team. That would have been unheard of in Rocco's outfit in the 82nd Airborne Division. There, the officers like Ed and the noncommissioned officers like Sam would never associate with lower-ranking enlisted men such as Specialist Four Rocco DeCalesta.

But it was different in the Green Berets where Ed and Sam were assigned. There, there were many such close relationships between Special Forces officers and the noncommissioned officers they commanded. The close-knit, twelve-man 'A' teams spent most of the time training together, living side-by-side during field training exercises, and sharing the work that needed to be done in garrison without regard to rank, and those things created a similarly close comradeship during off-duty time.

It was unusual that an officer as newly-commissioned as Ed Walker was, was assigned to Special Forces. Until very recently, an officer had to be a first lieutenant before he could get into the Green Berets. But there weren't enough first lieutenants and captains volunteering for the demanding assignment now that the Vietnam war was gaining momentum. So they were letting second lieutenants volunteer for the assignment, which suited Ed Walker just fine. And as Sam said, they'd much rather have second looies who wanted the job than the disgruntled captains who were being assigned against their will.

When Ed left to meet Mary up at the lighthouse, Sam and Rocco sat on the beach watching the remaining fishermen and drinking the last few cans of beer from the cooler.

Rocco sighed deeply and Sam looked at him, knowing what he was thinking about because Sam was thinking about the same thing. Vietnam. They would both be headed there soon.

Rocco slugged down the rest of his can of beer and looked at Sam and said, "You really looking forward to getting over there, Sam?"

Hagen nodded and said simply, "Yep," then reached into the cooler and pulled out another can of beer, and handed it to Rocco. "Thanks," Rocco said, then sighed again. "I wish to hell I was looking forward to going," he said. "I can't win. If I don't get my ass shot off, I'll have to come back home and marry my fat-assed cousin. And with my luck, I'll probably have that friggin' Lieutenant Black for a platoon leader. Jesus, I can't believe a guy like that could win a Distinguished Service Cross."

Sam Hagen had heard the story of Rocco DeCalesta's nemesis, who had left OCS after his conflict with Rocco, only to get to Vietnam and win the nation's second-highest medal for bravery shortly after his arrival there. "Well," Sam muttered, "they say you never know."

The two soldiers, as yet untested in combat, fell silent then. Each was wondering how he would behave in battle. Both had heard tale after tale of timid men becoming heroes in combat, and just as many of seemingly brave men turning into cowards under fire.

After awhile, Rocco said, "So, what about this party next weekend? You going to take my sister or not?"

"You wanna date my *seester*, senor?" Hagen replied jokingly. Rocco's sister Maria was coming to Fort Bragg to visit him the coming Fourth of July weekend, as it was probably the last chance she would have to see Rocco before he left for Vietnam.

"Well, OK," Sam said after opening the last can of beer for himself. "I had in mind one of the strippers from down on Hay Street. But I guess I can do one favor for a guy I'm about to go off to war with."

"Thanks, sarge," Rocco said. "I'll write Ho Chi Minh a letter and tell him to take it easy on you."

                    *   *   *

A week later Rocco DeCalesta was regretting ever having *met* Sam Hagen. "My old man will kill me, Ed," he said. "I was supposed to look out for her - you know, make sure nobody laid a hand on her or anything. Now she says she's not even going home until after he leaves for Nam."

"Well, you can't stop love, Rock," Ed Walker said. "Anyway, Sam's a damn good man. She could do a lot worse."

"Yeah, but he's not gonna be a North Shore lawyer like the guy she's supposed to marry. Hell, he's not even *Italian*, for Christ's sake."

Ed offered him a cigarette, but Rocco waved it off, so he lit one for himself. "I thought you were against those prearranged marriages. In fact, that's why you joined up, isn't it?"

"It's not the same thing. Not to my old man, anyway. I mean, this is a *disaster*, Ed! Jesus. How could Sam *do* this? *Love*? Shit, they only *met* three days ago!"

Ed pulled two bottles of beer out of the refrigerator, popped the caps off, and handed one to his distraught friend. "Don't lay all the blame on him, Rock. You're the one who suggested he take Maria to the party. And, after all, he was good enough to tell you that they wanted to leave together. You talked like you were all in favor of it, at the time."

"Yeah, but that was just because I had too many of *these* things," Rocco said, holding up his beer.

"Where are they now?" Ed asked. He had given Sam his car to use, since Mary had driven hers down to Fayetteville. She had started back to Virginia an hour earlier.

"I wish I knew," DeCalesta said, looking at his watch. "Damn! Her flight's gone anyway, even if she changes her mind. I should have just knocked the hell out of Hagen and sent her home."

Ed raised his eyebrows at Rocco. "Pretty big order, knocking the hell out of Sam Hagen."

A car pulled up, and Ed walked out onto the balcony that overlooked the parking lot of the apartment building. "Here they are now," he announced, then said, "No, wait a minute. It's Sam, by himself."

Rocco was standing with his fists balled up when Hagen walked in. "Where the hell's my sister?" he asked Sam.

Sam looked at him, then flopped into a chair and said, "She's on the way to Chicago."

DeCalesta looked toward heaven and said, "Oh, thank God. I was afraid she meant that bullshit this morning about staying here with you."

"She did. She's gone to Chicago to tell your father she's leaving home."

Rocco threw his hands up in the air and looked at the ceiling. "I'm dead. That's it, I'm a dead man."

He paced the floor several times, then banged his fist on the table. "How could you do this, Hagen? She was a *virgin*, for Christ's sake!"

Sam looked at him, then wiped his face with his hands, and looked at her brother again. "I'm in love with her, Rock. I don't know how it happened so quickly, but it did."

Rocco stared at him and lowered himself into a chair at the dinette table. "She's just a little girl, Sam," he said pitifully. "Just a little girl who's fallen for the first guy to get in her pants."

Hagen shook his head slowly. "No. No, she's a grown woman, Rocco. There's something about her, I don't know, something mystical. Like she's lived for a thousand years."

Rocco DeCalesta eyed his sister's lover strangely. He too had sometimes felt that way about Maria. She had always seemed more mature than many women he knew who were twice her age. And she was wise beyond her years and experience. He had told her once himself that it was as if she'd lived before, and she had shrugged her shoulders and said, "Maybe that's true, Rocco. Who knows about people's souls? Maybe I have." Now he raised his palms, surrendering to the reality of his sister's relationship with the Special Forces sergeant.

"Maybe she has, Sam," he muttered. "Maybe she has."

*   *   *

"Thank you," Maria DeCalesta said to the stewardess as she took the pillow and placed it in the corner made by her seat back and the window of the airplane. She lay her head against it and closed her eyes. She was tired, but she knew she wouldn't sleep; she had too much to think about.

Sam Hagen had changed Maria's life forever, and she still couldn't fathom how much. Within an hour after meeting him, she felt that he was someone she had known forever, or someone she had been looking for ever since she had become a woman. What was it he had said that described it so well?

I can't figure it out, Maria. It's like you walked in and before I knew it, there was this feeling that I had never really met anybody from my own species before.

Chemistry, that's what they called it. "Love at first sight," wasn't it? He was rugged and handsome, yes. But that wasn't the attraction. It was the things he talked about, the things he cared for. Most guys talked about music or the weather or money or, most often, themselves.

Or they fed her flattery about her looks. Frivolous things. Sam didn't care at all about things like that. He talked about mountains, and sunsets, and animals, and a sense of duty to his country. He wasn't worried about big houses and fancy cars and nice clothes. His concerns were about too many roads in national forests, too many people killing elk and just cutting off the hind quarters. About horses being forgotten by their owners when they got old, and fishermen keeping more fish than they would eat.

He was the kind of man she had always dreamed about raising children with, and once that realization struck her, there was no turning back.

Her father would be furious, of course. He would never understand, never agree to her abandoning a meaningless life of shopping and vacation trips to big hotels on Florida beaches, and a husband who felt that showering her with diamonds and furs would atone for extra-marital affairs with the sexually frustrated wives of Chicago brokers and shopping center owners. But this was her chance for a life with some meaning to it, and she wasn't going to be denied that chance.

Maria DeCalesta touched her abdomen, wondering if perhaps she was already pregnant. She hoped she was.

$$* \qquad\qquad * \qquad\qquad *$$

"Well," Doctor Smith said, flipping his glasses up so that he could better see the expression of the young woman across the room from him, "as they say, 'the rabbit died.'"

He saw the color drain from the young woman's pretty face, and she looked down at her hands, then back at him, her eyes misty at the doctor's confirmation of her pregnancy.

"You won't tell my parents?"

"No, of course not. That's up to you to do."

She stood and said, "What do I do next, Doctor Smith?"

"You start taking care of that little child inside you by taking care of yourself." He handed her the pamphlet on prenatal care he was holding. "This should cover everything you need to know, but if you have any questions, anything at all, you give me a call. Otherwise, I'll see you in six weeks."

She took the pamphlet and flipped absently through it. "That's all?" she asked.

"That's all. This is a pregnancy, not some medical emergency. Pregnancy and birth happen thousands of times every day, don't forget, and usually without interference from a physician."

She nodded. "Six weeks, then," she said.

She walked out into the bright sunlight and looked around, half expecting to see her father standing there glaring at her, but there was not even another patient going in to see Dr. Smith.

She got into her car and started it, then turned it off, lay her forehead against the steering wheel, and sobbed.

She wouldn't tell her father until she got back from Fort Bragg, or her mother either, for that matter. The baby's father deserved to be the first to know. What would he say? He had already hinted at marriage, but it was always in the context of "after I get back from Vietnam."

Suppose he wanted her to get an abortion? Should she? Maybe she should just have one without even telling him.

She wiped her eyes and started the car again. No, she decided, he wouldn't want her to do that. Not Ed. He would make her Mary McClanahan Walker. And then he would go off to war.

*   *   *

Second Lieutenant Edward Walker stood at the front of Abingdon Episcopal Church in his dress blue uniform. His best friend and best man, Sergeant Sam Hagen, also in dress blues, stood beside him.

As they watched James escort Mary's mother up the aisle, Sam studied the guests; on Ed's side of the aisle, his watermen friends and his myriad cousins, and a sprinkling of soldiers in uniform. And of course Maria DeCalesta, his own true love, seated beside her brother Rocco.

Many of the women among Ed's guests wore simple cotton dresses without hats or gloves, and an equal number of the men were without suit coats or sport jackets, and some had on no neckties.

Mary's side of the aisle held ladies in elegant dresses and fashionable hats, and men perspiring in the heat of the August afternoon beneath suits and ties. All but a few of these men were pallid, and Sam supposed that the ones with suntans had gotten them on the golf course, in contrast to the hard working watermen across the aisle from them, whose tans were deep on weathered skin. How much more sensibly the folks from Guinea were attired, he thought, for a hot and humid Gloucester County afternoon.

The organ music increased in volume, and Mary's maid of honor and former college roommate, Sharon Miller, glided slowly up the aisle. Ed looked at her, and then at Rocco DeCalesta, and smiled. The two of them had disappeared from the rehearsal dinner the night before, no doubt to make up for the time they had missed at the Blue Day formal. Blue Day, Ed Walker thought. God, it seemed so very long ago, and so much had changed since then.

The Wedding March began, and Mary appeared on her father's arm. Her wedding dress was the simple kind that only a beautiful woman could make look elegant, and its simplicity seemed perfect to bridge the difference in dress between Ed's guests and her own; that was why she had chosen it.

When she saw Ed standing there in his uniform, the sense of panic that had gripped her the last two days all but disappeared. A few minutes earlier, when her father had said, "It's still not too late to back out of this, you know," she had nearly given in to the panic, and fled. But it would be all right, now. He was no longer a poor waterman; he was a college graduate now. A commissioned officer, soon to be leading men to battle in an exotic, distant land. Even her father had acknowledged what that meant; he was of *their* class, now, or nearly so. And he was, after all, the father of the child she carried within her.

The reception at Broad Marsh spilled out of the big house and out among the old boxwoods below the veranda, down toward the spacious fields. The crop had long ago changed from the tobacco that made the original owners wealthy to the corn and soybeans that gave the current ones a good tax break.

"No horses," Sam Hagen remarked to Maria DeCalesta as they surveyed the spacious fields. "I'm surprised."

She looked at him, then at the big house, then back at the fields below. "What would you raise here, if you owned the place, Sam?" she asked.

He smiled at her, then put his arm around her and gave her a rough hug. "Boys," he said. "Boys and horses."

"Hey, Sam! Sis!"

They turned to see Maria's brother Rocco and his girlfriend Sharon waving them toward the house. "Come on. They'll be leaving soon."

A gauntlet of rice throwers was forming on the steps beneath the towering columns of the front porch, and the four of them joined it.

The newlyweds came out and, to the cheers of the well wishers, ran to the car as a storm of rice rained down on them. Ed helped Mary into the passenger side, then ran to the driver's side and waved to the crowd. Then he froze in place, and his expression became dark and serious. He was looking at Sam Hagen and Rocco DeCalesta. He walked back around the car to them.

"I'll see you guys in a couple of months, OK?" he said. "Just keep your heads down."

Sam nodded. "No sweat, sir. I'll drop you a line as soon as I find out which team I go to. You have a good honeymoon."

Sam held out his hand for Ed to shake, but the lieutenant ignored it and gave the sergeant a hug. Then he hugged Maria and said, "Give him a good sendoff, OK?"

"You can bet on it," Maria said, and kissed his cheek.

Ed turned to her brother Rocco. "Rock, you let me know where you are, too. I'll find some way to get to see you, hook or crook."

Rocco nodded, but said nothing, and Ed gave him a hug, then stepped back a couple of paces and saluted his comrades-in-arms.

They returned the salute, and the wedding party clapped and cheered, and the rice barrage began anew. Then Ed hopped into the car, and Lieutenant and Mrs. Edward Walker drove away, the horn blaring as they tore down the tree-lined lane of the old plantation.

"Are you sure you want to go to Ocracoke?" Ed asked, hugging his bride to him.

Mary had said she wanted to honeymoon in the little village on the isolated barrier island on North Carolina's outer banks. It was a five hour drive and a forty minute ferry ride to Ocracoke Island.

"I'm sure," she replied. "But not until tomorrow. Stop at the first motel you come to. Ocracoke can wait."

They got to the little fishing village the next afternoon, and checked in at the Bluff Shoals motel. It was the following morning before they ventured out.

The village of Ocracoke, with its charming white lighthouse that has stood as a beacon to mariners since 1823, forms a crescent around a little circular harbor. Just outside the harbor, where the water was deep enough even then, the pirate Edward Teach, better known as Blackbeard, used to anchor in the early 18th century when he wasn't preying on passing merchant ships. The channel there is still known as Teach's Hole where Blackbeard was caught and beheaded in 1717 by Lieutenant Maynard of the Royal Navy.

Ocracoke has long been a favorite stopover of sailors making their way along the east coast of North America.

It was to the little harbor that the newlyweds wandered after breakfast. They walked up and down the several docks where trawlers, working skiffs, and sailboats were tied. Ed looked at the transom of each sailboat to see where it was from. One of the boats was a new sloop of about twenty-eight feet, and Ed looked at the name. He stopped and pointed, and said to Mary, "Hey, look at that. *Mary Anne.* And she's from Gloucester Point!"

Mary was smiling broadly when he looked at her. "It's ours," she said. "My father's wedding present."

They took the *Mary Anne* on a trial run into Pamlico Sound that afternoon. She sailed well and handled easily, and, that determination made, they anchored to make love before heading back into the creek.

"Where do you want to keep her while I'm gone?" Ed asked his bride as he tied up to the dock. Ed was as pleased as he could be with the generous wedding gift. He avoided any mention of the fact that he thought it was unwise to give such an extravagant present to a man who would soon be off to war for a year. The wood-hulled boat would require a lot of maintenance, and he certainly couldn't saddle his pregnant bride with that responsibility.

"Dad says we should keep it at Gray's marina in Sarah's Creek. He said to tell you that you could either leave it here, and he'll have someone sail it up there, or we can sail up there, and he'll get the car brought up."

"Do you feel up to sailing for a couple of days?" Ed asked. They had plenty of time, as he had taken two weeks leave. He didn't have to be back at Fort Bragg for another week.

"A couple of days?" Mary asked. "What's the rush? We can just sail up to the bay, find a cove to anchor in, and try to figure out how many different ways there are to make love on a sailboat."

They checked out of the motel, bought several days worth of provisions at the community store, and checked the weather forecast. It looked fine for the next few days.

They made the most of it, and four days later, as Ed lowered the sails to put into Sarah's Creek under the power of the boat's auxiliary motor, Mary Walker looked at her husband and smiled. "About thirty-five, I figure," she said.

"Thirty-five what?"

"Thirty-five different ways to make love on a sailboat."

Ed killed the motor and tossed the anchor overboard.

"Because," he said, taking her by the hand and leading her down into the cabin, "we're going for an even three dozen."

PART TWO

FIRE

"When it has leveled everything, fire burns itself out, and so does a lie."

Samuel Shellabarger; *Lord Vanity*

FOUR

The Huey helicopter descended almost straight down toward the yellow 'H' on the landing pad. There was an increasing amount of enemy presence in the hills and jungle covered valleys around Camp Thuong Duc, and the pilot wanted to avoid being taken under fire from them.

Sergeant First Class Newton leaned over and yelled above the noise of the whining engine and beating rotor blades of the helicopter, to the other passenger sitting atop the pile of medical supplies, mail bags, and cases of patrol rations.

"Let's get this stuff off loaded in a hurry, sir. We'll get mortared for sure if we sit here for more than a minute."

Lieutenant Edward Walker stopped studying the little ridge top fortress long enough to look at Newton and nod in acknowledgment, then he looked back out of the open door.

Camp Thuong Duc sat on a knoll atop a long ridge between two valleys. The one to the north, covered in jungle, was between that ridge and a mountain that sloped up away from the valley. The valley south of the camp was broad and flat, and a wide, dirty brown river flowed through it from the mountains west of the camp; a chain of mountains stretching as far as the eye could see. Somewhere out there, not too distant, was the Laotian border, marked only by a dotted line on maps of the region. On the other side of the river valley, a huge cliff rose almost straight up to a high plateau. Atop the cliff, there were clumps of bushes and irregular fields of growth, not the seemingly impenetrable jungle like that to the north and west of the camp.

The helicopter settled with a jolt in a swirling cloud of red dust, and Ed hopped out to retrieve his rucksack and duffel bag. SFC Newton, assisted by the door gunners, was already slinging boxes and bags from the helicopter onto the landing pad. A moment later the helicopter lifted off. The storm of dry red clay it created filled Ed's eyes, ears, and the collar of his jungle fatigue uniform.

He wiped his eyes to clear them, and looked around. There was no one else in sight, just the piles of boxes and mailbags. Then there were two explosions just outside the camp's defensive wire, and Ed ducked to a squat.

"Lieutenant!" a voice from behind him yelled. "In here! We've got incoming!"

He turned and saw SFC Newton motioning him to a sandbagged bunker beside the landing zone. He ran to the bunker and ducked inside.

Newton pulled him away from the bunker door and said, "The next ones will be on target."

Ten seconds later, there were two more explosions so near the bunker that sand was jarred from the protecting sandbags of the bunker roof onto their heads. "Eighty-twos," Newton said. A few seconds later, another pair of mortar rounds landed in what seemed to be the same place as the last two.

"Cigarette?" the sergeant asked. Ed's eyes were becoming adapted to the bunker's darkness, and with shaking fingers, he took a Pall Mall from the pack that Newton held out to him.

After a couple of drags from his cigarette, Newton said, "Looks like that's it," and stepped outside the bunker. "Aw, shit," he said as Ed stepped out behind him. One of the rounds had impacted in the pile of medical supplies and mail. There were letters blowing all over the landing zone.

Two more Americans and a half-dozen stocky Orientals in striped camouflage "tiger suits" appeared. The latter were hill tribesmen of the Bru tribe of Montagnards, one of the ethnic minorities of Vietnam from which the Special Forces recruited their Civilian Irregular Defense Group soldiers. One American and the tiger suited CIDG soldiers began carting off the undamaged boxes. The other looked in the direction of Walker and Newton.

"Newt!" he called. "How was Bangkok?"

"Outa sight, sir," Newton replied. It was only then that Ed noticed the bareheaded man was wearing embroidered captain's bars on one side of his collar. The other side bore the crossed rifles of an infantry officer.

"And you're Ed Walker," he said to Ed, holding out his hand. "Welcome to Thuong Duc. I'm Snake Mullins"

"Thank you, Cap'n," Ed replied, shaking his new commander's hand.

"Grab your gear and I'll show you your hootch, Ed," Mullins said when they had picked up the last of the letters. "You'll be rooming with one of the medics, Pete Gregovich. *The* medic, for the time being. Our other doc and one of the engineers got nailed day before yesterday, and we haven't gotten replacements in yet."

"How'd they get hit?" Ed asked, swallowing. He had only been in the camp for a few minutes, and already he'd been mortared and learned of the loss of two of his eleven American teammates.

Mullins pointed to the plateau south of the river. "Ambush," he said. "Up there, trying to find the damned mortars you just got a taste of. Sticks - that's our intel sergeant, Sticks Howard - will brief you up on the whole situation around here. It ain't too pretty at the moment."

Captain Mullins led Ed into a bunker beside the camp dispensary. There were two bunks, two metal wall lockers that reached to the sandbagged roof of the ten-by-ten foot room, and a pair of folding chairs. One of the wall lockers was peppered with jagged holes. The room was lighted by a single, bare bulb hanging from the middle of the ceiling.

"I'm afraid this is it, for the time being," the team leader said. "The team house took a 122 rocket hit a week or so ago. Blew the place apart like a can of beans in a campfire. The XO was the only one in there at the time, thank God." He shook his head, remembering, then looked at Ed. "Real mess, what was left of him. That's why you're here. Welcome to Thuong Duc."

Ed swallowed again, then threw his duffel bag on the canvas cot, and dropped his rucksack beside it.

Master Sergeant Bruno Kadlewicz and Sergeant First Class Sticks Howard were waiting in the tactical operations center, or TOC, when Mullins and Walker arrived.

Kadlewicz and Ed had served together in the same company at Fort Bragg for several months, and when Ed recognized him, he said "Why, howdy there, Sergeant K!"

Kadlewicz, who was busy going over the operations summary he would use to brief the new lieutenant looked up, and when he recognized the dusty lieutenant, said, "Hey, it *is* the same Lieutenant Walker! Good to have you out here, sir." He glanced at Captain Mullins and nodded as if to say, "I know this one. He's OK."

They shook hands warmly, then Kadlewicz said, "This is Sticks Howard, sir. Best intel sergeant in I Corps."

Ed shook the hand of the intelligence sergeant, who said, "Welcome aboard, sir."

"Thanks," Ed replied, then looked around the TOC. It was an underground bunker constructed of four eight-by-eight foot corrugated steel shipping containers, with ten-inch thick wooden beams resting atop them to form a roof over the space between the containers. Piled on top of the whole thing were layer after layer of sandbags for protection from mortars and artillery. One of the containers held a bank of radios and space for a radio operator. Another had two field desks in it; one for Kadlewicz, the team sergeant, and the other for the intelligence sergeant, SFC Howard. On two of that container's walls were maps of the Thuong Duc operational area, some 1600 square kilometers, most of it mountainous jungle.

The third Conex container, as the heavy shipping boxes were called, served as an office for the team's two officers. It held a filing cabinet, a metal desk, and two chairs.

The fourth container was crammed with neatly stacked batteries, maps, water cans, rations, two footlockers of emergency medical supplies with red crosses painted on them, Coleman lanterns, ammunition, and other items that made it evident that the bunker was not only the camp's operations center, but its last-ditch-stand position, as well.

The open space between the Conex containers held ten folding chairs facing two easels and a chalkboard. On the easels were two map boards covered with acetate. On one, known enemy positions and recent activity were annotated with red grease pencil. There were numerous red boxes on the west and south sides of the map, and a few on the north.

The other map showed in blue grease pencil, the recent, current, and planned positions of friendly forces. Except for a pennant drawn in a small, irregular circle in the middle of the map - Camp Thuong Duc itself - there were only a few blue symbols drawn near the camp.

"We'll let Sticks brief you up on the enemy situation first, *Thieu Uy*," Sergeant K. said. *Thieu Uy*, Ed knew, was Vietnamese for second lieutenant. "Then I'll tell you what we have, and how we plan to deal with them."

Ed took a seat, and one by one, SFC Howard pointed out the enemy locations on the map and told what he knew or suspected was at each. As Captain Mullins had pointed out, it wasn't a pretty situation around Thuong Duc at the moment. It appeared that two North Vietnamese Army regiments, supported by local Viet Cong guerrilla units, were moving in to lay siege to the camp, probably in an effort to overrun and eliminate it.

"Problem is," Kadlewicz said when Howard had finished his briefing, "we've been having too much success hitting the troop units and supplies they're trying to move from the Ho Chi Minh trail in toward Danang, and they've got the ass at us. So they're going to try to get rid of us."

Ed shifted nervously in his seat and lit a cigarette as Kadlewicz got up and moved to the operations map, which listed the friendly units in and around the camp.

Including the new executive officer of the A team at Thuong Duc, Ed Walker, there were ten Americans assigned to the camp.

Their counterpart team of *Luc Luong Dac Biet* – Vietnamese Special Forces - consisted of one officer, one officer-aspirant, and four noncommissioned officers. The board showed, however, that only the aspirant and two NCOs were present for duty.

"Where are the other LLDB?" Ed asked.

Who the hell knows?" SFC Howard interjected. "Or cares, for that matter."

Master Sergeant Kadlewicz let Howard's comment slide and said, "Usually only about half of them are in camp at a time - except on payday, of course. And with the NVA moving in, I expect that'll drop to one or two."

The generally inferior quality of Vietnamese Special Forces - LLDB - was common knowledge among their American counterparts. Most of the LLDB officers were commissioned because of family or political ties to the South Vietnamese hierarchy, and their subordinates were often picked for their subservient qualities as opposed to their military abilities. But they were not *all* inferior, and Kadlewicz wanted to be certain that Lieutenant Walker understood that, so he said, "Aspirant Hung and Sergeant Tran are the two who will probably stay. I hope so, anyway. They both have their stuff together. Hung is a Northerner who really believes in what he's doing, and Tran is a fighter."

"They get along well with the 'Yards, too," Howard added. "That's unusual for any Vietnamese, especially LLDB."

The Montagnard tribesmen, though official residents of the Republic of Vietnam, felt no loyalty to their government. In fact, they considered themselves a separate nation, and had a well organized underground separatist movement. They had been fighting the ethnic majority, who still referred to them as *moi* - "savages" - since time immemorial in an effort to gain independence for their mountain tribes.

Kadlewicz moved his finger to the portion of the chart that showed the organization and number of Civilian Irregular Defense Group soldiers, the troops who were recruited, trained, paid, and ultimately led into combat by the American Green Berets.

"We have three companies of CIDG," he said. "'Camp Strike Force' companies, as group headquarters now calls them. 1st and 2nd Companies are Bru tribesmen, and 3rd Company is ethnic Vietnamese from the handful of villages in the district east of us."

Each unit had around 130 men assigned, and the Montagnard companies, the chart showed, had all but a few present for duty. The company of ethnic Vietnamese, 3rd Company, had only about half its members present.

Kadlewicz pointed to the 3rd Company figure and remarked, "They usually have about a hundred in camp, but when the NVA are around, that number drops off in a hurry."

"Second jobs with the enemy, probably," Howard added cynically.

"The ones that are left are pretty good, though," Kadlewicz said, "especially when Tran and Hung are around to lead them."

"How are the Bru companies?" Ed asked. He seemed to recall from premission briefings that the Bru were not the most highly respected of the Montagnard tribes.

"Well, 2nd Company is pretty good, but 1st Company is another story. They've only been around for a few months, and we haven't been able to keep the same Americans with them for more than a month or so, because of transfers and casualties. They're the ones who got ambushed up on the plateau the other day." Kadlewicz pointed to a spot on the map south of the camp. "Right here's where they got it," he said.

Just then, one of the radios in the commo room hissed, and a voice called, "Punchbowl, Punchbowl, this is Rattler. Fire mission, over."

Another voice on the radio responded almost immediately, "Rattler, Punchbowl. Send your mission."

Kadlewicz immediately headed for the bunker door, saying, "Let's go, Lieutenant! That's Carl Brown calling our four-point-two inch mortars for fire support. We'll help Nicholas shoot the mission!"

He grabbed two steel helmets from pegs on the wall near the entrance and handed one to Ed, then they ran to the sandbagged pits where the big mortars were going into action. Captain Mullins was already there, manning one of the mortars. SFC Newton was on the other. They were traversing the tubes in response to the data Nicholas was calling from the tiny fire direction center bunker between the pits as two Vietnamese soldiers prepared the propellant charges on the mortar rounds.

"You hang rounds for Newt," Kadlewicz said as he hopped into the pit with Mullins.

Ed jumped into the other pit, accepted one heavy round from the Vietnamese soldier who was cutting charges, and double-checked the charge and fuze, then waited for SFC Newton to level the bubbles of the mortar sight and call, "Up!"

When both mortars were ready, Nicholas yelled, "Hang 'em!" and Walker and Kadlewicz loaded the charged ends of the big rounds into the top of the tubes.

"Fire!" Nicholas commanded, and the men dropped the heavy projectiles. Kadlewicz ducked his head well beneath the level of the tube, but Ed did not. The concussion of the propellant's blast almost knocked his helmet off and sent him staggering back, holding his ringing ears. He looked at Newton, who was yelling something, but Ed couldn't hear.

"What?" he yelled back.

Newton put his face close to Ed's ear, "I said, get your head lower next time! Get some more rounds ready! Charge twelve!" Then he leaned over the mortar to level it.

Ed shook his head to clear it, straightened his helmet, and began taking the rounds the CIDG mortarman handed to him. He checked the charge and fuze of each, then lined them up on the sandbag wall of the mortar pit.

There were four rounds there when he heard, above the ringing in his head, Nicholas call, "Repeat! Fire for effect! Three rounds!"

"Hang one!" Newton said, and rechecked to ensure the bubbles were leveled as Ed hung another round in the muzzle of the mortar tube.

"Fire!" This time, Ed ducked his head well below the muzzle as he dropped the round into the mortar tube.

Twice more Newton quickly leveled the mortar and ordered, "Fire!" and Ed dropped rounds into the tube. There were six rounds arching toward the target now, and Ed pictured them impacting among the enemy mortar crew, hot shards of jagged iron ripping through the men as round after round exploded. And then Nicholas yelled, "Incoming!" and the image in Ed's mind changed to one of him and Newton and Mullins and Kadlewicz being subjected to the same sort of deadly barrage. He looked around to see where the others would run to hide, but all they did was duck a bit lower into the mortar pits, so he did the same.

Between explosions of the incoming rounds, Ed heard Nick repeat Rattler's radio transmission: "Target destroyed! End of mission, out!"

The mortarmen remained in the pits until they were confident that they had won the duel and the attack against them was over. Then Captain Mullins climbed out and looked around to see if it had caused any additional damage to the camp. Kadlewicz and Newton joined him, as Ed Walker watched them from the pit. He wondered how his teammates managed to take the incident with such matter-of-fact calmness. Could they really be used to this? Or was it that they had developed such fatalistic attitudes that they figured there was no use worrying about it; if their time was up, that was it. And where the hell, Ed wondered, were all of the CIDG soldiers?

Sergeant First Class Nicholas came out of his bunker and walked over as Ed climbed out of the mortar pit. "You must be the new XO."

"Yes," Ed replied, holding out his hand to the wiry mortarman. "Ed Walker."

"Nick Nicholas. You handled those rounds like you know what you're doing, sir."

"Well, other than nearly taking my own head off with the first one. What else do we have here in the way of fire support, Sergeant Nicholas?"

"Three eighty-one mortars and a pair of 106 recoilless rifles. You'll get plenty of practice using them all, the way its going around here these days. When you have some time, come see me, and I'll show you how we're set up."

Ed nodded then walked over to the others. An American he hadn't yet met was with Mullins and Newton. He hadn't been in the camp an hour - hadn't met even half the team - and already he'd been under attack by mortars twice. He didn't even know his way around the little fortress, yet. *What the hell would I do*, he wondered, *if Captain Mullins had gotten hit just then, and I had to assume command of the camp?*

Kadlewicz introduced Ed to the other Special Forces NCO, Sergeant First Class Farley. Farley looked down his bloated, red-veined nose at the lieutenant and said, with breath that smelled of whiskey, "*Second* Lieutenant Walker, huh?" Then, to the team sergeant, said, "What the hell are they sending us second looies for, when I need NCOs for my company?"

"We need an XO, too, Farley," Captain Mullins said. "You'll get some replacements in a day or so. Meanwhile, Howard and Saxon will go with you." Mullins looked at Ed, and added, "Lieutenant Walker can help you out, too."

Farley looked at the lieutenant standing there in his sweat-soaked, brand new jungle fatigues and said, "Yeah, sure," then walked away laughing.

Mullins looked at Walker. "Farley's got 1st Company," he said. "He's just frustrated, right now. He lost both his NCOs the other day, and he's had his nose in the jug. He'll be all right when he gets back out in the field."

"Maybe," Kadlewicz muttered, then said to Ed, "Let's finish getting you briefed up, sir."

As they walked back to the TOC bunker, Ed noticed a number of Montagnard soldiers in tiger suits emerging from bunkers around the perimeter of the camp. Many of them followed him with their eyes, wondering who this new "roundeye" was.

When they got back to the command bunker, there was a Vietnamese Special Forces sergeant there, and Kadlewicz introduced him to Ed. It was Sergeant Tran, one of the two LLDB - Vietnamese Special Forces - of whom the Americans had spoken highly. "A fighter,"Ed remembered one of them saying.

Master Sergeant Kadlewicz resumed the operations briefing by pointing out the one block on the organizational chart he hadn't covered before the mortar exchange.

"Headquarters company is Nicholas's. He has the heavy weapons platoon, the cooks, and supply room. You'll be dealing with him on supply matters, and me on admin."

Ed nodded in acknowledgment. As the team executive officer, he would have primary responsibility for administration and logistics at the isolated camp. In addition, he would be performing as an infantry unit leader on combat operations when it was his turn to take elements of the camp strike force to the field. He was also to be prepared to take command of the entire camp in the event that Captain Mullins became a casualty or was absent for any reason. Ed hoped that wouldn't be anytime soon.

Kadlewicz returned to the map, showing Ed where 3rd Company would set up ambushes on approaches to the camp that night, and where 2nd company would be operating for the remainder of the day and night. "They're moving down here to sweep along the river to the west to roll up any that may have moved in close to us."

There was a dashed circle of blue on the ridge west of the camp, about a kilometer away. Kadlewicz pointed to it and said, "We're getting a Mike Force company from Danang day after tomorrow. This is where they'll set up their patrol base, to block anybody from coming after us down the ridge line."

The Mike Force, short term for "Mobile Strike Force," was the reaction force that the Special Forces company in each of Vietnam's four corps areas maintained to counter such threats as the one now facing Camp Thuong Duc. In addition, there was a Mike Force at group headquarters to react to Special Forces needs throughout Vietnam.

"Is one more company enough to do any good?" Walker asked. The two enemy regiments believed to be moving against the camp gave the enemy a numerically superior force some five times that of the friendly forces there, even after taking into account the company of Mike Force, which had not yet arrived. Ed Walker didn't see how even the Americans' advantage of unchallenged air supremacy could possibly offset that.

"Hell no, it's not enough," Kadlewicz admitted. He looked around the TOC to make certain the LLDB sergeant was gone, then said, "What I'm about to tell you is secret info, sir. For God's sake, don't let the LLDB know."

Ed looked at him quizzically and said, "Not even Tran and the aspirant?"

"No, sir. Hell no. The VC will know within an hour, if they don't already."

The distrust of their LLDB counterparts by his teammates was disturbing to Ed, and he wondered if it was well-founded.

The team sergeant moved to the small safe in the corner, opened it, and withdrew an acetate overlay. He placed it over the map and aligned it with the grid lines. Ed moved closer so he could see it. There were two one-kilometer by three- kilometer rectangles on the overlay, each with a series of numbers in it. One covered a portion of the plateau to the south, the other the same ridgeline on which the camp was positioned, but well to the west.

"Arclights," Kadlewicz said, smiling. "B-52 strikes. Sixty tons of bombs each. The plateau tonight, and the troop concentration up the ridge tomorrow night."

He removed the overlay, placed it back in the safe, and spun the lock. Ed moved to the intelligence map and compared the locations of the planned airstrikes with the symbols depicting known and suspected enemy positions. About half would be covered by the twin rectangles of death. He had seen films of arclights at Fort Bragg. The exploding hailstorm of bombs would turn the earth to cratered moonscape, and even men hundreds of meters from its edges were likely to become casualties of the massive series of concussions it created.

"Jesus," Ed said softly. Now he understood why his team mates seemed fairly unconcerned about the enemy on three sides of them.

"You'll get to see the results up on the plateau yourself tomorrow, if you go with Farley," Kadlewicz said. Then he looked at his watch and said, "Let's grab some lunch, then I'll show you around the place."

The team mess hall served as both a dining hall for the Special Forces A detachment, and a bar and recreation area. Several men from Nicholas's headquarters company served as cooks and dishwashers. It was a room of about twenty by twenty feet in size, not counting the attached kitchen. There were two tables with six chairs each on one side of the room, and a bar with four stools at it, against the other wall. The walls were decorated with Playboy pinups and enemy flags and rifles.

"Air conditioning," Kadlewicz said as they entered, pointing to the ceiling. There was a large hole with smaller ones surrounding it in the tin roof - the results of a direct hit by an enemy mortar round.

Nicholas and Mullins were there, and a staff sergeant who stood up and introduced himself to Ed as Pete Gregovich. "We're roommates, I guess. Until we get a new team house built, anyway. I'm also the only medic we have right now. How's your health?"

Ed shook his hand and said, "Fine. No problems."

There were ten paper cups in a group in the center of the table, and Gregovich picked up one that had "Walker" written on it. He handed it to Ed and said, "Keep it that way, sir. Here's today's dose of pills - malaria prophylaxis and vitamins. I'll make sure you have what you need in here in your cup every day. If you're in the field, it's up to you to take 'em."

Ed nodded. It seemed that Gregovich, like every Special Forces medic he had met since he'd donned a green beret, had his stuff together.

Ed looked around the room then up at the ceiling at the "air conditioning" that Kadlewicz had pointed out when they entered.

"Y'all aren't worried about a mortar round hitting this place when everybody's in here?" he asked, trying to sound only mildly concerned.

"Nah," Nicholas said. "Somebody usually hears the rounds leave the tube and yells 'incoming,' so you've got ten or fifteen seconds to haul ass. And if it's too windy to hear 'em fire, it's too windy for 'em to get a first round hit, unless they're lucky. Getting mortared hasn't been a problem here until the last few days, anyway. We usually only get a few rounds every couple of weeks."

"Hopefully, it'll be like that again, after tonight's little surprise," Kadlewicz said. The others knew he was referring to the planned airstrike by B-52 bombers.

"What time's the show start, anyway, top?" Gregovich asked.

"0050 local time," Kadlewicz said. 12:50 AM.

An old Vietnamese man brought plates of food to Walker and Kadlewicz. "This is Pop," Kadlewicz said.

"Fought on the French side at Dien Bien Phu, right Pop?"

The wiry old Vietnamese nodded. "Maybe soon Thuong Duc same same Dien Bien Phu," Pop said worriedly. "Beaucoup VC!"

"I wouldn't worry about it, Pop," Gregovich said. "The French didn't have B-52s."

Kadlewicz glared at him. "Stow it," he said.

The medic shrugged, then slid a bowl of hot pepper sauce in front of Ed.

"No, thanks," Ed said.

"Eat some and start getting used to it, sir," Gregovich counseled. "It'll keep the parasites out of your innards."

Ed followed Kadlewicz's lead and spread a liberal amount of it on his meat and potatoes. After a couple of bites, he had downed all of his iced tea, and was looking desperately around for more, his eyes watering. "Whew!" he said, wiping the sweat from his brow. "That stuff will clean out your pipes, all right."

Nicholas grinned. "That's nothing," he said. "Wait till that big orange malaria pill you just took kicks in. You'll be shittin' like a goose eatin' Ex-lax!"

FIVE

Lieutenant Edward Walker, the executive officer of Special Forces Operational Detachment A-109, Camp Thuong Duc, lay on the bare mattress of his bunk in his drawers, smoking a cigarette and staring at the sandbagged ceiling of the dimly lighted bunker that was his new home.

He was frightened and he was lonely. The fear wasn't an hysterical sort, but the kind that lies heavily deep in one's belly in situations of unfamiliar danger. And the loneliness was not that of a person without friends, but of a young man with a beautiful wife that he wouldn't see, wouldn't touch, for a full year.

He looked over at Mary's photograph in the five-by-seven inch silver frame someone had given them for a wedding present. He had wired it to the door of his wall locker as soon as he returned from the damaged supply shed with his new weapon, ammo, bed sheet, and other items of standard issue at Camp Thuong Duc. It was a photograph he'd taken aboard the sailboat her father had given them. Her head was thrown back, hair blown by the wind, and she had a smile on her face. He had selected it because of the way it showed the color of her eyes, the speckles of amber in blue irises. It seemed as if a year had already passed since he had held her. And as if a lifetime would pass before he could do so again.

A lifetime. Out here, that could be no time at all. One well placed Katusha rocket, one lucky mortar round, was all it took. No amount of training, nor of dedication or sense of duty or bravery mattered, when the rounds rained down as they already had twice during his first day at Thuong Duc.

Maybe out there, out in the jungle, it was different. There, skill and training and even daring might make a difference, might give him the edge. But sitting here in this tiny outpost, surrounded by enemy forces bent on its destruction, only luck mattered, it appeared.

He hadn't written a letter to Mary since the day he had arrived in the coastal city of Nha Trang, where the 5th Special Forces Group headquarters was located. He had spent his first ten days in Vietnam there, processing in and attending the week-long Combat Orientation Course.

He had seen Sam Hagen at Group headquarters. After three months with little action at one of the sixty-odd Special Forces camps along Vietnam's borders with Laos and Cambodia, Sam was transferring to the Nha Trang Mobile Strike Force, the force whose mission was to react to major enemy threats in the Special Forces operational areas throughout Vietnam. It was a good assignment, Sam said. The troops were the best of the Civilian Irregular Defense Group. Most of them were Montagnards from the well-respected Rhade nation of the central highlands. The others were courageous, hard-fighting Chams, descendants of the fierce Champa who had ruled much of Southeast Asia for centuries before being overrun by Annamese from the north. As Sam Hagen put it, the Civilian Irregular Defense Group Mike Force were not *civilians*, but professional soldiers who had been raised as warriors. They were not *irregular*; they were better trained and equipped than most of the regular army units of South Vietnamese. And they seldom *defended*, instead, taking the fight to the enemy where he was strongest. They spent little time searching for an elusive enemy; when the Mike Force went in, it was against an enemy spoiling for, or already engaged in, a major fight.

Another benefit of Sam's new assignment was the fact that their base camp was in Nha Trang. There, like the staff at group headquarters, they lived in relative luxury: air conditioned quarters; ready access to supplies, including items such as fresh food and beer, for which they traded war trophies to the Air Force. In fact, the Mike Force even had a tailor in headquarters company whose sole function was to make bogus NVA flags, shoot a hole or two in them, and sprinkle them with a bit of chicken blood. One of those, appropriately garnished with a good war story, would trade for a case of steaks or a pallet of soft drinks at the big supply center down at Cam Ranh Bay.

And Nha Trang was on the coast. That fact meant little to Sam, but to Ed Walker, it was a bigger plus than all the steaks and air conditioning in the world. The beautiful South China Sea. From Nha Trang you could sail, with a couple of days of fair wind, to Hong Kong, or Taiwan, or Manila. Or south to Singapore or Borneo, or even around to Bangkok.

Maybe one day I'll do that, he thought. One day, after this war is won, Mary and I and our child - *children*, by then - can sail out here, and visit Nha Trang and Danang and those other places.

He got up and pulled a pad of writing paper from the shelf of his wall locker, then sat down on his bunk and wrote his young wife a letter.

He told her where he was, describing the surrounding terrain without mentioning the enemy with which it was infested. He told her that he hoped her pregnancy was proceeding without complication, that he had seen Sam, that his roommate was a good medic who would keep him healthy, that there were hundreds of CIDG soldiers in the camp to help defend it, that there was nothing to worry about. And then he wrote about the beautiful city of Nha Trang, and an imagined tale of them vacationing there someday, and sailing off with their children to all the exotic ports on the South China Sea.

It would be at least a week or ten days before the letter reached her, he knew. Perhaps by then he would have something more exciting to tell her. Meanwhile, please let James and Evelyn know his address, and that all was well with him.

Then he wrote a short note to let Rocco DeCalesta, somewhere down-country with the 25th Infantry Division, know where he was.

The mail drop was in the TOC bunker, where Ed's roommate, Pete Gregovich, was on duty for the night, so he pulled on his fatigue uniform and took the letters there.

He passed a few CIDG soldiers in battle dress on the way, en route to relieve others on guard duty around the camp's perimeter.

There was a light on in the mess hall as he walked by, so he stuck his head inside. Sergeant First Class Farley was sitting at the bar alone. Ed quietly closed the screen door and moved on. That guy's in trouble, he thought to himself.

Gregovich was sitting at the bank of radios in the commo Conex. "Hey, *Thieu Uy*," he said. "You still up? You ought to be getting some sleep, if you're going out with Farley in the morning."

"He's the one who should be in bed," Ed said. "I just passed the mess hall. He's in there by himself, drinking."

Gregovich shook his head. "He's gonna be a basket case if Snake doesn't get him transferred out of here. The C team sergeant major has promised he'll pull him back to Danang as soon as he can get somebody out here to replace him."

"What about you, Pete? I thought you were going out tomorrow, too?"

"I am. I'm just sitting in for Sticks while he goes around to check the perimeter and let the indig know about the arclight. If we didn't let 'em know ahead of time, they'd think it was the end of the world. Little jokers would probably haul ass all the way to Laos."

Ed looked at his watch. Almost half past midnight. Another twenty minutes until the airstrike. "Maybe I'll sit up and watch it," he said.

"Me, too," Pete said. "I'll join you at our chalet as soon as Sticks gets back."

While he waited, Ed checked his combat gear for the third time to satisfy himself that it was ready for the patrol up onto the plateau the following day. It was an awful lot to carry up such a steep hillside. He wondered how the others, especially Farley, were able to do so.

He checked his watch, then lay down on his bunk to rest until Gregovich arrived. He was asleep a minute later.

       *   *   *

The ground shook so violently that the bare bulb hanging from the ceiling came loose and smashed against the bunker floor. Ed Walker rolled from the bunk onto the floor and wrapped his arms around his head. A rocket attack? The earthen floor continued to reverberate beneath him, and outside the bunker door, the sky was alight with incessant flashes.

The arclight! He checked his watch. Yes, right on schedule. But obviously off target - right at the edge of the camp, instead of atop the plateau across the valley.

And then he heard, above the continuing rumble, Gregovich's voice. "All right! All right! Lay it on 'em, big boys!"

Ed scrambled to his feet and out the door, the vibrations of the trembling earth running up his leg bones and into his guts. Pete's face, eyes wide, was lighted by the flashes of the exploding bombs two kilometers away. Ed stared at the plateau, mouth agape, as it continued to be rent by the massive line of detonations. The strike was right on target.

"Oh, my God, my God," he mumbled. No one could survive that, no matter how deeply into the earth he might have dug. And still the line of explosions crept on to the west, as if it might never end. It did, but only after pounding the earth for another fifteen seconds, the sound not ending until several seconds after the flashes had finally ceased.

Both men stood in silent awe at what they had just witnessed, until Gregovich said, "Thank God we rule the air. Let's get some sleep, *Thieu Uy*."

*　　　　　　*　　　　　　*

The boy beside him was whining, and although Colonel Ngo Van Ngoc of the Peoples Army of Vietnam couldn't hear him above the thunderous hammering of the bombs' concussion, he could sense it. He put a hand on the boy's shoulder and squeezed it to comfort him. They were at least five hundred meters from the edge of the airstrike, but even so, the blasts were like continuous blows to their heads, and the ground did not just shake - it heaved beneath them.

Fools, Ngoc thought. Stupid, careless, American fools.

He had known for more than twelve hours exactly where and when the B-52s would strike, and he had not only had enough time to move his regiment out of the way, he had even had time to have the bodies of the men he had recently lost to battle wounds and disease dug up and moved to the area of the airstrike. He had ordered all damaged weapons and equipment to be moved into there, too. That way, the enemy patrols that came to assess the results of the strike, as they almost always did, would find enough human and materiel remains to report that the airstrike had been a great success. No doubt they would even count each piece of flesh they found and report it as a dead soldier.

Colonel Ngoc was the only member of his regiment who knew how they found out each time there was to be a B-52 strike, even though the enemy classified those bombing operations Top Secret. Because, in spite of that classification, the Americans invariably broadcast a warning to their pilots to stay out of a given area during a specific twenty-four hour time period. And, each time, the communist radio intercept operators heard them. The analysts had learned that all they had to do was take the center of mass of the designated area, and the midpoint of the time frame, and they would know the exact time and place of the massive bombing target. And because these notices were broadcast twenty-four hours ahead of time, there was plenty of time to let the affected communist units, or at least most of them, know that they were in danger.

At last it ended, and Ngoc stood and brushed the debris from himself, hoping that the enemy could somehow be kept from realizing that their giant bombers were usually wasting their time. Perhaps the ploy of sowing the strike area with the recent dead, as macabre and distasteful as it was, would continue to keep them fooled, and thus keep the units of the Peoples Army safe from the American bombers' potentially terrible destruction.

Ngoc reached down and helped the boy to his feet. He could feel him trembling with fright, and he said, "There. I told you there was nothing to worry about, didn't I?"

He called out for the other runners from his battalions, and when they were assembled, he issued terse orders.

"First, find out if we suffered any casualties from stray bombs or falling debris. Then I want 1st Battalion to move back into the bombed area to recover any unexploded bombs. 2nd Battalion will be responsible for moving to the new base area and preparing it for occupation. 3rd Battalion will position its elements in ambush sites around the bomb strike to deal with whomever the enemy sends to assess its effect. They may come in helicopters, or they may come on foot from the camp across the river. Whichever the case, the main object, especially if they come from the camp, will be to kill the Americans. Make certain that point is understood: *kill the Americans.* Without them, the camp's defenses will crumble when we attack. The fewer Americans, the fewer airstrikes they will be able to call. Understood?"

Each of the battalion messengers repeated the instructions Colonel Ngoc had issued, then disappeared into the darkness to relay them to their battalion commanders.

*   *   *

Thuong Duc's 1st Camp Strike Force Company left the ridgetop outpost in a column of platoons, well strung out to minimize the danger from mortar fire if they were spotted by the enemy on the ridge south of the river. They weren't really worried about it, though; after the previous night's arclight, they doubted there were any mortar crews left.

The fact that they weren't taken under fire on the way out of camp caused them to relax - all except the new XO, Lieutenant Walker, anyway. It was, after all, his first combat patrol.

"That's a mighty big rucksack you're toting, sir," Staff Sergeant Gregovich said as they moved down toward the river. They were between the two rear platoons, and Ed could see that all the men in front of him had much less in their rucksacks than he did.

"Well, all that's in it is the stuff the field SOP says we're supposed to have."

Gregovich chuckled. "I should have told you what to leave out," he said. "Whoever wrote that SOP must have thought he was going off to war alone for a long time. About half the stuff never gets used."

"Wish you'd said something before we left camp," Ed said, leaning forward and shifting the load up higher onto his back. But he wondered about the utility of standing operating procedures if they weren't going to be followed.

Ahead, Staff Sergeant Saxon and the lead platoon had reached the river, and the company was bunching up as the point element started across through the thigh-deep water. Farley made no effort to send the following platoons to either flank to cover the crossing, and once he got across, he continued on straight ahead instead of clearing the bank in either direction and covering the remainder of his company as it crossed.

Ed Walker started to say something about it, because he knew it was wrong. But he was the FNG - the "fucking new guy" - on his first patrol. Farley would be leaving soon, and Ed would have a little experience under his belt. Then, he could question such things. Meanwhile, at least for this first patrol, he would continue to make mental notes of things he felt needed to be corrected in the future.

It was a struggle climbing the steep, winding trail that led toward the plateau, especially with the overburdened rucksack. As they started up, he asked Gregovich if it was wise to use the trail. He had been taught that it was bad tactics to walk on trails, if it could be avoided.

"Probably not," the medic said, "but if we didn't, it would take all day just to get to the top."

It quickly became evident to the lieutenant that Gregovich was right. This was one of those times that the use of a trail couldn't be avoided, if the company was to complete its mission in a timely manner. The steep slope would have been nearly impossible to climb if it hadn't been for the winding trail. As it was, Ed slipped several times, once tumbling off the trail and rolling halfway back down the slope before getting his feet under him again.

Finally, though, they made it to the top, and stopped to rest from the exhausting climb. This time, Ed was glad to see, Saxon and SFC Newton, who was with Second Platoon, had spread their platoons out in a rough perimeter for security, in the absence of orders from Farley.

Ed had barely caught his breath when the company got back into a column and started west toward the bomb strike.

"The hard part's over now, *Thieu Uy*," Gregovich said, reaching a hand to the lieutenant to help him to his feet.

*   *   *

My Dearest Husband,

I can't understand why I haven't heard from you yet. Maria called to say that she'd had a letter from Sam saying he had seen you, and that you were going to some base up near Danang. I looked Danang up on the map, and it looks like a pretty big city. You haven't taken up with one of the townies, have you?

I miss you. We - the baby and I - both miss you.

I'm really sorry now that I decided to try to go back to school until the baby is born. It's hard driving back and forth every day, and I've about decided to either drop out of school, or to try to find an apartment in Williamsburg. The apartment is the best idea, I think, especially with mother being so difficult. She thinks I should sit at home, learn to play bridge, and act like some dumpy old married woman, studying recipes and sewing clothes for the baby. But you know me, Eddie. I'm not about to do that....

*   *   *

A sudden eruption of noise and flashes and smoke brought the reality of war to Edward Walker with the merciless abruptness of an enemy ambush.

He was supposed to be going along to see how the veterans of this war did things. But almost instantly, the veterans were lying about, dead or wounded and, he was in command of a company of infantrymen locked in a desperate battle with the enemy. Suddenly, more than a hundred under-trained, overly-young, anxious hill tribesmen were looking to him for those things they had gotten from the other "roundeyes" during the weeks and months they were under arms before Lieutenant Edward Walker arrived.

It had gone from a simple move toward the bomb strike to a raging battle in such a short span of time. Two minutes before, 1st Company had been an organized military unit, an experienced American with each of its three platoons. Staff Sergeant Saxon with the First Platoon, walking with his point squad. Behind them, with the Second Platoon, Sergeant First Class Newton. Between Second and Third Platoons, calling in a progress report to the TOC back at camp, the company's senior advisor, SFC Farley. Staff Sergeant Gregovich, with Third Platoon, examining a lesion on the neck of one of the Montagnard soldiers as he walked just in front of Ed.

But that was two minutes ago, before a rocket propelled grenade smashed into one of the Montagnards, blasting his rib cage open and heralding the initiation of the violent ambush. Two minutes ago, before an ounce of brass-jacketed lead breached the side of Saxon's skull at supersonic speed, shattering bone and liquefying brain tissue, then blasting out the other side of his skull, creating a hole ten times larger than the one it made on entry.

A few seconds later, Newton, standing frozen for a moment as he watched Saxon crumple, rushed forward toward him. He made perhaps ten meters when another bullet neatly split his sternum, passing between his lungs and rupturing his spinal column; nearly two minutes ago, but Newton was not dead yet; he would jerk and moan and roll his eyes a bit longer before his twenty-two years of faithful service ended, and his wife became his widow, and his two teenaged daughters, fatherless.

Farley was knocked down just seconds after Newton. He had dashed behind a tree beside the trail in those first moments of confusion, and was safe from enemy fire for a time. But one of his own soldiers, twenty yards behind him, took a round in the leg. It caused the man to accidentally fire his grenade launcher forward into the column. The forty millimeter grenade struck Farley in the wrist and detonated, blowing the flesh and bones of Farley's arm apart and sending dozens of small fragments into his face and neck and chest. Now Farley was slumped beside the tree, gazing dumbly at his severed hand lying in the trail several feet away while the stump of his forearm, torn and blackened by the exploding round, spurted a narrow, pulsing stream of blood into the air.

The medic, Gregovich, saw the detonation, and knew that Farley was badly wounded. He rushed forward and scooped the injured man up in his arms, then pivoted to run back to the rear of the column, where the hot steel hail had not yet reached. But a bullet tore into his belly, and knocked him from his feet, and before he even hit the ground, dropping Farley heavily onto the trail, a second bullet struck him in the hip, flipping him madly into the air before he crashed to earth.

All the other Americans were down now, dead or severely wounded, and Lieutenant Walker didn't know what to do. He should call the camp on the radio, have them summon air support, or a medevac chopper, or call for fire from Thuong Duc's mortars. But he didn't know where the radio operator was - the Montagnard RTO who, just a minute or so ago, was a half pace behind Sergeant Farley.

What spurred him to action was the raw courage of Gregovich and Newton - the bravery of the men who had dashed forward into a hail of bullets to assist their wounded team mates. That those men would unhesitatingly do that for their comrades in the face of almost certain death, overwhelmed Ed's rational fear, and before he realized it, he was rushing forward into the fire himself, toward his wounded team mates. The sharp rattle of bullets passing nearby made him aware that he would probably be hit, too, to lie bleeding in the dirt with the others. But at least he would be one of them, these veteran warriors among whom he had been cast.

He lifted Gregovich and spun, ran back toward the rear of the company past the little groups of 1st Company soldiers. They were beginning to recover from the initial shock of the ambush now, sending bullets back at the unseen enemy in an increasing stream of noise and flash.

Gregovich, as heavy as Ed, seemed to weigh almost nothing, and Ed heard him plead, "Get me out of here, lieutenant. I'm hurt bad. Don't let me die."

Ed realized he was out of the fire now. He heard himself say, "It's OK, Pete. It's all right now. You'll be OK." He laid the wounded man down in a shallow depression beside the trail, removed the battle dressing from the pouch on Gregovich's belt, and tore it open to cover the belly wound. He didn't realize that the medic was hit in the hip as well, and would bleed to death in a few minutes unless the flow of blood from it was stanched.

There was a lull in the firing as most of the Montagnard troops reloaded and tried to determine the sources of enemy fire, which had also lessened considerably.

Ed left Gregovich and ran forward in a crouch to the point at which he sensed the ambush killing zone began. Somehow, he knew that where he now was, he was safe, but that if he moved just a few feet forward, he would again be exposed to the deadly rain of steel that had already left eight or ten men dead or dying on the trail.

Farley lay on his back on the side of the trail twenty meters away, his remaining hand clutching his other forearm just above the shredded flesh and splintered bone of the stump, staring at it, scolding it as if it were a naughty child. A few feet away lay the severed hand, palm up and fingers curled.

This time Ed Walker didn't simply react. First, he rapidly sized up the situation: There was Farley, badly hurt, destined to die unless Ed quickly helped him. Between Ed and him there was an intermittent wall of death-dealing steel projectiles, cracking past unseen. He probably could not get safely through that wall to help Farley. He could crawl beneath it, perhaps, but he could not carry the man back through it without almost certainly being killed. But he could at least crawl to the dazed and bleeding man and put a tourniquet on the stump of his arm, Ed decided.

He took a piece of nylon parachute cord out of his pocket, then reached into his own battle dressing pouch and removed the bandage. Carrying those two items in his fists, he crawled quickly forward beneath the crackling rifle and machine gun fire until he reached Farley.

"OK, Sergeant Farley, I'm going to put a tourniquet on this arm," he said as he wrapped the parachute cord around the arm just below the elbow, a few inches above the wound. He knotted it tightly, and the spurting blood subsided to a trickle. Then he placed the battle dressing over the jagged stump and tied it there. That done, his problem now was how to get Farley - and himself - back out of the killing zone.

"Come on, Farley. Crawl with me now. Come on," he begged as he tried to drag the sergeant back down the murderous trail. Farley made a couple of kicks with his legs, propelling himself a few feet in the direction Ed was trying to drag him, then passed out.

It was no good. The only way to get him out was to pick him up and carry him.

Ed knew that other things had to be done now; find the radio, call the camp and inform Captain Mullins of the desperate situation. Order a medevac helicopter and some air support. Get the rate of fire of the Montagnard troops under control, for they were burning up ammunition so fast that they would soon run out. Those things had to be done, and done in a hurry, or the whole company might be lost. Those were the things he had gone to school for, had trained for.

But he couldn't leave this man in the killing zone to die. He had seen Newton's and Gregovich's unselfish examples, and he was the officer and, in spite of his inexperience and fear and almost certain death, he would have to try to carry Farley to safety.

So be it. If they get me, they get me. Haven't I already shown that I'm one of those destined to go unharmed? I've done it once, with Gregovich. I can do it again.

Ed Walker stood, picked the unconscious Farley up in his arms, and ran back toward the depression where he had placed Gregovich.

Bullets cracked and snapped past his ears, and some kicked up dirt in front of him. Each yard seemed like ten; each second an eternity.

But then it was all behind him. He was out of the killing zone, and safe. He was exhilarated, almost euphoric. He was untouchable. His heart no longer raced with fear, and he became the infantry officer he had trained to become - calm, confident, capable.

Farley's radioman had seen the new lieutenant carry the company commander out of the killing zone, and followed him. Now he was crouched beside Ed, holding the radio handset out to the only American left to use it. Ed took it and placed it to his ear. He heard Captain Mullins calling desperately. They could hear the firefight down in the camp, but had been unable to raise anyone on the radio. Ed couldn't recall the proper call signs, so he said, "Mullins this is Walker, over."

"This is Mullins," the detachment commander responded. "What's the situation up there, over?"

"Ambush," Walker responded. "We've got a bunch of dead and wounded. I need a medevac and some air support. Can you get the mortars up?"

"Roger. We've already got a pair of gunships on the way. They'll call this frequency when they get in range. What priority is the Dustoff?"

"Urgent," Ed replied. "Farley's lost an arm, and Pete's hit bad. Saxon's dead." He nearly retched as he recalled the sight of Saxon's head exploding from the bullet that breached it.

The fire had slackened somewhat, but there was still a lot of shooting going on up the trail, and some explosions. Then he realized that most of it was from the Montagnards. Two machine guns were in action, raking the area from which the ambush had come, and he could see several of his men throwing hand grenades in that direction, as well.

Another voice came across the radio. It was Nicholas. "Walker, this is Punchbowl. We're ready to shoot for you, champ."

Ed felt in the side pocket of his trousers for his map, but it was gone. He saw one sticking part way out of Gregovich's pocket, though, so he pulled it out. It was soaked with blood. He looked at his roommate's face. It was deathly pale, so he laid the handset down. He ripped Pete's bloody trousers open and found the gaping hip wound, then took the radioman's battle dressing, shoved it into the hole, and tied it there.

Then he briefly studied the map, made a quick check of his compass, and picked up the handset. He gave a quick and competent call for fire, and in what seemed but a few seconds, Nicholas called, "Shot, over."

"Shot, out," Ed said in acknowledgment.

"Splash," the mortarman called as Lieutenant Walker heard the whirring sound of the round passing a short distance overhead. It exploded in a shallow draw fifty meters behind the ambush site, right where Ed wanted it, right where he guessed the enemy would rally after their deadly work was done.

"Repeat," he called. "Fire for effect," and not long after, a quick series of bursting mortar rounds ripped through the draw.

The small arms fire had stopped now, and he could hear the sound of helicopter rotors beating the air in the distance. He grabbed the handset and put it to his ear. One of the pilots was calling him: "Walker, Walker, this is Spitfire, over," the pilot called.

"Spitfire, this is Walker, go ahead" Ed answered, surprised at the calmness of his own voice.

"Roger, Walker. We're a pair of snakes armed with miniguns and rockets, about two minutes east. Say your position, over."

Two minutes later, the Cobra gunships had located the company's position and were pouring deadly streams of rocket and minigun fire into the jungle around them. Ed was moving around the company now, positioning his soldiers for security against any further attacks by the enemy.

But the communists had done enough damage, killing or severely wounding all except one of the Americans, and they had their own problems, now. With uncanny accuracy, their rally point had been ripped by mortar fire, and they had several dead and wounded of their own to deal with.

Praying that the Cobra gunships would fail to spot them, the North Vietnamese ambushers melted back into the jungle away from the ambush site and the firestorm that now blazed around it.

Ed moved among the wounded, patching the injured as well as he could, and having them carried back to the depression where Farley and Gregovich lay.

"You need to get some IVs in us, sir," Gregovich mumbled weakly as Ed checked his wounds and those of the unconscious Farley. The lieutenant did so, consciously thankful for the cross training in medical skills he had gotten at Fort Bragg.

The Montagnard radio bearer moved everywhere Lieutenant Walker did now, and whenever he heard a voice on the radio, he tapped Ed and passed him the handset.

The gunships reported that they would remain overhead and continue to search for any signs of enemy movement, and the pilot of the Dustoff - the medical evacuation helicopter - called to say that they were nearly there.

Ed quickly had the wounded moved to an open area they had passed just down the trail after dispatching a platoon to secure it. A few minutes later, the Dustoff identified his smoke marker and landed. As Ed helped load Gregovich aboard, the young medic managed a faint grin and a feeble salute.

Ed Walker's worried look changed to a slight smile, and he said, "I'll see you before long, Pete."

The medevac helicopter lifted off, and the gunships called to say that there was another pair of Cobras on the way to replace them, and as their ammunition and fuel were low, they would escort the Dustoff to Danang.

It became eerily quiet when the helicopters were gone. Ed stood in the cartridge-littered trail, gazing at Saxon and Newton's bodies and those of four dead Montagnards sprawled on the ground in grotesque poses and, nearer to him, the macabre sight of Farley's severed hand clawing at nothing.

Ed reached into his jacket pocket for a cigarette, and as he lit it, saw the thick stains of blood on his hands. He rubbed them on his trousers and looked at them again. The blood was still there.

So this is war, he thought. All these men dead and wounded, and for what? We were supposed to go see how badly we had mauled the enemy with our bomb strike. Instead, we got mauled ourselves. Jesus. How close did I come to being killed? And yesterday, in the mortar attack. How close? How many days can you almost be killed before it catches up with you? Three? Three hundred?

He looked at Newton and Saxon and at Farley's dead claw of a hand and thought, I'll never see you again, Mary. I'll never know my child.

"I haven't even seen *one* of them," Ed said to his radio bearer, who understood nothing he was saying. "If I'm going to die, I want at least to see one of these people we're fighting."

The Montagnard thought the lieutenant wanted to use the radio, and gave him the handset again. Ed took it, and called Captain Mullins.

"I'm going to send a couple of squads back with the bodies while we move on to the arclight area, if that's all right," he said when the team leader answered.

"No need for that, podner," Mullins replied. "Your, uh, your roundeye situation's a little too slim, so you'd best head for the ranch."

"Roger, Dugout," he said, his voice showing the fatigue of his adrenaline-drained body. He gave the handset back to the radioman, then looked down the trail at the carnage again. A feeling of utter despair washed over him. He had failed. Failed his initiation to battle. Failed to correct the move across the river, failed to insist on avoiding the trail, failed to prevent the ambush that had killed his teammates and the boy soldiers of the Camp Strike Force company. And worst of all, he had failed to get to the objective of his first combat patrol. He felt such a sense of defeat that, if there had been someone else there to take over - another officer, another American - he might have just sat down in the trail and given up. But there was only him, and that fact steeled him enough to act now as he had been trained.

"Interpreter!" he called. He had seen someone translating for SFC Farley as they prepared to leave the camp, and that man now came to him.

The impulse to yell at the man, to strike him, rose up in Ed. Why hadn't the son of a bitch come earlier to do his job, to offer his help? But Ed just looked at him and thought, Who am *I* to be angry at someone for failing to do his job? "Get somebody to wrap the dead men up in ponchos," he said. "And bring the senior man from each platoon to me."

While he gave a patrol order through the interpreter to the Montagnard platoon leaders for the move back to camp, a squad of men wrapped the dead in ponchos, binding them in with the belts and harness of their combat equipment. Then they cut poles with the machetes some of the soldiers carried and tied them atop the ponchos. Walker looked at them, and it reminded him of his brother James and himself carrying the carcass of a whitetail deer out of the woods of Broad Marsh plantation. He called the interpreter and had him translate as Ed explained how to make a litter out of another poncho and two poles. Then he sent them off to make a litter for each body.

James. Now he understood about his brother, about his disgust for war. No wonder. But as he watched the men rigging the litters, he remembered James's comments about the lieutenant he had admired. What was his name? Granger. No, Grange. That was it. The one who had assembled his platoon for inspection after an all night battle. The one who had stuck to the basics. Yes.

He turned to the interpreter. "As soon as they're done with that," he instructed, "have one squad at a time report here to me."

"Why you do that, *Thieu Uy*?" the interpreter asked.

Ed looked at him through narrowed eyes. He didn't care much for this man, and he said, "What's your job in this company?"

"Interpreter," the tribesman replied. "You tell me in English, I tell CIDG in Bru language."

"Exactly," Ed said. "Now, do your job. One squad at a time, lined up right here."

The Montagnards mumbled among themselves as the first squad lined up. Ed went to each man, checked his ammunition, redistributed bullets and hand grenades as necessary, spot checked weapons, canteens, squad radios.

It made sense, especially the redistribution of ammunition, and the mumbling soon ceased. They sensed that this American knew what he was doing, and by the time he had finished with one platoon, the others were responding with respect. He asked each squad leader if his platoon leader had briefed him on the move back. If they said no, he sent for the platoon leader. Without scolding, he made them understand that any orders or information he gave them was to be passed to every man in the platoon.

By the time he had finished the first squad of the Second Platoon, he saw that the Third Platoon leader was already inspecting his own squads. He smiled and nodded at the Montagnard platoon leader, who smiled and nodded back.

The basics, he thought. The basics are the things that matter. The basics will keep you alive. The basics will get you home, will give you victory.

They were finished the inspections now. They understood the patrol order for the move. They were a military unit again. And now Ed Walker felt like a combat arms officer.

They moved off the trail and started back to camp, with Lieutenant Walker, his radioman, and his interpreter midway in the lead platoon, the litter bearers spread through the two following platoons. At the point, flanks, and rear, there were security elements. At the danger areas, there was a halt, the area was cleared, and the company moved on. Ed designated rally points along the way. He made corrections when faults were spotted. The company took on an attitude of seriousness. They began to follow the basics.

Mullins and a platoon from 3rd Company were waiting at the river. He hadn't even spotted the company with his new executive officer when Walker called him on the radio.

"What's your location?" Mullins asked, wondering why he hadn't seen the company coming off the plateau on the trail. They must be lost, he thought.

"Two hundred meters to your southwest," Ed replied.

Mullins scanned the terrain in that direction. "You sure about that? I don't have a visual on you over there."

"Good," was all Ed said, and a moment later, two squads appeared, moving along the riverbank in either direction to secure the crossing site. Then two more squads crossed the river, took up security positions, and covered the crossing of the remainder of the company.

Mullins turned to his team sergeant, Master Sergeant Kadlewicz, and said, "Damn, Bruno, look at that. You sure that's the same 1st Company we sent out this morning?"

Kadlewicz looked at the orderly crossing, and at the poncho-wrapped bodies being carried across. "No, sir. It's not the same company. And it's not the same company that got its ass whipped up on the hill, either."

"You're right," Mullins said. "It's not."

They watched their executive officer come across, the Montagnard element leaders looking over at him for any signals he might give, any guidance or corrections.

"That's not the same cherry lieutenant we sent out here this morning either, top," the Captain said.

"No, sir," Kadlewicz agreed. "It sure as hell ain't."

        *   *   *

...Anyway, if I can get a decent apartment for a reasonable price, I will, even if it's not right in Williamsburg.

Other than that, everything seems to be OK. I have good professors, except for political science. He's a real pinko who thinks he has all the answers. He never follows the textbook, just launches into these tirades about the government and the "unjust interference in

Vietnam's civil war," as he puts it. It's impossible to know how to study for his tests. Oh, well. I guess you don't want to hear about that.

I go back to Dr. Smith for a checkup tomorrow. I think I'm really *starting to show now, and it makes me feel so fat and unattractive, even though I've only gained a few pounds.*

Oh, Ed, I miss you so much. I can't believe you have to be away until after the baby is half grown. Please take care of yourself, and write to me. *You can't be too busy to at least write a note now and then.*

I love you and I miss you terribly,

Your Mary

SIX

Susan Charlotte Madison sat with her twenty-four Army Nurse Corps classmates and listened as her father's assignments and the medals he had won in the Korean War and recently in Vietnam were listed as he was introduced. She was proud of him, proud to be his daughter and proud that she had decided to be an Army nurse.

Harry Madison, a Colonel of Infantry, sat erect in his chair on the stage, the overhead lights reflecting off his highly-shined brass and silver insignia, his master parachutist's badge, his combat infantryman's badge with star.

He gazed intently at his pretty daughter, sitting there in her own officer's uniform of Army Green, his mind drifting back through the twenty-one years of her life, to its beginning at Fort Campbell, Kentucky.

He had thought at the time that he would prefer a son, but Ellen wanted very much to have a daughter to dress up in pretty frills and to raise to be a dainty young lady. So they were both happy when the doctor announced that they were the parents of a healthy baby girl.

It hadn't taken Lieutenant and Mrs. Madison long to realize, though, that this daughter of theirs was not to be a dainty little thing, but a rough and tumble tomboy who would rather wear a baseball cap than an Easter bonnet, and who, given the chance, would rather go fishing with her father than take the ballet lessons her mother had insisted on.

Harry Madison smiled at her now as he remembered her running into the house with a bloody nose, at age eight, not to fly weeping into her mother's arms, but to tell him that the neighborhood bully had been beating up on her friend Todd, and that she had jumped into the middle of the fight and split the bully's lip.

And then there was the time she broke her leg and, as Ellen later told him, had cried so desperately for him. That was the first time she had ever mentioned wanting to be an Army nurse, back in 1955, at Fort Benning.

She never had become the little lady her mother wanted her to be, but when she became an accomplished equestrienne in her early teens, Ellen finally accepted that as about the most ladylike endeavor she could expect from Sue.

Madison's face darkened then as he recalled the incident in the stables at Fort Bragg when, at age fourteen, she had nearly been raped by one of the stable hands. One of her friends heard her screams, and beat the young man with a rake. He ran away, and was never seen at Fort Bragg again. Thank God for that, Harry thought. I would have killed him.

Sue hadn't gotten over the incident for a long, long time.

Colonel Madison heard his name mentioned, and everyone was clapping. He rose and walked to the podium, surveying the young faces in the front rows of the auditorium, almost all of them young women, including his own daughter.

He thanked the other officer for the introduction, then looked at the new Army nurses. "In a few minutes, ladies and gentlemen," he said, "you will swear a solemn oath. It is the same oath that I and every officer with whom you will serve has sworn, and it is basically the same oath taken by every American soldier you will meet.

"It is an oath to uphold and defend the Constitution of the United States, to bear true faith and allegiance to the same. Yet most of you have probably read that great document only once, or perhaps twice, and then only because it was required for a civics course. Most of us, if we had to write all we could about this rulebook of our political system, this declaration of our rights, would probably fail miserably. Of the hundreds of thousands of men who have died to defend the way of life our Constitution outlines, very few would have even been able, I dare say, to recite the preamble, or list more than a few of the rights we, as citizens of this great nation, inherit from birth.

"So if I may, I will take a few minutes to refresh your memories concerning this document that you are about to swear to uphold, and to bear true faith and allegiance to."

Colonel Madison drew from the pocket of his beribboned blouse the page of paper on which he had made notes. He took his eyes from the paper and scanned the attentive faces before him. "The strange thing," he said, "is that those of us who swear to uphold these rights for our fellow citizens must put aside many of those very rights for the duration of our military service. It's just as important that you understand that fact, as it is for you to understand what you're about to vow to defend."

Madison quickly summarized what he felt were key points of the Constitution, particularly the Bill of Rights, then folded the paper and put it away. Many of the nurses were looking somewhat bored, but he found Sue's face, caught her eye, and continued in a tone that caused her and her classmates to know what he was saying was absolutely sincere.

"Now let me say a few words as a simple infantryman; a combat arms officer whose terrible duty it is to order men to risk, and sometimes lose, their lives. Young American men whose battle wounds it will be your job to heal."

The bored ones became more alert, and Madison noticed a number of them sit up straighter. That's better, he thought.

"I pray to God that none of you will ever have to give up life or limb in battle." He looked at his darling Sue, and the thought of it caused a pang in his heart. "But I'm afraid that many of you - probably even most of you - will suffer the wounds of war nevertheless. You will suffer wounds that will never completely heal - wounds of the soul. You will be handed, to do with what you can, once-fine young men. Many just boys, really. They will be shot and mangled and bleeding and burned. You will call upon your skills and your courage to save them, heal them, rehabilitate them. And you will, thanks to the skills you've worked so hard to learn, usually be successful, if not always in saving their limbs, at least in saving their lives."

Many of the young Army nurses' faces bore faint smiles as they pictured themselves as saviors.

"But some..." Harry Madison continued, "some you will be unable to save. Some will die. Before your eyes, and in spite of your best efforts, some of those young soldiers will die. And you will question the madness of war. You will wonder what sort of man could order young men into battles that produce such horribly wounded boys. How men such as I could live with themselves after perpetrating such slaughter and maiming. And you should - you *must* - question such things.

"Some of you will perhaps become numb to it, at least for awhile. But most of you will be haunted by it for the rest of your lives."

The thought caused many of them to drop their chins, and he paused to let his words sink in, because they were, he knew all too well, true words. "Forgive me for being so morbid on a day that should be a happy occasion for you. But I want you to understand the seriousness of this vow you're about to take.

"First, though, I have a different vow to make. A promise to you that I will always - *always* - do my best to care for those for whom *I* am responsible. A promise that I will never forget the awesome responsibility of my decisions, and that I will risk human lives for one reason, and one reason only. And that is for the cause of human freedom. So help me God."

There was a smattering of applause, though most of it was from the parents attending the ceremony, and not the nurses nor the other young people in the audience. He noted that Sue sat staring into his eyes, her hands in her lap.

No, they didn't believe in this war, Harry Madison knew. But they would do their duty. They would go, and they would do their best to save the lives of the soldiers, friend or foe, that they were handed. And that was all that mattered.

He respected them for that. And they would respect themselves, when it was all over. Maybe even more so than if the war had been a popular one.

He stepped from behind the podium and said, "Now please stand, and raise your right hands, and repeat after me.

"I - state your full name - do solemnly swear..."

Sue's eyes remained locked to his, and when the oath had been taken, he said simply, "Congratulations, and Godspeed."

After the benediction, Madison descended to the floor of the auditorium and gave his daughter a kiss and a hug, then held her at arms length. "Guess that was a bit heavy, eh, Suzy Q?"

She smiled and leaned against him, and said. "Yeah, it was kind of heavy, Dad. But you're a heavy guy. Anyway, most of us will forget it, until we experience it. Then we'll remember what you said, and what we swore to. And I suppose that's when we'll *need* to remember. Come on, let's go find Mom."

Lieutenant Susan Madison spent that night at her parents' home in Chevy Chase, Maryland. While she sorted through her clothes and the things she would take with her to Fort Sam Houston, Texas, the next day, her mother sat on the bed making small talk.

She looked at her mother and knew there was something more she wanted to say to her daughter. Sue sat down beside her, and took her mother's hand in hers. "OK, Mom. Out with it. What do you want to say?"

Ellen Madison looked away a moment, then faced her only child. "Sue, I'm worried about your, well, your relationship with men. Or rather, your lack of it."

"Oh, mother. Don't be silly. I don't have any problems with men. I know you think it's some hangup I have from that thing at Fort Bragg, but I've all but forgotten that. It's been, what, seven years ago? It's just... Oh, I don't know."

"Just what, Sue? My God, you're a full grown woman, and a darned attractive one. You should have fallen in love a half-dozen times by now. But you've never even dated the same man more than twice."

She knew her dating habits were unusual. Her classmates at nursing school had noticed, too. Most of them were gaining a practical education in sex along with their nursing degrees, and much of the dormitory talk was about sex. Sometimes her friends kidded her about being the only virgin over the age of eighteen in the whole Washington metropolitan area, and that sort of thing, and once there had been a rumor that she was having a lesbian affair with one of the other students. Her good friend Sally Blair had talked to her about it, and eventually learned about the incident with the stable hand. After that, the word got around that she had been raped as a child, and that she was still hung up about it. And of course she was affected by the assault. But she was over that, now. She enjoyed the company of men. Still, it did seem that all of them eventually got around to wanting to get into her pants, and forgot about everything else.

"Mother, I'm a *nurse*. I know about sex. I'm healthy. I like good looking men, and I fantasize about sex with them, all right?"

"Oh, Sue, I don't mean..."

"What *do* you mean, mother?" she said, standing and throwing the sweater she had been folding onto the bed. "That I'm abnormal because I don't want to screw some guy I'm not in love with? That *real* ladies are supposed to spread their thighs for every..."

"Susan!" her mother interrupted. "How dare you talk to me this way!"

She sat down beside her mother and took her hand again. "Aw, mom. I know you're worried about me, and you think I'm the only old fashioned girl around. But it's OK. I just don't want to fall in love yet, to get tied down. There's a big world out there, and I want to be free to experience it on my own terms for awhile, OK? I promise, when I fall in love, or even if I decide to yield my maidenly virtue before I do, you'll be one of the first to know. All right?"

Her mother smiled at her, then looked down at her hands and picked at her cuticles. "Look at me, Sue. All worried because my daughter seems to be the only one left who isn't lowering her knickers like the flag every time 'Retreat' sounds." She shook her head slowly, then smiled and looked at Sue again and said, "Ten years ago, bridge gossip would have been about the one kid who *was* being promiscuous. These days, it seems to be about the only one who isn't. Forgive me, dear. I feel like a silly old fool."

"Oh, mom. Look, if it'll make your bridge pals happy, just tell them that the last you saw of me, I was being serviced by the entire Old Guard in front of the Tomb of the Unknown Soldier."

They laughed together at that, then turned the conversation to Sue's coming trip to Fort Sam Houston.

*   *   *

"Do you think he's telling the truth?" Lieutenant Walker asked Sticks Howard. Walker had just finished reading the interrogation report of a North Vietnamese prisoner the Mike Force company west of Camp Thuong Duc had captured.

"I do," Howard replied. "There's no reason to doubt him, based on the way they were able to hit you up on the plateau the other day. They sure as hell didn't walk out of the arclight and do that."

He took the report from Ed, shaking his head. "No, we missed 'em, *Thieu Uy*. Somehow, they knew the B-52s were coming."

The prisoner had suffered the misfortune of being separated from his unit when the second B-52 strike went in to the west of Thuong Duc. He was on the edge of the bomb pattern, and had been so badly rattled by the nearby detonations that he was just wandering around in a daze when the Mike Force found him. He made no effort to resist interrogation, and he said that his unit had been warned, just as their sister regiment on the plateau to the south had, of exactly where and when the bombs would fall.

His regiment's mission, he stated candidly, was to attack and overrun the American Special Forces camp at Thuong Duc. As soon as they had stockpiled enough supplies, he said, they would wait for bad weather to minimize the Americans' use of air support, and launch the attack.

"What's the weather forecast?" Ed asked.

Howard looked at him with worry in his eyes. "Not good," he said. "It's supposed to cloud up tonight and really turn bad tomorrow night. My guess is, that's when they'll come at us."

Ed looked at his watch. "The old man should be back from Danang in about half an hour," he said. "Maybe he'll have some good news."

Captain Mullins had been picked up by helicopter several hours earlier to brief the commander of the Special Forces C team in Danang. Everything pointed to an imminent attack on the little camp by the enemy regiments now confirmed to be lurking nearby, untouched by the massive bomb strikes intended to decimate them. With any luck, Mullins should be able to arrange for more Mike Force reinforcements, and perhaps for spoiling attacks by conventional Army or Marine Corps forces against the massed communist soldiers.

"When was the last sitrep from 2nd Company?" Ed asked.

"About ten minutes ago," Howard replied. "They're moving toward an LZ to secure it for Snake when he comes in."

The enemy mortars had the camp's landing zone so well zeroed in now, that it was necessary to use random locations outside the camp for helicopter landings. Even then, they could only set down for a few seconds, or risk being mortared.

"I'm going to check the claymores and crew-served weapons on the perimeter, Sticks," Walker said. "We might well have to use them tonight, if that POW knows what he's talking about."

The claymores - electrically detonated, directional anti-personnel mines - were a key weapon for defending against assaults by enemy troops, and the defensive wire that surrounded Thuong Duc was covered by them in depth.

Walker found Nick Nicholas and a squad of his troops adding another ring of the deadly mines around the inner perimeter of the little ridgetop fortress. "This'll give 'em something to think about, if they get this far," Nick said as he aimed one of the curved claymores to cover the space between the outer trenches and the bunkers of the inner perimeter.

"How are you fixed for mortar and recoilless rifle ammo?" Ed asked.

Nicholas waited until he had screwed the electrical blasting caps into the claymore before he answered. "We're OK. I asked Snake to put in a request for more while he's at the C team."

Ed looked at his watch, then scanned the clouding sky to the east of the camp. "He ought to be showing up anytime now," he said.

Nicholas studied the executive officer for a moment, thinking, God, he's aged so much already. "I haven't had a chance to tell you, but you did a hell of a job up on the plateau the other day, Lieutenant," the veteran mortarman said. "A *hell* of job for a guy in his first firefight."

Ed involuntarily glanced to the south, to area of the high plateau where he had received his hellish baptism by fire. It seemed as if it had been weeks before, except sometimes when he lay on his bunk, and images of the chaotic violence returned. Then, it seemed as if it had just ended, and he would shudder. "Thanks, Nick," he muttered. "I should never have let us get in that kind of a fix, though."

Nicholas was the last of his remaining teammates to say something about his actions that day. And their praise meant more to him than any medal could, because when it really comes down to it, the respect of one's peers is what matters most to a man at war.

"Clouding up," he said, again searching the sky to their east for the sight or sound of Snake Mullins's helicopter.

"G'day, Lieutenant," a voice behind him said, pronouncing the rank "leftenant." It was Mick O'Day, the Australian warrant officer who commanded the Mike Force company up the ridge west of the camp. There were a number of Aussies in the I and II Corps Mobile Strike Forces, and they had earned a well deserved reputation as courageous and capable fighters. Ed turned to him and smiled. "Hello, Mick," he said. "Any more prisoners?"

"Christ, boss," the digger replied, "don't say that too loud, will ya? The Montagnards think it's a bloody disgrace to take a prisoner, especially the 'yards in the bleedin' Mike Force."

Ed chuckled. "Well, it's a damn good thing you did. Otherwise, we'd be sitting here drinking toasts to the Air Force, thinking everything was fine and dandy."

"Did Sticks tell you what we just got out of the dink prisoner a bit ago?" the Australian asked.

"No," Ed said, frowning. He didn't like to hear derogatory nicknames for the enemy. *I wonder why that offends me?* he thought, but said only, "What did he say?"

"The little punch up you had up there the other day," O'Day said, inclining his head toward the plateau. "Seems like you zapped one of their battalion commanders with mortar fire. Screwed up the whole bloody command group, as a matter of fact. Well done."

Ed glanced again at the site of the brutal ambush. The image of Sergeant Saxon's head exploding flashed in his mind, only this time it was the head of a North Vietnamese officer. "Good," he muttered in a tone of unmistakable rancor, then thought, *That sounded just like my brother.*

SFC Nicholas moved off, carrying several more claymore mines to emplace. O'Day offered Walker a cigarette and held his lighter to it, then to his own. Then the two men stood searching the eastern horizon for a sign of the helicopter.

"C'mon, mate," O'Day said toward the empty, darkening sky. "I need to get my arse back up the ridge."

As was the American beside him, he was anxious for Captain Mullins to arrive with any news of reinforcements or additional orders for the Mike Force company.

Ed Walker's thoughts, like his empty gaze, went far beyond the eastern horizon. He was thinking of his wife and their unborn child.

What would she be doing now? It was well into the morning back in Virginia. She was probably in class. He was glad she was pregnant. Maybe that would keep her fellow students at William and Mary from making passes at her. He immediately regretted even thinking about such a thing, and sighed.

O'Day gave him a glance, then looked behind them, up toward the ridge where his company waited for his return. The sun had already disappeared behind the jungle-covered mountains in that direction. "I'd better take the squad I've got with me and get back up to my company, before it gets dark," he said.

"OK, Mick. Stay ready. God only knows what might happen tonight."

The Aussie nodded. "Right," he said. "You lads keep your heads down. We'll keep the bastards from coming at you from down the ridge, at least." He threw Ed a palm-outward salute, then disappeared.

They will, too, Ed thought. If there's any way they can, they will. Then he tried unsuccessfully to return his thoughts to Mary.

They have two regiments, Mary. And we only have two effective companies in camp, and one up on the ridge. That means they outnumber us at least five to one. And the weather looks as if it's going to be on their side, too.

There were only seven men left in Thuong Duc's US Special Forces A team now.

Nicholas, approaching from the direction of the TOC, said, "Snake just called to say he ain't coming out tonight, sir."

"Not coming? Why?"

"We're getting a battalion from the Nha Trang Mike Force tomorrow, and he has to brief them. That's the good news. Well, part of it, anyway."

"That's *great* news," Ed said, hoping Sam Hagen would be among them. "What's the other part?"

"We're getting some preplanned airstrikes tonight; Navy A-6s. Bruno wants you to help him decide where to put 'em."

"OK," Ed said. It suddenly dawned on him that, with Mullins absent, he would be in charge of the camp that night. He peered up at the darkening sky. There were still enough breaks in the clouds that he could see the dim flicker of several stars. God help me, he thought, meaning it with sincerity, not self pity.

*   *   *

Mary McClanahan Walker closed her notebook and watched Professor Milton, barely listening to him. He was railing against the Republicans at the moment, saying that all Eisenhower proved was that the country could function without a president. It's too bad, she thought as she looked at the clock and saw that class was only half over, that such a good looking man has to be such an ass.

She opened her notebook again to begin a letter to Ed. She was beginning to worry now about not hearing from him. He'd been gone two weeks. Two weeks. Two into fifty two - God, that's only one twenty-sixth of the time. It already seemed like an eternity. Well, maybe it would be over before then, and he could come home.

"Miss Walker? Hello? Miss Walker, this is earth calling..."

Some of the other students were laughing, looking over at her.

"Oh," she said, feeling her face flush as she closed the notebook. "Were you talking to me, sir?"

Milton gave her a crooked smile and said, "Yes, I was. I asked what you thought of Eisenhower's handling of Korea as compared to Truman's."

Oh, hell. All she really knew about the Korean War was that it had started under Truman and ended under Eisenhower. That, and the fact that her brother-in-law James had served there. And there was something about MacArthur, but she couldn't remember what.

"Well, Miss Walker?"

She sat up straight and looked him in the eye. "It's Mrs. Walker, Professor Milton," she said. "And as far as Korea goes, I guess you could say that Truman handled it like a Democrat, and Ike like a Republican."

He was still staring at her, still wearing that crooked smile. "I see. Well, one could hardly argue with that, I suppose. Although, in those terms, it would seem to me to be more appropriate to say that Truman handled it like a Republican, and Eisenhower, like a golfer."

There were a few snickers from the class, but Mary and her youthful professor ignored them, their eyes still locked on each other's for a long moment more.

What is he thinking? she wondered. It has nothing to do with political science, I'll bet. She returned a faint smile and his gaze dropped momentarily to her shapely legs, exposed most of their full length below her hiked up skirt. Almost automatically, she stroked her thigh, where he seemed to be looking.

His eyes went back to hers for a brief second, just long enough for her to notice a new sparkle in them.

So, she thought. The Game. The Game of Men and Women. Yes, and why not? A little teasing might make this class a bit less dull and boring - at least until he notices I'm pregnant. That will be the last laugh in this little game, she thought, her mouth parting in a sensuous smile.

Whenever Milton looked in her direction after that, she shifted her legs, and she knew he noticed. And she would toy at her full lips with her pencil when she caught his eye.

When class was over, she sensed him watching her walk out, and she smoothed the back of her skirt with her hand and swayed out the door, thinking, Round one in the game goes to *me*!"

*   *   *

The class in which Lieutenant Susan Madison of the Army Nurse Corps sat at Fort Sam Houston, Texas, was worlds apart from the one Mary Walker had just attended in Virginia. It was entitled *Triage Practical Exercise*, and it was a class in the brutal realities of trauma medicine, as opposed to the theoretical science of politics.

"Make a decision, Lieutenant," the Army Medical Corps major said to Sue. "This is triage, not Scrabble."

She continued to study the three color slides projected on the screen at the front of the classroom; actual photographs of hideously wounded soldiers taken in field hospitals in Vietnam. One was a man with both legs blown off above the knees, one was a charred and oozing creature barely recognizable as a human being, and the third was a man whose bowels had spilled out of his torn abdomen. He was holding as much as he could of the glob of guts in his hands.

"All right," Sue said. She had made up her mind. "First priority, the gut wound. Second, the burn victim. Third, the traumatic amputation"

"Wrong,"the major said. It seemed to always happen this way. They wanted to save them all.

"While you're working on the burn victim, you're probably going to lose the amputee," he said. "Look at the slides again."

She wished she didn't have to, but she did. The major, an experienced physician just back from the carnage of field hospital emergency rooms in Pleiku and An Khe, walked to the screen with his pointer.

"You're right about the gut wound," he said. "He'll die from peritonitis if you don't get his guts washed and back in his belly. But look at the burns. This guy is completely fried. Totally. He's going to die, and there's nothing you can do about it. So don't waste time - precious time - on him. Say a quick prayer in your mind, if you want. But then get your mind, and your hands, on this guy." His pointer was on the man whose legs were missing.

He looked at the faces of all twenty nurses, all but one of them young women. They looked so young, so fresh. He wondered if they were really as beautiful as they seemed to him, or if he was only imagining it. He looked again. No, it wasn't their physical appearance that was beautiful. It was their concern, their attentiveness, their innocence.

God, I hope that filthy, stinking war is over before they get there, he thought, although he knew it would not be.

"One decision," he said, looking sadly at Sue Madison, "and you have two dead patients, instead of one. You just killed half of the men you might have saved."

She tore her eyes from the sight of the legless soldier, feeling as low as if her wrong choice had actually cost him his life. Her nostrils flared, and she tried her best to keep it from falling, but a tear spilled from her eye onto her cheek. The major wanted to reach out, brush it away, send her home. Or take her in his arms and say, "Don't worry, it's

OK." But it was not. So he asked the rest of the class, "How many of you made the same decision? Come on, be honest. Let me see your hands."

More than half of them slowly raised their hands, and the major nodded, then looked back at Sue and, for her sake, said, "More than half of you. Ten or twelve dead soldiers, then. Because you're still thinking like school nurses, damn it, not combat nurses."

Combat nurses. Some idiot in the Pentagon had sent a message to the whole Army medical community a short time before advising that the term should not be used. Females, the edict said, are by law disallowed from being placed into combat situations, therefore the term is inappropriate. *Well, screw him and the lawyer he rode in on,* the major thought.

"That's what you are, and what you'd better start thinking like. Combat nurses. This is combat," he said, flicking through more slides of savagely wounded soldiers. "Get your minds steeled to it. And think. Your decisions can kill them as surely as the bastards who send them out to be slaughtered. Think!" he yelled, and struck his pointer against the podium so hard that it snapped in two.

They were looking at him as if he were a madman, and perhaps, after eighteen months of almost daily scenes such as those he had just shown them, he was.

"If you think I'm kidding," he said softly, "or if you think I'm exaggerating, then consider this: All those slides I've just shown you are from my own camera."

He looked at his watch. "All right, that's all we have time for today," he said. "But tomorrow, when we do this again, I want you to come in here with one thing in mind. I want you to think of saving the living, not succoring the dying. You didn't wound them, you didn't make the decision to send them to be wounded, you didn't determine whether they got to you in a hopeless condition or not. So if they're hopeless, forget them. They're not your problem, not your responsibility. The dead are for parents and wives and politicians and morticians to worry about, not you. Salvage the salvageable. That's your responsibility."

His voice trailed off wearily. But he said it once more. "Save the living. They're all that matters."

SEVEN

It began with a thunderous hail of exploding mortar rounds, and when it did, Edward Walker looked at Sticks Howard and said, "I'll go help Nick with the mortars." He said it as calmly as if he had casually mentioned that he was going for a cup of coffee.

He pulled on his helmet, picked up his rifle, then turned back to Howard. "Let Danang know what's happening. If you need me, call Nick on the fire net."

He ran to the mortars and found the crews already there, hunkered down inside the sandbagged pits, waiting for the barrage to abate. He ducked inside the tiny fire direction bunker with SFC Nicholas. Nick scooted over to give him as much room as he could and said, "Looks like the shit's on, Thieu Uy."

The cramped bunker was lighted by a small bulb hanging from a battery in the rafters. It gave off just enough light for the mortarman to read the firing tables and his plotting board. Ed saw a drop of blood fall onto the plotting board, and looked at Nick's face. There was a battle dressing on his forehead, and blood was dripping from beneath it.

"What happened to your head, Nick?"

Nicholas pressed the bandage and said, "Just a scratch. No sweat."

Two rounds impacted nearby, sending shards of shrapnel zinging across the camp, then the voice of Warrant Officer Mick O'Day came across one of the two speakers on the wall of the bunker. "Uh, Punchbowl, this is Wallaby. We're in contact on our south and west. Can you get me some illumination, mate?"

As Nicholas grabbed the handset of one of the radios to answer him, Ed said, "I'll man one of the guns, if you like, Nick."

Nicholas answered O'Day before he said to Ed said, "No, sir. We'll handle the guns. You go on."

Ed understood the curt response to his offer. Nick was busy, and he didn't need the acting commander of the camp to man the mortars. Ed might soon be needed elsewhere, if a ground assault on the camp was coming.

Ed scurried out of the Nick's bunker and made a dash for the TOC. When he got there, he found Sticks on the radio to the Special Forces headquarters in Danang, apprising them of the enemy contact.

Ed studied the diagram of the camp taped on the door of the operations sergeant's Conex container. It was triangle-shaped at its outer perimeter, where tanglefoot wire covered the mined fields of fire beyond the outer trench line. Closer to the trenches, but beyond hand grenade range, was a wall of concertina wire. There was a machine gun bunker at each point of the triangle, and one midway of each side to which the claymore mine firing wires were strung.

The inner perimeter of Camp Thuong Duc was generally rectangular, the sides of the rectangle consisting of a second, irregular fighting trench, and just inside it, the plywood-sided, tin-roofed barracks of the Civilian Irregular Defense Group soldiers, and several other buildings. These included the dispensary, supply room, mess hall, and the ruins of the team house. Each building was sandbagged for three feet of its height, except for the dispensary, which was sandbagged to the roof. In addition, the dispensary roof was protected by a layer of bags, above which was suspended a canopy of chain link fencing material. The fencing was intended to cause shells falling on it to detonate before striking the roof, thus lessening their effect.

The exact center of the camp was a mound of dirt beneath which the tactical operations center lay. Clustered around it were the mortar pits; an ammunition bunker; the bunkers intended for additional ammo, fuel, and water but currently serving as living spaces for the A team; and a generator bunker. Between the inner and outer trenches was another ammo bunker, the helicopter landing zone, and the primary water supply for the camp, a deep well and pumping unit.

One point of the camp's outer triangle pointed up the ridge toward the west. 1st Camp Strike Force Company's positions ran from that point along the southwest leg of the camp's trenches. 2nd Company was on the northwest, and the understrength 3rd Company defended the eastern, downhill side, which afforded the best fields of fire, and was considered the least likely to be assaulted.

Ed Walker thought, It'll take an awful lot of men to get in here, even if we don't have air support. But the North Vietnamese *had* a lot of men, and they tried. They got between the camp and the Mike Force company, and probed in both directions. They were met by scathing fire from both points, but they were only sparring while they gave their mortars time to rake the camp before the main assault.

The mortars made a lot of noise, and holed the empty buildings, but did little damage.

When the fury of explosions shifted to O'Day's Mike Force company, one enemy battalion came up out of the low ground to the south and threw themselves against the southwest trenches. The camp's claymore mines shattered the initial surge, and a torrent of fire from 1st Company's rifles, machine guns, and grenade launchers caused the follow up assault to wither, as well.

Another battalion of NVA tried the northeast point of the camp next. Once more, the brutal claymore mines butchered them. And when they tried that corner a second time, Nicholas and his eighty-one millimeter mortars joined the rifles and machine guns until the communists had all they could bear from that quarter, and retired.

As they did, a fresh battalion rushed the 1st Company trenches again, and although another salvo of claymores staggered them, the North Vietnamese didn't break. Once more the mortars and Montagnards' small arms depleted their numbers, but still they came. Most of those who reached the concertina wire fell there, but a handful got through and into a section of the trench, trading hand grenades with the enemy soldiers on either side of them.

Lieutenant Walker went there, and with the two squads constituting 1st Company's reserve, annihilated them. Most, they killed with hand grenades. But one, though badly injured, rose to meet the American as he cleared a section of the trench in the eerie light of drifting flares. The enemy soldier raised a pistol as he struggled to his feet five meters away, and for a moment, Ed stood transfixed by the surreal sight of him. He looked so small and vulnerable. The urge to turn and run passed through Ed in a split second, and almost passively, he raised his CAR-15 and gave the man a burst that put him down for good.

The overhead flares of mortar illumination burned out temporarily, and Ed squatted in the trench, peering down it for any further signs of life. He noticed stars blinking through the broken clouds above, then Nicholas got more illumination up. The Montagnards with him bypassed Ed in the trench then, calling ahead to their comrades in Bru dialect to avoid a fight with their fellow tribesmen beyond. They gave each dead North Vietnamese an unnecessary burst of fire as they passed, then linked up with their comrades, and the camp's defenses were restored.

Ed Walker stood pondering the body of the man he had killed. A lieutenant, the same as me, he thought. He felt no remorse, no pity for the enemy soldier. But there was something. Respect? Yes, that was it, he realized. The NVA lieutenant had shown great courage, had led his men into withering fire, through the wire and into the trench. And he had not surrendered, as he might have. He had fought to the end. He had earned Ed Walker's respect, if not his pity.

His dead eyes were still open, and Ed reached down and closed the eyelids, then felt in the man's pockets. There was a little notebook, and nothing else. He took it, then picked up the man's pistol. The slide was bent. It could not have fired. Ed wondered if he had known, then threw the weapon back down beside the body.

There was no firing now except the occasional pop of illumination rounds from SFC Nicholas's mortars. He trotted back to the bunker where Bruno Kadlewicz, temporarily in command of the company in the southwest trenches, was located. "We killed all the ones who got inside the wire," Ed said in a matter-of-fact tone.

"OK. Good. I'll send a couple more claymores down there to cover the gap they got through. Jesus, I've never seen anything like this, sir," the team sergeant said, a hint of fear in his voice. "I'm lucky I only had a few guys wounded. They're already at the dispensary." He cleared his throat and spat a glob of bubbly spittle into the dirt, then looked out at the corpse-littered defensive wire. "God, I hope they're finished."

"Don't count on it," Walker said. "That was nowhere near two regiments. Stay ready." It struck him that he sounded the more experienced, and then he thought, This was nowhere near as bad as the ambush. Not yet, anyway.

There was the droning sound of an airplane overhead, a propeller driven one. Then came a flash of light and a loud pop, and the camp was lighted by a huge flare from high above. "Spooky," Kadlewicz said, the relief in his voice evident. "Thank God."

Spooky was the nickname of the AC-47 gunship, a World War II vintage transport that the Air Force had resurrected and converted to carry side-firing miniguns - rotating cannons that spewed forth a stream of bullets at the rate of hundreds per second. As long as the crew could see the ground, it was a terrifyingly effective weapon, especially against such targets as infantry massing for an assault.

"I'd better get back to the TOC, Bruno. If they come this way again, I'll be back." The team sergeant was the lone American with 1st Company. It was only right that he should have Ed's help directing the defense of that side of the camp.

"Yes, sir. I'd appreciate that, *Thieu Uy*. But I don't think they'll try as long as Spooky's around."

Walker looked up. The big flare swinging beneath a parachute was below the cloud bottoms now, and he could see only a few breaks in the clouds. It was doubtful that the old airplane could be much help if the clouds continued to close in, but all he said was, "See you later then, Bruno."

He was exhilarated by the fighting, Ed realized as he trotted to the underground headquarters bunker. Buoyed by the camp's success against the enemy's initial assaults, he almost hoped they'd try again. He was confident they would once more be massacred, and the sooner they were defeated, the sooner they would take their mortars and disappear back into Laos to lick their wounds. And maybe next time, they'd leave Thuong Duc alone.

* * *

Sue Madison walked into the officers club alone, drawing appreciative stares from many of the men, most of them Army physicians and Medical Service Corps administrators.

She looked around the crowded bar for a familiar face, but the only one she recognized was Major Draeger, the officer who had given the class in triage earlier in the day, sitting in the near darkness of the corner of the room. She got a drink, then walked to the corner where Major Draeger was, slumped in his seat and sitting alone. "Hello, Major. May I join you?" she asked.

He looked dully up at her, then heaved himself up from his chair, gestured to the seat across from him, and mumbled, "Sure. Lieutenant Madison, isn't it?"

"Yes, sir," she said. "Sue Madison."

He waited until she was seated, then flopped back into his chair.

"That was a good triage class you gave today, sir," she said.

Without looking at her he replied unenthusiastically, "It's Curt, not 'sir'. Glad you enjoyed it."

"Oh, I didn't enjoy it at all," she said. "But it was a good class."

Now he looked at her, and a weak smile showed on his face.

"Thank you," he said.

She studied the somber Army surgeon in silence for awhile. He had given the triage class in shirtsleeves that afternoon, but now he was wearing his Army Green blouse. It was ill-fitting and rumpled, but bore three rows of ribbons beneath a combat medical badge. The big black and gold patch of the First Cavalry Division was on his right shoulder.

One of his ribbons was the Bronze Star. There was also an Air Medal, which meant he had at least twenty-five combat flights, and three stars on his Vietnam campaign ribbon.

She found herself curious to know more about him. But first, she wanted to lighten his mood.

"Is the stripe really to separate the horse shit from the gun powder?" she asked.

"What?"

"The stripe on the First Cav patch," she said. "Is it really to separate the horse shit from the gunpowder?"

The unit patch of the First Cavalry Division is a yellow shield with a horse's head above a diagonal black stripe. She had once asked her father, who wore the same combat patch, what the stripe stood for, and that was what he had jokingly replied.

Major Draeger chuckled and said. "Used to be. Now it's to separate the horse shit from the aviation fuel."

The First Cav was the Army's first airmobile division, equipped with scores of helicopters to give it the mobility needed for the modern equivalent of cavalry.

"My dad was in the Cav," she said.

"Yeah? *Colonel* Madison?"

"Uh, huh. Know him?"

"Sure. Third Brigade commander," Draeger replied. "He used to visit his wounded more than any other commander I saw."

His brow furrowed, and he took a large swallow of whiskey, then stared darkly into the glass.

The levity was gone, and Sue wished she hadn't mentioned her father. She recalled what he had said at her commissioning ceremony. Something about wounds of the soul that never heal. This one had suffered more than the physical injury his Purple Heart signified, she was certain.

Draeger took another swig, then looked at her and said, "Did he make it home all right?"

"Dad? Yes. He's at the Pentagon now."

"Too bad," Draeger said, and Sue's eyes narrowed and shot his a searing glance.

Draeger caught it. "I meant, too bad he's at the Pentagon, not too bad that he made it home all right."

"Oh," she said, feeling foolish for thinking he meant the latter. "He feels the same way about being there."

"I'm going to have another of these," Draeger said, holding up his empty glass. "What would you like?"

"I know it's none of my business to say this, Major Draeger," she blurted, "but you can't drown it, you know."

"Can't drown *what*?" he shot back.

"Whatever it is you're trying to drown."

Draeger opened his mouth to say something, but suppressed it and studied Sue's pretty face a moment. He hadn't invited her to the table. He didn't even know her. And she was right when she said it was none of her business. He would have said something rude and asked her to leave, as he almost had just now. But he remembered her father, the colonel. He recalled the man's insistence on candor when he asked for the prognosis of one of his wounded soldiers, and the distress, the sadness in his eyes when it was bad.

She had those same eyes, that same sadness in them as she returned his gaze.

"Maybe not," he replied. "But sometimes it helps." He swished the ice around in his glass, drained the last of it, and said,

"Next time you talk to your father, tell him hello for me. Tell him I remember what he said to me once about oaths."

"Oaths? What do you mean?"

"Oaths. Vows. Promises. One time, he brought a bunch of wounded in on his own chopper," the major explained. "One of them was a VC. I happened to be the one who got the first look at them as they came off the helicopter. The Vietnamese guy was the worst of the salvageable ones, so I took care of him first. There was one American with most of his brains blown out. No hope, so I ignored him."

Sue noticed that Draeger's eyes had darkened at the memory and she said, "You don't need to tell me this. I can ask him."

"Yes, I do need to. It doesn't matter that he's your father. You're going to be a combat nurse. You need to hear it.

"Anyway, the brain guy died, of course, and another of the wounded troopers - his buddy, I guess - called me a few choice things that I won't bother to mention. But the gist of it was, I was a traitor for taking care of the VC first. Your father hated that his guy died, and he said something, too. So I asked him if he'd ever heard of the Hippocratic oath."

It is the vow of physicians to care for the sick, and Sue asked, "What did he say to that?"

"He said, 'You also took an oath as an American officer. You can't have it both ways.'

"I told him I'd taken the Hippocratic oath first, and he said, 'It doesn't matter which one you took first. What matters is what you believe in the most.' So I said, 'I know that, Colonel. That's why I took care of the VC.'"

"What did he do then?" Sue asked.

"He walked away. But then he came back and said, 'You're a good man, Draeger. But next time, I'll leave the communist son of a bitch on the battlefield.'

"I said, 'No, you won't, Colonel.' He asked me why not, and I said, 'Because you don't have to *take* an oath to believe in it.' He looked at me for a long time, but he didn't say anything. Finally, he just nodded. Then he left."

Sue could picture her father and Draeger standing there, and she wasn't surprised that the conversation had gone that way. "That sounds like my father, all right," she said.

The major nodded. He picked up his glass to go get another whiskey, then set it down and said, "I've had enough booze for one night. What are your plans for dinner, Sue?"

She shrugged her shoulders. "None, really," she said.

"Well, I'm going down by the river and stuff myself with Mexican food, as soon as I get out of this monkey suit," he said. "Care to join me?"

She liked this thoughtful but troubled surgeon. And after all, he was a friend of her family, of sorts. So in spite of the fact that it wasn't really proper for students to date faculty members of the medical school, she smiled and said, "Yes, thank you, Curt. I will."

*   *   *

The apartment was tiny, but it was clean and well-furnished. It was really all Mary Walker needed for the rest of the semester until she left school to have the baby, so she took it.

Anyway, she thought as she folded her clothes and arranged them in the dresser drawers, if it were any larger, mother would probably want to spend the night here half the time. And avoiding the drive between Broad Marsh and Williamsburg was not the only reason she had wanted an apartment near William and Mary College.

When her clothes were put away, she went to the Safeway and bought a few groceries for the little refrigerator. She was starting up the stairs with them when Professor Milton came walking down.

"Oh, hello, sir," she said.

"Hello, Miss Walker. What are you doing here?"

"I live here, as of today."

"Oh, really? Here, let me help you with those," he said, reaching for the bag of groceries.

She let him take it, and he followed her up the stairs. She glanced back at him, and caught him gazing at the rear of her snugly fitting jeans, the crooked smile on his face. As she unlocked the door, she said, "Are you just visiting someone, or do you live here, Professor?"

"I live here, right above you. And you can drop that 'sir' and 'Professor' crap. After all, we're neighbors."

"Well, this is the South," she said, "not California." She knew from his biography in the college catalogue that he was a native of San Francisco, and a graduate of Stanford and Berkeley Universities. With an exaggerated drawl, she said, "We're expected to show our professors the deference due their position."

"Oh, to hell with that Southern caste system bullshit!" he said, dropping the bag of groceries on the counter of the kitchenette. "You people act as if you *won* the fucking Civil War, for Christ's sake."

She glared at him, shocked at his language. Nobody ever talked to her like that. She wasn't sure how to respond to it. Then she recalled what one of her friends had said once when a Northerner had made a similar remark about the Civil War. "Really?" she blurted. "Well, who said it's *over*?"

His dark eyes darted angrily from one of hers to the other. He hadn't noticed the flecks of amber in the bright blue before. Then he threw back his head and laughed.

"Yeah, you've sure got that right," he said. "It *isn't* over." Then his eyes narrowed, and he said, "When some poor black family moves in and takes over the land you've hoarded from them all these years, *then* it'll be over. See you around the plantation, Miss Scarlet." With that, he walked out, leaving the door open behind him.

"Oh, screw you," she mumbled.

Milton stuck his head back inside her apartment. "The word is 'fuck,'" he said.

She glared at him and blurted, "Fuck you!"

His mouth formed the crooked smile and he said, "That's more like it," then closed the door between them.

Mary stood there a moment, frowning. At first she thought, How *dare* he! Then she considered her response, and smiled at herself. After all, what had he said that was really wrong? The fact that his values, his manners, were *different* from those she had been raised with didn't mean they were *wrong*. People like him were so open, so honest. And wasn't that better than the stuffy, frustrating way her parents had lived all their lives? Yes, and young people all over the country were beginning to realize that. Their parents were quick to write it off as rebellion, but so what? What was wrong with rebelling against tired, worn-out old values? After all, she thought, as she began to put her groceries away, this is Nineteen *Sixty* Seven, not Nineteen *Thirty* Seven.

EIGHT

Colonel Ngo Van Ngoc examined their faces for any sign of fear, any hint of defeat. There was none.

Ngoc was in command of both the North Vietnamese regiments around Thuong Duc, now, since the Americans had gotten lucky and hit the command post of his sister regiment with one of the bomb strikes they put in the night before. Or maybe it wasn't luck; maybe Colonel Vo had been transmitting over his radio from there, and the imperialists had fixed his position. Whichever the case, the bombs had killed Vo before his battalions had gone in.

They were supposed to pass through one of Ngoc's own battalions south of the camp, after their initial attacks there had weakened the enemy defenses. It would have been so easy. His own men had borne the brunt of the hellish mines, had depleted them with their fearless assault. They had opened gaps in the wire, even gained a foothold in the enemy trenches when Lieutenant Trung had valiantly led his men through the furious machine gun fire and into the camp.

But Vo's men never appeared. Instead of pressing on with the plan, they had hesitated, waiting for Vo's call, which never came. By the time Ngoc got a runner to them, it was too late. The gunship was overhead, the enemy had cleared the trench of Trung and his brave men, and the momentum was lost.

But never mind. They would go in next, and they would keep going in until they took the place, no matter how many of them went down. They were his men now, not Vo's. And they would fight like his men - like the intrepid Lieutenant Trung - or they would not come back. That would be the price of their earlier hesitation.

He recognized many of them, but not all of the battalion and company commanders of Vo's regiment were known to him.

"Which of you commanded 2nd Battalion?" he asked. His use of the past tense was not lost on the officers.

"I do," a major replied, defiantly changing the tense.

It was the wrong thing to do. As the others stood in stunned disbelief, Colonel Ngoc drew his pistol and shot the major in the forehead. "You *did*," Ngoc muttered to the officer as his body crumpled to the jungle floor.

His eyes burned into the others, waiting for one of them to dare to protest. None did, and he holstered the pistol.

"Today," he said, "you will not falter, you will not delay. You will not let the lives of your sister regiment's men be wasted again."

And then he turned away. There was a hole in the jungle canopy above him, and he looked up. Thick clouds lay heavily just above the trees, and he thought, There will be no enemy aircraft to interfere *this* day.

                    *   *   *

"I don't think we can get in until the clouds lift some," the helicopter company commander said over the intercom.

Captain Larry O'Neil, commander of the Nha Trang Mike Force, pressed the push-to-talk button on his headset and said, "You just find a hole and get us down through it, Major. Those guys are in deep shit down there."

Another burst of green tracers arched up through the clouds ahead. The NVA gunners around Thuong Duc were searching for the helicopters they could hear, but couldn't see.

The major led the flight in a wide, banking turn to the north. Behind him, the teenaged warrant officer flying the next helicopter said, "Now where's the son of a bitch going?"

Sam Hagen, on the intercom with the gum-chewing teenager, said, "I don't know, but look to your ten o'clock."

Through the open door of the Huey he could see a break in the thick clouds below, and the lush green of the jungle several hundred feet beneath it. The pilot saw it, too, and called his commander on the radio. "I've got a hole at ten o'clock, Six," he reported, banking his helicopter and descending toward it.

"Uh, where's it at?" the others heard the major reply. "I don't see anything big enough to get down through. Hold your position, Bearcat Two."

The youngster ignored him and continued his descending turn toward the hole. When he was above it, he said, "Plenty of room here. Follow me in."

The column of aircraft banked in his direction and the major, forgetting that the Special Forces officers were on the intercom, said to his copilot, "Reckless little bastard."

"You mean *brave* little bastard, don't you?" O'Neil retorted.

When they were beneath the cloud cover, Sam could see a ridge rising into the fog to the south. Thuong Duc was somewhere up there. Then he spotted a patch of grass to the right front and said, "Put us in that grassy spot by the stream, chief."

"Got it," the kid said, and made a flaring turn toward it.

Before Sam Hagen pulled the headset off to leap from the chopper, he said, "Good job, chief," and heard the young pilot reply, "No goal too bold, no spot too hot. You call, we haul, y'all!"

Sam jumped into the grass and fell several feet further than he had expected to, knocking the wind from himself. The Cham soldiers with him knew the height of elephant grass and were prepared for it, breaking their fall with flexed knees, and tumbling. Sam crawled away, gasping for breath, before the next load of men leaped into the grass. By the time he fully got his breath back, Mullins and O'Neil were at the edge of the stream, studying a map.

"We're right about here," Snake said, pointing to a spot some three kilometers southeast of the camp's location.

"Three klicks. All uphill," O'Neil said. "Well, maybe the next lift can get in closer."

Only one of the three Mike Force companies in the battalion could be lifted by the helicopters at a time. It would be late afternoon before the whole battalion was on the ground, providing they could find holes in the cloud cover to get down through. And the North Vietnamese were already pressing their attack.

Mullins was on the radio to Sticks Howard in the camp. He sent Sticks the encoded coordinates of the landing zone as the last of the helicopters lifted up through the heavy mist. Then he asked for a situation report.

"I can't really tell from in here, except that there's a lot of firing going on. Most of it seems to be on the south, though," Howard reported.

The noise of the helicopter flight was fading to the east now, and the men at the landing zone began to hear firing far up on the ridge to their southwest. There were muffled explosions, and the steady *thump, thump* of a heavy machine gun.

Sergeant First Class Ben Davan, commander of the Mike Force company that had just landed, reported to Captain O'Neil that they were moving out.

"A soldier goes to the sound of the guns," said O'Neil, quoting Murat.

Davan grinned at him and added, "...especially a Mike Force soldier."

Sam Hagen, leading the point platoon, turned and started toward the distant sound of battle, his well-trained troops following him across the stream and up the ridge.

Mullins and O'Neil watched the first two platoons pass, appreciating the disciplined interval, their attentiveness to the flanks, the readiness with which they bore their weapons. Their battle gear was uniformly clean, and well secured. There was an air of quiet competence about them.

"Good looking troops," Mullins said.

O'Neil nodded. "Chams," he said. "Warriors. Fierce, and tough. Soldiering is in their blood."

Atop the ridge, the fight was expanding in intensity. The claymores had almost all been fired now, even though at first light

Lieutenant Walker had seen that they were replaced where they had been depleted the night before. Now they were all but gone, scores of enemy bodies in the tanglefoot wire testifying to their brutal effectiveness.

The daylight attack had caught the camp's defenders by surprise. The North Vietnamese just suddenly appeared out of the heavy fog, coming up the hill from the south.

Nick Nicholas was supervising the transfer of the dwindling supply of ammunition from the bunker near the outer perimeter into the one beside the mortar pits when the attack began.

Staff Sergeant Carl Brown was at the gate on the eastern side of the camp with one of his 2nd Company platoons, about to make a quick sweep around the outside of the perimeter.

The other four Americans in the team were asleep, resting themselves for the battle they expected after dark, and most of their Camp Strike Force soldiers were either in their mess hall grabbing a meal, or asleep in their bunks. Only a third were in the trenches, awaiting their turn to eat or sleep.

The I Corps Mike Force company under the Australian, Nick O'Day, was moving closer to the camp and digging in.

Sergeant Brown reacted quickly when the first smattering of fire from the thinly-spread and sleepy soldiers in the southwest trenches signaled the enemy's presence. Immediately after, the NVA presence was confirmed by an incoming salvo of rocket propelled grenades and the crackling of machine gun fire across the camp.

Brown made a mad dash for the bunker in the center of the line, and fired a volley of claymore mines into the charging North Vietnamese. They reeled, but did not withdraw.

Nicholas and his crews were in action before the NVA recovered from Brown's brutal greeting, though. They used no formal gunnery skills, just turned the heavy 4.2 inch mortars to the southwest and dropped the big shells in the tubes at "charge zero." The internal charge was all they needed to propel them in a lazy arc the short distance to the massed formation of NVA troops. By the time twelve rounds had ravaged them in quick succession, the assault disintegrated into retreat, then into flight.

The next battalion of Ngoc's fresh regiment tried the northwest trench. But by then most of Thuong Duc's defenders were at their posts, and the assault on that side had begun to falter from the torrent of small arms fire even before the claymores ripped through it. What remained of the effort was dissipated by more 4.2 inch mortar rounds.

Colonel Ngoc had proved his point to his new regiment, and they to him. Now, with the cursed claymores gone, and the pressure mines and defensive wire scattered by the enemy's own heavy mortar rounds, it was time to maneuver his battalions for the final violent blow.

He looked up at the heavy clouds, pleased to see that nature was prepared to assist his effort. There was no way that the helicopters he had heard could get down through that, and no way that their jet fighters or their gunships could be used. Ngoc turned to the commander of his heavy weapons battalion. "Commence the rocket and mortar attack," he ordered.

Katusha rockets slammed into the ridgetop fortress, their big, 122 millimeter warheads creating six-foot craters where they exploded. One rocket found the trenches on the northwest side of the triangle. Four soldiers from 2nd Company were killed outright by the blast, and a half-dozen more were wounded there. Staff Sergeant Brown was among them, one lung badly holed.

Another rocket landed near enough to one of Nicholas's mortar pits to collapse it. Both men inside it were injured, and the mortar was damaged. A third Katusha destroyed the command bunker's generator and sent flaming cans of fuel spewing across the camp. The supply building was set afire by one of them.

Lieutenant Walker was in the tactical operations center when the rockets hit. He was on the radio to Captain Mullins, trying to determine when he and the Mike Force company from Nha Trang would arrive.

"We should be there in half an hour," Mullins was saying, "unless we run into..." Then the bunker shook, and the lights and radio went dead.

While Howard scrambled to get a Coleman lantern going, Walker tried to call his team leader back, but got no answer. So he tried Kadlewicz, then Brown. Neither man answered his call. He tried Nicholas's fire coordination net, but Nicholas didn't respond. He had no way of knowing it was because Nick was tending to his wounded.

Then Kadlewicz's worried voice came over the fire net. "They're coming up again," he cried. "Jesus, there's so many this time! Give me some support, Nick!"

Ed waited, thinking aloud, "Come on, Nick. Answer him." God, it was so confusing, so chaotic. And the team was stretched so thin. Nicholas was off the air. He couldn't raise Brown on the radio. He'd lost contact with Mullins. Kadlewicz's company was under attack and calling desperately for support. What the hell was going on out there?

You have to *see* the battlefield before you can influence actions on it, whether that means physically observing it, or envisioning it through the use of maps and accurate, timely reports. He was not getting enough of the latter, and anyway, the best way is to actually look at what's going on. And that's the only way to *feel* it. He decided to go see.

"Get everybody on the fire net, Sticks," he said as Howard placed a Coleman lantern in the commo Conex. Then he grabbed a backpack radio from the emergency supplies, turned it on, and set the frequency on the fire coordination net. As soon as he stepped out of the bunker, he called Kadlewicz.

"I can't raise Nicholas, and I need help bad," Bruno reported.

"I'm going there now," Ed replied. "Stay on this net. We're going to get everybody else up on it, too."

Specialist Link, the other American with Brown's 2nd Company, was the first to call when he got the word from Howard to switch to the new frequency. "Brown's down with a sucking chest wound, and I've got a bunch of other casualties," Link reported. "There's a lot of small arms fire, a lot of dinks over here."

Lieutenant Walker was at the mortar pits now. He found Nicholas trying desperately to keep one of his men alive with mouth-to-mouth resuscitation. The rest of the crewmen were hunkered down in the remaining mortar pits as enemy fire continued to sporadically rake the camp.

"Nick," Ed said calmly, "you've got to leave him and get on the guns."

Without looking up, Nicholas continued to press the heel of his hands onto the man's chest with rapid, hard shoves and said, "Go to hell, Lieutenant. He's not gone yet. I can still save him."

Ed recognized the badly injured soldier as the mortarman's constant companion. He'd seldom seen Nicholas without the man by his side. "Leave him and get on the guns, Nick, or we're liable to lose the camp."

Nicholas looked up at him, oblivious to the desperate battle that was underway around him, his eyes burning with frustration and rage. Then he looked back at his friend and said, "All right, then. God damn them, anyway. All right."

It began to rain as Nicholas barked commands to his crews, but it did nothing to stem the advance of the North Vietnamese against Kadlewicz's position. By the time Walker got to the bunker where Kadlewicz was, he found the team sergeant desperately trying to get the machine gun back into action. It was badly jammed, and its absence from the defensive fires was obvious. The enemy had reached the wire in several places between the bunker and the southeast corner of the camp. The mortar rounds from Nick's remaining 4.2 inch tube were landing beyond them. While Bruno continued to struggle with the gun, Ed called the mortar section and advised Nicholas of the problem, then headed down the trench line toward the enemy. He found the Montagnard troops there low on ammunition, and most were now heaving their remaining hand grenades at the approaching North Vietnamese.

A dozen of the Bru were dead or wounded, and Ed tore the unused magazines of ammunition from their combat gear and tossed them to the men who still were fighting. The hand grenades he found, he threw at the NVA himself. But it was not enough to stop them. He could see some of them jumping into the trench down near the corner of the triangle.

Then there was a blast somewhere behind him, and the air was filled momentarily with a strange kind of hum. A few seconds later, the blast and humming sound occurred again, and he looked back at the source.

Atop the command bunker, SFC Nicholas and some of his men were shifting their big 106 millimeter recoilless rifle and reloading it. And then they fired again, and once more the humming sound zipped past in a split second, and Ed understood what it was; it was a beehive round, and the sound was hundreds of flechettes, tiny steel darts from the big gun's anti-personnel round passing just overhead before ripping through the massed enemy approaching the trench line, mowing them down like an invisible scythe. But before the 106 crew could reload and fire again, a line of tracers from the bunker at the southeast corner of the camp sprayed their position, scattering them. The enemy had the bunker now, and had turned the machine gun in toward the camp.

"Aw, no! No!" Ed cried aloud. The North Vietnamese could not be allowed to control the crucial bunker. It would let them dominate the trench line in two directions, and open the corner as a main point of entry into the camp for the assaulting forces.

He looked around him. There were only a few Camp Strike Force soldiers in sight, popping up above the trench just long enough to throw a wild burst of fire at the enemy, who were now shifting toward the corner of the camp their comrades controlled.

Something had to be done about the bunker. Ed grasped the radio handset and pressed the button to inform the other Americans of the development, but there was a loud squawk in his ear. The handset had been short-circuited by the increasingly heavy rain.

Without the radio, he realized with a sinking feeling, he was in command of no one but himself. There was no organized defense anymore, just scattered pockets of men fighting for their lives. Maybe the best thing would be to pull everyone back to the inner perimeter and fight from there. But once they took that first step back, that unmistakable signal of retreat, the enemy would know. They would redouble their efforts and quickly take over the whole outer trench line, giving them cover from which to do battle. Their mortars would shift their full fury onto the remaining defenders concentrated within the tiny inner perimeter and massacre them. And the Mike Force battalion, if it ever arrived, would have to try to root the NVA from their entrenched positions. No, they had to try to hang onto the outer perimeter. Help would be there soon. At least one company from the Nha Trang Mike Force. And he could call the Australian with the company west of the camp and order him into the trenches, too.

If they could keep the NVA in the open, they could continue to slaughter them. If they could hold most of the camp, they could avoid the increased vulnerability to the enemy mortars. But first, something had to be done about that damned bunker at the corner of the camp.

Ed Walker sighed so deeply that it came out of his throat as a distraught moan, and he said aloud, "God help me." Then he moved alone on down the trench.

He found two hand grenades on the combat gear of the next Bru soldier he reached, a man who was shot through the throat and dying. Without taking time to administer to the man, Ed shrugged the radio off his shoulders, cradled his stubby CAR-15 rifle in his arms, and crawled down the trench toward the enemy with the grenades in his fists.

The trench was filling with water now, and the rain was turning the red clay of the hilltop into slippery mud.

A man in front of him was leaning over the top of the trench, firing rapid but well-aimed, single shots into the attackers. He turned and ducked down to reload, and Ed saw that it was Sergeant Tran, the Vietnamese Special Forces sergeant of whom his teammates spoke so highly.

"Many VC!" Tran said, quickly slamming another magazine into his rifle, then rising above the sandbagged top of the trench to pick off another dozen or so of the enemy. Ed crawled past him, but he had only gotten a few feet when he felt a tug at the leg of his trousers. He looked back and saw Tran, who asked, "Where you go, Thieu Uy?"

"The corner bunker," Ed answered. "The NVA are in it."

"OK," the Vietnamese said without hesitation. "We go."

Just ahead of them, three frightened Montagnards of 2nd Company's battered defenders were abandoning the trench to the enemy, crawling back toward Walker and Tran.

"No!" Ed ordered, stopping the first of the men and shoving him back toward the North Vietnamese. "We have to hold here! Right here!"

They were chattering in Bru and showing Ed that they were out of ammunition. He pulled his own magazines, six of them, from his ammo pouches and handed them to the men. Tran was speaking to them, and Ed had no idea what he was saying, but the men reloaded and stayed between the LLDB sergeant and him as he picked up the two grenades and began to crawl toward the enemy-held bunker once more.

He was filled with dread. How could he expect to do this? But what else could he do? Run somewhere and hide? Wait for them to come and kill him, while he hoped in vain that someone else's bravery would win the day? No, he had to try. He couldn't expect the others to fight, if he didn't. And anyway, the others were watching him now.

He halted, then peeked around a corner of the jagged trench. There was a North Vietnamese soldier there, peering above the trench into the camp. Walker backed off, put the hand grenades in the mud, squatted, and drew his rifle to his shoulder. Then he jumped around the corner and fired, and saw the enemy soldier collapse into the mud as he looked beyond for others. There were none in the short stretch of trench that he could see. He backed up, retrieved the grenades, and crept forward, past the dying man he had just shot. The North Vietnamese soldier, unable to move, followed the American with glazed eyes, until the Bru behind Ed smashed his skull with his rifle butt.

There was a helicopter high overhead somewhere, and Ed wondered what its purpose was. A single Huey, from the sound of it. Maybe a medevac trying to get in, responding to a call from Howard or someone else. He'd never get in through this mess, Ed knew.

He froze. Around the corner of the trench, someone was yelling in Vietnamese. Tran moved up beside him, listening. Ed held a grenade in front of him and grasped the pin, but Tran stopped him by putting his hand over Ed's, then put his finger to his mouth to signal Ed to be quiet and wait.

The LLDB sergeant listened for a few moments longer, then stepped past the American sergeant, leapt around the corner, and fired a long burst from his rifle. Ed followed him. There were two NVA lying in the mud, one holding a radio handset.

"He tell other NVA to move into trenches on east side," Tran explained in a whisper. "They decide to take that area first." Tran was smiling, as if he'd discovered some great secret, and added, "Now we know."

"So what?" Lieutenant Walker said. They had no radio to inform anyone else of the enemy's intention. What good did it do to know they'd take the eastern side of the camp first?

"Now we take bunker," the Vietnamese NCO replied, as if it were a logical answer. He pushed past Ed, taking a hand grenade from him as he did. He rushed down the trench and Ed followed, saw him pull the pin from the grenade and reach the bunker, then lean around the corner of it and dump it in through the firing aperture. Both men hugged the muddy bottom of the trench until it exploded, then Ed got up and ran to the bunker, throwing the other grenade around it and into the trench line beyond. He ducked back behind the bunker again and found Tran standing there, looking into the center of the camp and waving his arms to the men crouched behind the mound of dirt atop the TOC. They saw him, and scrambled to the big recoilless rifle. They swung it to the eastern trench line in response to Tran's mad gestures, and fired. The deadly hum of tiny steel darts filled the air once more, shredding the massed enemy swarming through the wire there.

Tran ducked down into the trench and grinned at Ed. "Get more soldiers, get more grenades," he said, still grinning. "We wait here." Then he began giving orders to the three Montagnards.

Ed stole a peek at the wire in front of the trench line to his rear. There were no NVA trying to come in that way now; the only movement was of several wounded men attempting to crawl away.

He started back down the trench as the boom and hum of another beehive round rent the air. He peeked around the first two turns of the twisting ditch, then decided his best bet to avoid being shot by some of his own men was to get out of the trench and run toward them. He did so, and when he had collected a squad of the Montagnards, he led them in a headlong rush back down the trench toward the bunker.

He turned them over to Tran and ran back to let Kadlewicz know what was going on. He got to the bunker in the center of the line and found Kadlewicz on the radio.

"I think we should pull back and hold the inner perimeter until they get here," Bruno was telling someone. Then he saw Ed, and paled. "My God," he said. "I thought you'd been killed." He said into the radio, "Wait one, Sticks. The lieutenant just showed up."

"They're in the eastern trenches," Ed reported. "What's going on over on Brown's side of camp?"

"Brown's been hit," Bruno said. "And Link says he can't hold on. The Aussie's company is headed that way, but I think we ought to pull in and defend the inner perimeter until Mullins gets here with the Mike Force."

"Where's Mullins now?"

"I don't know."

"Let me use the radio," Ed said.

Kadlewicz passed him the handset, but before he spoke, Lieutenant Walker took a moment to collect his thoughts. He had to change the situation from a series of scattered fights into a coordinated defense of the camp again. And then he needed to organize a counterattack to return the eastern trenches to friendly hands. It didn't seem impossible now; a quick and simple plan executed with boldness could do it. Tran had shown him that. He wished there were a dozen more men like the LLDB sergeant in the camp. Perhaps there were, but without direction, without some order imposed upon the madness that raged around the ridge top fortress, they could not be expected to spend their bravery successfully.

He called Link first and asked for his estimate of the situation on the far side of the camp, the northwest leg of the triangle. "It's pretty bad, sir," the young specialist replied with a quaver in his voice. "We've got a lot of wounded, and we're awful low on ammo."

"Roger," Walker answered. "Where are the NVA on your side? Are they still assaulting?"

"Uh, no sir, not right now. But there's still firing."

"Then send some men for ammo, right now, while you can. You copy?"

"We're getting ready to move back. We can pick it up then," Link replied.

"Negative!" Walker answered. "We're not going to give up any more of the outer line. Just hang in there. I'll get you some help. Break. Wallaby, this is Walker. What's your location?"

"We're just west of the wire. I've, uh, I've got a bit of a punch up going with the bastards in front of Link."

"Can you attack them?" Ed asked.

"Er, say again, mate?"

"I say again, can you launch a counterattack on the troops in front of Link?"

"Aren't we needed inside the camp?" O'Day asked.

"Negative. Not yet, anyway. Can you hit their flank on that side?" Ed inquired again.

"Ah, roger that, boss. I'd rather do that than get stuck inside the wire, anyhow," Mick O'Day said, and Ed thought, *That's more like it.*

Captain Mullins reported in. "Walker, this is Snake. We're almost there. Where do you want us?"

Thank God! Ed thought, then asked, "What's your location now, sir?"

"We're about two hundred and fifty meters northeast," Mullins replied.

Ed considered what he should ask Mullins and the Mike Force company with him to do. While he pondered the problem, he noticed that the rain had stopped. He noticed, too, that Kadlewicz was dispatching a squad to get a resupply of ammunition from the bunker in the inner perimeter and wondered, Why the hell didn't he do it before?

Nick Nicholas took advantage of the lull in radio traffic to report that he was going to continue to work the east trench line with the 106 millimeter recoilless rifle, and was ready to put the 81 millimeter mortars wherever anybody needed them.

Good, Ed thought. It's coming together, now. His troops still held two legs of the camp's triangle. The NVA had quit trying, at least for the time being, to take the southwest wall, where he now stood. The Camp Strike Force troops there were being resupplied with ammunition in case the enemy did try again.

The northwest side would be all right, too, since Mick O'Day's company was hitting the enemy from the flank on that side, now.

The NVA were in the trenches on the east, and they were liable to start pushing out along the other legs. Tran couldn't hold them off forever, and Ed didn't know if the bunker at the other end of the enemy occupied trench line was still in friendly hands or not.

"Walker, this is Snake. Where do you want this element?" Mullins asked once more, impatient for an answer.

Colonel Ngo Van Ngoc of the Peoples Army of Vietnam supplied the answer. He sent another battalion toward the eastern trenches. They appeared in an orderly line, coming out of the jungle and up the slope into the open area beyond the wire.

Lieutenant Walker saw them and decided what he wanted the Mike Force company with Mullins and O'Neil to do. "They're coming with an assault from the east!" he said over the radio. "Can you hit them over there?"

Larry O'Neil answered. "Walker, this is Crossbow. Affirmative! We'll hit them from the north!"

That was what the Mike Force commander wanted. He barked an order to the company commander, SFC Ben Davan, and Davan passed the order to his platoon leaders, and they to their fierce Cham warriors. The company moved out in a wedge toward the enemy, Sam Hagen's platoon at the point of the wedge.

Ed rushed to the inner perimeter trench on the eastern side of the camp. He found old Pop the cook, in the trench there. Pop had a case of hand grenades, and as he removed each one from its cardboard container, he would pull the pin, peer for a split second above the top of the trench, then hurl the grenade at the nearest enemy he spotted. When Ed crawled up beside him, the old man said, "Beaucoup VC, Thieu Uy! Same Same Dien Bien Phu!" Then he resumed his deadly business.

Ed peered above the trench. The ground between there and the outer trench line was littered with dead and dying NVA. It suddenly struck him that, had it not been for the old cook, the North Vietnamese would have taken the inner perimeter trench on this side. Thuong Duc had more than four hundred Camp Strike Force soldiers, but except for a few men like Pop and Tran - and, yes, Ed now realized, himself - except for those few, the camp might well now be in the hands of the North Vietnamese.

He joined Pop in repelling the few remaining enemy trying to reach the inner trench, wondering as he did so why they had come up one battalion at a time this way. Why piecemeal, instead of one overwhelming surge to begin with? They would own the camp by now, if they'd done that early on. He wondered who their commander was, what was on his mind. He wished that he'd been made to study the North Vietnamese senior officers more, instead of Clausewitz and Napoleon and Hannibal and Lee. Maybe then he'd understand. They were brave, these NVA. But their officers were either stupid, or they had no regard for the lives of their men.

He leaned across his stubby rifle, enclosed one of the enemy within the aperture of the sight, and squeezed the trigger. The man collapsed, and Ed moved the sight onto another, thinking, It's all right now. The Mike Force - Sam and his men - will be here soon.

NINE

"I, uh, I'd like to apologize for the way I acted this afternoon," Professor Sandy Milton said, bringing a bottle of wine from behind his back and holding it out to Mary.

She stood in the door of her apartment and clutched the front of her robe, glaring silently at him.

"It's California wine," he said, his mouth wearing its crooked smile. "Is that why you're hesitant to accept it?"

"It's nice of you to apologize," she said. "But it's awfully late."

"Not in California," he said.

"This isn't California."

He sighed and said, "No, it certainly isn't."

She noticed that his other hand held a corkscrew; he obviously planned to come in and share the wine with her. She wondered if he really thought it would be that easy to get next to her. It was amazing what showing a little leg to some guys would cause them to do. Still, it was nice to be made to feel attractive, even if it was in such a blatantly sexual way. Typical California attitude, though, she thought; first you say, 'fuck,' then you do it. Well, she was learning to rethink her values, but there were limits. She reached for the bottle with one hand and for the door with the other. The front of her robe fell open, exposing the lacy bra and panties she wore underneath, but Milton got only a brief glance as she said, "Thank you. I accept your apology," and quickly closed the door in his face.

Milton stood there a moment, then almost knocked on the door again before he stopped himself. No, he'd better let it go at that, for now.

His reason for apologizing had not been simply to try to make a move on this attractive, sexy student of his. There were plenty of other, openly-willing coeds, if that was all he had in mind. But he had looked up Mary's college application the previous day, and had learned, among other things, that her father was a man of considerable influence with the hierarchy of William and Mary College. If she were to report to her father that one of her professors had spoken to her as Milton had, it might well cost him his job at the conservative Virginia college. And that would be a disaster, because if he lost his deferment, he would, in all probability, be called up by the draft board. And Sandy Milton wasn't about to risk his promising life in the politicians' senseless, evil war in Vietnam. So he turned away from Mary's door, smiling to himself as he thought of the voluptuous body she had flashed at him.

I'll share that bottle of wine with you yet, Mrs. Mary Walker, he thought. And after I finish with you, you'll never want to be with that redneck soldier of a husband of yours again.

*   *   *

Ed Walker watched his good friend, Sam Hagen, with respectful awe as the Mike Force sergeant led his Cham warriors out of the jungle and into the flank of the staggering enemy. The NVA were still reeling from a furious and accurate barrage from the camp's remaining mortars and the grenadiers of the Mike Force company, which now shifted away from the flank and into the center of the enemy line.

As the Cham infantrymen assaulted into the North Vietnamese positions, there was Sam in the middle of his men, standing and waving them forward, looking for all the world, Ed thought, like the *Follow Me* statue at the Infantry School.

Ed could see that Hagen was yelling something to them, although he couldn't understand what it was.

The Chams couldn't understand Sam either, but they could hear him. They could not have understood what he was saying above the din of battle even if he spoke their language. But they heard him yelling, and they looked at him, and saw his gestures, the fierceness in his eyes as he went striding boldly into the fray, and it inspired them to act. They pressed the attack, overwhelming their foe and rooting them out of their hard-won positions.

Every man in the platoon was firing, Ed noticed from his position in the inner trench. And not haphazardly, but deliberately, pausing to aim each burst, reloading on the move. Ed noticed, too, that each Cham rifle bore a ready bayonet. He had read much about how ten percent of the soldiers in a unit do almost all the killing, much as ten percent of fishermen catch ninety percent of the fish, and he thought, Whoever wrote that was not writing about the Chams.

Nick Nicholas was still on the recoilless rifle, using the last of his deadly beehive rounds to ravage the enemy just forward of Hagen's assault. On either side of Ed Walker, 3rd Company's machine guns clattered in support of the attack, as well.

Ngo Van Ngoc made one last attempt to hold the eastern trench. He rallied one of the decimated battalions from his earlier attempts to storm the camp and led them out of the jungle toward the fight.

The company of Chams tore into them, and they staggered. Colonel Ngoc rushed forward in an attempt to maintain the attack, but Sam Hagen saw him, and put him down with a bullet to the brain.

The remainder of the North Vietnamese around Thuong Duc had borne all of the carnage they could stand, and under the onslaught of the Mike Force counterattack, they began to melt away, back into the sanctuary of the jungle. An hour later, they were gone, and Camp Thuong Duc was quiet.

"I'm worried about you, Sam," Ed Walker said the following day.

Hagen stopped cleaning his rifle and looked up at his friend. "Me? What do you mean, *Thieu Uy?*"

"Just that. You're going to get yourself killed, if you go charging into firefights like you did yesterday, standing up and acting like you're bulletproof, or something."

Sam turned his attention back to the weapon and said, "Not me. The way you keep from getting killed is to kill them *first.* Kick the hell out of them before they know what's hit them. And you don't lead the Chams from anywhere but up front."

He finished putting the rifle together, then put it aside and looked at Ed. "Anyway," he said, "from what Kadlewicz and Howard told me last night, you've got no room to talk. And you don't have the Chams to cover your ass like I do, just a bunch of sorry Viets and Bru. *You're* the one who needs to take care of himself, Ed."

It was the first time that Ed could recall Sam calling him by his first name. He was glad he did.

"What do you hear from Mary, anyway?" Sam asked. "Everything going all right?"

He was genuinely concerned. Maria DeCalesta had said, in her last letter to Sam, that she had spoken to Mary Walker on the telephone after Sam had written about seeing Ed in Nha Trang. Mary just didn't seem to grasp the fact that Ed was at war, she said, or that she was a married woman about to have a child. As Maria had put it, "she doesn't act as if Ed and their child are the most important things in her life, which they should be. I'm just afraid she'll let him down."

Walker shrugged his shoulders and replied, "Yeah, I guess everything's OK. The doctor said the pregnancy's going all right. She's talking about moving out of Broad Marsh and getting an apartment in Williamsburg, though."

"Why's that?"

Ed downed the last of the lukewarm coffee from his cup and replied, "Her parents are driving her nuts, I guess. Anyway, it would be better for her than driving back and forth to college every day. You ever stop to think how dangerous driving is, Sam?"

"Driving?"

"Yeah. I mean, when you think about it, we kill, what, fifty thousand Americans on the highway every year? Hell, we haven't lost half that many people in this whole damned war."

"Yet...." Sam added. "So, what does she think about you being out here in the middle of VC territory?"

"Humph," Ed snorted. "She thinks I'm in Danang. Said something about being worried I might take up with one of the 'townies.' I guess I ought to send her a picture of a couple of those old Bru hags down in the village, with their black teeth, and flabby tits hanging down to their waist."

Hagen laughed at the thought, then said seriously, "Well, you oughta tell her the truth about what it's like here. God knows, she won't get the truth from TV or the newspapers."

Ed Walker thought about the carnage he had seen since his arrival at Thuong Duc, about the nearness of death. His tour was not a tenth up, and already he had almost been killed in an ambush, and the camp had nearly been overrun by the enemy. If Sam and the rest of the Mike Force had not shown up the day before, God only knows what might have happened to him. He might even be dead by now.

Ed shook his head. "Nah," he said. "No use worrying her. There's nothing she can do about it."

Sam Hagen wasn't sure he agreed with that. She could do *something* for him. She could at least give him her moral support. Everybody needed somebody back there pulling for him. Somebody who believed in you, and in what you were doing. Somebody to live for. Sure, it was your buddies you fought for. You fought for their respect, and, if necessary, for their lives. But that wasn't what you lived for. If anything, they were what you died for.

Maria was the reason Sam Hagen wanted to live. In every letter that she wrote faithfully each day, she reminded him of the fact that she needed him. She needed him to live and to come home, because if he didn't, her life would be empty. Meaningless. Time and again, that was what she told him.

To hell with the craftily-worded aims the politicians gave for the war, and patriotism, and freedom, and all those lofty causes for which young men went into combat. Because once they got there, Sam Hagen had learned - once they had been dipped in the boiling cauldron that was battle, the idealism was scalded off. And what was left was the naked reality of war; the fact that you would either survive it, or you wouldn't. But you had to have a purpose to survive, and Maria

DeCalesta was his. He hoped to God that Mary would be a worthy reason for Ed to do so.

To Sam Hagen, the way you survived was by winning. To others, the way was by avoiding battle, but that was the coward's way, and Ed Walker was no coward. If the idealism wasn't gone yet, Sam believed, it soon would be. And if he lost the only remaining reason to survive this mess after that was gone - the love of a good woman - he was doomed.

He looked at Ed sadly, hoping Maria was wrong. But she did have this remarkable intuition about such things.

"Hey!" Ed said. "You look like you just lost your best friend, Sammy. What's bothering you?"

"Ah, nothing," Hagen said. "I was just thinking about you having to be over here when your kid's born."

Ed grinned at him. "Hagen, you're turning into a sentimental old softie. All I'm going to miss is being up to my elbows in baby crap, and having to get up at two in the morning to feed the little booger."

"Well that's better than being up to your ass in blood and getting awakened all night by mortar attacks, isn't it?"

That wasn't the sort of thing Ed Walker was used to hearing from Sam Hagen. Something was bothering him, and it wasn't the fact that the baby was going to be born before Ed got home. What was it? "How's things with Maria, Sam?" he asked, wondering if perhaps they'd had a falling out.

"She's fine. Writes every day. She's working at one of those kiddie places in Fayetteville where the wives take their children while they go play bridge or meet their boyfriends."

"Lieutenant Walker," someone called into the battered mess hall building where the two men sat. Ed turned and saw that it was one of the team's new replacements, Staff Sergeant Cal Wilkerson.

"Yeah, Cal. What's up?"

"Captain Mullins wants you, sir. He's in the TOC."

"OK. Thanks. I'll be right there." He turned back to Sam Hagen. "Will you be here when I get back?"

Sam looked at his watch and said, "No, I won't. I need to get my troops squared away. We're moving out in about twenty minutes."

The Mike Force battalion was going out after the remnants of the North Vietnamese regiments whose effort to overrun Camp Thuong Duc they had thwarted the day before. Captain Mullins would have been perfectly willing to let them stay in camp a day or so to ensure the enemy was gone, then head back to Nha Trang. But that wasn't the way the Mike Force battalion commander, Captain Larry O'Neil, did things.

"No, we're going after them," O'Neil declared. "If we don't, they'll just show up here again, or at some other camp, and we'll have to come back. And I don't want to come back here again. There's no women, and not a bottle of Irish whiskey in the whole damn camp!"

Behind O'Neil's banter was the serious motivation of an officer who saw as his mission the destruction of as many of the enemy as possible, because that was the way you won wars. And Larry O'Neil was going to do his part to see that this war was won. His reconnaissance platoon was already out tracking the battered NVA troops, who appeared to be hightailing it for Laos. The weather had cleared, and he still had operational control of the assault helicopter company. He wasn't about to miss such an opportunity.

"Well, if I don't see you before you leave, remember what I said, Sam," Ed told his buddy. "Keep your head down."

"You, too, Ed. For your kid's sake," Hagen replied, holding his hand out to the officer. Ed ignored it and gave the big sergeant a rough hug. "You sweet motherfucker, don't you never die," he said. The crude expression was probably the fondest thing one Special Forces soldier could say to another, in those days.

When he got to the tactical operations center, Ed found Snake Mullins and Larry O'Neil waiting for him.

"Sit down, Ed," Mullins said.

Ed looked at him curiously. The tone was one he would expect to hear when bad news was about to be issued. *Oh, God,* he thought, *Please don't let it be something about Mary or the baby.* "What's wrong?" he asked, still standing.

"Nothing's wrong," Mullins said. "It's just that we're getting more replacements in." He glanced at O'Neil, then back at Ed. "One of them's a first lieutenant, and you know what that means."

Second Lieutenant Walker nodded. "It means I won't be the team XO any longer."

"That's right. You'll be the CAPO officer."

The civil affairs/ psychological operations officer was a new position on the A team created for the Vietnam war. The primary duties of the CAPO officer were to attend to the morale of the Camp Strike Force soldiers and the welfare of their dependents, to foster a positive attitude among the soldiers toward the government of South Vietnam, and to use psychological operations against the enemy. It was not what Ed Walker wanted to do.

The arrival of another officer senior to him in rank also meant that Ed would no longer be the second in command at Camp Thuong Duc. From now on, the first lieutenant would assume command during Captain Mullins's absence from the camp. Ed said nothing, but looked at the floor and slowly shook his head.

"I don't want you to get the idea that this is some kind of demotion or something, Ed," Mullins said. "You did a hell of a fine job of defending this camp. In fact, we might well have lost the damn place, if it hadn't been for you. You're a fine officer, a damn good soldier, and..."

"Oh, quit beating around the bush, Snake," Larry O'Neil interrupted. "Do you want to be the CAPO officer here, Walker, or do you want to come down to the Mike Force with me? You're a fighter. We could use you."

Ed looked up at him, then at Mullins, then back at O'Neil. "Are you serious?" he asked.

"Yeah, I'm serious. They're about to expand the Mike Force to two battalions, and I'm going to need a couple of good lieutenants for XOs. The group adjutant's a friend of mine; he'll give me whoever I want. Do you want the job?"

Ed looked again at Mullins and said, "You don't think I'd be running out on the team, sir?"

"What team? Hell, Nick and I are the only guys left on the original team that came out here. And we're both short."

"So, what'll it be, Walker?" O'Neil said, standing and picking up his rifle. "You want to stay here and try to convince the Montagnards that the Vietnamese government's a wonderful institution, or do you want to go with me, and fight the war?"

Ed Walker looked at Snake Mullins. "I'm going to the Mike Force, sir," he said, then to O'Neil said, "I'll get my weapon and field gear."

O'Neil slapped him on the back and said, "Not so fast, son. I think we can handle one more operation without you."

"Anyway," Mullins added, "you and Sergeant Hagen have to be here when the corps commander shows up in a couple of hours. He's going to give you two an impact award."

"A what?" Walker asked. He'd never heard of an "impact award."

"A medal. Kind of a hip pocket award he's allowed to hand out on the spot, without paperwork."

Ed had never thought that what he did during the NVA assault on the camp might lead to his being awarded a medal.

"Why me?" he said. "Sam, sure, but what about Nicholas and Mick O'Day, and Pop and Tran? They're the ones who deserve medals. Are they going to get them, too?"

"Not today. They just wanted one name from me and one from Larry," Mullins explained. "The others will have to go through regular channels. That's one of the things you need to take care of before you leave here."

"Well, I've got to get going," O'Neil said. "Got to go give as many NVA as we can the chance to earn Purple Hearts or whatever they get for getting shot. I'll see you when we get back, Walker. Welcome aboard." He offered his hand, and Ed shook it and said "Thanks, sir. I won't let you down."

"Don't thank me yet, boy. I'm going to stick your dick so deep in the dirt that by the time you leave the Mike Force, you might wish you'd never seen me."

"We'll see," Ed replied cockily.

"Yep," O'Neil said, studying him through narrowed eyes, "we'll see."

*　　　　　　*　　　　　　*

Sue Madison drew a hot, bubbly bath in the tub and got in. She was tired, but sleep wouldn't come to her, and she thought that perhaps a warm bath would help.

She was unable to decide whether or not she was disappointed in herself for making love earlier that night to Curt Draeger.

He had revealed, during dinner, that he was a married man. The fact that his wife, also a medical doctor, chose to live apart from him while he was in the Army, should have made no difference to her. But it did.

He needed someone. He was a tortured, lonely man. How could his wife, if she loved him, fail to see that, and fail to deny him the shelter of her presence, her physical love? The gory memories from operating rooms of field hospitals seemed to possess him, and even his Stateside duties as an instructor would not allow him to escape them. Sue had asked him why he stayed in the Army, if it bothered him so, and he had said, "Because they need me. Because one of them may survive to be the President someday, and put a stop to this sort of madness. Because the wounded are the only ones who really understand it."

When he said that, she remembered what her father had said about wounds of the soul. This was a man with a wounded soul. And so she had followed the impulse to care for him, to draw him, for a time, away from the torture of his soul and into her. And it had been good for him, because he forgot the wounds and the misery and the pain, and lost himself in the consuming joy of their lovemaking for a time. How could she regret that?

She didn't, she decided. She came to the conclusion that her sleeplessness was not from the guilt of giving herself to a married man, but to the fear that her duties as a nurse - a combat nurse, as he so rightfully pointed out - might leave her wounded as Curt Draeger had been. And the fear of that was what disturbed Sue Madison deeply, and robbed her of sleep.

*   *   *

"Oh, hell! I don't believe it," Ed Walker muttered to Sam Hagen as they watched the corps commander's aide-de-camp lead him off the helicopter.

"What?" Sam said.

"The general's aide. It's Black, the son of a bitch Rocco punched out back in OCS."

Hagen looked at the officer. He was standing with his hands on his hips, surveying the damaged camp around him while Captain Mullins saluted the general and introduced himself. Black's uniform was starched and neatly pressed, and the leather part of his jungle boots was highly polished.

So, Sam Hagen thought, this is the man who accosted Maria at Fort Benning; the man who was the cause of her brother having been thrown out of the Officer Candidate School.

Lieutenant Black didn't look the way Sam would have imagined. He looked good; fit and tall and erect.

Black and the general approached the two Special Forces soldiers who were standing at attention in front of a platoon of Camp Strike Force soldiers, the honor guard for the ceremony. Ed made certain that Black recognized him before he faced about and called the platoon to present arms, then turned back to the general and saluted him.

The general returned the salute and said, "Give your men *at ease*, Lieutenant."

Ed put the platoon of Bru soldiers at ease, then returned to a position of attention in front of the general, avoiding looking at his aide, First Lieutenant Black.

Sam stood at attention, too. But he did not avoid looking at Black. Instead, Sam glared at him and surveyed him from head to toe, then fixed the officer with a look of unmistakable distaste.

Black returned the stare. Walker must have made some disparaging comments about me to the sergeant, he thought.

The general made a few paragraphs of rambling remarks about the heroic defense of Thuong Duc, then turned to Black, who broke off the glaring look he'd been trading with Hagen and handed the general one of the medals he held in his hand.

As he pinned the Bronze Star on Ed Walker's jungle fatigue jacket, he asked, "Are you married, Lieutenant?"

"Yes, sir," Ed replied.

"Any children?"

"One on the way, sir."

"Well, I'm sure they'll be very proud of you for what you did here."

Ed wondered if the general really had any idea of what he had done, or whether he was just using a standard remark he had for such occasions. "Well, I did very little, compared to Sergeant Hagen here, and some of the others."

"Indeed," the general replied. "Then, I charge you with the responsibility of making sure they're put in for what they deserve." He shook Ed's hand, then moved in front of Sergeant Hagen.

Before he could pin the medal on Sam, the copilot of his helicopter approached and said, "General, your deputy is on the radio. Says he has some urgent traffic for you."

The corps commander looked at his aide and said, "You go ahead and do the honors for this fine sergeant, Chuck," then turned and walked toward the helicopter.

Ed looked over at Sam Hagen, then stepped forward and snatched the medal from the box that Lieutenant Black had opened as he moved in front of Sam. "I'll pin it on him," Ed said, turning toward his friend.

Black made no move to stop him, but Snake Mullins saw what happened and reached over and grasped Ed's elbow.

"What's the problem here, Ed?" he asked.

"It's a long story," Ed replied. He passed the medal to Mullins. "You're the senior man, sir. You pin it on him."

Mullins did so, then shook Sam's hand and said, "Thank you for everything you did here, Sergeant Hagen. If it hadn't been for you and the Mike Force, some NVA officer would probably be standing here now, pinning awards on *his* men."

"I doubt that, sir," Hagen said. "Ed... Lieutenant Walker and your other troops nearly had their butts whipped when we showed up. All we did was speed it up a little."

"Well, you both deserve these. And more. In fact, you should just consider the Bronze Stars as interim awards. You're both being recommended for higher medals for what you did. Congratulations."

Black waited until Mullins had left, then looked at Ed and said, "Look, Walker, I know you're still holding a grudge against me for what happened in OCS. But that was a long time ago."

"Not long enough," Ed answered. "Anyway, I doubt that Sergeant Hagen would want to accept a medal from the officer who grabbed his future wife's ass, then lied about it."

Black's face turned deep red beneath his tan, and the muscles in his jaw tightened. His eyes darted from Ed's to Sam's, then back to Ed's again. Then they softened, and he nodded. "I understand," he said. "I'm sorry you feel that way, but I understand." He looked at Sam and said, "I learned a lot from that incident, Sergeant. I hope you'll be man enough to accept my apology on behalf of your fiancee."

Sam studied Black for awhile before he responded. It was really just a petty incident that got out of hand, as he understood it. And since then, Black had proved himself where it really counted, on the battlefield. He'd been awarded a Distinguished Service Cross - just one step down from the Medal of Honor. That was what mattered, not some meaningless tiff at a dance. Anyway, as Maria was fond of saying, things happen for a reason. If it hadn't been for the incident, he might never have met her.

Still, Black had lied about it, and officers shouldn't lie. Nevertheless, he held out his hand to the lieutenant and said, "To hell with that petty crap, sir. We've got a war to fight. That's all that matters, now."

Black shook Sam's hand, then held his hand out to Ed Walker.

Ed looked at it, then looked Black in the eye. "Well, maybe it's best forgotten," he said. "If it doesn't matter to Sam, why should it matter to me?" He shook the other lieutenant's hand.

"All right, then," Black said. "It's forgotten."

He turned toward the helicopter, which was starting to crank up. The general was already aboard, and the crew chief was motioning to the aide to come get on.

"Looks like we're leaving," he said. "Congratulations on your medals. I'll try to get out here to see you when we've got more time, Walker. Meanwhile, if there's anything I can do for you, let me know. About the only good of being a general's aide is getting things done for your friends."

Ed didn't bother to tell him he was leaving Thuong Duc. He just waited until Black left to board the Huey and said to Sam, "I still don't like the son of a bitch."

"Me either," Sam said. "And I wouldn't trust him as far as I could throw that chopper. But he does have a DSC."

"Yeah," Ed Walker said. "But I wonder if he earned it."

"Careful what you say about other people's DSCs, Lieutenant," Hagen said, then grinned broadly.

Ed gave him a look of curiosity, and Sam explained himself: "I heard Captain Mullins talking to Nick and some of your other team mates earlier. They're going to put you in for a Distinguished Service Cross, too."

TEN

James Walker stood on Fary's Point, the sandbar at the mouth of Sarah's Creek where it met the York River, and cast a lure into the deep water behind the point. He let it settle toward the bottom for several seconds, then began reeling it in, pulling the rod tip gently up each few cranks. Nothing struck the lure on his first cast, or on the second. But the third time, he let the lure sink a little deeper into the water before beginning to retrieve it.

There! He felt the fish hit, and snapped the light rod sharply to set the hook.

"Aw, you're a nice one, ol' fella!" he said, keeping subtle pressure on the line as he reeled it in. As he brought the fish in, James watched a sailboat pulling away from the marina into the broad creek, using its auxiliary motor, and thought, She looks a lot like the boat Mary's father gave Edward and her for a wedding present.

When the boat was passing the point, James looked over and saw that the sailboat was, indeed, the *Mary Anne*.

Good, he thought. Mr. McClanahan must be taking her out for a sail. And a boat, just like a man's body, needed to be used to keep it in shape. He tried to see who was at the tiller, but he couldn't tell, because whoever it was had on a slicker with the hood up.

James watched the boat move out past the channel marker and turn to port, his thoughts on his younger brother.

Edward seemed to be doing all right. The letter they had received from him about moving out of that jungle camp to a city on the coast had been a cheerful one. And he was with his cowboy friend, Sam Hagen. Hagen had impressed James, at Edward's wedding, as a good man and a capable soldier. As long as Edward had NCOs like him to work with, he should be all right.

The fact that his kid brother had already won a Distinguished Service Cross for something he did at the camp was worrisome, even though James was proud of him, and made sure everybody in Guinea knew about it. But you could get killed winning medals, and James remembered from his time in the infantry during the Korean War that, once they won the first medal, too many soldiers would then risk their necks trying to win a higher one. He hoped his brother had better sense than that; few men won the Medal of Honor and survived to collect it.

James's biggest worry, though, was that Edward had to depend on foreigners fighting beside him. It was one thing to fight alongside American boys, but he wasn't so sure about the Vietnamese. They were probably as useless as the Koreans had been in the last war; otherwise, why was it necessary for American boys to be over there fighting their war for them?

James gave one last glance at his brother's boat, now well out into the river and under sail. Beyond it, he could see the marble figure of "Victory" atop the Yorktown victory monument rising above the trees, and he remembered Edward as a little boy, playing beneath it.

Victory. They hadn't gotten a victory out of the Korean war, in spite of all the American blood spilled there. Maybe it would be different in Vietnam. He hoped so. And he knew that, if not, it wouldn't be because of a lack of effort or of sacrifice on the part of boys such as his younger brother.

*   *   *

"Bring that jib around as soon as we come about," Mary Walker said.

"What the hell does *that* mean?" Sandy Milton asked.

Mary laughed and said, "It means, as soon as I turn the boat, slack off that line on the right, and tighten up the one on the left, you landlubber."

"Hey," Milton answered, "don't denigrate your crew like that, or you'll have a mutiny on your hands."

Mary brought the boat around to a starboard tack and watched Milton fumble with the jib sheet, but he finally got it set.

Lord, this was a bad idea, she thought as she watched him. Why had she agreed to take him out on the boat for the weekend? It wasn't that she didn't want to spend the weekend with him. She wanted that very much, for she had learned during the several nights of lovemaking they had already shared in her apartment or his, that he could satisfy her sexual desires in a way that she had never imagined was possible.

It was the total lack of inhibition that he insisted on that made it so erotic. No holding back, no concern for anything except what felt good at the moment. And no concern about whether or not they might respect each other afterward, because that didn't matter. All that mattered was the raw, sexual enjoyment of the moment, with no commitment to tomorrow. That was the way it was in the progressive parts of the country, so why should it be any different for her, just because she was stuck here in the backward, conservative sticks of the South? Life was short, and if you didn't look out for your own needs, who else was going to? Certainly not Ed, who had run off to Vietnam in a silly, childish attempt to prove his manhood.

And, after all, as Sandy had said when he found out she was pregnant, it would be the last time in her life that she could afford to be totally selfish and enjoy the full potential of her sexuality without concern for a child and a marriage and, as he put it, "a society that stifles the natural impulse to fuck and feel good." When she had finally accepted that; when she had come to the realization that it could never be that way with Ed, or that way after she had a child to care for, she had let herself go. And it led to pleasures beyond the wildest fantasies she had ever imagined.

But it was foolish to take the boat out and risk being seen by someone who might mention to a member of her family that they had seen her sailing aboard the *Mary Anne* with a strange man. Yet, even the risk of that possibility contributed to the excitement of being there with him; made it more of the forbidden fruit that Mary Walker wanted to taste, while she was still able to do so.

    *   *   *

Ed watched as Master Sergeant Shumate finished inspecting the Montagnards' weapons, then dismissed 6th Company for their two-day pass.

Ed's primary duty since arriving in the Mike Force three weeks earlier had been to supervise the training of the newly-recruited company and although they were improving, he wondered if the two weeks remaining in their training period would be adequate.

They were good troops, these Rhade tribesmen of which the company was composed. They brought with them the cohesion of young men - teenagers, most of them - who had grown up together in the same, or neighboring, villages. And they knew the jungle, for they had lived in it all their lives. But they were slow to grasp the elements of fire and maneuver. When simulated contact with the enemy was made, they would hit the ground and return fire all right, but they wouldn't maneuver against the enemy unless one of the Americans physically led them. And there was only Shumate and two other Special Forces NCOs assigned to the company.

Shumate turned and walked to where Ed stood. "Well, that's that, for a couple of days. You going downtown with us, sir? We figured we'd go to La Fregate for lunch, then hit the Streamer Bar."

"Thanks anyway, Walt," Ed said. "But Hagen's company gets off standby at noon, and we're going fishing."

"Fishing?"

"Yep. We're going to take one of the assault boats down to the beach and launch it. Sam says there's a reef just south of here where he thinks there should be plenty of fish. Anyway, we're going to find out."

"But what are you going to use for tackle?" Shumate asked.

"Sam managed to, uh, 'liberate' a couple of rods from the R&R center down at Vung Tau the other day," Ed said, then reached inside his jacket pocket and withdrew a plastic soap dish. He opened it and proudly displayed its contents. There were several improvised fishing lures, and Ed withdrew one that looked much like a commercially-made Hopkins lure and held it out.

"This was the handle of a messhall spoon," he said. "I cut it off and hammered it into a lure that Mr. Hopkins himself would be proud of."

He put it back and withdrew another. It was a rifle bullet with a small hole drilled in it and a hook at the back that was covered with white hair. "This one," he said, "we call a Chucktail." It looked much like a commercial bucktail lure. "Chucktail instead of a bucktail, because the hair is from Charlie Norton's head."

Shumate chuckled. Lieutenant Colonel Norton, the group deputy commander, was one of Special Forces' most colorful characters. "How did you convince him to give you the hair?"

"We didn't, Ed explained. "O'Neil got him drunk on Irish whiskey, then we sneaked into his hootch and snipped it off. You sure you don't want to come along and see how they work?"

"Some other time, maybe," Shumate said. "What I've got in mind *smells* sorta like fish. But you can catch it down at the Streamer Bar with a five hundred piaster note."

Ed found Sam in the mess hall, huddled at a table in the corner with Ben Davan, who was the Cham company commander, and the Nha Trang Mike Force commander, Captain Larry O'Neil.

O'Neil saw him come in said, "Pull up a chair, Ed."

The captain and the two noncommissioned officers seemed to be in an unusually serious mood, Ed thought as he sat down, so he said, "Y'all seem awful serious. What's up?"

"A Shau," Davan said.

A Shau was the name of a valley northwest of Thuong Duc that was infamous among Special Forces soldiers. There had been a camp in the valley until about a year-and-a-half earlier, when it had been overrun by the North Vietnamese in the most desperate battle Special Forces had yet been involved in. The Mike Force, newly constituted at the time, had sent a company there to reinforce the besieged camp, and they had performed heroically. But they had suffered terribly. More than half the members of the company were killed, and of the remainder, most were wounded or missing in action. There were seventeen US Special Forces men in the camp. Five died there, and the rest were wounded at least once.

The most notable act of heroism among the many performed during the battle at Camp A Shau in March of 1966 was that of a young Mike Force medic, Staff Sergeant Billie Hall. Both of his legs were blown off early in the battle, and Hall put tourniquets on the stumps of his own legs, then dragged himself around to others who had been wounded, treating their injuries. Even after he was carried into the dispensary, he continued to advise the team on the treatment of other wounded soldiers, until he lost consciousness and died.

Ed Walker knew these facts about Camp A Shau, and when he remembered Billie Hall, he thought, There was a man. You can debate forever whether war is a necessary evil or not, and whether this government or that is right or wrong. But there could never be any doubt about a man like Billie Hall. Whatever side you found yourself on, whatever opinion you held about the profession of soldiering or about politics or about the meaning of the universe, you had to agree when it came to a person like Billie Hall: *there* was a man.

"A Shau?" Ed Walker asked. "What about it?"

O'Neil sat back and looked at Ed and said, "We're going back in and put another camp in there."

Ed nodded, and the four men sat in silence for awhile. Since the camp there had been lost, the North Vietnamese had ruled the valley unchallenged. It was now, they all knew, one of the enemy's primary strongholds. The Ho Chi Minh trail emptied much of its incessant stream of troops and materiel there, and it was vital to North Vietnam for its operations in the south. They would not yield to the reestablishment of a camp there without exacting a heavy price from anyone attempting to do so. They were all wondering if two battalions of hill tribesmen with a handful of American leaders could get it done.

"When?" Ed asked, breaking the silence.

"In about six weeks, it looks like," O'Neil said. "We were just talking about the reconnaissance mission to choose which site to go for." He looked at Sam Hagen after he said it. Hagen was grinning when Ed glanced over at him.

"I just volunteered for it," he said.

Ed raised his eyebrows, then looked back at O'Neil. "Wouldn't it be better to let one of the units that runs recon for a living go in there?" Ed asked. It wasn't that he lacked confidence in his friend. But there were outfits that were set up specifically to run long range reconnaissance missions. They had well-established procedures, highly trained and experienced reconnaissance teams, and even had their own aircraft and pilots for that particular role.

O'Neil shook his head. "We need to put our own people in there. Nobody else understands exactly what we need to know - what our own capabilities and limitations are. Anyway, whoever goes on the recon will lead us back in when we go in with the main body. It makes more sense for them to be our own guys."

That did make sense, as the recon teams would be the only ones familiar with the actual terrain.

"What size team?" Lieutenant Walker asked.

"Two roundeyes and four Chams, if I have my way," Sam Hagen replied.

Ed looked at Captain O'Neil. "Well, I'll take the other roundeye slot, then," he said.

Walker had less experience than anybody in the Mike Force, and Larry O'Neil needed experienced men on the ground for such a dangerous and vital mission. He had been thinking that one of the senior NCOs would be best suited for the task of team leader, but he had not been able to decide which one it should be. He hadn't even considered using the executive officer of one of his two battalions.

O'Neil looked at Sam Hagen to gauge the sergeant's reaction to Walker's offer. Hagen was looking at the lieutenant and nodding slightly. The two were friends, and they trusted each other. Maybe Walker and Hagen might be a good pair to lead the team, after all. They were young, but they knew soldiering. And they had guts; they'd both proved that already.

"You sure you want to do it?" O'Neil asked Ed.

"Yes, sir. If you can give us some time to train, to get our SOPs down and run a couple of practice missions, we can do it."

Captain O'Neil turned to the Cham company commander and said, "What do you think, Ben?"

"I think they'd make a good team," SFC Davan said. "And since the Chams are coming out of my company, I'll handle the reaction force."

It also made sense to let Davan provide the reaction force that would be on standby to pull the team's nuts out of the fire if they got into trouble, since Hagen and the four indigenous troops on the team would come from his company.

"All right, then," the Mike Force commanding officer said. "It's done. Walker, Hagen, and four Chams for the recon team, and the rest of 7th Company will provide the reaction force."

O'Neil looked at each of them as they nodded their assent to the decision. "We'll start working out the details in the morning," he said. "Meanwhile, enjoy your day off."

Hagen got the thirty-five horsepower Johnson outboard motor started, and turned the sixteen-foot fiberglass assault boat south toward the reef where they were going to fish.

"Take her slow, Sam," Ed Walker said. "We might as well troll on the way down there."

Sam slowed the boat to about two knots, and Ed tossed a trolling lure overboard. It was a wooden plug he had carved in the shape of a squid body, then wired strips of surgical rubber onto for tentacles. The large hook was made from the ring of a hand grenade pin that he had partially straightened and sharpened to a point.

Ed let a length of line off the reel, then locked it into place, as the two Cham soldiers they had brought along watched the activity with curiosity. There was a Navy supply ship anchored offshore between the US military installations south of the city and Hon Tre island, where there was an American air defense battery. Ed pointed at the ship and said, "Circle that big tub once, Sam. Might be some dolphin hanging around under her. Or mahi mahi, as they call them out here in the Pacific."

On the first pass alongside the ship, a big bull dolphin took Ed's lure, and he yelled "Fish on!" as the line dragged off the reel. The crew of the ship gathered alongside the rail to watch as Ed pumped and cranked to get the big fish landed. When it was near the boat, Sam grasped the leader and hauled him aboard. The big fish flapped and jumped in the bottom of the boat for awhile, then Sam held it up for the Chams and the ship's crew to admire. It weighed nearly twenty pounds, Ed guessed.

They hooked another dolphin, but lost the lure, so they moved down to the reef to try their luck there.

To get some smaller fish to use for cut bait, they dropped a hand grenade overboard. After it detonated, a number of fish knocked out by the grenade's concussion floated to the surface. The Chams chattered their approval of the method, and Sam said, "I think we may have just revolutionized the Cham fishing industry, sir."

The men moved in between the reef and the shore, and from the deep water there, managed to catch two groupers of six or seven pounds each, and several smaller fish of a type with which neither Sam nor Ed was familiar. Sam used the hammered spoon Ed had devised to land a small barracuda, as well. And then, as they had no ice to refrigerate their catch, they headed for home.

What a wonderfully relaxing day it had been, Ed thought. He had scarcely given the war a moment's thought all day, except to think how fortunate they were to be able to go fishing while so many thousands of other American soldiers were slogging through the mud of rice paddies, or humping up and down jungle hills. To most of them, a day off consisted of a couple of warm beers at some dusty firebase, and a game of poker or a scratchy movie they'd probably already seen in a real theater.

The Mike Force men cleaned their catch on the dock beside which they'd launched the boat. It belonged to the small Navy detachment that was responsible for the security of Nha Trang harbor, and Sam remarked, "If I had the job these guys do, I'd be fishing all the time."

"Yeah," Ed said. "This would be a hell of a good place to set up a charter fishing outfit after the war, wouldn't it?"

"Would that," Sam agreed. He looked to the west, out beyond the military installations to the mountain the French had named the Grand Summit, which rose to three thousand feet from its base on the South China Sea. It could be a real paradise, this country, if it weren't for the war. In fact, Nha Trang had been a resort during the days that Vietnam was known as French Indochina.

"You know," Sam said, "I wouldn't mind doing something like that after this thing's over. I mean, you could set up a resort down by the reef where we were today, over in that coconut grove. Run trail rides and camping trips back into the valley below the Grand Summit."

"Sure," Ed said. "It looked like a nice beach inside the reef there, too. Sailing, scuba diving, charter fishing. Hell, we might really be onto something, Sam. 'Course, we've got to win the damn war, first."

Sam continued to look at the high, verdant slopes of the Grand Summit for awhile, then said, "Nope. First thing we've got to do, old buddy, is survive the A Shau Valley."

*   *   *

Mary McClanahan Walker answered the knock at the door of her little apartment, expecting to find Sandy Milton there. Her smile turned to a look of surprise, then curiosity when she saw that it was not Sandy, but her sister-in-law, Evelyn.

"Evelyn! Hi. What a nice surprise."

The unsmiling Evelyn said, "Hi, Mary. May I come in?"

"Why, yes. Of course. Where's Sookie?"

Evelyn walked in and surveyed the apartment quickly before she turned around to face her sister-in-law. She saw nothing to indicate that Mary was not alone in the apartment.

"She's at home with her father. How have you been, Mary?"

"Fine. Just fine, Ev. Getting fatter every day, as you can see."

Evelyn Walker looked at the other woman's abdomen and said, "Oh, I couldn't even tell you were pregnant if I didn't already know it, Mary. Everything coming along all right?"

"Why, yes. Just fine, thanks." The older woman seemed somewhat aloof, and Mary wondered why. "Sit down, Ev. Can I fix you a cup of tea or something?"

Evelyn took a seat on the couch but said, "No, thank you. I can only stay for a few minutes. What do you hear from Edward?"

"Very little, I'm afraid. The last letter I had was, oh, a week ago, I suppose. He seems to like his new job. He's with his friend Sam Hagen now, you know. And I'm sure you know about his medal, since it was in the paper."

"Yes," Evelyn replied, the tone of coolness in her voice evident to Mary.

"Is something wrong, Ev?" she asked.

Evelyn eyed her for a long moment, then said, "I'm not sure, Mary. You tell me."

Mary sat beside her on the edge of the couch and thought, Oh God. She knows... "What do you mean?" she asked.

Evelyn reached over and took her sister-in-law's hand in hers. "The man you took out on your sailboat last weekend. It... well, I don't mean to be prying, Mary, but..."

Mary pulled her hand away and stood, her speckled eyes glaring at the other woman. "My God, Evelyn. He - he's just a friend! A professor of mine, in fact. We just went out for a sail, for Christ's sake. Are you insinuating that there's something wrong with that?"

Evelyn looked at the floor, shaking her head, then peered up into the other woman's face. "I'm afraid that won't cut it, Mary," she said. "We both know better. You don't go out on these waters, anchor in the Mobjack the whole weekend, and expect the waterman to let it go unnoticed - not when you're in a boat that belongs to one of their own."

Mary's defensive glare melted into a look of despair and she muttered, "The Guineamen. The damned, nosy.... What business is it of theirs, anyway?"

"Your husband is one of them, Mary. And, unfortunately, since you, like I am, are an outsider, they love nothing better than to get something on us to gossip about."

Mary flopped down on the couch, remembering now the way several work boats had passed close to the sailboat, even though she and Sandy had anchored in a cove well away from the channel. She looked at Evelyn and said, "So, I guess they're spreading it all over Guinea now? 'That slut from Broad Marsh is screwing off on her husband, while he's away risking his life and winning medals.' Is that it?"

Evelyn nodded. "That's about it. Only, it's not just confined to Guinea. James says he's heard about it from some people up the county, as well."

Mary sat silent, and Evelyn watched her for a time, then said, "Look, Mary, I'm not here to make judgements or to stick my nose into your affairs. I'm just here as your friend. I know it's difficult for you, with Edward being overseas and everything. It's just, well, you know how it is with them. I'm sure there are a lot of his so-called friends who can hardly wait until he gets home, so they can be the first to tell him."

Mary stood again, and paced the room in silence, until Evelyn said, "I have to get back across the river. I just thought I'd better let you know what was being said. If you want to talk or anything..."

"No," Mary interrupted. "I'll work it out myself. I... it's nothing I can't handle."

Evelyn stood and gave her sister-in-law a hug. "Well, if you need a shoulder, a friend, I'm always there, Mary. I hope you realize that."

"Thank you, Evelyn. I... I'll call you. OK?"

Evelyn Walker nodded, knowing from Mary's trembling lip that she was trying hard to fight back tears. "Yes," she said. "Please do. And take care of that little one, OK?" she added, glancing at the other woman's abdomen, still only slightly swollen from the child growing inside her.

Mary closed the door and rested her head against it a moment, then stumbled to the sofa and flung herself down on it. She began to sob, and cried, "Oh, damn it! Damn you, Ed Walker! Damn you and your nosy, hick friends! And damn your stupid, destructive war!"

ELEVEN

"Well, you're just in time, Sue," Major Westcott said as she walked Lieutenant Madison to her quarters.

Sue wiped the perspiration from her upper lip, shifted her clothing bag to her other hand, and said, "In time for what, ma'am?"

"The lunar new year," the Army Nurse Corps major said, "Tet, as it's called here, will be here in a couple of days. It's the biggest party the Vietnamese have. In fact, the *only* party time the Vietnamese have, as far as I know."

She opened the screen door to the wooden barracks-type building and held it open for Sue. "And please, don't call me 'ma'am,'" she said. "Call me Maggie."

Sue smiled and said, "All right. Maggie it is." She set the clothing bag down next to the one Maggie had carried for her from the administration office and looked around. So, this will be home for the next year, she thought.

The room held two army issue bunks, a mosquito net hanging above each. There was a wooden foot locker at the end of each bed, and two metal wall lockers against the wall. Two folding chairs sat at a small field table. There was a desk lamp on the table and in one corner there was a floor fan and a gray metal trash can. That was it.

"Don't let the looks of the place depress you," Maggie Westcott said. "I'm sure that, by the time you and your roommate scrounge around and fix the place up, you'll forget how empty and Spartan it was when you walked in."

Sue nodded and said, "Who is my roommate, Maj... Maggie?"

Major Westcott said, "I don't know, yet. Whoever the next nurse assigned here happens to be, I suppose. Now, let me show you the latrine and showers. I'm afraid they're probably a little more primitive than you're used to."

They were. The latrine was a canvas-enclosed room with a toilet seat above half a fifty-five gallon drum.

"The drum gets emptied daily by Vietnamese laborers," Maggie explained. "There's a couple of gallons of diesel oil in it. Theoretically, the oil, since it's lighter than water, sits on top of the excrement. But the way it smells... Phew! Oh, and by the way, if you smoke while you're sitting on the throne, be careful. The Vietnamese have been known to put gasoline in the damn things instead of diesel. There was a guy who threw a cigarette butt into one of them and *whoom*! Had to medevac the poor guy to Japan with flash-fried equipment!"

The shower was much the same - a canvas-enclosed shelter with drums of solar-heated water above it. The shower heads were standard ones with pull chain valves so that the water ran only while the chain was pulled down.

"We're having more hootches with indoor plumbing built," the major explained. "But the increase in troops over here, and the increase in casualties, has us behind the power curve, I'm afraid. We've had to convert what was intended to be hospital staff quarters into more wards for the patients.

"Now, you go ahead and get settled in, get some rest, and I'll meet you at the mess hall for supper. I'll show you around the rest of the place tomorrow," the major said. She smiled and held out her hand to Sue. "Welcome aboard," she said, and then her expression turned dark and she said, "It's a real challenge here, Sue. The wounds to the souls here are often worse than the physical ones."

Sue shook her hand and said, "Thanks, Maggie," and the other nurse turned and left the oppressively hot room.

Wounds to the souls, she thought. There was that expression again - the same one that her father and Curt Draeger had used. She wondered whether Maggie meant the souls of the wounded soldiers, or of the medical staff - or both. She turned on the big floor fan and stood in front of it, trying to get relief from the stifling heat, and looked out through the screened siding of the building at the sprawling hospital complex beyond.

The army hospital at Cam Ranh Bay was designated as an evacuation hospital, which meant that most of the patients there were the badly wounded whose injuries had been treated at outlying field hospitals. They were then transferred to Cam Ranh Bay for additional surgery or until their medical condition improved enough to allow them to be evacuated back to Stateside hospitals. The wards were largely filled with men who had suffered amputations, brain damage, paralysis, and other devastating injuries. Many would not survive, and a tragically large number would never be whole again.

"Wounds of the soul," Sue Madison muttered to herself, "No wonder."

She began unpacking her bags. After that, she'd have a shower, then go find Major Westcott and get straight to work. She could rest later. Right now, she just wanted to get a taste of what she had volunteered to come to Vietnam to do.

       *   *   *

"I just don't understand it, Sam," Ed Walker whispered.

Hagen didn't answer until he finished surveying the abandoned enemy base camp, lowered his binoculars and slid back into the dense jungle growth.

"Well, they've gone somewhere, that's for sure. All I can figure is that they must be massing somewhere east of here."

Ed Walker nodded. It was the third major base area they had encountered in the A Shau valley in as many days. But, like the other two, the North Vietnamese Army troops who had occupied it were nowhere to be seen. In all three cases, it was evident that the NVA troops had moved out several days earlier.

The only enemy the six man reconnaissance team - Ed, Sam, and four Cham strikers from Sam's Mike Force platoon - had encountered since their helicopter infiltration into the A Shau valley three days before, was a group of lightly-armed troops. Thirty men and women had been in the group, moving quickly northwest out of the valley toward the main supply route into Laos commonly referred to as the Ho Chi Minh trail. The Americans surmised that they were a carrying party probably headed to the trail to pick up supplies.

The Mike Force men had expected to find the valley crawling with enemy troops, because it was the main staging area of the North Vietnamese Army in the northern part of the Republic of Vietnam.

"Well, if they stay gone, it'll sure make it easy to get the new camp established, at least," Ed whispered. He checked his watch, then slid out of his rucksack straps and began erecting the whip antenna of the FM radio inside it. The radio relay aircraft would be in the area within the next five minutes to receive the recon team's latest intelligence report. The covey, as the aircraft was called, was the team's only reliable link with the outside world, as they were beyond radio range of their base camp. It flew above the valley at eight-hour intervals to receive reports from the team, and to ensure that they were still operating undetected. In the event the team had been compromised and gone into hiding, or was on the run from the enemy, the covey would remain overhead to coordinate their recovery by the reaction force, and to direct airstrikes in support of them, if necessary.

On occasion, in the dangerous task of long range reconnaissance, the covey would arrive over the recon zone to discover that contact with the recon team could not be established. In that event, a backup team would be infiltrated to try to find them or to attempt to discover what had happened to the missing men, not knowing whether some or all of the team had been killed or captured. As often as not, when a team became missing in action, no trace of them was ever found again.

Each of the Americans carried a small emergency radio that transmitted a distress signal that could be received by any aircraft flying nearby. But rarely were such signals heard when a recon team got into trouble, and on occasion, the enemy captured the little radios and attempted to use them to draw search aircraft within range of their anti- aircraft batteries.

Deep penetration reconnaissance missions into enemy territory was not a task for the timid nor the careless. It was the most demanding and stressful mission of American forces in the Vietnam war. But that was because it normally meant being surrounded by enemy forces. Except for the carrying party they encountered just after infiltration, though, the Mike Force team reconnoitering the A Shau valley could find no North Vietnamese troops.

The voice of Walt Shumate calling from the covey aircraft came across the handset as soon as Ed turned the radio on. Ed gave a terse reply; "Cowbell, this is Mickey Mouse. Go secure."

As he attached the speech security device in Sam's rucksack to the radio in his by means of the cable Hagen handed him, Ed wondered, How the hell do they come up with these call signs? Then he called Shumate on secure voice. "Cowbell, this is Mickey, over."

"Loud and clear, Mickey," Shumate replied. "What's your position?"

Ed passed him the team's location, then said, "Still no enemy sighted. We've found another big base area a hundred meters southeast of our current location, but nobody's home."

"Uh, roger," Master Sergeant Shumate answered from the airplane high above them. "I've got a change of mission for you, if you're ready to copy."

"Change of mission," Ed said to Sam as he reached inside his shirt pocket for his notepad and pencil, then said into the radio handset, "Send it, Shu."

Shumate read the recon team's new instructions from his own notebook: "Enemy forces appear to be moving east from the A Shau valley toward the Hue - Phu Bai area. Your new mission is to confirm or deny this movement, and, if possible, to attempt to ascertain the primary route being used for this movement. Your recon zone is modified as follows..."

He then gave Ed the team's new reconnaissance zone. Ed located it on his map and saw that it was a long, west-to-east rectangle ten kilometers high and twenty kilometers wide. He understood the obvious; that the team was to attempt to intersect the enemy's axis of movement and track them to the east, not attempt to cover the whole recon zone.

"Roger, copy," Ed said. "Continue."

"Your new exfiltration time is zero-six-fifteen hours on 31 January - just under four days from now," Shumate said. "Copy?"

"Solid copy," Walker replied. "Continue."

"Message continues: record and report any suitable landing zones you find en route. Emergency pickup zone will be last reported LZ. Covey flights will remain as scheduled. End of message."

Two minutes later, the team's radio equipment was packed up and Walker had Hagen and the four Cham troops gathered around his map, pointing out the new recon zone and showing them the route he intended to take to try to track the enemy forces thought to be moving east.

To the one Cham who spoke enough English to serve as the interpreter for the other three, Ed cautioned, "We're going to have to conserve our food now, if we're going to make it last for four more days." The team had brought enough rations to eat sparingly for five days. The remaining two-day supply would have to last for four days now, though. The Cham soldier translated Ed's remark for the others, who nodded their understanding.

They were good, capable men, Ed Walker knew. Sam Hagen had chosen them well. They would carry on with the new mission without complaint.

"All right," the lieutenant said, folding his map and placing it in the pocket of his tiger striped uniform, "everybody understand what we're going to do?"

The interpreter relayed his remark to the other Chams, and the three of them nodded. Hagen ran a forefinger across his mouth in the gesture he called, "zip your lip." The team would move in absolute silence until one of the Americans indicated it was all right to speak in a low whisper, relying until then on the hand and arm signals that Sam had drilled into every member of the team, including Lieutenant Walker.

They circled to a point east of the former enemy camp, found the trail the North Vietnamese had obviously used, and moved stealthily alongside it. The vegetation was thick off the trail, and movement was difficult. If they were to have any hope of making reasonable progress in their pursuit of the enemy, they would have to move on the trail itself. It would mean sacrificing security for speed, but the Americans agreed that it was necessary.

They moved stealthily down the trail for the rest of the day, making frequent listening halts. Toward the end of the day, they began to find indications that they were getting closer to the enemy - fresh feces beside the trail, leeches that had recently been burned to make them fall off, and footprint holes with muddy water in them. But as darkness approached, they had still not made visual contact with the enemy. Ed signaled the others to move north off the trail, and they picked their way through the thick vegetation in the fading light until they reached a bamboo thicket about fifty meters from the trail. There, they halted for the night.

Shumate passed nearby in the covey aircraft not long after, took their latest position and report, and, not wanting to risk compromising their presence, departed for the forward operations base. He would return to the area at first light.

The men ate a small amount of their rice-based rations as the thick darkness closed around them until the only thing visible was the faint glow of the luminous dots and hands of Ed's watch when he raised it, now and then, to check the time. The others slept while he stood guard, their feet together in a close circle and their bodies radiating away from the center, each man's head resting on his rucksack, his rifle at his side.

Ed fought the fatigue that tried to drag him to sleep, but he finally succumbed to it shortly before he was to wake one of the Cham soldiers to assume guard duty.

He was awakened by someone yanking on his trouser leg, and his mind snapped to consciousness when he heard voices nearby. They were Vietnamese voices, and for a moment, in the total darkness, he was confused about his whereabouts. The voices seemed much closer than they had been to the trail when he had dozed off, and he thought, How could that be? We couldn't have moved nearer the trail. But yes, the voices were unmistakably close. A deep breath was frozen in his lungs. He forced himself to exhale slowly, feeling his heart pound as he listened, trying to determine what the voices' owners were doing, and if the other members of his team were awake and alert.

A feeling of shame and fear gripped him. He had fallen asleep. He had let the others down, and failed to warn them of the danger now so obviously near.

He felt Sam's breath on his ear before he heard him say, in an almost inaudible whisper, "Stay still."

Without seeing him, he sensed Sam move himself with fearful caution next to one of the Chams, and knew he was telling the man the same thing.

Barely moving, Ed's hand crept to the stubby automatic rifle in his lap. He wrapped his fingers around the pistol grip and checked the position of the safety with his thumb, then slid his index finger into the trigger guard.

Now he could hear other voices - many of them - in the distance, near where he knew the trail to be. There was some clinking of metal now and then, as if the Vietnamese - North Vietnamese soldiers on the trail, he was now certain - were adjusting their equipment. No, they were probably taking a break there, he decided when it became evident that the voices he heard were not those of moving men. The nearer voices were probably soldiers who, like he and his men, had moved off the trail to rest.

Ed sat silent and motionless for what seemed an eternity, until his lower back began to throb with pain from the sitting position he maintained with absolute stillness.

He had been sitting up with his back leaning against a clump of thick bamboo stalks when he was supposed to be on guard. He leaned his shoulders back toward the bamboo a millimeter at a time until it made contact with the stalks once more, then relaxed against them, holding his breath until he was certain they would support him without making noise. Finally, he was able to breathe evenly.

As the endless minutes crept by, Ed heard the enemy voices go silent. Only an occasional muffled sound from someone stirring reached his ears and joined the sound of his own heartbeat.

Somewhere to his front there was a tiny, momentary flare of light; probably someone striking a match. Immediately, Ed heard an admonishing voice from someone near the flame, and it was immediately extinguished.

God, they're close, Ed Walker thought. Suppose they had moved all the way in here and stumbled across us while I was asleep? Again he was gripped by a feeling of guilt. But dwelling on it would do no good. Now what he needed to do was devise a plan for what to do in the event they were yet discovered.

They had plenty of time before it would start getting light - hours. But what then? Would the North Vietnamese discover their trail? Might one of the enemy wander off in their direction to relieve himself and stumble on them? Perhaps their best bet was to attempt to move west along the edge of the bamboo thicket now, slowly and carefully, while it was still dark.

*   *   *

Susan Madison stared up into the darkness from her bunk at Cam Ranh hospital. The combination of jet lag, the stifling heat of South Vietnam, and what she had seen on the ward of the hospital where she was to spend the next year nursing, prevented her from sleeping.

The ward was filled with men - young men - who were only the detritus of battle. There were amputees blasted into partial beings by mines and artillery shells; brain-damaged soldiers unable to comprehend their surroundings or to control the weakening muscles and organs of bodies that until recently had been athletic and strong and whole. And there was so little she could do for them, except to administer the medicines already prescribed for them. The intent was not to save their lives; that part had already been accomplished. Nor was it to rehabilitate them; to start them on the road to rebuilding their lives from what was left of their damaged minds and bodies. That would be done when they got to Veterans Administration hospitals and rehabilitation centers back in the States.

No, the ward was nothing but a temporary storehouse, a holding point at which they would stay only until they healed enough to enable them to stand the rigors of the long flight back to the United States. Or until, if the efforts to prolong their shattered lives failed, their weakened bodies or wills gave in to the inevitable, and they died.

It was not what Lieutenant Sue Madison had expected. She had pictured herself being there when the soldiers were first brought in, skillfully assisting surgeons in saving the lives of recently-wounded, gallant young soldiers; making them whole to return to the battlefield or to the homes where wives and mothers waited anxiously. She would turn their grimaces of pain to smiles, and they would wave goodbye as they left, whole men again, to return to heroes' welcomes at home, or to the hearty greetings and banter of their buddies in the fighting units. But there had been neither grimaces nor smiles on the ward where she had spent half of her first day in Vietnam; only blank stares and drooling mouths. And few of the men she found there would take part in any hearty banter for a long, long time - if ever again.

Sue Madison rolled onto her side. She curled up into a ball and, despite the heat, pulled the sheet up over her head, feeling completely helpless and alone, and dreading the long year ahead.

   *   *   *

Sam Hagen leaned forward in the thick darkness, straining his senses to try to determine what was happening. There was rustling in the jungle leaves, but what was it? He could see nothing. He sensed something close - very close. But what?

He smelled - what? - rotten meat? He reached a hand forward, when just to his left the stillness was torn by a blast of noise and light.

"Jesus!" he cried aloud. The flashes of light from the weapon gave him a brief glimpse of what he had heard and smelled. It was a tiger! A huge, stalking tiger, its mouth opened wide, his hand just inches from the big teeth in the animal's jaw.

Ed Walker saw the creature in the flashes of light also, and he flipped the selector switch of his assault rifle to automatic as he brought it to his shoulder. He put a burst of six rounds into the tiger as it made a wide swipe with its paw at the Cham who had fired first.

Walker quickly emptied the rest of the magazine of ammunition in the direction of the North Vietnamese soldiers who were yelling down near the trail. Then he dived to a prone position to change his magazine, and began barking orders to the rest of the team. "Move right!" he yelled. "West! Back to the last rally point! Move, Move!"

He heard the others scurry off to his right as he slammed a fresh magazine home and released the bolt. He yanked a hand grenade from his magazine pouch, pulled the pin, and, still lying on his side, tossed it in the direction of the nearest enemy voices. Before it even detonated, the North Vietnamese began raking the jungle around him with small arms fire. The grenade exploded, and in the momentary flash of light, Ed could see the huge tiger writhing just to his front, it's claws slashing wildly at the jungle growth. Ed began to scurry away, crawling blindly in the direction he thought the rest of his team had gone.

He could hear one of the Vietnamese bellowing orders above the continuing sound of rifle and machine gun fire crackling above his head and to his rear. There was a lull in the firing then, and he crawled as quickly as he could.

The last rally point he had designated was a fallen log beside the trail about three hundred meters back, to the west of the bamboo thicket. Christ, he hoped west was the direction he was moving. But the important thing now was to get some distance between himself and the enemy.

A tiger. Of all things, a goddam *tiger*! Wasn't it bad enough to have the NVA to contend with? For a moment Ed was gripped with the fear that he might stumble into another tiger, then that fear was surpassed by the more likely concern that he might not be able to find the rest of his team.

The firing was still continuing sporadically, but it was well behind him. He pulled out his compass and opened it. He couldn't make out the weakly luminous letters on the dial, but the north arrow was visible enough that he could see he was moving slightly south of west. He adjusted his direction of movement, rising to a crouch as he moved further away from the site of the bizarre incident. The North Vietnamese had ceased firing, but he could still hear their voices. He estimated that they were now seventy or eighty meters behind him. He would move another hundred and fifty meters or so to the west, then turn south to intersect the trail and find the rally point.

Sam Hagen and the four Chams were moving slowly, Hagen at the point of the team, with the Chams bunched up closely behind him to maintain contact. He was following his compass due west, and he estimated that they had moved about two hundred meters from the tiger.

God, it had been a near thing. The huge cat would probably have grabbed him, clamping him in its powerful jaws, if the Cham soldier hadn't fired when he did. Sam had seen films of tigers and lions clasping their prey in their teeth and shaking them madly. Even if he had survived the tiger's attack, the NVA probably would have killed or captured him.

When he had moved another fifty meters, Sam halted and sat down. Pulling the interpreter close to him, he whispered, "We'll wait here and listen for Walker."

"Maybe the Vietnamese kill him already," the Cham whispered in reply.

Maybe they had. Or perhaps Ed was lying wounded somewhere back there. Hagen momentarily entertained the thought of going back to see, then rejected it. Even if there had been enough light to see, it would have made no sense to go back. Perhaps, if Ed didn't show up at the rally point by daylight and the NVA left the area, they could backtrack and try to find him. But it would be foolish to try it now. No, they'd wait here a few minutes and listen for Ed's movement toward the rally point. If he didn't appear, Sam would move closer to the fallen tree beside the trail to try to find him.

Ed Walker held his breath and listened for any sound that would indicate the movement of the rest of the recon team, or of the enemy, but he heard absolutely nothing. He wasn't sure how close he was to the trail, or how much further he had to go to reach the rally point. He decided that his best bet for finding it was to move to the trail and inch his way west along it until he reached the fallen tree, then, if Sam and the others weren't there, move off into the jungle a short distance and wait until they appeared.

Ed checked his compass, pointed himself due south, and crept along toward the trail. He had gone just a few meters when he broke out of the vegetation onto the narrow but well-worn path. He slowly stood, peering into the almost total darkness ahead of him and began to creep along to the west.

Well, that's long enough, Sam Hagen thought. Ed must have passed them, or perhaps he was lying dead or wounded back there somewhere. It was time to move to the rally point and see. He didn't want to leave Ed there alone, if he had managed to get there. He pulled the Cham interpreter's ear near his mouth again. "I'm going to move to the tree and see if I can find the lieutenant," Sam whispered. "If he links up with you here, move to the tree. If not, and I don't come back by daylight, move to the last pickup zone we passed yesterday. Do you remember where it was?"

"Yes," the Cham replied. "About two kilometer back, just south of trail."

"That's right. Wait there until the reaction force comes. They'll get you out." He slid his arms from the carrying straps of his rucksack, then felt the left thigh pocket of his trousers to ensure he still had his little URC-10 survival radio, checked his compass, and moved slowly off toward the rally point.

Ed Walker froze, his pulse pounding in his ears. He had heard something just ahead. He stood motionless for a good half minute, peering into the darkness. He should be near the fallen tree by now, and the rest of his team. That must be the sound he'd heard.

"Sam?" he whispered softly. When there was no reply, he whispered again, slightly louder. "Sam?"

A light suddenly shone in his eyes from a few meters away, and for a second he was unable to move. Then he started to raise his rifle, but something slammed into his back, and he pitched forward, the rifle flying from his hands. He fell forward onto his hands and knees, and immediately there was a heavy weight on his back, then his face was in the dirt, the light still shining on him. He heard low, frantic voices - Vietnamese voices, and saw sandaled feet at his face.

"Arrr!" he yelled, trying to rise, then feeling heavy blows pummeling his head. "You bastards!" he screamed, before his face was pushed down into the dirt of the trail.

Sam Hagen saw the light come on twenty meters to his left and dropped quickly into the thick growth. He heard Ed yell, then heard the voices of the North Vietnamese soldiers.

Silently his mind cried, *No! Aw, Ed, goddamit, no!* Hagen almost sprang to his feet to rush the site, then decided against it. No, that would probably mean the death of Ed and him both. He could tell by the number of voices that there were more than a few of the enemy. No shots had been fired yet, so Ed had probably not been badly hurt. There was little Sam could do by himself. If the rest of the team were with him, they might stand a chance of taking on the enemy. They might yet, if he went back and got the others.

Hagen quickly made the decision to move back to the four Cham soldiers, believing the noise the NVA were making would cover the sound of his movement. He rose and moved quickly away. He used his compass and counted his paces, and when he figured he was almost to them he stopped and called softly to Khoe, the Cham interpreter.

Khoe answered immediately in a hoarse whisper. "Sam? What happen?"

Hagen moved to the sound of the voice and dropped down beside the others. "NVA on the trail," he whispered. "The sons of bitches captured Ed, I think."

Khoe told the others, and there were whispered curses, then he asked Sam, "What we do now?"

What *do* we do? Hagen wondered. Leave Ed and head for the last reported pickup zone? Move to the trail and attack the NVA; try to spring Ed, and then hightail it for the PZ? He weighed the options quickly, then said, "We move."

TWELVE

Ed Walker knelt gagged and bound as the North Vietnamese went through his rucksack. His hands, tied together behind his back, were lashed to the rope that also bound his ankles.

He felt no self-pity at having been captured; not yet. Right now all he could do was curse himself. He cursed himself for falling asleep when he should have been standing guard. He cursed himself for not keeping up with the others when they had fled, for moving on the trail, for not spraying the enemy with his rifle in that first split second and making a run for it.

His mind raced, remembering the principles of evasion and escape he had learned in the rigorous training he had undergone for just such situations. He remembered the frightening tales of torture and interrogation he was told he might encounter; that he would, sooner or later, be made to talk. Unless, that is, he died first.

Well, he had done enough harm to his team. The enemy wouldn't make him talk. That was that. Maybe a couple of days from now, but not until the team was safely extracted.

He began trying to recite the Code of Conduct in his mind: *I am an American fighting man. I will never surrender of my own free will...* But then the image of Mary appeared, her belly swollen with their unborn child. The child he might never now see. Oh, God. What is going to happen to me? Edward Walker wondered.

A painful kick to his ribs from one of his captors quickly changed Ed's mood from self-pity back to defiance. A man holding a flashlight in his eyes brought his face close, yanked the cloth gag from Ed's mouth and said, in English, "Where are the others?"

Ed said nothing, and this time the man struck him hard on the skull with his flashlight. His head began to throb with a sharp pain.

"Where are the others, and how many are they?"

Again Ed made no reply. The Vietnamese showed a pistol in the beam of light, cocked it, and held it to the American's head, pressing the muzzle firmly against his temple. "I will count to five. If you do not answer, I will pull the trigger. How many others are there, and where are they now? One...two..."

Ed thought, He won't do it. I know that. I'm of no value to them dead. He won't. But he squeezed his eyes shut, for he was not absolutely sure.

"...five!"

The pistol shot was so loud in Ed's ear that his skull seemed to ring like a huge bell, and the hot gunpowder from the muzzle burned his ear. But he thought, I knew it! They won't kill me - not for a long time.

Another Vietnamese was speaking roughly to the interrogator in a harsh, low voice. There was a brief argument from the other man, then another kick to Ed Walker's ribs. He fell over onto his side and groaned with pain.

The Vietnamese yanked Ed by the hair, pulling him back into a kneeling position, then onto his back. He stepped on Ed's forehead, pressing the back of his head hard against the ground. Then another man shoved the neck of a canteen deep into Ed's mouth. The water gurgled out of it into his throat. He tried to hold his breath, but another sharp kick struck him in the ribs, and he gasped. The water lodged in his throat, choked him, spurted from his nose. He tried to shake his head, to get the canteen neck out of his mouth, to keep from breathing the water into his lungs. Another kick jolted him, and again he gasped, trying to cough the water out of his mouth, but it kept flowing, still spurting from his nose and seeping into his windpipe.

Ed was drowning, and he knew it. And then the water stopped.

He coughed, gasped for breath, his nose and mouth burning. Again he was kicked in the ribs, and the voice asked, "How many? Where are they?"

When there was no reply, another canteen pressed against his lips. He clenched his teeth, but a hand closed over his mouth, and now the water was poured into his nose. He blew it out, blew again, and his breath was gone. He couldn't keep it from running into his nose, but he closed off his throat until something struck him in the mouth. Three times it smashed against his closed mouth, and he could feel the skin of his lip split, then another blow was delivered to his ribs. He opened his mouth enough to gasp in a short breath, and the canteen opening was thrust between his teeth. Again the water flowed, and this time he could not get rid of it. He tried to swallow, tried to breathe, but he no longer could, and the lack of oxygen to his brain and muscles caused him to give up. There was an image of red light in his eyes; glowing, red liquid, speckled with iridescent flashes, and then his vision darkened and he lost consciousness. His last thought before he did so was of Mary's amber-speckled eyes.

Sam shot the flare directly down the trail, and the Chams opened fire, their tracers sweeping through the men standing above the trussed figure lying motionless in the eerie light. Some ran, but most of the NVA went down. Sam put several rounds into the two men who were trying to bring their weapons up to return fire.

The flare was burning out, but before Sam fired a second one, he threw two hand grenades down the trail in each direction. Without waiting for them to detonate, he fired the second flare beyond Ed. As soon as he heard the grenades explode, he rushed directly to his friend, oblivious to the crackling of rifle fire - most of it from the Chams - that rattled the jungle trail. He scooped Ed up in his arms, one hand still holding the rifle, and turned back toward his men.

The flare went out again, but he charged on into the jungle growth, not worrying about the noise he was making. He tripped, falling heavily onto Ed. Behind him, the Chams were continuing to spray rifle fire down the trail, pausing now and then to add the blast of a hand grenade to the surprise assault.

Sam pulled his pen light from his pocket and examined his gasping comrade. He pulled out his trench knife and quickly cut the ropes binding Ed's wrists and ankles. He saw blood pouring from Ed's split lip, but ignored it.

Now free of his bonds, Ed rolled onto his hands and knees, trying to cough the liquid from his lungs. Sam gave him several sharp blows to the back to assist, at the same time saying, "We've gotta get the hell out of here, sir. Can you make it?"

"Yes," Ed gasped, not certain that he could.

"Break contact!" Sam called to the Chams, their fire now slackening. An increasing but ineffective volume of fire was coming from the NVA who were moving toward the sound of the firefight.

Sam could hear the Cham soldiers stumbling toward him, Khoe calling in a low voice, "Sam, where are you?"

"Here. Keep coming," Sam replied, then to Ed said, "We've got to move quickly, Ed." He pulled his compass from its carrier and handed it to Walker. "You take the point," he said. "Haul ass to the northwest as fast as you can."

Still coughing water from his lungs, Ed said, "OK. Jesus, Sam. I thought I was dead. You saved my life."

"Don't mean nothin'," Hagen said.

The four Cham soldiers caught up to them, and Khoe said, "They come after us. NVA commander very angry. Tell soldiers, 'Find them and kill them all.'"

The enemy had ceased fire now, and gone quiet. They were listening for the noise of the patrol's movement. Sam leaned over to Ed and said, "OK, move slowly for awhile. But if you hear them behind us, then start moving as fast as you can."

Walker stifled a cough and, without replying, began to move slowly off through the dense growth in the darkness.

Ten minutes later, Sam could still hear the North Vietnamese behind them, following their trail, so he said to Ed, "You need to pick up the pace a little, Ed."

Ed moved as quickly as he could for a time, and put more distance between his team and the enemy, then halted again. He waited for Hagen to move close to him, and whispered, "Sam, I can't go much further."

"Of course you can," Sam said with a hint of irritation. "You can keep going as long as you need to." He wondered whether the experience of being captured had weakened Ed's resolve.

"I - I've lost a lot of blood, Sammy," he whispered weakly. He felt for the sergeant's hand, found it, and held it to the front of his shirt. It was soaked with blood. He had been losing much more than Sam realized from the badly split lips. "Shit," Sam said. "I didn't know you were still bleeding. I'd better get a bag of Ringer's in you."

There was no doubt that he needed to start an IV in Ed to replace his lost blood with a bag of the Ringer's lactate that each man on the team carried. It would mean the loss of precious time and the possible compromise of their position. But it had to be done or Ed would collapse.

"No time," Ed replied weakly. "I'll find a place to hide, and start an IV myself. You can come back for me after you link up with the reaction force."

"Don't be stupid," Hagen replied.

"I'm not being stupid, Sam," Ed said. "I'm being realistic."

Hagen weighed the alternatives. Maybe it *would* be best to find a landing zone, bring the reaction force in, and come back to get Ed. The rest of the team would make a much more discernable trail than a single man moving stealthily into a hiding place, and the enemy would be almost certain to follow the heavier trail. And it was obvious Walker was getting too weak to carry on. Resting and replacing some of his lost fluids would keep him from weakening more. But he had no equipment. Sam could give him his, but how the hell would they ever find him again? Sam doubted that he could locate their position on a map within a thousand meters. No, if they left him, he'd either be captured by the enemy again, or he'd pass out and never be found. Or he might even end up in the belly of a tiger. Sam wondered if he'd ever be able to get the tiger out of his mind.

"No," he said. "We aren't leaving you, Ed. I'll carry you, if I have to. But we're not going to leave you."

"That's dumb, Sam," Ed said, as Hagen dropped his rucksack and felt through it for his medical kit. But he didn't protest. He'd go as long as he could, but if worse came to worst... The image of Mary carrying their unborn child came to him again, and he was filled with a sense of dread and hopelessness.

Hagen found the bag of fluid and IV needle and tube, and had Ed hold his penlight while he ran the tube down the inside of Ed's fatigue shirt to keep it from being snagged as they moved through the jungle. Something fell from Ed's shirt onto the ground and Sam saw it and picked it up. He held it in the thin beam of the penlight, and saw that it was a photo of Mary in a bikini. He handed it to Ed, and said, "*That's* why we're not going to leave you, lieutenant. Now, let me get this needle in you."

He found a vein and inserted the needle, taping it firmly in place, then made a collar with parachute cord and hung the bag of fluid around Ed's neck, tucking it and the excess tubing inside the shirt. Next, he examined the wounds to Ed's mouth. He used the rest of his adhesive tape to crudely close the bleeding wound, then helped Ed to his feet.

"Khoe, you take the point. Keep moving northwest," Hagen directed. "Ed, you move behind him. All right, let's go."

Before he gave the penlight back, Ed took another quick look at the photograph of Mary that Sam had picked up and handed to him. He wiped a smear of blood from it, and the sense of hopelessness he had been feeling lessened considerably then. Maybe they *could* make it. They *had* to.

Good old Sam, he thought, as he shoved the photo in his pocket and moved off behind Khoe. He knew nobody else who would have come back for him. How the hell did he ever do it? And the Chams - five men in the midst of the enemy, attacking against such odds, at such selfless risk to themselves, to rescue him. And all because he had failed them, falling asleep when they were counting on him to be alert. He felt cowardly and inadequate, compared to the brave young men around him.

One more hour. If he could just hang on for a little more than an hour, the covey would come, and Shumate could bring in the choppers to get them out. Maybe then he could make it up to them somehow. But first, he knew, they had to find a landing zone.

　　　*　　　　　　　　*　　　　　　　　*

The sky across the nearly calm South China Sea was just beginning to lighten when Sue Madison walked out of her sparsely furnished room and past the hospital buildings to the beach. She had given up trying to get any more moments of fitful sleep and decided to walk down to the water. The Vietnamese guard in the watchtower overlooking the beach gave her a curious stare, then turned his attention back to heating his small pot of coffee.

Sue had decided to ask for a transfer - now, before she got settled in. Surely there was a need for nurses at some of the remote field hospitals, where the wounded were first brought in from the battlefields.

She felt so useless here, where all that Vietnam's medical facilities could do for the wounded had already been accomplished. She hadn't come here to administer drugs to men for whom no more could be done while they awaited evacuation. Sure, there was an emergency room, but it dealt with a trickle of men whose injuries were mainly accidental ones - dropped tools on toes, sprained ankles from playing tennis, and that sort of thing. She wanted to be someplace like Curt Draeger had been; where men like her father - infantry soldiers, wounded in battle and fighting for their lives - needed a skilled nurse to assist in triage and to deal with the traumatic injuries of warfare. A *combat* nurse.

There was little chance of anything like that happening here. And what was worse, she didn't like the attitudes of most of her co-workers. All they had seemed to care about the afternoon before was what they were going to wear to the Tet costume party the hospital staff was having the following night. Partying, of all things, in the midst of these miserably wounded men, while their medical corps peers up-country were involved in desperate battles to save combat soldiers' lives.

She watched the orange arc of the rising sun appear above the distant horizon, then turned back toward the hospital. She would wait in Major Westcott's office until the head nurse appeared, and make her wishes known.

     *   *   *

They happened upon a small open area just as the darkness of the jungle began to give way to faint light, and Sam Hagen halted the team and moved them into positions around it.

As Walt Shumate had promised, the covey appeared overhead with the light of dawn. Sam apprised him of the situation, and Walt sent an urgent request to scramble the choppers for an emergency extraction of the team.

Twenty minutes later, Sam heard the sound of rotor blades beating the air in the distance. It gave him the greatest sense of relief he had ever felt, and he said to Ed, "Hang in a bit longer, buddy. We'll be out of here in a few minutes."

Sam put Lieutenant Walker and three of the Chams on the first chopper into the LZ, and he and Khoe boarded the second.

Larry O'Neil, the Mike Force commander, was waiting at the landing zone with the medics when they reached the forward operations base.

As he landed in the second chopper, Sam could see Ed being carted off toward the dispensary, and O'Neil leaving his side to come to Sam's helicopter.

"Sorry we screwed up the patrol, Captain," Sam said as O'Neil helped him with his rucksack.

"You did fine. They're blasting the shit out of the NVA you found with airstrikes as we speak. Looks like something big is cooking - a major attack on Hue, maybe."

"I thought there was supposed to be a Tet truce coming up," Sam said.

"There is. Starting tonight."

"How's Lieutenant Walker doing?" Hagen asked.

"He's fine. A fat lip, but he'll be OK. He said you really saved his ass, Sam."

Hagen shrugged. "We were lucky. Anyway, I owed him. He kept me from getting eaten by a tiger."

"A tiger?" O'Neil said, looking at him incredulously.

"It's a long story. I'll tell you about it later. I better go look after the Chams now, sir."

As O'Neil watched Sam Hagen walk away, he thought, There's a warrior, all right. With men like him, we're going to *win* this shitty little war.

　　　　　*　　　　　　　　*　　　　　　　　*

Major Maggie Westcott looked at the new nurse with surprise and said, "You're up and about mighty early, Sue. Couldn't sleep? Jet lag does that sometimes."

Sue Madison wrung her fatigue cap in her hands and said, "I, uh, I came to ask for a transfer, ma'am."

Westcott studied the lieutenant's pretty face for a moment, then said, "Sue, you've only been here half a day. What's wrong?"

"It's... I just... I think I can do more in a field hospital, ma'am. That's all."

The major gestured to the chair beside her desk and said, "Sit down, Sue," then poured coffee from the Thermos bottle she had brought with her into two paper cups, and handed one to Sue. "Now, tell me why you're already unhappy at being here. Are you homesick?"

Sue took a sip of the tepid coffee, then said, "No, I'm not homesick, Maggie. It's just not what I expected, I guess. I mean, it looks like all I'd be doing here is administering drugs and changing dressings. That's not why I came to Vietnam."

Maggie sat on the edge of the desk, considering the younger nurse's words. "Yes," she said, "that is largely what a ward nurse's duties are in this hospital. At least, that's the technical part, the easy part."

"Well, what other part is there?"

Major Westcott started to say something, then stopped herself. She stood, set her coffee down and said, "Come with me."

They walked onto one of the wards and into the nurses' station, where the night nurse was filling out charts before going off duty. Maggie introduced Sue to the night nurse, a first lieutenant named Lisa Strong, then asked, "Any problems last night, Lisa?"

Lieutenant Strong sighed and nodded. "We lost one. The brain injury in bed two. And Schneider, the double leg amputee, pulled his IVs out. Said he didn't want to go home half a man. I put him under, but he'll probably be coming out of it by now."

Maggie looked at Sue and said, "That's the third time he's tried that. What do you think we should do, Sue?"

Both of the other nurses were looking at her, waiting for an answer.

"I suppose he should be referred for psychiatric counseling," she said.

"The shrink talks to him every day," Lisa said. "Him and a hundred others. With some it seems to help a little. With others, it doesn't do shit. Like Schneider."

She picked up the charts one at a time, glancing at each and offering a sentence or two about each of the men they represented.

"Blackston. Newlywed with his dick and balls and one leg gone. All he ever wanted, he says, was to go back to the farm and raise kids.... Whiting, back of his head missing. Thinks he's in France. Keeps asking to see General Patton.... Stankovich, who lost both eyes. Volunteered for the army so he could go back to art school on the GI bill.... Johanssen, a ski guide from Colorado, paralyzed.... Rodham, a little gangrene. A real whiner. Lost a couple of toes, and thinks the only reason for the existence of the Army Nurse Corps is to look after his every personal wish and whim. He should be leaving today, thank God."

She dropped the rest of the charts on the pile and said wearily, "Welcome to Ward C, Sue. The home of broken dreams."

"That's the other part of nursing duty here, Sue," Maggie Westcott said. "The hard part. Caring for the wounded souls."

There was that term again, Sue Madison thought. The same one her father and Curt Draeger had used; *wounded souls.*

"Well, why don't you go get some sleep?" Maggie Westcott said to Lisa Strong. "We'll cover the morning rounds with the docs."

Lisa glanced up at the clock, happy to have an extra fifteen minutes off. "Thanks. I will." A faint smile came to her face when she added, "Gotta rest up for the party tonight. See you there, Sue?"

Sue shrugged and said, "I guess so."

"Well, I'd take every chance I could get to party here," the other lieutenant offered. "All work and no play, and you'll end up as crazy as - as Whiting, out there." She waved a weak goodbye and disappeared.

"So," Maggie said, "as you can see, there's a lot more to do here than handle drugs and dressings, Sue. A lot more. You'll end up being part shrink, part chaplain, part surrogate sister, or wife or girlfriend. Because that's what these men need, while they're here."

She put her arm around Sue's shoulder. "I know it's not as - as glamorous, maybe, as trying to put them back together when they first get flown out of the field," she said. "But it's damn well as important. And in a lot of respects, much harder. But if you still want field duty when your tour's half up, I'll see that you get a transfer. I'm sure there's a lot of nurses up-country who'd be more than happy to trade their jobs for one here."

Now Westcott's tone became somewhat stern, and she said, "Meanwhile, I'll expect you to do your best here. This is where the Army has sent you, because this is where you're needed. And the needs of the Army come first - just like they did for all those poor bastards out there on the ward."

Sue nodded slowly, and she said, "Yes. Thank you, Maggie. I'll do my best."

          *   *   *

Mary McClanahan Walker sat, pen in hand, staring at the wall of her apartment. On the table before her was a box of stationery, several crumpled pages lying beside it.

The baby in her belly stirred, and she set the pen down and felt her swelling abdomen. When the baby's movements ceased, she took another sheet of paper from the box, dated the paper January 29, 1968, and wrote, *Dearest Ed, I hope this letter finds you well.*

Again she raised her gaze to the empty wall, wondering how a woman should go about telling her distant husband that she had been having an affair while he was at war.

She had to do it, otherwise he would find out from someone else, either in a letter or, more likely, from his so-called friends when he returned to Guinea.

She could lie about it, of course. But it would always be there, even if he believed her. Her sister-in-law, Evelyn, knew. She was the one who had let Mary know that her tryst aboard the *Mary Anne* with Sandy Milton was common knowledge in Gloucester County. If Evelyn knew, then obviously Ed's own brother did. So even if Ed did accept her denial, the others would always know, always allude to it when they wanted some reason to hurt her.

No, it was best to make a clean breast of it now, in her own words. But how? What the hell was she supposed to say?

For many minutes more, she tried to think of how to do it, and now and then her eyes would fill with tears and spill over. Several times, she put the pen to the paper to write, but each time, the phrase she had in her mind seemed inadequate. Finally, she crumpled up the sheet of letter paper and tossed it beside the others, then put down the pen, pushed herself up from the chair, and went to bed. For a long time,

Mary lay on her back, staring at the faint grey of the ceiling, her thoughts a confused jumble of regret and self-pity and anger.

Eventually, she rolled onto her side, and mumbled "Oh, damn you, Ed! Damn the Army and this stinking war for taking you away when I need you the most! And damn you to hell for going!"

THIRTEEN

The Tet Offensive, the great battle of the Vietnam War, opened early on the morning of 30 January 1968. With blatant, calculated disregard for the truce to which both sides had agreed, the North Vietnamese Army regulars and Viet Cong guerrilla militias launched massive assaults throughout South Vietnam at the height of the Lunar New Year celebrations.

It was a devastating military defeat for the communists. Reeling from the initial series of surprise blows, most delivered in the midst of civilian populated cities, the United States forces and their allies quickly marshaled their strength and counterattacked. They rooted the enemy from the cities in difficult house-to-house combat, pounded them where they were massed in the countryside, and killed them in unprecedented numbers - scores of thousands, perhaps *hundreds* of thousands.

But the military successes of the US and her allies in the series of battles was not without great cost, for the unqualified military victory was turned into a devastating political defeat. Ignoring such atrocities as the mass murder of thousands of noncommunist intellectuals in Hue city, the news media instead concentrated on the stories they could capture on film; a Vietnamese policeman summarily executing a Viet Cong guerrilla in Saigon; US military policemen, ill-trained for organized combat, attempting to retake the US embassy compound; the stream of American wounded being brought in from the battlefields where they and their comrades-in-arms were annihilating the enemy regiments that had eluded them for so long.

The American public, fed these incessant, slanted images and increasingly disenchanted with the length and cost in lives of the war, began to turn against their government's ill-managed involvement in it.

And worse, they began to heap their frustrations on the conscripts and volunteers who, at the peril of their lives, followed that government's bidding into combat.

On the battlefields, the young men caught up in the cauldron of war were unaware that their sacrifices would come to nought. They knew only that the enemy had at last exposed himself in face-to-face encounters. All across South Vietnam, the Americans and their allies tore into the communists with wrathful fury.

It was not until years later that an American officer, during negotiations at the end of the conflict, remarked to his North Vietnamese counterpart, "You know, don't you," the American said, "that we never lost a battle."

"That may be true," the North Vietnamese officer replied. "But it is also irrelevant."

Lieutenant Susan Madison was already awake when Major Maggie Westcott burst into her room not long after daylight on that first day of the Tet offensive. Sue had stayed at the hospital party only briefly the evening before, the jet lag and culture shock of her arrival in Vietnam two days earlier finally catching up with her. It had been a good enough excuse to allow her to withdraw from the sexual advances of several of the male medical personnel, as well.

The scream of Phantom jets taking off from the adjoining airbase at Cam Ranh Bay, and the sounds of distant artillery had caused her to awaken at dawn.

"Up and at 'em, Sue," Maggie said when she burst in. "There's a country-wide alert."

"What do you mean?" Sue asked.

"There's fighting all over the place; Nha Trang, Saigon, Danang. Even in the village just off base."

Sue pushed her mosquito net aside and swung her legs out of her bunk. "Are you sure?" she asked. "I thought there was a truce."

"Yeah, so did everybody else. Everybody but the VC, apparently. Eighth Field hospital up in Nha Trang is under attack. They can't take any medevacs in there, so we're going to bring them in here. Jesus. Half the staff is hung over. I want you to go to the emergency room over by the LZ. Help with triage. And hurry; there's a couple of chopper loads already on the way in. Gotta go."

The major rushed off to alert more of her subordinate nurses as Sue dressed quickly in her fatigue uniform. By the time she left her room, Sue could hear helicopters approaching.

Well, she thought as she ran toward the landing zone, it looks as if I'm going to get my wish to be a real combat nurse a little earlier than I expected.

Not far up the coast, in Nha Trang, the Mike Force had responded quickly to the attack on the city that adjoined the base they shared with the 5th Special Forces Group headquarters. Two battalions of the North Vietnamese 18B Regiment had infiltrated the outskirts of the former resort city under cover of the truce. In a coordinated assault just after midnight, they seized several of Nha Trang's key installations, left lightly guarded by Tet celebrants.

Although two companies had been sent on leave to visit their home villages during the truce, the three remaining Mike Force companies, including the Cham soldiers of 7th Company who had just returned from the ill-fated reconnaissance patrol into the A Shau valley, were quickly assembled and rushed into town to deal with the invaders.

Their rapid response caught the NVA off guard before they were able to consolidate their gains. In fierce house-to-house fighting, the Mike Force troops routed the two North Vietnamese battalions, pushing the remnants into two small pockets. The third battalion of the NVA regiment, trying to reinforce them, was decimated when an AC-47 Spooky gunship caught them in open rice paddies between their staging area in the mountains and the city of Nha Trang. The survivors limped back into the hills.

Larry O'Neil and his deputy commanding officer, Joe Zamiara, were two of those who paid the price of the Mike Force victory. Zamiara was killed in the effort to retake the province headquarters, and O'Neil was severely wounded when a bullet smashed through his thigh, shattering the femur. Several other noncommissioned officers of the American Special Forces team were less-severely wounded, and several dozen of the Montagnard and Cham strikers were killed or injured.

O'Neil's absence left Lieutenant Ed Walker in command of the Mike Force elements engaged in the fierce battle. But Walker was tentative in his actions, hesitant in deciding how to maneuver his troops to deal with the remaining enemy.

Sam Hagen was greatly concerned, if not surprised, for Walker's mood had been one of depressed silence since their return from the A Shau valley. The young sergeant wondered whether Ed's ill humor was the result of his brief but frightening capture by the enemy - a newfound sense of vulnerability to the dangers of combat that, more simply stated, was raw fear. Or was it the fact that, once again, there was no letter from Mary? It had been weeks since Ed had heard from her, and he seemed to sense that her silence stemmed from something deeper than a lack of time to write or of interesting news to tell.

Perhaps, Sam thought, Ed's depression was the result of a combination of those factors, and the pain of his injured mouth. The slight case of pneumonia had quickly cleared up, so it wasn't that.

Whatever it was, Sam felt, the young lieutenant had better snap out of it, or turn the team over to someone with fire in his belly. The mood of a unit's commander is infectious, and Lieutenant Walker, like it or not, was the Mike Force commander now.

He showed up at Sam's position just as he was preparing to move his platoon to 7th Company's flank. They were going to try to maneuver around behind the enemy force that they had trapped in a cluster of houses at the edge of town. With their backs to the open rice paddies, over which American aircraft patrolled, the NVA had decided on the only reasonable course short of surrender; dig in and fight.

"What are you going to do, Sam?" Walker asked without enthusiasm, then touched the sutures in his sore, swollen lips with a fingertip.

"I'm going to move around their flank and get behind them," Sam replied. "We can't get at them from this side."

Ed nodded and looked around. There was a burst of machine gun fire from beyond the tin-roofed houses to their front, then a prolonged burst from one of 7th Company's guns as they returned the fire. Neither man flinched at the noise of the bullets cracking overhead.

"How many of them do you think there are?" Ed asked.

"About a platoon, I guess."

"Well, be careful," Walker said.

"Right," Sam muttered. Another burst of machine gun fire came from the enemy positions, and this time it was answered by the *thunk* and *boom* of one of the Cham's grenade launchers. A moment later, two Mike Force troopers scurried past, carrying a gut-shot comrade to the rear. Ed looked at the man with detachment, and shook his head but did nothing to assist.

"I'd better get going," Sam said, and turned to follow his troops around the flank of the cornered enemy platoon. He could use Ed's help in the assault, but the lieutenant just stood there.

Sam turned back to him. "You OK?" he asked.

Ed shrugged, and Sam said, "Look, Ed. I don't know what's bothering you, but we have a hell of a fight going here, in case you hadn't noticed. We could use your help."

"What do you want me to do?"

"*Some*thing," Sam said. "Anything. Christ, Ed! You act like you're on some other planet." He turned and moved off behind his troops.

Ed Walker followed him. They rounded the corner of one of the small buildings, and both Americans stopped. There, lying on the ground before them, was a young Vietnamese woman, her legs twisted beneath her, her mouth open and her eyes rolled back in their sockets. Across her belly lay a tiny baby girl. The back of the child's head was missing.

"Oh, you God damned sons of bitches!" Sam Hagen blurted to no one in particular at the sight of the two civilians.

Ed Walker only stared, open mouthed, in horror. Then he dropped to his knees beside them and closed the woman's eyelids over her dry, dead eyes. Next, he picked up the dead child, placed her face down on the mother's chest, and wrapped her thin, stiffening arms around the child.

He looked up at Sam Hagen, hate now burning in his eyes, and leaped to his feet. "All right, Sam," he said. "Let's go, now. Let's go root the fucking rats out of their holes!"

*   *   *

The wounded lay all around the entrance to the Cam Ranh hospital emergency room, not only American soldiers, but Vietnamese troops and civilians of all ages. Sue Madison, followed by two medics with a stretcher, moved among them, quickly deciding who needed to go into the operating room first, which ones could wait, and which others were, in her judgement, beyond help.

If it had only been the two helicopter loads of soldiers that landed just after she arrived, it would not have been so bad. But a truck, an army two-and-a-half ton filled with wounded from the fighting in a nearby village, had gotten there just after the medical evacuation helicopters took off. Now another medevac chopper was flaring in a swirl of sand and dust above the landing pad. Strangely, she felt grateful for the noise it made, for it drowned out the maddening cries and moans of the wounded.

"Take this one in, then hurry back to help with this chopper load," she ordered the stretcher bearers, pointing to a Vietnamese soldier who lay on his back, holding in his hands the guts that spilled from a gaping wound in his belly. Two other medics returned with a bloody stretcher from the operating room, and she yelled above the whine of the medevac helicopter, "Unload the chopper!"

An old man sat clutching a frail, elderly woman in his arms, and she reached down and felt for a pulse in the woman's neck. There was none, so she pried the woman from the old man's grasp and saw why. There was a ragged hole blasted in the middle of her chest. It was not even bloody, just a mass of torn flesh and splintered bone. Her dead heart was pumping no blood through it. She exchanged a brief look of despair with the old man, then turned to attend to the soldiers coming off the helicopter.

The first one off stumbled toward her, one of his hands clutching the other forearm, from which the hand dangled by a tendon. Someone had tied a tourniquet just above the elbow, and she thought, That will do for now. She said, "Sit down over there," pointing to a bare space along the wall.

"But my arm! Jesus, look at my arm, lady!"

"You'll be all right. Now, sit down over there! Move!"

The three other soldiers were carried from the helicopter, and one of the men who had unloaded them quickly collected three unused litters, threw them in and hopped aboard, and the chopper lifted off again. Sue strode to the new casualties to examine them. The first man had a mass of small wounds from his chest up, his face swollen and peppered with shrapnel. She slit his shirt open with her scissors. He was gasping with short, irregular breaths, and she noticed that several of the wounds were bubbling with bloody foam.

"Left lung's punctured," a man's voice behind her said.

"Yes," she said, turning to see who had spoken. A handsome face looked back at her with the brightest blue eyes she had ever seen. The soldier had such striking good looks that Sue involuntarily stopped her examination of the wounded man for a moment to stare at him.

He smiled briefly, then looked at the other two casualties. "The captain has a shattered femur," he said. "Nicked the femoral artery, I think. He's been down for awhile. Better get him in before he goes into shock. Nothing we can do for *him*," he said, nodding toward the third stretcher. "He died on the way here. Now, let's get the captain inside."

Without even bothering to confirm the man's diagnoses, she struggled to lift one end of the captain's stretcher as the man easily hoisted the other and moved into the crowded emergency operating room.

"What have we got?" a masked doctor asked, his hands washing the intestines laid out on the belly of the Vietnamese soldier who'd been brought in shortly before.

Before Sue could speak, the man at the other end of the litter said, "Gunshot wound shattered the left femur and nicked the femoral artery about an hour-and-a-half ago. He's had two bags of Ringer's and a hit of morphine just after he got shot. Pulse was starting to weaken on the flight in."

"Put him there," the surgeon said, nodding toward the only empty gurney in the crowded operating room. Sue helped the man place the litter on the gurney, and another nurse and surgeon came over, the doctor asking, "What do we have?"

The man, whom Sue now noticed was wearing a Special Forces patch on his uniform, repeated his diagnosis as the surgeon began to examine the wound. "Got it," the surgeon said. "What else have we got out there?"

"One guy with multiple frag wounds of the chest and face," the Special Forces man said. "One lung collapsed. We need to get a chest tube in him right away."

"Are you an MD?" the doctor inquired.

"No, a Special Forces medic," the blue-eyed man said.

"That's good enough," the surgeon replied. "Get the chest tube in. We're a bit pushed for hands, right now." He looked at Sue and said, "Give him a hand, lieutenant."

"Yes, sir," Sue Madison said. She looked up at the Special Forces medic and said, "I'll get the tube. Suction machine's over in that corner. What else do you need, sir?"

"Gloves, scalpel, hemostats, and a suture kit," the medic replied. "And it's 'sergeant,' ma'am, not 'sir.' Staff Sergeant Dick Chamberlain."

He got one of the hospital corpsmen to help him move the wounded man into a corner of the roomful of wounded soldiers and busy medics, then pulled on the gloves and knelt beside the gasping soldier. He cut the man's shirt off, scrubbed the dirt and blood from his ribs, and kneeled on one of the man's forearms to hold it down. "Sit on his other arm, ma'am," he directed Sue.

"What?"

"Just what I said. Sit on his arm, so he can't move it." He looked at the soldier and said, "This ain't going to be any fun, son. But you'll feel a lot better when I get done."

The injured soldier nodded his acknowledgment, and Chamberlain quickly felt for a spot just above one rib and sliced open the skin with the scalpel. Then he pressed the hemostat, a thin, scissors-like instrument similar to needle-nosed pliers, hard into the incision. The man gurgled deep in his throat at the pain, but Chamberlain ignored him, pressing harder until the point of the instrument punctured the muscle and entered the man's chest cavity. The man screamed in pain, but again Chamberlain paid him no heed, pulling the handles of the hemostat apart to rip a larger hole in the lining of the chest. Next, he shoved the half-inch thick plastic tube in through the opening and sutured it in place. The man's breathing grew slightly deeper almost immediately, and the Special Forces medic said, "Better?"

The man whispered, "Much better, doc. Thanks."

Chamberlain examined the other wounds with which the man was peppered, then ripped off the gloves and said, "No sweat, troop. Just be glad you have two lungs. The rest will be OK until the real docs can get to you. Hang in there."

He smiled at Sue Madison, who was again gazing at him with undisguised admiration. "We'd better see what we can do for the others out there, ma'am," he said.

She nodded, and they stepped outside again. Another nurse was ushering the man with the nearly-severed hand into the operating room, and Chamberlain said, "He had morphine, oh, forty-five minutes ago, nurse. The tourniquet was last loosened aboard the chopper around twenty minutes ago."

The nurse acknowledged his comments with a nod and a smile, and disappeared inside with the man.

The old Vietnamese man was still clutching the dead woman, and Chamberlain squatted before him and spoke softly to him in Vietnamese. Then the old man surrendered the body to the Special Forces sergeant, who gently wrapped her in a discarded poncho.

While Sue did what she could for the few remaining wounded, she occasionally glanced over at Chamberlain.

She felt remarkably attracted to this unassuming but obviously capable soldier. It was not just his handsome face and athletic build, nor his quiet confidence. There was something else; some aura about him. Some powerful attraction she couldn't really define.

One of the cooks from the mess hall came around with a big container of hot coffee, and Lieutenant Madison and Sergeant Chamberlain each accepted a cup. Sue took a sip, then said, "I don't think I had the chance to introduce myself, Sergeant Chamberlain. I'm Sue Madison." She held out her hand to him. He shook it firmly, and smiled. "Pleased to meet you, ma'am."

"Please, call me Sue," she said, grateful that he did not release her hand for awhile. "Where are you stationed?"

"Camp Duc Lap," he said. "A Special Forces camp over on the Cambodian border. I was on my way out on R&R when this big fight started. Don't know when I might get out, now. It looks like Charlie is going all out in this one, doesn't it?"

Sue sipped her coffee and nodded, then asked, "Where were you going?"

"On R&R? Hawaii," he said.

"Oh," Sue said. She supposed he was going there to meet his wife or a girlfriend, as did most of the troops who went to Hawaii instead of one of the more exotic ports of call such as Hong Kong, Taipei, or Bangkok.

"Don't know why," he said, as if reading her thoughts. "I'm not meeting anyone there. I've been over here for the last two years straight, and I thought it would be nice to go someplace where everybody speaks English, for a change."

She tried to think of something clever to say - something that would let him know the strong attraction she felt for him. But nothing clever came to mind, so she said, "You're really good at this medical business - Dick, is it?"

He nodded. "Well," he said, "you get a lot of practice out in the border camps. Everything from delivering babies to things like the chest tube there. And worse."

"Ever think of going to medical school?" Sue asked, but he ignored the question, his eyes fixed on a Huey helicopter flying fast and low toward the hospital.

"Looks like another load coming in," he said. "If he's going back to Nha Trang, I'd better go with him."

Sue wanted to say, No, don't. Stay here with me. But she didn't. She just looked at him until the helicopter was almost there, then said, "Dick, please come back sometime. I mean, just to visit. To see me."

She knew she was blushing at the forward manner of her words, but she didn't care. She only knew that she felt a strange and powerful attraction to this man. She wanted desperately to see him again, to be near him.

He fixed her with his steel blue eyes, then smiled warmly. "All right, Sue," he said softly. "Yes. I'd love to do that. Maybe I'll just save this R&R until later."

She nodded, a sheepish grin crossing her face at the realization that her unaccustomed boldness had succeeded. "Thank you," was all she could think to say.

The helicopter flared and landed, and they rushed forward through the swirl of dust around it as the doors of the aircraft opened. There were two patients, one American and one Vietnamese. As several corpsmen joined them to help off-load the wounded, she heard Dick yell to the crew chief, "You going back to Nha Trang?"

The crewman nodded, and Chamberlain jumped aboard as the wounded were carried away. She looked back at the helicopter from the door of the emergency room just as it lifted off. He was watching her, and he waved. Sue Madison returned the wave, and watched the aircraft pivot and fly away.

*   *   *

"I can get to them, if you lay down a base of fire to cover me," Sam Hagen told Ed Walker.

Ed peered around the corner of the building for a second and looked at the two children Sam was talking about, then ducked his head back just before a burst of machine gun fire crackled past. A boy of about ten was crouched behind the corner of a building just down the street and across it. He held a small girl between his knees, and the Mike Force men could hear her wailing.

"That damned machine gun will cut you down before you get halfway across, Sam. We've got to put him out of action first."

Now Hagen got down on his knees and took another quick peek around the corner. Again, a burst of machine gun fire from the house at the end of the street ripped past, tearing up the dirt inches from where Sam's head had been.

"She's hurt, goddamit!" Sam said. "I can see blood all over her legs. We've got to get her!"

"All right," Ed said. "Wait here a minute."

He scurried around the backside of the house and ran at a crouch to the wall where two of the Cham soldiers lay with an M-60 machine gun. He dived beside them and said, "I need that gun, men."

The Chams didn't understand the American's words, but they understood his intent when he handed one of them his CAR-15 rifle and reached for the machine gun. He ran back to Sam's position with it in time to see Hagen lunge around the corner and fire a forty millimeter grenade in the direction of the gun. The projectile detonated, but again the enemy weapon raked the street with a long burst of fire.

Ed made a visual check of the machine gun and belt of ammunition, then, leaning against the building, said, "OK, Sam. You ready?"

Hagen reloaded the grenade launcher and replied, "Ready as I'll ever be."

Ed Walker dashed into the street, the M-60 machine gun rattling a long burst toward the enemy gun as he dived into the dirt. Barely pausing, he got the gun up onto his shoulder and loosed an aimed burst at the doorway of the building fifty meters distant, then at one of the two windows, then back at the door.

Behind him, Sam aimed the grenade launcher at the center of the building, fired, and dropped the weapon, jumping over Ed and his barking gun as he sprinted toward the two children cowering behind the building across the street.

Now Ed saw the twinkle of the enemy machine gun's muzzle as it fired a long burst in his direction, and he shifted his aim there. He squeezed the trigger and held it, trying to keep the bucking weapon aimed at the source of fire. The belt of ammunition ran out just as Sam shuffled sideways past him, the children locked against his chest in his strong arms, his back to the enemy, shielding the kids with his body. Ed scooted out of the street after him, and they were safe behind the cover of the building once more.

The little girl was still wailing, and Sam quickly saw why. A bullet had pierced the flesh of both of her thighs, mercifully missing the bones. He tore open his battle dressing and began to patch one leg. Ed dropped to his knees beside him, using his own dressing to treat the child's other leg. That done, the men paused and looked at each other.

"Good job, old buddy," Ed said to his comrade-in-arms.

Sam reached a hand to him, and they shook hands warmly for a moment. "What a team, eh?" Sam said with a broad grin.

"Yeah," Ed Walker said, smiling for the first time since they had become separated in the A Shau valley days before. "What a team. Now, you hustle those kids off to the rear."

"What are you gonna do?"

"I'm gonna make sure that friggin' machine gunner down the street is done for," Walker replied, picking up the grenade launcher and cracking open the breech to load it.

*　　　　　*　　　　　*

The medical evacuation helicopters swept into the landing zone at Cam Ranh Bay hospital throughout the day and into the night, and Sue Madison met most of them. Each time, she hastily looked for Dick Chamberlain's face among those bringing them in before she turned her attention to the wounded, but he was never there.

There were wounds of every description, some of the injured young men unconscious, others moaning and crying with pain, others only cursing. A few, relieved to be out of the cauldron, even laughed. But most suffered silently as they awaited their turn on the operating table. Others, their torn bodies beyond repair, quietly died.

How could there be so many? the young nurse Sue Madison wondered. What in God's name were they doing out there? Surely they would all be used up soon, at this rate.

Finally, Maggie Westcott, her surgical apron covered in blood, came out and said, "Go grab a shower and get a little sleep, Sue. I'll take over here."

"No," Sue said. "I'm all right, Maggie. You're the one who needs to get some rest."

"Go on now," Major Westcott insisted. "There won't be many casualties coming in, now that it's dark. The medevac choppers will have to wait for daylight to go out after the wounded. We'll need you here again then."

"OK," Sue said, looking around the ground outside the emergency room in the dim light of the bare bulb above the door. Bloody bandages and cut up pieces of uniform littered the ground.

"Who was that gorgeous green beanie you helped with the chest tube, by the way?" Maggie asked as she lit a cigarette.

Sue looked at her and smiled. "Just a guy from up-country who was headed for R&R," she replied. "He got caught in Nha Trang by the fighting."

"Well, you should have kept him. We could use a guy like that around here. And not just to help with the casualties, if you know what I mean," Maggie said with a wink.

Sue felt a twinge of jealousy at the comment, then thought how adolescent that was. She felt like a teenager with her first crush. "Maybe he'll be back," she said, then, "If you're sure you won't need me, I'll be going."

"Yes," Maggie said. "Get going. And Sue, you did a hell of a good job out here today."

"Thanks," Sue said. "I hope tomorrow won't be so busy. Poor boys."

"You did your best, Sue. That's all anyone could ask for. And try not to think about them." She chuckled and added, "Fantasize about that Special Forces guy, instead."

Sue brushed her comment off with a wave and walked to her room. She switched on the light and looked at herself in the mirror. There were splotches of dried blood on her forehead and her hair was matted and in disarray, and she hoped vainly that she hadn't been such a mess when Dick Chamberlain had seen her.

She stripped her uniform off and threw it in the trash can in the corner, then pulled on her terrycloth robe and headed for the shower, wondering if she would ever feel clean again.

FOURTEEN

Sue Madison heard a helicopter landing at the emergency room pad as she scrubbed herself dry with a rough towel, and wondered if she should quickly pull on a fresh uniform and go see if her help was needed. No, she decided, there would be plenty for her to do in the morning. She'd better get some sleep while she could, as Maggie had ordered. She fluffed her hair, pulled on her robe, and walked back to her room. She thought about writing a quick note to her parents to let them know she was OK, then decided it could wait, so she removed her robe and pulled on the extra large T shirt she used for a nightgown, crawled beneath the mosquito net that covered her bunk bed, and closed her eyes.

Images of the gruesome wounds she had seen that day, that she had earlier been able to view in a purely clinical way, filled her mind. She forced them away, replacing them with the image of Dick Chamberlain, the handsome and capable Special Forces medic whom she had found so magnetically attractive. Would he really come back to visit her? Sleep came quickly as she thought of how it might be if he did.

*   *   *

"What do you hear from Maria, Sam?" Ed Walker asked as he opened a C-ration can of sliced peaches. The two men were sitting in a small house on the edge of the rice paddies near where they had rooted out the last of the North Vietnamese from Nha Trang. Now, all they were doing was waiting to ensure that no more of the enemy attempted to infiltrate the town from across the dark paddies, as they had done the night before. To assist them, an occasional flare from the Mike Force mortars in their compound a mile away popped overhead, lighting the rice ponds with a dim glow.

Hagen set aside the knife he was sharpening. "Not much in the way of news," he said. "She still hasn't been able to find time to get up to Virginia and see Mary." He knew there had been no letter for Ed when they got back from the A Shau valley, and he supposed that fact was weighing heavily on his friend's mind.

"I wish she *could* get up there to check on her, Sam. I'm really getting worried, man. I haven't had a letter from her in weeks."

"Yeah, I know. Look, I'll tell Maria to just find some time and get up there. I'm sure everything's all right, though."

"Yeah, I guess you're right," Ed said, sighing and lying back on the dirt floor of the house. "Otherwise, I'm sure I'd have heard something from Evelyn."

The room was dimly lighted momentarily as Ed struck a match to light a cigarette. "I think maybe I'll write to her, Sam," he said.

"That might help, Ed. I mean, hell, if you haven't been bothering to write to Mary, how can you blame her for doing the same thing?"

"Not Mary - Maria. I've been dropping Mary a line fairly regularly. Maybe if I wrote to Maria and asked her to go up there...." He let the thought trail off, inhaled deeply from his cigarette, and exhaled with a sigh.

"Lieutenant Walker," someone called softly from outside the building.

Ed pushed himself up to a sitting position and said, "In here," then lit a match to show the man where he was.

Master Sergeant Shumate stepped in. "You need to get back to the CP, sir," he said.

"What for?"

"New mission," Shumate explained. "The group operations officer came by. Seems the NVA have the north hill of the camp out at Duc Lap. They have some aircraft laid on to start lifting us out there at first light."

Walker got to his feet and picked up his combat gear. "What's the mission?" he asked.

"Pretty straightforward," Shumate answered. "*Go take it back.*"

*　　　　　　　　　*　　　　　　　　*

At first Sue didn't know why she had awakened. Then there was another knock on her door, and someone said, "Sue?"

"Yes?" She slid out from beneath the mosquito net and stumbled to the door, glancing at the luminous dial of her watch. It was almost midnight. She opened the screen door slightly, holding the baggy T shirt down with one hand, and said, "What is it? Do they need me at the E.R.?"

"No," the man's voice answered. "It's me, Dick Chamberlain."

She opened the door to him, and he stepped in, took her in his arms, and kissed her warmly. She wrapped her arms around his neck, pressing herself against him as he kissed her cheek, her ear, her mouth, his hands sliding down her hips to the bare buttocks beneath the T shirt.

"I - I don't believe this is happening," she whispered hoarsely. "It's - it's like a dream."

"It's crazy, I know," Dick said. "But I couldn't get my mind off of you, Sue." He moved his hands to her shoulders and held her at arms' length in the near darkness. "You don't mind that I'm here?" he asked.

She pulled his face to hers, her open mouth kissing his with undisguised eagerness as they pressed their bodies together. No words were needed to answer his question.

They expressed their passion with uninhibited physical fervor, their whispered words the only things they held back, to avoid being heard by those sleeping nearby. The bunk was creaky, so Dick pulled the mattress to the floor.

"I wish I could see you," Sue whispered at some point, and he said, "Yes. Next time, you will."

It was a long time before they lay still, curled up together on the mattress with a sheet pulled over them.

"I don't want tomorrow to come," she said.

He kissed her forehead. "No. But it will. Listen..."

In the quiet, when she listened intently, she could hear what he heard. Like distant thunder, the sound of artillery rumbled somewhere far away. "Is it going to be as bad tomorrow?" she asked. "There were so many boys today."

"I imagine so," he said, rolling onto his back. "It's about over in Nha Trang, but in some places - Saigon, Hue, Pleiku - it looks like just the beginning."

"God, don't tell me that."

"But maybe it's the beginning of the end. Maybe this is a last, desperate gamble. I don't know."

"You mean, you think we can win?"

"Maybe. If we can just hold on to them now. If they'll let us follow them back into Laos and Cambodia and up north."

She pictured him trudging through North Vietnam and into Hanoi, the enemy fleeing before him. "What will you do when it's over?" she asked.

"I don't know. Stay here, maybe. Join the Peace Corps again."

"Again?"

"Yeah," he said. "I spent a year in Thailand before I joined the Army." Somehow, she wasn't surprised.

"What about you?" he asked.

"I don't know, either. Getting here is as far ahead as I've thought."

Chamberlain rolled over onto his elbow facing her. He kissed her lightly, trailing his fingers along the soft skin of her breasts and belly. "Is there a man in your life?"

"Well, sort of," she said.

"What do you mean, 'sort of?'"

"There's this handsome, blue-eyed, ex-Peace Corps, Green Beret," she whispered, pulling him atop her.

Dawn's light was just beginning to show when she awoke to the sound of him coming back into the room. He'd been to the shower, and she quietly watched his shadowy figure as he pulled on his jungle fatigue uniform. She said nothing until he sat on the bare springs of the bunk to tie his boots.

"I'm glad you're still here," she said. "I was afraid I'd wake up and find out it was only a dream."

He finished tying his boots, then stood, came to her and lifted her up, hugging her naked body to him. "I have to go," he said.

"Where?"

"Nha Trang. Then back to my camp, if I can get there. God only knows what's going on."

"When will I see you again, Dick?"

"God only knows that, too. When things settle down, I guess. Not long, I hope."

"I - I don't know what to say, Dick. Except, hurry back to me. And, take care of yourself."

"You said enough last night," he whispered, then cocked his head to one side and, after a moment, said, "Here they come."

The sound of a helicopter's rotors beating the air reached them from the distance.

"I'll see you, Sue," he said, then kissed her quickly and released her.

She took one of his hands and held it as long as she could while he walked to the door and out into the dawn. Then she threw the mattress onto the bunk, slipped on her robe, and rushed off to the latrine. The first medevac helicopter of the day was almost to the hospital LZ, and Sue felt a twinge of guilt that she wasn't there to meet it.

         *   *   *

Lieutenant Ed Walker, the acting commander of the Nha Trang Mike Force, and the noncommissioned officers who commanded the companies and platoons of the unit's indigenous soldiers listened intently as the sergeant from Camp Duc Lap explained the layout of the camp and described the surrounding terrain.

"What about LZs, Sergeant Chamberlain?" Ed Walker asked when the medic had completed his briefing.

Chamberlain used a grease pencil to draw several large circles on the overhead photographs group headquarters had supplied for planning the mission to retake the camp's north hill. They were old photographs, and it was a fortunate coincidence that Chamberlain had been in Nha Trang en route to R&R when the offensive began. After briefing and assisting the Mike Force in planning the assault, he would accompany them out to the camp.

They would first fly to the American base at Ban Me Thuot aboard C-130 transport planes, linking up with the assault helicopters there.

The first helicopter lift, 7th Company's Chams, would land south of the camp and move inside it to reinforce the defenders and to provide supporting fires for the other two Mike Force companies involved in the operation, Walker decided. The other two companies would land to the east of the camp. One company would move to a blocking position to preclude further reinforcement of the North Vietnamese already on the north hill; the other would then conduct an assault to return the hill to friendly hands. A pair of helicopter gunships from Ban Me Thuot would be overhead to provide support.

"All right," he said, then checked his watch and gave a time check. "Any questions? OK, let's get moving."

On the flight to Ban Me Thuot, Ed looked around the crowded airplane, considering the awesome responsibilities with which he found himself faced. A lieutenant with less than two years in the Army, he was in command of a battalion-sized unit of infantry, more than four hundred men, en route to do battle with the enemy. In the regular army units, captains with twice his time in service were in command of understrength companies sometimes amounting to only sixty to eighty men. The officers of conventional units who commanded battalions were lieutenant colonels - three ranks higher and with many more years experience.

He looked at each of the Special Forces NCOs he now commanded. They, too, bore unusually great responsibilities for soldiers of their ranks, leading companies and platoons of larger size than the captains and lieutenants who were their counterparts in conventional infantry units.

Four hundred men. That was the same number that Alexander Hamilton, Edward Walker's boyhood hero of the battle of Yorktown nearly two centuries before, had led in an assault not unlike the one he was soon to lead.

He could do it. He was confident of that, now. The ambush at Thuong Duc, the battle to hold the camp there against desperate odds, yesterday's fight in Nha Trang - even his brief capture by the North Vietnamese in the A Shau valley - they had given him all the experience and the confidence he needed. And those experiences had given him something else, too, he thought. They had proved that he was invulnerable.

*   *   *

The U.S. Army hospital at Cam Ranh Bay was better prepared, on the second day of the Tet offensive, to handle the stream of casualties that continued to pour in. And now that the enemy had been cleaned out of Nha Trang, the field hospital there was fully back in operation, lessening the load at Cam Ranh.

At midmorning, Sue Madison found time to take a break and went into the mess hall for a hurried breakfast. She found Maggie Westcott there, and took a seat beside her.

"Did your, uh, visitor find you all right last night, Sue?"

Sue blushed, and Maggie chuckled. "He showed up on another medevac," the older nurse said. "I hope it was OK that I told him where to find you."

Sue nodded. "It was OK," she said, her eyes dancing.

"I thought it would be," Maggie said. "Just one word of caution, though."

Sue looked up from her tray of watery scrambled eggs and greasy bacon, prepared to be admonished for her fraternization with the NCO.

"Be discreet," the head nurse said, looking at her sternly. "We don't want the troops to get the wrong idea."

Sue nodded and mumbled, "I, uh... yes, ma'am."

Maggie stood and picked up her tray, then leaned over to the younger nurse and said, "You lucky girl. The only guy who ever makes a pass at me around here is that damn, fat supply sergeant."

Sue looked around at her, and Maggie gave her a wink and a smile, then hurried off.

*   *   *

Ed Walker and the Mike Force operations sergeant, Walt Shumate, circled high above the kidney-shaped Special Forces camp at Duc Lap in the command and control helicopter. Borrowed from an American infantry division, the cargo compartment of the modified Huey helicopter contained a console of radios from which the passengers could monitor and transmit on four separate frequencies simultaneously.

The whole area around the camp was visible from Ed's seat at the console, and at first he thought, What a great way to run a battle. Up here, you could see so much more of the battlefield than you could from the ground. But as the assault got underway, and he heard the breathless commands of the company commanders to their subordinates, bullets cracking and grenades exploding in the background of their transmissions, he realized what a false impression the view from the helicopter gave. Because you could only see the battlefield, not the real battle. You couldn't even hear it, couldn't *feel* it - the fear and the chaos and the loneliness - the desperate reality of the fight. Suddenly, the young lieutenant understood the look Shumate had given him when he said he'd command the battle from the C & C helicopter, and why the wise old master sergeant had insisted on bringing a backpack radio along.

Over the intercom, Ed said, "Put us down at the LZ to the east of the camp, pilot. You going to be the radio operator, Shu?"

Shumate looked over at him, twirled one end of his handlebar mustache, and smiled. Then he removed his headset, pulled on the radio backpack, and picked up his weapon.

The battle to retake the enemy-occupied hill was not a long one. The enemy had scant hope against men who led with hand grenades and followed up quickly with fire and movement and more grenades and more fire and movement, relentlessly.

Led by Sergeants Cooper, Hetzler, and Woody, that's what the Montagnard company assigned to conduct the assault did. They maneuvered forward through the wire and into the trenches under a furious hail of bullets and grenades. Methodically and mercilessly, they killed the trapped North Vietnamese where they were, for it was not the way of the Montagnards to accept surrender. There were no prisoners taken at Camp Duc Lap that day.

When it was over, and the remarkably light Mike Force casualties had been tended to, Lieutenant Walker made his way to the main part of the camp.

Sam Hagen, whose troops had supported the assault by fire from inside the camp, was talking to the medic, Staff Sergeant Dick Chamberlain, when he saw Walker and Shumate approach from the recaptured hill at the other end of the camp. "How'd you two get down here?" Sam asked. "I thought you were going to fight the battle from up there in the C and C ship?"

"I found out you can't fight an infantry battle from five thousand feet," Ed replied.

Sam Hagen looked at Walt Shumate and smiled, then said to his commander, "How'd you like to have another good medic on the team, sir?" and pointed his thumb at Chamberlain.

Ed looked at the medic.

"They way I figure it," Chamberlain offered, "these camps will be closing down before long, now that we have Charlie on the run. And they're bound to send the Mike Force over the border to finish him off. I'd like to be along. Anyway, I've been out here for two years. Nha Trang would be a nice change, when you're out of the field."

He didn't bother to mention that it was only a short distance from the hospital at Cam Ranh Bay, as well.

"Well," Ed said, "we could sure use you. Check with Sergeant Sharp, my senior medic. He..."

"Incoming!" Shumate yelled, and the men scurried for cover. From somewhere outside the camp, the North Vietnamese had launched a salvo of Katusha rockets in a final, angry response to their defeat at the hands of the camp's defenders and the Mike Force troops who had pushed them off Duc Lap's north hill.

The first rocket slammed into a perimeter bunker where several of the camp strike force soldiers had taken cover. The big 122 millimeter warhead left a smoking crater where the sandbagged bunker had been, its occupants scattered among the debris.

Chamberlain peered out of the door of the bunker to which he had led the Mike Force men. He saw several bodies and parts of bodies around the crater. One of the Montagnard soldiers, a leg missing from below the knee, was attempting to crawl away from the devastation. "Oh, Christ!" Chamberlain cried, and rushed out of the bunker to the soldier's aid.

The second rocket struck twenty meters away from the crater the first had made, just as Chamberlain reached the wounded man. As the Mike Force men watched in horror, they saw the medic blown tumbling across the red clay of the camp by the powerful concussion of the detonating warhead.

Shumate broke from the bunker door at a run, just as two more rockets slammed harmlessly into the ground outside the camp. He fell to his knees beside Chamberlain, and Hagen and Walker rushed out to assist him in attending to the injured Special Forces medic. "Get a medevac bird in here," Shumate said to Hagen. "Urgent."

Chamberlain didn't look badly hurt at Ed's first glance, but as Shumate rolled him over, he saw why the Mike Force operations sergeant had ordered an urgent medical evacuation. The handsome medic's skull had been sheared open by a fragment from the enemy rocket. A large chunk of scalp and skull were missing from the back of his head, and brain tissue was oozing from it.

"Ah, no," Ed Walker mumbled to himself, then said to Shumate, "I'll get Sharp," and ran off toward the north hill in search of the Mike Force senior medic.

Overhead, he saw the helicopter gunships swooping in toward the site from which the Katushas had been launched, spitting streams of rockets and machine gun fire.

"Get 'em!" Ed yelled as he watched the rockets slam to earth. "Blow them all to God damned hell!"

He found Sharp, who ran with him to the injured medic. Ed watched as Sharp's skillful hands worked to keep Chamberlain's promising young life from escaping his wounded body, but he knew it was no use.

Another one gone, Ed Walker thought, and his eyes moved from Chamberlain to the others. *Another one used up.* How many of them could you use up, before the rest would quit? Or did you reach a point at which it became *your* turn to be used up?

       *   *   *

Lieutenant Susan Madison moved among the beds, checking the tubes of life-sustaining liquid that dripped into the injured men, speaking softly to those who were able to reply, doing what she could to comfort their pain and their fears. She smiled at men whose condition made her want to weep, and touched their foreheads, not because she was checking their temperatures, but because she knew that a soft touch from a caring human being was good medicine for their wounded souls.

It was different now, somehow. She had seen most of them when they first arrived, still in bloody field dressings and filthy uniforms, just in from the fields of battle. They were no longer, as they had seemed before, only temporary occupants; transient casualties en route from one distant place to another. They were *her* boys, her men, comrades-in-arms from a war that was her own as well as theirs, now. And comrades-in-arms of Staff Sergeant Dick Chamberlain, her lover, and of Colonel Harry Madison, her father.

She was a combat nurse now, and proud to be serving with such men. And she wanted those two, above all others, to be proud of what she was doing.

At lunch time, when Sue had an hour-long break, she wrote a short note to Dick Chamberlain. It was just a few brief lines to let him know that she was thinking of him and to let him know how very much she looked forward to seeing him again. She put it in an envelope addressed to him at Camp Duc Lap, 5th Special Forces Group, and when she saw a Special Forces chaplain on the ward that afternoon, she asked him if he could see that it was forwarded.

The chaplain looked at the note's destination, and his face became troubled. He knew that there was a desperate battle underway at Duc Lap. But there was no need to let this pretty nurse know that, he decided, for it would only make her worry. "Of course," he said. "I'll see that it gets out there as soon as possible."

He smiled, but in his mind he gave a silent prayer for Staff Sergeant Chamberlain, and for all the other men at Camp Duc Lap.

When the Chaplain got back to Cam Ranh Bay hospital the following day, before he visited the wounded Special Forces men, he sought out Sue Madison. He found her in the mess hall, drinking coffee, and sat down beside her.

"Oh, hello, chaplain," she said. "Did you get that letter off to Duc Lap for me?"

The clergyman set the letter on the table beside her, then laid a hand on her arm.

Sue looked at him curiously, then at the letter, and suddenly she understood.

"I'm sorry, lieutenant," the clergyman said. "He died in the field hospital in Pleiku last night."

The color drained from Sue's face, and the energy from her body. She picked the letter up, stared at it for a moment, then tore it in half. I won't cry, she thought. Not here, in front of everyone.

She looked over at the chaplain, her lower lip quivering as she spoke. "Thank you for letting me know, sir."

She stood and walked out of the mess hall, then ran stumbling to her room. Only when she had reached her bed - their bed - did she let her emotions go.

The chaplain heard the wail all the way from the mess hall. He looked toward heaven for a moment, then picked up the torn letter and headed for the ward. There were living men there to succor; wounded, but alive.

*   *   *

"Try to get back here for a visit before you report in to the First Cav," Sam said. "Maybe we can go fishing."

"Yeah," Ed said. "That would be nice." He immediately regretted having said it, because he had no intention of coming back to visit Nha Trang when he returned to Vietnam in thirty days. He would go straight to the 1st Cavalry Division headquarters in An Khe, as his orders stated. "Or maybe I'll wait until my tour's almost up. Anyway, I'll keep in touch, for sure," he said. He looked around the Mike Force compound one last time. It was hard to believe he had been there for the better part of a year. Well, actually he had only been here, in the compound, for a few weeks of that time. Most of the time, he had been in the field; the A Shau valley, Camp Duc Lap, Camps Katum, Thien Ngon, Thuong Duc, Ben Het, Dak Pek, and a half dozen other Special Forces border camps that had been threatened by the resurgent Viet Cong and North Vietnamese Army forces.

It was difficult to believe, too, that only nine months earlier, they had all but written the enemy off. He still couldn't comprehend how, after the terrible beating the communists had taken during their surprise Tet offensive, they kept coming back. Again and again, they had massed around one of the little border camps, sometimes overrunning the sparsely defended outposts. And each time, one of the Mobile Strike Forces - either one of those organic to the four corps areas into which South Vietnam was divided, or the country-wide reaction force of which he was a member, the Nha Trang Mike Force -

each time, they had rushed to the scene of the battle. And each time, usually assisted by the overwhelming firepower of American aircraft, they had beaten the enemy soundly and sent him reeling back across the border to his sanctuaries. Well, almost every time, anyway.

Camp Lang Vei, seized months earlier by a force that, for the first time, had been supported by NVA armor, was still in enemy hands. But other than that, the enemy had always been rooted out and driven off. Every time.

"We never did get back into the A Shau, Sam," Ed said, recalling with a shiver the reconnaissance patrol on which he had been briefly captured.

"Nope. We never did, did we?"

The Tet offensive had caused the cancellation of the operation to rebuild a Special Forces Camp in the enemy-infested valley, and it had not been mentioned since.

Ed checked his watch. The C-130 that would take him down to Bien Hoa airbase was scheduled to depart in half an hour, and he knew he should get on over to base operations and check in. But he didn't really want to leave the Mike Force; or more correctly, his Mike Force comrades-in-arms, and especially his best friend, Sam Hagen.

Sam and his other Special Forces teammates had become closer to Ed than his brother was, although he felt a new kinship to James now, too, because of the distinction they shared as veteran combat infantrymen.

Ed glanced over at the little memorial the team's Americans had built to their fallen comrades. There were so many little brass plaques on it now, each one inscribed with the name of one who had given his life in the line of duty with the team. So many. And so many battles after which his own name, or Sam's, might well have ended up among them. He looked at the face of his friend and fellow soldier.

Hagen seemed so much older than he had during their days at Fort Bragg, his eyes so deep and distant. God, they had seen so much since then.

"I'd better go, Sam."

"Yeah, I know."

"You keep your head down, all right?"

"Sure. You have fun with that kid of yours. I'll see you when you get back," Sam said, then held out his hand.

Ed ignored the hand and hugged his burly friend. "I love you, you son of a bitch," he said.

"I love you too, bro. Now, get your ass going."

Ed Walker hopped into the jeep with the Montagnard driver and said, "OK, Fireball. Airfield base ops," and with a last quick glance and a wave to Sam Hagen, he started home on extension leave. Home to the son he had never seen, and the wife he had come to feel he hardly knew.

FIFTEEN

There was something about the young men Ed Walker saw arriving at Bien Hoa airbase for duty in Vietnam that disturbed him, but he couldn't tell what it was, at first. Then he noticed that the hair was a little longer than he was used to, the uniforms a bit more unkempt. But it wasn't just that. What was it, then? He watched them a while longer, and thought, Surliness. That's what it is. They're surly. Sullen. And no wonder. From what he had been reading in the news magazines that arrived a week or so after they were shipped from the States, the mood of the whole country with respect to Vietnam was one of disenchantment and surliness.

The Democratic National Convention in Chicago had been the scene of rebellious protests of unbelievable proportions, if what he had seen in the magazines was true. And the establishment's reaction to it - that's what they called the elements of government at every level, these days, "the establishment" - had been as uncontrolled as the dissidents' rioting had been.

Support for the war had been eroding since the Tet offensive and, in fact, the end result of the military victory that the allies had achieved had somehow been turned into a defeat in the minds of the American people. It just didn't make sense to him. Of course, neither did the decision to prohibit ground troops from pursuing the badly-mauled communist forces into their sanctuaries in Laos and Cambodia, to finish them off. If they had been allowed to, Ed Walker honestly believed, it might well all be over now. As far as he was concerned, they should have moved into North Vietnam after the communists, too. And if the Chinese and Russians didn't like it, so what? The whole Communist Empire would have to be dealt with sooner or later, so it might as well be sooner, while America was geared up for war. There was concern in some quarters that the Soviet Union or Red China might respond to such action with nuclear weapons, but Ed didn't believe it. They wouldn't dare, he felt.

His seat on the airplane was beside a boyish-looking Transportation Corps captain from the 25th Infantry Division. Fort Eustis, Virginia, the home of the Army Transportation Corps, was only a few miles from Ed Walker's home, so he said, "You headed back to Fort Eustis by any chance, sir?"

"Hell, no!" the captain growled. "I'm getting the fuck out of this fucking Army and going back to fucking Kansas."

Ed nodded and thought, Well, so much for a traveling companion back to Virginia. He was glad, though, that the man wasn't someone he wished to talk to. He wanted the time the long flight allowed him to try to think things through.

He hadn't told Mary yet that he had extended his tour in Vietnam for six months, and he had to try to figure out how to break the news to her.

It was a sensible move, since he had decided to make the Army a career - another fact of which Mary was not yet aware. He would soon be promoted to captain, for it was all but automatic after serving a year as a first lieutenant, now. And he had to have conventional unit command time to remain competitive. It made little sense that they considered his time in Special Forces to be detrimental to his career as an infantry officer, for even though Ed had led a battalion into combat time and again, the fact that he commanded only eleven other Americans made it, as one Infantry Branch representative put it, "the equivalent of squad leader time." It was ridiculous, but that's the way it was. Anyway, he was looking forward to leading a company of American troops into combat - especially a company in the world's first helicopter-borne division, the First Cav.

When the aircraft rose from the runway, most of the men cheered or clapped, and the captain beside him peered out of the window, mumbled, "Good fucking bye Viet fucking Nam. And good fucking riddance." Then he pulled the window screen down, curled up in his seat, and went to sleep.

Ed and most of the other men lit cigarettes, lowered their seat backs, and thought their own thoughts.

God, but he hoped Mary would understand. Her letters, that had begun arriving weekly about six months earlier, had been so void of references to the future. And so void of love; of passion. Yes, she ended each with "all my love," but there was no other reference to their relationship, no response to his occasional mention of some passionate memory or plan for a romantic reunion when he got home. Mostly, her one or two page letters just passed on news about their six-month-old son, Jimmy, or James and Evelyn's latest real estate acquisition or sale, or news of her own family. She had completed only one semester at William and Mary before she moved back to Broad Marsh prior to Jimmy's birth. About the only other news she had passed on was that Sam's fiancee, Maria DeCalesta, had come to visit her twice. But she didn't really seem to get along well with Maria, for some reason. That was a shame, because he hoped that the two couples could be the best of friends. Hell, Sam Hagen had even asked him to be the best man at their wedding in four months time, when Sam's extended tour in Vietnam was up. But with Ed's own decision to extend, it wouldn't be possible, now.

Old Sam. He sure hoped the guy would take care of himself. Four months in the Mike Force meant a lot more battles, the way things were going. And now that Sam was in command of 7th Company, he'd no doubt be with the most heavily-engaged platoon, the way he led from up front.

One of the stewardesses was reaching up into an overhead compartment for pillows, and Ed's eyes were drawn to the way her large breasts pressed against the fabric of her blouse, then his eyes traveled down to the long, stocking clad legs stretching beneath the hem of her short skirt. God, it was good to see a sexy, round-eyed woman again. He closed his eyes and thought of Mary, picturing her undressing for him, then coming to him, to their bed.

It had been a whole year since he had touched her, held her. The photos she had sent since the baby was born proved that she was as voluptuous now as she had been before her pregnancy. It would be heaven to make love to her again.

One whole year. They were supposed to have met in Hawaii after Jimmy was born, but Ed had canceled his R & R two days before they were to leave. Camp Thuong Duc had been under attack again, and his battalion had to go relieve the camp.

He lit another cigarette, not because he wanted one, but because it was less unpleasant than breathing the stale smoke the other young men throughout the airplane were creating. He took a drag, coughed, and crushed it out. What a stupid habit. He was going to quit when he got home, he decided as he slipped the pillow behind his head and shut his eyes to try to get some sleep.

*   *   *

Mary Walker gave her baby boy Jimmy another bottle of formula to try to quiet him, but the child would not take it. She had to get out of bed and walk around the room with him on her shoulder.

Maybe Maria was right, she thought. Maybe breast feeding would have been better, would have made him a happier child. Sure, it tied you down, kept you from being away from the child to do your own thing. But maybe that was the way nature intended it. Still, what did Maria know? She didn't have a child.

Well, it's too late to have regrets about that now, she thought. The Westminster chimes of the grandfather clock downstairs in the big plantation house rang. Four o'clock.

"Your father's coming home in twelve hours, little Jimmy," she said softly. "Don't you want to let mommy get some sleep?"

She had decided not to take him with her to Richmond to meet Ed's flight, but to leave him at Broad Marsh with her mother. She had made reservations at the Williamsburg Inn for the night - a night of uninterrupted lovemaking.

A twinge of fear grabbed her in the pit of the stomach. Suppose he knew, somehow, about her affair with Sandy Milton? What would happen if - no, *when*, in all likelihood - he found out from his Guineamen friends? Would he believe them, or her?

He'll believe me, she thought. After all, they had no proof. All they knew was that we were on the *Mary Anne* together, anchored in the Mobjack Bay overnight. They didn't know we were having sex.

She had long ago decided to lie, if she was confronted with it. She would admit to being on the boat with Sandy, but she would never admit to the affair, no matter what. Anyway, if she had her way, they would move to Florida or California, or maybe even Hawaii soon, before he got involved with that Guinea bunch again. Unless, of course, he still had that stupid idea about staying in the Army. He hadn't mentioned it in months, though. And he was bound to see, by now, what a despicable career the military was. The whole country knew it, especially after seeing the things they were doing in Vietnam. There was no way he could still want to be a part of that. He was too good.

She took the sleeping child from her shoulder and placed him gently into his crib, then climbed into bed. Sleep wouldn't come to her, so she lay thinking of Ed, imagining the passionate reunion they would share. She would show him sensual things they had never done before, things she had learned from Sandy. Or maybe not. Maybe that would make him suspicious. Still, she could claim she had read it in one of those books about sex that were so popular these days. Yes, that's what she'd do. Claim she had read about it. Anyway, who was to say he hadn't learned the same kinds of things from some Vietnamese bar girl? Everybody knew most of the soldiers in Vietnam went to whorehouses all the time. The Army even set them up outside of the camps; she had read about it in a newspaper article. And so what if he did? she thought, wanting to believe it was true to assuage the tinge of guilt she felt about her affair with Sandy Milton. As long as he doesn't bring home some awful disease.

Late that morning, Mary took a long, soaking bath before she left for Richmond to pick Ed up at the airport.

She looked at herself in the full-length mirror before she dressed, and was pleased with what she saw. He will be, too, she thought.

The only makeup she used was a bit of mascara and liner on her eyes, and a thin coating of glossy red lipstick. Then she pulled a flowered silk dress over head, added the faint scent of lavender he liked so much, and left for the airport.

When Ed saw her standing at the door of the terminal as he quickly descended the stairs of the airplane, all the doubts were washed away, for there she was, young and beautiful - more beautiful than she had been when he left a year earlier. Suddenly, that seemed like only yesterday.

She rushed into his arms, and they held a long, tight embrace, then kissed. She pressed herself against him and was surprised at how tall, how strong and powerful he seemed. She had forgotten.

"God, Mary," he said. "I'd forgotten how beautiful you are."

She smiled and kissed him again, then pushed him out to arm's length. He looked good in the khaki uniform, lean and tan and rugged. Older, yes; much older than he looked a year ago. It must be that the long trip from Vietnam had tired him out and made him appear so, she decided.

"Where's our son?" he asked, looking all around.

"At the farm with his grandmother," she said. "I'm sorry, darling. I just wanted you all to myself for the night. I've reserved us a room at the Williamsburg Inn."

His look of concern changed quickly to a lustful smile, and he said, "No way. That's too far. Let's get a room in the nearest motel. Where's the car?"

"What about your baggage?"

"I can come back and pick it up later," he said, then pulled her to him and kissed her passionately again.

"All right, then," she said breathlessly. "Let's go."

Soon after, they came together, their senses as closely meshed as their flesh, whispering to each other the utter joy they felt. They stayed that way for a time, fused together as they kissed, sharing endearments they had not shared for so very, very long.

*   *   *

"Mama said you're very brave, Unka Edward."

Ed smiled and glanced at Evelyn, who was pouring two bottles of beer into glasses for him and his brother James.

"Not as brave as your daddy is, Sookie," Ed said to his niece, who was balanced on his knees.

"Don't you listen to him, Sookie," James said. "Your Uncle Edward's the bravest man in the county. And he has the medals to prove it." He chucked his younger brother on the shoulder and said, "DSC, Silver Star... I'll land in hell if you ain't somethin', Bubba."

The two men's eyes held contact for several moments as images of war flashed through their minds; James's of hordes of Chinese infantry attacking in the bitter cold, Ed's of chaotic ambushes on jungle trails and bloody assaults at isolated border camps.

It was a look of comradeship and love that neither man would have exchanged for all the medals there were. There was a kinship between the two combat infantrymen now that was even stronger than their nearly-identical genes.

"You sure you don't want to hang up your boots and go into business with us, Bubbie?" James asked. He and Evelyn were making a fortune in the real estate market, now that Gloucester County was becoming a bedroom community for the military installations and growing industrial complex of the Virginia Peninsula. Ed and Mary had invested some money with them, and it was already paying considerable dividends. But it was not what Ed Walker wanted to do with his life.

"I'm sure, James. Not until we finish in Vietnam, at least. Anyway, from the looks of the property deeds Evelyn showed me, you've already made me rich. Why would I want to take a *real* job?"

"You don't have to get a real job, Unka Edward," Sookie said. "You can be a fisherman like me."

The three adults laughed, and Ed said, "Well, from the way you and your daddy caught all the fish this morning, I'd better keep my job in the Army, little darlin'."

"What does Mary think about your decision to stay in, Edward?" Evelyn asked.

His brow furrowed, recalling Mary's words when he had told her of his extension the evening before: "Jesus, Ed, no!" she had shot back. "You can't *do* this to Jimmy and me."

He replied, "I'm not doing it *to* you and Jimmy. I'm doing it *for* you and Jimmy," and she shouted, "Don't give me that bullshit! If you go back, it's because you're selfish, and because you don't give a damn for us! Christ, Ed! Haven't you done enough to prove your manhood, or whatever it is you're trying to do? Even my right wing father has finally figured out that it's a shitty, useless war!"

She had stormed out of the room with the baby then, and that night they slept on opposite sides of the bed at first. But then she rolled over to him, and their anger dissolved into passion. When it was over, she said, "Please don't go back, Ed."

"I have to," he had said softly to her. "I just have to, Mary."

Now he looked at Evelyn and said, "She wasn't real happy. But she'll get over it."

Evelyn made no reply, but the look in her eyes seemed to ask, Are you sure?

James and Evelyn exchanged a glance, and Ed's brother said, "Well, you'd better be careful, boy."

"Nothin' to worry about, James. They can't get me."

"I ain't talkin' about them. I'm talkin' about her."

Ed set his niece on the floor. "What the hell's that supposed to mean, James?"

James eyed him evenly. "She's young, and she's mighty pretty. You stay away too long, she's liable to end up with another mate for that fancy sailboat her daddy bought you."

Ed's eyes narrowed. "So *that's* it." He shot a glance at Evelyn and understood the look he had seen in her eyes moments before. "For your information," he said as he stood, "she told me about being out on the boat, and the rumor running around Guinea that she was having an affair with the old professor she took with her."

His brother and sister-in-law made no reply, so he just shook his head and turned for the door. Then he paused and looked back at them. "I can believe those shiftless jerks would spread rumors like that. But I can't believe you two would. You know the boat's got to be used or she'll go rotten. What the hell do you expect Mary to do, take her out by herself?"

"Aw, come back here and sit down, Bubba," James said. "Nobody's accusing her of anything. I'm just saying you ought to think about her before you go running back off to Vietnam."

Evelyn walked to him and gave him a hug and said, "Your brother - all of us, for that matter - are just worried about you going back, Edward. That's all. Lord, we see on TV every night what it's like over there. We just don't want you to end up like any of those wounded boys."

Sookie came and hugged her uncle's legs, and then she stood back from him, put her hands on her hips and said, "Unka Edward, don't you go runnin' back to that old Bietnam any more, you hear?"

He smiled, lifted her up, and kissed her cheek. "Sookie," he said, "if you'd been there when I was about to sign those extension papers, I'd probably have told them to, well, to keep their old papers. But I'll be back from that old Bietnam before you know it, OK? And then you and I can take little Jimmy out fishing."

The little girl wagged a finger in his face and said, "Well, OK!" Then she hugged his neck and gave him a kiss, and he set her down.

He looked at the clock on the wall. "I'd better get back up to Broad Marsh," he said. "See you tonight?"

Evelyn kissed his cheek. "We'll be there about six-thirty. Kiss that little boy, OK?"

His mood darkened as he drove away. The rumor about his wife and the man she'd taken sailing still gnawed at him. It wasn't that he believed there was any truth to it, but that wasn't the point. It was the fact that the Guineamen, men who were supposed to be his friends, many of whom were even his cousins, would exaggerate things to the point that people acted as if Mary had been screwing the guy.

Well, there was one way to put a stop to it. He'd just drive down there to the dock on Perrin Creek and wait for one of them to say something, then knock hell out of him, and anybody else who wanted to say anything. He pulled over to the side of the road to turn around. Then he thought, Look at you, Walker. You're acting like you're a damn waterman again, not an Army officer. There'll be plenty of fighting for you to do in a few weeks, when you get back over with the First Cav.

He pulled out onto the road and headed for Broad Marsh again.

Mary was sitting in a rocking chair on the porch of the old plantation house when he circled around the big boxwoods and stopped at the steps. God, she's beautiful, he thought. He hopped out of the car and said, "Hi, gorgeous."

"Where's all the fish?" she asked as she got up from the chair.

He bounced up the steps and hugged her. "Well, let's just say they preferred to be caught by James and Sookie. Where's that boy of ours?"

"Sleeping, finally," she said.

"Yeah? Everybody else gone?" he asked as he reached a hand around to her buttocks and squeezed.

She nodded and smiled, so he swept her into his arms and said, "Well, then. What are we doing out here instead of up in that big old bed?"

"You'd better call Fort Bragg first," she said. "Some sergeant called you. The number's on the pad by the phone."

He wondered who it was, then thought, Probably one of the guys who just got back, had a few beers at the Parachute Club, and got telephonitis, no doubt. He pushed the door open with his foot and started up the stairs with his wife in his arms. "Fort Bragg can damn well wait," he said.

It was well over an hour later that Ed Walker went downstairs to return the telephone call from Fort Bragg. Ten minutes later, he had not come back upstairs, so Mary pulled on a robe and went to see what he was doing.

She found him sitting on the floor beside the telephone table, his arms wrapped around his knees and his chin resting on them, his eyes staring blankly at the floor.

"Ed? What is it, darling? Is something wrong?"

He turned his head and looked at her with an empty, distant look.

"It's Sam. He was killed yesterday at Dak Seang."

"Oh, Ed. Oh, no. Not Sam," Mary said sadly. She knelt beside her husband and wrapped her arms around his shoulders, her cheek against his.

Ed Walker buried his face in her shoulder. He was trembling, and Mary held him tightly to her and wept softly with him.

Upstairs, their baby son began to cry, but she ignored him for awhile. When Ed finally heard him, he raised his head and wiped his nose and cheeks with his wrist.

"You'd better go get Jimmy," he said.

"Come with me."

"No. I've got to make a couple of phone calls."

"Maria?" she asked.

"No. She doesn't know yet, apparently. Or maybe she found out somehow. Anyway, they haven't been able to find her."

Jimmy was wailing now, so Mary stood and said, "I'll be right back," and went upstairs to tend to their child.

By the time she changed Jimmy's soiled diaper and came downstairs with him, Ed was on the telephone again, his voice businesslike, void of emotion.

"All right," he said, checking the time on his wristwatch. "I should be able to get down there by around twenty-one hundred tonight. I'll go straight to JFK Center and meet you there."

He hung up the telephone and turned to Mary. "We've got to get down to Bragg right away," he said.

She gave him a curious look. "Fort Bragg? Why?"

He gave her a look of surprise. "Because Sam is dead. Because I've got to go make sure the arrangements are made for his funeral. Because Maria needs us, Mary. Why do you *think*, why?"

"Ed, I can't just pick up the baby and run off to Fort Bragg on the spur of the moment. Anyway, Jimmy has an appointment with the pediatrician tomorrow. Can't it wait until after that?"

"Wait? Jesus, Mary. He's my best friend. He was our best man, for Christ's sake. No, it can't wait!"

"Ed, he's dead. You can't undo that by running off to Fort Bragg. Can't you let somebody else make the arrangements? Surely they must have people..."

"Mary, we're talking about Sam, not some guy I hardly knew. Come *on*, now!"

Jimmy began to cry at the sound of his father's angry voice, and Mary said, "You don't have to yell, Ed. I'm not one of your soldiers."

He lowered his voice. "Well, what about Maria? Don't you think she could use a friend right now?"

"We're not very good friends, Ed. To tell you the truth, I don't think she even likes me."

He shook his head in disbelief. "Well, I'm going, Mary. If you don't think you need to, fine. But, by God, *I'm* going, and I'm going right now."

"You'd do that, wouldn't you? You'd take the precious little time you have with your son and me before you go back to that damned place, and run off to do something for a guy you can no longer help, and his girlfriend - not even his wife, Ed, his girlfriend - and, and...."

He was nodding his head and looking at her with what she thought was a sneer. "Yeah. I would. I am. If you don't want to come tonight, I'll let you know when the funeral is, and you can drive down then. But yes, I'm going. Tonight."

"Oh, Ed. Be realistic. How am I supposed to drive all the way to Fort Bragg with Jimmy?" The boy was crying again.

"I don't know. Maybe you can get a ride with that professor friend of yours you took sailing."

Her face took on a look of hurt, then loathing, and she turned her back to him. "I think you should go. Go ahead. Go now, God damn you."

He despised himself for having made the remark about the professor. He was angry, that's all; angry about the death of his best friend. Angry that he wasn't there to keep it from happening. "Aw, Mary. I'm sorry," he said, and reached a hand out to her shoulder.

She recoiled from his touch, then turned to face him, holding their bawling child tightly to her breast. He had never seen such hostility in her amber-flecked eyes.

"Just go!" she spat, then turned and walked to the back door of the house, slung it open, and hurried down the boxwood-lined brick walk toward the spacious fields below.

He packed his uniform and a few civilian clothes in a suitcase, then went to look for her. He called her name, searching the fields and woods and outbuildings of Broad Marsh plantation for more than half an hour, stopping now and then to listen for her, and for his son's cry. Then he went back to the house, searched there again. But he could not find them.

Sadness and impatience filled him, and then anger. Finally he gave up looking for them and wrote a note that said, "I have to go, Mary. I'll call you tonight. I love you."

He walked out to the back porch again, stood on the steps, and called her name as loud as he could, searching the fields for a time. Then he threw his suitcase into the car and started down the tree-lined lane toward the highway.

Mary watched him pass from a spot in the woods beside the lane. "Don't do it, Ed. Don't leave us," she whispered as she watched the car through burning eyes. But the car moved on, gathering speed, and she said to her little son, "There he goes without us, off to spend his time with a dead man."

He was a quarter of a mile past her, almost to the highway, when she yelled after him, "What about us? What about the living? You bastard, what about *us*!"

SIXTEEN

Ed parked his car outside the John F. Kennedy Special Warfare Center and walked inside. He found Master Sergeant Bill Edge, whom he had known in Nha Trang, at the duty desk, studying a sheaf of messages from the 5th Special Forces Group in Vietnam. Edge peered up over his glasses and, seeing Ed Walker, stood and held out his hand.

"Hello, Lieutenant Walker. Or is it Captain by now?"

Ed shook the sergeant's hand and said, "Still lieutenant for a few more days. What happened to Sam, Bill?"

Edge handed him several sheets of paper he had laid aside for Ed to read after their telephone conversation hours earlier. One was a casualty report; the other, a situation report on the battle at Dak Seang. Ed scanned the battle report first.

The Dak Seang Special Forces camp had been besieged by two North Vietnamese battalions. Three Mike Force battalions - two from Pleiku and Ed's old battalion from Nha Trang - had been called in to relieve the pressure. Assisted by tactical airstrikes, they had made short work of the NVA, except for one company entrenched on a hill overlooking the camp. The Nha Trang battalion assaulted to push them off. Receiving heavy mortar and machine gun fire, they had been forced to withdraw while the hill was again hit by tactical air strikes. Then the Mike Force battalion assaulted again. This time, 7th Company - Sam Hagen's Chams - gained the top. After a furious NVA counterattack was repulsed, the enemy withdrew to the west, with one of the II Corps battalions from Pleiku in pursuit.

Ed studied the casualty chart at the bottom of the report. Five of Dak Seang's Camp Strike Force troops killed in action, one US Army Special Forces and eight CSF wounded. The Pleiku Mike Force lost six Mobile Strike Force troops killed in action, and twenty wounded, including two of their American leaders. Ed's battalion had nine MSF soldiers and one USASF - Staff Sergeant Sam Hagen - killed in action, and eighteen MSF wounded.

Ed traded a look of sadness with Bill Edge, then turned to the casualty report.

Hagen, Sam L., Staff Sergeant...Detachment A-503 (Mike Force)...During an enemy counterattack on hill 688, vicinity of Dak Seang...gunshot wounds to both legs...multiple fragmentation wounds to the head and chest...remains recovered to Pleiku graves registration for processing...

A few paragraphs of stilted phrases. A handful of words that sounded like a report on some barbarous sporting event, the dead and wounded mere statistics in the box score at the end. No words of sorrow, no prayer of mourning, just empty words. Where were the descriptions of the suffering, the heroism, the fear? Where was the crying out at the loss of life, the waste of one of the best young men in America? Where were the lofty words telling *why*, for Christ's sake?

Ed Walker could picture it all in his mind - the frightening uphill struggle toward the enemy, the deafening explosions of mortar rounds and five-hundred pound bombs, the crackling of rifle and machine gun fire and detonating grenades. The cries and curses of the wounded, and the moans of the dying.

"The mournful mutter of the battlefield," General MacArthur had called it in his famous farewell speech. What bullshit, Ed Walker thought. It was only a "mutter" from a distance; from a headquarters bunker or a command-and-control helicopter. Up close, where the man-to-man fighting went on, it was a chaotic, frightening, deadly cacophony. It was exactly as Sherman had described it, not as MacArthur had. It was pure and simple hell. And now it had claimed Sam Hagen, the best one of them all.

Ed handed the papers back to Master Sergeant Edge.

"He was the best, Bill."

Edge put his hand on Walker's forearm. "He was a warrior, sir. A good Special Forces soldier."

Edge's eyes moved to the big marble plaque on the wall behind them at the entrance to the Special Warfare Center. Both men silently read the words of President Kennedy inscribed there.

The Green Beret... a symbol of excellence, a badge of courage, a mark of distinction in the fight for freedom.

"Freedom," Ed muttered. "Freedom for what? For a bunch of hippie shitheads to degrade their soldiers, and this country, and everything it stands for?"

Bill Edge was never one to allow his fellow soldiers, commissioned or enlisted, to stray from the American warrior ethic, so he looked the lieutenant in the eye and said forcefully, "That's right, sir. And your job, and mine, is to make damned sure they keep that freedom, just as it is to make sure the good ones - the Jeffersons and Frosts and Edisons and Kings, and that great majority out there who get up and go to work every day - that they have those same rights, those same freedoms. Because if we ever lose that, Lieutenant, then Sam Hagen and all the thousands of others like him will have died for nothing. For nothing at all. Don't you forget that, sir. Don't lose it. Because that's all that makes it worth it."

Ed looked at him, wondering whether the stocky veteran of two thankless wars really meant it. Yes, it was there, in his fiery idealist's eyes. He meant it. He believed it with all his being. "I hope you're right," Ed said.

"I am, sir. By *God*, I am."

Ed telephoned Broad Marsh again. He had tried earlier, when he stopped in Petersburg for gas, but there was no answer then.

This time, Mary's mother answered the phone.

"Miss Carrie, it's Ed. Let me speak to Mary, please."

"Oh, Ed. She's not here. She's gone to Williamsburg to spend the night with friends."

"She has? I see. Well, let me have their number, and I'll call her there."

"I don't have it," Mrs. McClanahan said. "She just left a note saying she was going. Ed, did you two have a fight or something?"

"Oh, no, ma'am. Not exactly. I just had to rush off down here to Fort Bragg. Sam Hagen has been killed."

His mother-in-law remembered the best man in her daughter's wedding and said, "Oh, no, Ed. Poor Sam. How is Maria handling it?"

"I haven't seen her yet. Look, Miss Carrie, let me give you the number of the duty NCO here. When Mary calls or gets back, have her call, please. I'll leave the number where I can be reached."

"All right, Ed."

He passed her the number, and she said, "I'll tell her to call this number as soon as I hear from her. When can we expect you back here?"

"I don't know, yet. A few days, I guess. Did Mary say anything about coming down here for the funeral?"

"No, just the note saying she was going to Williamsburg to stay with friends for, let's see, 'for a day or so,' it says."

"'A day or so.' I see. All right, Miss Carrie. If she comes back, please ask her to call this number right away, no matter what time it is."

He pressed the hangup button, then dialed Maria DeCalesta's number. It rang unanswered ten times, so he hung up. Where on earth could she be? He decided to go to her apartment and ask her neighbors if any of them might know.

He apologized for disturbing the other occupants of the stairwell in the apartment building where Maria lived, and asked each if they had any idea where she might have gone.

None did, but one woman said, "I hope she's all right. My son goes to the kindergarten where she works, and he told me she wasn't there today."

"I see," Ed said. "Well, if you happen to see her before I do, would you please tell her that Ed Walker came by? Her fiance is a good friend of mine from Vietnam."

He got a hamburger, then drove back to the bachelor officers' quarters near the JFK Center where he had booked a room for the night.

It was almost eleven by then, so he decided not to call Broad Marsh to see if Mary had returned. Instead, he telephoned the Center duty desk. There were no messages for him.

He flopped back on the bed. On the wall was a framed print of Third Infantry Division troops fighting in Korea. The Gauntlet, they had called it. He stared at it, thinking of his brother and Bill Edge and all the others of that forgotten war. Then he thought of Sam, and of himself, and of their war. Would all they had done, all they had sacrificed, be forgotten so soon, as well? Did it take a Hitler, a Holocaust, a Pearl Harbor, for Americans to understand that war was sometimes necessary? Or was a clear victory, an unconditional surrender by the enemy, the only thing they would understand?

They would never get that in Vietnam. He knew that now. But the line could be held. The system of slavery the communists had made of the socialist ideal could be kept from spreading, as it had been checked in Korea. The Republic of South Vietnam could be maintained, improved, turned into a true republic, if only the United States would stay the course - stay the course and change the rules to let the Army pursue the enemy into their sanctuaries, their territory.

Look at West Germany, he thought. And South Korea, compared to the despotic regime in the north. And Taiwan.

Yes, they would do it. They would at least hold the line. *De Oppresso Liber*, the Special Forces motto read; "Liberate the Oppressed." Liberty. Freedom. What was it Bill Edge had said? Because if we lose that ideal, then Sam and all the others will have died for nothing. Because that was all that made it worth it.

He sat up on the side of the bed, bone tired but not the least bit sleepy. There was a pen and some notepaper on the desk. He got up, sat at the desk, and began to write.

My dear son,

Perhaps someday you'll read this. I may be there, or I may not. I may have fallen in battle, and if I have, and you want to know why, I'll tell you now. It was in the cause of freedom.

Freedom is all that matters. It is the one thing from which all else worthwhile springs. Without the freedom to think, to learn, to choose, there is nothing; no truth, no growth, no hope, no joy. Freedom is the only thing worth living for, creating for. And it is the only thing - the only thing - worth dying for.

Freedom. Take it. Use it. Sow it everywhere. And if someone tries to take it away, whether from you or from someone else, fight him. Fight him first, if you must, with words, with warnings, with the lessons of history. But if he persists in his oppression, attack him. Attack him with all the might and rage and courage you can muster. Because even if he kills you, you will have won. You will have won because you died a free man. And freedom is all that matters.

He stared at it awhile, wondering if he really meant it. He wasn't certain that he did. But he thought he did. Right now, he did. But would he always?

He folded the sheet of paper, shoved it in a corner of his suitcase, then removed his uniform to hang it in the closet. He looked at the rows of brightly colored ribbons for a moment. Then he took them off, dropped them into his suitcase, and repositioned his combat infantryman's badge where the ribbons had been. It said enough by itself.

     *   *   *

Ed Walker reached Maria DeCalesta by telephone at mid-morning the following day.

"Maria?" he said. "Hi. It's Ed."

"Oh, Ed. Have you called to tell me about Sammy?"

Then she had already found out. "You know, then," he said.

"Yes. He's dead, isn't he?"

What did she mean, *isn't he*? Maybe she had heard it through the Fort Bragg grapevine but wasn't certain.

"Er, yes. Did his sister let you know?"

"No. No, I just knew it. I felt it. It was the day before yesterday, wasn't it? On top of some hill."

He found himself unable to answer her for a moment. How could she have possibly known, if she hadn't been told? He had heard about premonitions, about people waking with a start, thinking that a loved one had been killed, only to learn that it had actually occurred. But those were only rare coincidences, weren't they?

"Uh, yes. Yes, Maria. It was the day before yesterday," he said. "Outside of the camp at Dak Seang. On a hill."

He heard her sigh, then she said, "I'm so sorry, Ed. I know he meant an awful lot to you. And he loved you too, you know."

"Yes. Are you all right, Maria?"

"I'm OK. Are you calling from Virginia?"

"No. No, I'm here, at Fort Bragg."

"Are Mary and Jimmy with you?" she asked.

"No. She'll probably come down when I find out, you know, the funeral arrangements and all of that."

"What *are* the arrangements, Ed?"

"I don't know yet. That'll be up to his mother and sister. Unless he made some special arrangements in his will, or something."

"No, he wouldn't have done that," she said, and sighed again. "But he wants to be buried with his father."

"Did he write you that?" Ed asked, and thought, So that's it. He had a premonition and wrote to her about it - one of those self-fulfilling prophesies that caused a man to get himself killed.

"No, he told me. Yesterday. At least, I think he did."

The poor girl is losing it, Ed Walker thought.

"I went out to the Uwharrie hills when I knew he had been killed," Maria continued. "I sat out there on this rock we used to go to for picnics now and then. I know it sounds crazy, but he was there - his spirit, or something was. I know it was. We - well, we communicated."

"I see," Ed replied, his voice empty of conviction.

He heard her chuckle and say, "I know you don't believe me, Ed. But that's all right. It's true, and I know it. Just like I know I'll see him again, someday. Be with him again."

Well, if she believed that, what harm was there in it? It was obviously a good defense mechanism that her mind had contrived. At least she was handling it well.

"How well do you know his mother and sister, Maria?"

"I don't know them at all. I wrote each of them a letter when Sammy and I decided to get married, but I never even got a reply from either of them. He wasn't particularly close to them, you know."

"Yes, I know. Well, I'll try to get hold of them and find out what's going to happen," Ed said. "What are you going to do? Are you going to work today?"

"No," she said. "I'm just going to take a hot bath and go to bed. But telephone me and let me know, as soon as you find out something, will you, Ed?"

"Of course. Say, how's your brother doing, Maria?"

"Rocco? I don't know. We've lost track of him, Ed, since just after Sharon left him. He was in California, last I heard. Drugs are easier to get out there, you know."

"He's still on the stuff, then?"

"I'm afraid so. Heroin, mostly. At least, that's what he was on before he disappeared."

"I'm sorry to hear that," Ed said, thinking back to his days in OCS with her brother, before he was dismissed. More and more young soldiers were coming back from Vietnam on drugs, it seemed. "And I'm sorry I wasn't there with Sam, Maria," he said. "Maybe things would have been different. Maybe I could have, I don't know, done something."

"No. It was his time, Ed. There's nothing you could have done. I'm glad you weren't there. I want you to remember him like I do. Alive."

"Yes. Well, you take that bath now, and get some rest. I'll let you know as soon as I find out something."

"OK. Thank you so much for coming down here, Ed."

He hung up the telephone, considering the strange conversation about Sam. Was it really possible that Maria had somehow sensed his death? The mind is a powerful thing. But that powerful? That bit about communicating with him on a rock out in Uwharrie was beyond reason, though.

Still, if man had a soul, did it just - what? - evaporate or something? Ed Walker shook his head. Who could say about things like that? Theologians and philosophers had been arguing them for thousands of years without reaching a consensus.

He telephoned Sam's mother next. She didn't recognize Ed's name, and wasn't even aware, until Ed told her, that Sam had been his best man, or that they had served together in the Mike Force.

When he asked Mrs. Hagen about the funeral arrangements, she said, "I suppose he'll be buried in the national cemetery here. The major, the one who's supposed to take care of all that, said that would be the best thing. Unless they find a will or something. Do you now if he had a will, Edgar?"

"Edward, ma'am. No, I don't know whether he did or not. He had an insurance form, I know, because we're all required to fill one out each time we transfer somewhere. But wills are optional."

"Well, perhaps you could talk to Major Johnston. He's the survival... whatever you call it. He's checking on it."

"Survivors' Assistance Officer," Ed said. "Yes, ma'am. If you have his telephone number, I'll give him a call."

He got the number from Sam's mother and called Major Johnston. After Ed explained that Staff Sergeant Hagen had been a subordinate of his in Vietnam, and was his best friend, the major said, "It sure would help if you made your troops have wills made, Lieutenant Walker. Anyway, it's too late in his case, isn't it? So it's up to the mother. I've recommended she just plant him in the nearest national cemetery, unless you know something I don't."

Ed felt his anger rising at the casual way the major was treating Sam's death and funeral arrangements, and he started to say something about it. Sam deserved better. And so did Maria. Then he recalled what she had said about the strange incident in the Uwharrie forest. "I know that he wanted to be buried beside his father in Wyoming," he told the major.

"Wyoming? Shee-it. That's just what I need. How do you know that?"

"He told his fiancee that's what he wanted."

"His fiancee? Is that this Maria Delacastro he has as his beneficiary?"

"DeCalesta. Yes, Maria DeCalesta."

"Well, I've been trying to get in touch with her out in North Carolina, but haven't had any luck. Do you know where she is? I need to let her know about the insurance."

"I just spoke to her."

"Yeah? Well, ask her to give me a call, will you? So I can give her the good news about her ten grand."

"I'll tell her myself," Ed said coldly. "What about his desire to be buried with his father in Wyoming?"

"Well, if he didn't put it in a will, that's tough geshitski, as the Russians say. It's up to his old lady, and whether or not she's willing to foot the bill. I guess if she is, I can get Sixth Army to push the burial detail duty on some poor son of a bitch out there."

Ed Walker shook his head in disgust at the major's attitude, then had an idea. "I'll tell you what, sir. I think I can arrange to get orders to handle it myself. Can I call you back and let you know?"

"Sure," Johnston replied, the tone of his voice making it evident he'd be glad for someone else to assume the responsibility. "But you still have to clear it with the family. Let me give you the funeral home number, too. If the old lady OKs it, you can deal directly with them about shipping the body out there."

He got the information, then called Bill Edge and told him about his conversation with the Survivors' Assistance Officer.

"Sounds like a real prick," Edge said. "But the key is, if the mother will consent to it. Somebody has to pay for it, don't forget."

"I'll pay for it myself," Ed said.

He called Mrs. Hagen again. She was hesitant to allow it, but when Ed explained that he'd make the arrangements and foot the bill, she said, "Well, if you're certain that's what he wanted...."

"Yes, ma'am. He told Maria, his fiancee."

Master Sergeant Edge went to the Special Warfare Center Sergeant Major after Ed informed him of the mother's consent. He arranged for the 20th Special Forces Group, a National Guard outfit with a battalion in Salt Lake City, to provide the honor guard and burial detail. "Better than having some route step outfit in LA give him a half-assed burial," Edge said when Ed thanked him for arranging it. "After all, he's one of our own, not some dope-smoking draft dodger."

When it was all arranged, Ed let Maria know.

"Oh, Sam. You're such a good friend," she said. "Like the brother he never had."

Now there was just one thing left for Ed to do; inform Mary. He called Broad Marsh to do so. Mary wasn't there, but she had told her mother that if Ed called while she was at the pediatrician's office, to tell Ed to let her know when the funeral was. She would leave Jimmy at Broad Marsh with her mother and fly down to Fort Bragg for it.

So, she had gotten over her anger and come to understand that it was important, then. "The funeral isn't going to be here though, Miss Carrie," he said. "It's in Wyoming."

"Wyoming? Oh, my goodness. What shall I tell her?"

"Tell her I'm leaving Fort Bragg now. I'll be home in about six hours."

"So, you won't be going to Wyoming for the funeral, then?"

He wanted to. He wanted very much to go. And he wanted Mary to go with him. But he had made certain that the arrangements - proper arrangements - for Sam's burial were made. And his extension leave seemed to be flashing by without spending much time at home. He would leave the decision up to his wife as to whether or not they went to the funeral. "Just tell her it's her call whether or not we go," he said. "I'll leave it up to Mary."

It was almost midnight when he reached the old plantation house. Mary was still up, watching the late show on television while she waited for him.

He went to her, knelt in front of her chair, and said, "I'm sorry, sweetheart. But I just had to go down there. I had to."

She pulled her husband's head to her bosom. "I know you did. You don't have anything to be sorry about. I'm the one who acted like a damn fool. Forgive me, will you?"

"There's nothing to forgive. How's little Jimmy?"

"He's all right. The doctor changed his formula, and he seems to like it better. I should have breast fed him, like Maria said. How is she taking Sam's death?"

"Fine. She's fine. She told me the strangest thing, though." He went on to explain to Mary about Maria's premonition, and about the communication she claimed to have had with him after his death.

"She is a strange one, isn't she?" Mary said. "So, they moved the funeral all the way to Wyoming based on something as eerie as that?"

Ed nodded. "I'm glad they did. At least he'll get the ceremony he deserves out there, thanks to Bill Edge."

"Well, I doubt that he'll know the difference."

"*I'll* know, though," he said with irritation in his voice. "And Maria will. And if what she says is true, maybe he *will* know."

"Oh, Ed. You don't believe in that hocus pocus, do you?"

"I don't know, honey. The more I see....I just don't know. Did you decide whether or not we should go out there."

She stood and walked to a nearby table, and handed him an airline ticket envelope.

"Then we are going?" he asked.

"Not we. Just you."

"Aw, Mary. I don't want to go if you're not."

"Yes. You need to. I understand. But I don't want to go. I don't want to be reminded that the same thing could happen to you."

"Hey, don't even talk like that," he said. "They can't get me. I've told you that. I know how to take care of myself."

"And Sam didn't?" They looked at each other in silence for several moments, then she said, "Oh, this came for you, too."

She handed him an envelope from the Infantry Branch of the Army Personnel Center, and he tore it open. There were two copies of orders promoting him to the rank of captain, effective the following day.

He smiled and handed Mary one of the copies. She read it, then looked up at him just as the grandfather clock began to strike midnight.

"Well, congratulations, Captain Walker," she said, moving to him and giving him a kiss. He held her pretty face in his hands, prolonging the congratulatory kiss, changing it to one of passion.

She responded, pressing hard against him, and whispered into his ear, "Take me out to the pool house and make love to me, Ed. I've never done it with a captain before."

He smiled weakly and nodded, then kissed her again and led her by the hand out of the room.

    *   *   *

It was clear, crisp day in Wyoming, and Ed Walker shivered, knowing it was not just from the cold as he watched the burial detail remove Sam's flag-draped coffin from the back of the hearse. Maria stood beside him, her hand in the crook of his elbow. There were a half-dozen cowboys there, too, the horses they had ridden to the grave site grazing nearby. One of the horses had been led there saddled but riderless, and Ed knew without asking that it was there as a tribute to Sam.

Off to the side, at parade rest, stood the firing squad and bugler. The only other people on the rocky knoll were the chaplain from the 20th Special Forces Group, a woman who had introduced herself simply as "Jeanne, a friend of Sam's father," and the men from the funeral home in Jackson Hole. Sam's mother and sister had missed their airline connection in Salt Lake City, and sent word to go ahead with the funeral, as they could not get another flight in until the following day.

The National Guardsmen were sharp and well-practiced, and Ed watched them appreciatively, thinking that they were as good as any Regular Army outfit, the only thing setting them apart from regulars being the teal blue flashes on their green berets.

The ceremony was brief and dignified, and as Ed looked around at the beautiful forested mountains, he was glad that he'd been able to arrange for his friend to be buried here. He could not imagine Sam being buried in Los Angeles by men like the snide major he had spoken to on the telephone, and without his cowboy buddies present. He looked at the rugged young men, their battered felt hats in their hands as they listened to the chaplain. They were so different from the hippie-garbed youths and the grey-suited young businessmen he had encountered in airports during his trip home from Vietnam, and the flight out here. The former seemed always to be slouching around looking as if the world owed them something, while the latter were hurrying to airline gates or blabbing into pay phones as if the world depended on them.

What the world *really* depended on, Ed Walker felt, was the sort of people assembled on the rocky knoll above the Wounded Elk ranch; good soldiers and reliable, hard-working men and loving, loyal women. Those were the kinds of people who had built this country and made it strong. Those were the ones who had heard Jack Kennedy when he said, "Ask not what your country can do for you...." The ones like Sam Hagen. And, yes, he felt with a deep sense of pride, like himself.

When the flag was folded and saluted and handed to Captain Walker, who was to see that it got to Sam's mother, the firing squad leader barked his orders and three volleys of rifle fire echoed around the hills above the Wounded Elk. And then the somber strains of *Taps* filled the crisp mountain air. The sad, mournful sound tore at Ed Walker's heart, not just for Sam Hagen, but for all his fallen comrades, and all who had gone before them, and he wept softly.

Maria DeCalesta did not weep, for she had already made her peace with the death of her friend and lover. She put her arm around Ed's waist, and patted him tenderly while he rendered the last salute.

As Ed had directed beforehand, the men from the funeral home did not wait until the mourners were gone to lower the casket and fill in the grave. They did so while Ed and Maria and the rest watched.

One of the men reached behind the pile of rocky dirt and held up the rusted remains of a shotgun. To Captain Walker, he said, "We found this at the edge of the hole."

Ed nodded, reached out and took it from the man.

"It was his father's," the woman named Jeanne explained. "Sam threw it into the grave the day his father was buried."

Ed smiled and looked at it. "Old Sam," he said. "He told me about that. Killed a grouse with it, and threw that in, too, didn't he?"

Jeanne turned and pointed to a clump of bushes up on the hillside. "Right over there," she said, then shook her head and added, "He was a lot like his daddy, young Sam was."

"Then his daddy must have been a hell of a man."

"Yep. That he was."

Sam threw the gun into the hole, then pulled the combat infantryman's badge off his uniform blouse and threw it in, too. Maria picked up a handful of dirt and dropped it in, and the others filed by and did the same.

One of the cowboys pointed to the folded triangle of the flag that Ed was holding under his arm. "That'd look mighty good flying over the Wounded Elk," the cowboy said.

"It would that," Ed agreed, handing the flag to the man.

Edward Walker snapped one last, sharp salute to his fallen comrade and muttered, "So long, old Sam." And it was over.

*   *   *

Mary McClanahan Walker thrust herself vigorously again and again as waves of delight surged through her and she wailed, "Yes! Oh God, darling, yes!"

When the waves subsided, she threw herself back onto the bed, panting from the exertion of the wildly satisfying sex.

"Oooh, how can it be so good?" she asked.

"It's the cocaine," Sandy Milton said, stroking her heaving breasts. "Marvelous stuff, isn't it?"

"Yes. It made me feel like a - a goddess or something."

"Made you *fuck* like a goddess," Milton said, surveying her beautiful, naked body. Having the kid had done nothing to detract from it, he thought. And if anything, she was hotter, wilder than before. Or maybe it was the knowledge that he could get her off like that, while her soldier boy husband apparently couldn't, that was so satisfying to him.

"Maybe I should give you a few spoons of coke to take to soldier boy," he said. "You know, to fire him up so he can give you what you need."

Mary rolled onto her stomach. "You promised me you wouldn't talk about him," she mumbled. But she was thinking much the same thing. What *did* Ed need to make her feel so - so sexually fulfilled? It wasn't that he lacked the body, for he was much more muscular and fit than the soft, pale professor. So why couldn't he satisfy her as Sandy could? Why couldn't he make her feel so delightfully wanton and uninhibited? He always treated her so gently, and while that was nice sometimes, at other times she just wanted to be ravaged. To be demanded, taken, to be treated like a whore instead of some fragile, medieval lady.

And why did he always seem so distracted? That was the worst part. She always felt as if his mind was only partly involved in their lovemaking, as if part of it was somewhere else. Not like Sandy. He was always totally involved, absolutely uninhibited, as if, for the moment, nothing else mattered.

It was that damned war. It had to be. Part of him was always there. Why in the name of God couldn't he just let it go for awhile, and involve himself totally in her?

But he was going back. He would always go back. He was corrupted by it now. Ruined.

She raised her head and looked at the clock on the dresser, then sat up and began collecting her clothes.

"I've got to get going," she said, more to herself than to her lover.

Ed would be arriving at Byrd Field from Wyoming soon, and she had stayed at Sandy Milton's apartment longer than she intended. She hurried into the bathroom, and as she showered, the glow of the sex and drugs she had shared with Milton faded, replaced with guilt. She thought, My God, what am I doing here? Why do I keep doing this? And now it's drugs, too, not just raw sex. And with Ed not even gone back to Vietnam yet.

She dried herself off and dressed quickly.

"Christ," she said when she came out of the bathroom and looked at the clock. "I'm going to be late."

"When did you say he's heading back to the slaughter?" Milton asked, and without waiting for her to answer, added, "I can't believe the stupid ass is going back for more."

Mary shot him a look of disgust and said, "Damn you, Sandy. I told you not to talk about him. Anyway, you should be thankful he has the guts to go. If it weren't for guys like him, you wouldn't have your precious deferment."

"Oh, I'm thankful, all right. Thankful that the dumb bastard doesn't have more sense. And thankful he's leaving his hot little wife behind."

"Fuck you!"

"Yeah, you will. While soldier boy is off killing people, you sure will."

"Oh, you think you're so damned irresistible, don't you? Well, I've got news for you, Sandy. I don't need you. You don't mean *shit* to me."

"Yeah, but this does," he said, obscenely grasping his flaccid penis in his hand and shaking it at her. "You can't live without it."

"We'll see about that."

He laughed and said, "Oh, you'll be back. No sooner than he gets on the airplane to go back to his Vietnamese whore, you'll be knocking on this door again."

"The hell I will," Mary shot back as she grabbed her purse and hurried out the door.

"Yeah, sure! That's what you said about eight months ago, remember?"

Ed was waiting outside the terminal when Mary got to Byrd Field. She slid over and Ed got into the driver's seat. She said, "I'm sorry I'm late, Ed. I got a late start."

"Oh? I called the farm, and your mother said you left hours ago."

"Well, I stopped by Williamsburg to do some shopping. I just lost track of the time, that's all."

"Don't mean nothing," he said. "What did you buy? Some more of that sexy, lacy stuff you had on when you picked me up here last time?" He reached over to pull her skirt up, but she pushed his hand away.

"Not now, Ed."

"Why not? Didn't you miss me?"

"Of course I missed you. How was the funeral?"

"How? I don't know. Pretty *final*, I guess." His mood went dark, and after awhile he said, "I still can't believe he's gone, Mary. It's going to be so different, without him there."

She reached over and took his hand in hers, squeezed it. "Do you have to go back, Ed? Can't you change your mind?" Maybe if he stays, she thought. Maybe he can get it out of his mind, and things will be different between us then.

"No," he said. "I'm committed to it now, Mary. I've signed the papers."

"My father might be able to do something. He knows lots of..."

"Forget it, Mary."

"Well, why not?"

"Because it's my duty, and I'm not going to be like those bastards who're pulling strings like that, or making college a profession just to avoid going. It's my duty like it was your father's and my brother's, and a hell of a lot of other guys' for the last two hundred years."

She pulled her hand away from his. "Jesus, Ed! What about your duty to *us*? To Jimmy and me? They're not even *drafting* men who have two dependents, like you do. You know that."

"That's different. I'm a captain now, honey. They need experienced officers to lead companies, so those kids over there carrying the load will stand a chance of winning."

"*Winning?* Good *God*, Ed, don't you read the newspapers?"

He glared at her, opened his mouth to say something, then thought better of it. She just doesn't understand, he thought. She sucks up all that bullshit from the newspapers and television like it's the truth.

"I read the newspapers," he said coolly. "That's how I know how full of shit they are."

They rode along in silence, until he said, "Sweetheart, I'm a career soldier now. A professional. You need to understand that."

"Some career," she said. "Some profession."

He slid over against the door to get as far from her as he could. She turned on the radio and twisted the dial until she found a screaming rock group, then turned it up.

Ed shook his head. "Listen to that crap," he said. "They've ruined rock 'n' roll now, too. There hasn't been a real singer since Buddy Holly died."

"God, you've gotten old," she mumbled. It was the last thing they said on the hour-long drive to Broad Marsh.

        *   *   *

Captain Edward Walker spent much of the remainder of his month-long extension leave playing with his baby son on the grounds of Broad Marsh plantation, or fishing with his brother James and his niece Sookie. Many nights he would go to bed late, watching the late news on television to see if there was anything about the Mike Force, or the 1st Cavalry Division. Then he would sit thinking about it, absent-mindedly watching the late show until he dozed off, eventually crawling into bed without waking Mary.

On other nights, one or the other of the young couple would make the effort to try again to revive the passion they had once known. But no matter how fervent their lovemaking might temporarily become, when it was over, the gap between them seemed still to be there, an emotional separation that seemed constantly to expand and contract, seldom shrinking enough to allow them to touch.

"What's happening to us, Mary?" he asked one night before he left.

"I don't know," she said, staring blankly at the ceiling. "I just don't know, Eddie."

He sat up on the side of the bed and lit a cigarette, then mumbled, "This extension leave stuff is a bad idea."

"What?"

He looked at the cigarette before he answered her and thought, What a stupid habit, and snuffed it out.

"I said that this extension leave is a bad idea. You can't get your mind off of the fact that you're going back. It ruins everything. They should give you the thirty days after you finish your tour."

So, that *is* it, she thought. Just as I figured. That damned war. Halfway around the world, and it's still messing up our lives, our marriage.

She rolled over, straddled him. "Yes," she whispered. "Then you'd have only five months left, and we could get on with our lives."

He said nothing, but a tear spilled out of his eye. She leaned forward and licked it from his cheek, then traced a line to his mouth, swaying her large breasts so that the nipples brushed against his muscular chest.

This time, Mary wanted to give herself to him gently and slowly, and he let her. It was tender, soul-soothing love that she gave, and he needed it, took it, let her love him. And when it was over, she stayed atop him for a long time, and he kissed her fingertips and stroked her hair, and said softly, "It will be all right, sweetheart. Once I get done with this tour, we'll be OK."

"It's got to end soon," she said. "It's got to, or they'll send you back again, won't they?"

"No," he said, knowing it was a lie. "It won't last much longer. I won't have to go back after this."

At the airport a few days later, when he pulled the ticket folder from his uniform blouse, a sheet of stationery fell to the floor. He reached down and picked it up, looked at it, then handed it to Mary.

"It's for little Jimmy," he said. "Something I wrote at Fort Bragg when Sam was killed."

His flight was being called, and he said, "I'd better go, honey. Take care of him, and of yourself."

"Oh, Ed. I'm sorry it wasn't..."

He put his fingers to her lips to silence her, then kissed her and held her in a strong embrace for a moment. "I'll be home before you know it, sweetheart."

He lifted her chin, studying her eyes, wanting to remember them. Then he kissed her and said, "I love you, Mary."

"Oh, Ed. I love you, too," she whispered.

She watched him go and said a silent prayer that he would come home safely, and that things would be different then. Several other servicemen climbed the stairs to the airplane, too, and she thought of all the airports all over the country where young men were doing the same thing every day; going off to war. They were only boys, really, most of them. Boys off to play a deadly game that would destroy them and so many others. Couldn't they see how wrong it was? Couldn't they hear the rest of the country, the rest of the world, crying out for them to stop? To resist the warmongers who were getting rich from the blood that flowed from their young lives, and the lives of Vietnamese children?

Ed waved from the top of the stairs, then disappeared inside. She stood and watched until the airplane taxied out of sight, then reappeared speeding along the runway, and lifted off into the Virginia sky.

She looked at the sheet of paper in her hand then; the thing he said he had written for their son:

> *My dear son,*
>
> *Perhaps someday you'll read this. I may be there, or I may not. I may have fallen in battle, and if I have, and you want to know why, I'll tell you now. It was in the cause of freedom. Freedom is all that matters...*

Mary Walker sighed, folding the paper and shoving it into her purse. He was so naive. A crusader flying off in search of a crusade. Freedom. When would he learn that he had it backwards? That freedom was all the Viet Cong wanted, too? Freedom. Both sides slaughtering each other in the name of freedom. It was time for the madness to end.

PART THREE
BLOOD

The thorns which I have reap'd are of the tree
I planted; they have torn me, and I bleed.
I should have known what fruit would spring
from such a seed.

George Gordon, Lord Byron
Childe Harold's Pilgrimage

SEVENTEEN

Lieutenant Mike Robbins stood second in the rank of six soldiers who were waiting for the assistant division commander to pin on their newly-won decorations. On his right was a major, a helicopter pilot who was being awarded a Distinguished Flying Cross. And on his left, Sergeant First Class Peters, a platoon sergeant from Mike's own infantry company who was to be awarded a Bronze Star for his actions in the same battle for which Mike was also being decorated with a Bronze Star.

Overhead, a Huey helicopter settled toward the airfield, its rotor blades making the distinctive *whop whop* sound with which every man standing there was intimately familiar.

Mike wished that his wife Penny could be there to see him receive the award, because maybe that would help her understand why he felt it was important for him to be there. She had never conceded that it was important for him to be over here, doing what he felt was his duty, and doing it well, although she was a good Army wife who took his long absences without falling apart, as he had seen many wives do. Perhaps one day she would understand.

Mike had met Penny Riley while they were both students at Ohio State. She was there one night when Mike and his date were sitting in the local tavern with several other couples, drinking pitchers of draft beer and discussing such matters as the good and evil of government, and of the responsibilities of governments to their people, and people to their government. As always, Mike's views on that subject were a cause for hot arguments and lively discussions. Unlike most of his peers, Mike believed that the United States was helping to thwart a communist takeover of South Vietnam. He viewed communism as the new form of slavery, because it took away choice, because the reality of it was, he knew, not the socialist ideal of everyone helping everyone else. The reality of totalitarian communism, Mike Robbins believed, was that the government ruthlessly ensured that everyone was working for the benefit of the government. He saw it as an evil not unlike the evil of the concentration camps of World War II, except that the Communist Party was in control instead of the Nazis, and the rest of the populace was enslaved as surely as the Jews had been enslaved at places like Dachau.

He believed that it was proper for the draft to be used as a means to keep the nation's armed forces up to strength, and that student deferments were terribly wrong. They created the opportunity for the wealthy to draft-proof their sons by making professional students of them, while the poor remained vulnerable. And besides, if college kids were supposed to become responsible people - the country's future leaders - why should they be exempt from that particular responsibility?

When he expressed that belief to the others, Penny Riley, in the moment of relative quiet that followed his argument while the others considered their rebuttals, looked at him from across the table and blurted, "Well, if you feel like you have such a responsibility to become cannon fodder, why don't you just join the stupid damned Army?"

He had been considering that very thing all year, because his beliefs had been increasingly drawing him to the conclusion that it was his responsibility to back up those convictions with action. And so he replied, more angrily than Penny's comment had warranted, "Maybe I will, goddamn it! Maybe I'll do just that!"

He visited the Army recruiters the following day, and learned that, if he finished earning his degree, he could probably earn a commission in the Infantry. The Army planners could plainly see that there was going to be a rapidly increasing need for Infantry lieutenants in Vietnam.

By a month before his final exams, his mind was made up; the day that he finished his exams, he would go back to the Army recruiter and sign up. It was time to put up or shut up. And he really did believe that it was his responsibility to serve the nation that stood above all others for the freedom of mankind.

The day he signed his enlistment contract, Mike Robbins was walking back across campus, full of the satisfaction of having made some commitment to the future and to his country, when he happened to meet Penny Riley.

"Bye, Mike," she said. "Have a good summer, OK?"

"We'll see, I guess," he replied. "I just joined the Army."

Penny watched him walk quickly on, a hint of swagger in his step, and slowly shook her head. "Too bad," she muttered to herself. "He might have amounted to something."

The general pinned on the major's Distinguished Flying Cross as the adjutant read the citation, then moved in front of Lieutenant Robbins. He surveyed the young officer with interest as the adjutant described Mike's actions of a month before.

It had been late in the day, and his platoon had just settled into a perimeter around a landing zone to secure it for the rest of the company to come in by helicopter, when the Viet Cong attacked the position. It had been a hot firefight for a time, and the communists were gaining the upper hand until a pair of Cobra gunships arrived and kept them at bay while the remainder of the American company landed in an alternate landing zone and came to the platoon's relief. Mike had lost four men killed and six wounded in the attack, and only his courageous leadership and skillful employment of the gunships and supporting artillery had kept the position from being overrun. Mike's company commander had recommended him for the award the general now pinned on him, the Bronze Star for valor.

"Well done, Lieutenant," the general said, then moved on to the next man in line.

As the other citations were read, Mike Robbins's thoughts returned to Penny. In a few weeks, he would fly to Hawaii for R&R, and she would meet him there. What a wonderful time that would be, lying on the beach all day, relaxing. And making love all night, every night, for a week. It would be as exciting as their whirlwind romance had been, when he had returned to Ohio State for homecoming just after he'd earned his commission.

"It was the uniform," Penny jokingly said later. "I just can't resist a man in uniform, and the mailman wouldn't have me."

She had gone with Mike to his motel room that night, after a homecoming party at which they sat together in a corner most of the evening, discussing the war and the Army and their hopes and fears of the future. And, though they were poles apart on many of the points they discussed, it was not with rancor, but with respect for the other's thoughtful opinions.

"Well, I really disagree with you on that," Mike said after some long-forgotten opinion Penny had offered.

"But you'll defend to the death my right to express it," she replied, echoing the quote she remembered he had once used when he was still in school.

He said nothing and only looked at her, and she said, "You really would, wouldn't you? You'd defend it to the death."

Still he said nothing, and so she leaned over and kissed him, and that was the beginning of a romance more heated than their discussions had ever been.

Mike and Penny saw each other as often as they could manage after that night, and when she went to Fort Dix to spend a week of her Christmas vacation with him, they decided to get married. They drove to Atlantic City that night, and did so.

They had four months together before he went to Vietnam, and settled into a warm and comfortable relationship, in which the beliefs and opinions of the other were usually respected, if not agreed with. And their passionate romance grew into maturing love.

The long and thoughtful letters they had exchanged in the five months he'd been gone had served to heighten that love, and now he thought, It will be so good to be with you again, my precious wife.

The ceremony ended, and the newly-decorated men went to the little officers' club to have a beer with the general; then Mike Robbins excused himself and walked down to the airfield to catch a ride back to his battalion firebase.

He checked to see which helicopter was scheduled to make the flight out, then went to sit in the shade of it while he waited for the crew.

There was a captain standing beside the helicopter. He was wearing new jungle fatigues, but he had the rawboned, tanned look of a veteran not long removed from the battlefield. Mike saluted him, then approached and asked, "You headed out to LZ Custer, sir?"

"Sure am," the captain responded. "Are you from the 2nd of the Fifth Cav, Lieutenant?"

"Yes, sir. B Company," Mike said.

The captain held out his hand and smiled. "Might as well get to know each other, then," he said. "I'm Ed Walker. I'll be your new company commander."

*   *   *

Captain Edward Walker settled in quickly as the new commanding officer of Company B, 2nd Battalion, 5th Cavalry Regiment. It was vastly different from the Special Forces teams he had served with his previous year in Vietnam. The unit was badly understrength, as were most of the companies in the division. And he'd had more sergeants in the thirteen-man Mike Force A team than he had in the whole infantry company he now commanded.

But the ones he had were good. The senior NCOs- the staff sergeants and sergeants first class - were solid, steady men from the same cut of cloth as Sam Hagen and Walt Shumate and Bill Edge.

The two platoon leaders who had been with the company for the last several months were good, also. He thought especially well of Mike Robbins, the one he had met at the LZ on the way out to the fire base. Al Wentzel was good, too; quiet, but good. He didn't seem as full of fire as Robbins, but Ed hadn't seen him in action yet. And you couldn't really tell about a man, a leader, until you saw how he performed under fire.

The biggest difference, though, was in the young enlisted soldiers who made up the bulk of the rifle and mortar squads of the company. They were a pleasant surprise to their new commanding officer. With few exceptions, the diverse group of American youths were competent and capable infantrymen who knew their jobs and seemed willing to take on their North Vietnamese and Viet Cong adversaries. At least, that was the attitude they displayed at the battalion fire base the company had been defending since Ed's assumption of command. He would have to wait until the following day, when he led them on a helicopter-borne assault for the first time, to see if they displayed that same attitude in the field.

There was little evidence of racial tension among the men. Ed had worried that it was a problem he would encounter. It helped, of course, that the first sergeant and two of the platoon sergeants were black. But even if they hadn't been, that wouldn't have accounted for the several examples he saw of blacks and whites or blacks and Hispanics hanging around together as best buddies. No, it was the bond among infantrymen who depended on each other for their lives that made them brothers-in-arms. No imposed directive to put aside their cultural and racial prejudices could cause that sort of closeness.

They bitched and complained a lot, of course. Soldiers always did. But their complaints were mostly about the chow, or not enough soft drinks of the type they preferred. It was the red clay dust and the mosquitoes they complained about, not each other, or their leaders, or the things that really mattered.

It would certainly be different, Ed Walker thought, being able to converse with each of them without going through an interpreter. He looked forward to leading them into combat.

Three replacements had just arrived at the fire base; a new second lieutenant platoon leader and two private first class infantrymen. First Sergeant Fraley left them standing outside the tent that served as the company orderly room and walked inside. "The new meat's here, sir,' he said. "The two PFCs claim to be the world's greatest machine gun team, and from the looks of the letters in their 201 files, they might be right. I'm going to put them in Lieutenant Robbins's platoon."

"OK, top," Captain Walker replied. "Let me review their files. I'll talk to them first, then I'll brief our new second platoon leader."

Fraley gave Ed the soldiers' personnel files, then stepped outside while the captain studied them. The files showed them to be of two totally different backgrounds. Henderson was a city boy who had nearly completed the requirements for a degree from a prestigious university, while Zeisman was a high school dropout and ex-coal miner from the rugged hill country of southwest Virginia. But Ed noted that both soldiers had been trained in the same basic and advanced infantry training units, and had served together in the same company in the 82nd Airborne Division before their assignment to Vietnam. And there was a letter of commendation from the 82nd Airborne Division commander in each man's file, lauding them for achieving the highest score in the division during the annual machine gun team competition.

They should be a real asset to the company, then, Ed thought. He handed the records back to the first sergeant, who ordered the two PFCs - Tom Henderson and Randy Zeisman - - to report to their company commander.

The machine gunners marched in, stood at attention, and in unison said, "Sir! Privates First Class Henderson and Zeisman reporting for duty!"

Ed returned their salutes and said, "Stand at ease," then grinned and asked, "Which one's which?"

"I'm Henderson," one of them said, and the other said, "I'm Zeisman, sir."

"Very well." He shook the hand of each of them and said, "Welcome to the finest rifle company in Vietnam. I hear you make a pretty good machine gun team."

"The best," Henderson said, and Zeisman added, "If this is the best company in Vietnam, we'll fit right in, Captain."

Ed grinned again. They had the spirit, at least. So many of the new replacements he had encountered en route to Vietnam seemed to be infected with the surliness that was spreading through the ranks of the Army these days. But not these two.

"We'll see," Captain Walker said. "Now listen up, and listen good. This is an infantry rifle company in a combat zone. Our mission is to close with and kill or capture the enemy by means of fire and maneuver. The enemy is sometimes hard to tell from the civilians over here. But in this company, we make sure we know first. We're not going to disgrace the American people and give ammunition to those mindless protesters back home by hurting innocent civilians. You got that?"

Both men responded, "Yes, sir," but Tom Henderson wondered if the captain really meant it, or was just covering his ass.

"Point two," Captain Walker continued. "This company is made up of men of various ethnic backgrounds from all over the country. But as far as I'm concerned, we're all OD in color. And we're all from the same place, the United States of America. I expect you to adopt that same attitude. Any racial slurs, any of this city slicker versus redneck bullshit, and I'll make you wish your tongue had been cut out... Where are you two from, anyway?"

Henderson had taken note of the company commander's accent, and the way he pronounced "out," and correctly identified him as being from Tidewater Virginia.

"God's country," Tom said, and gave the motto of the state, "*Sic Semper Tyrannis.*"

Walker smiled broadly. "Well, don't disgrace our good Commonwealth. And don't get into any pissing contests with all the damn Yankees in this outfit who still think the North won the war. And no rebel flags."

They both nodded, and Zeisman said, "Airborne, sir."

Walker glanced at the parachutist badges both soldiers wore and thought, Good, another indicator of esprit, and of guts. "Either of you married?" he asked.

"No, sir."

"Good. Write to your parents once a week. I'm going to write to them once, myself - to tell them how proud they should be that you're serving your country, and how proud I am to be serving with you. Don't make a liar of me."

Tom Henderson frowned and his company commander asked, "Is that a problem with you, Zeisman?"

"I'm Henderson, sir. He's Zeisman," Tom said. "There's no problem. I just thought that the only time a company commander wrote to anybody's parents was when they got killed."

"Yes. But that's not going to happen. Not if we do our jobs right, is it?"

This time it was Zeisman who answered. "God damn, I *hope* not, Cap'n."

"No drugs," Walker said, continuing his lecture to the men. "Leave that shit to the leg clerks and jerks in Saigon. I find any of that stuff in this company, and it's an automatic court martial. Either of you drink?"

Both men nodded. "A few beers, now and then," Randy said.

"Well, no harm in that, if you don't overdo it. No beer or booze in the field, though. Keep your weapons and ammunition and your other equipment clean and ready at all times, wear the uniform we tell you to wear, and maintain your personal hygiene. That includes malaria pills."

He eyed the men for a moment then said, "The only other thing is to stick to the basics, the things you've been trained to do, like well-aimed fire, noise and light discipline. You'll be all right. Help each other. Stick together."

The two young men looked at each other, and Ed could tell that there would be no problem in that regard.

"I'm proud to have you men in this company," he said. "Any questions?"

"Just one," PFC Henderson asked. "Why are we in Vietnam?"

Ed looked at him for a time before answering the question. Had he been wrong about this one? Was Henderson the type who was going to question every order he was given?

"'Because we will share any burden, pay any price, to ensure the success of liberty,'" Ed said, quoting the reason that President Kennedy had once given for America's involvement in Vietnam.

"JFK said that," Tom replied. "What's *your* reason, sir?"

Ed looked the replacement in the eye and said, "Because I believed him."

PFC Henderson nodded. It was a shallow, idealistic answer. But this captain seemed to be sincere about it, and that was all that mattered. "That's good enough for me, Captain," he said. "Let's get on with it, Randy."

       *   *   *

The long twin lines of Huey helicopters lifted slowly off the airstrip in a swirling cloud of red dust, then nosed over and headed toward the jungle-covered hills to the west.

Two Cobra gunships took up positions on either side of the double column of troop-carrying Hueys.

"Man, look at those snakes!" Randy Zeisman yelled to Tom Henderson, sitting in the floor of one of the Huey helicopters. "We're gonna bring some smoke on old Victor Charlie today!"

Specialist Gilstrap, one of the fire team leaders in their squad, shouted, "If Charlie don't smoke your ass first, cherries!"

The squad leader, Sergeant Whitehorse, elbowed the specialist and said, "Easy, Gilstrap. You were a cherry a couple of weeks ago too, don't forget. And if you think that piddlin'-assed little contact we had last time out was combat, you've got another think coming."

Henderson gave Whitehorse an appreciative nod, then looked at Randy, their M-60 machine gun cradled in his lap. How can he be so relaxed, Tom wondered, when I'm scared shitless? Doesn't he realize there are thousands of communist soldiers out there, just waiting to kill us?

For the tenth time, he checked to ensure that his rifle was on safe, and that his grenades were securely fastened to the sides of his ammo pouches, the snap straps routed through the pins to preclude them from being snagged and pulled loose accidentally. He was glad that the Old Man required the company to stand inspection shortly before loading aboard the choppers. Apparently, the previous company commander had not required it, because there was some complaining at first, until Top Fraley had put a stop to it with a glaring look, and the discovery of several deficiencies among the "old hands."

The jungle below was lush and verdant. It was difficult for Tom Henderson to picture the sort of mayhem occurring there that he had seen so often on the television news. The thick vegetation stretched unbroken for miles and miles in every direction, up hills and down them, and in the valleys between. Where are the landing zones we're going to? he wondered. There were so few open areas, and most of them seemed too small to land a helicopter in. Perhaps that was the reason there were so many stories about "hot LZs," where the enemy lay in wait to attack the helicopter-borne American troops as soon as they landed. Yes, he thought, that must be it. He swallowed hard, almost certain now that the enemy would be all around the landing zone they were headed for, waiting. Patiently waiting.

*   *   *

"That was a very interesting homily, Father," Mary said to the youthful priest, Father Riddell. They were standing in the parish hall of Abingdon Episcopal Church, just a few miles from Broad Marsh.

Riddell studied the woman's pretty, amber-flecked eyes. Her expression was one of sincerity.

"I believe very deeply in what I said," he replied. He was unsure what she meant by "interesting," for he knew that Mary Walker's husband was an Army officer in Vietnam, and his homily had been obviously anti-war.

"Yes," she replied. "I could tell you do. Did you know that my husband is serving in Vietnam?"

"Yes, as a matter of fact, I was aware of that, Mrs. Walker. I hope you weren't offended by my remarks."

As a visiting priest, he had toned down his anti-war message, which was usually much more direct and stronger. He didn't want to alienate members of a parish that was not his own.

"Not at all. And please, call me Mary."

"All right, Mary. I do hope your husband is well, and that he'll be home safely soon."

"Thank you," she said. Then she smiled and said, "I got the feeling, though, that you were beating around the bush a little; that what you really wanted to do was just come out and say that it's a terrible, tragic war, and that we in this country - our government, anyway - are primarily to blame for all the killing. That it needs to be stopped."

"Perhaps. Is that the way you feel about it, Mrs... Mary?"

"Yes," she said. "Yes, Father. I do."

"It's Jeff," he said. "May I ask why you feel that way?"

She shrugged her shoulders slightly. "Because of what it's done to my husband, I suppose. And because I don't want my son to ever be involved in such a thing. And of course, because of the things we all see on television."

Riddell sipped from his coffee cup, then set it on the table beside them. "And just what has it done to your husband? I'm told by Father Mueller that he performed rather heroically over there."

She smiled at him. "Do you priests always discuss your parishioners in such detail?" she asked.

"No. I just wanted to know my target audience, that's all. You and your husband were the first ones he mentioned."

"Target audience? That sounds awfully like a military term, coming from a priest, Jeff."

"It is," he said. "I was a Marine before I was a priest."

Her eyebrows arched. "Really? Vietnam?"

He nodded. "That's why I feel so strongly about it."

"Well," she said. "That's something. Why didn't you mention that fact? It would have made your message all the stronger."

"It makes no difference, if the message is true, does it?"

"No. I suppose not."

An elderly couple came by to pay their respects to the visiting priest. The parish hall was rapidly emptying, but Mary went to the coffee urn and drew herself another cup. After the couple had left Father Riddell, she walked back over to him.

"What are your plans for lunch, Father Jeff?" she asked.

He patted his flat stomach and said, "To tell you the truth, I try to avoid lunch when I can, Mary. Overeating is one of the risks of the priesthood. People are always inviting you to meals, and you hate to offend anyone by not having a little of everything they offer. Anyway, I need to get on back to Richmond."

"Well, all I was really going to offer was some tomato juice, a bit of Worchestershire sauce and Tabasco, and a squeeze of lime. With a little vodka, just for its medicinal value, of course. And my home - my parents home, actually - is on the way to Richmond."

Riddell laughed. "That's mighty hard to refuse, at least on the grounds that it would destroy my diet. But are you sure a radical anti-war activist would be welcome in your home?"

Mary's face took on a look of seriousness. "I'm sure," she said. "That's what I want to talk to you about. I think I'd like to become involved in the movement."

*   *   *

Tom Henderson could not bring himself to pull the trigger at first. He was supposed to initiate the ambush by raking the jungle trail with machine gun fire as soon as the first man in the enemy column reached a point twenty meters from him, but he could not do it; he could not begin the killing. It was only after the claymore mines had ripped through the North Vietnamese from the flank, and the rest of the squad, deployed along the trail on the long leg of the L-shaped ambush, began spraying the startled NVA with rifle fire, that Tom was able to join in the slaughter. Even then, he might not have taken part in it if Randy Zeisman, lying beside him to feed the belt of ammunition into the gun, wasn't yelling, "Come on, Tom! Get 'em! Get going!"

Tom closed his eyes and fired a long burst down the trail. When he opened his eyes again, he saw no one, for the dead and severely wounded had been flattened and were lying in the dirt beneath the view of his sights, and the living had dived into the jungle beside the trail.

"Swing right!" Randy was demanding. "In the bushes over to the right!"

Henderson shifted his aim to the thick vegetation along the right side of the trail then, and began delivering six-round bursts into it, glad that he could see only leaves instead of men beyond the sights.

"Too high!" Zeisman said, and Tom lowered the barrel of the weapon slightly and continued firing. Now the rest of the squad was tossing hand grenades across the trail where the NVA had fled, and after they detonated, Tom could hear the squad leader, Sergeant Whitehorse, yelling something, but he kept firing until Zeisman broke the belt of linked ammunition to cause the gun to stop.

"Cease fire, goddammit!" Tom heard Whitehorse shouting when the machine gun went quiet. When he was certain that the M-60 had ceased firing, the sergeant yelled, "Assault! Assault!" and he and the other men alongside the trail got up and swept across it, still firing bursts of rifle fire into the jungle where the enemy survivors had fled.

It was only then that Tom Henderson noticed that his finger was still squeezing the trigger of the empty machine gun. He released it and sat up.

"Jesus, Tom," Randy said softly. "Why didn't you start firing? And why didn't you stop when the sarge said to?"

"I don't know," he mumbled. "I guess the trigger was jammed, or something." He looked down at his hands. They were trembling, and he put them between his legs to hide them.

He looked over at his friend. Zeisman was eyeing him skeptically. "Well," Randy said, flipping the feed tray cover open and inserting the first round of the broken belt, "I'll take over for awhile, if you want."

After Randy slammed the feed tray cover shut, Henderson pulled the charging handle back, put the gun on safe, and moved back from it. Zeisman handed Henderson his rifle, double-checked the safety, then picked the weapon up and pointed it down the trail in the opposite direction, in the unlikely event the enemy might swing around and try to counterattack from there.

"You keep covering the ambush site," he said to Tom.

"OK," Henderson said. Whitehorse and his men were dragging bodies out onto the trail, and Tom watched them, wondering if he'd been responsible for any of the deaths.

"Eight," he heard Whitehorse say. "Shit. There must have been twenty of them. We should have had them all." He looked in the machine gun team's direction, then walked toward them.

"What the hell happened?" he asked.

Henderson just looked at him, but Zeisman said, "Damned trigger jammed, sarge. It won't happen again."

"We should have had 'em all," Whitehorse said. "So much for the world's greatest machine gun team. All right, saddle up. Let's get out of here before they come back with their buddies."

He called the platoon leader on the radio to render an initial report on the ambush, then formed the squad up for movement.

They linked up with the rest of the platoon a short time later, and Whitehorse reported to the platoon leader, Lieutenant Robbins. Then he came to the machine gun team's position and said, "The L.T. wants to see you two."

They temporarily turned the gun over to two other members of the squad, and went to see Lieutenant Robbins.

"Sit down, men," Mike Robbins said to them, then excused his radio operator. The lieutenant looked at each of the gunners. "Sergeant Whitehorse says you had a problem with your M-60. What happened?"

Randy waited for Tom to explain, but he was silent, so Randy said, "The trigger jammed, that's all. Won't happen again, sir."

"Who was behind the gun?" Robbins inquired. He was looking at Henderson.

"I was."

The lieutenant nodded. "Is that what happened?" he asked.

Tom shook his head. "No, sir," he said. "I froze, Lieutenant. There was nothing wrong with the gun."

"I see. Well, that happens to a lot of guys in their first contact. It happened to me, too," he lied.

The two enlisted friends traded a glance, and Robbins said, "But you did get the gun into action, finally, so I guess we don't have to worry about it happening again, right?"

Zeisman spoke. "Right, sir."

"Your buddies are counting on you, Henderson. Remember that," the platoon leader said. "That's the important thing. You know, we're lucky that they didn't return effective fire, that your squad didn't take any casualties."

Zeisman looked at Henderson, who was studying the dirt at his feet.

"Yes, sir," Tom mumbled, then looked up at the lieutenant. For the first time, he realized that his platoon leader was probably no older than Randy and he. *So, what makes him different from us?* he wondered. He had studied the officer every moment he had been around them. He seemed to be a competent, capable officer, not the callous, knuckle-dragging type who reveled in killing, or anything like that. *So, what makes him different? It isn't just the rank.*

"Do you believe in what we're doing over here, Henderson?" Lieutenant Robbins asked.

The question took Tom by surprise. He thought about it a moment, then said, "I don't know, sir. To tell the truth, I guess that's why I'm here. To try to find out."

Robbins nodded. "I see. Well, meanwhile, you just make sure you live to find out. You, and the rest of us who are counting on you. And the only way we can do that is to do our jobs the way we're trained to."

"Do you believe in what we're doing, sir?" Tom asked.

"Of course I do," the lieutenant said. "Otherwise, I wouldn't be here. I wouldn't be asking you to risk your lives for it if I didn't believe in it. I believe in it with all my heart, PFC Henderson."

He motioned to his radio operator to return then, and Henderson and Zeisman stood.

"All right," Mike said, eyeing both machine gunners, "I'm counting on you, men. We all are. Just remember that. Don't let us down."

"No sweat, sir," Zeisman said. "You'll see."

Henderson nodded. "I'll do my job, Lieutenant," he said.

"That's all I'm asking," Robbins said. He watched them walk away, and wondered. Then he turned to his radio operator and said, "OK, Pete. Call the Old Man and tell him we're on the way there."

    *   *   *

"The first thing you should understand is that only a small percentage - about fifteen per cent is my guess - really believe in what they're doing."

"Do you mean fifteen per cent of the soldiers, or of the protesters?" Mary Walker asked Father Jeff as she handed him the bloody Mary.

"Both," he replied. "The rest are either doing what they are because of peer pressure, or because someone they look up to told them to do so, or for their own selfish reasons."

"Selfish reasons?" she asked as she took a seat on the sun porch and gestured for the Episcopal priest to sit beside her. "What sort of selfish reasons?"

He sat and took a sip of his drink. "The protesters, many of them, do it for the social life."

She raised her eyebrows and gave him a look of skepticism.

"No, really," Riddell said. "Most protests are nothing but one big party. It's a pretty liberal bunch, you'll discover. A lot of marijuana, a lot of free love, a lot of self-indulgence. And shallow self-righteousness."

She nodded, thinking how well Riddell had just described Sandy Milton, and wondering how much the priest was involved in those aspects of the movement. "And what about the soldiers?" she asked. "I don't see how they could be risking their lives for selfish reasons. I don't believe that's why my husband is a soldier."

"Maybe not," Riddell replied. "Maybe he's one of the fifteen per cent who believes in what he's doing."

"And the other eighty-five per cent?"

Riddell took another drink and set his glass on the wicker table between them. "Well, as I said, a lot of it is because of peer pressure. In fact, that's why, in the end, most young soldiers and Marines fight so well. And they do, you know. At least when they're well-led, they do."

He supposed Captain Walker was one of those who led well, who made his troops willingly risk their lives to do what all their instincts told them was dangerously wrong. That's why winning this young woman over, making her one of the fifteen per cent on his side - on God's side - would be worth the effort. If he could make a believer of her, a true believer, then maybe she could convince her husband that what he was doing was wrong. And if not, then at least she might take away his will to fight, to lead. And that would be better for everyone - his troops, the innocent Vietnamese, and yes, for the captain as well. Because then he might turn his abilities, his leadership, toward some worthwhile goal, instead of killing his fellow human beings.

"And the others?" Mary asked.

"Medals. Fame. Promotion. And in too many cases, because they're sick, depraved killers. Or because the danger of combat is the ultimate high. That was my reason, until, thank God, I finally came to realize it."

She stared at him for a long time, thinking, What a deep young priest this is. Deep in his conviction that what he is doing is right. A lot like Ed, in that regard. Yet Jeff Riddell had seen it from both sides, and he had come to the conclusion that the war and the killing were wrong.

It would be hard to argue with such conviction, even if she were inclined to do so. "So, if my husband is not one of the selfish ones - and

I don't believe he is; I think he believes that what he's doing is right. If his reasons are unselfish, wouldn't it be, I don't know, disloyal of me to become involved in the anti-war movement?"

"No. Because if he is one of those fifteen per cent, then he's the real hope for the future. If he's a dedicated leader, and it sounds as if he is, then the world needs that leadership channeled in the right direction."

He leaned toward her, his eyes fixed on hers. "Can't you see how much it would mean if he would come to his senses and turn his energies toward the good of mankind, instead of its destruction, Mary? Especially in putting a stop to this evil war?"

It was true. He had only been a lance corporal, his one noteworthy decoration a Navy Commendation Medal with combat "V". This woman's husband was an officer. And according to the parish priest, he had already earned a Distinguished Service Cross and a Silver Star. What a powerful voice he might become, if only he could be made to understand.

"Anyway, Mary," Riddell said. "It might well save his life. Don't ever forget that fact, as well."

She stood and walked to the windows overlooking the wide fields of Broad Marsh plantation as she considered the priest's arguments. They were not the reasons she had been considering becoming an anti-war activist. She had been prepared to be one of those he called the eighty-five per cent; one of the followers, the seekers of the social life, of something to do. And yes, perhaps of the liberal environment of sex and drugs it offered, she had to admit.

But there were better reasons, perhaps. And one of the results might be to have her husband, her son's father, come home alive instead of in a coffin as Sam Hagen had.

She turned and looked at Father Riddell for awhile, the deep lines of sincerity still furrowing his brow, waiting for a response.

"All right, Father," she said. "Tell me what I can do to help."

EIGHTEEN

"Letter for you, sir," Mike Robbins said to his company commander.

Ed Walker looked up from the after-action report he was reading and saw that the letter Robbins held out to him was addressed in Mary's writing. He took it and said, "Thanks, Mike." It was thicker than most of her letters, he noticed. "Have you got a minute to proof-read the after-action report?" Ed asked.

"Sure," Robbins replied. Ed handed it to him, and Mike sat down in the chair in front of Ed's field desk. Ed opened the envelope and removed the four pages of stationery. He smiled when he saw that the letter began, *My dearest husband.*

Robbins found a mistake on the second page of the report and looked at Ed. He was frowning, shaking his head. When he'd finished reading the letter, he sighed and mumbled, "Man, I don't know where they get these screwy ideas."

"What do you mean?" Mike responded.

"Mary," Ed said, searching for a sentence on the second page. "Listen to this... 'I just hope the president will finally wake up and realize that it is unfair to us to be risking your life to impose his will on the Vietnamese. Regardless of whether the North or the South is right, it's their civil war, and he has no right to ask people such as you to die for his imperialist goals, like poor Sam did....'" He threw the letter on the desk and mumbled, "Sam Hagen must be twitching in his grave."

"Sounds like Penny," Mike said, smiling.

Ed nodded. Mike had told him, during their long chats in the field at night, about his wife Penny's frequent and thoughtful questioning of the American government's policies in Vietnam. But, as Mike had pointed out, she never questioned his motives, and her arguments were based upon the way the US was trying to check the advance of communism in Southeast Asia, not the fact that they were trying to do so.

"I don't know," Ed said. "I don't think she put the same amount of thought into it that Penny does. It's like she just accepts whatever pinko press reports she reads."

"And you still don't write to her about why we're over here?" Robbins asked. That was another difference between the couples, he had learned. Ed Walker didn't express his thoughts in his letters to Mary, his motivation for serving here, or his thoughts about the government's policies because, as he put it, it only seemed to start arguments.

"Nah," Ed said, then glanced at the letter and shook his head again. "'Imperialist goals.' I wouldn't waste my time answering such drivel."

"Well, I still think you ought to write to her about why we're here. I mean, what would you think, if all you had to go on was the news reports?" Mike asked. "Jesus, when I read what they wrote about Saigon during the Tet offensive, I thought it was a story from some other planet, for Christ's sake. And I was there, man!"

"Well," Ed said after a moment of retrospect, "You know the saying: 'Truth is the first casualty of war.'"

"Trite, empty phrase, sir," Mike shot back. "Trite, empty words. Anyway, that 'truth is the first casualty' thing; it refers to government reports, not the reports of a free press, doesn't it? Otherwise, how would anybody have ever known that truth had become a casualty? You see what I mean? Take the First World War, for example. The only way they ever knew that it was a bunch of bullshit, a friggin' slaughter, not some holy crusade - not 'the war to end all wars' - was because of the fact that whole villages - the whole young male population of entire *villages* - simply never came home. Well, that and the handful of poets who put it into words that were too poignant to be ignored. But except for that, the press, which didn't want to tell the *real* truth for fear of being accused of treason or something, backed up the party line; the 'war to end all wars' bullshit. So, is that what you want? Reporters who follow the party line, or guys who try to sort out the real truth? See what I mean?"

Ed smiled at Mike's fervent response, then said, "Maybe. The problem is, regardless of their intentions, they keep getting it wrong! And that - you know, meaning well but getting it wrong - is harder to see through than telling the obvious lie; than following the line that any thinking person can see is the party line. So, maybe a free press that everybody believes is worse than a government-controlled propaganda organ that everybody sees for what it is."

Mike shrugged. "Well, maybe. But we're just as much to blame as anybody else. We treat the press like the enemy; refuse to talk to them, or take them out in the field with us. So, how the hell are they supposed to get to the truth?"

"I don't know, Mike," Ed said. He picked up the letter and looked at it, then threw it down again. "Maybe one of these days I'll write a boo...."

Wham!

A loud explosion somewhere within the firebase interrupted his words, and men began yelling, "Incoming!" as more explosions shook the ground. Firebase Caballo was under attack.

Walker's was the only rifle company at the base. With the rest of the battalion deployed on search and destroy operations some distance away, and the battalion executive officer off in An Khe, it fell on him to command the defense of the firebase. He made a dash for the command bunker as Mike Robbins ran toward his platoon's perimeter positions.

The mortar rounds were falling with increased intensity and accuracy by the time Ed reached the bunker. Lieutenant Wentzel was already on the radio, reporting that the south side of the base was under attack by rifle and machine gun fire, and rocket propelled grenades.

"Are you sure?" the battalion operations sergeant responded over the radio. Like Ed Walker, he found it difficult to believe that the

enemy would be attempting a ground attack on the base in the middle
of the day.

Outside the defensive wire, trenches, and bunkers of the
Firebase Caballo perimeter, one of Mike Robbins's squads was
guarding the two medical evacuation helicopters that were sitting in the
cleared area that served as the base's landing zone. The choppers and
their crews were waiting there to respond to calls for the evacuation of
any wounded the rest of 2nd Battalion might incur during their search
and destroy operations well to the west of the firebase.

"Christ Jesus!" Randy Zeisman exclaimed as the mortar rounds
peppered the base to their rear. "What are we supposed to do, Tom?"

They and the rest of Sergeant Whitehorse's squad had been
given the mission of guarding the medevac choppers and their crews.
But the likelihood of anything occurring just outside the perimeter in
the middle of a clear and cloudless day was so remote that Whitehorse
had directed that only two men should man an observation and
listening post about fifty meters into the jungle at the edge of the
landing zone. Zeisman and Henderson, along with Whitehorse and the
rest of the squad, had been lolling around the helicopters, trading war
stories with the medevac crews.

Now the squad leader was on the radio, trying without success
to raise the two men in the listening post as the helicopter crews
scrambled to get their machines airborne.

"Come with me!" Tom Henderson said to Randy Zeisman,
grabbing their machine gun and rushing toward the edge of the jungle
with it. Zeisman picked up his rifle and the can of linked ammunition
for the machine gun and followed him.

When he got into the edge of the brush, Tom stopped and
waited for Randy to catch up.

"Where the hell are we going?" Zeisman asked.

"Stitch and Tooth," Tom said. "Sarge couldn't get them on the
radio. They're out here somewhere."

Randy licked his lips. "You mean we're going after 'em?"

"Hell, yes - if Charlie hasn't already got 'em," Tom answered in a loud whisper. "Follow me." He moved into the jungle at a crouch, listening intently for any sign of their fellow squad members, or of the enemy. Zeisman followed him closely, checking first one flank and then the other.

Tom thought he heard something and dropped to a squat, and Randy followed suit. Then Tom raised himself slowly up until he could see beyond the bush in front of him. There, not ten meters away, were six enemy soldiers. He acted instinctively, thumbing the gun's safety off and squeezing the trigger as he brought it up to shoulder level, pouring a steady stream of fire at the figures before him. Some of them crumpled to the ground immediately, while several others spun or were knocked backwards from the impact of the bullets that slammed into them. But eventually, they all fell. Tom lowered his point of aim when they were all down, and watched their bodies jerk as more of his bullets ripped into them, until he was certain that they were dead or mortally wounded.

He dropped back into a squat then, and called, "Stitch! Tooth! Are you all right?"

The response was a long burst of fire from some distance beyond the dead enemy.

Again Henderson called to his squad mates, and again he was answered by a burst of fire, this one coming close, the rounds rattling through the leaves just above his head.

He glanced back at Zeisman, who was squatting wide eyed and open mouthed behind him, and whispered, "All right, we'll move around them to the right. Let's go."

With that, he moved off at a low crouch with Zeisman obediently following. When they had gone about fifty meters, he stopped again and listened. The only sounds he could hear were mortar rounds exploding on the firebase, and sporadic fire from the perimeter, so he veered left and moved on.

He moved cautiously now, stopping every few paces to listen, raising himself from a crouch to peer ahead and to the sides. He sensed that the missing men were just a short distance ahead, wondering why he was so certain of it as he moved cautiously on. And then he froze. There they were. One of the Americans - Stitch, the black one - was on his back, and Tooth was kneeling as one of the enemy soldiers tied his hands behind him. Two others watched, their rifles aimed at Tooth. None was looking in Tom's direction. He crouched and whispered to Zeisman, "They're in front of us - Stitch, Tooth, and three NVA. Take the one on the right."

Randy swallowed and nodded, then both men slowly rose to a standing position. This time, Henderson brought the machine gun up to his shoulder, aiming it like a rifle. He killed one of the two men standing guard with a burst of six rounds as Zeisman's rifle dropped the other one. Tom followed the third NVA with his front sight as the man dived to the ground between Stitch and Tooth. His finger jerked three times, firing single rounds, and all three bullets found their mark. Then he ran forward toward his comrades, spraying the jungle all around them as he ran.

He thought Stitch was dead at first, and had almost decided to grab Tooth and run when he saw the black soldier's eyes follow him. His mouth was opening and closing like a beached fish, and it was only then that Tom noticed the long gash across Stitch's throat.

"Take care of Tooth!" he ordered Randy, and dropped to his knees beside Stitch. The gash was deep, the trachea and esophagus severed. He ran a finger into the hole to clear it of clotted blood and mucous, and immediately air began to pump in and out of the windpipe. He glanced over at the other Americans. Tooth was whining and crying, "Mama. Oh, God, I want Mama!" as Randy cut the rope from his wrists.

"Shut up, Tooth!" Tom said hoarsely. "Can you walk?"

Zeisman pulled the whining soldier to his feet, spun him around and slapped him hard. "Get ahold of yourself, mother fucker!" he demanded. Tooth put his hands in front of his face to ward off another blow, but Randy said, "You're all right, Tooth. You ain't even hurt. Now, pick up one of them rifles and let's get the fuck outta here!"

"Take the gun, Randy," Henderson said. "I'll carry Stitch." He picked the wounded man up, being careful to cradle his head in the crook of his elbow as he carried him. Stitch was looking up at him with wide eyes, his mouth still working open and shut.

"You'll be OK now, Stitch," Tom said. "I'll have you on the medevac before you know it." But he wondered if the man could survive long enough to get him back to the perimeter.

"Crazy bastards went after the two guys in the O.P." Mike Robbins reported to Ed over the radio. He had learned of Henderson and Zeisman's actions when Sergeant Whitehorse, their squad leader, returned to the platoon's position inside the firebase after the medevac helicopters had cranked up and flown away to a safer location.

"We need to get out there and find them," Robbins said.

Ed weighed the situation before he answered. It appeared that the enemy unit that had been preparing to attack the firebase in the vicinity of Lieutenant Wentzel's platoon had been beaten back by the 105 millimeter howitzer battery stationed at the base. Direct fire from the American artillery into the tree line where the enemy fire originated had quickly silenced the North Vietnamese attackers. Now the big guns were searching the jungle for the mortars that still spat an occasional round at Firebase Caballo. The enemy might attempt an assault on another part of the thinly-defended base, but having Robbins's platoon outside the perimeter would not necessarily be to the defenders' detriment; rather, it might enable them to spoil such an attempt by hitting the attackers on the flank.

"All right," Captain Walker said to his lieutenant. "Keep me advised of your movements, and don't get too far away. There should be a pair of Cobras out here to shoot for us at any minute. Call them direct if you need them."

"Wilco," Mike answered, then gave his platoon a quick briefing on their mission.

They were only a short distance into the jungle when the point element was spotted by a security team of the North Vietnamese company that was withdrawing from the vicinity of the firebase. The hammering by direct fire from the American howitzers had caused them to abandon the attempt to penetrate the base. Their intent had been to try to draw the rest of 2nd Battalion, 5th Cavalry back to the base, as it appeared to the communists that the American battalion was about to find their regimental base area to the west. If they did, it would be devastating to the regiment. The area contained caches of ammunition and other supplies the regiment required to sustain itself in battle.

When it was reported to the NVA commander that an American platoon was approaching his position, he saw it as a stroke of good luck. If he could hit them hard, and prevent them from getting back into the firebase, it might result in several things. First, it would exact revenge for the beating his company had taken from the howitzers. More important, it might yet achieve the result of having the American battalion abandon their operation to the west, to return to the firebase to defend it. If not, and the platoon could be destroyed, the American defenders of the base would be hard pressed to hold their perimeter against a determined attack, especially if the supporting mortars could hit the artillery and prevent it from again beating back the attack.

The North Vietnamese captain ordered his company to form a wedge shaped ambush ahead of the Americans' advance, so that, if they continued on their present course, the platoon would move into the open end of the wedge. Then, when they were near the point of the wedge, he would open fire on them, and they would be trapped within the sides of the ambush, and destroyed. And he wouldn't have to worry about the American artillery, either; the adversaries would be too close to each other for the big guns to respond without risking the destruction of their own people.

Quickly and silently, the company deployed ahead of the Americans - every man, wounded included, who could fire a weapon. The others were left just beyond the point of the wedge and cautioned to be silent. Those who were too badly wounded to stifle their moans were administered morphine from the precious few supplies of the company medics.

The NVA officer could already hear the rustle of the enemy soldiers approaching when his platoon leaders relayed the signal that they were prepared to initiate the ambush. He peered into the jungle ahead, then brought his assault rifle to his shoulder and prepared to begin the destruction.

Randy Zeisman froze and dropped to his knees, looking wide-eyed back at Tom Henderson. He peeked around the bush in front of him a moment, then crawled back to where Tom was gently placing Stitch down. Tom scooped more blood and mucous from the wounded man's throat with his finger, then turned to Randy and whispered, "What is it?"

"More NVA," Zeisman whispered. "A bunch of wounded, just lying there."

With Randy following, Tom crawled forward past Tooth to the position where Zeisman had seen the enemy, and stuck his head around the bush. Yes, there were a half-dozen badly wounded enemy soldiers lying there. Perhaps it was a medical collection point or something. He raised his eyes slowly above the top of the bush for a better view, and beyond the wounded men he now saw several more North Vietnamese. They were all facing away from him, guns at the ready, as if they were about to open fire. When he saw an American approaching them, Henderson understood what was about to happen. He grabbed the machine gun from Randy Zeisman and began spraying the jungle beside the approaching American, yelling, "Ambush! Ambush!" at the top of his lungs.

The North Vietnamese were caught by surprise. The confusion brought by a gun opening fire on them from the rear caused many of them to turn that way, and caused others to hesitate in opening fire. Only a few thought it was the signal to initiate the ambush and began shooting into Mike Robbins's platoon.

Robbins dived to the jungle floor at the sound of the first of Henderson's rounds cracking nearby, and heard him yell, "Ambush!"

He quickly determined that the platoon was under fire from both flanks, but it sounded as if there was less from his right. "Flank right!" he ordered. "Flank right and assault!"

Tom Henderson heard his platoon leader's order as he saw one of the enemy soldiers swing his rifle around to bring it to bear on the machine gun that had spoiled his ambush. Henderson cut him down. Randy was beside him now, firing single, well-aimed shots at any enemy he saw. He stopped to reload, looking back at Tooth cowering in the dirt behind him, and Tom heard him yell, "Get up here, God damn you, or I'll shoot you myself!"

"Loading!" Tom yelled as the belt of machine gun ammunition ran out, and he dropped to the prone to reload. Randy flipped his rifle to automatic and continued to fire into the enemy flank as Tom quickly reloaded. Tooth was lying beside Randy now, firing blindly ahead.

The rest of the platoon followed Lieutenant Robbins's order and flanked to their right, firing, rushing forward, throwing grenades ahead of them, then rushing forward again. Their hand grenades and aggressiveness quickly broke the enemy ambush on that flank, and the NVA began to die or withdraw before them. But they were still taking heavy fire from the other leg of the wedge, now to their rear.

Henderson knew it, and when his gun was back in action, he stood and began walking, firing from the hip, down along the line of enemy. He was on their flank, and he took them one at a time, Randy walking beside him, shooting any of the enemy Tom failed to kill. Now Tooth came up on his other side and joined in the killing until an enemy bullet smashed into his face and he collapsed backwards.

The belt of ammunition was nearly gone now, and Tom yelled to Randy, "I'm out of ammo!" as he fired the last burst into the jungle ahead. They quickly moved back along the line of enemy they had killed, and Henderson was astounded at how many there were.

When they got to Tooth, they found that he was already dead.

The fire had slackened now, and only an occasional burst from one side or the other could be heard. Above them, they heard the sound of approaching helicopters.

"What should we do?" Randy asked.

"Get to the platoon," Tom said, "then go get Stitch."

They could hear someone yelling their names from some distance away now; "Z-man! Hendo! Can you hear me?"

It was Sergeant Whitehorse. "Comin' in!" Tom yelled. Quickly, the men moved off in the direction of their squad leader, calling out now and then to avoid being fired on by their comrades.

The platoon moved out toward the badly wounded Stitch as soon as Lieutenant Robbins learned of his situation from the two machine gunners. A pair of Cobra gunships guarded them from above, ready to respond instantly to any enemy foolish enough fire on them. Only the mortar crews made that mistake, though. When they did, the Cobras rolled in on them and silenced them forever.

They weren't certain whether Stitch was alive when they placed him on the medevac helicopter with the several other casualties the platoon had suffered in the disrupted ambush. Tom watched the aircraft lift off as Randy Zeisman said to him, "I ain't sure Stitch is gonna make it, Tom."

Henderson shrugged and said, "We did our best, Randy."

The platoon moved along the line of dead enemy then, in search of Tooth's body. Lieutenant Robbins was just behind the two machine gunners. As they passed more and more enemy dead, he said, "Jesus, men. You slaughtered these bastards."

Zeisman grinned and said, "Ripped 'em a new asshole, all right. 'Course, Tommy did most of it with the M-60."

Henderson glared first at the platoon leader, then at Randy Zeisman. The sight of the twisted bodies caused him to feel only revulsion for what he had wrought, and the words of the other men only served to heighten that revulsion. "It's not funny, Z," he said. "And it wasn't a case of slaughter, sir. I just did what I had to do."

Mike Robbins looked at him and saw the anger in his eyes. "I didn't mean to make light of it, Henderson. I just meant that you did a hell of a good job."

"Good job? Shit, Lieutenant, what's good about killing a bunch of people who... who were just trying to do *their* jobs, too? It's fucking *sick*, that's all it is."

They reached Tooth then. Sergeant Whitehorse was spreading his poncho out on the ground to wrap the body in it, and they watched him. Tom took one glance at his dead squad mate, then looked away. The way his face was distorted from the shock of the bullet slamming into its bony structure made him barely recognizable.

A tear rolled down Henderson's face and he turned his back to the dead man, then turned again when he saw other men searching the bodies of the dead. "That's it," he mumbled. "That's all I'm going to do. Never again." He threw the machine gun to the ground and put his face in his hands.

Lieutenant Robbins put his hand on Henderson's shoulder, but Tom jerked away and walked a short way into the jungle. Robbins followed, and said softly, "It's all right, Hendo."

Henderson shook his head, his face still buried in his hands.

No," the gunner replied. "It's not all right, God damn it. It's *murder*, that's all it is."

"It's war."

Tom dropped his hands and turned to the lieutenant. "Yeah, sure. Murder, war; what the hell's the difference?"

"Not much, really," Robbins replied. "Not much, except for the reasons."

"Yeah, right. 'Insure the success of liberty' and all that bullshit, right, Lieutenant? Please, save the lecture for somebody who believes that crap."

Robbins stood in silence for awhile, then said, "No, I'm not going to give you a lecture, Henderson. But I want you to turn around, and look around you."

Tom stood with his back to the officer, head bowed. "Come on, turn around," Mike said. "I just want you to look at something."

Henderson turned to face his platoon leader, and Mike pointed to the men of the platoon, several of them tying the body of the dead

American into the poncho, while others stood or knelt, peering into the jungle. Several were looking at Tom and Mike.

"You see that? You see your buddies standing there? Zeisman and Whitehorse and Shelton and Brown, and the others? They wouldn't be there if you hadn't done what you did. They would be dead, most of them. They would have been killed by the enemy you jumped and killed first. And that goes for me, too. We'd probably all be dead, if it wasn't for you and Z and Tooth. That's reason enough, isn't it?"

Henderson looked at the other members of his platoon, at Tooth's shrouded body, at the grotesquely twisted enemy dead lying about, then back at his platoon leader.

He said nothing, but the look in his eyes softened.

"It was a brave thing you did, Tom; you and Z," Mike said. "Going after Tooth and Stitch in the first place was brave. A little foolhardy, maybe, but brave. And I'm proud of you. We're all proud of you. Maybe that's another difference between war and murder - the fact that good men can be proud of what you do in battle."

Henderson's eyes moved from the other men of the platoon to the lieutenant's face. He studied the officer for a moment, then nodded. "I hope you're right, sir," he said. "God, I hope you're right."

"I am. I know I am. Now, let's get back inside the wire before it gets dark."

The assistant division commander, Brigadier General Casey, arrived by helicopter at sunset while the platoon was standing inspection, as Captain Walker required of each of his platoons whenever they returned from the field. Walker turned the inspection over to Lieutenant Robbins and went to report to the brigadier. They conferred for a few minutes, then Walker sent for Robbins.

"And he wants you to hold the platoon here in formation for now, Sergeant Fraley," the messenger said to Mike's platoon sergeant.

The general, the captain and Lieutenant Robbins walked over to the platoon two minutes later. Fraley called them to attention, and saluted the general. Leaving the platoon at attention, General Casey said, "Specialists Henderson and Zeisman, front and center."

The two friends glanced at each other for a moment with a look of slight confusion, partly because they were still privates first class, not the next higher rank of specialist. They shrugged, then moved in front of the platoon and stood before the general.

Casey grinned at the young machine gunners, then said, "Captain Walker and your platoon leader tell me you two are the best machine gun team in Vietnam. Is that right?"

Without hesitating, Randy Zeisman said, "You bet your... uh, yes, sir, General."

"Well, that being the case, you deserve to be promoted," Casey said. "And since it's in my power to do so, you're both hereby promoted to the rank of specialist four." He looked from one of the men to the other, then said, "They also told me that you proved that claim today in a very courageous way. Lieutenant Robbins says, in fact, that if it hadn't been for you two, your whole platoon might have been wiped out in an ambush."

Zeisman pointed a thumb at his friend and said, "Tom is the one who deserves all the credit, General. He kicked ass out there."

Tom Henderson was still uncomfortable with the fact that killing people could be considered a laudable deed. He shot Randy a glowering look, then gazed at his feet.

"I just did what I had to do, that's all," he mumbled.

"I see," General Casey replied. He sensed the young trooper's discomfort with his newly earned reputation as a noted warrior. "But that's all we can hope to do when the time comes, all of us; to do what we have to do. That's what this business is all about, in the end; doing what has to be done. At least, that's the way it is for any soldier who's worth his salt. Nobody likes it; nobody whose head is screwed on right does. But we do it, because the nation, the free world, needs us to. And when a soldier does it at the risk of his life, when he's able to control his fear and overcome the natural selfishness that tells him not to risk his life for somebody else, or in pursuit of some principle he believes in, then that's what we call valor. And valor deserves to be recognized."

Without waiting for a response from the reluctant hero, the general turned to his aide.

"Attention to orders!" the aide called. He handed two small, blue boxes to the general then glanced at the page of notes he had taken during Casey's conversation with Captain Walker and Lieutenant Robbins. "The following impact awards are announced. The Bronze Star Medal with 'V' device is awarded to Specialist Four Thomas Henderson and Specialist Four Randall Zeisman, Company B, 2nd Battalion, 5th Cavalry, 1st Cavalry Division, for heroism in ground combat in the Republic of Vietnam...."

With Lieutenant Robbins's assistance, General Casey pinned a medal on each of the machine gunners.

Ed watched the troubled face of Tom Henderson and thought, I know what you're feeling, Henderson - as if you've traded your soul for a piece of ribbon. But that's not what you've done. You've lost your youth, that's all. You've become a man, whether you were ready for it or not. All the boyish things you looked forward to are gone now; meaningless. You'll never be the same.

Ed felt sorry for the young soldier, he realized. Here he was being presented a medal for valor, being recognized as a hero in front of his peers and his superiors, and all Ed Walker could feel for him was sorrow. There must be something wrong with that, he thought, but that's what he felt - sorrow as deep as that he felt for Tooth and the other dead men.

NINETEEN

Father Jeff Riddell watched the parishioners file to the front of the church and kneel at the communion rail to receive the sacrament. When he saw that one of them was Mary Walker, his eyes widened and he wondered why he had not noticed her before. Their gazes met and he acknowledged her presence with an almost imperceptible nod of his head, then he turned his attention back to his priestly duties. When he reached her and said, "This is my blood, which was shed for you," she took the base of the chalice and tilted the cup of holy wine to her lips, and drank. He touched her forehead with his thumb, making the sign of the cross, and again their eyes met. The brief glance seemed much longer than it was, and as he saw the shine in her amber-flecked eyes, Riddell thought, God forgive me, but I love you with such passion, Mary.

It had happened so quickly. They had only seen each other three times since their first meeting at the old church near Broad Marsh. She had come to Richmond the following Saturday, when he was helping to organize an anti-war demonstration at Richmond Professional Institute.

She had said little, watching him as he manipulated the young college students into making decisions they thought were their own: no radical dress; no use of drugs at the demonstration site; no obscenity on the signs they would carry; no references to the establishment or the troops as "pigs" or "baby killers" or such. There would be no burning of the flag or draft cards. Instead, they would stick to the things that were acceptable to the citizenry of the conservative southern capital. "War is unhealthy for children and other living things," and "Thou shalt not kill," and other familiar, inoffensive phrases would be used. And instead of fiery speeches denouncing the government in harsh terms, they would simply read the names of the American battle casualties of the last month.

There were more than five hundred names, garnered from the casualty lists in the newspapers. When one of the students remarked that it would take only about an hour to read the names off, much less time than the demonstration was planned for, Mary spoke up.

"Then, why don't we read their hometowns, too?" she said. "The ranks, names, hometowns, and states. That should take about three times as long, don't you think?"

They all agreed it was a good idea.

"Besides," Mary Walker said, "people who hear the names of towns they're familiar with will be touched by that, even if they don't know anyone from that town."

Jeff Riddell was beaming at her, she noticed when she looked to him for approval.

She had agreed to read fifty of the names, and she returned to Richmond the following Friday to do so.

She came early and met Jeff at the rectory. It was a nice old home, well appointed with antique furniture but lacking hominess, as one might expect of a place occupied by a bachelor priest. She accepted his offer to go out for brunch, and they went to a little restaurant in the Fan. On the way back, she stopped at a supermarket and bought a large bundle of cut flowers, several potted plants, and a quantity of colorful fruits. When they got to the rectory, she arranged the fruit in a bowl and placed it on the dining room table, decorated the house with the plants, then, with Jeff's assistance, arranged the flowers in several vases. Their hands touched as they arranged the flowers, and they allowed the physical contact to linger for a time, until Jeff pulled his hand away. It was not unusual for attractive women - married women included - to want to touch him, he had learned since donning the collar of a priest. But he had never before wanted them to, not until Mary McClanahan Walker came along.

He looked around the rectory when they were finished. The little splashes of color made a remarkable difference, and he said so, and thanked her.

"Well, they won't last long," she said with a smile. "I'll have to come back now and then to give the place a woman's touch, I suppose."

His face was serious when he responded, "Yes. That would be kind of you, Mary."

It would have been a fairly innocent comment, had he not been a priest, and she, a married woman. But those facts and his sincerity made it something other than innocent, and they both knew it, both felt it. Their eyes locked for a long moment, and he said, "Your eyes are so beautiful, Mary. The color is so, well, so...."

They were close enough that she had to take only one step forward to kiss him. She did. It was a soft, short kiss that he made no effort to avoid. They were both aware of that fact, too.

He put his cheek against hers for a moment, then turned away and said, "I'm sorry, Mary. I, uh, I shouldn't have let that happen."

She said nothing until he turned back toward her and they looked into each other's eyes a moment. Then she leaned forward to kiss him again. This time he took her by the arms and gently held her away from him.

"We'd better get over to R.P.I." he said softly. She nodded, but there was a slightly seductive smile on her face, and her eyes darted from one of his to the other as if to say, You know that you want me, and I know you know.

He stayed in the background at the demonstration. It was fairly orderly, and the policemen sent to observe it and maintain order dutifully protected the demonstrators from confrontations with the small number of hecklers who turned up.

When it came time for Mary to read the list of fifty names she was handed by one of the student organizers, she stepped up to the microphone and slowly, clearly, began to read them off: "Specialist Anthony L. Trotter, Bell City, Texas... Second Lieutenant Santos J. Rodriguez, Salinas, California... Sergeant Sam L. Hage..."

The name caught in her throat. She stared at the list for several seconds, then dropped the two pages of names and covered her face with her hands.

Jeff Riddell looked at her from beyond the crowd, wondering what was wrong. Was she ill? Had she suddenly been gripped by a sense of guilt? What was it?

The student beside her put his hand on her shoulder and asked, "What's wrong? Are you all right?"

Mary pulled away from him and ran down the marble steps, pushing her way through the silent, staring crowd. Jeff caught up with her and grasped her by the arm. "What is it, Mary?"

She wiped her eyes and nose with her hand and looked at him. "Take me away from here, Jeff. Please."

"Why, Mary? What's wrong?"

She shook her head and put her hands over her face again and began to sob.

His arm around her shoulder, Jeff Riddell led her to her car and let her in the passenger side, then went around and got in. He watched her wipe her nose with a tissue, then look up at him.

"I'm sorry," she said. "I'm such a baby. It's just... I couldn't fin...." She leaned across the seat and hid her face against his chest.

Riddell stroked her head and said, "I know it was a difficult thing for you to do, Mary. Don't worry. It's all right."

She put her arm across his chest. "It was the name," she mumbled. "Sam Hagen. He... he was the best man in my wedding."

Riddell stopped stroking her head and sighed. "Oh, no. Ah, Mary, I am sorry. What a horrible way to find out."

"No. I already knew. It happened while Ed was here on leave." She sat up and wiped her nose again. "It's just so sad, that's all. Such a terrible waste of a man who could have done so much more with his life. I'm sorry I lost control, Jeff." She put her hand on the back of his, and he turned it over and clasped her fingers with his.

"But that's just proof that what we're doing is right, isn't it?" she asked. "Trying to stop the loss of men like Sam, I mean."

He brought her fingers to his mouth and kissed them. "Yes, it is," he said.

She smiled at him, then leaned forward and kissed him lightly on the mouth. "Take me to your house, Jeff," she whispered. "Help me forget things for awhile."

Riddell sighed. "Mary," he said, "I... I just can't. I think you know that I want to. I want to very much. But it would be wrong; a... a terrible sin."

"God will forgive you," she said. "He's the only one who will know."

He released her hand and shook his head. "No," he said, and thought, If only you weren't married, Mary. "It would be wrong, Mary. Awfully wrong."

She took his hand and covered her breast with it. He made no effort to pull his hand away, but only looked at her, wanting her.

"It would be much less wrong than what you did in Vietnam," she said. "He forgave you for that. And He brought us together for some reason."

"He brought us together to help end this war."

She nodded, and squeezed his hand against her breast. "Yes. But is that the only reason, Jeff?"

Now he pulled his hand away. He was aroused. He had been without a woman for so long, and the temptation was great. Too great. His conscience struggled with itself, and he was silent, brow furrowed, for a time. If it was wrong - truly wrong - he would not feel such a need for her. And if yielding to her and to his own desire was unforgivable, then the things he had done as a Marine had surely already damned him. And unless he made love to Mary Walker, and discovered whether he felt unforgiven afterward, he would never know. It was not an uncommon thing for priests to yield to sexual attraction. It was not uncommon at all. And it was not unforgivable.

He reached his fingers to her lips, and she opened her mouth and took the tips of them between her teeth and touched them with her tongue.

Riddell looked deep into the amber and blue of her eyes, then pulled his hand away and started the car.

Their time together that first day was brief; a short half-hour of passion that left Jeff Riddell feeling torn between joy and remorse. But then the joy faded, replaced by guilt, and he climbed from the bed, wrapped a towel around his waist, and stood with his back to her. After a while he said, "Mary, that was wrong. Beautiful, yes. But wrong. Forgive me. You'd better go now. And I... I think we had better not see each other anymore."

She looked at him in silence for awhile, then, when he turned to face her, she said, "That's not the way I feel about it, Jeff. Not at all. It was a wonderful act of sharing we just experienced. It was... it was loving, unselfish sharing of feelings that we can't help feeling. There's nothing wrong with that. Oh, maybe it's not... what? Socially acceptable because of our situation? But that doesn't make it wrong. Not in my mind. And I doubt that it is wrong in the sight of God. Not the loving and caring God I believe in."

He stood there with a towel covering him, shaking his head. She was so lovely to look at. Too lovely, so he turned away from her again. "No, Mary. It was wrong. We both know that. Please go now. Please, I need to think."

She climbed from the bed, picked up her clothes, and went into the bathroom. After she dressed she found him downstairs in the dining room, leaning forward on the table with his head in his arms. She walked to him and laid her hand on his shoulder.

"I'll stay away from you, Jeff, if that's what you really want. But it's not what I want. And not what I feel inside me is right. Not for either of us."

She leaned over and kissed the back of his head, then started for the door. But she stopped there, turned back to him and said, "I've gained so much from you already, Jeff. So much meaning. I wish you wouldn't deprive me of that, but it's up to you. Think about it. I'll be at Broad Marsh if you decide I'm right."

She turned away and opened the door, then paused again and looked back at him. "But whatever you decide, at least I had this brief time with you, Jeff. And I'll always cherish that."

And then she was gone.

It was two weeks before she saw him again. She was at home by herself at Broad Marsh when the doorbell rang, and she went downstairs from the nursery where she had just put Jimmy to bed for his afternoon nap. She opened the big front door and there he was. They said nothing for several long moments; instead they studied each other's eyes in an attempt to see what the other might be thinking, feeling. And then she moved into his arms, and he wrapped them around her and kissed her warmly, passionately.

She clung tightly to him and whispered, "There's no one here but us and the baby, and he's asleep."

He nodded, so she took him by the arm and led him upstairs to her bedroom.

A week had passed since then, and although she had phoned him several times since that passion-filled afternoon, he had no idea that she would be coming to Richmond this Sunday.

After the service, when the parishioners had cleared out and he had put things away, he found her in the church parking lot, sitting in her car, parked next to his. He got in beside her and she reached her hand to his. He took it and gently squeezed it. "I've missed you, Mary," he said. "It was a wonderful surprise to suddenly look up and see you like that." Then he leaned toward her to kiss her, but she pushed him gently away.

"No," she said. "Someone's liable to see us here." She reached her other hand to him and gave him a key. "I have a room in the Williamsburg Lodge," she said. "I'll see you there in an hour."

He looked at the key, then at the enchanting colors of her eyes. "Yes," he said, and his face was brightened by a broad smile. "In an hour, then. At the longest."

       *   *   *

"Well, this *is* cause for a party!" Maggie Westcott said, looking up from the sheet of paper First Lieutenant Susan Madison had just handed her.

Sue smiled and held the palms of her hands out to her sides. "What can I say? I figured if it was good enough for you, I might as well do it, too. Anyway, by extending, I'll have a better shot at getting assigned to Walter Reed when I leave."

"You're sure you want to do this?" Maggie asked. She wondered if Sue's decision to extend her tour was for the right reasons. Was it just the fact that she didn't want to leave this place where her Prince Charming had so briefly appeared? That's what she had said about the Special Forces medic who had been in her life so briefly: "It was like a fairy tale, Maggie. Like Prince Charming. Every woman's dream. I could have spent the rest of my life with him." That's what she had said shortly after he'd been killed. Was she waiting for it to happen again? It wouldn't.

"Yes," Sue said. "I'm sure."

Maggie pulled the pen from her pocket and wrote *Recommend approval*, then signed her name. It didn't really make any difference why Sue was asking to extend her tour. So few nurses were volunteering for the Army now because of all the disenchantment with the war back home. They desperately needed nurses; especially ones as capable and experienced as Sue Madison.

*　　　　　　　*　　　　　　　*

Lieutenant Wentzel halted the platoon and called Captain Walker forward.

Ed joined him at the point of the company column. Ahead, where a large area of jungle was cleared away beside the river, was the remains of what had been a village. The frames of some of the thatch houses were still smoldering, and the men could see the stiff and bloated bodies of several water buffalo lying in a field beside the ruins. The hot, still air stunk of death.

Ed surveyed the scene in silence for a minute, then turned to Lieutenant Wentzel.

"Take your platoon around to the left and secure from here to the river. Third platoon will take from here to the right."

The two platoons moved off in files to secure the flanks of the area. Mike Robbins came up and stood beside Ed, his platoon behind him, awaiting orders.

"What do you want me to do, sir?"

Without looking at him, Ed said, "One squad around each flank and secure the riverbank on the far side. Bring your other squad with me." He stood there awhile longer, his jaw muscles flexing as Mike dispatched his squads.

Someone had destroyed the village. Totally destroyed it, and killed the livestock. There were no villagers in sight, but Ed Walker knew their fate. He knew by the stench of death. He wondered who had done it; his side or the other. He prayed to God it was the communists, but he was afraid of what he might discover, so he stood awhile longer staring at the ruins, then sighed and walked forward into them. Mike Robbins and Sergeant Henderson's squad followed.

They found the bodies in a low area beside the riverbank. The old men and women were at the edges; frail, wrinkled things too skinny to bloat except for their bellies. The younger women and the children were in the middle in a tangled mass, most of the youngest ones locked forever in the arms of mothers or older sisters.

Ed estimated that there were about sixty altogether, and he noticed that only a few were military-aged men.

Not far away, Mike Robbins found four teenaged girls. They were nude, lying on their backs, each shot once in the forehead.

There was a chorus of mumbled curses for a time, then all the soldiers fell silent. Ed turned around and looked at each of them, standing there stunned and stoop-shouldered. Some were shaking their heads, a few weeping silently. Ed noticed that Tom Henderson was doing both.

"Look for expended cartridges," Ed ordered in a low voice, for he had seen none lying around. "Or any other signs of who did this." The men gladly turned their backs on the carnage and did so.

Ed could not take his eyes from the children nor his mind from his wife and baby son for several minutes, and his jaw was clenched so tightly that it made his teeth ache. Finally, he turned to Tom Henderson and said, "Check to see if any of 'em are still alive."

Tom nodded, wiped his eyes, and moved toward the children as Mike Robbins walked up to his company commander. He held out his hand to Ed. In the palm were three expended M-16 cartridges. Ed glanced at them, then at Mike's face.

"And there's jungle boot prints down by the river. Not many, because they tried to obscure them. But they're there."

Ed nodded and took the cartridges. "Show me."

Mike led him to the riverbank and pointed at the footprints he had found. Ed Walker put his size eleven boot next to one of them. It was at least as large as his own, and the faint hope that all of the footprints would be the smaller footprints of Vietnamese, vanished.

"That's it, then," he mumbled. He walked back to where Henderson was checking the last of the bodies for any signs of life. There were none, and Tom looked up at him and shook his head.

"They'll pay for this," Walker said to no one in particular. "God *damn* it, the sons of bitches will pay."

He turned to Joe Guitteriz, his radio operator, and growled, "Get battalion! I want to talk to the colonel."

While he was waiting, he said to Tom, "You still want to be an officer, Henderson? Some so-called officer is probably responsible for this, you know."

Henderson surveyed the bodies again for a time, then looked at Ed and nodded. "Yes, sir. I do. More than ever, I do."

"Good," Ed said. "Find a camera. Take pictures, lots of pictures. Then bring me the film."

Guitteriz handed him the radio handset. "The colonel, sir."

Ed explained to Lieutenant Colonel Chapman, the battalion commander, what his company had found. Chapman got the details and ordered Ed to have his company secure the site until he could report it up the chain of command and get someone to investigate. He didn't question Ed Walker's judgement about what had occurred in the devastated village, nor which side was responsible for it.

First Sergeant Fraley came up. "Want me to organize a burial detail, sir?"

"No, top. No, what I want you to do is bring every squad in the company by here. Every man. Bring them by here and tell them that this is what can happen when hate overcomes a sense of duty. This is what can happen when leaders - squad leaders, platoon leaders, company commanders; *any* leaders - this is what can happen when they forget they're Americans, and what that means."

He paused and looked back at the twisted bodies, then at Fraley again. "And tell them that if any leader they have ever orders something like this, allows something like this to happen, tell them to kill the son of a bitch. Kill him, and cut his fucking heart out, and burn it. Tell them *that*."

He turned and walked away, kicking at the dirt and cursing under his breath, and the others left him alone.

Guitteriz, Ed's radio operator, found him a short time later sitting on the bank of the narrow, muddy river. "Battalion called, sir. They're sending the new brigade XO out to do an investigation. An article thirty-three, or something."

"Article thirty-two. A formal investigation. Good."

Guitteriz lit two cigarettes and handed one of them to Ed.

"Thanks, Joe. Have a seat."

Guitteriz dropped his heavy load, sat down beside his company commander, and leaned back against his rucksack.

"What the hell would cause somebody to do that, Joe? To let it happen? Americans, I mean."

Joe took a deep drag and exhaled, and a long drink of water from his canteen before he answered. "Racism."

"Racism?"

"Yes, sir. You see, everybody - every race - either thinks they're superior to everybody else, like most of you Anglos do, or they feel like they're inferior. Tell a man long enough that he's inferior, and treat him like shit, and after awhile he begins to feel that way. Or he realizes it's a bunch of crap, and he rebels. That's what a lot of the brothers are doing now. Anyway, if a man feels inferior, he looks for somebody inferior to him."

He took another drag from his cigarette, flicked it into the river, then locked his hands behind his head and exhaled.

"Yeah," Guitteriz continued, "and that's where the Vietnamese come in. Everybody thinks they're inferior. But that's just because they don't have shit. And because they're the race we're here to kill. So there it is. Some people kill them because they feel superior to them, and that's the best way to prove it. Some guys waste them just because they can't tell one from the other. And some of them, like they probably did here, kill them just because it's easy to do, and they can get away with it."

He looked at his company commander, who was contemplating his explanation with a furrowed brow. "But none of those fit you, captain. So, why is it *you* kill 'em?"

Ed took a drag and exhaled. "Because they're communists, Joe. Communist soldiers."

He heaved himself up onto his feet, took another drag, and tossed the cigarette into the water. "And because I thought *they* were the ones who were the murderers. Not us."

Joe got up and swung the heavy rucksack onto his shoulders, then reached over and put his hand on Ed's arm. "They still are, sir. Most of the time it's them, not us."

They could hear a helicopter in the distance, headed their way. The investigating officer, they assumed.

"That's not good enough, Joe," Ed replied as he moved toward the field they would use as a landing zone. "*Most* of the time won't cut it."

TWENTY

The new brigade executive officer sent to investigate the massacre under the provisions of Article 32 of the Uniform Code of Military Justice was none other than Major Chuck Black. When Ed saw him step off the helicopter in pressed jungle fatigues and spit-shined boots, he spat on the ground, then walked briskly forward and threw Black a half-hearted salute.

Black's eyes narrowed, his return salute crisp and quick. Then his face cracked in a toothy, exaggerated smile.

"Well, well. Walker. We meet again. So you've given up your little green beanie for the *real* Army, eh?"

Ed's eyes locked on Black's. "Special Forces soldiers sweat and bleed and die just like the rest of the Army, sir. And they don't slaughter civilians like somebody in the *real* Army did here."

Major Black's chin raised slowly until he was looking down his sharply-chiseled nose at Walker. "You would be well advised to withhold such opinions until the completion of this investigation, Captain. And until you've been advised of your rights under the provisions of Article 31 of the UCMJ."

Ed nodded and said evenly, "Oh, I know my rights, Major."

"Perhaps. But as investigating officer of the alleged events that took place here, I will advise you when your testimony - fact, not opinion - is required. *After* you've been sworn in, I might add."

"I see. Well then, would you like to see the alleged bodies before or after you swear me in, sir?"

Black shot him an icy glance but made no reply. He turned toward his legal assistant, a pot-bellied specialist five in a sweat-soaked uniform. He gestured to the man, who came to where Black and Walker were standing. Black pointed to some of Henderson's men who were sitting on their rucksacks watching the officers. "Have those men put up some ponchos for shade for us, Specialist Grisham," he said. "And tell them to find us something to sit on."

"Just a minute," Ed said to Grisham. "Tell my first sergeant what you need. He'll handle it. We use the chain-of-command in this company."

Grisham looked at Major Black as if to ask which officer's instructions he should follow.

Black flashed his phony smile and said, "Go through the first sergeant, then. And tell him to make it snappy."

"Yes, sir."

Ed stifled a laugh at what the response would be if a spec-five told his crusty first sergeant to "make it snappy." Tom Henderson walked up. He nodded at Black and handed a roll of film out to Ed.

"Don't you salute field grade officers in this company, sergeant?" the major asked Henderson.

Ed pocketed the film and put his hand on Henderson's wrist to preclude him from saluting. "I don't require my men to salute on combat operations," he said to Black.

"Oh?"

"No, sir. It makes it too easy for snipers to identify the officers."

Black threw back his head and laughed snidely. "Yes. Very well, then." He looked down his nose at Ed's pocket. "Is that film of the alleged incident site?"

"Yes, sir," Henderson said, and Ed added, "And the alleged bodies of the women and children who were slaughtered."

Major Black's eyes narrowed to dark slits and he held out his hand. "Then let me have it, please. I'll need it for my investigation."

Ed took the canister of film from his pocket and handed it to the investigating officer. Then he took out the expended M-16 cartridges Mike Robbins had given him and said, "I suppose you'll want these, too, then."

The major looked at them and his eyebrows raised slightly.

"Evidence?"

"Yes, sir. I believe so."

Black frowned and shook his head. "You mean you found what you think is evidence of a crime, and you removed it from the scene?" He placed his hands on his hips, his thumbs hooked in his immaculately clean pistol belt. "You should know better than that, captain."

He called over his shoulder to his assistant, "Grisham! Bring me an evidence bag." Then he looked at Ed and shook his head once more. "You realize, of course, that you've obscured any fingerprints that might have been used for identification."

Damn, Ed thought. Black was right. You didn't expect to encounter a crime scene on a combat operation, but he was right about the fact that the fingerprints of the men who had handled the cartridges might help to determine who had committed the massacre.

"I didn't think about that, sir," he said, dropping the cartridges into a plastic bag that Grisham held open for him.

Black frowned at him a moment, then flashed his irritating artificial smile. "No, you didn't. Think, Walker. *Think!* Now, please raise your right hand and repeat after me."

Ed slowly raised his hand and the major swore him to the fact that the evidence he was about to give in this matter was the truth.

While Henderson's men constructed a poncho shelter and fashioned a makeshift desk from the remains of the village, Major Black began his interrogation of Captain Walker. Specialist Grisham held a small tape recorder near the men's mouths as they spoke.

When Ed had summarized what the company had discovered at the site of the village, Black said, "I must remind you that what you say at any time during the course of this investigation will be under oath. Now, let's look at these bodies you've described." He turned to Grisham. "Bring the camera with you."

Ed led them to the tangle of bodies, and when he saw them again - the women and children and the frail old men - the anger and sorrow that gripped his heart were so strong that tears fell from his sad, green eyes. He wiped them away and looked at Black, who was studying the corpses. The major's face was cold and without expression. It showed no emotion, no surprise, no revulsion or disgust. Grisham moved among the dead taking photographs.

Black turned toward Ed and watched him wipe his cheeks, and he shook his head almost imperceptibly. Too emotional, the major thought. He was a good man in battle, they said, at least at company level. But too emotional. And all of his loyalty seemed to go down, not up. Otherwise, he wouldn't be stirring up trouble like this for the brigade and the division. Or at least trying to.

But I know what to do, Black thought. That's the reason they made me the investigating officer. I'm sure of it.

"The ones who were raped before they were killed are over here," Ed said, walking toward the bodies of the four young women.

Black's eyebrows arched slightly and he followed Ed to where the corpses lay.

Mike Robbins had ordered his men to cover the bodies with ponchos. He was sitting on his rucksack at the riverbank, and he stood when Major Black and Captain Walker approached.

"Were these bodies covered like this when you found them?" Black asked Ed.

"I covered them," Mike Robbins said.

Black peered down his nose at the lieutenant. "And did you *otherwise* disturb them?"

"Yes," Mike said. "I tried to straighten their legs and fold their arms over their breasts. But I didn't do a very good job of it. They were already too stiff."

The major stared at him through narrow slits, then looked at Ed and flashed the fake smile. "More evidence disturbed? Have your men remove the ponchos so that Specialist Grisham can photograph the bodies. And have your medic take vaginal swabs."

Ed's brow furrowed. "Vaginal swabs? What do you mean?"

"Exactly that. For evidence of semen in the event they were, as you assert, raped."

"It was pretty damned *obvious*, major," Mike interjected. "Is that really necessary?"

Black shot a cold glance at him, then asked Ed, "Is your platoon leader a trained pathologist, Captain Walker?"

"Of course not. And my medic's not a gynecologist, either. Get the battalion surgeon out here if you want vaginal swabs, major."

"Or better yet," Mike offered, "get a pathologist from graves registration. Someone who can tell how long the villagers have been dead. Then all you'll have to do is go to division G-3, find out which unit was operating here at the time and bingo, you'll know which murdering bastards are responsible for this."

Black's face was expressionless for a time, then the smile appeared. "Yes, well, unfortunately, lieutenant, I don't have access to the tactical operations centers of North Vietnamese regiments. Or are you, like your company commander, already prepared to accuse one of your sister units? On the barest of circumstantial evidence."

Mike wiped beneath his nose with his forefinger and said, "Yeah, maybe I am. Based on what I've seen here, my guess is that an American unit did this. But you're right; it's only a guess, so far."

"Quite right," Black replied through the phony smile. "Now, Captain Walker, I'd like to examine the weapons of your men."

Ed gave him a quizzical look. "Sir?"

"Your men's weapons. I'd like to examine them. As I understand it, you haven't made contact with the enemy since you departed your battalion firebase. Is that not correct?"

"Contact? No, but..." Black's implication suddenly dawned on him; if they hadn't been in a firefight since departing Firebase Caballo, and their weapons had been fired, then it might be assumed that they had taken part in the carnage at the village.

The thought that Black would even consider such a thing caused anger to surge through Ed Walker. His hands balled into tight fists and he said, "Exactly what are you implying, major?"

The fake smile appeared momentarily, then melted into an icy mask. "I'm not implying anything, captain; merely gathering facts. And so far, your company is the only unit I am able to place at the scene of this incident. And since you claim you've had no contact, if your men's weapons show evidence of having been fired..."

Mike took a step toward the major. "Why, you God da..."

"Mike!" Ed admonished, cutting off his platoon leader's curse. "Go check the perimeter. Move out!"

Robbins was glaring at Black, his hand tightly clutching his M-16 rifle. Without taking his eyes from the major's frigid face, he muttered, "Yes, sir, captain," and moved away.

Ed Walker watched him go, then turned back to face Black. His hands were shaking with adrenaline-fired anger but he controlled his voice and said evenly, "Major Black, if you want to inspect my men's weapons, go ahead. But I can tell you exactly what you'll find. You'll find that every God damned one of them's been fired."

Black's eyebrows arched and he said, "Oh?"

"Yes. They'd *better* have been. Because I require every weapon in my company to be test-fired before we move out on combat operations. So there's no need for you to waste your time or theirs inspecting them. Now, if we could get on with obtaining statements from those of us who discovered and reported this massacre, I'd appreciate it. We have a combat operation to conduct, and I'd like to get on with it."

For a long time, the major stood stock-still and said nothing. His eyes did not even blink, Ed noticed. Then the irritating smile appeared for a moment and he said, "Very well, captain. I'll start with Lieutenant Robbins. Have him report to me immediately."

He looked Ed up and down, then pivoted and walked off.

*   *   *

"But sir, it's wrong! Damn it, it's dead wrong and we both know it."

Ed Walker's battalion commander, Lieutenant Colonel Chapman, took the thick report from him and dropped it into his out box. He wiped his face with his hands, sighed, and pushed himself up from his chair.

"Of course it's wrong. But the brigade commander doesn't want to hear it, Ed. He says that Major Black's investigation was thorough, and his conclusions valid, and that we should get on with killing the enemy."

Walker shook his head, shoved his hands into the back pockets of his jungle fatigues and kicked at the dirt floor of the tent.

Black had done it. He had so managed to manipulate the facts and shade his conclusions that the truth would never be known, not now that the bodies were buried. He had even managed to convince the G-3 Air to put an airstrike in the area of the massacre the night after the investigation. "To punish the NVA who murdered the villagers in the event that they're still bivouacked nearby," Black had said, Ed learned from a friend in the air operations section.

One of the companies from another battalion had been in the area the day before Ed and his men discovered the carnage. Major Black had pointed that out in his report. But according to the sworn testimony of the officers he had interviewed from that company, they had not committed, nor had they knowledge of, any massacre. They had received fire from enemy troops in the village, returned fire, then pursued the enemy across the river, leaving one platoon behind to sweep through the village. Unable to reestablish contact with the NVA after the river crossing, they had called the other platoon forward and continued the mission to the west. The only member of the platoon that had been in the village that Black had bothered to interview, Ed noticed from the report, was the platoon leader.

Black's conclusion was that the North Vietnamese or Viet Cong had returned to the village and committed the atrocity "...probably as retribution for not warning them of the Americans' approach, which is common *modus operandi* of the communist forces."

He further concluded that the NVA apparently had, for purposes of propaganda, collected their spent ammunition and obscured their footprints in an attempt to make it appear as if an American unit had perpetrated the murders. He went on to say that, "unfortunately, the occupation of the village by Company B, 2nd Battalion, 5th Cavalry, and the subsequent disturbance of certain physical evidence by Captain Walker, Lieutenant Robbins, and others prior to the arrival of the investigating officer makes it impossible to fully verify this conclusion."

And that was that. No criminal charges were filed against any member of the United States Army, Vietnam.

Someone had gotten away with murder.

"I spoke to the division commander," Chapman said.

Ed looked up at him. "And?"

"He said that he respects your effort to do what you thought was right."

Ed nodded. "But?" he said, then waited for Chapman to complete the sentence.

Chapman shrugged his shoulders and sighed. "But he says that he has to accept Major Black's report."

Ed shook his head slowly. "They really don't want to know, do they, sir? The truth, I mean."

"'Truth is the first casualty of war,' as they say," the battalion commander replied softly.

"So I've heard."

"Well, we'd better get the operations officer in here, Ed. We've got an airmobile assault to plan," Chapman said, flopping into his chair.

"Yes, sir," Walker replied, throwing a salute and turning away. He started out of the tent, then stopped and turned back to his battalion commander. "Sir?"

"Yes?"

"Do you think I did the right thing?"

Chapman rose, walked over to Ed, and placed his hand on the captain's shoulder. "Of course you did. You're a fine officer, Ed. I know that. And your officers and men do, too. A lot of them have told me so."

Ed searched Chapman's eyes for sincerity, and found it. He nodded and said, "I guess that's all that matters then."

"No, it's not *all* that matters. But it matters a lot."

"I hope you're right. Thank you, Colonel Chapman. I'll go find the S-3, now. We've got a war to fight."

      *   *   *

It was an instant after the explosion - Ed thought it was a B-40 rocket that landed between them - that he first realized the kid was there. He looked strangely comical at first, a puff of filthy gray smoke surrounding his mud-splattered face, which bore a look of utter surprise, like a fall guy for some comedian, whose cigar had just exploded and who had been hit in the face with a chocolate meringue pie at the same time.

But then the smoke drifted away and the kid's lower lip quivered. He blinked and a droplet of something fell from his eyelid onto his cheek and slid down alongside his nose. He looked incredibly young, Ed thought. Twelve years old; or, at the most, fifteen.

The boy soldier wiped his cheek and looked in amazement at his hand, testing the texture of the goo between his finger and thumb. As he did, Ed realized suddenly what it was; it was the blood and brains of Joe Guitteriz, his radio operator.

Ed looked down and saw Guitteriz's left arm twitch twice as a last, fleeting signal that the soldier had once been alive. His face was half gone, the one remaining eye wide open in horror, as if he had seen the rocket just before it blew his brains out.

Ed's mind somehow filtered out the depravity of the sight. God, or something, had by now given him the ability to instantly reject such ungodly sights as being other-than-real, as if a circuit breaker tripped in his brain and caused such images to bypass his soul and prevent it from short-circuiting; from going up in smoke.

He reached to Guitteriz's face and closed the eyelid over the terrified eye, and brushed what was left of his radio operator's cheek with the back of his hand, feeling the short stubble of his thin beard.

"Good-bye, Joe," he mumbled, meaning it as sincerely as if the boy were going home to finish out his life in a normal fashion.

By the time Ed Walker thought of him again, it would be as he had seen him several nights before, back at the battalion firebase, laughing and sipping on a beer and talking about the girls who would be his conquests when he got back to Texas.

The kid on the other side of Joe leaned forward and retched twice, but nothing came up. Then he looked up at Ed Walker with a look that had turned from the one of innocent trust he had given Ed when he had climbed off the helicopter with the other replacements, to a look of naked hate. Yet he still looked incredibly young.

"Are you hit?" Ed asked in a voice so low and calm that he surprised himself.

"No, sir," the kid replied with equal calm.

"We're lucky," Ed muttered. He saw tears well up in the kid's eyes, and the look of hate melted into one of bewilderment.

Ed Walker found himself staring at the kid, unconscious of the incoming rifle fire cracking past nearby, his mind ignoring its duty to spur him into action. He watched the boy lean over his rifle and begin firing methodically into the tree line from which the enemy fire was coming. His teeth were clenched, and he gripped his weapon so tightly that his knuckles whitened. There was still a droplet of Guitteriz's blood and brain on his nose, and each time he fired, the rifle's recoil caused it to slide a little farther down his nose until it finally fell off the end. Only then did the circuit in Ed's mind trip and jolt him back to the reality of the firefight.

He picked up the radio handset to call his platoon leaders, but the radio was dead. As Ed threw it down in disgust, Lieutenant Robbins dived into the dirt beside his company commander, his radio operator right behind him. One glance at Guitteriz told Mike why he'd been unable to contact Captain Walker on the radio.

"Oh, Christ!" he said. "Are you hit, too, sir?"

"No, Mike. I'm all right," he answered with detachment as he watched the kid load another magazine, release the bolt, and resume firing. "Give me the handset," he said to Mike.

His ears were ringing loudly, and he wondered how he'd been able to hear the kid and Lieutenant Robbins so clearly. He checked with Lieutenant Wentzel about Second Platoon's situation. They had two slightly wounded. No sweat.

Sergeant Yost's Third Platoon was about 150 meters to the rear of Ed's position, so he told Yost to maneuver left and try to get on the enemy's flank. He gave Robbins the handset back and told him to place mortar fire into the tree line until Yost called him off.

It was at times like this that Guitteriz had always lit two cigarettes and handed one to his company commander. Ed reached over and unbuttoned the dead radio operator's bloody breast pocket and pulled out a half-empty pack of Lucky Strikes. He took two of them out, placing them side-by-side in his mouth. As he searched Guitteriz's pockets for his cigarette lighter, he noticed the kid staring at him in open-mouthed disbelief.

Ed found the lighter and, without taking his eyes from the kid's, he lit both cigarettes, then took one and held it toward the boy.

The young soldier narrowed his eyes in disgust, turned back to his weapon, and resumed firing into the tree line.

"Hey, kid" Ed called. The soldier ignored him.

"Hey, kid!" he called again, and backhanded the boy on the shoulder. The youngster ceased firing and slowly turned his head and fixed his eyes on the company commander's.

Ed Walker wanted to say, What the hell's with you, kid? You want instant credibility, don't you? Well, I can't give you that. You've got to trust me, to believe that I wouldn't be here crawling in the mud with you, flinching at the same explosions, ducking the same bullets, if I didn't have reasons that are very important to me - as important as your reasons are to you. I don't like this part of it any more than you do - the killing and the dying and the fear. But I'm not going to let it warp me, drive me insane, destroy me.

That was what Ed Walker thought, but it wasn't what he said. "Guitteriz and I have been together a long time," he said. "I've always bought the smokes, and he's always carried them."

The kid studied him for a moment, then stretched his hand toward the captain, the index and middle fingers forming a narrow 'V'.

Ed placed the cigarette there, and the kid took it, stuck it between his lips, and went back to firing his rifle.

"Battalion, sir," Robbins's radio operator called, as he held the handset out to Ed. He took it, but before he answered the call, he thought, Please, God, spare this kid. Don't let him lose his disgust for all of this.

And then he got back to the business of war.

*　　　　　*　　　　　*

Two days after Joe Guitteriz died, Captain Ed Walker wrote the dead soldier's mother a letter of condolence, and then he accepted his battalion commander's offer of a night of R & R in Saigon. Mike Robbins went with him.

"Come on, *Dai Uy*," Mike said late that night. "We have to get back."

His company commander shook his head from side to side and said, "No way, ol' fella. I'll land in hell, there ain't... Hey!" He grabbed the leg of a passing bar girl and said, "Bring us two more of them rot-gut Ba Muoi Ba's, darlin'. You *biet*? *Hai Ba Muoi Ba, co dep.*"

Mike looked at him and shook his head in disgust. Ed had been talking in that strange waterman's accent and rudimentary Vietnamese since he got drunk. That had been several beers and an hour or so earlier.

"You buy me one Saigon tea, *Dai Uy*?" the bar girl asked Ed.

"No, we're leaving," Mike said to her but she ignored him and Ed said, "Why, hell, yes, darlin'! I'll go to Hampton if I won't buy you a hip boot full of Saigon-fuckin'-teas!"

The Vietnamese teenager smiled and went to get two beers and a so-called Saigon tea - the watery drink the prostitutes sold to GIs, charging them whatever exorbitant price they thought they could get away with. For that, the soldier got a quick feel-up and a few minutes of meaningless conversation in pidgin English.

"Sir, we need to get going," Robbins insisted.

"Aw, sit down, Bubba," Ed said, holding his watch up and trying to see the time. He couldn't focus on it, but he said, "It's early yet. We got all night."

"We have to catch a chopper back to the fire base first thing in the morning, sir. Anyway, it's almost curfew. The MPs will be in here soon."

Ed reached up and took his platoon leader's wrist, and said, "Aw, hell, Mike. Awright. Jus' sit down, then. We'll go after this one. I promise."

Mike pulled his arm away and slumped down in the seat of the booth across from his captain.

The girl brought two bottles of Bier 33 - *Ba Muoi Ba*, in Vietnamese - and a shot glass of Saigon tea, and said, "Seben hunded fipty pee, *Dai Uy*."

Ed pulled his wallet from the front pocket of his jungle fatigues to get some Vietnamese piasters. All he had was military payment certificates, though, so he took out a ten dollar certificate and held it out to her. She took it, but when he pulled his hand back, it hit the shot glass, spilling the contents onto the table. "I'll land in hell..." he mumbled.

The girl looked at him and shook her head, shoving the ten dollar certificate down the front of her low-cut mini-dress, "You drunk, *Dai Uy*. I no can sit down now."

Ed grinned at her and squeaked, "'I no can sit down now,'" then waved her away, saying, "Don' worry 'bout it, darlin'. Go buy your mama a new water buffalo or somethin'."

He gave the frowning Mike Robbins an exaggerated wink, then picked up one of the bottles of beer and took a long drink. He was still holding the wallet in his hands, and he looked at it a moment, then pulled out the plastic photo holder. He held it out toward Robbins and pointed to the photograph of Mary in her bikini aboard their sailboat. "See this, *Thieu Uy*? I ever tell you about it?"

Robbins glanced at it and said, "Yes, sir. You've shown it to me before. Your wife on the sailboat you got for a wedding present."

Ed nodded, studying the picture, trying to focus the image in his drunken brain. He couldn't, but it didn't matter. He had long ago memorized every detail of it; the long legs, the way the hair was blown to one side by the wind, the tanned globes of flesh above the little bikini top. And the smudge of blood in the corner of the picture. He held it out to Mike again and mumbled, "Blood."

"What?"

"I said, 'Blood!' It was on there when Sam gave it back to me."

Mike nodded. "You told me."

Ed looked at the other side of the plastic holder, at the photo of his son Jimmy. He couldn't focus on it either. And he couldn't draw the image out of his memory to remember what the boy looked like. He sat back and squeezed his eyes tightly shut, trying to remember. But he couldn't, so he opened his eyes wide and looked at it. It wouldn't come into focus, and he couldn't remember.

He picked up the bottle of beer and drank another long swallow, then set the photos on the table to light a cigarette. After he took a drag, he picked up the photo of his son, again looking wide-eyed at it. He still couldn't see, still couldn't remember. He looked at Robbins, who was yawning and checking the time on his watch, then he looked back at the photo. He shook his head and turned it over, rubbing the corner where he knew the blood was. "Ol' Sam," he mumbled, and Mike saw Ed's bleary eyes cloud up, then saw him turn the photograph over again, his forehead wrinkled.

And then he saw Ed lean forward and bury his head in his arms. At first he thought the captain was passing out, but then he saw his shoulders shaking as Ed Walker began to sob.

Mike got up and walked around the table and put his arm around Ed's shoulder. "It's all right, sir. It'll be all right. You've just had too much to drink, that's all. Come on, we'll get back to the transient barracks and get some rest."

As they waited at the LZ to fly back to the battalion fire base early the next morning, Ed squinted at Mike Robbins through bleary eyes and said, "I, uh... I'm sorry about that little display, last night, Mike."

Robbins looked at him without smiling. He was worried. Ever since they happened upon the massacre, Walker had not been the same. And the death of Joe Guitteriz, his radio operator, had left him sullen, moody, too ready to lash out at the troops for any little mistake. And that sort of attitude was infectious, dangerous.

This wasn't the same Captain Walker whom Mike Robbins had first met right here, on this same landing pad. And he was worried about him. But he forced a smile and elbowed his commander and friend and said, "Don't worry about it, sir. Don't mean nothin'."

TWENTY ONE

It seemed to Ed Walker to happen in slow motion - *Deja vu* in slow motion, he thought when the point platoon came under fire from the tree line across the rice paddies to their front.

Lieutenant Wentzel threw himself to the ground beside his company commander as his troops began to return the fire.

"Get the mortars on the tree line," Ed directed. He was the only one standing now, looking into the trees in an attempt to fix the exact locations of the enemy soldiers. As usual, you just couldn't tell. He dropped down beside Wentzel, listening to him give the mortar section its fire mission.

When he heard Wentzel repeat, "Shot, out," he got to his knees to watch for the first round to impact, so that he could adjust the fire. As he peered at the trees, he saw one of the enemy soldiers pitch forward out of the shadows, no doubt struck by a bullet from one of Ed's men. A moment later, another communist soldier appeared, reaching for the first man in an apparent attempt to grab him and pull him back into the trees. Ed snapped his rifle to his shoulder, placed the sights on the man's chest, and with a sinking feeling in his heart, squeezed the trigger. He felt the recoil and the slap of sound as his weapon fired, and watched the second man jerk, then fall lifelessly forward.

There was a sudden flash of white light. Ed's head felt as if someone had yanked it backward by the hair, and his face felt numb; surrealistically large, and completely numb.

An iron fragment had torn through the bridge of Ed Walker's nose, ripping out a hunk of cartilage, then slicing across his eyelid and lodging in the bone beneath his eyebrow. A smaller shard ripped through his bottom lip, shattering two teeth and tearing a hole the size of a nickel from his left cheek.

For a moment, he sat there dumbly, unable to comprehend what had happened. Something, or someone, fell against him, bumping him back to reality. Blurred though his vision was, he could see that it was Lieutenant Wentzel. Wentzel, who a moment before had been on the radio to the company mortars, calling fire on the enemy positions.

That's what it was, a mortar. A mortar round had exploded almost on top of them. Their own, or the enemy's?

He could see an ugly hole above Wentzel's ear. He could feel the body tremble against his own, and he could see that the platoon leader's eyes were already rolling back in their sockets.

Dead, Ed Walker thought, not certain whether or not he'd actually said the word. He's dead. He called the round right on top of us.

His eyes burned with a searing pain, and he could feel blood running down the back of his throat. He suddenly wondered if he was going to die, too. Die, like Sam and Newton and Guitteriz, and now Wentzel. And all the others - little boys playing a stupid, deadly game of cowboys and Indians. Cops and robbers.

He could hear someone moaning loudly beyond Wentzel, and looked in that direction, trying to see with blurred vision who it was. It was the platoon radio operator, writhing in the mud and holding his gut.

Ed thought, I've got to help him. He started to climb across the dead platoon leader's body, but something smacked hard into his shoulder and knocked him on his back. He heard Mike Robbins's voice, he thought, and he tried to say, Get them, Mike! but then he felt as if he were spinning through space, and Mike's voice turned to that of a woman. He tried to open his eyes, but the light was too bright, and he couldn't tell whose voice it was. She was speaking softly but urgently to someone.

"Mary?" he tried to ask, but could not. And then there was nothing.

*   *   *

Mary opened the door, and when she saw the expression on Evelyn's face, she thought, *Oh, God. Not again.*

"Hello, Mary. How are you?" Evelyn said, and then Sookie jumped from around the corner of the porch and said, "Boo! Did I scare you, Aunt Mary? Where's Jimby?"

Evelyn smiled broadly, and Mary thought, No, she must not know. Thank God. "Gosh, Sookie! You scared me silly!" she said, throwing her hands to her cheeks and looking as surprised as she could. "Jimby is right in here, playing. Come on in and see him."

Evelyn laughed and said, "Have we caught you at a bad time, Mary?"

"No, not at all. I'm glad to see you. I just finished feeding Jimmy, and was about to put on a pot of coffee."

Sookie ran off to play with her cousin, and Evelyn followed Mary into the kitchen.

"What do you hear from Edward, Mary?"

Mary smiled at the fact that Evelyn called Ed by his full name, just like a Guinea gal would, then said, "I haven't had a letter in weeks, Ev. Have you?"

"No. It seems like months. I hope he's all right," Evelyn said.

"I wouldn't worry. If anything happened to him, they'd let me know. They're very efficient about that sort of thing, you know,"

Evelyn watched her fix the coffee and said, "Yes, I suppose so. James is worried, though. He says it's the medals; that they get one, and it makes them want to get a higher one."

"Humph," Mary snorted. "He's got just about all the damned ones they have." She knew it sounded frivolous, so she said, "I'm sure he wouldn't do something stupid to try to get a medal. He didn't even wear them when he was home. Not even to Sam's funeral, or when he left to go back over there."

"Well, I hope you're right," Evelyn said, then she shook her head. "Do you think it'll be over soon, Mary?"

Mary finished with the coffee pot and turned to face her sister-in-law. "With Richard Nixon in the White House? No, not until he's used them all up. Or until we throw him out on his fascist ass."

Evelyn didn't even raise an eyebrow at the comment. She was used to it, and not only from Mary. It seemed that almost everybody was talking that way now, including James. Just the night before, he had jumped up and turned the TV off when it showed its nightly footage of the slaughter in Vietnam, and mumbled, "Enough is enough. Bring 'em home." Still, she wondered if it was really right for Mary to be going off to these protests, with Ed still being over there. No doubt he knew, and that's why he wasn't writing.

She sighed heavily, and Mary looked at her and said, "What is it?"

"Oh, I don't know. It must be very difficult for you, that's all."

"He'll be back soon. They all will, if I have anything to do with it," Mary said.

"Well, that's sort of what I mean; that it must be a pretty tough choice, deciding whether to go to those protests, or to support your husband."

Mary Walker looked at her sister-in-law and shook her head. "No, it's not. It's no choice at all. It's the same thing. Don't you see that?"

Later, when Evelyn and Sookie had gone, Mary sat sipping coffee and looking at her son. He was what mattered most, now. Every day, he brought her more and more joy. Every new sentence he put together, every new way of getting into mischief, every new discovery he made was hers, too. Hers and Jimmy's, alone, because there was no one else to share them with.

She seldom saw Jeff Riddell anymore - once every couple of weeks, or less. And their relationship had turned into a largely platonic one. She sighed at the foolish idea she'd entertained for a time, that she would divorce Ed and marry him. Because once the newness of their passion had worn off, she found that he was, sexually, much like Ed had become - distracted, and increasingly inhibited.

If she did love him, as she still claimed whenever he hinted that he wanted her to say it, it was because of the passion he showed for what he believed, not the passion he showed her in bed.

She walked over to her little boy, picked him up, and hugged him tightly to her, showering his pudgy face with kisses as he giggled. "Oh, I love you, little guy," she said. "And guess what? When you grow up, you're not going to be any soldier or priest or anything silly like that. No, sir. You're going to be a famous doctor."

*   *   *

Ed Walker stood on the beach in blue hospital pajamas, looking out across the South China Sea. A mile or so offshore, a rusting freighter headed slowly out to sea.

Two Phantom jets, flying low and slow, swooped in from the north, wingtip to wingtip, dark plumes of fuel smoke trailing some distance behind them.

The midday sun was hot on his head and shoulders. He could feel sweat breaking out on his forehead, even through the bandages that covered all of his face except his one good eye. His jaw ached with a dull throb and he ran his tongue lightly over the sutures where his teeth had been. He realized suddenly that he was very hungry, and wondered if he'd be able to chew with one side of his mouth when the doctors finally unwired his jaw. His shoulder ached, too, and he wished it were his left arm in the sling instead of the right. He was so useless with his left hand.

The hot breeze from offshore caused him to try to imagine himself sailing past aboard the *Mary Anne*, but he could not imagine that without thinking of Mary leaning back against the mast in her bikini, her willowy legs stretched out on the foredeck.

He didn't want to think of Mary, so he turned his thoughts to his troops, instead. He wondered if they had been lifted back to the battalion firebase yet, or if they were still out in the bush, perhaps in another firefight. He imagined Mike Robbins on the radio, calling for fire support as he led the company in an avenging assault against the communists. But then the memory of the exploding mortar round returned, and he could feel Wentzel fall against him, the last act the young platoon leader had performed in life.

He still hadn't written Wentzel's mother a letter yet - not that he would have been able to do so with his useless right arm, anyway.

Then he imagined a letter arriving from Mary, one full of tenderness and concern and love. But there hadn't been any letters of that sort - not in a very long time. They had turned from ones full of invective against the government and the war, to no letters at all. And that was worse. Much worse. Where did I lose you, Mary? he asked her in his mind. Where are you now, and where is our son?

First Lieutenant Susan Madison stood in the shade of the tin-roofed walkway that connected the low cinder block wards of the sprawling hospital. She saw Captain Walker standing on the beach, and started to call to him to get his attention. But she had been in the Red Cross lounge a short while earlier when he tried to get a telephone call through to his wife.

The ham radio operator - one of many in the States who, working with the Military Affiliated Radio System, or MARS, linked soldiers in Vietnam by radio and telephone to their families back home - had apparently gotten through to the number Walker had asked for. He had difficulty speaking through his clenched teeth, but she heard him say clearly enough, "Let it ring a few more times. She's probably asleep." Half a minute later, though, he said, "OK. Thanks for trying, anyway. Out."

Sue had seen him get slowly to his feet then, and walk over to the time zone map that was thumbtacked to the wall. With his left index finger, he counted the time zones from the east coast of the United States across the North American continent and the Pacific Ocean to Vietnam. "After midnight," she'd heard him mumble.

What does a guy think, Sue Madison wondered, when he calls halfway across the world to tell his wife that he's been wounded, and that he's coming home, and it's after midnight, but she's not there?

She had gotten used to the physical wounds people suffered in this wretched place - the gunshot wounds, the burned bodies and faces, even the missing limbs. She'd had to, or it would have overwhelmed her. But she couldn't get used to their wounded souls, whether it was a frightened young private who has seen his best friend blown to bits, or a guy who lay in his bed staring blankly at the ceiling after receiving no mail from home day after day. Or the young captain who calls his wife at midnight, and she isn't there.

Her father had warned her about wounds of the soul, yes. But he had been talking about her own soul. And because of that early warning and what he had taught her about duty and its price; about self-worth, and the satisfaction of doing the best you could, she had remained unscarred. But she just couldn't seem to get used to the wounded souls of others.

She walked down near the Infantry officer and stood behind him. "Captain Walker? Sir, you shouldn't be out in this heat."

Without turning around, he said something that, because of his wired-shut jaw and bandaged mouth, she was unable to understand. When she made no reply, he turned and surveyed her face with his unbandaged eye. "Have you ever put a note in a bottle and set it adrift?" he asked.

"No," she said.

"I did once, when I was eight or nine. Set it adrift on the York River. Found the damn thing myself a couple of weeks later, not half a mile from where I'd thrown it overboard. I was surprised when I found it didn't have an answer in it, just the same note I'd written."

"What did it say?" Sue asked with genuine curiosity as she took his arm and urged him gently away from the beach toward the ward.

"Hell, I don't remember. 'Hi, my name's Ed Walker. What's yours?' or something like that."

"Sue Madison," she said. "Pleased to meet you, Ed Walker."

It looked to her as if he was attempting to smile through the bandages around his mouth, and his one eye fixed hers and he replied, "I wish you'd found the friggin' note."

"Come on, Ed Walker," she said, smiling at him. "Let's get you out of this heat and back to the ward."

That night, before she went off duty, Sue went to see Ed to pass on some unpleasant news she'd gotten from another nurse. She found him sitting in the near-darkness on the bed of a young black soldier who had been told that day that he would never see again. Ed was holding the other man's head against his good shoulder and stroking the stubble of hair atop the blind youngster's head.

He looked up at Sue when she approached, and she could see rage in his unbandaged eye. "Fuckin' war," he muttered.

Sue sighed softly, took his hand from the soldier's head, and replaced it with her own. "He's asleep now," she said. "Come on. I'll buy you a Coke."

He followed her through the ward past the nurses' station, where she stopped long enough to tell the nurse who had just come on duty, "I'm taking old cyclops here over to get a Coke and ogle the donut dollies,"

He opened the door for her with his good arm, and as she brushed past, Ed thought he noticed a faint scent of perfume above the medicinal smell of his own bandages.

She was wearing men's jungle fatigues, and they were baggy on her. Her blond hair was rolled into a knot and pinned to the back of her head, and Ed wondered how long it would be if it weren't pinned up.

She was an attractive woman, this Lieutenant Madison. Kind of short - five foot three or four, he guessed - and perhaps a little heavy beneath those fatigues, although with their bagginess, he couldn't really tell. And she had a cute face - not strikingly beautiful like Mary's, but cute, with large blue eyes, a turned up nose, and cupid's bow lips.

She opened the door to the Red Cross lounge and held it for him. As he walked past her, he made a conscious effort to catch another whiff of her light perfume, and did so.

The lounge was almost empty, as it was late. The "donut dolly," as the Red Cross girls were affectionately known, was at her desk writing a letter, and didn't look up when Sue and Ed entered. A nurse in a surgical cap and gown was sitting on the pool table in the middle of the room, her hands on the shoulders of a young medic who stood facing her, his own hands on the nurse's knees. They glanced at Ed, then resumed their flirting.

"Let's sit here," Sue said, pointing to a settee facing the window that looked out onto the searchlight-bathed beach. "Coke?" she asked.

"Please. Need a straw," Ed replied. He sat down and adjusted the sling on his right arm, and a flash of pain shot through the gunshot wound he'd taken in the shoulder.

He watched the insects flitting around in the spotlight outside the window, then thought for a moment about having the Red Cross girl try again to get a call through to Mary. He had to let someone know he'd be coming home in a few days. He could call James and Evelyn, but that would be avoiding the real issue.

You're afraid, damn you, he thought. Afraid that Mary won't care, or worse, that she'll feel obligated to do so. He was more afraid of that, than of calling and not getting an answer again.

Why wasn't she at Broad Marsh, though? Evelyn had mentioned in her last letter that Mary's parents were going to Europe on vacation about now. But where was Mary?

Well, it's early morning there now, anyway, he thought. Too early to try calling again. Anyway, maybe it would be best to wait until he found out when he'd be arriving in the States, before he called anyone.

By the time Sue Madison returned with two cans of Coke and a straw for him to drink through, Ed had decided to wait until knew when he would be getting home. Hell, it might even be that they would change their minds and decide not to medevac him from Vietnam at all.

Sue handed him a can with a straw in it, and he mumbled, "Thanks." He raised it toward his mouth, but the gauze bandage had ridden up over his lower lip, so Sue reached over and slipped the bandage down, then guided the straw into the corner of his mouth opposite the wound, her fingers touching his lips as she did so. He sipped through the straw, studying her face.

It made her self-conscious, that single, deep green eye gazing at her from among the bandages. She reached into her waist pocket and pulled out a pack of cigarettes and a lighter. She held them out to him, but he shook his head and said, "Can't," his eye still fixed on hers.

She sat back, lit a cigarette, and inhaled deeply. She looked at it as she exhaled, and thought, I might as well tell him now, and get it over with.

"One of your men was asking about you tonight, before he died," she said, then looked at him.

He turned his face away for a moment, then looked back at her, the eye now barely visible behind his narrowed eyelid.

"Who?"

"Lieutenant Robbins."

He closed the eye and sat there for a moment, then got up and walked to the window. She followed him and stood next to him. She could hear him breathing deeply through his clenched teeth.

"I don't know what happened, Captain Walker. Dottie Fletcher, one of the OR nurses, said he was pretty badly shot up. She said he asked if you were here. She checked and told him, yes, you were. He said to tell you to tell Penny, I think it was - he said to tell her to marry a used car salesman next time. That's all he said, and then he died. I'm sorry."

Ed turned his face toward hers, his unbandaged eye darting angrily back and forth from one of her eyes to the other. "Used shoe salesman!" He spat the words, then turned and walked quickly past the couple still flirting at the pool table, and bumped the door open with his wounded shoulder. He ignored the pain and walked out toward the beach.

So now it's Mike Robbins. Robbins, Hagen, Guitteriz, Wentzel, Saxon, Newton and Christ only knows how many others, all too young to die, but all dead. Dead as - as the dirt they were buried in. Mangled and lifeless and rotting in the darkness under well-kept plots of grass, with nothing but a piece of cheap granite to show that what's down there was once a living, laughing young man. Oh, Jesus, why? What was it all for?

Well, to hell with it. To hell with this war and this Army. To hell with all of it. They'll never get me back out there to lead them to the slaughter again; to fill those kids full of God and motherhood, duty, honor, country, and all that meaningless bullshit that only leads, in the end, to a hail of bullets. And to death.

He stumbled in the sand and fell. Unable to break the fall, he struck the ground with his wounded shoulder, sending a shock of hot pain through him and showering sand into the bandages on his face.

He groaned with hurt, but struggled to his feet and spit the sand out of his wounded mouth. He cursed the sand, his wounds, the war, his God, and he stumbled on to the water's edge. He looked up at the blurred stars, and thought of Mike. The good officer, the good friend. He thought back to their long conversations about the war, about life, about the future - a future that had suddenly become meaningless.

It had all seemed so simple to Mike Robbins; the enemy was not difficult to define, as far as he was concerned. He was the armed soldier who fired at you in the jungle, or the one you ambushed on trails at night. The fact that the farmer you passed as he planted rice in the daytime might become that armed enemy at night - that fact never bothered Mike. He would wait until he met him in the jungle, and deal with him there. So simple to him. The communists were evil enslavers of free men who had to be stopped, he had said so often. Enemy sympathizers, whether Vietnamese or American, were only victims of propaganda; mistaken souls who would be brought to their senses once the enemy was defeated on the battlefield. And that was his job. His only duty. The rest of it - the complex political considerations, the civil affairs, the formulation of policy - that was all someone else's job, and he had refused to concern himself with it.

His only complaint was that some of his fellow officers and his troops, and especially his beloved Penny, didn't share that same commitment. He used to remark, "Maybe she'd be happier if she'd married a used shoe salesman."

Maybe she should have, Ed Walker thought. She'd sure as hell be better off today.

Lieutenant Madison was beside him on the beach now. "Come on, Captain," she said softly. "You can't bring him back. You've got to take care of yourself, now."

He turned toward her, and spoke angrily to her through his wired-up teeth. "Hell *no*, I can't bring him back! *Nobody* can bring him back. Does that mean it's right for him to be dead? He's just another God damned 'X' on your 'died of wounds' chart, isn't he? 'Pull out the needles and shove him in a body bag. Maybe we'll get it right with the next one!' Is that it?"

"Now, just a minute, Captain Walker!" she shot back, as disappointed in him as she was angry at his remarks. "It's *your* God damned war! It's guys like you who send us the business. And we do a pretty damned good job with the half-dead boys you send us. And if you're not satisfied with what we try to do, then go find some other combat arms hero to patch you up. We could use a day off around here, anyway!"

She turned and walked away then, as furious with herself for losing her temper as she was with him for being so insensitive. It had been a long, hard day, and she was exhausted, both physically and emotionally.

Ed hit her with a bitter parting shot as she stormed off. "Go fuck a used shoe salesman!"

By the time Ed stumbled back to his bed, the head nurse, a matronly major named Westcott, was waiting. He took her admonishment without comment as she supervised the cleaning and redressing of his wounds, a process that the nurse accomplished in a manner seemingly intended to give him as much pain as possible. It hurt terribly, so badly that he wanted to scream. But he didn't. He refused to flinch, refused to whimper, and he refused the painkiller that one of the younger nurses offered when the others had finally finished with him and left the ward.

For the next two days, except when he was taken to the operating room for the debridement of his wounds, and his occasional trips to the toilet, Ed lay sullenly in his bed. He tried to use pain to distract his mind from other things. But it didn't work.

Sue Madison had not reappeared on the ward before he learned that his evacuation to Walter Reed Army Medical Center in Washington, DC, would begin the next day. He had hoped she would, because he wanted to apologize to her, and thank her for what she'd done for him, and for all the other wounded soldiers.

He didn't bother trying to call Mary again. He decided to wait until he had gotten to the States.

That night, just before lights-out on his last night in Vietnam, Ed handed a note to one of the medics on duty. He had laboriously printed it with his left hand and addressed it to Lieutenant Sue Madison.

Dear Lt. Madison, the note said.

> *I just want to apologize for making an ass of myself and to thank you for the things you did for me, including letting me know about Mike Robbins.*

> *I have a great deal of respect for Army nurses - all soldiers do. I wouldn't like to think that a stupid remark from someone like me would cause you to think otherwise.*

> *I hope, for all our sakes, that it will soon be over, and you can go home knowing that, without your help, there would be a lot more of us going home in body bags instead of bandages.*

> *Thank you,*
> *Edward Walker*

Captain, Infantry

"She's gone, sir," the medic said when he saw who the note was addressed to.

"Gone?"

"Yes, sir," the medic replied. "Gone to Hawaii. R&R."

"Oh," Ed said. "Then, give it to her when she gets back, will you?"

For a time, Ed Walker lay awake thinking of the future, imagining how it would be. He was out of the war now. It was over. He had done his duty, and in a few days, he would be home - at least home in the broad sense of the word. The rumor among those scheduled to be evacuated was that they would stop in Hawaii so that those who did not fare well on the long flight across the Pacific could be hospitalized there, if necessary. He briefly entertained the thought of seeing Lieutenant Madison there, so that he could apologize to her in person, then dismissed it as improbable and turned his mind to the hope - the dream - that everything would be all right with Mary and him; that his physical wounds would somehow bring them together. Not out of pity; he didn't want that. But that it would bring them back together as a result of the realization that they had almost lost each other. Forever, as Mike and Penny had, and as Sam and Maria had.

It wasn't unreasonable to hope for that, he believed. Yes, because, if he had he been killed, as he so nearly had, wouldn't it have been a terrible, regrettable thing? Hadn't their love given them a son; Blood of our Blood and Flesh of our Flesh, making them forever a part of each other?

Yes, he thought before he fell into a restful sleep. It will be all right, once we're together again.

*   *   *

Vo Tu Trung was so frightened that he was trembling. It became so bad that the excused himself on the pretense of having to defecate and moved just out of sight in the bushes beyond the small perimeter that the eleven other North Vietnamese formed as they awaited darkness and the execution of their awesome mission.

Trung had not wanted to be a swimmer-sapper in the first place, for he was afraid of unknown waters. But he was a good swimmer, and smart, and small of stature. He had all the right attributes for the job, and he was told that being a swimmer-sapper was what the People needed him to do in their just struggle against American aggression. So that was what he had become.

There was incongruity in the coming mission, and that bothered him. He understood revenge, and he had heard of many cases of the Americans attacking North Vietnamese hospitals, bombing them to rubble while his helpless, ill and wounded countrymen died in their beds. But if it was so wrong for them to do so, how could it be right for his own sapper platoon to attack an American hospital? Wouldn't the Americans make a propaganda issue of it?

What was it Lieutenant Cam, the political officer, had said when someone in the platoon asked that question after the mission briefing? "It is right," Cam had said, "because we must make these dogs understand that they cannot build sanctuaries on our soil which are immune to their own tactics. My only regret is that we cannot be making the attack against a hospital in the heart of the United States."

That's easy for Cam to say, Trung thought: He isn't taking part in the attack.

"Trung," his friend Luan called softly. "Come on. We are going now."

An hour later, Trung entered the dark waters of Cam Ranh Bay wearing nothing but a pair of shorts and a small rucksack inside which was a tightly sealed plastic bag containing the satchel charges he would employ during the attack. His AK-47 assault rifle was strapped to the outside of his rucksack. A mile away, across the bay, the lights of the hospital and the other American installations south of it were plainly visible.

Once he was in the water and swimming slowly toward the target with his comrades, Trung's fear left him. Soon it would be over, and he would either be dead, or he would still be alive. Either way, he would have repaid a just debt for his countrymen.

It seemed to Edward Walker that he had just fallen asleep and was having a nightmare when he awoke to chaos. There had been an explosion. There was shooting, and it was not a bad dream, it was real. What the hell was happening? Had someone gone berserk? No, it was more than one person. Jesus, we're under attack! We're being attacked, right here in the hospital!

Suddenly he felt strong. Whole. He was being challenged, and all his training and instincts as a soldier and a leader took over. Amid the screams of panic around him, Ed jumped up from his bed and dived for cover under it to assess the chaotic situation around him.

The lights blinked off, then on again. He saw two pair of skinny legs, rubber sandals on their feet, as one sapper pulled the fuzes on two satchel charges and hurled them down the ward, while the other North Vietnamese sprayed the building with bursts of automatic rifle fire.

"Bastards!" Ed cried, and he scooted from under the bed and attacked. With nothing - no weapon, no hope of winning, with only his wounded body - he attacked, leaping up and running toward the enemy sappers.

He caught one of them in the small of the back with his knee as they neared the door, and the man collapsed to his knees. Ed kicked him in the face, and the sapper fell onto his back, and the Ed thought, Good! Now I can stomp him to death! And he began trying to do so.

But there was an explosion near him then, so close that he felt it more than hearing it. He saw a flash and felt a heavy slap, and went down. He didn't know that the explosion had broken his ankle, and that a fragment of debris had penetrated between his ribs and entered one of his lungs. He struggled to his feet and saw the other sapper, just a few feet away, raise his rifle. Ed lunged at the man, and felt the top of his skull smash into the enemy soldier's face.

Then he felt another slap, and the world turned dark.

TWENTY TWO

For days after the sapper attack on Cam Ranh hospital- the intermittent periods of pain-wracked semiconsciousness when Ed Walker's mind tried to function, it projected strange images; supernatural visions that seemed real, before they dissolved into confusion or dark emptiness.

During one of those episodes, he was above a modern hospital room, looking down at it. Sunlight poured into the room with such intensity that he had to squint to look at it. There was someone lying in the bed, so badly injured that he was covered in a mass of bandages, and filled with needles and tubes running to plastic bags hanging all around him, dripping and draining in no apparent order. He watched the scene for hours, it seemed, until the bright sunlight faded into a soft glow, then began to disappear. Just when it seemed that the darkness was becoming so thick that it was almost tangible, a heavy liquid that would smother the broken body on the bed, the door opened, and from it came white, warm light which burned the darkness away. Then, silhouetted in the bright light from the door, a familiar figure appeared - a soldier in battle dress, the dark figure's ammunition pouches and steel helmet and rifle clearly outlined by the bright light behind him. The soldier stood in the doorway for awhile, then approached the bed, and stood staring at the injured man, surveying the bottles and tubes and plastic bags. Then he reached out and took one of the tubes that hung between a suspended bottle of liquid and the broken, bandaged body, and yanked it away. The dark soldier went mad then, wildly knocking over bottle stands, ripping at the tubes, throwing plastic bags aside, snatching bandages and props and wires away from the bed and the man upon it until there was nothing left except a naked young man, his trunk and limbs sliced here and there with gunshot wounds and fragment holes.

Then the shadowy figure leaned over the bed and gently lifted the naked, wounded man from it. He placed him down, feet first, and made him stand. He began to coax the man toward the glare of the open door, and with each step, the injured man seemed to gain strength, and to become better able to walk on his own. Just before he reached the door, the intruder released him, and the wounded man stood there a moment, straightening up and surveying his wounded body. And then he limped unassisted through door and into the sunlight.

And then Ed saw that the wounded man was himself, and he turned and looked back into the darkening room, trying to see who it was who had come for him, but he couldn't tell. So he turned and walked away from the wrecked hospital room and into life.

It was at that moment that Ed's mind shook off its fear that he would die, and he awoke to full consciousness for the first time since the sapper attack.

Pain shot throughout him, and he realized that his body was still hurt and bandaged. But his mind was lucid and clear. His first thoughts were of the shadowy figure from his dream. Who was it? Mike Robbins? Sam Hagen? Or was it his own spirit? Or all of them - all his soldiers.

He wondered how long he had lain there, drifting back and forth between semi-conscious pain and unconsciousness, but he had no way of knowing; he knew only that he was still alive. He realized that he had thought, during those earlier, brief moments of semi-consciousness, that he was going to die. Or had he died, and somehow managed to return to life? No, that was impossible. Or was it?

He looked around. He was in a room with another injured man, who had several tubes running beneath the sheet on his bed. The sheet was flat where the man's legs should have been. He was lying still, staring at the ceiling.

Ed tried to say something, and discovered that his jaws were still wired shut. Through clenched teeth, he asked, "Where are we?"

The other man rolled his head toward Ed and studied him, but said nothing.

"Where are we?" Ed asked again.

The man said, "That's the first time you've spoken to me. We're in Japan. Camp Zama."

How was that possible? How could he get all the way from Vietnam to Japan without being aware of it?

"Are you sure?" Ed asked.

The man managed a faint smile and said, "Yeah, I'm sure. We've been here together for two weeks. My name's Joe Keach. Fourth Division."

A nurse came into the room then, and smiled when she realized that Ed was awake and conversing with his roommate.

"Well, well! Look who's decided to return to the living," she said, moving to Ed and checking the fluid level of the bottle from which something dripped into his arm. She left, and Ed began to recall the attack on the hospital at Cam Ranh, and wondered whether Mary knew about it. Of course she would have been notified. After all, Keach said they'd been there for two weeks.

He noticed that his right eye was no longer bandaged, and closed his left eye. The vision in his right one was somewhat blurred, but he could see with it.

A doctor and the nurse were hovering over him now, shining a light in his eye, checking his pulse and blood pressure, listening to his lungs through a stethoscope. They asked how this felt, and that, and had him wiggle his fingers and toes. Pain shot through his ankle when he wiggled the toes on his right foot, but they moved; they were all there.

He looked at the table beside his bed and saw a stack of letters. He tried to reach for them, but his right arm was still bandaged to his chest, and his left was taped to a board to keep the intravenous needle from being pulled out. But the letters were there, and he was alive and healing. He would be all right, now. He lay in silence, staring at the ceiling, knowing for certain now that he would live, and that he was out of the war.

When they were finished examining him, he asked the nurse to open the letters for him and put them on his chest so he could read them. She did so, but by then Ed had fallen back to sleep.

When he awoke later, the letters were on his chest. He used his left hand to pick them up one at a time to see who they were from. There were four from his sister-in-law, Evelyn, one from Mary's parents, and one from Lieutenant Susan Madison. Only two were from Mary, and he read those first.

One had been written a couple of days after he'd been wounded the first time. It was full of sympathy and thankfulness that he hadn't been killed, and of questions about what had happened and when he would be home. But it was nearly void of love.

The second was much the same, except it included a great deal of invective directed at those whose responsibility it was to guard the hospital against such an attack. Again, there was only a brief, "I love you" at the end.

The lack of affection was demoralizing, dashing his expectant hope that he would find the letters full of love and passion and hopeful plans about the future.

Ed put the other letters aside without reading them, and rang for the nurse to give him something for his pain. It did little to ease the real hurt; the hurt deep inside him.

He didn't wake up again until the next day, and the first thing he did was to read Mary's letters once more, hoping to find more love in them than he had found the day before. It wasn't there.

He read Sue Madison's letter. It was dated several days after the sapper attack.

Dear Captain Walker,

I got your note the day after the attack on the hospital, as my R&R was canceled because of it.

I'm sorry we had to send you off to Japan in even worse shape than you were in when you got here, but the

*doctors assure me that you should be in pretty good
shape in a month or two.*

*You're quite the hero with everyone on the ward -
me included - chasing after the VC like you did.*

I'm sorry about Lieutenant Robbins, Captain Walker.

*Now, get your brain unscrambled and your body
healed, and go on home. You've done enough. And thank
you for what you said in your note. It means a lot.*

Bless you,

It was signed *Sue Madison*, and had a brief post-script:

*"I'm so short that I'll probably be back in the Land of the
Big PX before you are! Ten days and a wake up!"*

He looked at the date again. Yes, she was right about that last comment. She was back in the States by now. He wondered where she would be stationed next, then supposed that, like most soldiers, she would be leaving the Army after her Vietnam tour.

There were times during the next ten days that Ed wished he would lapse back into unconsciousness, because the pain was constant. And each time it seemed to be abating, medics would come and stick him for more blood, or nurses would fiddle with the needles and tubes running into his body, or a doctor would adjust the plastic chest tube that ran into his lung through the hole between his ribs while sharp, white pain slashed through him like a hot knife. Every few days, they would roll him onto a gurney for another session in the operating room, and the pain was at its worst during those times. They would put him under each time, and it would seem as if he were spinning through the air, faster and faster. Then he would remember nothing until he awoke to new pain.

Finally one day they didn't come for him. A Medical Corps colonel came, and after he examined Ed he said, "Well, Captain, I think you're going to be all right. The ankle was a little worrisome, but I believe you'll get nearly its full range of mobility back. The nose and jaw will need a bit more reconstructive work, but the shoulder's healing well. The main thing we need to do is get you out of this bed and onto your feet."

Ed just looked at him, his drug-dulled brain trying to assimilate it all.

"You'll probably even be well enough to stay in the Army, if that's what you want to do," the man said, and patted Ed on the chest. "You're a fighter, son. You've proved that the way you battled back against these wounds."

He smiled now, but Ed just stared at him in silence. "We were worried as hell about you for awhile," the doctor continued, "everybody was. But next time they ask about you, I'll say, 'Walker? He's gone back to the World.'"

Still Ed said nothing, so the colonel took his hand and said, "Good luck to you, Captain Walker."

When he was gone, and what he had said sunk in, Ed's mind began to clear.

The relief of knowing that he'd be whole again, and the sadness of leaving the others further behind - Sam and Mike and the others, and the living soldiers still struggling through the jungles and the mud - and the thought of going home, of seeing Mary and his son; it all combined to cause him to weep softly.

The tears were still running down his face when a nurse, a pretty lieutenant named Williams, came in. She saw him weeping, and she took his hand in both of hers. He tried to stifle the tears, but she said, "It's all right. Go ahead and let it out. You're going to be all right, and that's all that matters."

In a while, he regained his composure and said to the nurse, "Sorry. Don't know why I did that."

"Yes, you do," Lieutenant Williams said, and she leaned over and kissed his forehead.

                    *   *   *

He was squirming from the pain and discomfort of the long flight on the litter when he noticed the big C-141 Starlifter power down and finally begin to descend. The Air Force medical personnel were working busily to get their patients ready for the landing. Some were ensuring that IV bottles were full enough to last the rest of the way to Andrews Air Force Base, and from there by ambulance to Walter Reed Army Medical Center. Others made certain that the litter straps were secured, and some were administering drugs to keep the wounded men comfortable during the jostling they'd have to endure during the unloading and transfer to the ambulances.

A chubby redhead with a hypodermic needle came to Ed, but before she injected the drug, he asked, "Is that dope, nurse?"

"Well, it's something to help keep you comfortable until you get to the hospital."

"Wait a minute," he said. He wanted the drug - wanted it badly - because he knew his fidgeting would stop, knew the euphoric glow would come over him again, and the pain would go away. In fact, he hungered for the drug. He had decided while he was at Camp Zama that he was hooked on whatever the narcotic was, and it worried him.

"I don't want it," he said.

"You're certain?" the redhead asked.

"Yes. Might as well start kicking it now."

"Good for you," the nurse said, smiling and patting his leg. She moved on to administer to the other patients.

He heard the whine of the big transport's flaps being lowered, and soon there was the whine and *thump... thump* as the landing gear was lowered and locked into place.

They were almost there, now. Almost home. Away from Vietnam, from the stink and noise and fury of that place.

He thought of Mike and Sam again. Of Guitteriz and Wentzel dying beside him, their innocent souls flying from their torn young bodies. He flinched at the memory of the exploding mortar round, the bullet slamming into his shoulder, the horror of awaking to the attack on the hospital. For the first time, he remembered clearly the North Vietnamese sappers running through the ward, flinging their satchel charges among the helpless wounded and shooting at them. He recalled his anger, his pursuit of the sappers, his attempt to kick in the skull of one of them. He felt again the heat of the blast against his face, and he realized that it had made no sound that he could remember.

He was trembling now, and he wished he'd allowed the nurse to give him some narcotics.

But then there was the sound of the airplane's engines being cut, and then a thump as it touched down.

A cheer, weak but heartfelt, came from the wounded soldiers, and those who were capable of doing so clapped their hands. The engines reversed, the aircraft slowed. The red haired nurse unbuckled her seat belt, stood, and leaned over Ed Walker, smiling. "Welcome home, soldier," she said.

He looked her in the eyes and nodded. He wanted to say thanks for all that she and the rest of the crew had done for them during the long flight, but the words hung in his throat, and he could only say one word.

"Home."

       *   *   *

At Walter Reed, Ed was put into a room with a Cobra gunship pilot who had been severely wounded when his helicopter was shot down. The crash had smashed the man's face, nearly ripped one arm off, and crushed his feet and ankles. He would have burned to death if his copilot had not hacked his feet off at the ankles and pulled him from the burning wreckage.

Ed learned this from the man, Warrant Officer Avery Smith, as he waited for word from Mary on when she would arrive. None came that day, so when a Red Cross volunteer stopped in that evening to see what needs the men might have. Ed asked if she would check to see if his wife had been notified of his arrival.

It was not until the next morning, after he and Smith had been awakened for breakfast, that Ed learned that the Red Cross lady had returned the previous evening. Finding Ed asleep, she told Smith to inform him that she had contacted his wife and learned that she had indeed not been notified of his arrival at Walter Reed. She had been informed that he was hospitalized in Hawaii. "Turns out they were talking about some other Walker who was on the same medevac flight you were on," Smith explained. "Unbelievable, isn't it? 'Situation normal, all fucked up.' Anyway, the Red Cross gal spoke to your wife, and she said she and your kid will be up here to see you sometime this afternoon."

Ed nodded and thanked him for the information, then drew within himself, pretending to sleep as hope and then fear and then hope again struggled for control of his senses while he awaited the arrival of his wife and son.

*   *   *

Mary awakened early that morning, well before daybreak, and for a long time she lay motionless in bed, thinking. She thought of her past, and of Ed's. She thought of how they had arrived at this day, of how the paths of their lives had been so divergent most of the time, barely touching for brief periods, then veering off again for long periods before coming together again. It seemed more by accident than by design that they were ever together. Their world - their separate worlds, really - had changed so much in the time since she had first seen him. Sometimes it seemed only yesterday, and sometimes so long ago that it was as if it hadn't really happened at all. But it had.

Had she really ever been in love with him? She didn't honestly know. She had respected him, yes. His courage, and his willingness to sacrifice so much for his naive idealism - those things were worthy of respect. But were they a basis for love?

Maybe she had loved him as a friend, and later as the father of her child. But not passionately, not as a lover. Yet she was a woman of passion, and she needed someone to share that side of herself with.

He is a crusader without a cause, and I am a lover without a love, she thought. And now it's time to get up out of this bed and face this day.

I have to be honest with him, but not cruel. I must make no commitment that I'll later regret. But I am his son's mother, and I'm still his wife, at least for now. He needs me, if only because he's badly hurt and unable to do things for himself. I have to be his nurse, and try to be his friend. But not forever.

She bathed and dressed herself and Jimmy, and drove through the morning to Walter Reed. By the time she got to the sprawling hospital complex, she thought she knew what she had to do, had to say.

She tried to explain to little Jimmy that his father would be in bed because he was hurt, so that the child wouldn't be frightened by what he might see, but she knew his young mind failed to comprehend. When they reached the hospital, she began to regret that she had brought him along.

Well, it's too late now, she thought. She went to the information desk for directions and headed for the ward. On the way they passed a number of injured men, most of whom were in blue pajamas and seersucker hospital robes. Some were in wheelchairs, others on crutches, or walking with canes. A few of the men were missing limbs, and others had their heads bandaged. Young Jimmy stared wide-eyed at each of them and clutched tightly to his mother. When she reached the nurses' station on Ed's ward, the sergeant on duty there directed Mary down the hall to her husband's room.

She was not prepared for the sight she encountered when she entered, because the first thing she saw was the raw stumps of Warrant Officer Smith's legs. A nurse was changing the man's dressings, her body hiding his face. Stunned, Mary stood at the door for a long moment before she realized that there was another bed in the room, and a man lying in it, his face bandaged, staring at her with sad, green eyes. Ed.

She stood motionless for a time, her eyes locked on his, and there was some unspoken communication between them. It was not the first time that Ed and Mary had experienced this silent exchange of thought. In some of the more exquisite moments of lovemaking they had shared early in their marriage, this same thing had occurred, this exchange of unspoken emotion. Then, it had been a communication of the pleasure they were sharing; now, it was an understanding of the unshared pain each of them felt. Not sympathy, not love; but an awareness by each that the other had suffered greatly.

Jimmy saw his mother staring, and sensed the emotion she was feeling, because somehow children are able to do that. Mary approached the wounded man, and the boy began to whimper; a pitiful, animal-like whimper of fear. She stroked his hair and whispered, "It's all right, Jimmy. It's daddy. It's OK, honey. Here's your daddy."

It wasn't enough. When his father reached out and touched his arm, Jimmy screamed and clutched desperately to his mother.

The nurse who had been attending Mr. Smith came over and offered to take the boy from Mary, but he wouldn't allow it. He clung to his mother and continued to wail.

"Is there a nursery?" Mary asked. The nurse said there was, and told her how to find it. Mary took Ed's hand for a moment and squeezed it, then let go. "I'm sorry," she said. "I'll be right back." And she turned and left the room.

While she was gone, Ed began to realize what he had seen in her eyes, what they had communicated to him in the moments they had looked so deeply into his. It was loneliness, he thought. It was the hurt and confusion of being left alone and unprepared to raise an infant son, never knowing, from day to day, if they would ever again see the husband and father who had abandoned them for so long; abandoned them to pursue, with his life, abstract ideals that most Americans no longer felt were valid. He understood, now. It was not just his own life he had risked, but theirs, too. Suppose he had - as he so nearly had - been killed? What sort of life would they have been left with? What would his widow, his fatherless son, have done? He could control the risks he took on the battlefield; they could not. They couldn't even understand why he took them.

He had his fellow soldiers to turn to with his doubts and his fears, when they surfaced. And they would understand, console him, encourage him. She had few, if any, people around her who would understand, or even care.

He also came to realize, in those few minutes, how that must have made her feel betrayed, uncertain of his love for her, and of hers for him. And now here he was, injured and helpless, lying in a hospital bed, expecting all of that suddenly not to matter anymore; expecting her to not only forgive him, but to love him.

How unfair I've been, he thought. And how unfair it is to expect still more from her.

By the time Mary returned to the room, the nurse had finished with Smith's dressings and given him a shot to ease his pain, and he was asleep.

Mary walked to her husband's bed, leaned over his face, and kissed his cracked, dry lips. "I'm sorry about Jimmy," she said, but Ed said, "Shhh. I understand. I should have told you not to bring him yet."

"How are you feeling?" she asked.

"Much better, now that I'm home," he said.

"How long do they think you'll have to stay here?"

"I don't know. They haven't said yet." He looked away from her and said, "There's a whole lot I just don't know right now."

"What do you mean?"

He looked back at her, at those beautiful, speckled eyes, and said, "I mean there's just a lot I don't know yet. Whether I'll heal completely from all this mess, or how long it'll take. Whether I'll stay in the Army, or even be allowed to."

He was avoiding the real issue they needed to face, and that was their relationship; they both knew that.

Neither of them spoke for a time until she said, "Well, the main thing to do now is to get yourself healed and out of this bed. You... we can worry about the rest of it later."

No, he thought, we need to get it out in the open. But not yet, not at this moment. "The boy looks good, Mary," he said, avoiding for a while longer things he needed to say.

She smiled and nodded. "He's quite a little character. Smart as can be, too. Of course, all mothers feel that way about their kids."

Ed's mouth was dry, so he reached for the glass of water beside his bed. Mary took it and held it for him while he sucked from the straw. Then he said, "I don't want him to see me like this again, Mary."

"What do you mean?"

"I mean, I don't want him to see me helpless, lying in bed and all bandaged up like some damned monster. I don't want him to remember me like this. I want him to think of me as... Hell, I don't know. But not like this."

Mary nodded. She didn't think it was good for the boy to be here either, but it wasn't so much seeing his father like this as it was seeing all of them; the wrecks of men such as those they'd seen on the way to the ward, or the one lying over there with no legs. But it would have to be Ed's choice. "Well, if that's the way you really feel, Ed, I understand. But if you change your mind, all..."

"I won't," he interrupted. He was suddenly filled with despair. He wanted to be with his son, but now he wished he'd stayed in Japan or Hawaii until he was well enough to be a real father to him. And well enough to say to her what was on his mind, and to hear what was on hers. He had seen it in her eyes a little while ago. It had to be said.

"Look," he said, and she sensed that it was coming. Involuntarily, she stood and looked into his eyes. "They're taking good care of me here, Mary. There's really no reason you should have to come all the way up here to visit me. All it'll do is remind me how unfair all of this is to you and Jimmy. Do you know what I mean?"

She said nothing, so he continued. "I've got a lot of thinking to do, Mary. A lot of things to sort out in my mind."

She nodded in agreement. "That's true."

He stared at the ceiling, not wanting to finish. But it had to be done. Sooner or later, it had to be said.

"The thing is, I can't sort any of it out until I know how things are between us, Mary."

"How do you think they are, Ed?" she asked.

"I don't know. I don't even know how I feel about us, except that I feel guilty," he said.

"Guilty?"

"Yeah," he said. "Guilty. For what I've put you through. For giving you so little to say about it. For making all the decisions that should have been ours, not just mine. I've... I've taken your choices away, haven't I?"

She thought about it before she answered, wondering if he really felt guilty. Hadn't he only done what he thought was right? And hadn't he done it unselfishly, and, in the end at such... such brutal cost?

Guilty. No, if anyone should feel guilt, it was she. Yet she didn't. No, she had made her choices, too. And she would continue to do so. He needed to realize that. "You don't have anything to feel guilty about, Ed. And you haven't taken away all my choices. I've been making choices, too. And I... we, both of us, still have some more to make."

Mary sighed. She knew he wanted to get it out in the open, and so did she. But they were on different wave lengths. He was lying there feeling guilty because he thought she had been sitting at home alone, with a life of emptiness, when that was not the case at all. If only he were strong, standing on his feet, so that they could just say it, and be done with it.

Ed knew she was holding back, so he said, "Look, Mary. The war's over for me. That's all behind us. I'm going to be all right. But what about our marriage? Is it behind us, too? I've got to know how you feel about that, Mary."

It's time now, she thought. Just get it out. She took his hand in hers, and tried to choose her words carefully.

"I have a lot of feelings about you, Ed," she said. "I have great respect for you. For your courage, your... your willingness to risk your life for the things you believe in. I think they're foolish, sometimes. But you already know that. Still, I respect you for it. And I'm... I'm proud that you're the father of my son."

His hand gripped hers weakly, and she looked down at it. It was pale, and so weak, and she felt her own hand trembling slightly. She thought the squeeze was because of what she'd said about their son, but it wasn't. It was because the things she was saying were such empty phrases, leading up to something he knew he didn't want to hear. He barely heard them, waiting for what would come at the end.

"I'm sorry - terribly sorry - that you've been wounded so badly, Ed. And I'm thankful to God that you're alive, and that you're home. Thankful and relieved, especially for Jimmy's sake. But I've been wounded by this damned war too, Ed. And I just don't know if my wounds will heal."

She let go of his hand and wiped tears from her cheeks, and he thought, wounded... won't heal, and he knew that whatever it was, it was coming soon.

She took his hand again and said, "And you have to know this, Ed. When it got too lonely, and I couldn't stand the hurt any longer, I turned to somebody else to... to soothe the hurt."

He tried to pull his hand from hers, but she grasped it tightly and wouldn't let it go. He closed his eyes, and he thought, Oh, Jesus. It's true, then. I should have known.

"How long?" he asked, jerking his hand from hers.

She looked at him, at the flexing of the muscles in his bandaged face, the loss of what little color he'd had.

Just answer vaguely, she said to herself. Don't lie, but don't make it worse than it has to be. "What does that matter?" she said.

"Then, who?" he demanded.

"No one you know, Ed."

"God damn it, *who*?"

"It doesn't matter!"

He opened his eyes now. They were full of fire, and Mary wondered if it was the fire of anger, or hate, or both.

"Doesn't matter," he said. "No, I guess it doesn't, does it?"

She slumped into the chair beside his bed, not knowing what to say. But it was done. Now he knew. They could begin to make their decisions.

"I'm so fucking blind," he mumbled. "I should have seen it."

Mary made no reply.

"Are you still seeing him?" he asked calmly.

"Yes."

"I see. Do you lo..." He stopped himself, and rolled away from her, staring out the window. It looked so peaceful out there.

"Do I love him?" she said, finishing the question for her husband. She stood and took one of the cigarettes from his bedside table and lit it, then rested herself on the bed and answered the question. "No, not really. I thought I did, but no, I don't love him. But I think he loves me. He's been kind to me, Ed. Caring and good. If I thought we could be like that, if we could recapture what we had, build on it..."

"Who the hell are you trying to convince!" he said. "Me? Yourself?" He rolled back to face her, and said, "You're still seeing this son of a bitch, and you talk about trying to recapture something? You know what you can do? You can just keep yourself out of my life, Mary. You took yourself out of it, so *stay* the fuck out of it!"

His eyes burned into hers, and she began to weep, so he turned his face away from hers again. If only she weren't still seeing the guy. But she was. Their marriage was a failure - an unquestionable failure. And if he had learned anything in war, it was that reinforcing a failed effort was nothing but a waste.

Images of her that he'd had so often in Vietnam came into his mind. But instead of him making love to her, it was someone else. It first sickened him, then made him angry. He wanted to run at her, hit her, knock her down. He wanted to kick her face in, as he had tried to do to the sapper in Cam Ranh hospital. He fought to control his rage, and then he turned and faced her again, his eyes dark slits. "I can't stand the sight of you," he said. "You make me sick! Get out. And God damn you, don't come back!"

She felt more drained than she had ever felt in her life; even more than after the birth of their child, and she looked at him, wondering how it might have been if she had only fought her needs until he returned. Maybe they could have found the passion they knew so briefly. Maybe they could still, if they both tried. Oh, God, why had she told him? It was so different, now that she saw him, now that he was here, near enough to touch. "I'm sorry things are like they are, Eddie. Sorry I wasn't strong, like you. But those are the realities. I wish to God they weren't there, but they are." She dropped her head into her hands then and sobbed; lost control of herself, and cried, "Oh, God. What have I done?"

He pulled himself to a sitting position and lit a cigarette, watching her, hoping her pain was as great as his own. He felt no sympathy for her, no desire to ease her guilt. He felt used, and cheated out of a mother for his son. And that was all he felt about the woman who had been his wife. "You're a pitiful, worthless cunt," he said, because it was the worst thing he could think to say to her.

A nurse heard the sobbing and stuck her head inside the door. "You folks all right?" she asked.

Mary wiped her face, and Ed said, "She's just leaving," so the nurse nodded and said, "OK," then closed the door.

Mary stood, and without looking at Ed asked, "What should I do?"

"I don't care what you do," he said evenly. "I'll send for Jimmy when I get better. He can come up with James and Evelyn. If I have anything to say, I'll write. Otherwise, just leave me the hell alone."

He snuffed out the cigarette, slid back down in the bed and turned away from her once more.

Mary regained her composure somewhat and said, "Ed, I..."

"That's all I have to say," he interrupted. "Please leave. Just... just leave me alone."

"I'll wait to hear from you, then," she said.

"You do that."

Mary Walker walked to the door, then turned and looked back at her husband. She started to say once more that she was sorry, then decided against it. There would be time for that when he was better, when he was over the initial pain of her confession. She walked slowly to the nursery to get her son, feeling old and tired and confused; confused about herself, and about life, and where it all led to in the end.

The pain Ed Walker felt in his body and in his soul was so strong and deep that he thought it would overwhelm him, and he didn't care whether he lived or died. There is a defense mechanism in the mind for such times, and if it works, it allows one to switch off his consciousness for a time. Ed's worked, and he fell asleep. He didn't see or hear Mary return to the room just long enough to place a small silver frame on his bedside table. In it was a recent photograph of their son, smiling happily.

For days after Mary's visit, Ed lay silently in bed, plunged into a deep depression. And always, there was the presence of his physical pain. The doctors and nurses worried about the depression and noted it on his records.

Evelyn phoned to ask when James and she should come to visit, and whether they should bring Sookie, but Ed had the nurse who took the call tell her that he didn't want any visitors. He would call when he wanted them to come, he said, but it would be a long time before he did.

One of the hospital chaplains came in one day when Ed was picking at a meal, and he asked questions that Ed found irritating; questions about his wounds, and about his family. He picked up the photo of Jimmy and remarked that he was a fine looking boy.

Ed reached over and snatched it from him.

Do me a favor, will you, chaplain?" Ed asked.

"Yes?"

"Get the fuck out of here and leave me alone!"

The man gave him a startled look, but left immediately.

The next afternoon, while Ed was asleep, another chaplain, a Catholic priest, came into the room that he and Warrant Officer Smith shared. The priest was a small, dark man in a wheelchair. His skinny, useless legs were clutched by baggy black trousers, and from the right sleeve of his suit jacket protruded not a hand, but a hook.

Mr. Smith was awake, and the priest looked at him as he wheeled himself in and in a loud, high-pitched voice said, "You're Smith, right? And he," nodding toward Ed, "is Walker?"

"Yes, sir," Smith replied, and the priest said, "I'm Father Frank Fallon, here to see Walker."

He paused at the foot of the warrant officer's bed and asked, "How long before they're going to give you some new feet and let you get your ass out of here, chief?"

"A couple of more months before they get around to it," Smith said. "Real problem's the damned arm. There's not enough muscle left to do anything with, it seems."

"Well, don't worry about it, son," Father Fallon said as he wheeled over to Ed's bed. "There's plenty of good a one-armed man can do for the rest of his stay in this world."

Without waiting for a response from Smith, the priest poked the sleeping infantry officer in the ribs with his hook.

"Walker! Wake up!"

Ed awakened, and rolled toward the disturbance that had aroused him from his sleep. He rubbed his eyes with the heel of his hand, noticing the priest's collar, his wheelchair, and then the hook Fallon now used to pull a pack of cigarettes from his breast pocket.

Holding them out to Ed, he said, "You're the one who told Chaplain Stevenson to fuck off the other day, eh? Don't blame you. He's a pious little son of a bitch. Means well, but doesn't understand people. Especially guys like us who've had their shit blown away."

He continued his chattering without interruption as Ed took a cigarette from the pack. The priest produced a lighter and held it out to him, still talking. "My name's Fallon, Father Frank Fallon. The docs tell me you're in some sort of depression, Walker, and I'm here to tell you to snap the hell out of it. Look out of that window, boy! What a beautiful day! 'This is the day which the Lord has made; let us rejoice and be glad in it.'"

He crossed himself with the hook and said, "Thanks be to God," then rattled on. "The war ain't here, son, it's half way around the world, and by God, you're out of it. And from the looks of it, you're out of it for a long time, unless the Chinese or Russians jump in. We'll all get nuked if they do, anyway, so what the hell?"

He picked up the photograph of Jimmy, still chattering in his high-pitched voice. "Good looking kid. You can thank God for that, too. One reason I'm a priest is, I can't *have* kids. Got my balls blown off in Korea, same time as my arm."

He set the photo back on the table, still talking without interruption. "I understand your wife came to see you a few days ago and hasn't come back yet. Give her some time, son. She's been through hell, too, you know. She'll come back. But if she doesn't, well, tough shit. Hell, you're a hero, Walker; DSC, Special Forces, First Cav, and all that. You still have both arms, both feet - even though you might lose that damned foot if you don't kick this depression and start fighting back. You still got your dick and balls, too. I checked your record. Hell, you've got it made, brother! And you've still got your liver and kidneys; I checked on that, too. So I'm going down the hall to Sergeant O'Rourke's room and get us a jug of Bushmills. He's blind - unlike you and me, thanks be to God." Again he crossed himself. "So he'll never know who snitched it."

Father Fallon spun the wheelchair and headed for the door, still rattling on. "If you don't snap out of this depression crap by the time we polish off O'Rourke's whiskey," he said, pausing long enough to raise his hook, "I'll rip your balls off with this here hook, and you'll end up with a squeaky voice like mine." And with that, he was gone.

Warrant Officer Smith laughed aloud and said, "Feisty little son of a bitch, isn't he?"

"Yeah," Ed Walker had to agree, smiling for the first time in days. "Feisty Father Fallon." As he said it, he knew that would be the way he'd always remember the unforgettable little priest.

After a minute, Smith looked over at Ed and said, "You know, Captain Walker, the guy's right. You've got to snap out of this blue funk you're in. You're gonna be OK, man. We're lucky to be alive. Both of us are."

Ed stared at the ceiling, so Smith rolled his torso toward his roommate as best he could and said, "I've done a lot of thinking about it. We've paid a hell of a price, and a lot of people out there don't give a damn. But a lot of them do care, too. But most important, we know why we were there. And when our buddies finish kicking their little dink asses all the way back to Hanoi, it'll all have been worth it. And that's all that matters."

Ed looked over at Smith and studied him for awhile. He wondered how this maimed soldier, who had sacrificed so much, could show such an absence of self-pity. He wondered if he could be so positive, if he'd been as badly mauled as Smith. The old axiom crossed his mind about the man who felt self-pity because he had no shoes, until he met a man with no feet. He thought of the feisty little priest who had blazed in in his wheelchair, fired a verbal barrage at him, then dashed off in search of a bottle of Irish whiskey. And his self-pity began to turn into shame. Both of the other men were right. He would be whole again, with or without Mary. They never would. His own self-pity was unmanly.

Father Fallon came rolling back into the room, a bottle of Bushmills in his lap, and launched into another non-stop monologue. "Damned O'Rourke caught me! Made me promise to pay him back with a full bottle. I told him he was acting like a damned Scotsman, being so tight. He said I must be an Englishman, stealing whiskey from a blind man. Should have ripped his tongue out for that!"

Holding the bottle up to Ed, he said, "Well, uncap this damn thing, Walker, and let's get on with it."

Ed reached over and screwed off the cap. Father Fallon raised the bottle, said, "*Silange*," then drank deeply from it. "Ahhh!" he said. "Good stuff. Here you are, my son."

He handed the bottle to Ed, who took it, guided it to the corner of his mouth, and poured a bit in. His jaw was still stiff, and he sucked it in between his teeth and swallowed. It burned down his mouth in a warm trickle and made his good eye water. Some of it ran along his lips to his jaw, stinging the still-raw wound.

Father Fallon continued to rattle on. "Nothing like a bit of the ol' medicinal to turn the happy cells on, and the sad ones off, know what I mean?" he said as he took the glass of water from Ed's table, dumped it into the trash can then poured it half full of Bushmills. He replaced the straw, handed the glass to Ed, and said, "You know why God invented whiskey? To keep us Irishmen from ruling the world. Couple more weeks, when they get that jaw squared away, you can throw back your whiskey like a real man. Meanwhile, you'll just have to suck it up. Now, what's got you down?"

Ed sucked a sip of the tasty liquid into his mouth and swallowed it, then looked at the priest. He was grinning at the odd, whirlwind of a man now, and he said, "By the time I finish this, Padre, it won't really matter. I guess you're right, you and Mr. Smith are. I've got nothing to feel sorry for. I just need to get my shit together, get out of this rack, and get on with life."

"Now you're talking, son," Fater Fallon said, poking Ed in the ribs again with his hook and winking at Warrant Officer Smith.

"Now you're talking."

TWENTY THREE

"What you need, Walker, is some beauty," Father Fallon said as they sat sipping coffee in the hospital cafeteria. "American beauty. And this town has it."

Ed sat stoop-shouldered, staring into the mug he held in both his hands. He was tired of the hospital, tired of the miserable sights and the medicine smell and of the pain that kept coming back. He wanted to be completely whole again, back on the Chesapeake, sailing carefree and alone toward Tangier Island or Lighthouse Point or the Guinea marshes.

Then, as always happened when he had self-indulgent thoughts, guilt grabbed him, and images appeared of thin-mustached young men halfway around the world, cursing and sweating, struggling through leech-ridden rice paddies or bamboo thickets until the world around them erupted in the crack and thump and rattle and blast of heavy contact. Men fell, and moaned, and....

"I *said*, Walker, that what you need is some American beauty!" The priest was scowling at him. "I'm going to get you a pass for the day, and you're going to get your sullen ass out of here and into town to visit the Smithsonian, or the memorials. Or a 14th Street strip joint, if that's what you consider beauty." The little priest wheeled himself back from the table and spun away. "So, what are you waiting for? Go get dressed, boy!"

Ed turned and looked out of the window. It was a bright, sunny morning. Yes, it would be nice to get into Washington and visit a museum, or to just lie on the grass of the Mall and soak up some sunshine. He pushed himself back from the table and hobbled to his room.

He had a pair of slacks that he had split at the bottom to fit over his cast, so he pulled them on, then buttoned on a shirt. He was tying the shoe on his good foot when Father Fallon wheeled in.

"There's a shuttle bus to the Smithsonian in ten minutes, so get a move on." He held out a pass card, and Ed took it and put it in his wallet.

"Thanks, Padre. You going to come along?"

"I'd love to, Walker. But as you've no doubt failed to notice, it's Sunday, and I have to put some of your comrades-in-arms in touch with their God. See you," he said and wheeled quickly away.

Five minutes later, Ed was sitting on the bench at the shuttle bus stop, looking at the toes of his foot as he tried to wiggle them in the open-toed cast. The latest surgery on his ankle - the last, he hoped to God - had been done six days before. Another week or so, and he should be able to leave the hospital on convalescent leave, and he sighed at the thought.

Behind him, he heard a strangely-familiar feminine voice chatting lightheartedly, then laughing. He turned to see two nurses in white uniforms, and the first thought that flashed through his mind was *American beauty*.

The voice was Sue Madison's, and she glanced at him, then stopped, uncertain at first that it was he. Then her eyes met the deep green of his, and she saw the scars and heard him say, "Hello, Lieutenant Madison. How are you?"

"Why, Captain Walker!" she said, and her face lit up with a smile. An even prettier face than before, Ed thought. It was void of the strain of combat that he hadn't realized until this moment lined the faces of women soldiers as it did their male counterparts.

He struggled to stand with his crutches, the memory of their brief meeting in the hospital at Cam Ranh Bay coming to him, and of the letter she had written to him in Japan. He had never written a reply, but her letter to him was in the packet of personal papers that had accompanied him from Japan to Walter Reed.

"Oh, don't stand up, Ed," she said, placing a hand on his shoulder to prevent him from rising from the bus stop bench. To the other nurse, she said, "Angela, this is Ed Walker. He was at Cam Ranh hospital when...." Remembering, she stopped.

"Hi," Ed said and shook hands with Angela, then glanced at Sue's face as, for a moment, they both recalled those painful days.

"Are you waiting for someone?" Sue asked, her face relaxing once more into a smile.

"No, just the shuttle bus. I've got a pass for the day, and thought I'd visit the Smithsonian."

"Well, it sure is good to see you up and about. I was worried about you after you got hurt so badly in the attack on the hospital. We were really busy there for a couple of days, until I finally got away on R & R. When I got back, you'd already been evacuated to Japan... Did you get my letter?"

"Yes, I did, Sue. Thank you. Sorry I didn't get around to answering it, but...."

Sue's hand was still resting on his shoulder, and she squeezed it lightly. "Oh, don't worry about it. How much longer do you suppose you'll have to stay here at Walter Wonderful?"

"Not more than another week or so, I hope," he replied, glancing at the ankle that was the cause of his continued hospitalization.

"Well, listen," she said, "I'm working in the emergency room from midnight to eight these days. Drop in and see me, Ed. Really."

"I will, Sue. Thanks."

She moved her hand from his shoulder to the scar on his face, and they looked into each other's eyes. He saw again the strained look of a soldier not long back from combat, and he reached up and gently touched her hand, feeling a sense of comradeship with her, and with all the nurses along the way who had been so good, so competent and cheerful in spite of the rigors of dealing with wounded and dying men.

"Have a nice time today, Eddie. See you soon?"

"Sure," he said. "Nice to meet you, Angela."

She smiled, and both women said, "Bye."

He watched them walk away. They looked good in the white skirts and hose of their nurses' uniforms. Sue appeared taller and more shapely than she had in the jungle fatigue uniform she wore in Vietnam, and he felt a stir low in his belly as he watched the sway of her hips. He looked away and saw the shuttle bus approaching, and after one last glance at Sue, he pulled himself up onto his crutches as the bus braked to a halt.

"Eddie, wait!" It was Sue, walking quickly back toward him. "Forget the bus," she said. "I'll give you a ride."

"Oh, you don't need to..."

"Yes. I want to."

She leaned into the door of the bus. "Go on," she said to the driver. "He's going to ride with me."

A young soldier in the front seat yelled, "Take me! Take me!" causing laughter and whistles from the other GI passengers.

"One at a time, honey," she remarked with good natured humor, bringing more laughter and hoots from the young men.

The door closed, and the bus pulled away.

"Sue, really," Ed said. "You don't need to..."

"Oh, hush. The Smithsonian sounds like a good idea to me. I'll go home and change, and go with you. Come on."

She turned, and he hobbled down the sidewalk beside her.

"I'm living with my parents in Chevy Chase," she said as they walked toward the parking lot. "My dad's a grunt like you. 'Paying penance in the Pentagon,' as he puts it. I'm sure he'd enjoy trading you a cup of coffee for news from the front, while I change clothes."

"I'm afraid my news is kind of dated, Sue. Hell, you left Vietnam after I did."

"Not the same as one grunt to another. And he's been back for more than a year now."

They reached her car, an old red Volkswagen beetle, and he opened the door for her, then went around and got in, sliding his crutches into the back seat. She watched him, remembering how he had been wounded pursuing the enemy sappers in the attack on Cam Ranh hospital.

"Eddie," she said as she started the car, "that was a brave thing you did in the hospital attack. I'm sorry you were hurt again."

He searched her eyes for sincerity, and saw it.

"Instinct, that's all," he replied.

They fell silent for awhile, each thinking their own thoughts, feeling somewhat awkward. After awhile, Sue asked, "What part of Virginia are you from, Eddie? On the Bay, you said, didn't you?"

"Just off the Bay. Gloucester County, on the York River."

"That's right. I remember that's where you said you threw in the bottle with a note in it."

After a moment's silence, Ed smiled and said, "Yeah. I still wish you'd found the friggin' note."

She laughed, remembering his remark when she had found him standing on the beach in Vietnam. She remembered, too, the unanswered telephone call to his wife. Without looking at him, she asked, "Is your wife able to visit you often?"

He looked at her. "No," he muttered, then after awhile added, "We've decided to - well, to be separated."

"We?" she asked.

He didn't answer her, but turned on the car radio, and they rode along listening to the Beatles sing *Strawberry Fields Forever*.

She pulled into the elm-shaded driveway of an old, three-story white Victorian house and said, "Here we are."

They got out, Ed struggling somewhat to get his crutches from the back seat. They went up the steps to the front porch and when they entered the front hall, a man's voice from somewhere inside called, "Sue? That you?"

"Yes, Dad. With company."

Her father appeared; a tall, lean man with close-cropped gray hair who, even in the jeans and gray sweatshirt he wore, had the bearing of a seasoned professional soldier.

"Dad, this is Captain Ed Walker. We were in Vietnam together."

The fresh scars on Ed's face and his crutches led Colonel Madison to quickly understand how Ed and his daughter had met in Vietnam. He held out a hand to the other officer and said, "Harry Madison. Nice to meet you, Captain Walker."

Ed balanced himself on his crutches and exchanged a firm handshake with the colonel, saying, "My pleasure, sir."

"Ed and I are going to the Smithsonian, Dad," Sue said. "Would you get him a cup of coffee while I change?"

"Glad to. Come on in the kitchen, son, and get off that broken road wheel."

Ed sat in a chair at the kitchen table while Colonel Madison poured a mug of coffee for each of them. A copy of the Washington Post was on the table, and Ed glanced at the headlines; *Heavy Fighting at Khe Sanh. 12 Marines KIA.*

Madison set a mug in front of Ed and took a seat across the table from him. "Smoke if you got 'em," he said in the age-old words of leaders giving their troops a smoke break.

Ed fished out a Lucky Strike and offered one to Sue's father, who waved it off.

"Hell of a mess at Khe Sanh," the older man remarked.

"Yes, sir. I'm not sure I see the sense in sitting there holding a piece of terrain like that. Seems to me that all it does is give a fixed reference point for raining artillery on you. Of course, we did the same thing at a lot of Special Forces camps."

"Well, the plan is to draw Charlie in and attrit him with airstrikes. But it's become a matter of pride, now."

Ed sipped his coffee and thought, Pride. How many Marines were being killed, cramped into that red dirt Hell to satisfy the 'pride' of someone who wasn't there to endure it?

Madison was thinking much the same thought, and said, "I don't see a hell of a lot to be proud about in sacrificing troops inside the wire. That's the difference between Khe Sanh and the Special Forces camps, where they call in their reaction force to deal with the NVA outside the wire. Old George Patton must be twitching in his grave when he sees the Marines just sitting there."

Both men pondered the thought for a moment, then the colonel asked, "What unit were you with?"

"The Cav, sir. B Company, Second of the Fifth."

"Damned good outfit," Madison said. "The whole division is. Served with them myself. Were you on your second tour?"

"I extended for it. Special Forces before that - the Mike Force. Charlie cut my extension a little short, though."

"So I see. Everything healing up OK?"

"Yes, sir."

"That's good to hear. Are you on convalescent leave?"

"No, sir. I'm just on pass from the hospital. I should be released in a week or so, though."

"Good. That's a Tidewater accent you have, isn't it, Walker?"

"Yes, sir. Gloucester County, Virginia."

"Beautiful area. Is your family there?"

"A brother and two sisters. Both my parents are dead."

He thought for a moment about not mentioning Mary and Jimmy, afraid that Colonel Madison might not care to have his daughter spend the day with a married man, separated or not. But that would leave his answer a half-truth, so he looked at Madison and added, "I have a wife and son there, too."

He waited for Madison to make some comment; to ask why Ed wasn't spending the day with them, then, instead of Sue. But Harry Madison knew his daughter, and knew what war so often does to men and women. He would leave that for his daughter and this young infantry officer to sort out.

"Let me get you some more coffee," he said. As he poured it, he asked, "Do you know what your next assignment will be?"

"Yes, sir; the Advanced Course at Fort Benning, when the medics get done with me."

Madison placed the mug in front of Ed and sat down again. "Hmmph," he grunted. "It didn't even cross my mind that your next job might be in civilian life. What makes you want to stay in the Army, Walker? I mean, you're a young man, and it's an unpopular thing to be these days; a soldier is. And you've been shot all to hell."

Ed considered the colonel's question. There were a lot of reasons, right and wrong, that a man would want to be in the Army, and Ed knew that Madison had weighed them all many times. The answer he gave was simple and honest. "Because it's the only place American soldiers are, sir."

Madison searched his face, then grinned. So often when he asked young officers that, he got answers about duty or job security or family benefits or education. This Walker, though, had the only answer that really mattered.

"Soldiers," the colonel said, and raised his mug in a salute to them, and to Ed.

Sue showered quickly, feeling suddenly refreshed. It had not been very busy in the emergency room, not for the morning after a Saturday night; a couple of drug overdoses - an increasingly frequent problem these days both among young GIs and teenaged military dependents. And there was the usual complement of not-so-ill infants brought in by overanxious young mothers, most of whose husbands were away in Vietnam.

Sue usually came home and went straight to bed when she was working the midnight shift, but the last couple of days she had waited until mid-afternoon to sleep, more as an excuse to have for refusing Doctor Hannis's pleas for another date than anything else. She was off duty tomorrow, so she could sleep as late as she wished.

She pulled on a cotton mini-dress, light sweater, and loafers, checked herself in the mirror, and went down to the kitchen. Her father and Ed Walker were discussing the latest lunar orbiting mission that the Apollo astronauts were conducting in preparation for man's first landing on the moon later that year.

"I used to think that a night carrier landing in a jet was about the neatest thing a man could do," Ed was saying, "but putting that frail little LEM down on the moon... That's *really* going to be something."

The three of them sat there, chatting over coffee, and Ed felt more relaxed than he had since he could remember.

Madison asked him if he had ever visited the Smithsonian before, and Ed said that he hadn't, but that Father Fallon had suggested it. He laughed when he thought of the feisty, crippled priest, and told Colonel Madison about him.

Sue had met Father Fallon, and she told a couple of tales about him, as well. Her father added a story about two chaplains in his division in Vietnam; one Roman Catholic, one Methodist. They cross-trained each other so that, if necessary, one could substitute for the other in his denomination's ritual in their ministry to the soldiers.

They got on well together, these three Army officers, and Sue Madison took notice of that fact. It was not often that she heard her father laugh these days, and it was the first time she could remember seeing Ed Walker laugh, too.

Ed excused himself to go to the toilet. When he was gone, Harry Madison said, "He seems like a nice young man."

"Yes, he is," she replied. "Do you remember the sapper attack on Cam Ranh hospital?"

He nodded. Of course he remembered. He'd read about it in the morning intelligence reports at his Pentagon office, and worried all that day until he was able to find out that Sue was unharmed.

"He was there," Sue continued, "already hit in the face and shoulder. When they came in, he jumped out of bed and attacked them barehanded. It nearly cost him his life."

Harry Madison studied his daughter's face, suddenly dark with the memories of that night. It saddened him each time he thought of her amid the gore and carrion of war, his carefree little girl turned now into a serious woman, all innocence gone. It was not like the loss of sexual innocence to a lover, he thought. It was more like rape. He wondered whether she had ever had a lover, or many lovers, for that matter. She had mentioned a Special Forces medic she met in Vietnam; a sergeant who was killed not long after they met. But he didn't know if they had been lovers. I hope so, he thought. For both their sakes.

Ed came back into the kitchen and the colonel got to his feet and said, "Well, I've taken enough of you youngsters' time. Get yourselves on into town and have some fun."

"OK, Dad. I won't be late," Sue said, kissing her father.

Madison held out his hand to Ed. "It's a pleasure to meet you, Walker," he said. "No doubt we'll meet again."

"Thank you, sir. No doubt we will," Ed said.

Sue and Ed chatted easily on the drive into Washington. Each answered the other's questions about childhood, family, school days. Sue spoke of her years as an Army brat; Fort Benning, Germany, Fort Bragg, Fort Campbell.

Ed spoke mostly of Tidewater Virginia and his family's long history of fishing and crabbing there.

They progressed to the subject of marriage, and although the tone was less lighthearted, he opened up to Sue.

"I had this foolish idea that Mary was all that mattered to me," he said. "That there could be no wrong in the world as long as we loved each other. I suppose I really believed that. And the fact she was going to have a baby, well, that just made it seem even more so."

He lit a cigarette, and was silent for awhile, detached from Sue and thinking of the past. He sighed.

"Then I got orders to Vietnam, and suddenly there was a real world, full of all sorts of wrongs that needed correcting, and rights that needed to be upheld. It was still idealism, but a different set of ideals. Those ideals became my mistress. And my buddies, my fellow soldiers, became my brothers."

He looked over at Sue. "Then I got over there, and all those lofty ideals got hammered into reality."

Sue glanced at him for a moment. "But you're still an idealist, aren't you, Eddie? Even though real life ideals are tougher than those early, naive ones?"

He shrugged. "Maybe. But all my noble ideals did for Mary were to rob her of her youth."

Sue considered his remark for a moment, then said, "Well, the loss of youth is the price of maturity. Just ask me."

"The loss of dreams, too," he said.

They were silent again for awhile, until Sue said, "She'll catch up to you soon, Eddie. Everything will work out. Don't turn loose of the dreams."

He studied her, then slowly shook his head. "No, it will never be the same again, Sue."

"*Nothing* will ever be the same again," she said. "Life's a struggle that continually changes everything. You know that. It's a struggle between reality and hope, and all you can do is keep hoping and keep struggling, and they'll reach a balance. But not if you give up the hopes and the dreams. Do that, and the struggle will get the best of you. Anyway, you have a son to dream dreams for. He's worth the struggle, isn't he?"

He thought of little Jimmy, and wondered what the boy must think. He'd never had a father. One short leave from Vietnam and a visit to the hospital were all the time they had ever shared. He wondered if the child had nightmares of his visit to the hospital, of the frightening sight of the father he didn't know, battered and bandaged and lying among mutilated men. Unconsciously, he reached up and fingered the scars on his face. "Pull over a minute," he said, and when Sue had done so, they looked at each other and he asked, "Do I look frightening? Would my face frighten you, if you were a child?"

She studied the scars, one an indented welt on the bridge of his nose, one running through his left eyebrow, the other a mottled, inch-wide patch on his left cheek, sunken in as a result of the bottom teeth on that side having been blown away. They had not yet lost their purplish color.

She was used to seeing men with such scars, and with much worse ones. But what would a child think? She looked into his green eyes. "Maybe it would be frightening at first, Eddie. Until I got used to it; until I learned what kind of man was beneath the scars."

She took Ed's face in her hands, leaned over and lightly kissed his cheek, then gently touched each scar with her fingertips.

It was a more tender moment than he had known for a long, long time, and his sad eyes showed it as they searched hers. She kissed him softly on the lips, and he reached up and held the back of her head in his hands for a moment to prolong the kiss. Then he moved his hand, and they sat back in their seats. She put the Volkswagen into gear and pulled away from the curb.

They were silent as she turned left onto Constitution Avenue from 23rd Street, just up from the Washington Monument.

"Thank you for that," he said quietly after a time.

Her reply was a look of softness and a tender smile.

They went to the National Gallery first, because Ed said that Father Fallon's mission to him was to see some American beauty.

"Then Mary Cassat and John Singer Sargent are for you," Sue said. "And Winslow Homer. You'll like his *Breezing Up*, for sure."

She was right about Homer's painting of a man and three boys in a sailing dory. Ed especially liked the fact that "Gloucester" was painted on the transom of the little sailboat, even though he knew that it was for the Massachusetts port, not his native Virginia county.

When he saw Sargent's painting of *The White Girl*, he stopped and stared at it.

"Do you like that one?" Sue asked.

"It looks just like Maria DeCalesta," he said, "the girl who was going to marry my best friend, Sam Hagen. He was killed at Dak Seang while I was home on extension leave."

His best friend. A chill coursed through her, and she wondered why, then realized it was because he had said it so casually. Her mind flashed back to Cam Ranh hospital, and the news he'd gotten about another friend there; one of his officers. She recalled his pain on hearing the news, his angry outburst at her.

Ed studied the life-sized painting of the girl in a floor-length white dress. Her long, dark hair, dark eyes, and full lips looked remarkably like Maria's.

"She looks just like that," he said. "It's uncanny."

"Whatever happened to her?" Sue asked, wondering what had become of his lieutenant's wife, as well, and of all the other wives and fiancees of Vietnam's casualties. She supposed that most of them had done as she had upon learning of Dick Chamberlain's death; grieve briefly for their fallen warrior as if it were the end of the world, then realize it wasn't, and get on with their lives.

"I don't know," Ed said. "I've lost track of her."

What *had* become of Maria? he wondered. Had she gone back to Chicago and married the lawyer her father had arranged for her to wed; the one who had promised to keep her in diamonds and furs? He doubted it. She had probably gone to Wyoming to live in the shadow of the Grand Tetons Sam had loved nearly as much as he had loved her.

"And your lieutenant's wife?" Sue asked. "Robbins?"

His brow wrinkled and he gave Sue a curious look before he remembered how she knew about Mike Robbins, then his eyes softened, and he said, "Penny? I don't know. Maybe she got lucky and found a used shoe salesman, like he said."

She started to say something about Dick Chamberlain, and what his loss had meant to her, then decided against it. He hadn't come here to be reminded of war and death and lost friends, and neither had she. "Let's look at some more paintings," she said.

They lingered long among the impressionists' works, and she spent much of the time watching him, his face brightening when he saw a painting he particularly liked. Eventually, he said, "Sue, this is wonderful, but I've got to get off this leg for awhile."

"Why don't we get some bread and cheese and a bottle of wine and go down by the Reflecting Pool for a picnic? It's such a nice day out there. You could lie back and rest that leg of yours."

"Sounds good to me," he said. "'A loaf of bread, a jug of wine, and thou...'"

She drove to a delicatessen and they got French bread, sliced ham and cheese, a bunch of grapes, and a chilled bottle of Riesling.

They parked on Constitution Avenue. Sue had an army poncho liner in her car, so they found a grassy spot beneath the trees and spread the quilted nylon liner there.

They had gotten two cheap wine glasses and a corkscrew. Ed opened the wine and poured them each a glass, then raised his glass to her and said, "Here's looking at you, Lieutenant Madison. Thanks for a wonderful day."

"I'll drink to that," Sue replied, and did so.

They nibbled on their food, watching the people who strolled by and enjoying the warm sun and each other's presence.

After awhile, a couple in hippie garb walked near, their bare-bottomed little daughter toddling ahead of them. Ed watched the child, thinking how nice it would be to have Jimmy here, enjoying a picnic and watching his son play.

The long-haired man noticed the army poncho liner, then Ed's short hair, and his scars. He stopped and stared a moment, then snorted, "What happened, killer? One of the babies shoot back?"

Ed gave him a look of incredulity and propped himself up on his elbows, then said, "You talking to me, buddy?"

"Don't 'buddy' me, you fucking, baby killing pig!"

Ed grabbed for his crutches to get to his feet, but Sue restrained him with a firm hand on his shoulder.

"Look, mister," she said, her voice clear and firm, "we're going to sit here quietly and talk about everything but war and politics. So, we'd appreciate it if you'd go somewhere else, all right?"

Sue's remarks disarmed the man, and as his female companion tugged his arm to lead him away, the only response he made was to give Sue the finger.

She felt Ed tense up and try again to get to his feet, and he said, "Why, you... I'll..."

"No, Eddie. Leave it be," she said softly.

Ed stared hard at the other man, anger and self-discipline competing for control of his emotions. Discipline prevailed, though barely.

The woman looked sadly at Ed, her expression seemingly one of apology, so in spite of the loud, phony laugh the man gave, Ed only stared at him as he turned and walked on. Ed flopped back onto the ground, his burning eyes staring blankly at the bright blue sky.

"Son of a bitch!" he mumbled. "Dirty, no good son of a bitch. I... I just can't believe that actually happened!"

"Forget it, Eddie."

"Forget it, my ass!"

"Forget it. It doesn't mean anything. It doesn't matter," she said and touched her fingertips to his lips.

But it did matter, people like that, and the rest of them; the increasingly loud and numerous mobs, most of them around his age and Sue's, whose only occupation seemed to be protest of the war. It wasn't that he disagreed with their right to protest. It was the empty rhetoric they used - the lack of depth, of thought, in their arguments.

Oh, God, if they could only see what it was doing to the young men who were there in their stead, facing the fear and filth of it day-to-day. It turned their soldier-peers into such cynical young men, when what they needed was to be idealists.

But worst of all, it robbed them of their dignity. It made them feel guilty, as if they were wrong, when they had nothing to do with the right or wrong of the policies that put them there. Most were not even old enough to vote, although there was much talk from the guilty consciences in the government to lower the voting age to eighteen, so that those old enough to die for their country might at least have the right to help determine who their politicians would be.

And this feeling of guilt that was pressed upon the troops by their unthinking peers in the universities, where they were exempt from their country's call to arms - this feeling of guilt added to the heavy burden of fighting the war. It was more than those young men and women should be expected to bear. It would crush them, if they didn't have leaders who could lift at least that part of the burden from their shoulders - young, tough, honest leaders who still retained the ideals, who cared for them, for their dignity, their hearts, their souls. Someone who could make them believe in themselves and what they were trying to do, as Jack Kennedy had done, and who could make them believe in each other, because that was what would keep them alive - that belief in each other, regardless of what girlfriends or school chums or even siblings pretended to believe.

But if they were made to feel that what they were doing was immoral, then they *became* immoral. That was how it really hurt them, because then they would do things that would give them a reason - a personal misdeed - to feel guilty about, so that when it was proved, in the end, that their motives were right, and their sacrifices were noble, that guilt resulting from some personal misconduct would still be there.

That's why it was so wrong, and that was why Ed Walker couldn't leave them. Oh, God, how he hated the mindless mobs of protesters - self-righteous without reason to be so, and destructive of the souls of the less fortunate.

He wondered what his reaction might have been if Sue Madison had not been there, or if he had been whole, or if Sam or Mike had been there when the man called him a "baby killing pig."

He picked up his glass of wine and drained it, then poured himself another, his hand trembling from the adrenaline released in the struggle for control of his anger and hatred.

"It *does* matter, Sue," he said. "The troops - those kids you just spent a year trying to keep alive - deserve better than that. It's not like that son of a bitch was one of a tiny minority."

She knew that was true. But she also knew nothing was to be gained from a violent response to such indignities.

"Maybe when he gets up there, up to the Washington Monument, he'll think about the fact that George Washington was a soldier, too," she said. But she said it without conviction.

"Oh, sure. Fat chance," Ed growled. He watched a Boeing 727 climbing out from National Airport, and wondered how many soldiers might be aboard, headed for the West Coast and on to Vietnam. He wished that hippie bastard were among them, head shorn, in a khaki Army uniform, the fear beginning to gnaw at him. No, the woman and child were probably his wife and daughter, so he was immune to the draft. He dismissed the thought from his mind.

The two young officers lay there and made small talk, and sipped their wine. During one lull in the conversation, Ed lay back and smoked a cigarette. When he turned to Sue to say something, he found that she had dozed off, her head resting in the crook of her elbow and the fingers of her other hand clutching a corner of the poncho liner.

He propped himself up on one elbow and studied her. She reminded him of one of the paintings they had seen in the National Gallery.

He reached over and lightly brushed the hair from her cheek, not wanting to disturb her but unable to resist the urge to touch her, to assure himself that she was real.

Her eyes opened slightly at his touch, and she took his hand and laid it on her shoulder. Ed lay back and pulled her gently toward him until she rested her head on his chest, her arm across his stomach. The weight of her head caused some pain in his injured shoulder, but he ignored it. He savored the feel of her against his chest, the clean scent of her shampoo, the soft sounds of her breathing, until he, too, dozed off.

The sun was noticeably lower in the sky when Ed awoke. He turned his head toward Sue and found her sitting with her legs pulled up beneath her, watching him.

"Hi," she said, smiling. "I need to find a restroom."

Ed laughed. "Me, too."

They got into her car and drove the short distance to the Lincoln Memorial, and when Ed came out of the men's room, he found Sue talking on a pay phone.

"OK, sweetie. Thanks," she said, then hung up.

Oh, hell, Ed thought. I've probably kept her from a date. "Sue, I guess I should be getting back to the hospital," he said as they walked back to the car.

"Why? Is your leg bothering you that badly?"

"No, it's just... well, you probably have better things to do."

"Than what?"

"Than spending your time with a beat up old war horse."

"Oh, just get in," she said.

They got into the car and drove out of the parking lot, and Ed said, "It was really nice of you to do this, Sue. The nicest day I've had in a long time... well, except for that long haired... Anyway, thanks. Uh, why don't you just drop me off at the shuttle bus stop?"

"Oh, I couldn't do that, Eddie."

"Sure you can. There's no need for you to take me all the way out to Walter Reed."

"I'm not taking you to the hospital, Eddie. We're going to Angela's apartment. I just spoke to her on the phone. She's working tonight. She's going to sign you out on overnight pass when she gets to Walter Reed."

He looked at her quizzically, unsure of exactly what she meant, what she intended.

"Unless you'd rather go to the hospital, Eddie. I'm sorry. I should have asked you, first."

"No. I mean, yes. Hell, what I mean is, I'd love to... to go to Angela's place with you, Sue."

She reached over and took his hand in hers, and said, "I thought all you wounded soldier boys were supposed to fall in love with your nurses."

Ed squeezed her hand and said, "There's a lot of truth in that, you know. But most of them never see the ones they really fall for again; the ones they see when they first look up from the litter or the recovery ward, and realize that they are going to live, after all. They dream about those nurses for the rest of their lives, I imagine."

She looked at him and intertwined her fingers with his. "Well," she said softly, "tonight one of you, at least, is going have that dream come true."

He closed his eyes and leaned his head back. So she *did* mean that they were going to spend the night together; become lovers. Long dormant feelings stirred in him. Sweet Jesus, how long had it been? How long since he had known the warmth of an embrace, the caressing, the passion?

"Lord, listen to me, Eddie. I sound like some Fourteenth Street hooker. You must think I'm terrible."

He stroked her cheek with the back of his hand. "No, Sue," he said. "I don't think that at all."

After a time, she said, "I still have that letter you wrote to me in Cam Ranh hospital, Ed. It means a lot to me."

He smiled. "I still have the one you wrote to me, too."

"Really?"

"Really." Again, he stroked her cheek, then toyed with the back of her hair. "So, maybe this was meant to be."

"Yes. Maybe it was."

They found the key that Angela had left beneath the door mat, inside a folded note that read, "Booze in the bar, food in the fridge, bed in the bedroom... LOVE! Angie"

They went inside, and Sue pointed to the makeshift bar and said, "Would you like to fix us a drink? I'll have a gin and tonic. I've got to phone my dad."

As Ed fixed two gin and tonics, he heard her on the telephone. "Dad? Hi. Listen, I'm going to spend the night at Angela's, OK?... Yes, we had a wonderful time, Daddy. The National Gallery, and a nice little picnic beside the Reflecting Pool... Yes, he's a very nice guy, Dad... OK, I'll tell him... All right. Love you, Dad. Bye."

She hung up the telephone and took the drink Ed handed her. "To us," she said softly.

"Yes. To us. To soldiers and their nurses."

"To this soldier, and this nurse. Now, wasn't there something in Angela's note about a bed in the bedroom?"

"There was. And 'LOVE,' in capital letters."

She led him to the bedroom. He sat on the bed and put his crutch aside, and she sat beside him. They kissed a gentle kiss, and he lowered himself onto his back, the only way he could lie comfortably because of the cast on his leg. She lay down next to him, her face close to his ear, and said, "It looks as if I've found the note you put in the bottle after all, doesn't it, Eddie Walker."

"Yes," he said, drawing her mouth to his, "it does."

Their loving was gentle, tentative at first, she above him, obeying his hands and his whispers. There was tenderness, then passion, then satisfaction, and more tenderness. There was no one else, no other thing that mattered, at least for that one night.

Sue awoke early the next morning to the sound of water filling the bathtub, and soft music from the little living room, and the smell of coffee brewing. For a long time, she lay there quietly, remembering the joy of the night before. She thought briefly of Curt Draeger, the Army doctor who was her first lover, and of Dick Chamberlain, who had been her only true love until now. She recalled the days at Cam Ranh Bay, where she had first seen despair and fear and courage, and utter hopelessness. Where she had met Dick, and lost him, then Ed, and nearly lost him, too. And so many others so much like them, and so much different from them. She recalled Ed's anger at the news of Mike Robbins's death - how that anger had caused Ed to lash out at her, just because she was there, and how she had lashed back at him.

She imagined him during the sapper attack just after that. Hadn't someone put him in for a medal for what he did?

She remembered the sadness and the anger in the one deep green eye that had been unbandaged at the time; the same anger and the same sadness she had seen yesterday when that fool of a man made the remark about killing babies.

She recalled the chance encounter at the bus stop, when she found him sitting there, knowing at first only that he was someone familiar, then recognizing the eye, both eyes, repulsed at first because he reminded her of that awful place. Then she had remembered his letter; "...without your help, there would be a lot more of us going home in body bags instead of bandages..." Words that made her recall the moments of love and of valor amidst the carnage.

Then a song came drifting in from the radio. *Where have all the flowers gone? Long time passing...*

Twenty-one years of carefree youth had passed without meaning, it seemed, and then her twenty-second year and half of the next had been spent in Cam Ranh Hospital. Eighteen months that aged her beyond measure.

Where have all the young men gone? Gone for soldiers, every one. When will they ever learn? When will they ever learn?

Sue Madison wept, and wondered why. Was it for herself? For Dick Chamberlain? For Ed? For all of them?

The bathroom door opened, and Ed stood there on one crutch, a towel wrapped around his waist. He saw that She was weeping, and limped to the bed and took her in his arms. She made no effort to stop her tears, because she knew he understood them. He held her close against him, gently stroking her hair, and she realized that she had fallen in love.

She had promised herself never to do so again; not after the pain Dick's loss had caused her. And especially not with another soldier, not while there was still war. But she knew all along that she hadn't meant it. She knew deep inside herself that she would fall in love again. And she couldn't imagine falling in love with anyone except a soldier. They were the only ones who could possibly understand her, and she knew that Ed Walker did.

And so she wept until the pain was all washed away for awhile, and then her soldier made love to her again.

TWENTY FOUR

Ed was released from Walter Reed Army Medical Center for ten days of convalescent leave a week after he and Sue became lovers. After his leave, he was to return to the hospital to determine if further surgery would be required to repair his ankle, and to complete the reconstructive surgery on his jaw.

He couldn't decide whether to spend his leave in Washington so that he could see Sue during her off-duty time, or to go home to Guinea and spend time with his brother's family. There, he would be able to see Jimmy, too, although he was apprehensive about how the boy would react to him. Perhaps it would be better to wait awhile longer before trying to establish a relationship with the son he barely knew. Or was that just a cop out, an excuse to avoid the possible rejection the child might show him? he wondered.

Sue solved his dilemma when she learned he had been granted convalescent leave. "I have about three weeks of leave time coming myself, Ed," she said. "Why don't I take a week? We can go somewhere together, if you'd like."

They left the next day in Sue's little Volkswagen, crossing the bay bridge at Annapolis and driving down the Delmarva peninsula to Virginia's Eastern Shore.

There were quite a few watermen on the bay, and Ed explained to Sue what the men on each boat were doing.

"You miss that, don't you?" Sue asked.

Ed glanced back at the boats and the watermen, then shook his head and said, "Not really. What I really miss is Sam and Mike and men like that. Not just the dead ones, but all of them. The soldiers. That's what I really miss."

She took his hand in hers and squeezed it. "If the war were over, would you stay in?" she asked.

"The war won't end," he said. "This one might, but there will be others. There always will."

Yes, she thought. And good men like you will always go. And she wondered if that was *why* there would always be war; because of good men trying to right wrongs.

They spent the night in a cheap motel in Norfolk. Their lovemaking was tender, but he seemed detached, as if his mind was somewhere else. Ed slept fitfully, and Sue noticed, because she barely slept at all herself.

They spoke little the next morning as she drove through the farmland that led toward North Carolina's Outer Banks.

Near Currituck Courthouse, there was an old Chevrolet beside the road with a flat tire. Two elderly ladies stood beside it, looking perplexed. "Pull over and let me help them," Ed said. Sue braked and pulled off the road and Ed got out and hobbled back to the car.

Sue watched him in the side mirror of the Volkswagen as he changed the tire, the women looking curiously at the fresh purple scars on his face as he did so.

What is it about you, Edward Walker? she wondered as she watched him. What is it that makes being with you, loving you, so bittersweet? How can you make me so happy and so sad all at the same time?

She sucked in a deep breath for a heavy sigh, and pain shot through her chest. There was something about all of this - about Eddie Walker and love and war; about the future and what it held. Something that left her with a sense of foreboding. She loved him. She could not deny herself that fact. But she could never really have him; not as long as there was war, and there were soldiers to be led. So she would share him; share him with war and with his soldiers, and try to give him moments of beauty amid the pain and despair that was so much a part of soldiering.

She thought of Mary Walker. She knew so little about her, the woman who was still his wife. But Sue knew enough to hate her. If it weren't for Jimmy, their son, Sue thought. *If, if, if...*

He was finished with the tire now. While he lowered the car and put the jack away, one of the women came up to Sue's car, and Sue hopped out to talk to her.

"I just wanted to tell you, honey," the elderly woman said, "that we're sorry to bother you like this. I don't know what we'd have done if weren't for you and your husband stopping to help us. Thank you so very much."

"Oh, you're certainly welcome, ma'am. It's no bother at all," Sue said.

"I don't mean to be personal, miss, but his scars - are they from the war?"

"Yes, ma'am."

"I was afraid of that." She looked back at Ed and shook her head. "They put up with so much, our boys do in this one. And then they come home, and people treat them the way they do. These protests and all of that. It's a crying shame."

"Yes, it is," Sue answered, watching Ed struggling to put the flat tire in the trunk. She thought of the man who had accosted them with such cruel words while they were picnicking on the grass in Washington. And she thought of Mary again. "It's a crying shame."

"He won't have to go back, will he? After his wounds are healed, I mean."

"No," Sue said. "He won't have to go back." Then her eyes misted and she said, "But he probably will. He's that kind of man."

The stranger placed her aged hand on Sue's arm. "Oh, I'm sorry, honey. Now I've upset you. Don't you worry. We'll pray for him. And for you, too."

Sue wiped her tears away and nodded, and the elderly lady patted her arm, then walked back toward her car.

Sue heard the other old woman, who had been chatting with Ed as he changed the tire, say, "Frances, these young folks - he's an Army captain and she's a nurse - are going to the Outer Banks for a week. There's nobody in your beach cottage in Nags Head, is there?"

Frances looked back at Sue and smiled. "No, there certainly isn't. In fact, there hasn't been anyone there in quite some time. It would be good if somebody stayed there for a change. Air the place out and run the water so the pipes won't get rusted." She looked at Ed and said, "I wonder if you youngsters would be interested in staying there? It would be doing me a real favor."

Ed looked at Sue, who smiled and nodded. "That would be very kind of you," he said. "Are you sure?"

"Of course I am, son," the elderly lady replied, digging into her purse for the key. "It's the least I can do."

*   *   *

The Atlantic Ocean off Nags Head was unusually clear and the surf was nearly flat and full of Spanish mackerel.

In a corner of the porch, Ed found a rod and a reel spun with eight or ten pound test line. There was a small tackle box there, too. He dug through it until he found a little gold-colored Hopkins lure.

He left his crutches on the porch and limped through the soft sand on his plaster cast. The damp sand at the water's edge would probably ruin it, but Ed didn't care. He was tired of the thing, and anyway, you couldn't fish on crutches. The wound was nearly healed and didn't hurt much any more.

He didn't get a hit on the first two casts although he could see several of the sleek, fast Spanish breaking the surface of the water near the lure. He cast again in front of them and reeled the lure in quickly. *There*. One of the fish - a nice sized one, by the feel of it - took the lure.

Sue walked out onto the porch of the little beachfront cottage and watched him. Beyond him, the huge orange ball of the rising sun climbed above the bare horizon.

It was so beautiful, so peaceful, she thought. And so different from the last time she had stood like this looking at him standing on a beach. A very distant beach.

He got the fish in, and she could see him deftly remove the hook and hop closer to the water. When the next swell washed up, he raised his cast and leaned over, releasing the fish into the receding surf. Sue found it strangely sensual, and thought, Perhaps it's the gentleness. Yes. That's what he showed me last night, and again early this morning when we made love just as dawn was breaking.

Ed looked back toward the cottage and saw her standing on the porch sipping coffee from a mug. There was a look of happiness that she had not seen before on his face.

He started limping toward her, so she went out to meet him, intending to help him back to the cottage. But when she approached him, he reached out and held her away from him at arm's length. "I've never been happier than I am right now, Sue. Never."

She slid against him, her arms around his waist and her head against his chest. "Neither have I, Ed," she said softly. She knew that something else was coming, something she wouldn't want to hear; some but or if.

"If it weren't for little Jimmy. If it weren't for my son, I..."

She stopped his words with a kiss, but she couldn't stop her tears. He was going to leave her. Not now, not this week. But someday, someday soon, because of the sense of obligation he felt toward his child, he would go away from her, back to his son, and his son's mother.

He touched her cheek with his fingertips and felt the tears, held her away from him and looked at her. "I wish he was yours, Sue. Ours."

She laid her head against his chest again, tears flowing from her eyes. Bittersweet tears. "I do, too, Ed," she tried to say, but the words caught in her throat, and she thought, I wish it with all my heart. But he isn't.

They spent three days there. He taught her to fish in the surf, and she taught him to play cribbage. Twice, they went to restaurants for dinner, but the rest of the time they spent at the cottage the elderly woman had let them use, making love or playing cribbage or fishing from the beach in front of the place.

Early on the fourth morning, when the wind had risen and driven the fish away, he said, "Sue, let's go to Ocracoke Island."

"Where's that?"

"It's south of here," he said. "Nothing there, except beach and marsh and a little fishing village. That's what I love about the place. We can spend the day, and come back tonight."

But they didn't come back that night. Sue fell in love with the quaint little village and the old lighthouse and the spectacular sunset they watched that evening across the island's snug harbor.

They stopped by the commercial fish house, South Point Seafood, and Ed spoke to the fishermen there. She listened in fascination as he spoke to them with an accent like their own. They asked him about his wounds, but all he said was, "Don't mean nothin'," so the subject was dropped.

One of them handed him an onion bag as they were leaving. It was half-full of clams, and he looked inside and said, "Top necks. Much obliged, Bubba."

"Well, you enjoy 'em, Buck. You, too, young lady. And y'all come on back and see us."

"Thank you," Sue said. "We will. I love this place."

When they were in the car, Ed said, "I love this place, too."

She smiled and thought, We could be happy here. If I could only keep him here, away from the war, away from her... "Then let's stay," she said. "Let's stay as long as we can."

They rented a cottage on the harbor; one with a kitchenette. Then they went to the community store, and Ed bought a bulb of garlic, a hunk of salt pork and some potatoes, celery, onions, and fresh, ripe tomatoes.

They had brought two bottles of red wine with them, and while they drank one of them, Sue helped Ed make clam chowder his favorite way. While he scrubbed the small clams - there must have been about fifty of them - she peeled and chopped the onions and potatoes and some celery. "Shall I chop the tomatoes, too?" she asked as he browned the pork and onions and a smashed clove of garlic in a big pot.

"No," he said. "Just hand me that glass of wine."

She did, and Ed fished out the remains of the garlic and threw it away. He poured his wine into the pot, and it crackled and spattered in the melted pork fat. Then he threw the clams in, covered the pot, turned the gas burner down some, and poured himself another glass of wine.

He sat down beside Sue to rest his injured leg, and she said, "Won't it burn?"

He shook his head. "The clams'll start opening in a minute, and there will be lots of juice."

Ed told her some of the island's history while they waited, then he got up, checked the pot, and said, "Look at this."

The clams had nearly all opened, and the ingredients were steeping in the greasy juice. He dropped the celery and potatoes in, then held the tomatoes over the pot and crushed them with his hands, so that their juice was added to the stew. After he pulled the tomatoes apart with his fingers and dropped them in, he added a palmful of black pepper, then covered the pot.

"It'll take awhile to cook," he said, and she said, "Good," then took his hand and led him to the bedroom. He paused just long enough to lift the lid from the pot and pour in the rest of his wine.

Later, while Sue was in the shower, he fished the clam shells out, then poured the chowder from one pot to another several times to remove the grit. "There," he said to himself. "It's ready."

Sue thought it was by far the best clam chowder she'd ever eaten, with the little, succulent whole clams and delicious broth.

"Too much wine," Ed said, but he ate two-thirds of it.

The next day, they drove halfway up the narrow, sixteen-mile-long barrier island. There were no beach houses to spoil it, because it was a national park now, except for the little fishing village near its southern end.

The small nor'easter that had spoiled the fishing at Nags Head was gone, and the surf was nearly flat again. Ed fished while Sue jogged a mile along the beach. She didn't see anyone else or even a footprint. There were shells along the high-tide line, and she stopped on the way back to pick some of them up.

When she reached Ed, he was sitting on the sand, leaning back on his elbows and watching her. His fishing rod was in a rod holder, but the line was in the water, and she knelt beside him and kissed his scarred cheek.

"Bottom fishing, huh?" she said, and he nodded and grinned at her newly-acquired fishing term.

She showed him the shells she had collected, and he told her what each of them was; scotch bonnet, olive, cockle, tulip, and whelk. "They're my treasures," she said, placing them in one of her shoes. Then she lay back on the sand and said, "This whole island is a treasure. Thank you for bringing me here, Eddie."

He didn't answer her, but he heard her, and thought of his son, and how much he wanted to teach Jimmy these things - surf fishing, and the names of seashells. And to show him places like this, and America's other national treasures. And he thought of divorce, and lawyers, and knew that he would never get custody. Visitation rights, yes. But he would always be somewhere far away.

The tip of his fishing rod was dancing, and when he saw it, he dropped the subject from his mind and pushed himself up from the sand to reel in the line and see what he had caught.

*   *   *

Father Fallon noticed that Sue Madison was gone from Walter Reed at the same time Captain Walker was away on convalescent leave. When Ed returned from the evaluation of his ankle the day after his leave ended, the priest was waiting for him in his room.

"Come with me, Walker," Fallon said, and Ed followed the wheelchair down the hall to an unoccupied room.

They went inside and Fallon wheeled about. "Close the door and sit down," he said.

Ed did so, sitting on one of the beds with his legs dangling over the side, wondering what Fallon wanted of him.

The priest studied the infantry captain for awhile, then pulled out his flask of Irish whiskey, took a slug, and handed it to Ed. Ed took a drink and asked, "OK, what is it, Padre?"

"You're feeling a hell of a lot better, aren't you?"

He smiled warmly at the strange priest, the good friend who had done so much to lift him from despair. "Yeah, Padre, I really am. I found some of that American beauty you sent me out to look for."

"Yeah, so I've noticed. You'll be getting out of here soon."

"Thank God for that."

"*You* thank Him, boy. Make sure you do. Formally."

Ed pondered Fallon's words. He supposed that's what this was all about, a "go to church" lecture.

He hadn't really given much thought to religion lately. But yes, he believed in God, and in the teachings of Jesus Christ, if not necessarily in the way the various churches interpreted them.

"OK, Father. I will."

"Good. And while you're at it, ask Him how to help you figure out how to salvage your marriage."

No, Ed thought, *that's* what this is all about. He reached out toward the flask the priest held. Fallon took a swallow before he handed it to Ed, who drank deeply from it, then passed it back.

"I'm not so sure it can *be* salvaged," Ed said.

"Bullshit! It can if you want it to, boy. If you're willing to put the necessary effort into it, willing to make the sacrifice of a little of your God-given time."

Ed gave an insincere laugh. "Sacrifice?" he said. "Haven't I sacrificed enough already, Father?" He immediately regretted having said that to the wheelchair-bound man in front of him.

Fallon looked at him with a mixture of sadness and disgust. "Son, when they shame you and forsake you and nail you up on a cross, and you die - *then* you'll have sacrificed enough."

"Oh, Padre. I know what you mean. But I didn't abandon Mary. I wanted more than anything in the world to come home to her, to love her and take care of her. She's the one who... who wants to be rid of *me*!"

"And rid of the Army?"

"Yes, and rid of the Army."

"Then the Army may be what you have to sacrifice, Walker."

Ed lay back on the bed and lit a cigarette. "No way, Padre. No way. It's destructive, and it's fucked up, and it's unpopular as hell these days," he said, and thought of the long-haired man who had disturbed the picnic he and Sue were having two weeks before. "But it's necessary. "It's, it's good. Hell, it made a man of me, Padre. It's given my life meaning. And besides, I'm damned good at it, I think."

He took a long drag of his cigarette, exhaled, and said, "I'm meant to be a soldier, Father."

"Yeah, well, you're also a husband, and you're a father, Walker - whether you *meant* to be or not."

"I can have my son without having my marriage."

"I doubt that. But it's not the point anyway. Your wedding vows are just as important as your oath of commission, Captain. More important, because you swore your marriage vows to God."

"I swore my oath of commission to God, too; 'I solemnly swear... blah, blah, blah... so help me God.'"

The crippled priest's voice took on a softer tone. "Yes, you did, Walker. And you've upheld that oath well - damned well. Nearly died doing so. But your obligation to that oath ends when you leave the Army. Only death terminates your wedding vows."

There was truth in that, if one believed vows were more than mere words parroted after an officer or a minister. And they certainly were to this priest of the Roman Catholic Church. But Ed and Mary were not Catholic.

Ed sat up and clasped the priest's shoulder. "I know you mean that, Father. And that you believe it. But I'm not certain that I do." He snuffed his cigarette out in a bedpan and looked into Fallon's fiery eyes.

"I'll think on it. I'll really think it through. One way or the other, I have to get it settled, anyway, don't I?"

"Yes, you do, Walker. And you have to do it before you hurt Lieutenant Madison. She's in love with you, you know. And she's been hurt enough already, hasn't she?"

"What do you mean?"

"I mean the Special Forces sergeant she lost in Vietnam. I mean a year and a half of hell patching up guys like you and me, and watching the ones who weren't as fortunate as us die. I mean the fact that you're married, and that she knows, in the end, you'll do what's right and go back to your wife and son. So do it now, before you hurt her even worse."

Before Ed could reply, the priest backed his wheelchair away and left the room.

Ed lay on the bed chain-smoking Lucky Strikes and thinking. The light-hearted happiness that had been building inside him the previous two weeks had suddenly been crushed. He recalled a line of graffiti he had seen on a latrine wall in Vietnam: "*Life's a bitch, and then you die.*"

It had been two wonderful and happy weeks. It was a time that he would always remember as a time of love and healing, regardless of what might happen in the future; a time for which, he knew, Sue Madison would always have a special place in his heart. And he in hers. She had said so. She had said that she felt renewed, and that, because of him, she had finally been able to rid herself of the pain she had felt since the loss of Dick Chamberlain.

But she's never said that she loves me. She is my lover, yes, and she even said that she wished Jimmy was her son. But this is the Sixties, for Christ's sake. Just because you screw somebody doesn't mean that you have to spend the rest of your life with them, does it?

Was Sue in love with him? he wondered.

No, there was still some gap, some uncrossable line between them. Sometimes it seemed to be uncertainty or fear, sometimes a mood that's just a little too light, some slight distraction. He couldn't quite nail it down, but it was there. And since it was, the priest must be wrong. It wasn't really love. Not the kind that he and Mary had known.

Mary. She had strayed, but what the hell did he expect? He had left her pregnant and alone, and had showed up on leave only long enough to tell her that he had extended his tour, and to run off to Sam's funeral. And then he came home like this - all shot up and scarred and unable to even help her care for their son. And then what did he do? Instead of trying to make that lost time up to her, he ran off to the beach with another woman. A wonderful, caring woman, yes. But not his wife. Not the mother of his son.

Ed Walker lit another cigarette, conflicting loyalties and emotions storming in his brain. He smoked the rest of the pack, then opened another, weighing his feelings for Mary and for Sue and for little Jimmy, and weighing the words of the strange, crippled priest.

Finally, as his hospital room began to lighten with the dawning of a new day, Ed Walker realized what he had to do.

He had to try.

They might not be able to make it work - Mary might not even *want* to try. But he had to try. And if it didn't work, then maybe it wasn't meant to be. Maybe that would prove he belonged with someone like Sue. Someone who understands that life is a struggle. A painful struggle.

Sue stood with her back to him and bit down hard on her lip, fighting to keep the tears from falling. She had known all along that it was coming, but that didn't help. "I understand, Ed!" she said as angrily as she could. "It's no big deal. I had fun. I learned to fish. I discovered Ocracoke Island. Don't worry about it. I knew all along it would come to this."

'No big deal,' he thought, and the words angered him. He didn't want it to be this easy. Then he realized it was selfish to feel that way, and he said, "Well, that's that, then."

"Yes, that's that," she said.

"But if it doesn't work out, Sue, I..."

"God *damn* you, don't say it!" she yelled, turning to face him. She bit the gum inside her lower lip to keep it from trembling. "Just... just don't say anything else. Just go. I understand."

He sighed, then shrugged. "I want us to be friends, though, Sue. I... you've done a lot for me. You'll never know how m..."

"Don't mean nothin'," she said before he could finish.

He was wearing his Army Greens, and he had put his ribbons on because Mary was coming to pick him up, and he wanted her to see them.

Sue looked at them, knowing how much they meant when they'd really been earned, as his had. Then she said, "Damn, Captain," shaking her head in mock disgust. "You could at least get your ribbons on right."

"What do you mean?"

"You've got your campaign ribbon on the wrong side of the NDSM. Didn't they teach you anything in OCS?"

He laughed, as much with relief as in amusement, glad that there was something frivolous to talk about, and to bring their farewell to an end. "I'll get 'em straight before I sign in at Fort Benning," he said. "Those damn civilians at home will never know the difference."

There was nothing more to say after that, except "Goodbye, Sue."

"Goodbye, Eddie."

She watched him limp away, leaning on his cane.

She wanted to just go somewhere and die, but she didn't. She went back to her duties and tended to the suffering of others, ignoring her own deep hurt.

Father Fallon was waiting at the entrance to the ward when the shift changed, and when Sue walked out, he said, "Madison, I want to talk to you."

She gave him a puzzled look, but he had already spun his chair around, headed for an empty room on the next ward. She followed him, and when they were in the room, he held up a bottle of Irish whiskey he had produced from somewhere and said, "You look like you could use a drink."

For a moment, she thought it was the ploy of a crippled, dirty old man. Then he said, "Walker's not the only one out there, Lieutenant. And he's not the best one, either. Not for you, at least. Now, get the cap off this God damned jug, and let's talk about it."

   *   *   *

Ed entered her gently, trying to be as tender with her as he could, whispering softly, "Oh, God, Mary. I've missed you so much."

But she dug her fingernails into his back, and bit his shoulder until he gasped with the pain of it.

He pulled his head back to look at her, to ask what he was doing wrong that would make her want to hurt him like that. And then he saw the look in her eyes; the amber flecks as clear as hot stars, the expression on her face one of animal desire.

He thrust himself hard into her, and her mouth opened and she sucked air deep into her lungs, her eyes wide, staring beyond him. He thrust again, and her eyelids closed and she moaned, "Yes!" Again, and she pulled his mouth to hers. And again, even harder, and she bit his lip until it bled and they both tasted his blood.

He reached beneath her and dug his fingernails into the firm flesh there, and she cried out - *yes* and *me* and *harder*, and words that he had never heard her use before, and it was like nothing he had ever known.

TWENTY FIVE

It was raining so hard as she crossed the long bridge across Currituck Sound that Sue Madison down-shifted the little Volkswagen and crept along at twenty miles an hour. It was too early in the Spring for there to be much traffic between the mainland and the Outer Banks of North Carolina, the thin chain of long, barrier islands that run from the Virginia line, most of the way down the Carolina coast.

When she reached the end of the bridge she pulled off the road to wait for the thick, pelting rain to subside. She shifted into neutral, pulled up the emergency brake, but left the engine running and the windshield wipers on.

She leaned back against the seat and flinched at the sharp pain in her neck, took a deep breath - as deep as she could, at least - and felt the now familiar tightness in her chest, and the dull pain that seemed to radiate from between her breasts. She was so very tired.

She reached up and adjusted the rear-view mirror so that she could look at herself, and studied her thin cheeks and tired eyes with the dark lines beneath them. They looked sunken and ugly. She grasped the top of the steering wheel tightly with both hands and leaned her head forward against her knuckles.

"Dear God!" she cried aloud. "Why do I have to die?" Why do I have to die?"

But Susan Madison *was* dying; slowly but certainly, and with ever-increasing pain.

She had feared so, long before she mustered the courage to admit that something was wrong, to submit herself to the examination that she knew in her mind would prove the ugly truth. She had cancer, and she would die from it while she was still young.

It had been two weeks since Sue sat nervously in Tom Goldson's office, waiting for him to finish with another patient, hoping against hope that he would say it was something else - something operable, something curable. But she was a nurse. She knew better. He pulled up a chair beside hers, sat down, and took her hand in his. He said nothing for awhile, simply studying her face with undisguised sadness in his eyes. She knew, then. Without a doubt, she knew.

Finally Tom spoke. "It's the worst, Sue."

That was all he said at first, ensuring that it sank in, that she understood fully before he bothered to explain the extent of it, what could and could not be done.

"How long, Tom?" she asked, a sickening, sinking feeling engulfing her as if it would swallow her up.

"Oh, Sue, Sue. You know I can't tell. We'll have to do some more tests, and... ."

"How *long*, Tom?"

He still studied her face, and she let go of his hand.

He looked down at both of his hands, clasped them together, then looked at her again. "A few months, maybe a year. Probably something in between."

She felt nauseated now, sitting in the little car, and she opened the door and hung her head out in the downpour. She retched, and retched again. Nothing came up, and she sobbed, feeling miserable and hopeless and utterly alone.

She sat up, leaving the door open and feeling the rainwater run from her hair down her face. A car approached from the other direction, lights on. It passed, leaving a bubbly wake in the road.

She pushed her hair back from both sides of her face, then leaned forward, shifted into first gear, and pulled slowly out onto the road. The thundershower was abating now, and she shifted through the gears and drove on toward Cape Hatteras, and Ocracoke Island.

*   *   *

"Gentlemen, as we have seen this hour, the Mechanized Infantry Combat Vehicle will add a new dimension to the modern battlefield," the major behind the podium of the big classroom said.

Ed Walker yawned, thankful that this was the last hour he would have to spend in the classroom this Friday afternoon. He closed his notebook and listened to the instructor summarize the period of instruction on the soon-to-be-fielded combat vehicle.

"Goddam squad coffin, that's what they should call it," mumbled Hank Wittenberg, sitting beside Ed.

Hank had sat beside Ed throughout the thirteen weeks they'd been in the Infantry Officers' Advanced Course. The two captains had become friends during that time, frequently drinking a few beers together in the Infantry Bar after class.

Hank had served in the First Cav his last tour in Vietnam, and the two men discovered that they had a number of mutual friends.

The instructor dismissed the class, and the room was filled with the hubbub of a hundred and sixty young officers, all recent veterans of combat, now finished with another boring week in class. They gathered up their books and handouts and began filing out.

"Hey, guys," Bill Garrison said. "What say we hit the I bar for a couple of beers?"

"Why not?" Hank answered. "We owe it to our bodies. How about it, Ed?"

"Sure," Ed replied. Mary played bridge on Friday afternoons, and Jimmy was at the baby sitter's house.

As they walked out into the corridor of Infantry Hall, Hank stopped to look at the next week's training schedule on the class bulletin board.

"Hey, Ed," he said. "There's a note here for you." He pulled out the thumbtack and handed Ed a folded piece of paper with Captain Edward Walker, IOAC 6-70," printed in bold letters on the outside.

Ed took the note, unfolded it, and read, *Captain Walker, Call Colonel Madison, HQDA, at the following number...* It gave Madison's duty numbers at the Pentagon.

What the devil could this be about? Ed wondered. Maybe Madison is coming to Fort Benning and wants to get together, or something. "I'll meet y'all in the bar in a little while," he said to his friends. "Gotta make a phone call."

"Trouble at home?" Hank called after him.

"Negative. Some colonel in the Pentagon. Probably wants my advice on how to win the war," he joked. Curious, he went to the reception office and called Madison's number. A sergeant answered after one ring. Ed identified himself and asked for Colonel Madison.

"Ed? Harry Madison here."

"Yes, sir. I had a note to call you."

"Yes. Listen, Ed, have you heard from Susan lately?"

Ed's brow furrowed, puzzled. "No, sir. Not since I was at Walter Reed about three weeks ago. Is anything wrong?"

"No. No, Ellen and I just wondered if she might have said something to you about going somewhere. You know, going to visit friends or something."

"No, sir. Not that I can recall."

"Well, if you hear from her, give me a call, will you?"

"Of course. How is Mrs. Madison, Colonel?"

"Well, a bit panicked right now, son. Ed, listen. Did you know that Susan is ill?"

Ill? She had looked a bit pale when he saw her last, three weeks earlier during a trip to Walter Reed to finish the last bit of surgery on his jaw. He recalled that she kept reaching back to rub her neck. Yes, she had looked ill. In fact, she had said that she must be getting the flu. "She did look kind of sick the last time I saw her, now that you mention it, Colonel Madison. She seemed to think that she might be coming down with the flu, or something."

"The flu. Jesus, how I wish.... She's a very sick girl, Ed. She's - well, she's dying," he said, his voice cracking. "She has bone cancer."

The words first stunned Ed, and then they nauseated him. Revulsion welled up from deep inside him, then turned to anger. Oh, God damn it, *no*! Not Sue.

The image of Sue when he had first seen her came into his mind. He saw her standing on the beach at Cam Ranh Bay, then pictured her walking toward him at the bus stop at Walter Reed. He saw her on the beach at Ocracoke, laughing, and he saw her lying beneath him, her eyes fixed desperately on his as they gave their physical love to each other. Then he pictured her turning away from him, disappearing. Dying.

Ed's hand, holding the telephone, had drifted away from his ear down to his side. He returned the telephone to his ear, his hands trembling now.

"Walker?" her father was saying.

"Yes. I'm here, Colonel. I'm... I just can't believe it, sir."

"Where do think she might have gone, son?" Madison asked. "I know she wouldn't... wouldn't take it on herself to... to end it."

"No, of course she wouldn't," Ed mumbled. "Let me think about it for a few minutes. I'll call you back."

"All right then, Ed. Try your best to think of where she might have gone."

"I will, Colonel. I'll call you back in a few minutes."

The telephone went dead, and Ed slowly hung it up.

His mind began to rage. It just doesn't make any sense, he thought. It can't be true, because there's no *reason* for it. No God would allow it. Not Sue.

He walked out into the spacious lobby of Infantry Hall and stood looking out of the tall windows past the statue of the World War One Doughboy, perpetually leading his infantrymen out of the trenches and into the storm of battle, silently calling *Follow me!*

Ed felt deceived. If Sue was dying, then there was no justice in the world, no fairness. He shook his head and thought, It just *can't* be true. They've made a mistake. Still, they *think* it's true; *she* must think it's true.

After all she has done. It was as if she were out there somewhere wounded, now; lost, wandering around in the jungle alone, as he once had. Alone. Would she *want* to be alone? Or would she go to someone. There must be someone she would turn to. Perhaps she'd gone to Angela. They shared no secrets, it seemed. But wouldn't her parents have called Angela first? If not Angela, then who? Is there any man she's that close to? Father Fallon?

No, he's gone. Retired and gone to Hawaii.

Who, then? Me? Possibly. Maybe she *is* on the way here to see me. We're good friends, now. We laughed and had lunch together and acted as if that was all we'd ever been, the last two times I went to Walter Reed. Even Mary understands that's all we ever really were. "Like Sam," she'd said. "A war buddy you love like you loved Sam."

What other man does she care as much for? Her father, certainly. Yes, she told me once that when she was a kid, here at Fort Benning, she broke her leg, and that the thing that hurt her the most was that her father was not there. But she hasn't gone to him. Where else would she go? Where the hell would I go, if I were Sue; if I were dying and alone and wanted to think it all out? The water. That's where I'd go. A beach.

He remembered standing on the beach at Cam Ranh hospital, staring out to sea on the day they met.

God, it seemed so long ago. If only she were standing here now, and he could take her arm and lead her to the hospital, as she had done for him... They would heal her, make her well, as they had healed him.

No. No, her father knew what he was saying when he said she was dying. Bone cancer. Jesus. You can't sew up bone cancer. You can't repair it the way you can a gunshot wound - not yet. Maybe soon, though, maybe before it gets so bad that it kills her. Yes. They've found a cure for nearly everything else, so why not cancer? Some of the best doctors in the country, in the world, are working on it. Maybe soon they'll find the cure.

But they haven't found it yet. Right now, the thing is to find Sue. The beach; the Outer Banks. *Ocracoke!* That's where she would go. Her treasure, Ocracoke Island.

He called Harry Madison's Pentagon office again.

"Sir, it's Ed. Have you checked with Angela?"

"Yes, we did, Ed," Madison said. "She hasn't seen Sue since the day before yesterday."

"Do you think she'd come here to Fort Benning, sir? "

"I don't know. Maybe. We've thought about it, and you would be... I mean, we think she'd go to you, if anyone, Ed. Or maybe she'd just go off somewhere alone, to think things out."

Ed sighed. He felt unworthy of the trust or the love or whatever it was that caused her father to think that Sue would turn to him at a time like this. "Maybe she *would* want to go off somewhere to think things out, sir," he said to her father. "If so, my guess is that she'd go to the Outer Banks."

"Yes, she might well do so," Madison replied. "I'll check with the sheriff's office down there, and...."

"Sir, let me go look for her. I can be there sometime tonight."

"No, you don't need to do that. I can have the sher..."

"Please, Colonel Madison. I want to. Really. Christ, it's the least I can do. I'll leave right away."

He was certain now that he was right. She was somewhere on the Outer Banks, probably Ocracoke Island, trying to sort things out. Trying to justify how - why - this should happen to her. He didn't know why he was so sure, but he was.

"I know she's out there, sir. I'll call as soon as I find her. I'll call when I get out there, anyway, to see if you've heard anything."

"Well, I'd be deeply indebted, son."

"No, sir. I'm the one who's indebted. Me and a hell of a lot of other shot-up guys. I'll find her, and bring her home. Oh, one more thing; the disease; what has it done to her? So far, I mean."

He heard Madison sigh deeply. "It's a thing called TCL or CTL. Hard to detect at first. It causes aching in the bones, like flu sometimes does. But if it isn't caught early... well, it goes pretty quickly after that. For a few months you don't see anything, though. If you saw her, and hadn't been told, you probably wouldn't know."

"I see. Well, I'm going to get a move on, sir. I'll be in touch when I get out there. Thank you for calling me, Colonel Madison. It means a hell of a lot. Goodbye, sir."

He hung up the telephone and stood there a moment collecting his thoughts. *OK, there's nothing I can do for her until I find her. That's the mission, now; get up there and find her. Worry about the other bridges after you cross that one.*

He glanced at his watch as he walked quickly out the side door to the big parking lot where his Mustang was parked. He wondered how Mary would take the news that he was rushing off to find Sue. *Would she understand? Probably not, at first. She would be angry, and they would part on bad terms. But she would understand later, after he had gone, like she had when Sam was killed. Things would be OK when he got back. Jesus, she has to understand. Sue is dying, for Christ's sake.*

In the distance he saw a C-130 transport, wheels down, on final approach for landing at Lawson Army Airfield, which the military aircraft supporting training at Fort Benning used.

Wait a minute, he thought, and stopped in his tracks, watching the airplane disappear behind the trees in the distance. He had run into some of the C-130 pilots in the Infantry Bar two nights earlier. The ones who were currently supporting the airborne school at Fort Benning were from Pope Air Force Base, adjacent to Fort Bragg. Their mission would be completed and they would return to Pope this afternoon. *If he could catch a hop with them, he could rent a car at Fort Bragg to drive to the Outer Banks. That would save him five or six hours driving time.*

He hopped into his Mustang and drove to Lawson Field. He was wearing his Army Greens, but he had a pair of jeans and a polo shirt in the trunk of his car, along with his running gear. He drove to the base operations building at Lawson Field, stuffed the jeans and shirt into the athletic bag with his running gear, and walked into the building.

An Air Force captain and a lieutenant were standing at the flight planning counter, and he walked up to them.

"Excuse me. Are you guys going to Pope?"

"Yep," the lieutenant replied. "Looking for a hop?"

"Sure am."

"Just in time," the captain said, reaching into the leg pocket of his flight suit. He handed Ed a passenger manifest and said, "Just put your name and service number on here, and we'll be ready to go.'

"Got time for me to make one quick phone call?" Ed asked as he wrote his name and service number on the manifest.

"Sure."

Mary was still at her Friday bridge game. Sue Stiner was hosting bridge today, he recalled, so he dialed the Stiner's quarters.

He got Mary to the phone and said, "Listen, honey, Colonel Madison called awhile ago. Sue is real sick. She's gone off to the Outer Banks, we think, and I... he wants me to go find her."

"What? Oh, Ed, come on now!"

Goddamit, he thought. I knew it! "Mary, I'm going. I've got to. I'm at Lawson..."

"Shit, Ed! Tell Colonel Madison to go find her himself. What the hell does he think you..."

"Oh, for Christ's sake, Mary. She's dying!" he said bitterly, then his voice softened. "Look, I'm catching a hop to Bragg. I'll call you when..."

The telephone went dead, and he thought, To hell with you, then. He slammed the telephone down hard into its cradle and turned to the two Air Force officers, who were staring curiously at him. "Ready?" he said, and led them out of the door toward the aircraft.

They landed at Pope Air Force Base a couple of hours later, and he thanked the airmen for the ride.

"No sweat," the pilot said. "There'll be another couple of aircraft going back to Benning late Sunday afternoon if you want a ride. Just check in at base operations."

An hour later, Ed was on the way up I-95 in a rented car. He would drive up to Wilson, then head east toward the coast. Damn, he thought as he pushed the rented Chevrolet Nova up to 75 miles an hour, I forgot to call Mary. Well, that would just have to wait now, until he stopped for gas and coffee somewhere up the road.

       *   *   *

Sue stood holding tightly to the railing on the upper deck of the ferry boat as it pulled away from the Hatteras dock into Pamlico Sound. Seagulls darted and screamed astern, waiting for crumbs to be tossed to them by some of the passengers.

She watched them for awhile as a pair of twin girls tossed bits of bread up toward the birds. She had done the same thing when she and Ed had come to Ocracoke, and she recalled that he watched awhile and said, "Survival of the fittest. Nature's way. You see that? The same birds - the already strong ones, or the quick ones - get most of the bread. You'd think that they'd catch it and give it to their mates. Or their offspring. It doesn't work that way though, does it?"

Survival of the fittest, she thought. The healthy. Ed, I need you so much right now. Just to talk to, to lean against, to escape reality with for awhile.

She turned around and watched the sun setting behind a pink and purple and orange cloud bank over the mainland.

Sue had decided to go to Ocracoke and get a motel room for the night. She would decide tonight whether or not to take the early ferry to Cedar Island and drive on down through the Carolinas to Georgia. To Fort Benning, and Ed.

What could she tell him, though? And what if he isn't even there, or has something else planned? And Mary - what about Mary?

All she wanted to do was see him, talk to him. Or did she? She couldn't tell him that she was dying, or even that she was ill. Should she call? Yes, of course she should. Then she could be sure that he would be there. Or that he wouldn't be. She could make up some story about being on her way to the Gulf Coast to see friends. But suppose he didn't want to see her? Friendship was all that was left between them now, as far as he was concerned. She had no right.

Oh, God, what am I doing? Why can't I face reality? I'm alone. Ed doesn't need this. I'm such a fool, a desperate fool. I just want to go home. Home to Dad, to curl up in his lap and cry.

She looked down at the dark water of Hatteras Inlet. What would it be like to drown? she wondered. People who had actually done so - drowned and then been revived - said that it wasn't so bad at the end - that once you resigned yourself to it, there was a feeling of peace, then nothing. Nothing at all.

   *   *   *

Ed spent the four hour drive to the Outer Banks thinking of Sue. He remembered their every moment together, from that day on the beach at Cam Ranh Bay to the tender lovemaking and the fishing and the misplaced ribbons on his uniform. And the laughter the last time he saw her, when she told him about Father Frank's retirement ceremony and how he got drunk and pissed in his pants.

But now she was dying. Dying of a cruel, hopeless disease that neither he nor she nor anyone else could do anything about. He remembered the cancer patients he had seen at Walter Reed, many with their hair falling out, or completely bald as a result of the chemotherapy and radiation treatment that, at best, only slowed the disease's wretched progress.

Sue would hate that part of it. Would she even allow them to treat her? Ed wondered. Would she even be so distraught and filled with hopelessness that she might end her life before the disease did? Had she already done so, for that matter?

Please, Sue, don't do that. They'll come up with something soon. They're bound to.

He thought of death, of the horrible, sickening amount that he had seen, and had caused. He could justify the deaths of soldiers - of some of them, at least. You killed, and risked being killed, to stop the killing. To right wrongs, when nothing else would work. A sacrifice; a shitty, too-often-needless loss of life sometimes. But at least it seemed to have some purpose behind it.

But what, in the name of God, could be gained from the death of a caring young woman like Sue Madison? There is no sense in it, no reason. And there must be no God, either. There can't be.

He said aloud, "God damn you and your God, Frank Fallon!" and didn't even consider the contradiction in that.

It was dark now, nearly ten o'clock, and he strained to identify each approaching car. He stopped for gas in Manteo, cursing himself for not having asked Colonel Madison about the car. He assumed she was in the little red Volkswagen, but he would look for any car with a Maryland license plate and a Walter Reed sticker on the bumper.

He grabbed a cup of coffee, then pulled out onto Route 64 again and crossed over the bridge from Roanoke Island to the long, narrow stretch of islands of North Carolina's Outer Banks.

He turned south onto Route 12, between the myrtles and marshes of Bodie Island, over the towering Bonner bridge to Hatteras Island. There was a ferry schedule sign at the foot of the bridge, and he stopped to see when the last Hatteras-to-Ocracoke ferry ran.

Eleven o'clock. "Damn," he said aloud, and smacked the steering wheel with the heel of his fist. He couldn't get there in time to catch it now. If she was on Ocracoke Island, he wouldn't be able to find her until the following morning. That's that, then, he thought. He would look for her between here and the ferry dock at Hatteras village, and if he didn't find her, he'd park there until the following morning, sleep in the car, then take the first ferry to Ocracoke. But he'd stop in the village and call Colonel Madison to see if he had heard anything. And Mary; he'd have to call Mary.

When he reached Hatteras village, Ed pulled off at a phone booth and called Colonel Madison. Her father had heard nothing from Sue, so Ed explained the situation and promised to call again in the morning, in case Madison had heard something during the night.

He called Mary then, collect. When the operator asked if she would accept the charges, Mary said, "Of course," with a softness that caused Ed's tenseness to ease. "Ed, are you all right?"

"Yes. I'm OK, honey."

"Did you find her?"

He sighed. "No. Not yet, anyway. I'm at Hatteras, but too late for the last ferry to Ocracoke."

"Ed, I'm sorry I was such an ass when you called before you left. Please forgive me?"

"Ah, Mary. Of course. It's just that I... You know I owe her an awful lot."

"Yes, I know that. Like Sam. Poor girl. What, exactly, is wrong with her?"

"It's some kind of cancer, Mary. Apparently, it doesn't give much indication that it's there until it really takes hold, and then it's too late... a matter of months."

"Oh the poor girl. Find her, Ed, and take her home. I know you have to do that. I just feel like such a fool about this afternoon."

"Forget about it, Mary. I'd have done the same thing, I guess."

"No, Ed, you wouldn't have. You're not that way; that's why you're there."

She asked how he had gotten there, where he would stay, how he would get back. He answered her questions, then Mary said again, "Poor girl. At least she doesn't have a family - you know, children and all."

Unpleasant memories came to Ed's mind, and he shuddered, a deep sense of revulsion seizing him. He wanted to go now, to find Sue. More than ever, he wanted to find her. There was a slight tremble in his voice when he said, "Yes. Look, Mary, I'm going to go on, now. Thank you for understanding. I know it's difficult..." He wanted to add, But *you* of all people should understand. He didn't, though.

"I'll call you tomorrow. Goodbye, Mary."

Words, he thought as he hung up the phone, staring at his reflection in the cramped phone booth. Words are so meaningless without honor behind them. And honor comes from deeds, not words. It isn't what you *say*, it's what you *do* that matters.

He stepped out of the booth, his head and shoulders drooping, his eyes on the ground. He felt helpless, weary, torn. He hadn't felt this way since Mike Robbins had been killed, since Sue had told him so just after they first met, now so long ago. He recalled what he had said to her about Mike being just another statistic. And now it was Sue who would soon be what he had so cruelly called "a statistic."

Words. He heaved a deep sigh, straightened up, and looked toward the sky. "Please, God," he said aloud. "Let me find her."

There was a break in the clouds overhead, and he saw a star and thought of Sam and Mike and all the others, and again he said aloud, "Please."

He was hungry. There was a little restaurant at the charter boat marina where he could get some crab cakes and a beer, so he climbed into the car and headed there.

TWENTY SIX

Sue sat holding a half-empty coffee mug in both hands, staring at the dark liquid as she had earlier at the water of Hatteras Inlet from the deck of the ferry.

She felt like such a fool for having run away like this. Her parents must be worried sick. She turned again and looked at the pay phone on the wall. A chubby ferry crewman was still leaning against the wall, the receiver to his ear, smiling and carrying on a conversation in low tones.

She would telephone her father, then drive as far north as she could tonight, she had decided. When she got too tired, she would get a room, sleep awhile, then drive the rest of the way home to Maryland. It was the best thing.

She'd made the decision on the ferry. Her parents were what mattered now. Their worry and suffering would only be made worse if she did foolish things such as she had done today.

She was going to die. Everyone dies. Her time was just going to come earlier than most, that's all. Just as it had for all those thousands of boys in Vietnam, scores of whom she herself had seen die during her time there.

What mattered now was to try to put things in order before it happened to her, and to be as little bother as possible to other people. People such as her parents and Angela. And Ed.

How foolish it was, she thought now, to think of going to him, disturbing once more the life that he was trying so hard to make work for his family. Perhaps, before the disease ravaged her too badly, she would be able to see him. As an old friend. He wouldn't have to know that she was dying. She could go to visit friends at Fort Benning, and see him there. That's all I want, she thought; just to see him, to touch him one last time before...

"More coffee before we close, honey?" the portly waitress asked, pouring some into Sue's cup before she could answer.

"Oh. Yes, thank you." She needed to get going, but the coffee would help her stay awake until she got some distance up the road. She supposed she could at least make it to Virginia before she had to stop for the night. If she hadn't taken the Ocracoke ferry earlier in the evening, she would have been able to make it all the way home tonight, but she was nearly to the ferry dock on Ocracoke Island when she made the decision to turn around and go home. So she'd had to drive off, get into line for the return trip to Hatteras, and drive back aboard the last ferry of the night from Ocracoke. She had only stopped in the cafe to call her father and to get a cup of coffee.

Sue glanced at the telephone again. The ferry crewman was hanging up, so she took a last sip of coffee, and went to the phone.

Ed signaled and pulled into the parking lot of the little restaurant. It was still open, although he could see through the window that the waitress was sweeping up.

He didn't see the faded old Volkswagen sitting on the other side of the entrance until he was out of his car. He stopped a moment, then walked toward it. Yes. There was a Maryland license plate and an officer's sticker from Walter Reed Army Hospital.

Ed turned to the door of the restaurant and opened it. There she was, on the telephone, her back to him.

As Sue waited for the operator to answer, a hand reached over her shoulder and took the receiver from her. She turned and saw the scarred face, and those deep green eyes.

"Hello, Sue."

She turned away from him, startled and confused. Why was he here? What did he know? *How* did he know?

Ed hung up the telephone, then took her gently by the shoulders and turned her toward him. He looked into her eyes, studying them for a moment. "Sue, I... I talked to your father this afternoon. He told me."

He pulled her into his arms and she clung tightly to him. She sobbed, the strain and anxiety pouring from her. "Oh, Eddie," she cried, "I'm so afraid."

"It's OK, Sue. Cry all you want to, now. Let it all out, Sue."

The waitress and the ferry crewman looked at them, aware only that a man and a woman were having a tearful reunion.

"Come on, we'll go outside," Ed said.

They walked slowly around the side of the restaurant, clinging to each other. He felt suddenly strong and buoyant, as he had when he'd reached Gregovich and carried him to safety in the midst of his first firefight two years earlier.

The side of the restaurant opposite the road faced Pamlico Sound, and there was a deck there that served both as an outdoor cafe and as a dock for small boats. There were several picnic tables and benches on it and Ed led Sue to the one nearest the water.

They sat on the bench, his arm around her shoulder, hers wrapped around his waist. She leaned her head on his shoulder and they sat silently for awhile listening to the water lapping at the pilings and gazing across the sound. Far off to the southwest they could see the lightning flashes of a distant thunderstorm, too far away for the sound of thunder to reach them.

Ed took his arm from around her and pulled hers from around his waist, then took both of her hands in his.

"Sue, I want you to understand something," he said softly. "I'm not... I haven't come to you out of any sense of... of pity. To hold you and pat the back of your head and say, 'Poor Sue.' I've come because... well, just because I want to be with you. Because I want to share some time with you. Some talk, some thoughts. Do you understand that?"

She looked up at him with puffy eyes and said nothing, but her hands squeezed his.

"If you want me to stay, I will," he said. "If you want me to leave, I'll go."

She answered him by moving her hands around his waist again, and clinging tightly to him.

He watched the distant thunderstorm, searching for words to comfort her. Honest words.

After a time, he lifted her chin and said, "I love you," and they both knew he was telling the truth. "I'll always love you, Sue, long after we're both gone from this life."

She took one of her hands from his waist, touched his lips with her fingertips and, lips trembling, tried to say something. But more tears came instead - tears of joy and love this time. She knew him, knew that he was saying what he felt within himself, not saying it because he thought it was what she wanted to hear, but because it was true.

A light inside the little restaurant went out.

Ed looked at the cafe and said, "They're about to close, Sue, and I need to call your father from the pay phone."

She nodded, holding his hand. "I have to get my purse, too."

"Come on, then," he said softly, brushing her damp cheeks with the back of his hand.

They walked hand-in-hand around to the front of the cafe and went inside. The waitress and a man were facing each other across the counter, a bottle of beer in front of each.

"Do we have time to make a phone call before you close?"

"No hurry, ol' boy," the Hatterasman said.

While Sue got her purse and paid her bill, Ed made a collect call to Colonel Madison. He quickly accepted it and asked, "Have you found her, Ed?"

"Yes, sir. She's OK. We're on Hatteras Island."

"Thank God," Colonel Madison said, and Ed thought briefly of Father Frank and said, "Yes."

"Are you sure she's all right, Ed? For now, I mean?"

Ed glanced over at her. She looked tired and her eyes were puffy from crying, but she was all right, for now. A dull pain gripped his heart at the thought of the insidious disease gnawing inside her. But she was all right for the time being, and he was there with her.

"Yes. She just needed to get away for awhile, I think. Wait, I'll get her to the phone."

She was collecting the change the waitress counted out to her. She dropped it in her purse, turned to Ed, and managed a weak smile.

He held out the receiver to her and she came and took it from him as if it were a precious thing. She turned her face away and spoke softly to her father.

"Dad?... Yes, I'm all right. Daddy, I'm so... I'm sorry about going off like this. I just needed some time to... to think things out."

She looked over at Ed as her father continued to ask her questions, reassuring himself that his daughter - his one precious possession - was all right, was doing what she wanted to, and that she would be home safely soon.

"Don't wake mother," she said. "Just tell her that I'm fine, and that I love her, and I'll see her in a couple of days... I love you, too, Daddy. I love you very much."

She gave the telephone an almost loving look, then hung up. She moved to Ed, put her arms around his waist and hugged him gently.

They got Sue's suitcase from her Volkswagen and drove north into the village in Ed's rented car. They were silent, but they held hands and reached across to touch each other's face now and then.

Ed found a motel with a vacancy sign and he went in and got them a room, registering as Mr. and Mrs. Edward A. Walker.

It was a room with knotty pine walls and a few pieces of pine furniture. It had the musty, salty smell that every Outer Banks building seemed to have. There was a print of Cape Hatteras lighthouse above the double bed, and blue curtains with red and white anchors on them, that matched the bedspread.

Sue went straight into the bathroom and Ed went back to the car to get his cigarettes.

It had gotten chilly, and when he came back in, he was rubbing his arms with his hands to warm them. Sue had opened her suitcase on the bed and was taking her toiletries out. When she straightened up, Ed saw her wince with pain and place her hand on her aching hip to relieve it, and he felt a pang of sadness.

"Come on, Sue. Lie down awhile, and rest."

He moved the suitcase onto the floor, then took her hand to coax her to lie down.

"I really should clean up first," she said. "I know I must look a real mess."

"I've seen you look a worse," he said, sitting on the bed beside her as she lay face down on her stomach, cradling one of the pillows beneath her head. He stroked her hair, then rubbed her shoulders tenderly, wondering about the pain, not wanting to put pressure on the bone, afraid that it might hurt her.

"Ed?"

"Yes?"

She rolled onto her side, still cradling the pillow, and looked up at him, at the scars of the battle wounds that had first brought them together. "Thank you for coming," she said.

He stroked her cheek. "I'm just glad I found you, Sue."

She rolled back onto her stomach and asked, "How did you know where to look?"

"Where else would you have gone?" he asked.

"Ocracoke."

"Yes. That's where I was headed."

She lay silent for awhile, then said, "I want to go tomorrow."

"We will, then," he said.

She lay there studying him, thinking how natural it felt for him to be there. Nothing else mattered to her, not right now. But what about him? There must be other things that mattered to him. Jimmy, certainly. Mary? And always, his soldiers. But just this once, she would be selfish with his time. For one day. She might never see him again after this. It was her turn to be selfish. Still, she couldn't let it go at that.

"Does Mary know where you are?"

"Yes."

"Shouldn't you go home in the morning?"

"No."

She rolled back onto her stomach. Those short, matter-of-fact answers of his. There was such straightforward honesty in them. She hoped he would never change. But she would not be around to know, would she? Would he change? Of course, she thought. But how? She wished she could know, could be around to see. But she would not, and no one could change that.

Oh, God, that's the worst part of it, she thought. Leaving him, leaving her father, not being a part of their future - of *anyone's* future - whatever it might bring.

How long will he live after I am gone? she wondered. Will he become an old, old man? Will he be killed in some horrible war? In a car wreck on the way home to Mary?

Will he have more children? Grandchildren? Will he have to see Jimmy die before he does?

No, God. Please don't put him through that.

How much longer will I live? she wondered. How long? What will it be like?

He felt her tense up, and he eased her onto her side once more. "You all right?" he asked softly.

"No. I'm dying."

Yes. That was the truth of it. It had to be said, didn't it? It had to be talked about - talked all the way through. Now. "Yes, you *are* dying, aren't you, Sue?"

She drew her knees up and sunk her neck into her shoulders.

He propped himself up on the bed beside her, then asked, "Are you afraid, Sue?"

She lay with her back to him. "Yes," she admitted. She was afraid of the uncertainty of what came after death. What is it like? she wondered. Is there some existence after life on this planet? Does one become a spirit of some sort, drifting through space; a mind with no body attached, observing the lives of those left behind? Or is it simply nothingness?

She rolled toward him. He looked at her, awaiting some further response, but she only turned onto her back, her arms at her side, staring at the ceiling.

"Do they give Army nurses full military honors at their funerals, Ed?" she asked after a time.

"Of course," he said. "Is that what you want?"

"I don't know. I suppose I do. Isn't that strange?"

"No. You'll be in worthy company that way." He imagined her funeral then, and it sent a sharp pain through his chest.

"What do you suppose it's like, Ed?"

"Death?"

"Yes."

"I don't know. I've often wondered." He recalled the strange dream - or vision, or whatever it was - that he had just before he regained full consciousness after his injuries in the sapper attack on the hospital. Was that death? Or was it a *return* from death?

"Peace, I hope," he said. "What do *you* suppose it's like?"

"I don't know. I just don't know," she said, then sighed deeply. "I hope... I hope it is what I've hoped it is for other people."

"And what's that?"

She slid her arm across his chest, and one leg across his knees. He ran his arm beneath her shoulders, gently pulling her toward him until her head was resting on his chest. He twirled a strand of her hair around his index finger as she picked at the hem of his shirt sleeve.

"Peace," she said. "I've hoped it was real and lasting peace. Not 'nothingness,' but a real feeling of peace, somehow. Do you think that's possible?"

"Anything's possible, Sue. I mean, man's soul must certainly exist in *some* form after his body dies."

They considered that for a time, then Sue said, "Do you believe in reincarnation, Ed?"

"Reincarnation? I'm not sure. I used to think that I was once a Spitfire pilot in the Battle of Britain. I really believed it, at times. I had gone off to Canada and joined the RAF, then been shipped out to

England. I was shot down off the cliffs of Dover in a dogfight with an Me-109. If it didn't actually happen, then it was an awfully vivid daydream. Awfully vivid."

Her leg jerked, one of those involuntary reflexes that occur when one is falling asleep and isn't quite ready for it. He nestled her more closely to him.

"Sorry," she mumbled. "So tired. Want to sleep now."

Ed brushed her hair back from her forehead and kissed her lightly there. He slid away from her, got up and pulled the covers back from the other side of the bed. He wondered if she would be more comfortable without her jeans. He decided she would, and gently rolled her over enough to unfasten them, then pulled them down from the ankles, folded them and placed them on the dresser.

He lifted her gently over onto the sheet and covered her up to the shoulders, then stood over the bed and looked at her, aching in his heart for this young woman who had helped heal so many others, but couldn't be healed herself.

Oh, God, he thought. If it could only be me, instead.

He thought of Mary and Jimmy. What if it *were* him? What would they do? Why did it have to be *anyone* he cared for? Why couldn't it be some North Vietnamese bastard? Or the one who was responsible for the massacre that he and Mike had discovered? Why not some Nazi, or William Calley, or the Imperial Wizard of the Ku Klux Klan? It's just not *fair*, God! Heartless, mocking... *God*!

He began to tremble with anger and frustration at being unable to do anything about the miserable situation. How do you fight *this* enemy, you gun-toting son of a bitch? he asked himself.

He went into the bathroom and sat on the lid of the toilet. He buried his face in his hands and silently cursed, his mind raging with frustration and sorrow for the young woman in the next room whose life was to be taken from her so cruelly, without reason; and at his inability to do anything - anything at all - about it.

The bathroom door opened suddenly and he quickly tried to disguise the fact that he had been crying, but he knew it was useless.

"Oh, Eddie. No, darling," Sue Madison whispered. "It's all right. It's all right." She took his head in her hands, pulled it against her belly.

"Ah, Sue," he groaned, clasping her around the waist. "Sue, I'm so sorry."

"Shhh," she said, stroking his head. "Don't mourn me yet, Ed. I'm far from gone yet. I'm more alive, now that you're here, than I've been for a long time."

She took his arms from around her waist, grasped his wrists, and moved his hands to her breasts.

"Feel that?" she whispered. "That's me. Alive, Ed. And that," she said, moving one of his hands down to her bare thigh.

He stood and held her to him, and she kissed his throat and whispered, "Make love to me, Ed."

He carried her to the bed and they made love, slowly and tenderly and for a long time. And they proved to each other that she was, indeed, still very much alive.

Later, as she lay curled up asleep against him, he lay awake and thanked whatever God there might possibly be that he had found her, and that they loved each other.

No one had ever loved him as she did. No one. And he had never even loved Mary the way he now loved Sue. And he never would, never could.

Damn you, Frank Fallon! he thought, because he didn't want to blame himself for leaving Sue. Then he curled up beside her, trying to make sense of it until sleep finally came.

The next morning they went back to the little restaurant near the charter fishing docks and had breakfast, then took both cars across to Ocracoke Island on the ferry.

They checked into the Lakeside Cottages again, and then they toured the little village just as they had on their first trip there together. They went down old Howard Street and over to the lighthouse and out to Springer's Point.

They stopped in at South Point Seafood again, where one of the Ocockers had given him clams for the chowder he made. The fishermen remembered him, and again they spoke of peelers and sooks and jimmies, of drum runs and bluefish blitzes.

Sue listened and thought, This is where he belongs. Here, where they deal in crabs and fish, not there, where they deal in firefights and death. Inevitable death. She sighed a tired sigh, and Ed heard her and broke off his visit with the fishermen.

He took her back to the cottage and put her to bed, holding her gently, then sitting beside the bed and watching her sleep.

Sue. Ah, Sue, what have I done? I should have stayed with you. I thought I had to try, for Jimmy's sake. Was that so wrong? And what about now? What should I do *now*, before it ends? Before... before you die?

Suppose they just went together to the beach? he thought. What if they simply walked together into the surf, swam out as far as they could, and never came back?

He stood and walked to the window. Beyond the cedars he could see the harbor, Silver Lake. A sloop was coming in under sail, and it reminded Ed of his honeymoon. Things were so different, then. It had been barely three years ago, but it seemed more like a hundred. He had been so young, so naive.

How different would things be if he had not married Mary? He turned and looked at Sue. She would still be dying, regardless of what he had done. And other things would be different - just different enough that he probably would not have even met Sue. And he would not have a son. Not Jimmy, anyway. Maybe that was the purpose in all of this. *Does* everything happen for a purpose? So many thoughtful people seemed to think so.

Perhaps. Perhaps that's what this was all about, why he found himself here with this precious woman whose brief life would soon be over. There must be *some* reason for it; some reason beyond his understanding. There must be.

He turned back to look at her. She had awakened from her nap. She was lying there watching him and when she saw the sadness in his eyes, she held out her arms to him and he went to her.

They feasted on oysters and crabcakes and beer that evening, then went back to the cottage and made love with the gentle desperation that only star-crossed lovers on their last earthly night together could know.

The next morning they both fell silent. He would have to leave in a few hours - they both knew that without either having to say it. There was a ferry to Cedar Island at mid-morning, and he would have to take that one, if he were to get the rental car turned in and catch a flight to Fort Benning that night.

They drove to the north end of the village, stopping at the Variety Store to buy some things for breakfast - orange juice, a half-dozen doughnuts, a few pieces of fruit. Sue had a thermos bottle that they filled with hot coffee.

Halfway up the island, at the bridge over Parker's Creek, they pulled off the road. Ed took the paper bag of food and a blanket and they walked through the wax myrtles and yaupons and sea oats to the tall dunes above the beach.

They slid down the soft sand on the face of the dunes, and Ed spread the blanket out on the beach while Sue kicked off her shoes and walked to the water's edge, looking out across the Atlantic.

The morning sun was warm on her face as she stood watching the swells roll in, building up and up until they tumbled over in the shallows. Inevitably, she thought again of the day that Ed had stood on a beach like this halfway around the world, wounded in body and soul.

She looked back at him. He was sitting on the blanket looking off to the northeast. He looked at her, then pointed toward the spot he had been watching a moment before. She turned and saw two dolphin's backs and dorsal fins rise gracefully from the surface of the water, then disappear.

Freedom. The word sprang into her mind as she saw three more dolphins break the surface just behind the others.

She watched them awhile longer and when she looked at Ed again, he was standing, pointing to a spot near the surf.

She looked, and saw a patch of churning water with flashes of silver in it a few yards offshore. Terns and seagulls swooped above, darting down to the water to pluck glistening slivers from just below the surface.

"Blues, feeding on a school of baitfish," Ed said as Sue moved beside him.

They stood side-by-side for a time, Ed drawn by old feelings to the medium that was so much a part of his past, his heritage. He could picture exactly what was going on in the shallow water near them - a school of silversides, darting desperately along the thin seam of water between the ravaging bluefish and the surging wash of the waves, trying by instinct to avoid the voracious bluefish without being washed up onto the shore by the waves. More would be lost to the blues than to the waves, he knew, for that was nature's way of both feeding the bluefish and controlling the numbers of baitfish.

Sue watched the churning schools of fish, then looked at Ed. He was studying the scene intently, like some ancient hunter waiting until the moment was right to leap into the fray between the two lesser species, and take advantage of their struggle for his own ends.

Still watching intently, he spoke. "Look at them, Sue. Nature at work. For thousands of years, fish have lived like that. They're hatched, they feed, they mate, they're devoured. That's all life is for every creature but man."

He looked into her eyes. "Life and death don't mean a damned thing to any creature but us. And they don't mean a hell of a lot to us. But it's really all that matters, in the end; to have lived a belief, or died for one. To have contributed to something - some ideal - or to have struggled trying to contribute. Even if we're wrong, to have at least *tried.* Somebody - Dante, I think it was -once said that the worst place in Hell is reserved for those who fail to take a stand when great moral decisions have to be made. I believe that, I think."

She stood motionless looking at him, at her lover, who always seemed to be wrestling with life and its meaning.

He was still staring at the sea where the rippling swarm of feeding fish moved slowly offshore. And then they disappeared, gone deep beneath the surface.

The seagulls turned their attention to the baitfish that had been forced too close to shore, and now flipped and fluttered where the waves had washed them up onto the beach.

Ed hadn't intended to mention death, and now he tried to lighten the mood. "Anyway, the blues, like the rest of us, need to eat. Let's have some breakfast."

They sat on the blanket gazing at the broad expanse of the ocean and nibbling at their food. After awhile, Sue said, "If I could live my life again, do you know what I would do differently?"

"What?" he responded, giving her his full attention.

"I would have become a mother." She turned her face toward him. "A mother of sons like you, or of daughters like you. People who care about life, who try to understand it, and act according to what they believe, instead of what other people *tell* them to believe."

He thought about that for a moment, then said in a bewildered tone, "I don't know *what* I believe, Sue."

"No. You know what you believe, Eddie. Oh, your beliefs change sometimes. I know that - I've seen it. But you don't sit around waiting to sort it all out. You act on your beliefs of the moment, instead of waiting for some great revelation. That's why you're extraordinary."

He laughed. "Extraordinary? Hell, I'm just a misplaced waterman, caught up in things I don't even understand." His brow furrowed. "I'm confused, Sue. I don't know right from wrong. I can't understand the why of things. Why, *why*?"

He pushed himself up and walked to the water's edge, his hands balled into fists and shoved into the back pockets of his jeans.

Oh, Eddie, she thought. Eddie, stop struggling. Do what seems right at the time, and let it go at that. That's all you can do. That's all. I know that, now.

She stood and walked up behind him, held him by the elbows and placed her forehead in the cleft between his shoulder blades.

"Eddie," she said, "all we can do is what seems most right - least wrong - at the moment. Promise me you'll do that for one year after I'm gone. Just one year. Without asking why, except that it seems right. In your own mind. Based on your own values."

He turned toward her, his eyes roving her face. She tried to determine what was happening in the mind behind them. There was depth, as always. And restlessness. But there was something else.

All right, they seemed to say. All right, so that's the covenant of this moment. That's the "why" of now; the message. All right. I'll do it. For one year.

"We're saying goodbye, aren't we?" he asked.

She hadn't thought of it as that. But yes, they were.

"Yes, Eddie, we're saying goodbye."

For a few moments longer his eyes probed hers.

Resolve, she thought. That's what I see. No pity. A sense of sadness, perhaps. But mainly resolve.

"Then there's a couple of things I want to say first," he said.

She waited, telling him with her silence that she was listening.

"I'd die for you, if I could."

Her eyes misted and she said softly, "I know you would."

"I'll keep that promise to you, Sue. I'll try. In all I do, I'll try."

She knew he meant it, and hoped it was the right thing to have asked of him.

"And I'll come to you whenever you want, Sue. When it begins to get worse, I'll come to you, be with you, whenever you want, wherever you want, for as long as you want."

He thought awhile, then continued. "I won't forget you. Ever. What you are, what you stand for, what we were, what we had. And have. I mean that, Sue."

He walked away several steps, then stopped and turned back toward her. "And I'll see that you get a soldier's grave, because you deserve one. More than I believe anything else about what comes after, I believe that the souls of soldiers fly together somewhere. In Valhalla, or Hell, but somewhere."

He walked back to her, held her by the shoulders and looked deep into her eyes, and she heard him say, "And I'll love you until the day I die, and after, if it's possible after..."

He's almost finished, she thought, and said, "After death, Eddie. Say it. 'After death.'"

"After death."

He pulled her lightly against him, a loving, caring embrace, and they rocked gently from side-to-side, like the sea oats that clutched to the sand dunes behind them.

He had nothing more to say now. They both knew that. And they both knew that it was time for him to leave. He released her and she went to the blanket and folded it up as he watched her.

Ed picked up the bag of groceries and cradled it in his arm. He helped Sue up the steep sand dune, and they walked in silence through the cedars and wax myrtles and yaupons back to the car.

On the drive to the village, neither of them spoke, except once when Ed slowed the car and said, "Look." A great blue heron was rising from the marsh, his legs folded back and his broad wings undulating with slow, powerful strokes. Then the magnificent bird glided, coasted back down toward the marsh, his legs coming down and forward; long, spindly landing gear. He landed in the shallow water of Molasses Creek and watched the car pass by.

They pulled into the village and Ed parked beside Sue's car. They looked at each other for a moment; a long, thoughtful look. Then she opened the door and got out, and he did the same.

They stood in front of the car and Sue held out her hands to him. He took them in his and said, "Goodbye, Sue."

"Goodbye, Ed. I love you."

He nodded, and they shared one last, long, penetrating gaze. Then he released her hands, and he was gone.

Sue sat on the end of the long pier that jutted out into Silver Lake.

The ferry *Carteret* gave a blast on her air horn and rumbled, backing out of the slip and turning toward the narrow channel that led from the harbor into Pamlico Sound. Her screws reversed, water churned at her stern, and she headed out of Silver Lake.

Sue saw Ed appear on the upper deck, looking toward her.

She raised her hand in a feeble wave, and he saluted her, then the big boat turned to port and disappeared from Sue's view.

Ed Walker stood motionless, heedless of the gulls that darted and screeched around him, oblivious to the squeals of laughter of the children who tossed them bits of bread.

Goodbye, Sue, he said in his mind. *May whatever God there is be as good to you as He knows how.*

He stood there, silent and still, until the Coast Guard station and the old lighthouse disappeared behind the horizon. And still he stood there, saddened by unfathomable hurt, feeling as if his life was draining from him as it had drained from Sam and Mike, and his parents, and all the others it seemed he had ever loved. And now from Sue, the one he loved the most of all.

Sue didn't wait for the ferry to reappear on the other side of the clapboard Coast Guard station. She swung her legs onto the pier and pushed herself up, wincing at the pain deep in her bones. She walked into the village, crossed the road, and headed down old Howard Street. She walked along the narrow sand and oyster shell road beneath the big live oaks and old frame houses, past the weedy little family cemeteries filled with the graves of Howards and Austins and O'Neals. At the end of the ancient village street, she turned left to the little Methodist church.

She tried the door and, finding that it opened, walked in and went up front to the wooden communion rail.

She knelt, feeling the ache in her hip again, and gazed at the wooden cross. Ed had told her when they first visited the church, that it came from some old shipwreck.

Sue clasped her hands and bowed her head and said a prayer of thanks. Thanks for all that she had seen, all she had felt. For her parents. For having been allowed to serve as she had chosen. For having given her the opportunity to be a comforter; one who had helped ease the pains of war.

She gave thanks for Edward Walker. For creating him, for leading him to her, for allowing her to share his love.

And thanks for all of Your works that he showed me, she prayed. The sunrises and the sunsets, the horseshoe crabs and bluefish and the great blue heron. Keep him from harm, from any more hurt of body, or of soul. You've given him enough of that already, God.

And Mary - help her be what he needs. And let his son Jimmy grow up to be strong and good.

And finally, God, take me soon, swiftly. I'm ready now. I'm ready to go with them - his friends, brothers, kindred spirits - to wait, with them, for him to come to Valhalla. Or Hell. Somewhere.

She knelt awhile longer and thought of the great blue heron, imagined herself riding on him as he glided over the marshes. She wondered if he would be in Heaven, too.

And then Sue Madison smiled and stood up. She left the church and started home, to die.

PART FOUR

EARTH

"The earth belongs to the living, not to the dead."

Thomas Jefferson

TWENTY SEVEN

"So, that's it, then," Ed Walker said, a sad and distant look in his eyes. He shifted his gaze from the general's face to the window beyond it and stared out across the parkway and the Potomac River to the tall spire of the Washington Monument. "That's it."

Lieutenant General Harry Madison looked at him - at the battle-scarred face that had been so young when he first saw it, and at the blouse of the Army Green uniform where a single row of ribbons between a shiny Combat Infantryman's Badge and the wings of a master parachutist were pinned. The old general smiled. It was typical Ed Walker, that single row of ribbons - an understatement of the sort that he had come to expect from this good soldier whose service had now nearly reached its end. If Ed Walker had worn all the ribbons he had earned in his career, they would have reached from his pocket nearly to his shoulder. But instead he chose to wear only three. Even so, to someone who knew what they stood for - not only their ranking as three of the top four medals the United States awarded for heroism, but the actual deeds he had performed to win them - they were more impressive than the row-upon-row of brightly colored ribbons that most of his peers wore on their uniforms.

"Yes," Harry Madison said. "That's it."

The image of his daughter's face, forever young in his memory, came to the general, for this was the man she had loved before she became ill and died. His brow furrowed and he sighed, and Ed shifted his gaze from the Washington skyline back to Madison. He thought the sigh was for him.

"I've had a good run, sir. Hell, I only came into this Army to see what it was like, you know."

Madison smiled and nodded slowly. "Yes," he said, "you've had a good run."

Ed wiped his forehead with his hand. He should leave now, he knew. The Deputy Chief of Staff for Operations had better things to do than make small talk with a colonel whose Army career was at its end. It was good enough of General Madison to take the time to inform him personally that he had been passed over again for promotion to brigadier general.

General Madison was his mentor and his father figure, but more than that, he was a friend - a friend of many years. But he had a job to do, one that consumed most of his waking hours, so Ed saluted him and turned to leave.

Madison said, "You don't have to leave the Army, Ed. You know that."

Ed turned back to face him. "We've already been through that, sir," he said, managing a weak smile. The two men had discussed that fact a year earlier, when Ed was turned down for advancement by the generals' promotion board the first time. He would have left back then, if Madison had not convinced him to stay one more year to give another of the annual promotion boards the chance to promote him to the rank of brigadier general. "A second opinion," Madison had said. But the prognosis remained the same, and Harry Madison knew that, such being the case, Ed Walker would retire as soon as he could.

"What are you going to do, Ed?"

"Go to work on the water," Walker replied. "As soon as possible. And I look forward to it, sir; I really do."

"Where are you going to retire?"

"Guinea, I guess."

Madison grinned. "I meant, where are you going to have the ceremony? I'd like to be there, to pin your last medal on you."

Ed managed a weak smile. "I don't want a ceremony, sir. Or another medal, either. Don't need 'em, where I'm going."

The intercom on Madison's telephone set buzzed. It was his staff director, reminding him of a meeting with the chief operations officers of the other services. "Be right there," he said, then walked around the desk and held his hand out to Ed. "I've got to go. Can you come to my quarters for dinner tonight?"

Ed took the general's hand and shook it. "Thank's anyway, General. But I'm afraid I wouldn't be very good company tonight."

"Well, think about it before you say no," Madison said. "Let my secretary know." He clasped his protégé on the shoulder and said, "Unless you get a better offer, of course." He hoped that there was a woman in Ed's life again.

"All right, sir," Ed said. "And, General, thanks for being the one to let me know."

"Well, I wish the news had been better," Madison replied.

"Yes, sir. I do, too. Goodbye, General."

Madison walked out into the corridor with him then watched Ed Walker stride away. No hint of the dejection he was bound to feel showed in the colonel's bearing.

We used him up, the aging general thought. We took a fine young man, stretched him to - perhaps beyond - his limits, and now, because he wasn't perfect, we're casting him aside. There were so many who had never been tested time and again as Ed had, so their flaws had never shown. And we all have flaws, he thought. There must be a better way.

He shook his head once, then turned and moved off down the corridor to join the other senior operations officers of the U.S. military services.

    *   *   *

The Union Street tavern in Old Town Alexandria was, as usual on a Friday night, crowded with yuppies and bureaucrats and tourists and servicemen, and a scattering of off-duty waitresses and bartenders from other establishments.

Colonel Edward Walker, still in uniform, was among them.

It's been a miserable year, he thought as he stared into his drink. A miserable *two* years, for that matter.

He had spent them in the Pentagon, mired in budget planning while his peers led their troops to the swift, decisive victory of the Gulf

War, then came home to the parades and flags and welcoming arms of their countrymen. Not like his war. The parades he had come home to face were parades of protesters, and the welcomes were Mary's words of infidelity, and being called "baby killer" by men like the hippie who interrupted the picnic he and Sue Madison were having on the day they became lovers.

Sue. He had never seen her again after they parted on Ocracoke Island. And he had not been back to the place since.

She went off to Hawaii to die, to spend her last months in a hospice there, helping others who were terminally ill. He wanted to go see her when he finished the Advance Course, but she didn't want him to come. He didn't understand why until he saw Tom Henderson just before he died of cancer. It was horrible, because Henderson was wasted away to almost nothing, bald and hollow-eyed, and slurring incomprehensible words. No, he was glad he'd never had to see her like that.

Her parents had never seen her again after she went to Hawaii, either. They were planning to go, Harry Madison later told Ed. She had seemed to be doing so well, he said, and was looking forward to seeing them. But just before they were to leave for Hawaii, she suddenly died, and the closest they ever came to seeing her again was the cheap, flag-draped coffin where she lay as it was about to be lowered into the volcanic ash of Punchbowl Cemetery, behind Diamond Head. Not even Arlington, where Ed would have been able to go to say a last farewell, because Arlington National Cemetery was running out of space, and you had to have a Silver Star or higher award to be buried there. Vietnam had almost filled it up.

Ed took another swallow of his drink and mumbled to himself, "Not even that, after all she had done."

The bartender heard him say something, and asked, "Another gin and tonic?"

"Yes," Ed said, and then his thoughts turned to the year after Sue's death; the year that he had promised her he would do whatever seemed right.

He asked to go back to Vietnam, but his request was denied. Instead, they kept him at Fort Benning as an instructor, and it had been disastrous for him and, in the end, for his career. He deviated from the doctrinal manuals when he disagreed with what they taught, because it seemed the right decision at the time, and that was what he had promised Sue he would do. He preached leadership instead of management, and that was heresy in those days. He taught the lessons of Vietnam, even though it was all but forbidden to even mention the place back then.

And then the RIF began; the reduction-in-force. He saw many of the best of his students begin to disappear from class; stripped of their commissions not because they had violated the Honor Code, or failed to display courage, or mistreated their troops. But only because they had no college degrees. They had forgone that to go to war, while so many of their peers had stayed in school, avoided the draft, and protested. Or even organized protests overseas, as the Democratic Party's nominee to be the next president had done.

The RIF. All those good men sent away, when men like Chuck Black were allowed to stay.

He had gone to the Infantry Bar with the ones he knew before they left. And he got drunk with them, because it had seemed like the right thing to do at the time, also, but all that did was cause him more trouble with his superiors.

But the final straw came the time they were all in the big auditorium of Infantry Hall, and a general was responding to their questions, and one of them was, "What are you going to do to clean up the Army, General?"

He still couldn't believe the answer the general gave. But he said, "First, we're going to get rid of some of this OCS scum."

There was a murmur in the auditorium for a moment after that, and then Captain Walker stood up and yelled, "Fuck you... sir!" and walked out.

He had nearly been court-martialed for that - that and the other things that had seemed right at the time. But in the end, they only gave him a letter of reprimand, because enough of them agreed with him, and because of the medals he wore - the medals, when they probably didn't even know whether he had really earned them or not. He didn't even know himself whether or not he had.

He drank deeply from the drink the bartender set in front of him, then looked at it, remembering that there had been too much of that back then, too. In the end, it became enough of an excuse for both of them, and he and Mary went their separate ways. Ten years. He suddenly remembered that she would be entitled to part of his retirement because they had been married for so long, but he didn't care. The paperwork would be a pain in the ass, that's all. But he would take care of it Monday, when he went to the personnel center to put in his retirement papers.

He finished his second gin and tonic and, after giving momentary consideration to sitting at the bar and getting drunk, he pushed the glass away, paid his tab, and left.

He went to the parking garage and got into his car, then decided he'd had too much to drink, so he got out and pocketed the keys. He walked back out to the street and stood on the sidewalk waiting for a taxi.

The day was dying, the last rays of the sun reflecting off the clouds above the Potomac.

Dusk was a lonely time for Ed Walker these days. It usually, as now, signaled another lonesome night about to close in on him. The few friends he had in the Washington area were all married, and there was no woman in his life at the moment. His friends' wives were always trying to fix him up with available women, and occasionally Ed would take one of them to dinner or to some military social function held by his office in the Pentagon. Now and then, he would spend a night with one of them, but none of them ignited in him the desire to establish a relationship of any depth.

Maybe it was his age, or his attitude; he had become a cynical man. He hated his job in the Pentagon, pushing meaningless papers and watching blindly-ambitious young officers become self-serving bureaucrats in their efforts to make names for themselves or to win promotions or plum staff assignments. The better ones he encouraged to go back to troop units, and did what he could to assist them. The rest he ignored, or encouraged to leave the Army for some other endeavor; law school or business was their usual preference.

An increasing number of the better officers were women, and he wondered why. Maybe they weren't really better. Maybe it was just that he hadn't expected them to be as good as men in the profession of arms. The Nurse Corps, yes. But not the other branches. The idea of women commanding men in the armed forces still seemed strange to him, but he knew why. It was because he still saw the Army not as the huge, multi-faceted, increasingly-technical mega-business that it was, but as rifle companies and platoons and Special Forces A teams; small units of young, hard, sometimes frightened, often courageous, always vulnerable men whose lot was to be bored most of the time, and to fight desperate, cacophonous battles in mud and dust and storms of fire the rest of the time. Men like Sam Hagen and Mike Robbins and Walt Shumate.

The Army was right. He wasn't fit to be a general. Because the big picture wasn't important to him; not when it was compared to the thousands of little pictures of young men struggling and bleeding and killing and dying to support what someone else saw as the big picture. And the medics and nurses were important, too; up to their elbows in blood and gore, trying to keep the combat troops alive. The ones like Sue Madison and Dick Chamberlain. All the little pictures; the privates and sergeants and lieutenants in the combat arms and the field hospitals, and everything they did and thought and sacrificed - that was all that really mattered.

A taxi finally showed up, and Ed flagged it down and got into the back seat.

The images of Sam and Mike and all the others were still on his mind, still alive, laughing, forever young. God, how he missed them. And how he longed for Susan Madison.

"Where to, Colonel?" the cabbie asked.

Ed gave the driver the address of his apartment, then changed his mind. He would go see Harry Madison, Sue's father, and tell the old general how much he had loved his daughter, and how much he missed her, and how sorry he was that she was gone - sorry for both their sakes.

"Never mind that address," Ed said, his voice tired and weak. "Take me to Fort Myer."

The driver looked in the rear-view mirror and saw the aging soldier's eyes staring blankly off in the distance. He had seen that look before, and he thought, The thousand yard stare. Then he considered the ribbons and the First Cav patch the man wore, and he understood. He started to say something to try to cheer the colonel up, then changed his mind. Instead, he reached out to the dashboard and touched the Americal Division patch he had carried with him for more than twenty years.

As they were passing through Crystal City, Ed sat up straight and said, "Change two, driver. Take me to the Vietnam Memorial."

"Yes, sir," the cabbie replied. "Glad to."

They drove past the Pentagon - repository of the "big picture" - and past Arlington National Cemetery. In the fading light they could see the neat lines of simple white tombstones climbing in long, orderly rows up the hillside, most of them marking the remains of soldiers who had only seen the "little picture" of war - every American war that had ever been fought.

Thank God, Ed thought, that Jimmy will never have to be one of them. The Soviet Union was gone. The Berlin Wall was down. And not only was the draft gone, but it appeared that a draft-dodger from the Vietnam war - his war - might become the next commander-in-chief.

Maybe Mary had been right all along. Maybe, if they had just been left alone, the communists would have simply self- destructed. Vietnam would be no different whether or not he had fought there; whether Sam and Mike and all the other tens of thousands had died there or not.

Or maybe those repressive, evil regimes *wouldn't* have collapsed if men such as those hadn't held the line; men like his brother James, and Sue's father, and those who manned the Fulda Gap in Germany and the DMZ in South Korea, the B-52s in the dark skies and the guided missile submarines in the depths of the oceans. Maybe, unchecked, that evil system of neo-slavery might have prevailed. Maybe that effort, those sacrifices, had been just enough to cause Krushchev's missiles to be withdrawn from Cuba; just enough to keep some foolhardy finger off the nuclear trigger.

Maybe that was what had given the *mujahadeen* the will to prevail against the Soviets in Afghanistan, and the contras in Nicaragua. Maybe that was what had given hope to the Czechs during the Prague Spring, and to the students in Tienanmen Square, and had finally inspired the youth of Germany to tear down the Berlin Wall, and the Russians to embrace democracy.

Maybe so, maybe not. There had to be some reason for those sacrifices, though. There had to be.

They crossed Memorial Bridge, and the cabbie pulled over near the Lincoln Memorial. Ed looked at the taxi's meter. It was turned off.

"What's the charge?" he asked.

"No charge, Colonel. Just say hello to them for me."

Ed started to protest, then noticed the blue patch with the white stars of the Southern Cross taped to the dashboard of the taxi.

"Americal Division," he said. "I will." He reached his hand over the seat to the other veteran and said, "Thanks."

"Don't mean nothin'," the cabbie mumbled, but he took Ed's hand and gripped it firmly.

"Yeah, it does," Ed Walker replied. "It means a lot."

"Take care, Colonel," the other man said.

Ed got out of the taxi and watched it drive away.

He walked to the path that led to the black granite wall where the tens of thousands of names - each a little story, a little part of the big picture - were inscribed. He paused as he passed the bronze statue of the three young Americans who represented them all. It stood near -

perhaps even on - the very spot where he and Sue Madison had once picnicked. Had it really been more than twenty years? Yes. More than twenty-two, in fact.

That was longer than most of the men whose names were etched into the granite wall had lived. Almost as many years as Sue had spent alive.

He had lived twice as long as most of them, now. Why? What had he ever done to deserve twice the time on earth that they had lived? Was it only luck? Was there some reason for it?

If there was, Ed Walker couldn't understand it. He had accomplished no great deeds, no thing of timeless importance, no lasting accomplishment that would matter after he was gone. Nothing except his son Jimmy, and he had done little to mold the young man. And even if he had died over there it would have made no difference, really, for Jimmy would have been born without him.

No, there was nothing. Nor would there be, now that he was leaving the Army. No reason not to join them now.

He walked to one of the black granite panels near the center of the memorial, and looked up just above eye-level. Sam's name was there, he knew. He saw it, stared at it for a moment, reached out and touched the first three letters.

The granite was cold to his touch, and he held his hand there until the stone beneath it warmed slightly. He smiled, remembering the young cowboy who had been his best friend, and his most trusted comrade-in-arms. And then he walked further along the slate path to Mike Robbins's name.

He got down on one knee so that he could touch it, too. He did so, then stood and touched the names of Jose Guitteriz and Al Wentzel, killed when he had been spared, dead when he had only been wounded, and again he wondered, *Why?*

His thoughts turned to other things. Fishing was one of them. He had that to look forward to, now. No more of the stress of staff work and Washington traffic and having to associate with people he didn't wish to. That would all be behind him soon. That, and war, and the responsibilities and heartbreak that went with it.

He was walking away from the monument when he remembered the taxi driver and the promise he had made. He walked back to the center of the wall, pulling the combat infantryman's badge off his uniform as he did so. He placed it on the ground at the center of the monument, and said, "This is for all you guys from the Americal Division, from a cabbie who served with you over there."

That done, he stood erect, saluted the long wall, and walked away.

Half an hour later, Ed walked into his little Alexandria apartment, took off his uniform jacket and tie, and threw them across the back of a chair. He switched on the television, which was tuned, as it nearly always was, to Cable News Network. Then he went to the kitchenette and opened the refrigerator door. He saw nothing to his liking except a six-pack of beer, so he took one, twisted off the top, and drank a swallow of it.

The lead news story was about the civil war and famine in Somalia. Walking skeletons filled the television screen - human beings on the brink of starvation, some carrying children too weak to crawl or cry or brush away the flies that gathered on their dying eyes. Ed Walker watched the images and wondered, Why? Why is this still happening? Isn't the UN there? And what about the airlift effort? The United States Air Force had been there since August, he knew, along with air transportation assets from other nations - or rather, they had been in Kenya, flying relief supplies from there to a number of airstrips in famine-ravaged southern Somalia.

The news correspondent partially answered Ed's questions when she went on to explain that the airlift was helpful, but could bring in only a fraction of the necessary supplies. And further, she explained, the airlift was frequently interrupted for days at a time when the aircraft were fired upon. When that occurred, air operations would be shut down until it was determined that it was once again safe for the airlift to continue.

Now the television screen showed an emaciated man carrying two tiny, rag-wrapped bundles toward a field filled with small mounds. Burial mounds, the woman noted with a cracking voice, beneath each of which lay the remains of a human being who had starved to death. The little rag bundles held two more.

Ed Walker found himself enraged at what he was seeing. It was not that he was shocked that such starvation was occurring; little of what occurred in the so-called Third World shocked him anymore. But the fact that a few rounds from some bandit clansmen would cause the US Air Force to interrupt operations for days - that he found incomprehensible. The Gulf War celebrations were barely over, for Christ's sake. The United States was now the world's sole superpower. It had proved that beyond question. And the Air Force, with its incredible technology, was the undisputed proof.

Will, Ed Walker thought. That's what was lacking. Will. What was the old saying? "The people do not lack ability; they lack will." Something like that.

The phone rang, and he answered it. It was General Madison.

"Sorry to bother you so late, Ed. Do you have time to talk?"

"Yes, sir. Of course." He supposed Madison meant that, if he had a woman there, he might wish to wait until the morning to talk.

"Good. Listen, Ed. After you left this afternoon, we had a meeting about the situation in Somalia. We don't know what the hell, if anything, we should be doing over there."

He paused, and Ed said, "It's a mess over there, all right. I was just watching a piece about it on CNN." He didn't know what the deputy chief of staff for operations expected *him* to do about it, though.

"Yes," Madison said. "As you know, we've had a few aircraft out there for the past couple of months, delivering food to several feeding centers."

"Yes, sir." Except when they get a couple of pot shots fired at them, Ed thought.

"Well, they're not getting the job done," Madison said. "Since they're basically working for the UN, they have to operate under their rules. And the UN, some of us feel, is too cautious. Or too non-committal. Anyway, it may be time for the US to do something more. Unilaterally."

Madison paused, and Ed said, "I see. But, uh, what's that got to do with me, sir?"

"I thought maybe you'd like to go see. Find out what, if anything, we should be doing. And who should do it."

Ed didn't respond for a moment. He was trying to figure out why he should be the one to undertake such a potentially important mission. Wasn't it Central Command's duty to evaluate such requirements in their area of operations? And didn't they already have a task force there, headed by a brigadier general, to coordinate the airlift effort?

General Madison anticipated Ed's questions and said, "The problem with CENTCOM is that they're operating out of Kenya. They don't actually have anybody on the ground in Somalia, except for a couple of guys who go in to each airfield during the day to manage the airflow. There's nobody who's living there; nobody who has a feel for what the situation is really like - who can look at it with a trained eye and see whether or not military intervention would really do any good."

"What about the CIA, General? Surely *they* must have somebody in Somalia."

"Oh, they have some people in there, Ed. But they're not reporting what we need to know from a military point-of-view."

Ed said nothing, wondering what value the opinion of a washed up colonel could have in comparison to the staffs of the Central Intelligence Agency and the Defense Intelligence Agency and United States Central Command.

At the same time, Madison was wondering if perhaps it had been a mistake to ask Ed to go in and have a look. Maybe Madison had done so just to try to give his protégé something positive to do as a last assignment before he retired; one last, worthwhile mission. But Ed's apparent reluctance made the general wonder if perhaps it was unfair to ask him to go when he had just been passed over for general again, and had made up his mind to retire.

But "unfair" was a word that the old general had little tolerance for, so he said, "It needs to be done, Ed. And it needs to be done by somebody I can trust. I could get somebody else to do it, but it's important, and you haven't really been in the harness for awhile. I thought maybe something like this to do as a last assignment might leave a better taste about the Army in your mouth."

Ed thought about it for a moment, the images he had seen on television a short time earlier returning to his mind.

Yes. After all the years of being involved in killing and planning destruction for political ends, it would be good to be involved in something like this; something with a fairly simple, definable goal; delivering food to starving people. Yes, that would be good. Even if it had to be done by force, it would be good.

"When do you want me to go, sir?" he asked.

"Well, it'll take a few days to get it set up. Why don't you take a few days off? Go fishing - whatever you want to do. We'll shoot for having you go in a week from today."

It was sunset on the following day when Colonel Ed Walker turned onto the wooded Colonial Parkway between Williamsburg and Yorktown. A few minutes later, he broke out of the woods and was greeted by the sight of the broad York River, and on the far side, Gloucester County; his family's home for ten generations.

The sight never failed to move him, regardless how long he had been away. He turned into the parking area and studied the river and the far shore.

The view had changed little, he was certain, in a thousand years. There were a few houses visible among the trees beside the far bank a mile-and-a-half away. But very few. Other than that, it must have looked the same to Captain John Smith when he first sortieed out of the newly-established Jamestown Colony almost four hundred years earlier. Just over there was Wicomico, shortened from Werowocomico - "village of the chief," in Algonkian – Chief Powhatan, the father of Pocahontas. It was there that she saved Smith's life when Powhatan's braves had captured him upriver and brought him there. And before Powhatan, ten thousand years of habitation by his ancestors. Ten thousand years they had lived there, reaping the bounty of the river and the woods and fields, until men with names like Smith and Rolfe and Walker had shown up with their guns and axes and European diseases. And their slaves.

It all belonged to them, now - the descendants of the European colonists and the Africans they had enslaved.

Other than a handful of Powhatan's miscegenated descendants on a few acres of reservation along the Pamunkey and Mattaponi rivers, they were all gone from Virginia now. And with them, much of the bounty of the river; delicious sturgeon and sheeps head, the huge beds of succulent oysters, the plentiful scallops, the schools of herring. And soon, the rockfish, and then what? The few remaining flounder, the little spot and croakers? And finally, the blue crabs and the clams?

It didn't have to be, Ed Walker thought as he sat there pondering the river he had always known and loved. Not if you could get the watermen to help; if you could reach the right balance between allowing them to earn a living on the water and letting them help rejuvenate it.

It wasn't enough to just pass legislation restricting the catch of the endangered species of marine life. That hadn't done a damn thing to bring back the once-plentiful oysters. And academically devised solutions, such as trying to seed the bottom with disease-resistant Japanese oysters, hadn't worked either.

The ban on the taking of rockfish - striped bass - was another example of the folly of the academicians looking for simple solutions without tapping the generations-old expertise of the watermen. The ban had brought back the rock, all right. But it was at the expense of the declining shad population. As one old watermen had said when the rockfish ban was announced, "The favoritest thing in the whole damn world for a rockfish is shad fry. Let us catch 'bout half the rock of a year, and the shad will be all right, too. But turn them damn rockfish loose for a few years without cullin' 'em, and they'll go through the shad fry like Grant went through Richmond. There won't be 'ary a shad left from here to the White House!"

And he was right. The shad population had dropped off drastically as the rockfish made a rapid recovery.

The watermen were the rightful stewards of these waters; with a little help and reasonable legislation, they'd figure out a way to bring back the bounty of the river so that their sons and their sons' sons could earn a living from it as they had once done. But you couldn't do that by running them off the water.

Ed Walker thought of these things, and about what he'd do when he retired from the Army. He decided he wouldn't return here to contribute to the river's rape; he would return to use the knowledge he had gained from working on it in his early years, and studying marine biology in college, and the considerable amount of money he had managed to put away, and he would make it his wounded mistress; help to heal it, rejuvenate it.

But first there was Somalia to help heal.

He shifted into gear and headed down the parkway.

"Somalia?" Sookie said as she poured her uncle a cup of coffee. "Why, that's wonderful, Uncle Edward. I'd go with you, if it weren't for little Edward, here." She patted her pregnant belly and smiled warmly at him.

Ed looked at his niece and returned the smile, and thought, Yes, you probably would, Sookie. She had matured into a beautiful woman, and her pregnancy gave her a vivacious glow that only made her more attractive. "You're not really going to name him Edward, are you?" he asked. "What if it's a girl?"

"It's a boy, according to the ultrasound scan," Sookie said as she took a chair across from him. "But enough about me. Exactly what are you going to do in Somalia?"

"Oh, just have a look, try to figure out what we ought to be doing over there, and report it back to the Pentagon."

"Good," she said. "Something has to be done for those poor, miserable people. Especially the kids. And what about you personally, Uncle Edward? How's your love life?"

He smirked and sipped his coffee. "Non-existent, I'm afraid."

She studied her fingernails a moment, then looked up at him and said, "I saw Aunt Mary the other day."

Ed looked into his coffee cup and mumbled, "That's nice."

"She asked about you. I said she should call you and ask you herself. Did she?"

He shifted in his chair and shook his head, still staring at the coffee, and said, "Nope." Then he looked up at Sookie and asked, "What was she doing here? Visiting her mother?"

Sookie shook her head. "She's moving back to Broad Marsh."

Ed raised his eyebrows. "With her husband?"

"Yes. He's retiring," she said.

"Oh," Ed said. He stared into his coffee, surprised at the feeling that had gripped him a moment earlier. Back to Broad Marsh; that's all Sookie had said, and something had stirred in his guts, some feeling. Hope? Lust? Something. Images of a man and woman making love went through his mind. Violent sex, and the taste of blood, and *yes* and *harder* and other words. And the same man and woman, but a little younger, the man without scars. Gentle.

"Did you stop in Richmond to see Jimmy on the way down?" Sookie asked, bringing him back to the realities of the present.

Ed shook his head. He should have stopped, but he didn't. The new bypass around Richmond was a poor excuse, but that was what he used to justify not stopping to see his son at the Medical College of Virginia. But that wasn't the reason. He wouldn't have been able to avoid making some biting comment about the fact that Jimmy was campaigning for Governor Clinton, and he knew it would have ended in an argument. He didn't want that. He'd wait until he got back from

Somalia, because it wouldn't matter then, and there would be plenty of time to try to finally become his son's friend.

"You must really be proud of him. Just a few more months, and he'll be a full-fledged MD," Sookie said.

"Yes. He's worked hard at it. And it's such a worthwhile thing." He smiled at his pretty niece and said, "But you're not bad yourself, Sookie. Almost a Masters in marine biology. What's your thesis on?"

"Arster farming."

He chuckled at her Guinea pronunciation of oyster, but said, "Oyster farming? How does that work?"

"Pretty simple, really. Come on. I'll show you."

They walked out of the house and down to the dock on Perrin Creek, and she hauled in one of several tubes of fine-mesh plastic floating near the surface at the end of the dock. The inside of the tube was covered with scores of little seed oysters, and she said, "This one's only been in a few weeks. But because these little floats keep it near the surface, where most of the nutrients are, and where they can get some sunlight..."

She interrupted her explanation long enough to throw the tube back into the water and haul in another one, then showed it to him and said, "...the arsters grow this big in less than a year."

"Well, I'll land in hell," he said. The oysters were almost big enough to sell.

"Two years from seed to harvest," she said. "Perfect size and clean as a whistle."

"Beats the hell out tonging all day for next to nothing," Ed said appreciatively. "All that's left is figuring out a way to make 'em shuck themselves."

Sookie threw the tube back into the water and wiped her hands on her hips. "Well, you come on back from Somalia and retire, and we'll get together and figure out a way to do that, Uncle Edward."

Ed spent much of the rest of his leave with his niece. Her husband was offshore on a trawler, so she had plenty of time to discuss with her uncle all the things they might do to revive the depleted bounty of the bays and rivers. She had an old Hampton One Design day-sailer, and they sailed around to James and Evelyn's new place on the North River to visit them, and all around the Mobjack.

By the time Ed kissed her goodbye and got into the car to go back to Washington and on to Somalia, he felt twenty years younger than he had when he arrived. He could hardly wait to retire.

He stopped by Jimmy's apartment in Richmond, and he didn't even care that there was a Clinton-Gore sticker on the door; he would avoid mentioning politics and talk about the future instead.

Jimmy wasn't there, though, so Ed decided he'd go on to Washington, and call him from there, or write him a letter when he got to Somalia.

TWENTY EIGHT

The US Air Force cargo plane made a low pass over the Soviet-built airfield at Baidoa, Somalia, while the crewmen checked to make certain there were no camels on the runway and no Somali militiamen intent on opposing the landing. There were none, so the pilot swung the aircraft around and brought it in smoothly for a landing.

Colonel Ed Walker, peering at the town through one of the portholes in the fuselage of the aircraft, noticed that many of the buildings in the regional capital were roofless, and wondered why. As the aircraft taxied past the abandoned fighter base, he noticed, too, that the hangars and other buildings on the airfield had been stripped of roofs, siding, and even doors. Several obsolete Soviet fighters, corroding with disuse, sat abandoned in earthen revetments along the airfield, goats grazing the brown grass around them.

The ramp of the cargo bay opened, and the airplane was immediately filled with a blast of stifling hot air. The pilot turned onto a taxiway just off the long runway and braked to a halt. A moment later, a battered Toyota truck with a World War II vintage machine gun mounted on it pulled up just behind the ramp. A half dozen Somali militiamen were standing in the truck, dressed in a motley assortment of old uniform trousers and faded T shirts, and armed with a variety of rifles. Ed noticed that none of the men were the walking skeletons of humanity he had expected to see based on the images shown on television newscasts.

Hanging from a stick on the side of the pickup was a tattered CARE flag. The passenger door of the truck opened and a tanned and lanky Caucasian man in shorts and a T shirt climbed out. He walked to the ramp, hopped up onto it, and entered the aircraft, studying the four pallets of rice and wheat that were strapped to the floor. He shook hands with the loadmaster and after a brief conversation with him, looked back out the door and motioned for an ancient Italian-made cargo truck to pull behind the airplane. Four lean, tall Somali men jumped out of the back and began unloading the 50 kilo bags of rice and wheat from the airplane onto the old stake bed Fiat truck.

Ed hefted his rucksack onto his back, picked up his water bottle, and walked to the ramp.

"G'day," the CARE man said to him as Ed approached. "Name's Merv Chambers, CARE A'stralia."

Ed shook his hand and said, "Ed Walker. Pleased to meet you."

"Welcome to Baidoa. You'll be staying with us for a time?"

"Yes, until the UN decides to put an observer team in here, at least."

Since there was no UNOSOM - United Nations Observers, Somalia - team in Baidoa yet, it had been arranged with the CARE office in Nairobi for Ed to stay with their team of Australian relief workers who had been in Baidoa for the previous month.

Ed had been instructed to avoid mentioning that he was actually in Somalia to assess the requirements for a possible American military intervention. Not even the United Nations personnel were aware that his instructions went beyond simply making observations on the security situation in southern Somalia and reporting those observations to the UN headquarters in Mogadishu.

Chambers studied him a moment, taking in the well-worn civilian rucksack with rolled up sleeping mat, faded jeans, hiking boots, and long sleeved, light cotton shirt that the American wore. And he had water with him, and no camera; this one's here to work, the Australian thought. And it's obviously not his first time in the field, from the looks of him.

"You got any other kit?" he asked the American.

At the embassy in Nairobi, Ed had asked what the team he was going to stay with might like for him to bring them, and the answer had been "They're Australian. Take 'em some beer."

He pointed to the two cases of Kenyan beer he'd brought and said, "Just those cases of Tusker."

Chambers smiled broadly and said, "Ah! Good on ya, mate!"

As they loaded the beer onto the truck, Ed said, "I really appreciate you folks allowing me to stay with you. I'll try to keep out of the way."

"You won't be in the way, mate. We can always use an extra hand, so if you get bored, just let me know. There's plenty to do."

They climbed into the battered pickup truck. The six young Somali men eyed Ed curiously, chewing on little green stems of some plant as they did so.

At the gate of the airbase, the truck was halted by a group of Somali men in fairly uniform military clothing. As they inspected the contents of the truck, Ed could not help but notice the glares exchanged between these men and the motley bunch in the truck with him. There was a sort of respectful fear of these men by those aboard the truck, for some reason. He noticed, too, that the men manning the gate of the airbase wore web gear bearing extra ammunition, and that their weapons appeared to be better maintained. Remnants of some regular army outfit from the past, he deduced.

Once they were waved through the gate, the pickup sped away from the airbase and into the town of Baidoa. And suddenly, there they were; walking skeletons in tattered rags, standing in a line with beat-up bowls or makeshift containers at the gate of a small compound. A Red Cross flag hung from the gate, and two men with sticks stood guard there, yelling and gesturing at the emaciated specters. As they passed, Ed noticed that, alongside the building, several of the skeletal creatures, too weak to stand, sat against the wall or lay motionless in the dirt. There appeared to be no young men among them; only children and women and a few elderly men. Here and there along the street, amid the debris of stripped vehicle chassis, corpses lay, ignored by the shuffling creatures making their way to the feeding station, and Ed Walker thought, *My God. This cannot be real.* But it *was* real. He felt he was seeing the image of Hell come to earth.

The CARE truck met several other beat-up vehicles as they passed through the center of the town, each vehicle manned by five or six scurvy militiamen, and each mounting a machine gun of some description. Each was also flying the flag of one of the relief agencies; the Red Cross or the International Medical Corps or *Medicins sans Frontieres* or CARE.

How, Ed wondered, could there be so many relief agencies here, and so many people apparently starving to death? The answer, he would soon learn, was fairly simple: the town was swollen with refugees from all over southern Somalia who were flocking there by the thousands in hopes of getting some of the food being flown in on American, Canadian, German and Russian cargo aircraft from the port city of Mombasa, Kenya. But the meager amounts were simply not enough. It would not have been enough even if most of it had made it to the feeding centers scattered about the town. But most of it did *not* make it there, for even after the thirty percent or so that the "militias" demanded for "administration and security" was handed over to them at gunpoint, and the rest placed in warehouses, much of what remained was taken in armed night raids by competing subclans. At best, Ed would learn from Merv Chambers over a lunch of "salad sandwiches," perhaps twenty percent of the relief supplies actually reached the battered bowls of the starving refugees.

Ed was barely able to get the sandwich - a bit of lettuce and tomato on a buttered hard roll - down. But he would have felt guilty if he had not finished it, so he did so, thankful that he was here. Because he could - he *would*, he decided then and there - do something. He didn't know what, yet. But something.

After they'd had their lunch in one of the three small buildings the CARE Australia team occupied, Merv Chambers showed him around the place. Two of the buildings were in adjoining, walled-in compounds. One was living quarters for half of the team's six members and also had the kitchen and dining room. The small room with a long, communal table was also used for team meetings and other get togethers. There, the team's high frequency radio, its only direct link with the outside world, was also housed.

"No telephone?" Ed asked.

"Humph," Merv snorted. "There's not a working telephone in all of southern Somalia, mate. These bastards have stripped every centimeter of wire off every pole in the country. And they've shipped the wire and the telephones and the roofs and doors and every other bloody thing they could dismantle off to Ethiopia or the Yemen. Everything."

"Unbelievable," Ed muttered.

"Well, you'll see a lot *more* here that you won't believe, before it's all over," Merv said. "C'mon. I'll show you around the place."

The rest of CARE's holdings in Baidoa - all guarded by a few aging Somali men with a mixture of obsolete weapons - were the five-room house next door, used as an office and for the storage of the precious few medical supplies the team had; and a walled-in house across the street, which was living quarters for three of the team's members. There was a spare bedroom there, and Merv said, "This is where you'll be staying, Ed. I'm across the way there, and the two nurses, Cheryl and Katherine, have the other two rooms. The girls use the bath in Kathy's room, and we use the one at the back, there... when it works, that is."

Ed looked around the sparsely furnished house. The center hall surrounding the four small bedrooms obviously served as a common living area for the occupants, as there was an old couch and two chairs around a small table there, and against the wall was a small refrigerator. Atop it was a portable tape player with built-in speakers, a ten-cup electric coffee maker, and an empty charger for hand-held radios such as the one Merv had been carrying at the airfield. At the end of the hall opposite the front door was another small room, once the kitchen, but now with only a frame where the sink had been, and no stove. The only thing that cooled the house was an overhead fan above the sofa. Between the two rooms across from his was a stairwell leading up to the flat roof.

Ed peered into the room that was to be his. There was nothing in it but a bed, with a mosquito net hanging above it, and a rough table made from a couple of wooden crates. Ed threw his rucksack down on the bed and thought, It isn't much, but I've lived under a hell of a lot *worse* conditions.

There was one window in the room, but when he opened it, the noise and fumes of the diesel generator used to provide power to the house filled the room, so he closed it.

Merv was loading the little refrigerator with a case of the beer Ed had brought. "Better cool this beer while the generator's on," he said. When he finished, he looked at Ed and said, "You look tired, mate. Why don't you get your head down for awhile? You can meet the rest of the team at dinner."

'Good idea," Ed said. "Between the jet lag and the heat, I could use a nap."

He flopped down on his bed, using his rucksack for a pillow.

When he closed his eyes, the sight of the starving Somalis he had seen earlier came to him, and he sat up.

Hundreds of them were dying in Baidoa each day, he knew. And in Bardera and Belet Huen and Mogadishu and Kismayu, as well. Thousands dead each day simply because there was nothing to eat. How could it be? Why didn't the Defense Department just send Special Forces teams to each of the population centers, begin immediate and massive airdrops of food and medicines, and put an end to it? Who the hell was going to stop them? Not the rag-tag militiamen he had seen at the airfield and in town. That's what he would recommend for starters. It wasn't that hard, if only the politicians had the will.

He lay back on the bed again to compose in his mind the message he would send to General Madison the next day. The next day. Another thousand would be dead by then.

Only a few lines of his proposed message passed through his mind before he fell asleep.

He awoke to the sound of music. It was coming from the room outside his door; a song he vaguely remembered having heard before.

A woman's voice, off key, sang along; *"...and if I had a boat, I'd go out on the ocean; and if I had a pony, I'd ride him on my boat...*

That country singer from Texas with the high hair, Ed thought. He smiled at the sound of the woman still trying to sing with him; *"And we could all together go out on the ocean; me upon my pony on my boat..."*

Ed sat up, pulled on his shoes and shirt and opened the door. The woman was standing at the refrigerator, looking inside it, her back to him. She was wearing nothing except shower shoes on her feet and a bath towel wrapped around her, wet blonde hair hanging at shoulder length, and slender but muscular legs showing nearly to her buttocks.

Ed ducked back inside his room and coughed loudly, and the woman turned off the music and said, "Hullo? That you, Merv?"

"No," Ed replied, staying inside the room. "It's Ed Walker. I'm an American. I'll be staying here for awhile."

The woman appeared at his door then, holding the towel with her left hand where it was tucked in above her bosom. Her eyes passed briefly over his face and then locked on his eyes as if she hadn't noticed the scars.

"G'day, Ed," she said, holding her right hand out to him and smiling. "I'm Katherine Norris. Welcome to Baidoa."

Ed took her hand, and she shook it firmly.

"Hi," he said. "Hope I didn't startle you."

"No. I was afraid it was one of the bloody Somalis lurking about, that's all. You responsible for the Tusker beer in the fridge?"

"Well, yes."

"Good. I'll have one, if I may."

"Of course," Ed replied, smiling at the attractive Australian.

"Lyle all right with you?" she asked as she pulled a bottle of beer from the little refrigerator.

"Pardon?"

"Lyle Lovett," she said, gesturing at the tape deck from which the voice crooned. "You mind listening to his music?"

"Oh," Ed said, "not at all."

Katherine turned the tape back on and disappeared into her room, and Ed sat on the couch, listening to the music. She reappeared before the song ended, dressed in a T shirt and a pair of shorts, singing along with the song as she walked over, beer in hand, and sat in one of the chairs across from the American.

"The mystery masked man was smart;
He got himself a Tonto,
'Cause Tonto did the dirty work for free.
But Tonto, he was smarter,
And one day said, 'Kemosabe,
Well, kiss my ass, I bought a boat,
I'm goin' out to sea."

"He's coming out here for Christmas, you know," Katherine said with a smile.

"Lyle Lovett? Really?"

She gave a hearty laugh and took another swallow of beer. "Wish he would, but no, not really. But you know how rumors are; you start one, and after awhile everybody expects it to happen, and eventually somebody thinks they're the one responsible for making it happen. Now and then, they do."

Ed smiled and said, "'The wish is the father of the deed.'"

"Exactly," Katherine said as she slipped off her shower shoes and put her feet on the table.

"Home for Christmas," he said. "That was the rumor I always heard in the Army in places like this. Never happened, though."

She laughed and said, "The wish was a bastard, I guess. There's a rumor the Yanks are going to come sort this mess out," she said. "Is that one going to come true?"

He raised his eyebrows and said, "Maybe," then sat back and looked at her a moment as she combed out her hair. "*Should* it happen, Katherine?" he asked.

She shrugged her shoulders and thought about it as she ran the comb through her hair several times. Then she said, "I don't suppose there's any other way to keep them from looting all the food before we can get it distributed," she said. "I'd hate to think it's necessary, but I suppose it is, at least for awhile." She studied him for a long moment, then asked, "Is that why you're here, Ed?"

There's no use lying, he thought, so he said, "Yes. But no one's supposed to know it."

Katherine nodded, but said nothing.

Merv Chambers came in then, waved, and headed straight for the refrigerator. There was a young woman with him. She looked at Ed and said, "G'day. You must be the American who's come to stay with us."

Ed stood and said, "Yes. Ed Walker. How do you do?" He held out his hand to her.

She took it and introduced herself as Cheryl Terry.

"What's chef preparing for dinner, Cher?" Katherine asked.

"Dunno. Smells like donkey."

"Rice and donkey, or spaghetti and donkey?" Katherine asked, then grinned at Ed. "Don't look so horrified," she said. "He's actually quite a good cook. Used to be the chef for the American ambassador, he claims. Of course, so do the ones at IMC and Concern and..."

A burst of gunfire not far away silenced her, and Ed sat up, startled.

"Christ! What now?" Merv mumbled. The girls glanced at each other with a look of concern. There was another burst of automatic fire, followed by an explosion. It sounded to Ed like a grenade, and no more than a couple of hundred meters away. He stood and started for the door. "I'll have a look," he said.

"Might be able to see more from the roof," Merv said.

Ed nodded and turned toward the stairwell that led up there.

There were no multi-story buildings to block his view, and Ed could see quite well down the road that led into the center of town. Less than a quarter of a mile away, he could see a dozen or so armed men milling around a pickup truck. There was a body lying in the road near it, and the driver was hanging out of the door from the waist up.

Several of the men were holding a man while another beat him with a rifle butt. Then the beaten man crumpled to the ground. The man who had been beating him pointed his rifle at his head and fired a burst, then slung the weapon over his shoulder, kicked the body, and swaggered away.

Merv was standing beside Ed now. Ed glanced at him, then back at the scene.

The men pulled the driver's body from the cab of the truck, and one of them got in. He apparently tried to start it, but couldn't, so several of the men got behind the truck and began pushing it. The man at the wheel turned it into an alley and it disappeared. The three bodies were left in the street.

"What do you suppose that was about, Merv?"

"Dunno. Probably just changing ownership of the truck."

Ed shook his head and muttered, "Anarchy."

"That's the right word for it," Chambers agreed, then turned and walked down the stairs.

Ed stood watching for awhile longer. Katherine appeared in the courtyard below. She had pulled on a loose fitting dress over her shorts, and was carrying a backpack over one shoulder. Ed thought she must be going to the other house across the road, but she turned and walked quickly toward the scene of the firefight.

Ed hurried downstairs. Cheryl was on one of the hand-held radios, saying, "Kathy's on the way there now to see if any of them are still alive. If so, could you send a vehicle to take them to the dispensary?"

Ed rushed out after the pretty nurse. He caught up with her just as she reached the first of the Somali men. She glanced at Ed, then checked the Somali for any sign of life. Ed looked nervously in the direction the assailants had gone. Down the alley, he could see two of them watching Katherine and him.

"This one's gone," she muttered, then moved to the second man. He was obviously dead, his eyes open and unmoving, a large portion of the top of his skull gone. He was the one, Ed realized, whom the assailants had beaten before one of them finished him off with a burst from his Kalashnikov. Katherine only glanced at him, then went to the third man. This one was still alive. His legs were drawn up, and he was clutching his abdomen and moaning softly.

Katherine knelt beside him and pulled his hands away from his gut by the wrists. There was a long gash across his belly, and his intestines were spilling out.

"Oh, God," the nurse said, then replaced his hands. She stood and looked down the road to the east to see if anyone else was coming to help. No one was in sight, so she turned to Ed and said, "You take his shoulders. I'll take his feet."

Ed nodded and moved to the man's head. He clasped the Somali under the armpits and as Katherine lifted his legs at the knees, they raised him from the ground. Immediately, a burst of automatic rifle fire cracked above their heads. Ed dropped the man and dived for cover, but Katherine set the man's legs down gently and stood up. For several seconds, she glared down the alley from which the firing had come, then squatted, clasped the injured man beneath the back and knees, and lifted him into her arms.

Ed stood and looked at her as she began to walk up the road to the east. He had seen such bravery in the past -had even exhibited it himself, on occasion. But he had never seen it from a woman before, and that fact froze him in awe for several seconds. Then he got in front of her and took the frail Somali from her arms into his.

"Thanks," the Australian nurse said softly. She went back to get her little backpack, then caught up to Ed. There was a pickup coming toward them, a white flag with a blue symbol on it flying from a staff on one fender, and Katherine said, "Good. Here comes someone from IMC."

"IMC?"

"International Medical Corps. Americans. They'll take him off our hands."

The pickup - a Somali driving and three others with guns in the back - skidded to a halt, and a man jumped out of the cab. He was wearing cut off jeans and a Grateful Dead T shirt. He looked at Ed and said, "Put him in the back," then asked, "What have we got, Kathy?"

"Gut wound, Raymond" she said. "Not too bad."

"All right," the man replied. "We'll take him to the hospital, then. Any more survivors?"

"No," Katherine said, as Ed laid the man in the bed of the truck while the Somali gunmen watched without helping.

"OK, the man said, "we'll take it from here. Have a pleasant evening."

With that, Raymond jumped in the cab of the truck, and said, "Hospital, Abdul. Pronto." The transmission ground into gear and the pickup truck sped away.

Katherine started walking back toward the CARE house as Ed Walker stood for a time gazing at the two bodies lying in the road.

"What about them?" he called after her.

She stopped for a moment and looked at the dead men.

"Someone will collect them tomorrow, along with all the others," she said, and walked on.

He followed after her, glancing back from time-to-time at the bodies in the road. *My God*, he thought. What kind of place *is* this?

TWENTY NINE

The dinner meal that evening at the CARE house in Baidoa was actually quite tasty; spicy, roasted goat meat on rice, a salad of lettuce and tomatoes, hot buttered bread, and for dessert, banana pudding and coffee.

All six of the CARE Australia team were there, along with Ed Walker and an American nurse from IMC named Diane Williams.

Merv Chambers introduced Ed to Diane, and to the three members of the CARE team he had not yet met: Lowell Morrison, the team leader, a former Australian Army officer in his late thirties; his assistant, Jane MacArthur, a young woman in her mid-twenties who seemed to Ed mature beyond her years; and a self-taught electrician and plumber of about thirty named Richard Disney.

All of them treated Ed Walker cordially, if not warmly. Except for Katherine, who was the only one who smiled, they all seemed rather tense.

After his dinner conversation with Lowell Morrison and the others, which was mainly a briefing on the team's activities since they had arrived in Somalia a month earlier, he understood why. They had plenty of reasons to be tense.

When they arrived in Baidoa, hundreds of people there were dying daily of starvation and disease, the emaciated corpses left to rot in the streets. Armed gangs of young men were ransacking helpless villagers' homes and refugees' huts for anything of value they could take to Mogadishu or up to Ethiopia to trade for food, or for more guns and ammunition to protect what they had and to loot still more.

The meager crop of sorghum being grown in the outlying hamlets was stolen as soon as it was harvested. And while the bandits were plundering the scattered settlements of their inadequate crops, they would steal anything else of the least value that they came across, including the few remaining animals, simple farming tools - even the pumps from the sparsely scattered water wells on which the daily lives of the hamlets' inhabitants relied. Anyone who resisted was mercilessly shot.

As a result, the parched and starving villagers began flocking to the places their stolen grain and livestock had been taken; Mogadishu, Baidoa, Bardera, and a half-dozen other towns.

As soon as the word spread that relief agencies were arriving in those towns to bring in food for the starving, the desperate Somalis began migrating there by the thousands, although many died on the arduous marches en route.

But when bulk foodstuffs finally did arrive, warehouses were fought over and looted by the armed thugs of competing clans and subclans.

The relief agencies' next move was to hire, at extortionary cost, local gunmen to guard the warehouses. What *they* didn't steal finally got to the feeding stations.

Then, however, the small convoys of foodstuffs were being ambushed and looted on the roads from the port of Mogadishu, where a large percentage had already been extorted for loading, transportation, and ineffective security, before it ever got to Baidoa or the other feeding centers.

The emergency airlift was started then, but it couldn't keep pace with the huge numbers of refugees pouring into the regional capitol.

"We're going to try again tomorrow to bring a big convoy up from Moga," Lowell Morrison explained. "About fifty trucks full of Australian wheat. Something around a hundred tons. We've gotten the clan leaders and the so-called governor to agree to provide safe passage for it, for a price - albeit a rather *large* price."

Katherine began collecting plates from the table. When she reached for Ed's, she placed her hand on his shoulder to lean over him, and they exchanged a brief smile. Then Ed turned his attention back to Morrison.

"Where do you fit in, Lowell? You relief workers? What keeps these bandits from coming in and taking all you have?"

Morrison sat back in his chair and eyed Ed. "We're the only currency they have," he said. "They don't want to kill the goose that laid the golden egg, that's all. That's why, anytime we're physically threatened - shot at or roughed up or our personal kit robbed - we pull out. We just shut down, bring in an aircraft to take us to Nairobi, and stay away for awhile. No food comes in to be stolen, no money is paid to the gangs for guarding the facilities, no technicals are hired at extortionary prices, no petrol flown in, no landing fees paid at the airfield."

"Technicals?"

"That's what all these armed vehicles are known as. Don't know why they're called that. Probably the corrupted translation of some Italian term into Somali, then into English."

Ed nodded and considered Lowell's explanation about the non-government agencies (NGOs) and their relief supplies being "currency." Perhaps that explained why the airlift was halted for days every time the aircraft were shot at. But such interruptions, with the numbers of starving being so great, must have horrendous ramifications. "But when you leave like that, or the airlift is interrupted, what happens to the refugees?" he asked.

Morrison looked at him evenly and said, "They starve. The death rate soars."

Katherine and Diane came in then, and Kathy set a cup of coffee in front of Ed.

"It's tough to do," Morrison continued, "but it's necessary. Otherwise, they'd either kill us, or the relief effort would totally collapse."

"I see," Ed muttered, but thought, Not if the troops were here, by God.

"That's the rational explanation he just gave you, Ed," Diane offered. "It assumes the Somalis - the ones with the guns - will act rationally. But there's no guarantee of that, especially now that the *khat* trade is flourishing again."

"Do you know about khat, Ed?" Katherine asked.

"No. What is it?"

"Surely you saw most of them chewing on those little green stems," she said. Ed nodded, so she went on to explain, "That's khat. It grows in the highlands of Kenya and Ethiopia. It's a mild amphetamine."

"Mild unless you chew it all day, like these jerks do," Diane interjected. "Hell, by mid-afternoon they're all absolute, raving speed freaks."

"They start winding down about nine o'clock," Lowell said. "After that, it's usually quiet. Unless a gang shows up who haven't been on khat. If they get here and start a punch up before their cousins have really crashed after chewing the stuff all day, then they're in for a fight. A hell of a fight, because until these guys unwind off the stuff, they're absolute maniacs. Once they're down, though, you couldn't get them going with a horde of naked amazons."

"How do they get it here?" Walker inquired.

"They fly it in," Morrison said. "Tons of it every day. Aidid, the leader of the Hawiyeh clan that covers Mogadishu, Baidoa - most of the upper half of southern Somalia - has it flown in daily on charter aircraft from Nairobi. Hell, over at Mog West airfield, the relief aircraft can't even land until the khat planes, usually about eight of them, have come and gone. It's the way Aidid finances most of the guns, ammo, and technicals that give him sway over southern Somalia. Without it, he'd be just another in a gang of minor warlords."

"Is khat addictive?" Ed asked.

"Depends on whom you ask," Katherine said. "I'll tell you this, though; they'll kill each other for the stuff."

"Humph," Diane said. "They'll kill each other for a cheap watch. That's no news."

As if to accentuate the statement, the sound of gunfire from somewhere in town reached them above the noise of the compound's generator. The three veterans of Baidoa glanced nervously at each other but said nothing. Ed Walker swallowed a sip of coffee and looked at them. Yes, they have good reason to be tense, he thought.

Lowell Morrison rose from his chair. "Well, the generator will be shutting down soon," he said. "I guess I'll get my head down."

The American officer nodded, and the CARE team leader waved to the two women and left the room.

The generator quit just then. Ed would learn that Morrison's departure from the dining room at night was the Somali staffs' signal to shut it down. Katherine moved with familiarity in the darkness to the cupboard near the door and lit a candle, then placed it on the table in front of Ed. Then she returned to the cupboard and opened the door, and produced a nearly empty bottle of Scotch whisky. She brought it to the table and set it in front of the others.

"Would you like a wee dram in your coffee, Ed, or would you prefer it straight up?" she asked. Without asking Diane, she poured half an ounce into the IMC nurse's coffee.

Ed slid his nearly empty cup over to her. "In the cup, please," he replied.

She poured him a full ounce, and put just a splash into her own coffee, then raised her cup.

"To Ed Walker," she toasted. "May you find the answers you came here seeking."

"To Ed," Diane said. "And whatever the questions are."

The others sipped their drinks and Ed watched them in the dim light of the candle. What remarkable women these are, he thought. Out here in this godforsaken place, trying to make a difference. Then he wondered why; why were they here? They weren't "do-gooders," as he had expected relief workers to be - not with the connotations that such a term had always brought with it, in his mind. He sipped his whisky-laden coffee, then asked them, "Why *are* you here?"

The women glanced at each other with a look of seriousness for a moment, then smiled.

Diane said, "I'm here because it's as far away as I could get from the jerk I married."

"And I'm here for the money," Katherine said, smiling.

"So, there you have it, Ed Walker," Diane said, then leaned across the table and looked him in the eye. "Why are *you* here?"

Ed took another sip of his coffee. He tried to think of something cute to say, but instead he thought, They remind me of Sue. His face darkened, and he wondered whether, if she were still alive, she might be sitting at this table. Somehow, he believed she would.

Diane drained the rest of her coffee, then took the bottle of Scotch and poured Ed and herself each a small shot before emptying the last of it into Katherine's cup.

"C'mon, Ed," she said. "The question wasn't *that* hard, was it?"

His intuition told him that he should not be totally honest with her, so he said, "I'm just a soldier boy who couldn't keep a real job. So I'm just over here to see what's going on." Then he realized he had spoken the absolute truth.

"Well," Katherine said, clinking her cup against his, "I'm pleased that you are, Ed. Thanks for going out there with me to check on those men who got shot today."

He knew that she meant it, and smiled warmly at her. There was something about this Australian nurse that was very familiar. It was as if he had known her for a long time.

Diane finished her coffee and said, "Well, I guess I'd better call for my ride and get on home." When she called the IMC base station for a ride, though, the American man on the other radio said, "There's no driver and guard available, Donna. They're all crashed."

"Don't worry," Katherine said. "Ed and I will walk you down there."

Ed raised his eyebrows, and she said, "It's only a quarter of a mile. Nothing to worry about."

"If you're sure you don't mind," Diane said.

"I'll find a torch," Katherine said. She took the candle and located a flashlight in the cupboard.

They walked out through the pedestrian gate of the CARE compound, past the sleeping Somali guard. It was almost totally dark, and Katherine shone the light down the road for a few seconds. When they got their bearings, she turned it off. "No need to make our presence known," she said. "One of these lovelies might decide to loot our torch."

"They wouldn't, would they?" Ed asked. "Not something as minor as a flashlight."

"Ha!" Diane said. "I've seen them *kill* each other for less."

If that was the case, Ed wondered, what the hell were they doing walking down the road?

Katherine turned the light on now and then to ensure they were still in the middle of the road. Here and there they could see a candle glowing in one of the huts alongside the road. Ed looked up at the stars. It was amazing how many stars were visible when there was no ambient light to interfere with one's ability to see them.

The generator at the IMC compound was still running, and there was a dim light at the pedestrian gate.

"It's right up there," Diane said, inclining off the road toward it. She called to the guard as Katherine shone the light on the gate.

A moment later, a flashlight came on behind the gate. It shone through a viewing slot on their faces a moment, then the gate creaked open.

"Thanks for the escort," Diane said to Ed and Katherine. She gave the other woman a peck on the cheek, and did the same to Ed, then she stepped inside.

Katherine lit the way back to the road with the flashlight, then turned it off when they were headed back toward the CARE house.

They walked along in silence for awhile, bumping gently into each other in the darkness until Katherine took Ed's hand in hers to prevent it. He recognized it as a gesture of convenience, not affection. But it was nice to hold a woman's hand, he thought. This woman's hand, in particular.

"Oh, look," he said softly as he glanced at the stars to the south. "The Southern Cross."

"Sure," Katherine said, then chuckled and added, "That's right. You can't see it in America, can you? I forget that. We Australians take it for granted. Did you know that you can see Ursa Major from here, as well?"

Ed looked to the north for the Big Dipper, but if it was there, it was blocked by the buildings on the slight rise in that direction. Katherine was looking there, too. "I'll show you from the roof when we get to the house," she said. She tripped on something, and nearly fell. She turned on the flashlight to see what had tripped her. It was one of the frail Somali refugees, little more than a pile of bones.

"Oh, no," she said, and knelt in the dirt road beside the woman. She felt for a pulse, but there was none, so she stood. "Nothing to be done for this one, I'm afraid," she said sadly.

"At least let me move her off the road," Ed said.

Katherine put the light on the corpse, and Ed lifted it. He was shocked at how very little the starved woman weighed. It couldn't have been more than fifty or sixty pounds. He carried her off the road and laid her gently in the dirt, then straightened her body and folded her hands across her bony chest. Then he sighed and wiped his hands on his jeans.

"God, I hope that convoy arrives tomorrow," the nurse said as they continued down the road.

"It better," Ed said. "God damn them, they'd *better* let it through."

Katherine took his hand again. This time, she gave it a squeeze before relaxing her grip and walking on.

When they turned off the road and approached the gate to the wall around their house, she called to the guard. He opened the gate and let them in, and they walked into the house. Katherine lit a candle and placed it on the table in the hall. The doors to Merv and Cheryl's rooms were closed.

"You'd better have a wash," she said to Ed. "No telling what you might have picked up from that poor woman."

When he came out of the bathroom, Katherine was sitting on the sofa. She was wearing a sarong wrapped around her, her feet up on the table, drinking from one of the bottles of Tusker. She had poured half of it into a glass for Ed.

"Have a nightcap," she said.

"Thanks," he said, and sat across from her. He studied her pretty face in the soft light of the candle, and she said, "You never did answer her."

"Who?"

"Diane. You never said why you're here."

He smiled. "Sure I did. I told her I was just over here to see what's going on. It's the truth."

"But why *you*, and not someone else?"

Ed sipped his beer. "The truth?"

She nodded, so he said, "Because I was passed over for promotion, and an old friend of mine, a general, wanted to give me a chance to do something worthwhile before I leave the Army."

Katherine eyed him and said, "What will you tell him?"

"What do you think I should tell him?"

"Whatever you think the truth is," she said.

He leaned forward with his forearms on his knees.

"You've been here long enough to know, Katherine. What *is* the truth?"

She sipped from her bottle and set it down before she answered. "We're not getting the job done," she said. "There's just too much looting. But we would resent the military coming in."

"Why? How else is the food going to get to the people who need it?"

She sighed and said, "I suppose it won't. It's just that we hate to admit we've failed, that's all."

"We military guys think that you relief workers have some sort of an aversion toward us. Is that true?"

She raised her eyebrows at his comment, then sat back against the sofa and stretched her legs out. "I guess there's some truth to that," she said. "But not in CARE Australia. Lowell's an ex-officer. So is Bob Ashton up at Bardera. Still, the two - relief work and the military - don't seem to go hand-in-hand, do they? I mean, the principal job of the one is to save lives. The other is to *take* lives, isn't it?"

The comment didn't surprise him. He had seen animosity and distrust between the military and relief workers in nearly every conflict since Vietnam. The armed forces didn't trust the NGO's because they usually refused to take sides in such conflicts, and when they did, it was invariably toward the left-leaning elements. The NGO's, on the other hand, had a stereotypical view of the military as knuckle-draggers with itchy trigger fingers, anxious to solve every problem with violence. It had always disappointed him that the two seldom seemed willing to work together. There was so much that could be done if they did. The relief effort to assist the Kurds in northern Iraq after Desert Storm was the best and most recent example. And Somalia - based on his initial impressions, at least - seemed an ideal situation for such cooperation. A few Special Forces and civil affairs teams, backed by the necessary muscle and mobility, could do wonders, he thought. He explained his views to Katherine.

"Well," she said, raising her knees and wrapping her arms around them, "I hope you're right. I just hope that if there *is* an intervention, it won't be heavy-handed."

"I do, too, Katherine."

She finished her half of the beer and got up to put the empty bottle away. "Would you like another?" she asked.

"No, thank you."

"OK, then. Good night, Ed."

"Good night, Katherine."

She walked to her door, then turned and looked at him. "I didn't show you the stars from the rooftop," she said.

"No, you didn't. Some other time."

"Yes. Tomorrow night, maybe - after we're done with the convoy."

"Sure."

THIRTY

The convoy left Mogadishu at dawn, and the CARE office there notified Morrison over the radio of its departure.

"Forty seven trucks," he informed the other Baidoa team members at breakfast. "A hundred and twenty metric tons of Australian wheat."

While Jane figured out how many of the 50 kilo bags would go to each distribution site, Cheryl, Richard and Merv went to the office to brief their Somali assistants. Ed did some calculations in his head. There were about sixty thousand people in Baidoa. If everyone got an equal amount of wheat, each would receive two kilos - about five pounds. That wasn't much - not when one considered there hadn't been a convoy make it there in more than a month.

"Two kilos each," he said to the others. "How long will that last them?"

Morrison looked at him, scratched his head, and said, "Well, in the first place, they won't each get that much. About thirty tons will go as payoff to the gunmen for security and transport."

"Thirty *tons*?" Ed asked incredulously. "Hell, Lowell. That's a *fourth* of it!"

Morrison nodded. "Yes, it is. But we have no choice. It's either pay what they ask, or it doesn't get through. So, anyway, that will cut it back to a kilo and a half. Since it's unmilled wheat, they'll have to give up about twenty percent to pay for having it milled. So that's less than one and a quarter kilos per person, in the end."

Ed shook his head. Less than three pounds per person, then. The equivalent of three or four loaves of bread, he supposed. Christ. It would take two convoys a week of that quantity just to stem the starvation, not to mention the medical problems. And many more refugees were staggering into the filthy, overcrowded town daily.

Katherine studied the American's scarred face, his brow furrowed deep with thought. The look was a familiar one; everyone had that look when they first got to Baidoa, it seemed. All the Westerners, anyway. The look on the gaunt faces of the refugees, if they survived the trek from their distant hamlets, was one of utter relief at the fact that they had survived the journey.

"When you have nothing - absolutely nothing except a rag on your back - a kilo and a half of wheat seems like a lot," she said.

"Yes," Ed said. "But all that amount could possibly do is prolong the misery, isn't it?"

"It's a start."

"A start isn't enough," he replied.

She gave him a look that was half sneer, half smile. "Well," she said, getting up from her chair, "the convoy won't be here for a few more hours. I'm going out to Bay One camp and try to prolong a few refugees' misery till then."

She left, and Ed sensed Lowell Morrison glaring at him.

"We're doing the best we can, Colonel," he said.

"Hell, Lowell. I know you are. I sure as hell didn't mean to denigrate your efforts. I just meant that something's got to be done, that's all. Something to keep these bastards from starving their own people to death."

"Yes," Morrison said. "In the meantime, we're going to do what we can. It may not be much, but it does a hell of a lot more for them than noble thoughts and words." He stood to leave, then turned to Jane and said, "Why don't you take Ed down to Bay One, Jane? He hasn't visited a refugee camp, yet."

"I'd like to do that," the American said. That's where Katherine had said she was going; it would give him the opportunity to explain what he had meant, and to apologize if she had misinterpreted his comment.

Bay One refugee camp was the most squalid place of human habitation Ed Walker had ever seen. It was acre upon acre of little hemispherical huts, each constructed of a few sticks holding up a small square of plastic material that served as a roof. The stench was unimaginable.

The first inhabitants Ed saw weren't as bad off as he had expected, for as they reached the edge of the camp and he and Jane got out of the beat up Land Cruiser, a dozen children gathered around them. Half were smiling and playful, and though skinny, looked nowhere near starvation. The others, several barely more than skin and bones, were at least walking, and apparently without difficulty.

Then, behind them, Ed saw a tiny, frail child squatting outside one of the huts. As he watched, a watery fluid squirted from the child's bowels onto the ground. A look of horror crossed his face, and he ignored the other children and walked to the little girl. She cowered as the big white man approached and she fell back into the liquid feces. He reached down for her, and the child tried to scream, but a weak squeal was all she could manage.

Ed brushed at the flies swarming around her eyes, but they flew away for only a split second, then landed on the tiny girl's face again. He looked up at Jane, his face pale and drawn in anguish.

"She's beyond help, Ed," the Australian said softly.

His brow furrowed. "What do you mean?"

"I mean, she's going to die."

He stood and glowered angrily at her. "How can you *say* that?" he demanded. "Come *on*, Jane. We've got to get her to the hospital or something."

Jane looked at him with pity, but shook her head. "No," she said in a hoarse whisper. "Look." She reached down and grasped the little sticks that were the girl's arms. There was a plastic band on each wrist; one white, the other red.

"She's been seen by Katherine. The white band shows that she's undergoing the special feeding regimen. The red one means she can have no more medicines. What there is, is needed by those who have a reasonable chance of surviving. This one has missed that chance." She looked at Ed with an expression of pain and frustration as deep as his own and said again, "She's beyond help. She's going to die." Then she turned, knelt in front of the child, and lifted her against her breast. She stroked the little girl's filthy face, then set her down away from the pool of runny feces.

The dying child immediately squatted, and again a squirt of the undigested porridge issued from her, her fly-encrusted eyes following Jane as she turned away.

Ed stared pitifully at the child, a chill coursing through him.

"There's hundreds of them like that here," a voice said. It was Katherine. He turned and looked at her.

Their eyes locked for a time, and he said, "Hundreds?"

She nodded, then shrugged her shoulders. "Well, maybe only scores, by now. The rest - thousands - have already died. They're the first to go, you know - the little children. Those under five."

She turned and walked down one of the narrow paths that ran among the squalid huts.

He followed and clasped her gently by the arm, and she stopped and looked at him.

"Katherine, I... I 'm sorry for what I said back at the house."

She shrugged her shoulders again. "I don't know," she said. "Maybe you're right; maybe all we're doing *is* prolonging their misery. Maybe we should just... just shoot them. Get them out of their misery."

She turned away again, and he said, "That sounds like something I would say. Something stupid. Like somebody who has been here one whole day and has all the answers."

She turned back to face him, studied his eyes, then said, "Yes. It does, doesn't it?"

He smiled weakly and nodded. "Will you show me around?" he asked. "Explain things to me?"

She stared at him for several seconds, then her face melted into a warm smile. The expression reminded Ed so much of Susan Madison that it startled him.

"I'll try," she said.

She stopped to look into each hut, and Ed began to understand what a false impression his first sight of the refugee camp had given him. Inside most of the huts were one or two, sometimes up to four or five, ill and starving human beings. Or dead ones. Probably a fifth were either dead or so near death that he couldn't tell they were still alive by looking at them. Most of the others were too weak to do anything except lie there, awaiting the word to go to the next feeding session. Katherine checked each, explaining to Ed Walker about the facts of life - and death - in Baidoa, Somalia, as she did so. Ed began to appreciate the news media characterization of Baidoa as "the City of Death."

"About three quarters of the ones below the age of five have died," she said.

She found an elderly man who had died alone, and pulled his featherweight corpse from the hovel into the narrow path.

Ed tried to straighten the body out and fold the arms across the emaciated chest, as he had done with the woman in the road the night before.

Katherine put her hand on his arm and said softly, "You needn't do that, Ed. They'll wash him and put him in a shroud and bury him."

He looked up at her and nodded.

"What happens," she said as they walked to the next hut, continuing her earlier explanation about the infant mortality rate, "is that the villi - the little finger-like projections in the small intestine that absorb nutrients - wither. They cease to function, and the result, unless you can put them in a sterile environment and feed them intravenously, is what you saw back there. The food goes through them without being used, and they still starve to death. Unless measles or pneumonia or something else kills them first."

"But, why can't you make the IV fluids, and the necessary equipment to give it to these children, first priority, then?" Ed asked. "I mean - and this is just a question, not a criticism - why couldn't the airlift concentrate on things like that? Instead of bulk foodstuffs, like they brought in on the flight I took from Nairobi?"

Katherine looked at him and shook her head. "You tell *me*," she said. "I've been asking for medical supplies since the day I got here. I haven't gotten a tenth of it in. What *has* been sent has been looted. Once the looters find out what isn't marketable, or good for getting high, they put it on the market. I buy back what I can, but once they find out I want it, they raise the price so that it's cheaper by far to have it sent in again. Anyway, most of it has been ruined by then. It... It's just not that simple, Ed."

She wiped the perspiration off her brow with her shirt sleeve, then smiled at him. "Beware of simple solutions to complex problems, Ed Walker," she said.

He stopped and thought about her last comment as she looked into another hut. Someone else had said that to him, once. He couldn't remember who, but it made sense.

By the time they made their way to the looted shell of a building that Katherine Norris used as a dispensary, Ed had gained a much better understanding of the actual nature of the starving Somalis' problems, and of the problems faced by CARE and the other relief agencies.

The problem was not a lack of generosity on the part of donors; there was more food in the ports of Mogadishu and Mombasa, and en route to the Horn of Africa, than could possibly be consumed by the starving masses of the famine and anarchy-ravaged region. But the relief effort was layered, as all bureaucracies are, and it took time to adjust to the actual needs of the workers on the ground. That, coupled with the interference of the so-called warlords - Ali Mahdi Mohammed and Mohammed Farrah Aidid and the others - disrupted the effort to the point that it was still costing hundreds of lives daily. The shallow solution that most of the world held was that, since people were starving, sending food to the region was all that was necessary.

Colonel Edward Walker was rapidly learning that the problem was much more complex than that. But he was increasingly convinced that the best and quickest solution was the unilateral intervention of the United States - not just with combat troops to protect and effect the shipments of relief goods, but with the right *kinds* of troops; Special Forces and civil affairs and engineer teams to reestablish and run essential elements of the dismantled infrastructure of Somalia, and to train Somalis - not the lawless thugs who now controlled life and death there - but the more stable and caring Somalis who deserved the opportunity to reestablish a working government. Medical teams, secured by combat troops, .should be brought in to help the relief agencies establish hospitals and dispensaries and roving medical patrols until the crisis was thwarted and they could operate alone.

Katherine's pitifully under-equipped dispensary was filled with miserable slivers of humanity. Tropical and equatorial diseases of every sort ravaged the Somalis. Most pitiful of all was the fact that so few of the patients were babies and little children; most of them had already succumbed to starvation or disease.

Ed Walker made up his mind what he would do. Once the convoy arrived and the meager allotment of food was distributed, he would catch the CARE courier aircraft to Bardera, verify for himself that the conditions there were as bad as those here in Baidoa, then travel on to Nairobi. He would use the secure communications of the American embassy to speak directly to General Madison and explain what he had learned - how critical it was to do something now, before there were no children left to save.

Katherine was showing Ed the grossly inadequate supplies and facilities she had to work with, when there was the distant sound of machine gun fire to the southeast - down near the point at which the Mogadishu Road entered Baidoa, where Lowell Morisson and Merv Chambers were waiting for the arrival of the convoy of wheat.

Katherine quickly turned on her radio and called Lowell.

"What the devil's going on, Lowell?" she asked. "Are you all right?"

"We're OK, but the convoy is buggered. There's a hell of a firefight down the road. A lot of the lorries are turning back."

Now Ed could hear an increasing amount of fire, including the sounds of explosions - rocket propelled grenades and recoilless rifles, it sounded to his experienced ear. The firing was heavy for several minutes, then slackened to infrequent bursts from individual machine guns.

"Looks like it's finished," Morrison reported over the radio. "We're headed back to the compound."

"OK, be careful," Katherine replied. "Any of the convoy get through?"

"Not one lorry. Not a single bag," Morrison replied. "Everyone get back to the compound. Richard, get on the radio and inform CARE Mogadishu of what's happened. And make sure the other NGO's are aware. And while you're talking to Moga, tell them to get a charter plane out here as soon as possible. I'm going to send the girls out to Kenya."

By the time Katherine and Ed got back to the compound, the rest of the team was already there.

Morrison looked at them and asked, "Everybody all right?"

They all nodded, but no one spoke as he thought for half a minute, then asked, "Any of the other NGO's have any information, Merv?"

Chambers shook his head slowly, then said, "They all say they are either going to thin out, or evacuate everybody."

"So are we," Morrison said. "I'll stay. I need one other." He looked at Merv and Richard. Neither volunteered.

"I'd be glad to hang around, if I can do any good," Ed offered. He needed to get out and talk to General Madison, but he wasn't going to leave Morrison there by himself.

"No," the team leader replied. "Richard will stay. There won't be any flights coming in for a few days anyway, after this cock up. So Merv will go out. We need to keep the water supply flowing , and that's Richard's job."

"I need to stay," Katherine said.

Morrison looked at her and smiled momentarily, but shook his head. "No. We have to show the bastards that nothing's going to happen in the way of relief as long as they act this way. Nothing; no food, no medical care, no pay for the cars and drivers. Nothing. The only reason I'm keeping Richard is that I need some relief at the radio, and someone to keep an eye on the other house."

The others were silent, resignation on their faces.

"What are you going to do, Ed?" Morrison asked.

The American pursed his lips and thought a moment, then sat back in his chair and said, "I'm going to the embassy in Nairobi and try to convince the US Department of Defense to get off its ass and send some troops out here," he said.

Lowell Morrison nodded, then smiled. "Good luck," he said with a hint of sarcasm in his weary voice.

      *   *   *

The charter aircraft did not come that afternoon to take the CARE workers or their guest, Colonel Edward Walker, away from the chaos of Baidoa to the safety of Nairobi, Kenya. The security situation in Baidoa made it questionable whether the aircraft would be allowed to land the next day, either. So the relief workers returned to their houses and nervously waited to see what the night would bring.

There was scattered firing throughout the town from dark until around midnight. But almost none of it was in the northeastern part of town where the CARE houses were located, so while the others slept or sat sipping the Tusker beer Ed had brought, he joined Katherine Norris on the roof.

She had her cassette player with her, and one of Lyle Lovett's songs issued softly from it.

She was sitting on a foam rubber mat, leaning back against the concrete wall of the staircase that ended on the roof, gazing up at the stars and singing softly with the music. Ed sat beside her, placing the bottle of Tusker he had brought for her between her feet.

There was a half moon, and it reflected enough light for him to see that she looked up at him and smiled.

She turned and pointed behind her. "There it is," she said softly.

Ed looked back where she was pointing. The seven stars of Ursa Major, better known to Americans as the Big Dipper, twinkled near the horizon to the north.

"It sure is," he said, then turned and looked to the south and found the five stars that comprised the Southern Cross, and said, "So this is where north meets south."

Katherine looked at his profile in the dim light of the moon and said, "Yes, I suppose it is."

He turned his face toward hers, and they studied each other, then she reached out and touched the scars on Ed's face, and said, "This isn't the hardest place you've ever been, is it?"

He took her hand and moved it from his face, but held gently onto it. "No," he said before he thought about it, then changed his mind and said, "I don't know. Maybe it is."

She sighed and said, "Sometimes I wonder if it's worth it. This is one of those times."

Ed smiled and said, "I thought you were only in it for the money."

She laughed softly. "Money. If I had any, I wouldn't be here. I'd be in the Mediterranean, sailing my yacht around the Greek islands. With Lyle Lovett. And his pony."

"I doubt it."

"No? In fact, I've been thinking that, when he comes for Christmas, I'll take one of these donkeys to Mogadishu, and we can sail around the harbor in one of those old Yemeni dhows. Lyle upon his donkey on his boat. With me in his lap."

A donkey brayed in the distance just then, and she sat up and said, "See? Did you hear that? A volunteer! Did you hear it?"

Ed laughed, but before he could reply, a stream of tracers arced across the sky from the center of town, followed a moment later by the muted sound of the weapon that had fired them. "No," he muttered. "But I heard *that*."

Katherine picked up the bottle of beer Ed had brought her and took a long drink from it, then asked, "Will you be coming back here, Ed?"

"To Baidoa? I have no idea. I suppose I will at some point, but I'm not certain."

He saw her nod, then he asked, "How long do you think you'll be in Kenya, Kathy?"

"Just a few days, I hope," she said. "There's so much to do." Her gaze shifted to the east, toward the squalor of Bay One refugee camp, and again she said, "So much to do...."

Ed leaned back and stared at the Southern Cross, enjoying the feel of the woman's hand in his. The skin was rougher than his own, calloused from hard work and a lack of lotion to combat the effects of the harsh, dry climate. But that discovery only made the courageous and dedicated young woman more attractive to him.

"How old are you, Kathy?" he asked.

"I'll be thirty next week," she said. "Why?"

"Just wondered." He hadn't thought about the fact that there was such a difference in their ages. Still, Katherine was older than Susan Madison had been when she died, and he still loved her as the young woman she was then, in spite of the fact that his own age had doubled since Sue's death.

Then a twinge of guilt pinched him, and he thought to himself, Christ, Walker; what are you *thinking* about? You should be down there composing the message you're going to send to the general. *Doing* something, not sitting here holding hands like some teenager with a crush.

He let go of her hand and pushed himself to his feet.

"Off to bed?" Katherine asked.

"Yeah... well, no, actually. I've got to make some notes about this place. Do you think we'll be able to get out of here tomorrow?"

"I hope not," she said. "In my case, at least. Too much to do at Bay One."

He recalled what he had seen there earlier that morning and wondered how she thought she could actually accomplish anything with the pitiful amount of medicines and supplies she had to work with. No, what was needed was massive aid; the sort of effort that could only be accomplished in a place like this by the force of arms and a logistical organization such as the US military could provide. But he didn't say so. Instead, he said, "Well, maybe things will settle down soon."

"I hope so," she said. "Sleep well, Ed."

They got out of Baidoa the next day. At mid-morning, a small twin-engine airplane buzzed the CARE house at about twenty feet, then climbed quickly and turned toward the airfield that lay on the other side of Baidoa.

"Mad Tom," Lowell Morrison said as soon as he heard the aircraft roar dangerously low over the house where the team sat waiting. "Let's get to the airfield."

"Who's Mad Tom?" Ed Walker asked as they climbed into the two Land Cruisers that would take them there.

"The best charter pilot in East Africa," Merv Chambers declared. "He'll fly anytime, land anywhere, and carry anything."

On the way to the airfield, as they passed through the center of town, they saw a large truck stopped in the street.

"Death truck," Merv muttered when he saw it.

Two men were picking up an old man's body by the arms and legs. As the Land Cruiser passed, the men tossed the body onto the pile of other emaciated corpses in the truck. It looked exactly like a scene from a Nazi death camp.

A few minutes later, Ed studied the town as Mad Tom's aircraft climbed out past Baidoa's mostly roofless buildings and littered streets. All around the edges of the regional capital were clustered acres of tiny, plastic roofed huts, crowded together without order; the squalid, stinking refugee camps with deceptive names like Granada, Finland, Bay One and Bay Two. And nearby to each, fields dotted with earthen mounds that were the graves of those for whom arrival at the camps had come too late.

The camps of Baidoa should be named *Hades* and *Purgatory* and *Misery* and *Despair*, he thought. *The City of Death* - that's what the news media had taken to calling the place. For once, they had it right.

He closed his eyes and thought of the incredible things he had witnessed the previous couple of days - so incredible, in fact, that after he dozed off for a few minutes, he awoke wondering if he had only dreamed them. Then he opened his eyes and looked at Katherine, seated facing him, and knew that, yes, they were true.

Merv Chambers was looking at him. When he caught Ed's eye, he asked, "So, who's going to win the election, Yank? It's tomorrow, isn't it?"

Ed glanced at the little window of his watch that gave the day of the week and month. It was indeed the day before the election that would decide whether President Bush was to serve for a second term, or Governor Clinton would unseat him.

"Bush," the American officer said. "Unless Perot gets so many votes that it goes to the House of Representatives. But I doubt that will happen."

"The BBC claims Clinton's ahead in the polls," Cheryl said, sitting up in her seat to join the conversation.

Ed Walker sneered. "Polls..." he scoffed.

Katherine opened her eyes and looked at him, but said nothing.

Ed turned his head and looked at the barren landscape four miles below. The election was one thing he had failed to consider in trying to estimate the probability that the US government would intervene in Somalia. It could only serve to complicate the issue. If Bush were indeed defeated, he might well decide, as a "lame duck" president, that he might have to leave the decision up to Clinton. Then, it would have to wait until the inauguration in late January; almost three months.

If more than two-thirds of the children were already dead, as Katherine claimed, then by January, there would be hardly any left.

His face was dark with gloom when he looked at Katherine Norris and asked, "Will there be any children left by the end of January, Katherine?"

She gave him a curious look and thought about his question for a time, then said, "Yes, unless things get worse. Most of the ones who've made it this far will survive. We're inoculating them for measles as soon as they're strong enough, and if their digestive tracts aren't already ruined, they're getting enough Unimix and biscuits through the airlift to survive."

"Unimix; that's the enriched stuff they serve kids at the feeding centers?" Ed asked her.

"Yes. 'Porridge,' we tell them. That, and the high protein biscuits we try to dole out to them all day long do wonders. It will keep them alive unless some other disease ravages the camps."

"Such as?" Ed wondered aloud.

"Such as bubonic plague," Katherine said with a visible shudder. "Or a new stain of malaria when the rains come, to name a couple of possibilities."

Ed Walker nodded, praying silently that no new disease would sweep the wretched camps and destroy more of the helpless Somali children.

A CARE representative met the Australians at Nairobi's Wilson airport, from which most of the charter outfits operated, and while they were filling out their customs forms, Merv asked Ed, "Where will you be staying, mate?"

"Don't know," Ed said. He was counting on the Defense Attache's office at the American embassy to make those arrangements once he contacted them.

"Well, we'll be at the Fairview. The rates are cheap, the beer's cold, and the grub's not bad. Stop by, and I'll buy you a pint."

"Thanks, Merv. Maybe I'll see you there, then."

The others passed through immigration without incident, but as Ed had departed on a military flight and had no exit visa to show that he'd departed from Kenya three days before, the official stopped him for questioning.

Katherine noticed, and came back to where he stood waiting. She held out her hand and said, "Come by the Fairview if you can. If not, well, maybe you'll make it to Baidoa again sometime."

He shook her hand and smiled. "I'll try. And thanks for everything, Kathy; for showing me around Bay One and explaining about dried up villi and all that. And showing me the Southern Cross and Big Dipper at the same time."

She smiled and nodded, then leaned forward, pecked him on the cheek, and walked away.

He watched her go, then remembered one other thing she'd told him. "Kathy!" he called after her. She stopped and turned around.

"If I don't see you, have a happy birthday," he said.

The pretty nurse smiled warmly said, "'The wish is the father of the deed.'" And then she waved and walked away.

General Harry Madison listened in silence as Colonel Ed Walker read to him the notes he had prepared before calling on the embassy telephone in Kenya.

It was an impassioned plea - perhaps a bit too impassioned - but what he said made sense to the old general, at least as a rough plan for how the situation could be handled if the decision was made to intervene. The troop mix made sense, too; Special Forces, civil affairs, and field medical teams, backed up by helicopter support and a brigade of infantry from the 101st Airborne.

But in spite of the fact that there were as many as a thousand Somalis dying of starvation every day, nothing was going to happen as quickly as Ed was recommending.

President Bush was going to lose the election the next day; Madison had no doubt of that now. And that meant weeks of inaction on such matters.

It wasn't going to happen, Harry Madison also knew, based on the recommendation of an Army colonel who had only been there for a few days, no matter how right that recommendation might be.

Ed finished his plea and said, "So, there it is, General Madison. What do you think?"

"That's an awful lot to have learned from visiting one town for a couple of days, Ed," he replied candidly.

Ed was silent for several long seconds, then said, "I didn't learn all of it in a couple of days, sir. Some of it I learned a long time ago on Special Forces A teams. And at other times and places during the last twenty-five years."

Touche', Harry Madison thought, and smiled.

"Anyway, like I said, sir; we're talking about a thousand people a day. We're late already."

"Yes," Madison replied. "Well, it's a start, Ed. A damn good one. Clean up your notes, get them into hard copy, and fax them to me right away." He started to add, *and take some of the emotion out of them,* then changed his mind. He would do that himself, once he got them. "What do you intend to do next, Ed?"

"I thought I'd head for Mombasa in the morning and coordinate with the airlift task force there, then catch a ride with the next food shipment back into Somalia. Go to Mogadishu, Hoddur, Bardera; wherever they're flying. Spend a few days at each place learning what I can, then update my recommendations to you."

"All right. But don't give anybody the impression that we're seriously considering any intervention beyond the airlift that's already there."

"I don't understand, sir," Ed said, a tone of bewilderment in his voice. "If we're not seriously considering doing something, what the hell am I *doing* here?"

Ed immediately regretted saying it.

"What I mean," General Madison said with a hint of irritation in his voice, "is that the administration isn't seriously considering anything - not with the elections tomorrow. Maybe it'll change after that. Meanwhile, we'll be doing some contingency planning, of course. Central Command will, at least, since it's their area of operations."

"I see," Ed said.

Neither man spoke for several seconds, then Ed said, "General, just between you and me, what do you think the chances are of us coming in here and doing something like I've outlined? And if we were to, when would it happen?"

"The chances? Not better than fifty-fifty, Ed. A lot of it depends on what happens tomorrow at the polls."

"I see... But if we should, how soon, at the earliest?"

Madison already had a general idea of the answer to that question. "I'd guess about two months, at the earliest."

"Two months," Ed Walker repeated. "That's sixty-thousand lives, sir... More than all the names on that black granite wall across the river from you. Remind them of that, will you, General? And that a lot of them will be children."

"That's fair enough. I will."

"And one other thing, sir," he said, the images of Bay One refugee camp and Katherine Norris running through his mind. "I hope this isn't out of place, but... well, if Sue were one of those nurses out there, sir - and she might well be, if she were still alive - you wouldn't accept somebody telling you there was only a fifty-fifty chance that we were going to do something to help her."

The mention of his dead daughter's name and the shock of his subordinate speaking to him like that took Harry Madison aback for a moment. Then he reached out and picked up the picture of Sue that was always near him, and studied it. The anger he felt at Ed's remark softened to understanding, because he knew it was true.

"General," Ed was saying, "that was out of line. I'm sorry."

"No," Harry Madison replied softly. "You're right. I *wouldn't* accept it. I'll see what I can do, Ed."

"That's all that matters then, sir," Ed Walker replied. "Goodbye, General."

THIRTY ONE

When Governor Clinton of Arkansas was elected to the office of President of the United States, Colonel Edward Walker of the United States Army was in the town of Bardera beside the Juba River in southern Somalia.

He had spent the day before - election day - flying first to the port city of Mombasa. Once there, he briefed the officers and senior NCOs of the Special Forces company supporting the airlift task force that was based there, repeating the recommendations he had made to General Madison the night before. The Special Forces men agreed that the plan was reasonable, and Major Carroll, the company commander, promised to study it in detail with his subordinates and see if they could come up with recommendations to improve it.

When they came out of the meeting, some of Carroll's men were waiting outside the little conference room. They sensed that something was afoot; that there was a mission coming that was more important than the one they currently had of flying around all day, waiting to react in case one of the cargo planes went down.

Ed Walker looked at them and knew he was right. *These* were the men who could get it done in Somalia. His eyes caught those of one of the younger soldiers, and for a moment the two of them stared at each other. There was something familiar about the boy, but Ed couldn't put his finger on it. He looked like someone, but who? And then the aging colonel thought, He looks like *all* of them. Like Mike Robbins and Sam Hagen and Jose Guitteriz and a million others. Young. Vulnerable. Determined. He nooded at the young sergeant, then left to catch an Air Force cargo plane headed to Bardera with a load of Unimix and wheat.

Ed heard the results of the election on the world service of the BBC the next day while he and the members of the CARE team in Bardera were having lunch. It was the same meager fare that had been served for lunch in Baidoa - salad sandwiches. But it made no difference to Ed Walker what the lunch consisted of, because when he heard the news, he lost his appetite.

He listened, and shook his head and thought, How could this be? How is it possible that a man as devoid of courage and character as Bill Clinton could be elected to the office of President of the United States? Dear God, had it really been so long since this man was at Oxford University organizing anti-war protests, while Sam and Mike and Joe and all those thousands of others cursed and sweated and bled and died, that it didn't *matter* anymore? Or was it simply that it hadn't really mattered then, either?

Was it that the American people felt it didn't matter *what* you did when you were young? No, that *couldn't* be. Because it had mattered what Sam did when *he* was young, and what Mike did. It mattered what Buker and Sisler and Zabitoski and all the other young Americans who won the Medal of Honor did in those years, while this man languished at Oxford, shirking his duty. You're damned *right* it mattered what you did when you were young, Ed Walker reasoned. Especially if you died. Then it was *all* that mattered.

He lightly touched the scars on his face, half expecting that they might not really be there. But they were.

"So, what does his election mean, mate?" John Brien, the Australian engineer on CARE's Bardera team, asked.

Ed looked at Brien and shook his head. "I don't know," he said. "Other than that it's been a long time since Vietnam, I guess."

"Change," said Jenny Davies, the sole CARE nurse in Bardera, "that's what it's all about. The people want change."

"Speaking of change," Ed said glumly, "let's change the subject. Now, what about these mines you mentioned, Bob?"

Ashton walked to the map taped to the wall of the house the CARE team in Bardera occupied. He traced his finger along the roads leading south beside the Juba River, and east toward Dinsoor, and said, "They're here on the roads to the south and east. When Hershel Morgan - the local warlord - and his boys overran the place a few weeks ago, they apparently laid them to keep Aidid's forces from counterattacking and taking Bardera back."

"Do you know what type they are?" Ed asked. "Anti-tank, anti-personnel, or what?"

"Both."

Mines. Ed hated mines, and it wasn't just because he viewed them as soulless substitutes for soldiers - indiscriminate murderers whose employers took no risk upon themselves, but left them hidden to kill or maim whoever happened to stumble upon them, whether it was the enemy or unwary friends or even innocent civilians. They were all over the world now, killing and maiming innocent people years after most of the conflicts that led to their employment had ended.

"Are they metal or plastic?" Ed asked. If they were metal, it would be much easier to detect them with mine sweeping equipment when the time came.

"I don't know," Ashton replied. "But whatever they are, they're effective. We've lost two trucks and three Somali staff members trying to supply the villages south of here."

"And God knows how many refugees who were only trying to get here to keep from starving to death." Jenny added.

"Morgan's people must know where the mines are," Ed said, thinking aloud. "Would they agree to guide you through them, so you could feed the people down there?"

Ashton shook his head. "Wrong clan," he said. "He couldn't give a damn if the whole lot of them starved to death."

"What about airdrops?" Ed asked. "You given any thought to parachuting the stuff in?"

"We have," Brien said, "but your Air Force refuses to fly airdrops unless they have their own guys on the ground ahead of time to mark the dropping zones. And since they're not allowed to put people on the ground in Somalia, they can't drop."

"Afraid they'll hit some poor starving bastard on the head with the bundle," Ashton said with undisguised sarcasm. "So instead, they follow regulations and let a hundred starve to bloody death."

Ed hoped the Australians were misinformed, but it was probably true. That was just the sort of Catch 22 that peacetime staff officers and bureaucrats were famous for. He made a mental note to speak to someone on the joint task force about it at the first opportunity. "How many people are you losing here each day?" he asked.

"In Bardera? Ask Jenny," Ashton said.

Ed turned to the nurse. She looked tired and pale, and said wearily, "About sixty, on average. But it's not starvation that's killing them now. It's disease. This place is so bloody crowded and full of so many diseases that I wouldn't believe it if I hadn't seen it. And if we can't get food to the outlying villages, it'll just get worse. More and more refugees coming in every day."

Ed scratched his chin and studied the map. Even more than Baidoa, this region was suited to operations by Special Forces teams. There were hamlets all along the Juba which a split A team - six men - would be ideal to assist. They could bring in airdrops of food and medicines, operate dispensaries, help them purify their water supply - even arm and train them to protect themselves and their villages, if necessary.

He spent the rest of the day with John and Jenny at the growing refugee camp the Bardera NGO's had established outside of the town. Its squalor was comparable to that of Baidoa's Bay One, some ninety miles to the east.

There were some major differences in the people who inhabited it, though. The level of starvation had not reached that experienced by the wretched skeletons of Baidoa's refugee camps; these people at least still had a bit of meat on their bones.

But Ed quickly learned that the same abundant supply of water that provided enough plant and animal life to sustain the Juba River Valley inhabitants also carried every imaginable sort of disease. And these were killing people at a rate nearly as bad, per capita, as starvation was killing their countrymen in the areas away from the river.

It soon became evident that the disease was taking its toll on the relief workers, as well. That evening, Jenny Davies, after struggling with chills and fever all day, collapsed on the floor just as she, Bob Ashton, and their American guest were sitting down for supper. John Brien was already in bed, badly dehydrated by dysentery.

She was burning up with fever, and Bob Ashton called on the radio for a doctor from the small *Medicines Sans Frontieres* team in Bardera to come. A French physician arrived five minutes later. After he had examined her, he looked at the others and shook his head. "Very high fever," he said with a worried look. "We must get the temperature down and get her to Nairobi as soon as possible. It may be cerebral malaria."

He ordered Ed to get some wet towels as he stripped the unconscious nurse, then began to bathe her with the towels that Ed got. Bob Ashton radioed CARE Nairobi to inform them of Jenny's condition and order a charter flight to come in at first light in the morning. It couldn't come before then, because the poorly-maintained dirt air strip at Bardera had no lights.

"I will go get some medicines and ice," the physician said. "Keep her wet, and fan her."

She was curled up in a fetal position, shaking visibly from the fever that ravaged her, her skin hot to the touch as Ed bathed her.

The French physician came back after awhile, and the nurse with him took over the job of bathing Jenny with crushed ice wrapped in wet towels.

Some time later, the doctor examined her again, then stood back, shaking his head. "She may not live until tomorrow," he said sadly.

Ed looked at her, wondering how it was that these people could be left out here like this. How could civilized Western governments allow their relief workers to be left in hell holes like Bardera without protecting them, without ensuring that, at times like this, there was a means to evacuate them to safety, and modern medical care? This woman might well die as a result of their neglect. Yes, there was death all around her, and scores of others would die in this town tonight. But *they* had no government to blame. And it made no difference that Jenny Davies was Australian; it could just as easily be one of the American girls from the International Medical Corps.

He remembered what he had said to Harry Madison the night before; "You wouldn't accept it, if it were Sue...."

He went to the radio and asked the CARE radio operator in Nairobi to telephone the American joint task force in Mombasa.

"Tell them to have the duty officer contact Colonel Walker at CARE Bardera on this frequency. Tell them it's urgent."

Five minutes later, an American's voice came across the radio: "CARE Bardera, this is Provide Relief Mombasa, over."

Ed answered him and explained doctor's prognosis of Jenny's condition. "Can you evacuate her? It's urgent."

"I understand your request," the man said, "but we're prohibited from flying into Somalia at night. We'll be prepared to evacuate the patient on the first flight in there tomorrow."

"She may not make it until then," Ed said. "We need to get her evacuated immediately."

The other man said, "I'm sorry, Colonel. Those are the rules. Anyway, it's hard enough getting a C-130 down on that strip in broad daylight, much less at night. You don't even have portable airfield lights there, do you?"

Ed looked at Bob Ashton, who shook his head and said, "We had them when we first got here, but they were looted."

Ed thought a moment, then said into the microphone, "If you can get a bird in here, Mombasa, we'll have the field lighted by the time you get here. We can use fire pots."

"We can't do it, Colonel," the man replied. "Even if the rules allowed us to, we couldn't risk a whole crew for one medical patient."

"Bullshit!" Ed shot back. "Who *is* this, anyway?"

"The task force chief of staff," the man said.

The chief of staff was an Air Force colonel, Ed recalled. "Colonel," he implored, "I'm telling you that this woman is probably going to die if we don't get her out of here."

"I understand that," the man said, "and I wish we could help. But we can't do it. We'll have a medic on the flight there tomorrow to do what he can while we fly her back here. But that's the best we can do."

"God damn it, that's not good enough!" Ed shot back.

"I understand your frustration, Colonel," the other American replied. "But I couldn't do it even if she were a member of my family."

Then you're a sorry son of a bitch, Ed thought. But he was not going to get the US Air Force to evacuate her tonight. He would raise hell the next time he got out of Somalia, but that wouldn't help Jenny Davies.

Ed gave Bob the handset back and went into Jenny's room.

The Frenchman had just taken her temperature, and he frowned as he looked at the thermometer. "Still too high," he said.

Ed looked at the naked woman, wondering if she would survive the night, and even if she did, what the brain damage resulting from the exceptionally high fever might be.

So much death, he thought. All around him, starvation and disease and death. And there was so little he could do about it. He thought about the millions of people sitting in the security and comfort of their spacious homes, snacking on sweets and watching football on television and comfortable with the feeling that they had done their part in the war on hunger by donating a few dollars to the United Way.

And then there were people like these; the Jenny Davieses and Lowell Morrisons and Katherine Norrises - the ones who were the soldiers in that war. Soldiers deserved better than to be abandoned on the battlefield when they fell. You didn't just use them up and throw them aside.

"Call Nairobi again, Bob," he said. "Ask them to call the Fairview Hotel and get Merv Chambers or Katherine Norris on the phone. Tell him to let them know about Jenny, and have them try to track Mad Tom down. If we can find him, maybe he'll fly."

Ashton's eyebrows raised. "Mad Tom. You might just be right!" He turned to the radio and called Nairobi.

Ed looked at his watch. It was twenty past eight. If they could get to Tom in, say, half an hour, and he took off an hour after that, then he should be landing in Bardera before midnight. By two AM, Jenny could be in the hospital in Nairobi.

Bob Ashton sent one of the Somali guards off in search of one of the warlord Hershel Morgan's officers. An English speaking militiaman arrived at the CARE house a short time later and introduced himself as Captain Abubakr, then said, "What is it you want?"

Bob explained, and Abubakr listened, then asked, "Why should we do this?"

"Because she will die if you don't. And if she dies, we'll pull out of here. And that will mean no more food or medicine, no more hiring of technicals, no more payment of landing fees."

Abubakr considered Ashton's threat, then nodded and said, "Very well. We will take you there when you are ready."

Ed got busy making fire pots - cans filled with a mixture of diesel oil and sand, which he would use to light the runway. As he had agreed to do, Abubakr took Ed, Bob, Jenny, and the French physician to the airfield as soon as they were ready. Bob and Ed laid out the fire pots, and when John Brien called Bob on the hand-held radio to report that Mad Tom was ten minutes from landing, they ran along the length of the runway lighting the fire pots.

Mad Tom made one low pass over the lights, then landed and taxied to the end of the runway where Ed stood flashing his light on and off.

The door of the airplane opened, and Katherine Norris climbed down the built-in stairs.

"Hello, Yank," she said. "Where's the patient?"

*   *   *

Katherine stayed in Bardera after her gravely ill counterpart, Jenny Davies, was evacuated with cerebral malaria. She stayed for ten days, waiting for another CARE nurse, previously airlifted from the disease-ridden town with amoebic dysentery, to return to the Bardera team.

Colonel Ed Walker spent the days assessing the military capabilities of the warlord who called himself Hershel Morgan, whose Somali National Front troops had seized Bardera from Aidid's United Somali Congress militia a month earlier. Ed also gathered what information he could on the mined roads to the south and east of the town, and on the desperate plight of the settlements that could not be reached by the relief effort because of those mines.

He attempted to get the American aircraft stationed in Mombasa to make emergency drops to those outlying hamlets, but failed; the US Air Force was prohibited from making such drops without American ground controllers on the intended drop zones, and those controllers, although eager to do so, were denied permission to go into Somalia. Ed offered to go to the villages himself - on foot, if necessary - to set up the drop zones. But in spite of the fact that he had organized scores of paradrops during his career, he was not considered qualified to do so under the peacetime regulations by which the airlift task force was required to abide.

Ed sent a letter by one of the aircrews to the US defense attache in Nairobi to be faxed to General Madison in the Pentagon and the airlift task force commander in Mombasa. It was full of frustration and anger about the lack of badly-needed airdrops and the bureaucratic regulations that prohibited them. But it got no results, except one of which Ed Walker was not made aware. It was a heated request from the task force commander to his headquarters, US Central Command. It asked to have Colonel Walker stop meddling in the task force's business or be withdrawn from the country. "Fails to see the big picture," was one of the phrases used by the task force commander to describe Ed Walker in the message. "Politically naive," was another.

Only the close personal relationship between Harry Madison and the commander-in-chief at Central Command enabled Madison to keep Ed Walker in Somalia.

"He reminds me of you, old buddy, when you were a battalion commander in Vietnam," Madison told the other general when he called. "He's going to do and say what he thinks is right, and to hell with those tired old generals sitting on their dead asses in a headquarters somewhere."

The other general laughed, and Madison added, "Besides, we both know he's telling the truth. And he's sending us some good information that we just might need soon."

"Well, all right, Harry. But I still don't see how you got him in there in the first place without going through me."

"I didn't go through anybody," Madison admitted. "I just sent him. You're not the only one to ever do what he thought was right, even though some tired old general might disagree."

The nights at the CARE team in Bardera were quiet ones. John Brien's medical condition had improved, but he was still weak, and spent most of the evening hours in bed. Bob Ashton's evenings were usually spent at the other non-government organizations in Bardera, coordinating the relief effort with other NGO team leaders. Ed and Katherine sat together in the CARE house most evenings, monitoring the radio and talking, or sitting silently, each with his own thoughts, as they listened to Katherine's music.

The more they learned about each other from the talks they had, sometimes lasting until late in the night, the more the attraction between them grew. But as strongly as Ed Walker found himself drawn to the remarkable young nurse, he tried to avoid showing it. She was too young, for one thing. And he was there to assess the need for military intervention in the humanitarian relief effort, not to become involved in romance. Anyway, Katherine had made it plain that this was her life - serving as a nurse to desperate and innocent people in war- and famine-ravaged corners of the earth. His life, once his duty in Somalia was done, was going to be on the waters of Virginia.

The last night they were in Bardera together, as Ed sat preparing a report of what he had learned during his ten day stay there, Katherine said, "Ed, do you know this song?

He listened a moment and said, "Sure. The Eagles. *Desperado*."

He seldom listened to music. Most popular music was nothing but a raucous jumble of electronic noise and meaningless screaming, as far as he was concerned. But he liked the Eagles' music all right, because you could understand the words.

"It reminds me a lot of you," Katherine said.

Ed put down his notes and listened to the song, watching Katherine's face as he did so. He could tell from her expressions what parts of the song she felt applied to him.

Desperado, oh you ain't gettin' no younger,
Your pain and your hunger are drivin' you home.
And freedom? oh, freedom,
That's just some people talkin';
Your prison is walkin' through this world all alone...

Katherine sang along with the last verse of the song, looking him in the eyes as she did so.

Desperado, why don't you come to your senses?
Come down from your fences - open the gate.
It may be rainin', but there's a rainbow above you.
You better let somebody love you; let somebody love you;
You better let somebody love you, before it's too late.

She turned off the tape player, and for a long time they sat apart looking at each other, until he said, "Kathy, I'm old enough to be your father, for heaven's sake."

She said nothing, and her expression remained unchanged as she continued to study the battle-scarred face with its sad, green eyes, until he got up and went to her. She rose from the chair, and he took her into his arms and kissed her.

She felt smaller in his arms than he thought she would. And softer, too, as she leaned into him. Then she broke off the kiss and rested her head against his shoulder.

"We'll both be in Mombasa tomorrow night," she said softly.

"Yes. We will."

They were both going there on the relief flight scheduled to land in Bardera the next afternoon. From there, Katherine would be returning to the Baidoa team in a couple of days. Ed would speak to General Madison from the airlift task force headquarters, fax him his written report, then fly to Mogadishu to assess the situation there for a time. After that, he would fly to Hoddur and Belet Huen for a few days each, then back to Nairobi and on to the States. There was no plan for him to be in Baidoa again.

"Will you stay with me tomorrow night, Ed?"

He knew that she was aware of his plans; that it was unlikely that they would ever see each other again after they left Mombasa. So it would only be - what? A night of recreational sex? An intimate goodbye between two people who had become good friends, but for whom there was no hope of a real relationship? He wanted to say, "Yes." She was soft and young and beautiful, and he had not been intimate with a woman in so long. So why not?

Because somehow it just didn't seem right. Maybe it was the fact that he didn't want the relationship to change, or maybe he was afraid that he'd lose sight of why he was in Somalia. Or that he didn't want to complicate things, or even that he was just getting too old. But whatever the reasons, he felt that it was a bad idea.

"No, Katherine," he said. "It... It just wouldn't work."

She pushed away from him, but gently, and searched his eyes. "Come down off your fence, desperado," she said.

He drew her against him again and stroked the hair on the back of her head. "I'm no desperado, Kathy. I'm just an old fashioned soldier. You're the best friend I have out here, Kathy. Probably the best friend I have anywhere, for that matter. I don't want to ruin that."

She pushed away from him again and looked at him with a look he didn't understan. She was about to say something when Bob Ashton walked in from the NGO team chiefs' meeting.

"Bloody hell," Ashton said, hardly looking at the couple as he went to the refrigerator for one of the team's last bottles of Tusker beer. "Looks like we're in for some rain."

Katherine looked at Ed a moment longer, then turned to Bob and said, "Rain? That means no flight tomorrow, then."

"I reckon not," Ashton said. "The Hercs won't be able to land until the runway dries out, and that usually takes two or three days."

Ed turned his attention from Kathy to the team leader. "Two or three days?" he said.

"Yep. The courier might be able to land in a day or so. But the 130's are too heavy for this dirt strip. They'd get bogged down."

"But suppose somebody needed to be evacuated, the way Jenny did?" Ed asked.

Katherine answered the question. "They wouldn't get out," she said without looking at him. "Maybe that's why you have to do what you can *when* you can, around here. Before it's too late."

Ed lay in bed listening to the rain pound the tin roof of the house that the CARE team in Bardera called home. At least it was cooler when it rained. But he thought of the refugees huddled inside their pitiful huts and wondered how many of them would die that night. Katherine had expressed concern for them before she went to bed.

Katherine. Why had he refused her suggestion that they spend the night together in Mombasa? It wasn't really the differences in their ages, or that it might cause him to lose sight of why he was here. It wasn't really even that he was afraid he might lose her friendship if they became lovers.

A line from the song that she had played for him ran through his mind: *Freedom; that's just some people talkin', your prison is walkin' through this world all alone...*

That was what he feared for; his freedom. If he became involved with Kathy, it would mean a loss of freedom.

He was comfortable, now, with being alone. He was no longer responsible for anyone except himself; Jimmy was grown, Mary was remarried. And Sue was dead. And there were no longer soldiers for whom he was responsible, either. After this assignment, he would be completely free to do as he wished.

Yes, that was it. He was free, and he didn't need a long distance relationship with Katherine Norris or anyone else to rob him of that freedom.

THIRTY TWO

It was raining again when Bob Ashton woke Ed Walker early the next morning.

"I need your help, mate," he said. "Rene just called. Kathy's been trapped between here and the refugee camp by a flash flood. I reckon we'll have to get a rope across and haul her back, or something."

When they got there ten minutes later, they found that the stream near the refugee camp, which the day before had been but a trickle, was now a raging torrent twenty meters wide, and probably two meters deep. Rene, the MSF doctor who had treated Jenny Davies, was standing on the near side with one of his nurses, Michelle. Katherine Norris and several Somali staff workers stood helplessly on the other side. She waved feebly to Bob and Ed.

"Hang on, love! We'll get a rope over to you!" Ashton yelled, and she nodded in acknowledgment.

"I think I'd better swim a rope over to them," Ed Walker said, but Bob said, "Nah, no need for that. They can tie it off to that tree over there, and pull themselves across."

"Well, let's get it across to them, and let 'em tie it off. I'll test it out by going over to give them a hand crossing back, then," Ed said.

They secured one end of the half-inch-thick rope to a tree, tied a weight to the other end, and tossed the weighted end over to Kathy. She looped it around a tree on her side, and tied it off.

Ed sat down to take his hiking boots off, but as he got the first one off and looked across, Kathy was holding the rope and moving out into the water. He stood and yelled, "Wait, Kathy! Let me come across and give you a hand first!"

"I'll be all right!" she called back, pulling herself hand over hand out into the torrent.

"No!" Ed yelled, pulling off his other boot. "Wait! I'll be right there!" But she ignored him, and pulled herself further out into the swift, muddy water, her feet now washed out from beneath her.

Ed grasped the rope on his side, and began pulling himself out into the water to meet her.

The force of the water was unbelievable, and as he hauled himself across, he knew there was no way Kathy would be able to make it across without his help. She realized the same thing, and started back toward the bank, the raging water dragging hard on the material of the long cotton dress she was wearing.

The powerful water rushing around her dragged her head under momentarily, and she surfaced gasping for air.

"Hang on, Kathy!" Ed yelled. He was nearly to her now. But her grip weakened, and again her head went under. The raging water was too strong. She let go, and immediately disappeared.

"Ah, Jesus!" Ed said, turning loose of the rope and searching desperately for sight of her in the rampaging water as they were washed quickly downstream toward the Juba River. The power of the water sucked him under as it passed beyond some submerged obstacle, then washed him to the surface again. Fighting to keep his head up, he spotted her downstream from him. He stroked through the filthy water as hard as he could.

He reached her as the water made a bend, then seemed to slow somewhat. He grasped her wrist, and said, "It's all right, Kathy. We'll be all right, now."

The water to their right seemed calmer, and he said, "Swim for the shore! Swim hard, Kathy!"

She tried, but she was exhausted, the muddy torrent dragging her and her heavy dress down. She couldn't swim in it, so she tore it off over her head. Ed grasped her wrist again, reaching for the bottom with his feet. At last they touched, and he pulled her with him through the calmer water until they reached the shore.

They grabbed the bushes along the bank and held on, gasping and coughing and trying to catch their breath.

"We made it," Ed panted. "I wasn't sure we would, for a minute there." He pulled himself the rest of the way out of the water, then helped her to climb up beside him. She was wearing only panties now, so he took his muddy T shirt off and pulled it over her head. Then he drew her against him and hugged her. She raised her head to him, and he kissed her.

"You saved my life," she said. He tried to deny it, but her mouth covered his again, and this time their kiss was one of passion.

"It's not exactly Mombasa, is it?" he said.

"Not by a long shot," she said, snuggling her exhausted body against him. Then she laughed softly and said, "I didn't intend for you to see me naked unless you met me there."

They had no idea how far they had been washed down the swollen river, but a minute later they heard Bob Ashton and the others calling desperately to them.

They stood, and Ed yelled, "Over here! We're OK!"

Michelle had her camera, and she took a photograph of Ed and Kathy beside the raging water. They were covered with mud and scratches, but they were safe, and what had nearly been a tragedy became a matter for laughter once they all realized that. They posed, arms around each other, for another photo; Ed wearing only muddy camp shorts and Kathy in nothing but his wet, clinging T shirt.

They were soon headed back to the town, and as they turned off the muddy track from the crossing site onto the single road that ran through Bardera, they got behind an old flatbed truck carrying some Somali National Front militiamen. Stacked in the back of it was a pile of dark green metal discs. Ed Walker recognized them as anti-tank mines, but he was uncertain exactly what type they were.

"Do you have any more film in your camera, Michelle?" he asked. She said she did, and handed it to him, and he took several shots of the pile of mines. The military photo interpreters at Central Command would be able to tell what type they were from the film.

He asked if he could take the film and Michelle agreed, and he removed the film canister from the camera.

After they got back to the house and cleaned up, they learned from John Brien that CARE Nairobi had radioed to say a courier aircraft was going to try to land at the muddy airfield late that afternoon. It was bringing in the nurse who had previously left with amoebic dysentery, and a new nurse to replace Jenny Davies, whose medical condition had necessitated her evacuation back to Australia. Katherine was to leave on the courier for a brief stay in Nairobi before going back to Baidoa to resume her duties there.

"There's room on the plane for you, Ed, if you want to get out of here," Brien informed the American.

Ed nodded. "Yes," he said. "I need to get to Mombasa. I can catch a commercial flight down there from Nairobi."

*   *   *

At Wilson airport in Nairobi, after they had passed through customs, Katherine asked Ed, "Are you going to try to get a flight to Mombasa tonight?"

"I don't know," he said. "I'm going to the embassy first. I have to send a fax and make a phone call. It depends on what the results are."

"I see," she said. "Well, if you decide to stay in Nairobi, dinner's on me."

"You'll be at the Fairview Hotel?"

"Yes."

"Then I'll call you there later, and let you know my plans."

"All right," she said. She kissed him and climbed into the car that was waiting to take her to the CARE office in Nairobi.

He watched as it drove away, and stood there for a time thinking about her; about their conversation when she had asked him to stay with her in Mombasa, and their desperate plight as they were washed down the river, and the long talks they had shared those nights in Bardera.

They had told each other a great deal about themselves; his early days on the water, the Army, Mary and Jimmy, and Sue.

And Katherine had told him about her own brief marriage. Her husband had been an abusive drunk. She left him six months after they were married, and joined CARE. She had decided that relief work was her life's calling after a short time in Cambodia, and had never looked back. Since then, she had been to Niger, Uganda, back to Cambodia, to Pakistan, and most recently, to Iraq, assisting the Kurds in the marshes along the Euphrates.

"Have you ever been in love?" Ed had asked her one night.

"Yes," she said. "With a Norwegian soldier in Cambodia. But he already had a wife, as it turned out. Since then, I... well, I haven't always been chaste, but I haven't been in love."

He smiled now as he went to the taxi stand to catch a ride to the American Embassy.

General Madison was not there when Ed telephoned the Pentagon. He was at Central Command Headquarters in Tampa, his executive officer said. But he had left instructions for Ed to remain in Nairobi until Madison returned from Florida and contacted him through the defense attache's office at the embassy.

"When's he expected back?" Ed asked.

"Tonight, our time. So you can just hang out in Nairobi, as long as we can get in touch with you through the embassy there."

"All right," Ed said. "I'll go ahead and fax my report to you now, so it'll be there when he gets back."

He did so, then told the Air Force lieutenant colonel in the attache office, "I'm expecting a phone call from the Pentagon tomorrow morning, Washington time."

"That will be tomorrow afternoon our time, then," the other officer said. "Where can we get hold of you?"

"The Fairview Hotel," Ed said.

He called Katherine's room from the hotel desk.

"Where are you?" she asked.

"In the lobby," he said.

There was a moment of silence, and then she asked, "Will you be staying here?"

"That's up to you."

Again there was a brief silence, then she asked, "Coming down off your fence, desperado?"

"Yes," he said. "I guess I got washed off the fence during that wild ride down the river."

"OK," Katherine said. "I'll open the gate for you. Room 208."

When she opened the door, he stood looking at her for a time before he walked in. Her blonde, shoulder-length hair was brushed and shiny, and she had put on a touch of makeup. She was wearing a silk blouse and short, pleated skirt, and she looked beautiful.

He told her so, and she took his hand and said, "Thank you. I thought sure you'd come."

      *   *   *

"That's great news, General," Ed said to Harry Madison. Central Command was sending the J-3, their senior operations officer, to Kenya. His mission was to plan for a unilateral intervention by US forces to end the suffering in Somalia.

"It's highly classified, of course, Ed," Madison said over the embassy's secure telephone. "I'm sure you realize that."

"Of course, sir. I won't discuss it with a soul. What do you want me to do, sir?" he asked.

"When the J-3 arrives, you'll be working for him. The task force will remain as it is and continue the airlift mission, at least until after the intervention. But that's where the J-3 will hang his hat while he's in the area. He wants you to show him around Somalia."

"Glad to," Ed said. "Who is he, anyway?"

"Chuck Black, an Army major general. He says he knows you."

Ah, Jesus Christ, Ed said to himself. Of all people. "Yes, sir. He knows me. He was one of the tactical officers in my OCS class, and I've run across him a few times since then," he said, thinking of the massacre Black had covered up in Vietnam decades earlier.

"That's what he said," Madison replied. He didn't like Black, personally. And from the tone of Ed's voice, the colonel didn't seem to care much for the man, either. But at least it wouldn't be necessary to tell him to watch his back around the overly-ambitious, self-serving young general. Instead he just said, "You don't sound too pleased, Ed."

"Well, I've just never gotten along with him very well."

"I see," Madison said. "But it's only for a couple of weeks. So bite your tongue and do what you can to help him. And try to influence his decisions so he doesn't turn the damned operation into World War III."

Ed laughed. It sounded as if General Madison knew the man pretty well, too. The rapidly-rising Black no doubt saw the coming intervention as an opportunity to advance his stature in the military by involving as many forces as possible. As the J-3, he would be largely responsible for the operations they conducted.

"All right, sir. But why only a couple of weeks? I'd kind of like to stick around and see this thing through, at least until my retirement the first of the year."

"I have your orders right here, son," Madison replied. "Your retirement date is 1 January all right, but you have some terminal leave coming. You're supposed to report to the retirement branch at personnel on 23 November for out-processing."

"I had forgotten all about that, General," Ed said. He hadn't considered the fact he would be allowed to leave the Army earlier than his actual retirement date because of the leave time he had accrued.

Madison said, "Of course, you can always cash your leave in and stay till the first of the year, if that's what you really want to do."

"That's what I'll do, then, sir."

"All right. But I'm surprised to hear it. Your last fax made me think you'd had enough of Somalia."

"Things have changed, now that the troops are coming," Ed said. "And I, uh, I've met this nurse. She reminds me a lot of Sue."

Harry Madison smiled to himself, and looked at the photograph of his daughter on his desk. "The one you were referring to when you told me I wouldn't accept a fifty-fifty probability that we'd intervene, if my daughter were there?"

"No, sir. I was thinking of Sue then, not Katherine."

"Well, it doesn't matter which one you were referring to when you said it. It worked. So, I've done my part. Now it's up to you to help General Black plan and execute it."

"I'll do my best, General."

"I know you will. We'll send you his travel plans when we get them."

"All right, sir. And General, thank you for whatever you did to get this thing going. It needs to be done."

"Yes, but it needs to be done right. Well, you work for CENTCOM now, Ed, so you don't need to send anything else through here. Unless, of course, there's something that affects the Army I need to know about. But stay in touch, and come see me when you get back."

"I'll make it a point to, General Madison."

Ed hung up the telephone, then sat thinking about all the old general had done for the Army over the years, and for him, personally. If only there were more like him, and fewer like Major General Black....

He pushed himself away from the desk and went down to the embassy photo lab to pick up the photos he asked the technician there to print from the film that Michelle had given him. Then he hurried back to the Fairview, where Katherine was waiting.

He hurried to the door of the room and opened it with the key she had given him. He called to her, but she didn't answer. There was a note on the bed, addressed to him.

Dearest Ed,

    I've had to rush off to Baidoa. They had to get some money there to prevent the national staff from quitting, so the courier is going in today at 2 o'clock instead of tomorrow. Please come to Baidoa when you

*can. Otherwise, I'll let you know somehow when I'm
coming out again. Perhaps you can manage to be here or
in Mombasa then, as well.*

> *Last night was wonderful. I'll miss you
> terribly until I see you again.*
> > *With love,*
> > > *Katherine*

Ed sat down on the bed, his shoulders stooped in disappointment, and re-read the note. Then he looked at his watch. It was five after two. He flopped back on the bed and stared at the ceiling.

Katherine Norris looked back at the little passenger terminal of Wilson airport as Mad Tom taxied the King Air away. She was hoping that Ed would get the note in time to come to Wilson to say goodbye. But either he hadn't returned from the embassy in time, or he simply had not wanted to come. She closed her eyes, wondering which was the case.

He had been so gentle with her the night before. So loving. She had never known that before. The other men she had known - her husband, and Rolf in Cambodia, and the handful since then - had been sometimes rough, sometimes just hurried. But not Ed. His lovemaking seemed geared to her satisfaction without regard for his own. Unhurried. Unselfish.

She had told him that, too, because such was their relationship; they had been friends before they became lovers. "Good," was all he said when she mentioned the satisfaction his selfless lovemaking had given her. So she kissed him and got on top of him and said, "But now it's your turn, desperado. You are my master, and I am your slave."

"Then I free you," he said, and again they made love as if her satisfaction was all that mattered to him. But she had not stopped until he was satisfied, and when he came, she did too, and that made it the best she had ever known.

Later, when they were having a late dinner in the hotel restaurant, she asked him why he had been hesitant to stay with her when she first asked him to, and he was honest.

"I was afraid it would cost me my freedom," he said.

She remembered an earlier conversation they had shared about freedom on one of their first nights in Bardera together. It was a sentimental discourse about why he had become a soldier, and why he had remained one for so long. At the time, it had struck her as idealistic and naive. But he was sincere, and idealistic or not, he had put his life on the line for that ideal, time and again.

She looked at his scars, and into his sad, sincere eyes and said, "Freedom is important to you, isn't it, Ed?"

He thought in silence for a long time, slowly chewing his food as he contemplated her simple statement. Then he swallowed a sip of wine, and said, "Yes, Kathy, it is. But not just mine; mine had already been earned when I was born. By the men at Yorktown and Bull Run and the Somme and Normandy. And Gallipoli and New Guinea, too," he added in deference to Australia's soldiers.

His brow furrowed in thought, and he was silent for a time before he said, "You know what this trip has done? It's made me realize that America doesn't have a monopoly on making people free. It's stupid, but I hadn't realized that before. And it doesn't just take soldiers, does it? It takes people like you, and those kids at IMC, and Rene and Jenny."

She didn't say anything. There were still some thoughts running loose in his mind, she could tell. So she said nothing, and let them find their way into words.

"But sometimes, there's still a need for soldiers," he said. "And sometimes, they still need to fight. And this is one of those times. They need to come in here and fight Morgan and Aidid and Ali Mahdi, and the rest of those so-called warlords. Kill them, if that's what it takes. Because they're the bastards who have caused all of this. They're the ones who haven't just taken freedom from those kids at Bay One and Bardera and places like that. They've taken their lives. And all the food and medicine in the world won't stop them. But, by God, bullets will."

She poked at the food in her plate with her fork and considered his disturbing words. How could a man who was such a gentle lover, she wondered, espouse such acts of violence, such brutality?

Was it true? If, as he said, they went for the heads of the beasts - Aidid and Ali Mahdi and Morgan and the handful of others - would that be enough? Or would somebody else just take their places?

Maybe it was worth a try. After all, those were the men who claimed the leadership of the clan militias. But it never worked out like that, did it? It was always the crusaders who fell, not the kings who sent them.

She looked at him and shook her head. "It doesn't work that way, Ed. It never has."

He was about to take a drink, but he set his wine glass down and said, "What do you mean?"

"I mean that they didn't kill Hitler; he committed suicide. I mean Saddam is still alive, even though you killed a hundred thousand of his men. I mean that, in spite of all the Yanks and Diggers who fell in Vietnam, Ho Chi Minh died of old age. It just doesn't work that way, that's all."

His eyes took on a fiery look, but he didn't say anything, so she voiced the thought she'd had a moment before; "It's always the crusaders who fall, Ed. Not the kings who send them."

He looked at her without speaking, and filled her wine glass and his own. Then he raised his glass in a toast and said, "Here's to the crusaders, then. The Yanks and the Diggers. The Sam Hagens and the Mike Robbinses and the Billie Halls and all the rest of them."

He tilted the glass to his mouth and drank it all. Katherine watched him, then did the same. And then she took his hand and led him to her room, and again they shared each other's love.

THIRTY THREE

The following night, while Katherine Norris was back amid the squalor of Bay One refugee camp, Ed Walker was standing before Major General Black's desk at the joint task force headquarters in Mombasa.

Black finished scanning the four-page paper Ed had prepared for him on the need for military intervention to assist the relief effort in Somalia, and laid it aside.

Ed handed him two more pages and said, "And this is a recommended mission statement and the critical tasks that need to be accomplished, and my thoughts on what the forces should consist of to get it done."

Black took the pages, glanced at them, and smirked. "Special this, special that," he said. "Where are the *real* troops, Colonel Walker? This looks like a troop list of US Special Operations Command forces."

"A lot of them *would* come out of USSOCOM, sir. Because they're the one's best trained to do the job. But there's also an infantry brigade and some additional helicopter units from the 101st. And some engineer, transportation corps, and medical assets."

Black tossed the pages onto the other paper that Ed had spent most of the time preparing since Katherine departed unexpectedly for Baidoa. Then he leaned back in his chair, still smirking, and said, "Still think you're wearing that green beanie, eh, Walker?"

"No, sir," Ed replied. "I just think those forces are the ones best suited for the job, that's all."

"Well, Central Command has been given the mission to conduct this operation, Colonel. Not Special Operations Command, with a mish-mash of the so-called elite running all over the place, doing their own thing."

He pointed to the papers and said, "You made a note that you had photos of the mines around Bardera."

"Yes, sir," Ed said. He pulled an envelope of photographs from his pocket and sifted through them, looking for the ones of the mines in the SNF truck. He found them, set the others on Black's desk, and leaned forward to point to the mines in the pictures in his hand. "I'm not certain, but they look to me like Soviet TM series anti-tank mines."

Black ignored him, and reached for the rest of the photos.

"Those are just some photos taken by the girl who loaned me her camera," Ed said.

Black studied the photographs of the relief workers taken the day of the flash flood. He removed one from the pile and looked at it awhile longer. It was one of Ed and Katherine as they emerged from the river, wet and smiling, holding hands.

"So, this is how you've been spending your time in Africa, eh, Walker?" He held the photo toward Ed and pointed to Katherine, the wet shirt clinging to her so that she might as well have been nude. "Who's this, your expert adviser on military matters in Somalia?"

"She's a civilian nurse, General. We were just coming back across the river after a flash flood."

Black snorted, and said, "Right," then handed the photographs back to Ed. He put them back in the envelope and shoved it into his shirt pocket.

Black leaned forward across the desk and looked Ed in the eye. "They tell me you're retiring soon, Walker."

"Yes, sir. One January."

"I see. Well, once you do, you can resume playing around with those leftist do-gooders. All they've done so far is support the so-called warlords by handing over relief supplies intended for the starving. But until you retire, I want you to avoid them. A little slip of the tongue, and the next thing you know, they'll be telling Aidid and the others our plans. Am I making myself clear?"

He was making himself clear, all right. Ed leaned forward and stared him in the eye. "General Black, I'm a colonel in the United States Army, and I know full well what my responsibilities are with regard to classified information. I'm not about to jeopardize the lives of the soldiers who'll be coming out here by divulging operational plans."

He was agitated now, and when Black did not respond immediately, Ed continued: "I've given up a month-and-a-half of terminal leave, God damn it, so I could try to help get this thing done. But it's not too late to change my mind, so if you don't feel I can do that, then by God, I'll go ahead and retire. And what I do after *that*, with all due respect, General, is my own damned business, and nobody else's."

He sat back, then, peering at the other man through narrowed eyes, waiting for a response.

Black continued to glare at him, weighing what that response should be.

Walker was General Madison's darling, Black knew. The old general was the one who had sent him out here, after all. If the rumors were true, and Madison was to be given a fourth star and perhaps made the Army Chief of Staff when the new administration swept away the general officers from the Reagan and Bush era, then he was someone Chuck Black wanted to stay on the good side of. Anyway, judging from Walker's reports that the Pentagon had forwarded to Central Command, the man's assessments of the military situation in Somalia could be very helpful. They didn't give the big picture - the international political aspects of a unilateral US intervention. But they were good for tactical planning. And if he sent Walker into those wretched, filthy places, where you never knew if some khat-crazed gunman might blow you away, then Chuck Black could do his planning without having to risk his life by going to see for himself.

So he sat back in his chair and gave Ed Walker a toothy smile. "You don't need to get hysterical with me, Colonel," he said. "You've been assigned to help me, so I'll play with the hand I've been dealt."

Ed started to respond by telling the general to shove the hand he'd been dealt up his arrogant ass, but Harry Madison's earlier advice came to him: *"Bite your tongue and do what you can to help,"* the old man had advised. So Ed said, "Just tell me what you want me to do, General, and let me get on with it."

Ed left Black's office in the airlift task force headquarters at Mombasa airport in a happy mood. The major general who had once been his peer reluctantly paid him a compliment about the reports he had been sending out of Somalia. And instead of giving Ed some menial task to perform at the headquarters or having him carry his briefcase around Somalia as Ed had feared he might, Black had given him the best instructions he could have hoped for. He was to spend his time in southern Somalia on his own, assessing the military situation at the places he had not yet visited, and occasionally reassessing the situation in the places he had already been. That meant he could go back to Baidoa now and then. And going to Baidoa meant seeing Katherine Norris.

He caught the first relief flight out of Mombasa the next morning, and spent two days in Belet Huen with the UNICEF team there. From there, he went to Mogadishu, where he stayed for almost a week. The situation in the ruined capital city was so chaotic as to make the other locations he had visited seem almost peaceful, and it was all he could do in six days to make a realistic appraisal of the situation there.

He learned from the CARE office in Mogadishu that the team in Baidoa had been issued a satellite telephone since he was last there, and he got permission to make a brief call to Katherine. She was well, and they made plans to meet in Kenya the next time she was due for a break, just before Christmas.

Next he went back to Mombasa, and passed his reports to Major General Black, before flying on a UN courier to the ports of Merca and Kismayu. The only ride he could get out of Kismayu was going to

Mogadishu first before returning to Kenya. There, he found Mad Tom refueling his King Air.

While he waited for the UN plane to refuel, Ed went over to say hello and to pick Mad Tom's brain, since he usually knew more about the situation in the various towns than any other pilot involved in the relief effort.

"How's the situation in Baidoa?" Ed asked first.

"Why don't you see for yourself?" the pilot responded. "I'll be stopping by there for a couple of hours this afternoon before I go back to Nairobi, and I've only got one other passenger."

      *   *   *

Merv Chambers' replacement in Baidoa, Warren Pastorini, was at the airfield when they landed. Ed introduced himself and got a ride into town with the new CARE logistician.

Baidoa had changed little since Ed's last visit there, except that the few children he saw on the streets looked healthier than they had before. He mentioned that fact to Warren, who said, "Yes. That's largely thanks to the Muslim orphanages, and to Kathy Norris. She's been taking the worst ones to them for care, orphans or not. But the orphanages are the only places not getting looted, so it seems to be working."

It was lunchtime, and most of the team was assembled in the dining room, but Katherine wasn't among them.

"She's at Bay One," Jane MacArthur told Ed after giving him a hug. "We've just had several more families show up from all the way out near Bardera. What's left of several families, anyway."

"I'm going back out to the airfield to meet a Herc that's due in here," Warren Pastorini said, grabbing a salad sandwich and a bottle of water, "but I can drop you off at Bay One, if you'd like. Kathy has a car and driver there. She can get you back out to the airbase."

Bay One had changed somewhat. It didn't smell quite as bad. There were donkey carts carrying away half-barrels of human waste to a pit away from the camp, and the pitifully small huts were more fully covered by new plastic. And other donkey carts were carrying drums of water from the well to more conveniently located points around the camp.

Most of the children seemed healthier than they had appeared to Ed during his last visit, too. But, God, there were so few of them.

He saw one child who had the look of death cradled in the arms of his emaciated mother just outside the dispensary. The flies knew, as they always did, and were gathering on the tiny boy's eyes. Ed stopped and went over to him, and brushed his cheek with his hand while the infant suckled futilely at his mother's withered breast.

"Hang in there, son," he said to the child. "Just a while longer, that's all. Help is coming."

"It won't be soon enough for him," Katherine said softly from the doorway.

Ed stood and looked at her. There were dark circles under her eyes, and her hands were covered with purple medicine stains. And some of the scratches on her arms from the thorn bushes of Bardera had still not fully healed. But to Ed Walker, she was as beautiful as anything he had ever seen, and he smiled and said, "Hello, Kathy."

"Hello, desperado. You look well," she said, her tired face breaking into a smile.

"I've missed you," he said.

"And I've missed you, Ed."

He walked to her and hugged her against him, and she put her head against his chest. She inhaled and said, "You smell good. How long can you stay?"

"Just a little while," he said. "Mad Tom's waiting at the airfield. But I'll be coming back here soon."

She nodded weakly, then stifled a sneeze.

He said, "You don't look healthy, Kathy. Are you sick?"

"No," she replied. "Just a bit of a cold. And I'm tired. And frustrated. We just can't manage to get enough food and medicines in here to keep up. And now people like these starting to turn up here all the way from out near Bardera." She looked at the skeletal mother sitting on the ground with her dying child, then up at him, her brow wrinkled. "Are your Yanks really going to come sort it out?"

"I think so," he answered.

"To kill Aidid and Hershel Morgan and the others? Or to escort the convoys in here so we can save lives?"

"Both, I hope."

She knew he was sincere. "I hope it's soon, then," she said.

They heard an airplane, and looked up. An Air Force C-130 Hercules was descending toward the airfield. "Speak of the devils," Katherine said.

One of her Somali assistants came to her and said, "A baby comes to one of the women, Sister Katherine."

"I'll be there in a moment, Siana." She turned back to Ed. "Life goes on. You'd better get back to the airport. Deggie will take you. He's up by the water tower."

"All right," he said. She stepped toward him and he took her shoulders and kissed her gently.

"I'm sorry I can't stay longer, Kathy," he said.

She smiled forlornly and said, "Next time, maybe."

"Yes. Take care of yourself, OK?"

"I will. You, too." She turned and followed Siana, and Ed went to the driver who was to take him back to the airfield.

He found Mad Tom, Warren Pastorini, and another man from one of the Baidoa-based NGO's huddled in the front of the airplane, listening to the BBC news broadcast on the plane's radio.

"What's going on?" Ed asked.

"It's President Bush," Pastorini said. "He's sent the UN an offer to have American troops come see that the aid gets through."

"Thank God," Ed Walker said sincerely.

Major General Black was gone when Ed got to Mombasa that night. "He's gone back to CENTCOM to brief his plan, I guess," Major Carroll, the Special Forces company commander said.

"Did he leave any guidance for me?" Ed asked.

"Not with me, he didn't," Carroll replied.

Ed checked with the task force chief of staff, who shook his head when Ed asked him the same question. "What did you think of his plan?" Ed asked.

"Didn't see it. The general kept it close to his chest. Sent the faxes back to MacDill himself, and always locked them up when he left his office. We're as much in the dark as you are."

Ed went back to the Special Forces company and found the sergeant major, Harry Lloyd. The NCO net was bound to have found out something about Black's plan.

Lloyd didn't have any information, either. "But I found out from the group sergeant major at Fort Campbell, who checked with a buddy of his at CENTCOM J-3 that there's apparently no Special Forces in the plan."

Ed was sure that couldn't be right. Black was obviously keeping details of the plan close-hold. "Well, we'll find out soon enough, Sergeant Major," he said.

The fact that Black had left no guidance for him made Ed free to follow the last order he had been given, which was to go to Somalia and assess the situation there. But now, he decided, he would go to the two places most critically in need of armed security to protect the relief effort; Mogadishu and Baidoa.

He went to the airlift scheduling board to see when the next flight to one of those places was planned. There was nothing scheduled to either place the next day, but there were two relief flights into Baidoa and one to Mogadishu on the day after that.

He caught a ride to the Mombasa Intercontinental hotel, where the members of the airlift task force were quartered.

It was incongruously plush compared to the places that he had been staying in neighboring Somalia, but he didn't complain. It would be a pleasant change, and as he had nothing to do the next day, he offered to treat the Special Forces company commander and his sergeant major to dinner and drinks. They accepted, and while the others ate sensibly, Ed gorged himself on Mombasa's small, succulent oysters, grilled tuna, and South African wine.

He felt a momentary twinge of guilt after the first dozen oysters, when he thought of Katherine and the other relief workers making do with goat and rice, or goat and spaghetti, but it quickly passed when he decided he would take a cooler to the fish market before he went back to Baidoa and load it up with fresh seafood for the team.

He awoke in the middle of the night in a cold sweat. He had dreamed he was drowning in cold, deep water. He decided it must have resulted from a combination of the seafood on which he had over-indulged, and the hotel air conditioning, so he turned the air off and went back to bed, but he couldn't sleep. Something was bothering him, but he couldn't put his finger on it. Then he remembered; it was Jimmy's birthday. He had forgotten all about it.

He put in a telephone call to the States, and the hotel operator rang back shortly afterwards. All he got, though, was his son's answering machine. He left a happy birthday message and promised to write, then hung up.

No doubt Jimmy was at Broad Marsh with his mother. Ed briefly considered telephoning there, then rejected the idea and sat down at the desk to write the promised letter.

He wrote, *Dear son*, then sat staring at the paper for a long time, thinking of his only child.

James McClanahan Walker was twenty-four years old now. It hardly seemed possible to his father. Where had the time gone? And how had he let the years roll by without spending more time with his son? He would be out of medical school in just a few more months, and then he was going to Colorado. Orthopedics was his chosen field. And ski injuries were what he intended to specialize in, he said. At Aspen or Telluride, one of the resorts for the wealthy where he would not have to worry about his clients paying their bills, and where he could spend some of his own time on the slopes, pursuing the sport that had become almost a passion for him.

Ed had been elated when learned that his son wanted to become a physician. He envisioned Jimmy ministering to the needy, saving lives and curing illnesses. Or perhaps even accepting a commission in the Army, caring for battle casualties with skill and compassion - doctoring the young men who risked their lives for the principles of freedom and democracy, men like his father had once been, brought back from the edge of death by the capable hands of dedicated doctors and nurses. Not setting fractured legs for the wealthy so they could go back to their law firms and stock brokerages. And chasing ski bunnies in his spare time.

Oh, well. He was young, and his goals could change. Perhaps one day he might even end up in a place like this, caring for the starving and the helpless, desperately ill children, as the medical people in the NGO's were doing, Rene the Frenchman and Katherine and Cheryl. Perhaps he should even say so in this letter, now. Tell his son about Katherine, and about Diane at IMC, and the things they were doing; things that mattered. Challenge him to do the same.

But that wouldn't be fair in a birthday letter, would it? No, he would do it when he got back home. He would go see the boy - the man, now. Spend some time with him, talk about things man-to-man. Make up for lost time.

He looked at the hotel stationery and his son's name, then folded it neatly and set it aside. He just didn't feel like writing a letter now. Instead he went to the window and pulled back the curtains, pressing his face against the glass and shielding his eyes from the reflected glare of the desk lamp.

The moon, nearly full, was up, and he could see its light dancing on the waves of the Indian Ocean. He recalled the dream of drowning, and shuddered, wondering why his mind was so often on death.

THIRTY FOUR

Ed read the fax again. The task force duty officer had handed it to him as soon as he'd arrived from the hotel, still tired from an almost sleepless night.

Secure a satellite radio and proceed immediately to UNOSOM headquarters, Mogadishu, to serve as US Central Command liaison officer to Commander, UN Forces, until arrival of CENTCOM advance party.

"How the hell am I supposed to serve as the CENTCOM liaison officer, when I don't even know the plan?" he said as much to himself as to the Marine Corps major who had given him the fax.

"The warning order is over there," the man replied, pointing to a folder bordered in red, with SECRET in bold letters at the top and bottom.

Ed folded the fax and slipped it into his pocket before he opened the folder. He read the warning order twice, and sighed, shaking his head.

The units that had been alerted for the Somalia mission consisted primarily of the 1st Marine Expeditionary Force and the Army's 10th Mountain Division. A reinforced battalion of Marines already aboard ships steaming in the Indian Ocean, the 22nd Marine Expeditionary Unit, was to land first to secure the port and airfield at Mogadishu to enable the landing of the follow-on forces, which would then spread out to the population centers of southern Somalia.

The 10th Mountain Division. How did that make sense? There were no mountains in Somalia, and the division's training at its upstate New York base was geared primarily to operations in extreme cold weather. They would be ideal if the humanitarian mission was to be conducted in Bosnia. But the Horn of Africa, where the temperature frequently soared above a hundred degrees?

Sending Marines to operate near the ports made sense, and they would be excellent for escorting the aid convoys from those ports to the inland centers, but Ed wondered if there was a need for so many of them.

It was not as if there would be major battles to fight. A light strike force of helicopter-borne troops from the 101st Airborne or from the Ranger Regiment would be all that was needed to support the Special Forces teams sent in to reestablish the ravaged nation's infrastructure and to train the Somalis to become self-sufficient and secure again. But there were no Special Forces teams. Not one. There was a smattering of psychological warfare teams, and some civil affairs units. But there was no plan to employ the highly-skilled nation building talents of the Army's Special Forces A teams.

And there was no plan to remove the evil, murderous warlords from power and bring them to justice before the eyes of the world. They were the ones responsible for the rape of Somalia and the starvation of her people - a whole generation of her children. And for that, they should be removed in a quick and immediate series of savage blows.

Perhaps there *is* such a plan, Ed thought. After all, the warning order was only classified "secret." The raids to bring quick justice to Aidid and Ali Mahdi and Morgan and their peers were no doubt classified "top secret." Yes, that must be it.

Ed laid the warning order aside, then pulled out the fax that ordered him to Mogadishu. There was a C-130 going there just after noon. He would need a couple of uniforms for his duties as liaison officer, and he was badly in need of a haircut. He could get both here at the task force headquarters, though.

He did so, but before he put on his uniform, he bummed a cooler and caught a taxi to the seafood market in Mombasa. He loaded the cooler with oysters and rock lobster tails and filets of fish, then bought a case of wine and took them back to the airport and marked the items CARE Baidoa. Once he got them aboard the relief flight there, he went back to the headquarters, put on his uniform, and procured the satellite radio, cipher tapes, and the necessary signal instructions from the task force communications officer.

He barely got it done in time to catch the flight to Mogadishu.

The Somali capital was unusually quiet. News of the impending arrival of American forces had sobered the lawless city and created trepidation in the minds of the young thugs of Aidid's militia, and hope in the hearts of their victims. At least for now.

By the time President Bush announced the actual decision to initiate Operation Restore Hope, a host of other nations had pledged forces as well, and Mohammed Farrah Aidid called a news conference to say, as if he had any other choice, that the troops would be welcomed with open arms.

Ed Walker listened to the despot and thought, It's too late for you to try to establish yourself as a legitimate, benevolent leader, you murdering bastard. You'll get yours, you son of a bitch. And soon.

Ed spent day and night coordinating with the multi-national officers of UNOSOM - the United Nations Observers to Somalia - and with the military liaison officers who began to appear from the countries that had pledged support for the unprecedented humanitarian mission. Much of it was politics, not the actual coordination of the military operations that would at last ensure that the desperately-needed aid got through. The multi-headed monster of the United Nations Command was incapable of coordinating a fast-moving operation like the coming one, and the American government, well-schooled by the Gulf war, took charge.

It was with a great sense of relief that Colonel Ed Walker relinquished his liaison officer duties to Central Command's advance party in the first week of December, 1992.

That was it, then. His military duties were finished at last, or nearly so; a blizzard in the American northeast caused Major General Black to pass him one more assignment.

The snowstorm had, with the irony that only Mother Nature can conjure up, paralyzed the 10th Mountain Division's cold weather troops, bottling them up in their base at Fort Drum, New York, and delaying their deployment to the hot, dry climate of the Horn of Africa. They would be unable to meet the planned operations schedule, and the first phases of Operation Restore Hope would have to be changed.

Instead of near-simultaneous landings in Mogadishu and Baidoa, the plan was changed to have the Marines secure Mogadishu first, then move on to Baidoa and subsequently west to Bardera, with the 10th Mountain Division troops and equipment catching up when they could.

Colonel Walker's new mission was to return to those interior towns with small advance parties of State Department and intelligence gathering teams to provide last minute tactical information and to serve as guides for the forces when they finally arrived. It was an assignment he accepted gladly, and he changed into civilian clothes and went to the airport to catch a flight to Baidoa the day before the Marine Expeditionary Forces came ashore in Mogadishu. All the news teams in the world were at Mogadishu airport, it seemed. But when he got to Baidoa, he found still more of them there.

At the CARE house, he was nearly run over by Dan Rather as he was leaving, and Ted Koppel came in immediately after to get a quick interview, then rushed away.

Ed found Lowell Morrison and Jane MacArthur laughing about the fact that both newsmen had rushed in, conducted an interview of the first CARE employee they found for his "expert" opinion on the Baidoa situation, then sped off to get his comments on the air. The man they had interviewed was a visiting CARE press relations officer, who had not been in Baidoa more than fifteen minutes when the American news anchors had arrived. And he left again on the heels of the men who had interviewed him.

"So the Marines will be here tomorrow, then?" Lowell asked after they had a laugh about the newsmen.

Ed shook his head. "Not right away," he said. "Too much snow."

Morrison looked at him curiously, and Ed smiled and said, "It's a long story. I'll explain what's going on later. Where's..."

"She's over in the other house," Jane said before he could ask the question. "In bed with a bug of some sort."

Ed's smile turned to a look of concern, then he looked at Morrison. "Would it be all right if I hang my hat here for a few days again?" he asked.

"After that load of seafood and wine you sent?" the team leader replied. "Certainly, mate. If you can find a spare bed that some news person isn't already in."

"I think he'll manage," Jane said as they watched the American hurry away.

Katherine was awake, listening to the BBC news, when Ed knocked on her door. Probably another newspaper reporter, she thought when she heard the knock. The place was full of them, now that the Americans were coming, and most ended up staying anywhere they could find a spare bed. She reached over and turned the radio down.

"Kathy?" he said when there was no response, and cracked the door open slightly to look in.

She saw who it was and smiled. "Come in, Ed," she said, sitting up and reaching her arms out to him.

He dropped his rucksack, came to the bed, and sat beside her, leaning his face toward hers to kiss her.

"Not now," she said, turning her head. "You might catch whatever it is I've got."

He kissed her neck instead, and she tilted her head back, cradling his head in her hand and holding him there. Then she pulled away and looked at him.

"Nice haircut."

He rubbed the stubble on his head and chuckled. "Worst damn one I've ever had," he said. "I got it from the Marine barber in Mombasa."

"Mombasa. What I wouldn't give to spend a few days there while I got rid of this bug," she said, wrapping her arms around his shoulders and pulling his head against her neck for him to kiss her there again. He did, and ran his hand beneath the T shirt she was wearing, stroking the soft skin of her back.

"You don't feel like you have a fever. What do you think it is?" he asked. Then suddenly he pulled his head back and looked at her. "It's not morning sickness, is it, Kathy?"

She laughed. "No, just a virus of some sort, I think." She pulled him to her again. But suppose it were? she thought. What *would* he say if she had been pregnant from their time together in Nairobi?

He was wondering the same thing, and wondering what she would do, if that had been the case.

"Anyway, whatever it was, it's about gone by now," she said. "I feel much better, now that you're here." She looked up at him and asked, "Will you be staying for awhile, or is this just another lightning raid?"

"I'll be here for a few days, I think. The troops should be here by then. Then on to Bardera."

"I was listening to the news," she said. "Aidid is going to cooperate, and so is Ali Mahdi. That should make it much easier."

"I'll believe it when I see it."

"And after Bardera?" she asked.

"I don't know," he said. "I'll be finished with the job I was sent here to do, so I guess I'll be going back to the States."

"To get out of the Army."

"Yes. You should be going out on R & R to Kenya about then, shouldn't you, Kathy? I was hoping we could spend some time together. Before I have to leave."

So that was it, she thought. He's going to leave, and that will be the end of it. A few days in Mombasa or Nairobi together, and after that, she might well never see him again.

She lay back on her pillow, and tears came into her eyes, so she turned her head away from him and wiped them. "No, I won't be going out, Ed," she said. "Not till my contract is up in February."

"But I thought... I mean, we talked about going to Mombasa."

"There's too much to do, now that the soldiers are coming. The convoys will be getting through, and we can start resettling the refugees back into their villages. That's the most important thing, in the long run - to get them back to their homes to rebuild their lives."

He sighed and his shoulders drooped. Then he said, "You'll be taking some time off after you finish in February, won't you? Maybe you could come to the States, and..."

She interrupted him and said, "I'll be going straight to Vietnam after I leave here, it appears. There's an opening for a nurse in one of the CARE Australia projects there. For a year or two."

Ed stood and turned to the one window of the room, and pulled back the torn sheet that Kathy had hung there for a curtain. An old Somali man was walking past leading a donkey with a load of long sticks tied in a bundle on its back. Off to build one of those stick shelters, he supposed. And then in the distance, he saw several technicals speeding down the road toward town. Two had machine guns mounted in their beds, and the third was carrying a recoilless rifle. He didn't recall seeing those vehicles in Baidoa before.

He turned his thoughts back to Katherine. He didn't want their relationship to end; he wanted it to grow. He hadn't cared this much for a woman since he'd fallen in love with Susan Madison. He turned back to face Katherine.

"Forget Vietnam, Kathy," he said. "Take some time off. Come with me to Virginia."

She sat up on the bed and reached for a pair of baggy pants from the floor, then pulled them on.

"No. The chances for these long-term jobs only come once in a while. And I like that part of the world. I'm tired of these short contracts in desperate, filthy places like this."

"Damn it, Katherine!" he said, flopping onto the bed beside her. "Don't put me off like this. I want to be with you - for us to spend some time together. Alone, somewhere nice."

"Then come with me to Vietnam," she said.

"Don't be silly."

"Hello!" someone called from the hall of the house.

Katherine stood and buttoned her pants. "We'll talk about it later," she said to Ed, then called to the person in the hall. "Just a minute! Be right there."

As she had suspected, it was a reporter. The attractive woman introduced herself as Sarah Armstrong. She was doing a piece for a Canadian women's magazine, she explained, and wanted to get some views on the relief effort and the coming military intervention from a woman's perspective.

"Lowell suggested I speak to you, Katherine," she said. Ed took the hint and excused himself, then asked, "Will you be coming down to dinner later, Kathy?"

"I don't think so."

"Then I'll bring you a plate," he said.

As he neared the road between CARE's houses, he saw another technical approaching from the direction of Mogadishu. This one was mounting a US made .50 caliber machine gun. When the Somali gunner saw him, with his military haircut, he spun the weapon in Ed's direction. Ed froze, and the vehicle rattled on by, the Somali militiaman laughing at the startled American.

There was a tea stand beside the road now, set up by some enterprising Somali to take some of the earnings of CARE's national staff. Katherine's driver and interpreter Deggie was there, and saw what happened.

"Hello, Ed," he said.

"Hello, Deggie," Ed replied.

Deggie nodded in the direction the technical had gone. "They're all getting out of Mogadishu before the Americans come," he said. "That makes eight technicals we have seen pass here this afternoon. Do you know what was written on the side of that one?"

"No," Ed said.

"It was, 'Looting and killing is our religion,'" Deggie said. "And they mean it. There will be trouble here, if the Americans do not arrive soon."

Ed eyed his gaunt face. "Where do you think they're going?"

"Ethiopia. They will stay there until the Americans leave, and then they will come back. Two months, two years; it doesn't matter. They will be back, and they will not have changed. Looting and killing will *remain* their religion."

Ed nodded. This young Somali was so different from most of the others. He was the sort of man who could be developed to replace the corrupt, murdering men currently in positions of authority in the town. Maybe so, when the troops arrived and dealt with the others.

The raids will probably occur tonight, Ed thought. Teams from the Delta Force would sweep in aboard special operations helicopters while the warlords and their thugs slept off the effects of chewing *khat* all day, and spirit them away to stand trial. Or, if they resisted, kill them.

Ed took Katherine a plate of food, and one for Sarah Armstrong, who was still interviewing her.

Katherine was feeling better, and the trio sipped from one of the bottles of wine that Ed had sent from Mombasa earlier, and had a lively conversation that covered things far beyond the relief effort in Somalia.

They got around to the President-elect of the United States, and Ed said, "No politics."

"But it's important," Sarah replied. "After all, he's the one who's going to have to decide when the job here is finished, for one thing."

"No politics," Ed said again, but Sarah challenged him. "You're not going to get off that easily, Yank," she said. "It's easy to see that you don't care for him, and I want to know why."

Ed shook his head, but she wouldn't let go. "It's Vietnam, isn't it? You disagree with what he did a long time ago, and you refuse to put that behind you and give him a chance to do what - after all - your own citizens have elected him to do. Isn't that it?"

Ed thought of Sam and Mike and the others and he said, "It wasn't a long time ago for the ones who died. For them, it was only yesterday."

"Well, isn't that all he was doing, anyway? Trying to stop the killing and dying in a war that, in the end, was all for nothing?"

All for nothing, Ed thought, and it angered him, but all he said was, "I don't know. Just let it go, Sarah. Please. No politics."

She smiled and gave up then. "All right," she said, "then let's talk about men and women."

Katherine looked at him for a long moment, then she said, "I'm afraid neither of us knows much about that subject, either."

Ed had been sitting on one end of the couch while Katherine sat at the other, with Sarah in the chair across the table from them. Now he slid halfway down the couch and reached his arm behind Katherine's head and pulled her to him. She resisted at first, especially when he tried to kiss her, because of the illness she was just getting over. But then she yielded, and opened her mouth to his.

"My goodness, look at the time," Sarah said, getting up from her chair. "I guess I'd better get across the road."

As the Canadian reporter left, Ed lifted Katherine from the couch and carried her toward her room.

THIRTY FIVE

The raids that Ed Walker expected to be conducted to capture the vicious warlords of Somalia did not materialize. Instead, the American government decided to negotiate with them. The result was that, instead of bringing them to justice for the rape of Somalia, it gave them legitimacy in the eyes of the world. It turned Ed Walker's stomach, but it was beyond the scope of things he could influence.

Instead, the Marines were ordered ashore in the face of lights from television cameras and flashbulbs. The port and airfield at Mogadishu were soon secured, while the astute Aidid, who had controlled those parts of the city, organized demonstrations to welcome the Americans for the benefit of the TV cameras and his own political stature.

The US forces didn't make it to Baidoa right away, as had initially been planned. They didn't get there until a week later. And once the bandits streaming out of Mogadishu toward the sanctuary of Ethiopia realized that they were in no immediate danger, they began to terrorize Baidoa as they passed through, looting what they could while they had the opportunity. There was a major battle between competing militias in the marketplace that left more than twenty dead, mostly innocent women and children.

Lowell Morrison responded to the increasing violence by sending the female members of the team out to the safety of Kenya for a few days, in spite of their pleas to stay. Most of the other NGO team chiefs did the same.

The advance team of State Department men came to Baidoa a couple of days before the Marines appeared there. Ed met them, and showed them to the rooms in the CARE offices that Lowell Morrison had consented to let them use.

One of the men looked familiar to Ed Walker, and he said, "We've met before, haven't we?"

"I was in the A team outside of Nha Trang when you were in the Mike Force, Colonel," the man replied, offering his hand. "My name is Larry Freedman."

Ed briefed the men on what he knew of the tactical situation in and around the town, then they struck out on their own to collect the other information they had been tasked to provide.

The night the Marines finally arrived, Freedman and his men guided their advance elements to the airbase on the southwest side of Baidoa, using a dirt road that Walker and Morrison had shown them that bypassed most of the town.

The Marine commander, Colonel Greg Newbold, had a message for Colonel Walker from Major General Black, which he gave to Ed as soon as they were introduced at the airfield the morning after the Marines' arrival. He was to remain there, assist Newbold and his men in coordinating with the relief agencies for the commencement of relief convoys into Baidoa, then accompany the Marines into Bardera to do the same.

The women returned from Kenya the afternoon of the troops' arrival. Ed saw little of Katherine Norris, however. He spent most of his time at the airfield with Newbold's staff, planning for the first convoy of two hundred metric tons of supplies that would bring relief, at last, to the infamous City of Death.

It was not a difficult task. The Marine Colonel and his able staff proved to have the flexibility to adjust to the varying needs of each non-government organization, and by the time the convoy arrived on the 20th of December, the Marines had reconnoitered each of the twenty-odd distribution sites. As soon as the convoy arrived at the airbase, they began to lead each truck to its preassigned distribution point.

Ed Walker stood at the airfield, watching, studying each young Marine's dirt-streaked but determined face. He would miss men like these - just boys, really - most several years younger than his own son.

He would miss sharing with them these little moments of victory, and while the world's press took on its self-appointed role of judging their success by the political consequences of how it all turned out - the big picture - he was content with the knowledge that each of them had done his duty as it was given to him.

Maybe he was right - that the job could have been done best, in the long term, by the older professionals on Special Forces teams. But at the moment, it didn't matter. These were the ones who had been sent, and they were accomplishing their assigned mission.

He thought, They're American servicemen. American troops have always done their duty, and always will.

Katherine showed up at the airfield with the other CARE team members to meet this first convoy to make it through. She saw Ed standing off to the side, watching the food-laden trucks go, each led by a fire team of Marines, and she came and stood beside him, her arm and hip touching his.

"There go your boys, Yank," she said.

"Yep," he answered, and his nostrils flared with emotion, "there they go."

*   *   *

"The Ninth Marines will be here in the morning," Colonel Newbold told Ed that night as they stood beside the airfield, looking at the Southern Cross. "One battalion will be pressing on to Bardera right away."

Freedman had already passed him that information, and Ed said, "Yes. I'm going with them. And you'll be heading back to Mogadishu to board the Tripoli, I understand."

"Yes, we will," the Marine said. Then he sighed, and thought aloud, "I wonder if this will all be worth it, in the end, Ed, or whether we're just saving the next generation to grow up and do the same thing to Somalia their fathers did."

"It doesn't matter," Ed replied. "You and your Marines did what you were told, and did it well. That's what matters."

"Yes," the other man said, pulling on his helmet to return to his headquarters, "I suppose it is."

"Well, I've got some unfinished business at the CARE house to attend to," Ed said. "If you don't mind, I think I'll catch a ride with the next patrol headed to that part of town."

Newbold had seen him with the attractive Australian nurse earlier, when the convoy was dispatched to go to the distribution sites, and understood what that unfinished business was. "Go ahead," he said. "We know where to find you if we need you."

Ed found Katherine on the roof, listening to her music. She saw him come up out of the stairwell, and moved over on the foam rubber mat to make room for him, but he reached down, took her hand, and pulled her to her feet. She slid into his arms, and they kissed, then danced on the flat rooftop to the gently haunting music.

"I've been thinking, Ed," she said quietly.

"About what?"

"About us."

He kissed her again, then said, "And?"

"It looks as if things will go all right here, now. The Diggers are coming here, they say, and I'm sure they'll do all they can to help their fellow Aussies. So maybe I can leave early, after all - take a little time off before I go to Vietnam."

"And come to Virginia?" he asked, stroking the back of her hair as they danced.

"Yes, if you'd like."

"I'd like that very much," he said.

They danced in silence until the song ended. Then he stood slightly back from her and said, "I have to go to Bardera tomorrow, at least for a couple of days. Then I'll be finished."

"Will you be going back to the States from there?"

He smiled and said, "And miss the CARE Christmas party? No way! But after that, yes. I have to get myself mustered out of the Army by the first of the year."

He didn't have a place to live in Guinea, yet. But James and Evelyn still owned the old home place. He could always stay there.

"Can you come to the States with me when I go?" he asked.

"No, not that soon. But I should be able to come around the middle of January. That's not so long."

"No, it isn't," he said. "But I'll miss you, Kathy."

"I'll miss you, too, desperado."

          *   *   *

Two days later and ninety miles to the east, Ed stood beside Bardera's dirt airstrip with Larry Freedman and said to a Marine Corps engineer, "Well, that should make it all right to run convoys from Baidoa to here, then, is that right?"

"As long as they stick to the tracks the amtracks made," the captain said. "We've swept the road twenty kilometers out, and all we found were a few metal mines. Of course, that doesn't guarantee that there aren't any plastic mines, but we haven't seen any. And the amtracks didn't hit any."

If the heavy amtrack armored personnel carriers hadn't set off any mines during their run from Baidoa to Bardera, then there shouldn't be any danger to lighter vehicles. Ed turned to Freedman and asked, "What do you think, Larry?"

Freedman shrugged. "Makes sense," he said. "And it'll be a lot quicker than the northern route we took out here."

"OK, then," Ed said, smiling broadly. "We'll head out first thing in the morning."

The State Department team was moving from Bardera on to Hoddur the next day. Since the road was clear, that meant they could take the shorter route, through Baidoa, instead of going all the way north along the Juba, then east to Hoddur. And it meant that Ed could be in Baidoa before Christmas Eve.

He walked from the airfield into Bardera and went to the CARE house to say goodbye to John Brien and Bob Ashton.

John was gone, but Bob was there, sitting in the radio room. He greeted the American warmly. "I heard you were out at the airfield with the Marines, mate. Glad you dropped in. How have you been getting on?"

"Good," Ed said. "Busy as hell. How are things with you? You should be heading back to Oz soon, huh?"

"Yep. I'll be back down under by the new year."

"Then what?" Ed asked.

"Dunno. I've just been scanning the job openings," he said. He picked up several sheets of paper that listed the openings for employment with CARE and flipped through them.

"Here's one that's tailor-made for you, cobber," Ashton said. "Some fishing project supervisor's job. You may not care for the area, though; it's Vietnam."

Ed snatched up the paper and looked at it. Yes, Bob was serious. They were looking for someone to head a program aimed at assisting the Vietnamese in improving their commercial fishing and fish processing techniques. He studied the prerequisites intently, and Bob noticed.

"You look like you might actually be interested in it, mate," he said.

Ed nodded, still studying the job description. It was to be in Phan Thiet, one of the towns in the south from which the Chams came. And it wasn't far from Saigon - now, Ho Chi Minh City - where Katherine would be. It was almost too good to be true.

"I really would like to apply," he said. "Is that possible?"

"Sure," the Australian replied. "In fact, I'd be glad to write you a letter of recommendation for the job. Lowell would too, I imagine."

Ed could hardly sleep that night, hardly wait to get back to Baidoa and tell Katherine. He finally did fall asleep, only to awaken in a cold sweat in the midst of a nightmare. It was the drowning dream again, but he quickly dismissed it. No doubt it was from thinking about the fishing project before he fell asleep.

He said goodbye to the Marines in the morning, and to Major Dave Currid, the personable Army officer attached to the Marines who had worked so tirelessly and done such an excellent job of dealing with the NGO's. He returned Currid's farewell salute and climbed into the Toyota four-by-four with the State Department men.

The first stretch of road was little more than a muddy track, but he knew from flying over it that once it got away from the gullies leading to the Juba River, it straightened into a wide road that ran straight to Dinsoor, and from there to Baidoa.

Freedman looked back at him from the front passenger seat and said, "Have you decided what you're going to do after you retire, Colonel?"

Ed leaned forward, his face beaming with a broad smile. "Yes, I sure have," he said. "I'm going fishing. In Vietnam."

He watched through the windshield as the driver fought to keep the vehicle from slipping off the road at the bottom of a slight depression. He got the right front wheel back up onto the drier part of the road, between the muddy ruts the Marines' amtrack had made.

"Vietnam?" Freedman asked.

It was the last word he ever said. The blast of an Egyptian-made Bakelite mine killed him instantly.

It went off under the right front wheel. The explosion of the anti-tank mine blew a huge hole in the roof and blasted Larry Freedman and Ed Walker through it as the whole vehicle was lifted from the road and tumbled off to the side, the other three men still inside it.

When Ed's blast-numbed mind regained a degree of confused consciousness, he had no idea where he was, or what had happened, and everything was deadly still. And then he thought, *The sappers. That's right, they attacked the hospital. Ah, Jesus. Don't put me through this again.*

There was a woman's face in front of his - a woman with specks of amber in her eyes, and he said, or thought he said, "Mary?" And then saw that, no, it was Sue Madison, not Mary. He smiled, and tried to get up, but he could not. His legs were numb - all of him was. He pressed his chin down on his chest, and looked at his legs. They were not there. There were only ragged stumps of flesh where they had been, and beyond them, the pitiful remains of Larry Freedman. He laid his head back and said, "Oh, no."

He blinked his eyes wide, trying to clear his mind, but he was spinning through a narrowing tunnel now, the darkness closing in on him. He thought, Sam will get me out of this. But hurry, Sam, old friend. Hurry.

It was dark now, and cold. He was in the ocean, sinking quickly through cold, dark water. There was nothing he could do, so he gave into it, and relaxed. It was over now. It was all right. He would be with the others soon; with Sue, with Sam, with all of them.

"My God," the cameraman said as he zoomed in for a closeup on the scarred face of the one with close-cropped hair. "He had a smile on his face. No legs, but he's smiling."

"That's enough tape of him," the TV correspondent said. "Here comes the helicopter. Get some shots of them loading the wounded ones, then wrap it up. We can send it over the satellite unedited in time for the last segment of the morning news, if we hurry. Man, they're gonna *love* this back in Atlanta!"

*   *   *

Lowell Morrison found Katherine in the dispensary at Bay One refugee camp. It had a roof now, thanks to the US Marines. But the generator hadn't made it there yet, so there was still no electricity, and it was somewhat darker in the unlighted building than it was outside. There were boxes of medical supplies stacked neatly against the walls, and at first, before his eyes adjusted themselves after coming in from the harsh sunlight, Lowell thought she was sorting through some of them. Then he saw that she was hanging things on a scraggly little bush she had put in a corner of the room.

Katherine saw his shadow and turned.

"Oh, hello, Lowell," she said. "Here's my Christmas tree. How do you like it?"

He walked to her and put his arm around her shoulder.

She turned her face toward his, and asked, "What is it, Lowell? What's wrong?"

"I've just had a call from Bob Ashton over in Bardera," he said softly. "I'm afraid I've got bad news about Ed, Kathy."

He felt her stiffen, and heard her breath rush from her lungs, and then she let him clasp her to him as her shoulders began to shake from her almost silent sobbing.

*   *   *

Harry Madison was in his Pentagon office when he got the news by secure telephone from Chuck Black in Mogadishu.

He had heard about the deaths earlier from the public affairs office. One of the TV networks had announced the first American deaths of Operation Restore Hope. And they had tastelessly shown the bodies, so it was apparently true. A land mine near Bardera, they said.

But TV news traveled so much faster than most reports did through military channels, so that it was afternoon by the time Black called him with the details.

"Colonel Walker was one of them, Harry," Black said. "I thought you would want to know that right away."

Madison let the news sear his mind quickly without dwelling on it. "Ah, no," was all he said, then asked, "And who else?"

"A Special Forces type on loan to State," Black replied, wondering as he did why the news of Walker's death seemed to have so little effect on the old general. Maybe they hadn't been as close as he thought. He read the name to Madison; "Sergeant Major Lawrence Freedman."

"And it was a mine?" Madison asked.

"Yes. An anti-tank mine on the road between Bardera and Baidoa."

"Jesus, Chuck, I thought that road had been reported cleared?"

"Yes," Black said. "I'm trying to track down whoever said it was. I'll have their ass, when I do."

"Never mind that," Madison said. "Just do what you can to make certain no one else gets hurt. It may have been planted after the road was cleared. Were there any other casualties?"

"Three wounded. They're aboard the *Tripoli* off Mogadishu. All State Department types. You should be getting the hard copy details shortly."

Madison sighed and said, "All right, then. Oh - who's listed as Ed's notification next-of-kin?"

"Let's see... James M. Walker. Relationship: adult son. Medical College of Virginia."

"I see. All right, Chuck. I'll let you get back to work. But no more casualties, you hear?"

"Not if we can help it," Black said. "Goodbye, Harry."

Black hung up the telephone and thought, No more casualties? This is the guy who wanted to go in, guns blazing, and capture the warlords, and he's telling me 'no more casualties'? He's like Walker; a relic of wars past. It's time for the old bastard to retire.

Harry Madison gently put the telephone in its cradle and walked to the window. He stared blankly out as he let the news loose in his mind.

Ed Walker, dead. Killed on his last mission - a mission I sent him off to do, when I should just have let him retire and go fishing.

What was it he said when I told him he hadn't been selected for promotion? *I've had a good run*; that was it. But now it's over. He's been used up. Completely used up.

Maybe it's best for it to end like that for men such as Ed Walker, Madison thought, trying to justify it in his mind. He would probably have spent the rest of his life alone, and no doubt wondering all the while why the Army had not made him a general, when he had given so much.

Or he might well have gone back to drinking heavily. So many of them did.

But then he thought, No, not Ed. He would have found something to do. And someone to do it with him. Yes, of course - the nurse in Somalia he said reminded him of Sue.

Madison went to his desk and picked up the framed photograph of his daughter, and looked at it, at the always young and smiling face above the Army nurse's uniform.

Ed was with her now, if what she believed was true. And she had believed it strongly. That was why she had wanted to go to Hawaii to die.

There was a retired chaplain there whom she had known at Walter Reed - a crippled Catholic priest. She had moved into the hospice he ran, and spent her last months there helping the other dying for as long as she was able, and strengthening her faith. Her letters about that experience and about her imminent death were strangely full of humor and hope, and life. And then suddenly, she was gone.

And now Ed was, too - the one man she had ever seemed to truly love.

Well, they were together now, if she was right about what happens after death.

He touched the image of his daughter's smile with his fingertip, then set the photograph back on his desk, hoping with all his being that what she believed was true.

     *   *   *

Jimmy Walker looked with a mixture of irritation and curiosity at the woman in the Army officer's uniform who had interrupted his studying. He was trying to get the day's notes assimilated in his mind before he left in the morning for a Christmas ski trip to Breckenridge. He thought she must be at the wrong apartment until she asked, "Are you James Walker?"

"Yes," he replied. "What can I do for you?"

"May I come in?" she asked, and he noticed that she was clutching an envelope to her chest and her hands were shaking.

When she was gone, Jimmy crumpled into the old easy chair he had bought at a thrift shop when he was a freshman, and he picked at the tattered fabric of its arms with his fingertips.

So, he was dead. All that time, and it had finally caught up with him. Such a waste. A whole life spent chasing lofty-sounding ideals that, in the end, only meant young men going off somewhere to die. And now and then, an older one, like him. And in Somalia, of all places, where it seemed that they might finally do some good.

He sighed, and looked at the clock. It was late, but he would have to drive to Broad Marsh to let his mother know, before the name was released to the news. The officer had said that they would do that in the morning, now that his next-of-kin had been notified.

Mother can tell Uncle James and Evelyn, he thought. And Sookie.

No, that's my responsibility. I'll do it myself.

He pushed himself up and closed the notebook he had been studying when the woman arrived, and turned off the desk lamp. Then he turned it back on, remembering that somewhere in the desk drawer was a letter his father had written him when he was only a baby. His mother had found it among her things when she was moving back to Broad Marsh, and sent it to him.

He hadn't read it then, because when he scanned it, he saw that it was full of words about freedom and fighting and rage. And dying.

Now he sat down and dug around in the drawer and found it. He sat back and unfolded the single page.

He shook his head when he finished reading it, then read two of the last sentences aloud:

"Because even if he kills you, you will have won. You will have won because you died a free man."

"Ah, God damn it, Dad," he muttered, shoving the piece of paper into his shirt pocket.

THIRTY SIX

Harry Madison stirred the hot, red coals in the fireplace of his Fort Myer quarters and picked up a log to put on top of them. Then he changed his mind and put it back in the log rack. He would finish his glass of port and go upstairs to join his wife, who had already gone to bed.

The house looked nice, as it always did at Christmas time, with holly sprigs stuck everywhere and an electric candle in each of the front windows.

He inhaled, savoring the smell of the cedar tree. It was decorated with the same German lights and little wooden figures that he and Ellen had used every year since their first Christmas together in Heidelberg more than three decades earlier.

He was sipping the last of his glass of port when the haunting strains of *Taps* began to roll across the old Army post, drowning out the distant sounds of traffic and reminding Harry Madison and all the other old soldiers who heard it that they were still among the living, but that they would not always be.

He sat still until the last note died away, then pushed himself up, stretched, and walked to the front windows to unscrew the bulbs in the candles.

There was a taxicab stopping in front of the house, and a military police sedan, its blue lights flashing, was pulling up behind it. Another one caught speeding on post, no doubt, Madison thought.

He loosened the bulbs in the living room and dining room windows, and went into the den to unscrew the one in there.

The MP car's lights were still flashing, so he looked out between the curtains for a moment. One of the military policemen was speaking to the passenger in the back seat of the taxi. Not a fun job, Christmas Eve patrol duty.

He closed the glass doors of the fireplace and took his empty wine glass into the kitchen. He had just started up the stairs when there was a knock at the door.

He opened it to find a military police sergeant standing there at attention.

"I'm sorry to bother you so late, especially on Christmas Eve and all, General Madison," the man said.

"No, it's quite all right, Sergeant. What is it?"

The MP looked around and gestured toward the taxi. "There's some old guy in the taxi who insists on coming in to see you, sir. He said it's about Colonel Walker, one of the guys who got blown up in Somalia yesterday. We tried to get him to move on, but..."

Madison interrupted him. "Who is he?"

The soldier looked at the blue military identity card in his hand and said, "Retired Captain Fallon, sir. Francis X. Fallon."

Fallon. Frank Fallon, the priest who ran the hospice where Susan died. "Yes," Madison said. "I know him. I know of him."

"Shall we bring him in, then, General? He's, uh, he's got a wheelchair."

"Yes, I know. Help him in here, will you, Sergeant?"

He watched them take a folding wheelchair out of the taxi and lift a frail, white-haired old man into it - the man who had watched his daughter die. But the sergeant said it was about Ed Walker, not Sue, Madison thought as he watched the MPs wheel the man up to the front steps.

He walked down to help them get the wheelchair up the steps, and noticed that the man had a hook in place of one of his hands. Fallon eyed him in silence, and Harry waited until they got him up the steps and through the door before he spoke, then he said to the MP, "Thank you, Sergeant. I can handle it from here."

"Should we ask the taxi to stay, sir?"

"No, thank you. That'll be all."

The soldier saluted and said, "Merry Christmas, General."

"Merry Christmas."

He closed the door, and Fallon wheeled the chair around to face him. His clothes were rumpled, his white hair unkempt, and he smelled of sweat and liquor. "My name is Fallon, General. Frank Fallon."

"Yes," Madison said, offering his hand. "You run the hospice where my daughter died."

"Ran," the old priest replied, weakly shaking Harry's right hand with his left. "That was a long time ago."

"Yes, it was. Come in. I'll put another log on the fire."

Fallon wheeled into the living room. Madison went to the fireplace and threw two logs onto the dying coals. "Can I get you a glass of port, Father?" he asked as he did so.

"Frank," Fallon said. "And I'll have an Irish whiskey, if you have any. No ice."

Harry went to the bar and dug a bottle of Bushmills out from behind the other bottles. As he did so, he said, "You wanted to speak to me about Ed Walker?"

He poured Fallon a large shot of whiskey, and an ounce of port for himself while he waited for an answer. There was none, so he turned back and faced the other man.

Fallon was sitting with his arms around his chest, shivering. He was wearing only a light, frayed shirt.

"You're cold," Harry said. He handed him the glass, then pulled the Afghan off the back of the couch and wrapped it around the priest's shoulders.

"Thank you," Fallon said after he took a large swallow of whiskey. "Damned cold Mainland weather."

It appeared that the strange old man wasn't going to say anything, so Madison stirred the fire and said, "Colonel Walker was killed by a land mine yesterday morning in Somalia. He and another man. Did you know him, Father Fallon?"

"Frank," the man said again. "Yes. I was a chaplain at Walter Reed when he was evacuated there from Vietnam. That's also where I met your daughter."

"I know," he said. As odd as this man was, he was the one Sue had turned to in her dying days. "I hope you got the letter I wrote you after she died," General Madison said. "It meant a lot to her, being there with you those last months, judging from her letters. I had hoped to be able to tell you that in person, at her funeral."

"I didn't go," Fallon grumbled. "There were others to care for. The living." His eyes went to the picture of Sue that hung beside the fireplace, and Harry's followed them. Fallon stared at the photograph and said, "She was a fine young woman, Madison."

"Thank you," Harry said. "She was." Then he turned to face the priest and watched him take another long drink of whiskey, still looking at the picture.

"Why are you here, Frank?" he asked.

Fallon's dark eyes shot to Madison and studied him for a long moment. Then he threw the glass to his lips, drained it, and held it out. "Get me another drink and sit down, Harry," he said.

Madison did so, sitting back in the winged chair beside the fireplace and crossing an ankle onto a knee as Fallon took another swig of Bushmills.

Then Fallon said softly, "Your daughter had a child before she died."

"*What?*"

"I said your daughter had a child before she died!"

Madison's jaw dropped and his hand jerked, spilling some of the port onto his leg, and he thought, The poor man is insane.

"You're out of your mind," he said, pushing himself to his feet. "You're a drunken fool who's wormed his way into my house for a free drink." He pointed to the door and said, "Get out of here!"

Fallon eyed him through narrow slits, his head wagging. "For God's sake, Madison, I was *there*. A boy. Walker's and hers. *He* never knew about it, either. Now sit down and *listen* to me!"

Harry stared at him for a time, mouth agape, then he slumped down into his chair. He still didn't think it was possible, but he stuttered, "Wh... what happened? W... where is..."

"I'll tell you, if you'll shut up and listen," the priest said, then his voice softened. "She called me from here, from Washington, before she even knew she was pregnant...."

As the inconceivable story unfolded, Madison began to believe him, and when he did, he heaved himself up from his chair and said, "How could you, Fallon? How could you do this to my wife and me? And the boy! And to Ed, for Christ's sake!"

His voice woke his wife, and she came to the top of the stairs and called to him. "Harry? Harry, what is it? Is someone here?"

"It's all right, Ellen. Go back to bed. I... I'll tell you about it later."

"All right. But don't stay up too late," she said. "We're still going to early church, aren't we?"

"Yes. Please go back to bed."

He waited until he heard the bedroom door close, then he buried his face in his hands for a moment before he looked up at Fallon again with burning eyes.

"God damn you, why have you *done* this?" he said in a hoarse whisper. "All these years. *Why*?"

"Because I thought it was the right thing to do," the priest answered. "In the eyes of God, I thought it was right."

Fallon's whiskey glass was empty again. Without asking, Harry reached down and took it from him. He filled it half full, then poured the same amount into another glass for himself.

"You still haven't told me where he is now," he said after he flopped down into the winged chair again.

Fallon drank a swallow and said, "Put another log on. I'm coming to that."

As the priest neared the end of his astonishing story, Harry paced back and forth in front of the fire. The old clock on the mantle began to strike midnight, and Fallon stopped to listen. When it was finished, he crossed himself with the hook and mumbled, "The day we celebrate the birth of our Lord, Jesus Christ. Thanks be to God."

Harry Madison stared at the shabbily dressed, withered old man. He looked like an exaggerated character from some Dickens Christmas tale. Then the skin wrinkled at the corners of the general's eyes and he smiled and said, "I have a grandson, Frank. It's Christmas, and I have a grandson. Yes. Thanks be to God."

It took a long time for Mrs. Madison to fathom what her husband was telling her. And when it finally struck home, she wept, then laughed like a mad woman, then wept again. In the end, he had to give her a tranquilizer so that she could sleep.

When Harry went back downstairs, Frank was slumped over in the wheelchair in front of the fireplace with his chin on his chest. At first glance, he wondered if the priest was dead, then realized it was only the long trip he had endured to come here, and the Irish whiskey.

He got a pillow and comforter, and laid the frail priest on the couch, the wheelchair right against it and the downstairs bathroom light on, in case Fallon awoke and needed them. Harry wondered if he should unstrap the hook, but Fallon stirred and snorted just then, and reached up to brush his nose with the hook as naturally as one would do with his hand, so Harry left him as he was.

Then he went to the phone in the kitchen and called the Army operations center at the Pentagon.

"Merry Christmas, Colonel," he said to the man. "This is General Madison. I need you to locate a soldier for me...."

*   *   *

Of all Ed Walker's kin, his niece Sookie Hogge took the news of his death the hardest. She wailed and held her swollen abdomen, then ran out onto the dock in the freezing weather to cry. Her husband

Michael went to get her and she came back in, still weeping at the terrible news.

But she was pleased that her cousin Jimmy was the one who came to tell her. After she had regained her composure, she said, "I had a dream about him the other night, Jimmy. I dreamed that he was drowning. I was near, but there was nothing I could do to save him. It must have been about the time he died."

Jimmy patted her arm. "Stranger things have happened," he said, then sighed. "I guess it's like Mom said, Sookie. At least he died doing what he wanted to do. You know, off somewhere making the world safe for freedom."

Sookie glared at him with her puffy red eyes, because he sounded as if he didn't believe it.

"That's right," she said. "He *was*, you know. He sat right here and told me before he left. Freedom from hunger, freedom from want; that's what he talked about. That's why he was going, he said."

Jimmy picked at his fingernails, thinking about his father's letter. He hadn't changed.

He sighed heavily and said, "Well, I've got to get to Broad Marsh, Sookie. Then I have to go up to Washington tomorrow. They're going to bury him in Arlington the day after tomorrow, but I'm supposed to see some general tomorrow evening."

"For what?" his cousin asked.

"I don't know. But they were pretty insistent. Will you all be able to come up for the funeral?"

"Of course," she said. "I'm only pregnant, not dying."

"All right. I'm sorry to ruin your Christmas like this, Sookie."

"It's not your fault. Anyway, there will be plenty more Christmases," she said, then kissed him on the cheek. "I'm sorry, Jimmy. I loved him a lot."

"I know you did, Sookie," he replied. He looked at her swollen belly and said, "You wouldn't be planning to name your kid after him, if you hadn't."

         *   *   *

When young Sergeant Michael Fallon was summoned to the 5th Special Forces Group headquarters, he was afraid it was to notify him of Frank Fallon's death, because he could think of no other reason they would call him in on Christmas Day.

The retired chaplain who had adopted him was the only father Michael had ever known. His mother, he'd been told when he was old enough to ask his adoptive father, had been an unmarried nurse - an orphan like him. He didn't know who his real father was, and he supposed that perhaps his mother hadn't even known, herself.

He had not seen the old priest since he joined the Army and left Hawaii after high school. They had never been particularly close, and as young Michael grew up, his interest in surfing, mountain climbing, and other physically challenging activities had been something his wheelchair-bound father could not share with him. Anyway, it seemed to Michael that everyone around the old man was either drunk, or dying, or both, and he had just wanted to get away.

So when Sergeant Fallon arrived at the headquarters, he was shocked to learn that his crippled stepfather was there waiting for him, and equally surprised to learn that he was there with a three star general named Madison.

       *   *   *

Jimmy Walker was less shocked to learn of his father's illegitimate child than he was amazed and interested by the medical aspects of the birth, and what the woman must have endured to see it through.

He turned back to the paraplegic, one-handed old man who had been telling him about it and asked him, "And she wasn't on any sort of radiation or chemotherapy regimen?"

"No!" Fallon shot back. "She wanted the child, I said. Of course she wasn't."

"God," the aspiring physician muttered, "she must have been in incredible pain."

"You have no idea."

Jimmy glared at him a moment. Of *course* he had an idea what she must have gone through. He was almost a fully-qualified medical doctor. He started to say so, then decided against it. He didn't *really* know, because even though he had seen a lot pain, he had never experienced much. The old cripple obviously had.

"Was she taking anything for it?"

"The pain? Yes, but it didn't do much good."

"What was she taking?"

"Hell, I don't know, Walker!" Fallon said, his eyes darkening to tiny slits. "She was a nurse. I'm just a God damned priest."

And a strange one, Jimmy thought.

"What difference does it make to you anyway?" the old man grumbled. "She was no kin to you; the boy *is* - he's your half-brother, for Christ's sake. I would think you'd show a little interest in that fact."

Jimmy Walker sat down in General Madison's winged chair and looked at Fallon, wanting to hear it all and get it over with. "All right," he said. "Tell me about him."

Fallon shook his head. "No," he said. "I'll let him do that. He and Madison will be here soon."

"Just tell me one thing, then, Father Fallon," Jimmy said. "Why did you keep it a secret? Why didn't you tell my father?"

Fallon looked at his bony, shriveled hand for a time, then back at Jimmy. "She didn't want me to," he said. "Not until he retired, or unless he was divorced from your mother. She was afraid it would screw up his career, give him too much responsibility. I didn't give a damn about his career, but she was sure it would break up your parents' marriage, too. So I promised to keep it a secret."

"I don't buy it," Jimmy said. "My parents have been divorced for years, for God's sake. Didn't you know that?"

"Yes, I knew it." Fallon mumbled.

"Then, damn it, why didn't you tell him?"

"Because by then, he was *my* son. I didn't want to give him up."

The men stared at each other until Fallon finally said, "I didn't really like your father, Walker. By the time Susan died, I hated him, in fact."

"Why?"

"Because of what he put her through. Because of her pain. Because he wasn't there."

Jimmy felt tears well up in his eyes. He pinched the corners of them with his fingers, but the tears fell anyway when he thought, *He wasn't there for me, either*. He put his face in his hands and cried for a time, while it all sank in.

When he was able to speak calmly again, he said, "He told me about you once, Father."

The priest's shaggy eyebrows raised skeptically.

"He did," Jimmy said. "When my parents finally got divorced, he told me about the crippled chaplain at Walter Reed who had convinced him to try to make the marriage work. And he tried, I think. For a long time, he tried."

Tears began to fall from his eyes again, but this time he ignored them, and said, "I always thought it was for my sake. But it was for yours, too, Father. You didn't need to hate him. All you needed to do was tell him. He would have been there. You *know* he would have."

Frank Fallon had not wept since Susan Madison died, but now his chin drooped onto his chest, and a single tear fell from one of his bleary eyes. He nodded, then brushed at his cheek and said, "I suppose you're right. He was the kind of man who couldn't have done otherwise. But it doesn't matter, now. We can't undo the past - none of it."

He watched the young man stand and pull a handkerchief from his pocket and wipe his face and then his hands. He heard him blow a long stream of air through his lips, and saw him look at the photograph on the wall beside the mantle of the general's house.

"Yes, that's Susan," Fallon said without waiting to be asked.

He let Jimmy study it for a while longer, then he said, "Did your father believe in God, Walker? He said he did, way back then. But did he really?"

Jimmy turned from the photograph and looked at him, his brow wrinkled with thought as he considered the question.

"I don't know. I know he believed in freedom," he said, recalling the letter his father had written to him long ago, but he had only recently read. "But God? I don't really know."

A car door slammed outside, and Fallon spun his chair and looked out. "Here comes my son... here comes your brother, now," he said. "And his grandfather."

    *   *   *

The four of them stayed for a time after everybody else had gone, all of them silent. The only sound was off in the distance, at another grave site somewhere in the sprawling cemetery; three quick volleys, and after that, a bugler mournfully playing *Taps*. Harry Madison was the only one who seemed to hear it, and he looked in that direction thinking, That will be Sergeant Major Freedman. But when it was over, he noticed that Frank Fallon had heard it, too, and was still looking that way. Their eyes met for a moment, and Madison thought the priest had what might be a faint smile at the corners of his lips.

Jimmy Walker was the first one to speak. He patted the breast of his suit once, then reached inside and withdrew a sheet of paper from an inside pocket. He handed it to his half-brother and said, "He wrote this to me a long time ago."

Michael Fallon took it and unfolded it. He read it slowly, the muscles in his jaw flexing as he did.

Freedom....

When he finished it, he folded it and held it out to Jimmy.

"No, you keep it," Jimmy said. "He would... Just keep it."

The young sergeant nodded, and slipped it into a pocket of his uniform. Then he looked at the simple Army coffin in which his father lay and inhaled deeply through his nose. He could smell the freshly-dug dirt of Arlington, and it smelled rich.

He came to attention and saluted. It was not the slow, mournful salute that the Old Guard used, his brother noticed, but a sharp, crisp one; one that seemed to indicate a sense of purpose, as if he had places to go, and battles to fight.

"I saw him once, not long ago," he said, and Jimmy squinted and asked, "Where?"

"Mombasa," Michael replied, turning away to walk back up the hill to Fort Myer.

Jimmy put his arm on his brother's shoulder and walked with him. Michael looked over at him and smiled faintly. "It was just for a minute," Michael said. "It was last election day, after a meeting he had with my company commander. He was going back into Somalia, and I remember that he had this really determined look in his eyes, and I thought, That guy's going off to do something important, and we're going to be a part of it. We *all* thought that, at the time...."

Harry Madison and Frank Fallon watched them walk away.

"Do you know what the boy told me when he left the house last night, Frank?"

Fallon glanced at him for a second and shook his head once, then went back to watching them.

"He said that you were still the only father he had ever known, and that nothing could really change that."

The priest didn't acknowledge the old general's statement, but Harry knew he heard; he saw the stooped shoulders come back slightly, and saw the barely perceptible nod of Fallon's head.

Harry watched them, too; his grandson, Michael, whom this odd but strangely lovable old chaplain had accepted from the womb of Madison's own, dying daughter and raised into a man. And Jimmy, the doctor; the other son of the man they had come here to bury - the man who, from among all the thousands he had known in his long Army career, had been the one Harry Madison had most regarded as a son of his own.

"Have you ever read Sun Tzu, Frank?"

"Of course I have, Madison. And I know what you're thinking: *"Regard your soldiers as your children, and they will follow you into the deepest valley; look on them as your own beloved sons, and they will stand by you even unto death."*

They looked at each other, and Fallon's mouth opened in a dirty-toothed smile. Harry Madison returned the smile, then he went to the back of the wheelchair and began pushing it up the hill.

"Why did Susan decide to name him Michael?" he asked.

"She didn't. She wanted him to be called Harry Edward. But *I* named him." He turned his head and looked back at Harry with a scowl on his wrinkled face. "It's from a book you should read instead of wasting your time on that damned Chinaman's crap," he said.

Harry returned the scowl, wondering if Fallon was capable of civility for more than a brief moment now and then. How could Sue have possibly been happy around a man like this? Or was it just a long-practiced act the priest had developed - some gimmick to get the attention of the soldiers he had ministered to for so many years? Something to deflect their self-pity when they had been maimed, as he had been. Or when they were dying. And then he understood.

"Aw, blow it off, you tired old relic of the Chaplains Corps," Madison said.

Fallon's dirty-toothed smile appeared again, then they both broke into a spell of hearty laughter.

The two young men up the hill from them stopped and looked back. Harry Madison threw a wave of dismissal at them, and thought hard before he said, "OK, Fallon. Michael. The archangel. Let's see... the Old Testament? No - Revelations. That's it. *And there was war in heaven: And Michael and his angels fought the devil...*

"'...fought against the dragon...' But that's close," the priest said, scowling again. "And not bad for a tired-assed old infantryman. But, no. You have to read the whole chapter – Revelations, chapter twelve - to understand why I named your daughter's son Michael."

Madison tried hard to recall it, but he could remember only that it was about war in heaven, and the archangel Michael leading his angels against those of Satan. But he remembered that Michael *won* the battle, and that was good enough.

It wasn't enough for Frank Fallon, though, and he said, "Read it, Madison. Read it twice. And while you're at it, flip back a few pages and read Jude's epistle, too. And not just because Michael is also mentioned there. You might learn something about things that need your attention before you turn this Army over to your grandson, there."

Then he cocked his head and looked at the general again, his face still wrinkled and serious, but the eyes brighter, it seemed to Harry, than they had been at any time since he appeared on Christmas Eve.

"Did you know that Saint Michael is the patron saint of paratroopers?" Frank asked, his voice unusually soft.

"Of course I did, you sentimental old fool," Harry growled.

Fallon nodded, his furrowed brow indicating that he was still contemplating something serious. Then, for the second sentence in a row, he spoke softly.

"We didn't drink all that Irish whiskey the other night, did we, Harry?" he asked.

Madison chuckled. He was beginning to like this obscene old, worn out chaplain; beginning to understand what Sue had found in him near the end of her short life. But he drank too much. It was going to kill him, sooner or later.

"Not quite," he said. Then he thought, maybe he drinks to dull the pain of the injuries he suffered all those years ago; a mine explosion, like the one that killed Ed Walker.

For a moment, Harry Madison wondered at the irony of that, and how it was that Fallon had survived his wounds, and Walker had not. And why. Then he looked up the hill and saw his grandson, his half-brother's arm still resting on the shoulder of his uniform.

"No, Frank," he said, patting the old chaplain on the shoulder, "we didn't quite finish it off. But we'll need to get another bottle or two before we welcome in 1993."

EPILOGUE

October the Third, 1993

Doctor Jimmy Walker wiped the sweat from his brow with the sleeve of his shirt and muttered, "Damn, it's hot," then continued placing the neatly-folded clothes in the dresser drawer.

He unfolded the towel in the bottom of his suitcase and looked at the four small photographs he had wrapped in it to keep the glass frames from getting broken.

He picked up the one of his mother first, and wiped his brow again with the sleeve of his other arm as he looked at it, then glanced around the room. The dresser top was the only place he could put them.

He set the one of his mother there, then picked up the others one at a time and did the same; his half-brother Michael in his green beret; Sookie, holding her baby son on her hip; and the one of his father, taken long ago, before the battle scars had ruined his handsome face.

There was a knock on the door, and a pretty woman stuck her head in and said, "Hi. May I come in?"

"Sure," he said. He had met her when he arrived an hour earlier. She was one of the nurses he would be working with; Diane something.

"Getting all settled in OK?" she asked, moving beside him and watching him arrange the photographs atop the dresser.

"Yes, thanks," he said.

She studied one of the photos with a slightly puzzled look for a moment, then she shrugged her shoulders and smiled. "Well," she said. "If there's anything I can do to help, Doctor, just let me know."

"You can start by calling me Jimmy," he said, returning the smile.

"OK," she said. "Jimmy, then. Well, I have to go. We just got a truckload of supplies in that need to be put away. But I'll see you later.

Anyway, welcome to the International Medical Corps, Jimmy," she said, still smiling warmly as she flitted away, "and to beautiful Baidoa."

*   *   *

Katherine Norris lifted the newborn child, still attached by the umbilical cord to its mother in these first seconds after birth, and cleared his mouth and nostrils of mucous. The baby began to wail and Katherine smiled and said, "Life goes on." Then she tied and snipped the cord, and wiped the baby dry, and handed him to his sweat-drenched Vietnamese mother.

After she washed up, Katherine walked out of the dispensary and crossed the quiet street to the house she shared with the other CARE nurse in Phan Thiet.

A minute later, she stepped out onto the flat rooftop and looked out across the beach to the South China Sea. The moon reflected off it in a sparkling path from the horizon to the shore, and she stood there for awhile enjoying it. It was so much more pleasant here than in Ho Chi Minh City, with all its raucous traffic noise, and its smell of diesel fumes and burning garbage. And the Chams who comprised much of Phan Thiet's population were such lovely people to work among. No wonder Ed Walker had spoken so highly of them.

She looked out across the water for awhile longer, then set the bottle of *Bier 33* beside the lounge chair, and sat down with her compact disc player in her lap. She heard the wail of a high-pitched note from somewhere, but couldn't tell if it was the newborn child, or the call of some night bird.

She checked the disc in the CD player and selected her favorite song from it; Lyle Lovett's *Simple Song*, then sat back to listen, enjoying the quiet peace and the ballad's poignant message:

It's a simple song for simple feeling
You see the moon and watch it rise
Across the continent the night bird sings
And somewhere someone hears its cry...

...So hear my words with faith and passion

For what I say to you is true
And when you find the one you might become
Remember part of me is you...

*   *   *

Staff Sergeant Michael Fallon looked down at the ravaged Somali capital from his seat in the Black Hawk helicopter, wondering how long it would take to rebuild the ancient city once the warlords were gone and peace was restored.

Maybe the beginning is about to come, he thought.

They were going after Mohammed Farrah Aidid and his top lieutenants - Michael and the other Delta Force men were, and the tough young Rangers supporting them. And when they were finished with Aidid, maybe they would go after the other murdering bastards; Ali Mahdi and Omar Jess and Hershel Morgan. But first, Mohammed Farrah Aidid.

Aidid and his top thugs were reported to be in a building near the one that had once been the Olympic hotel, and the elite American troops were headed there now, even though it was broad daylight.

That fact was bothersome, because the men of Task Force Ranger - the Delta Force soldiers and Rangers and 160th Special Operations Aviation Regiment aircrews - operated best at night. They were trained and equipped to make darkness their ally; to *own* the night.

It was also worrisome that the bandits the warlord called his militia - the ones protecting him, and the thousands of others wandering the streets in search of something to steal - would be high on *khat* at mid-afternoon. By late evening, they would be sleeping off the effects of the drug, most of them.

But the Americans' elusive target was there *now*; by nightfall Aidid would no doubt be gone, hiding elsewhere in the rat warrens that had once been Mogadishu. So they were going after him now.

Fallon looked at Griz Martin, his team leader. Martin returned his gaze, his scarred and serious face reminding Michael of his own father's face in that brief moment in Mombasa a year before - the only time that he had ever seen Edward Walker.

Griz is worried, too, Michael thought. But then Martin's face broke into its usual, cheerful smile. Fallon returned it, and thought, *We'll be all right.*

He looked around at the others; at Shughart and Gordon, at Fillmore and Busch and the rest, and he thought again, *Yes, with men like this, we'll be all right.* Still, he touched the pocket that held the old letter about freedom his father had written, and the small photograph of his mother in her nurse's uniform.

They were his amulets; they and the medallion his grandfather, Harry Madison, had given him. It was a little medal of Saint Michael slaying the dragon, and Michael Fallon reached inside his fatigue shirt to touch it as the Black Hawk pilot, Chief Warrant Officer Durant, looked back and called, "One minute!"

> *And there was war in heaven: Michael and his*
> *Angels fought against the dragon; and the dragon fought*
> *and his angels, and prevailed not...*

www.specialops.org

Made in the USA
Lexington, KY
03 July 2013